RIVEN ROCK

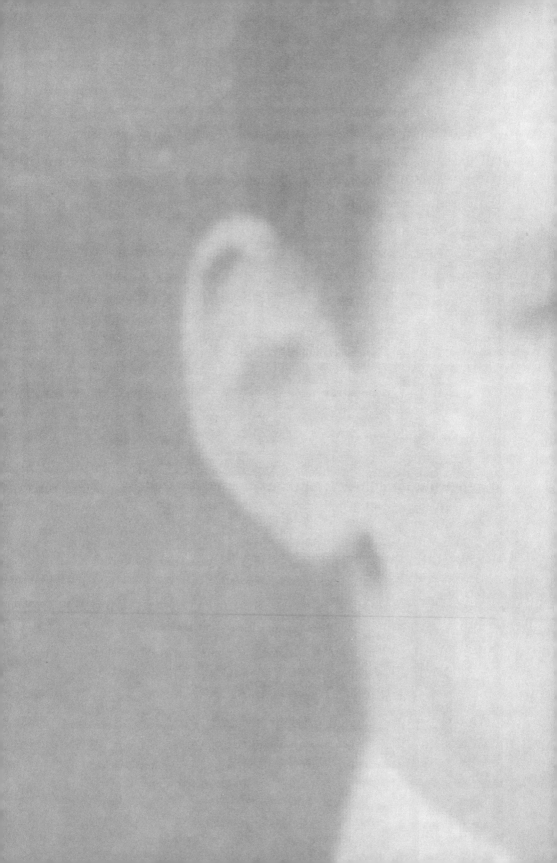

RIVEN ROCK

T. Coraghessan Boyle

VIKING

VIKING
Published by the Penguin Group
Penguin Putnam Inc., 375 Hudson Street,
New York, New York 10014, U.S.A.
Penguin Books Ltd, 27 Wrights Lane, London W8 5TZ, England
Penguin Books Australia Ltd, Ringwood, Victoria, Australia
Penguin Books Canada Ltd, 10 Alcorn Avenue,
Toronto, Ontario, Canada M4V 3B2
Penguin Books (N.Z.) Ltd, 182–190 Wairau Road,
Auckland 10, New Zealand

Penguin Books Ltd, Registered Offices:
Harmondsworth, Middlesex, England

First published in 1998 by Viking Penguin,
a member of Penguin Putnam Inc.

1 3 5 7 9 10 8 6 4 2

LIBRARY OF CONGRESS CATALOGING IN PUBLICATION DATA
Boyle, T. Coraghessan.
Riven rock / T. Coraghessan Boyle.
p.   cm.
ISBN 0-670-87881-2
I. Title.
PS3552.0932R58   1998
813'.54 — dc21   97-34632

This book is printed on acid-free paper.
∞

Printed in the United States of America
Set in Cochin, Nicholas Cochin, and Bembo italic
Designed by Jaye Zimet

FOR KAREN KVASHAY

ACKNOWLEDGMENTS

The author would like to thank the following for their assistance in gathering material for this book: Armond Fields, Frank and Sheila McGinity, James Emerson, and Cindy Knight.

CONTENTS

CONTENTS

SEX IS A TALENT,
AND I DO NOT HAVE IT.

—Gabriel García Márquez,
Of Love and Other Demons

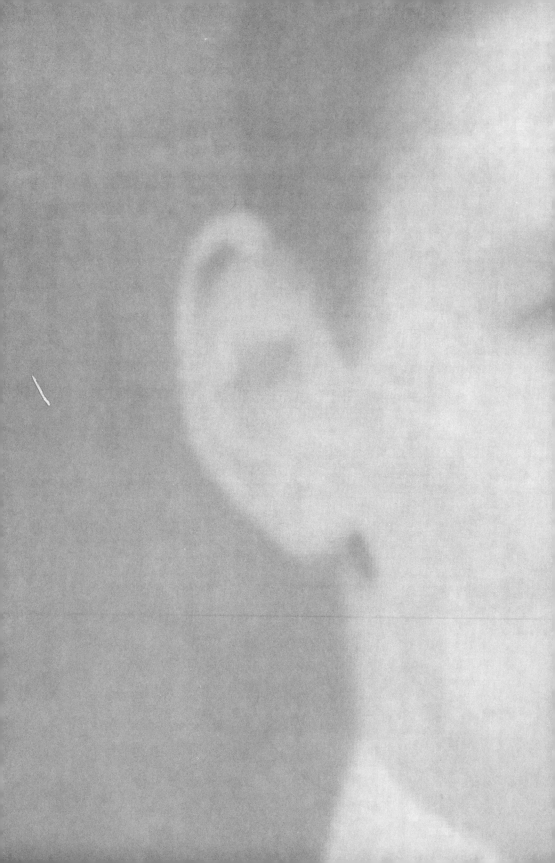

PROLOGUE

1927,

World Without Women

For twenty years, twenty long dull repetitive years that dripped by with the sleepy incessant murmur of water dripping from a gutter, Stanley McCormick never laid eyes on a woman. Not his mother, not his sisters, not his wife. No nurse or librarian, no girl in pigtails on her way to school, no spinster sweeping her porch or housewife haggling with the grocer, no slut, flapper or suffragette. It wasn't a matter of choice. Stanley loved his mother, his wife, his sisters, he loved other people's mothers, wives, sisters and daughters, but he loved them too much, loved them with an incendiary passion that was like hate, that was indistinguishable from hate, and it was that loving and hating that fomented all his troubles and thrust him headlong into a world without women.

He was twenty-nine when he married Katherine Dexter, a woman of power, beauty, wealth and prestige, a woman as combative and fierce as his mother, with heartbreaking eyes and a voice so soft and pure it was like a drug, and he was thirty-one when he first felt the cold wolf's bite of the sheet restraints and entered the solitary world of men. He went blank then. He was blocked. He saw things that weren't there, desperate, ugly things, creatures of his innermost mind that shone with a life more vivid than any life he'd ever known, and he heard voices speaking without mouths, throats or tongues, and every time he looked up it was into the face of masculinity.

The years accumulated. Stanley turned forty, then fifty. And in all that time he lived in the company of one sex and one sex only—men, with their hairy wrists and bludgeoning eyes, their nagging phlegmy voices and fetid breath and the viscid sweat that glistened in their beards and darkened their shirts under the arms. It was like joining a fraternity that never left the house, entering a monastery, marching in step with the French Foreign Legion over the vast and trackless dunes and not an oasis in sight. And how did Stanley feel about that? No one had bothered to ask. Certainly not Dr. Hamilton—or Dr. Hoch or Dr. Brush or Dr. Meyer either. But if he were to think about it, think about the strangeness and deprivation of it, even for a minute, he would feel as if a black and roiling gulf were opening inside him, as if he were being split in two like a Siamese twin cut away from its other self. He was a husband without a wife, a son without a mother, a brother without sisters.

But why? Why did it have to be like this? Because he was sick, he was very sick, he knew that. And he knew why he was sick. It was because of them, because of the bitches, because of women. They were the ones. And if he ever saw his wife again, if he saw his mother or Anita or Mary Virginia, he knew what he would do, as sure as the sun rises and the world spins on its axis. He would go right up to them, Katherine or Mary Virginia or the president's wife or any of them, and he would show them what a real man was for, and he would make them pay for it too, he would. That was how it was, and that was why he'd lived for the past nineteen years at Riven Rock, the eighty-seven-acre estate his father's money had bought him, in his stone mansion with the bars on the windows and the bed bolted to the floor, within sight of the hammered blue shield of the Pacific and the adamantine wall of the Channel Islands, in the original Paradise, the lonely Paradise, the place where no woman walked or breathed.

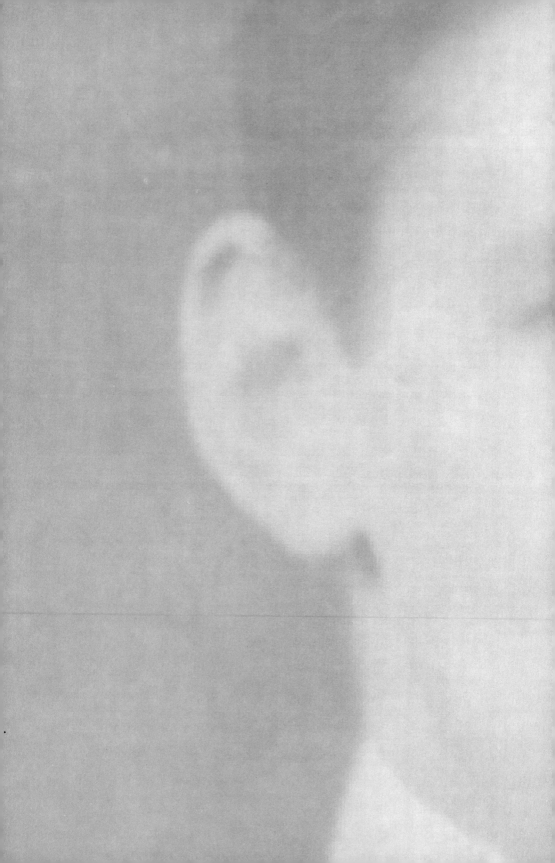

PART I

Dr. Hamilton's Time

1.

HOW HIS HAND

How his hand came into contact with her face—her sweet plump irritating little burr of a wifely face that found a place beside his each night on the connubial pillow—was as much a mystery to O'Kane as the scalloped shell of the sky and the rain that fell as one angry inveterate thing over all this weary part of the earth. It wasn't late—not ten o'clock yet. And he wasn't angry. Not yet, anyway. On the contrary, he'd been celebrating—polluting himself, as she would say, living it up, for he's a jolly good fellow and three cheers for this one and that one and rah, rah, rah—celebrating with Nick and Pat and Mart, and with Dr. Hamilton, yes, with him too. Celebrating the rest of his life that had just been turned on like an electric switch, flooding him with light, light that poured from his nostrils and ears and his mouth and no doubt his rectum too, though he hadn't yet had occasion to look down there, but he would, he would eventually. And then he had come home, and there she was, stalking the sitting room like a bristling tireless little rat-gnawing thing, all primed and ready to pounce.

He hadn't meant to hit her—and he'd hit her only once, or maybe

---

twice, before—and the thing was, he wasn't even angry, just . . . irritated. And tired. Drained to the core. The noise she made, and the baby squalling in the back room, and the way she kept thrusting her face at him as if it was a volleyball, tanned, stitched and puffed up to regulation pressure, and she wouldn't let him have this, not even this, after all the gut-wrenching and indecision it had cost him over the past two months, and when the inflated ball of her face had come at him for maybe the fiftieth time he slammed it right up and over the net, just as if he was still in school and diving for a low one on the hard foot-compacted turf of the volleyball court. That opened her up, all right, and there was no peace for him after that, she was like an artesian well, a real gusher, tears and blood and rage exploding at him, and all he could think of, dodging away from that streaming face till he was so drained and exhausted he toppled into a blackness deeper than the last dying wink of consciousness, was Mrs. McCormick—*Katherine*—and what a lady she was, and Rosaleen stuck to him like flypaper and howling till the windows went to pieces and the roof collapsed and the whole drugged and dreaming town fell away into some deep fissure of the earth.

Earlier that day, in the morning, it had been different. He'd awakened at first light and saw her there beside him, the soft petals of her eyelids and her lashes and lips and the fragile composition of her face, and he thought about kissing her, leaning over and brushing his lips against the down of her cheek, but he didn't. He didn't want to wake her—or his son either. It was too peaceful, the submarine light, the stealthy tick of the clock, the rudiments of birdnoise, and he didn't want to have to talk to her about the McCormicks and the meeting and what he feared and what he hoped—he hardly knew himself. He stripped off his flannels at the side of the bed and slipped naked into the sitting room with his good Donegal tweed over one arm and a fresh suit of underwear over the other, and dressed like a thief of clothes. Then he was out the door and into another life.

The year was 1908, and he'd just turned twenty-five. He was a hair under six feet, with the pugilist's build he'd inherited from his father (who'd put the prototype to good use in a series of mostly victorious bare-knuckle fights in the nineties), and his mother's wistful sea-green eyes with the two hazel clock hands implanted in the right one, inflexibly pointing, for this lifetime at least, to three o'clock. His mother had always told him that chronometric eye would bring him luck—great luck and fortune—and when he questioned her, skeptical even at ten and eleven, she just pointed to the proof and insisted that the hour was preordained. But what about you? he would say, lifting his eyes to the colorless walls of the four rooms they shared with his grandmother, his uncle Billy, his four sisters and three cousins, where's your three o'clock luck? And she would frame his face with her hands, the softest touch in the world, and whisper, "It's right here, right here, between my hands."

The morning flew. He'd started off at the White Street house, where they'd installed Mr. McCormick to get him away from the disturbing influence of the other patients, and then he'd gone on to McLean and now he was late, cutting across the lawn out front of the administrative building on a day that was like a wet dishrag, though it was the last week of April and he would have sacrificed to the gods to see a ray of sun—he was late and hurrying and he didn't give a damn for the fact that he'd left his hat and overcoat back in the nurses' common room and the cuffs of his good Donegal tweed trousers were soaking up the damp like a pair of fat swollen sponges tied to his ankles. He should have, because when the tailor came over from Ballyshannon and settled into the rooming house down the street from them and his mother said he should take advantage of the opportunity and have one nice suit made because if he ever hoped to work with his brains instead of his back he'd have to look like one of the quality, he'd laid out eighteen dollars for it. Eighteen dollars in good hard Yankee coin he'd earned at the Boston Lunatic Asylum scraping blood, vomit and worse off the walls. And here it was, wet through in the shoulders and crawling up his shins and sure as the devil it was going to shrink, but what did he care? It was two minutes to eleven, the hair was hanging wet in his eyes and Dr. Hamilton was waiting for him. If things worked out, he could buy six suits.

It wasn't like him to be late—it was unprofessional, and Dr. Hamilton was a stickler for the "three p's," as he called them: punctuality, propriety and professionalism—and O'Kane, already wrought up, felt like a piece of fat in the fryer as he charged across the wet lawn. He was sweating under the arms and the hair was dangling like rope in his face. It wasn't like him, but he was behind his time because he'd gotten distracted over at White Street, and then in the back ward, and all because of the apes. Apes and monkeys, that is. They were all he could think about. And it was funny too because this was the kind of day that got the violents stirred up — it wasn't just the full moon, it was any change in the weather, even from perpetual gloom to a driving downpour — and as he hurried across the lawn he could hear Katzakis the Mad Greek and the one they called the Apron Man hooting at one another from the maximum ward, hooting just like apes. Violents he knew inside and out — he ought to after seven years in the profession — but his experience with hominoids, as Dr. Hamilton called them, was limited. And why wouldn't it be? South Boston, Danvers and Waverley weren't exactly tropical jungles.

In fact, aside from the usual boyhood encounters with the organ-grinder's monkey, the sideshow at the circus, the zoo and that sort of thing, he'd only come within spitting distance of an ape once, and that was in a barroom. He'd gone into Donnelly's one afternoon for a pint and a chat, and when he looked up from his beer there was a man sitting beside him at the counter with a one-eyed chimpanzee on a leash. For a shot of rye whiskey and a beer chaser the man got the chimp to pull out his organ and piss in a beer glass and then drink it down as if it was the finest eighty-six-proof Irish — and smack his lips to boot. When the man had chased his third shot he gave a look up and down the bar and said he would challenge anybody in the place to arm-wrestle the thing for half a dollar — this scrawny half-bald one-eyed little monkey that stank like all the souls in hell boiled in their own juice and then left out in the sun for a week after that — and there was a lot of elbowing and obscene commentary from the patrons as they worked themselves up to it. Finally, Frank Leary, a big squareheaded loudmouthed bull of a man who worked for the railroad, took him up on it, and the thing pinned Leary's wrist to the bar in half a second and wouldn't let go of his hand till there were tears in his eyes.

The experience didn't exactly qualify O'Kane as a hominoid expert, as he would have been the first to admit, and he'd spent a painful hour in the library after work yesterday squinting into an encyclopedia in the vain hope of learning something — anything — that might impress Mrs. McCormick. Or, if not impress her, at least keep the level of humiliation down to a minimum if she suddenly took it into her head to grill him on the subject. The library was an alien place to O'Kane, damper than a Chinese laundry and three times as cold, the lighting hominoidally primitive and the illumination offered by the encyclopedia on the subject of apes nearly as dim. "Apes," he read, "are intelligent animals and are more closely related to man than any other living primates. They are popular zoo and circus animals. They also have figured widely in the legends and folktales of many countries." After a while he pushed himself up, replaced the book on the shelf and ambled over to Donnelly's to fix this vast reservoir of knowledge in his brain with the aid of a mnemonic whiskey or two.

And now he was late and his one good suit was crawling up his shins and he was wondering how he was going to break the staggering news to Mrs. McCormick, the Ice Queen herself, that apes were popular zoo and circus animals. But as he reached the verge of the lawn and vaulted the retaining wall there, crossed the flagstone walkway and started up the steps of the ad building, the multifarious marvel of his congested brain surprised him—the apes flew right out of his head and he was thinking about California. Or he wasn't thinking about it, not exactly—he had a vision, a sudden vivid recollection of a place there, date palms shimmering beneath the golden liquefaction of the sun and orange trees with fruit like swollen buttocks and a little bungalow or whatever they called it snug in the corner—and this was odd, more than odd, since he'd never in his life been west of Springfield. It took him a minute to realize it must have been one of those orange crate labels he was calling up, the ones that make you want to throw down the snow shovel right that minute and catch the next train west. But there it was, real or illusionary— *California*—hanging in his head in all its exotic glory where the apes had been a moment before.

And then finally, as he stepped through the big beveled-glass doors and into the dim paste-wax-and-coal-dust-smelling hall, he thought of his own Rosaleen, his sorrow and his joy, his sweet, randy, pugnacious, clover-lipped bride of three months and mother of his green-eyed boy, Edward Jr. What was she going to think when he told her they were moving to California for the sake of Mr. Stanley McCormick, late of the McCormick Reaper Works and the International Harvester Company, Mr. McCormick and a troop of apes? And what was her mother going to think and her cauliflower-eared brothers and her quibbling old stump of a father who'd wanted to skin him alive for getting her in trouble in the first place? As if it was all his fault, as if she hadn't seen her chance and taken it—and hadn't he done the right thing by her, and wasn't she at that very moment sitting snug in the walkup on Chestnut Street with her baby and her new curtains and everything else a woman could want?

He passed by Dr. Cowles's office at a stiff-legged trot, swiping at his hair and wrestling with his tie and trying to contort his shoulders to fit the sodden confines of the suit, and it was all he could do to flick a little wave at Miss Ianucci, Dr. Cowles's typewriter. Miss Ianucci was a spaghetti twister from Italy who couldn't seem to find a shirtwaist big enough to accommodate her appurtenances and who never ceased touching her lips and crossing and uncrossing her legs whenever O'Kane got a chance to stop in and chat with her—which was every time he passed by unless he was on his way to a fire. People were always grousing about the immigrants—the I-talians this and the Polacks that, the Guineas and wops and bohunks, and his father was one of the most vocal and vehement, though he'd come over himself in an empty whiskey barrel aboard a transatlantic steamer not thirty years ago —but for his money they could let in all the Miss Ianuccis they wanted. And wouldn't that be a job, standing there at the bottom of the gangplank, and passing judgment on this one or that: *Nah, send her back—she's flat as an ironing board. Her? Yeah, we'll take her. Come on over here, miss, and step into the examining room a minute won't you?* A man could create an entire race, a whole new breed based on tits alone — or hips or legs or turned-up noses and pinned-back ears. Look what they'd done with dogs. . . .

Anyway, he had to content himself with a wave this time because he knew how much this meeting meant to Dr. Hamilton—and to himself, himself and Rosaleen—and he hustled down the hall while Miss Ianucci stuck a finger in the corner of her mouth and sucked on it and crossed and uncrossed her legs and gave him the richest smile in all the world. Two doors down, three, and it was all he could do to keep from breaking into a run. He glanced up as he hurried past the portrait of John McLean, the decidedly unsmiling and bewigged philanthropist who'd given a hundred thousand dollars back in 1818 to open the doors of this fair institution, and though he was late, though he looked like hell and the smells of fear and hope were commingled in his sweat and his sweat was flowing as if it were the middle of July and he was carrying the entire McCormick family up a hill on his shoulders, apes and all, he couldn't help thinking, for just the fleetingest instant, of what he could do with a hundred thousand dollars —and it wouldn't be to endow any charitable organization, that was for sure, unless it was the Edward James O'Kane Benevolent and Fiduciary Fund. But enough of that. Suddenly he was there, at the far end of the hallway, breathing hard, three minutes past eleven, half-soaked, sweating and wild-eyed, tapping respectfully at the smooth varnished plane of Dr. Hamilton's door.

He could detect the purl of conversation from within, and his heart sank. This was what he'd been fearing since he'd slipped out of the house and into the festering gray maw of the dawn, what he was afraid of as he emptied bedpans and jerked rigid lunatics and simple morons down from the barred windows and up from the beds: she was there already. Which meant he was late. Officially. He cursed himself and tapped again, this time with a little more vigor, and felt even worse when the murmur broke off abruptly, as if he were interrupting something. There was an agonizing silence during which the wild thought that they were conspiring to leave him out of it altogether raced through his head, and then he heard Dr. Hamilton murmur, "That must be him now," and any trace of composure he might have been able to muster evaporated in that instant. "Come in," the doctor called, and O'Kane felt his face flush as he pushed open the door and entered the room.

The first thing he noticed was the fire—a lavish crackling devil-may-care blaze that played off the paneled walls and cast a soft glow on the doctor's collection of wax impressions of the human brain, the first fire O'Kane had ever seen in this particular fireplace, even in the dim frozen mists of January or February. But there it was, a fire to take the dampness out of the air and create a relaxed and cozy atmosphere, as Dr. Hamilton had no doubt calculated. It was a surprise, a real surprise, as was the tray of finger sandwiches, a teapot and the decanter of sherry set out on the low table in front of the settee, and O'Kane's estimation of Hamilton, already high, shot up another notch. "Oh, hello, Edward," the doctor purred, coming up off the edge of his desk to take O'Kane's hand and give it a squeeze. "We were just about to begin."

Anyone watching this performance would have seen nothing but good nature and cordiality in that hand-squeeze, but O'Kane felt the black blood of anxiety and irritation pulsing through the doctor's flesh-less fingers and the damp recess of his palm: O'Kane was in the wrong, he was late, he'd violated the dictum of the three p's and put everything in jeopardy. Despite all the doctor's warnings of the previous day, despite skipping breakfast and leaving the house early and wearing his tweeds and collar under the hospital whites to save time and keeping the apes hurtling through the crowded jungle of his mind, limb by limb and minute by minute, he was late. He'd gotten off on the wrong foot. Already.

Awkward, red-faced, too big for his shrinking suit and towering over the room like some club-wielding troglodyte, O'Kane could only duck his head and mumble an apology. He saw that Mrs. McCormick was already there—the younger Mrs. McCormick, the wife, not the mother. She was running the show now, and the older Mrs. McCormick, Mr. McCormick's mother, was back in Chicago, sitting on her golden nest and laying her golden eggs and counting up the dividends. As far as Stanley's—Mr. McCormick's—care was concerned, she'd left the field to the younger woman. For the moment, at least.

Since O'Kane wasn't wearing a hat or overcoat, it was just a matter of giving his tie a quick twist and bending from the waist to greet Mrs. McCormick and the woman who seemed at that instant to have sprung up beside her on the settee. He was momentarily confused. It seemed he was always confused in Mrs. McCormick's presence, whether he was holding the door for her like a lackey as she stepped regally into the front hall at White Street or trying his aphasic best to respond to one of her multitiered questions about her husband's progress—or lack of it. She was a society lady, that's what she was, cold as a walking corpse, all fur, feathers and stone, and O'Kane wasn't part of society. Not by a long shot. He wasn't even part of the society that aspired to be part of society. He was a working man, son of a working man, grandson of a working man, and on and on all the way back to the apes—or Adam and Eve, whichever you believed in. Still, every time he saw her, locked in the cold hard glittering shell of her Back Bay beauty, it made him ache to be something he wasn't, to impress her or make her laugh or lean in close and whisper something filthy in her ear, and it took a tremendous effort of will simply to bend forward and touch his fingertips to her gloved hand and then turn to the older woman beside her, a woman with a face like a squashed bird framed in the riot of feathers that was her hat, a woman he knew as well as his own mother but couldn't . . . quite . . . seem to—

But then he was seated—in the chair closest to the fire—an inoffensive smile attached to his face, the sweat already starting up again under his arms, and he had a moment to catch his breath and let recollection come roaring back at him. This older lady, the one dressed like a funeral director's wife, was Mrs. McCormick's mother, Mrs. Dexter. Of course she was. Dr. Hamilton was saying something now, but O'Kane wasn't listening. He worked his neck muscles and twitched his shoulders till he caught Mrs. Dexter's attention and broadened his smile to a kind of blissful grimace. "And a good morning to you, Mrs. Dexter," he said, hearing his father's Killarney brogue creeping into his own booming, baleful voice, though he tried to fight it down.

Dr. Hamilton paused in the middle of whatever he'd been saying to give him an odd look. "And to you, Mr. O'Kane," the old lady returned cheerily, and this seemed to reassure the doctor, so he went on.

"As I was saying, Mrs. McCormick, if the terms are acceptable to you—and your mother, of course—I think we have a bargain. I've spoken to Mrs. Hamilton and to the Thompson brothers, and they're all committed to the move—and to Mr. McCormick's care and welfare, of course. Edward, here, can speak for himself."

O'Kane shifted in his seat. He hadn't understood till that moment just how much this whole thing meant to him—it was a new start, a new life, in a part of the country as foreign to him as the dark side of the moon. But that was just it—it wasn't dark in California, and it didn't snow, and there was no slush and drizzle and there were no frozen clods of horse manure in the streets and life there didn't grind you down till you barely knew you were alive. A single acre of oranges could make a man comfortable— oranges that practically grew by themselves, without even the rumor of work, once they were in the ground—and ten acres could make a man rich. There was gold. There was oil. There was the Pacific. There was sun. "Oh, I'm committed, all right," he said, trying to avoid the wife's eyes.

How old was she, anyway? She couldn't have been much more than thirty, and here he was, a lusty strong big-shouldered hundred-and-ninety-pound Irishman from the North End who routinely stared down the craziest of the crazy, and he was afraid to look her in the eye? He made an effort and raised his head to take in the general vicinity of her. "Even if it means forever."

"And your wife—Mrs. O'Kane?" At first he thought the voice had come out of the ceiling, as voices tended to do for so many of the unfortunates on the ward, but then he realized that the old lady was moving her lips. He tried to look alert as the birdy face closed on him. "How does she feel about it?"

"Rose?" The question took him by surprise. He saw his wife in the kitchen of the walkup, stirring a pot of broth and potatoes, ignorant as a shoe, contentious and coarse and loud—but goodhearted, as good-hearted as any girl you'd find, and the mother of his son. "I—I guess I haven't told her yet, but she'll be thrilled, I know she will."

"It'll mean leaving behind everything she knows—her parents, her relations, her former schoolmates, the streets where she grew up," Mrs. Dexter persisted, and what did she want from him anyway? They were both watching him, mother and daughter, and they were two birds—both of them—beaky and watchful, waiting for the faintest stirring in the grass. "And where did you say she was from?"

He hadn't said. He was tempted to say Beacon Hill, to give an address on Commonwealth Avenue, but he didn't. "Charlestown," he mumbled, staring down at his wet and glistening shoes. He could feel the eyes of the younger one boring into him.

"And for you too," the old woman said. "Are you prepared to say good-bye to your own mother and father—and for as long as it takes for Mr. McCormick to be well again?"

There was a silence. The fire snapped, and he felt the heat of it chasing the steam from his cuffs and flanks and the shrinking shoulders of his jacket. "Yes, ma'am," he said, darting a glance at the younger woman. "I think so. I really do."

And then, thankfully, Hamilton took over. "The important thing," he said, or rather, whispered in the narcotic tones he used on his charges, "is Mr. McCormick. The sooner we're able to move the patient and establish him in the proper way in California, the better it will be for all concerned. Especially the patient. What he needs, above all, is a tranquil environment, with all the stresses that led to his blocking removed. Only then can we hope to—" He faltered. Mrs. McCormick had cleared her throat—that was all: cleared her throat—and that stopped him cold.

Dr. Hamilton—Dr. Gilbert Van Tassel Hamilton, future author of *Sex in Marriage*, as well as "A Study of Sexual Tendencies in Monkeys and Baboons"—was a young man then, just thirty-one, but he cultivated a Vandyke and swept his dun-colored hair straight back from his brow in an attempt to add something to his years. He wore a pair of steel-rimmed pince nez identical to the president's, and he always dressed carefully in ash-colored suits and waistcoats and a tie that was such an unfathomable shade of blue it might as well have been black, as if any show of color would undermine his sense of duty and high purpose. ("Avoid bright clothing," he'd admonished O'Kane on the day he hired him; "it tends to excite the catatonics and alarm the paranoics.") Young as he was, he was a rock of solidity, but for one disconcerting little tic that he himself might not have been aware of: every thirty seconds or so his eyes would flick back behind his upper lids in a spasm so instantaneous it was like watching a slot machine on its final revolution. Needless to say, when he was nervous or wrought up the tic became more pronounced. Now, as he looked expectantly at Mrs. McCormick, his pupils began a quavering preliminary little dance.

O'Kane was looking at her too. He couldn't help but look at her, as long as it didn't involve eye contact. She was fascinating to him, a real specimen, the kind of woman you saw only in glimpses—a silhouette behind the windowscreen of the long thrusting miracle of a Packard motorcar, a brisk commanding figure in a cluster of doormen and porters, the face of a photograph in a book—and how could he help contrasting her with his own Rosaleen? Sitting there perched on the very fractional edge of the settee with her finishing-school posture and her cleft chin stuck up in the air like a weathervane, wearing a dress of some satiny blue material that probably cost more than he would make in six months, she was like an alien, like the shining representative of some new and superior species, but for one thing: her husband was mad, as mad as the Apron Man or Katzakis the Greek or any of them, and all the manners and all the money in the world couldn't change that.

"About the apes . . . ," she said, and O'Kane realized it was the first time she'd opened her mouth since he'd entered the room.

Hamilton's voice fell away to nothing, the whisper of a whisper. "Yes?" he breathed, lounging back against the corner of the desk and resting his weight casually on his left ham, the doctor in his office, nothing the matter, nothing at all. "What about them? If there's anything that you—"

"They are necessary, aren't they—in your estimation, Dr. Hamilton? I understand that in order to lure such a promising young psychologist as yourself all the way out to the West Coast and uproot your family and your practice here at McLean, there has to be a quid pro quo"—and here she held up a finger to silence him, because he was up off the desk again and his mouth was already working in the nest of his beard—"and that your hominoid laboratory is a major part of it, in addition to your salary considerations, relocation expenses and the like, but is there really any hope of these *apes* figuring in Stanley's cure?"

This was Hamilton's cue, and with barely a flick of his eyes, he launched into a speech that would have done a drummer proud. He made no promises—her husband's case was more complex than anyone had originally believed, far more complex—but he'd personally supervised dozens of cases just as severe and he'd seen those patients make huge steps toward recovery, even complete recovery, with the proper care. New advances were being made not only in the treatment of dementia praecox—or schizophrenia, as it was now more commonly called—but across the whole spectrum of human behavior and psychology, and new figures like Freud, Jung and Adler had begun to emerge to build on the work of Charcot, Krafft-Ebing, Havelock Ellis and Magnus Hirschfeld. O'Kane had heard it all before, and he found himself drifting, the heat making him drowsy, the heavy material of his trousers adhering to his flanks like a second skin—and itching, itching like the very devil. Hamilton's voice droned on, hypnotic, soporific, the gloom beyond the windows like the backdrop of a waking dream. He came back to himself when the doctor finally got round to the question of the apes.

"—and while the behavioral sciences *are* in their infancy," Hamilton was saying, "and ours will be among the first hominoid laboratories in the world, Katherine" (*Katherine*, he was calling her *Katherine* now), "I really and truly do expect that my intensive study of the lower primates will lead to any number of breakthroughs in human behavior, particularly with regard to sexual tendencies."

Ah, and now it was out of the bag, O'Kane thought, the crux of the matter, the subject you don't discuss in mixed company, the thing men and women discover together in the dark. He watched the wife's perfectly composed face, with its stingy lips and little turned-up nose and sculpted ears, for a reaction. There was nothing. Not a flicker. She was a scientist herself—the first female baccalaureate in the sciences from the Massachusetts Institute of Technology—and no quirk of the human organism could ruffle her. She was made of ice. Layers of it, mountains—she was a glacier in human form, an Ice Queen, that's what she was.

"Yes, I understand," she said, pursing her lips and shooting a look at O'Kane that wilted him on the spot, as if he were the one who'd brought up the subject, "but apes are one thing and human beings quite another. I really don't see how any discovery you make as to the"—and here she paused, for just a beat—"sexual proclivities of apes and monkeys can be applied to my husband's case. I just fail to see it."

This was a critical juncture, and O'Kane, impelled by the heat of the fire, the closeness of the room and the sudden fear that the whole thing—orange trees, bungalow and all—was about to collapse like a house of cards, suddenly plunged in with a speech of his own. "But we'll take the best care of him, ma'am, I and the Thompson brothers and Dr. Hamilton and Dr. Meyer too. He asks for us specially, you know, and we feel a real . . . a real compassion for him that we don't always feel with the other patients . . . he's such a gentleman, I mean, and bound to improve. And I admit I don't know the first thing about apes—hominoids, that is—but I'm young and willing and I can learn, I can. You'll see."

There was a silence. Mrs. McCormick—*Katherine*—looked startled, as if the chair or the hat rack had suddenly begun to speak, but the old lady seemed satisfied—she had a sort of fixed benevolent old lady's smile pasted to her lips—and Dr. Hamilton, his eyes jumping, paused only to stroke his beard for effect before coming in with the heavy artillery. 'That's right, Edward: it will be a learning process for all of us, and for the sciences in general, and beyond the good we'll do for Mr. McCormick, we have an excellent chance of doing something good and valuable for all of humankind, and, what's more"—spreading his hands wide with the flourish of an old character actor—"for every poor unfortunate sufferer like your husband, Katherine." His eyes held steady. He was slowing down, decelerating his delivery till every word could have been a paragraph in itself: "And for every wife that suffers with him."

The doctor's words hung there a moment, the rain beating at the windows, the wax impressions—corpus callosum, medulla oblongata, pineal gland—glowing as if they'd come to life. Very faintly, so faintly O'Kane couldn't be sure he'd actually heard it, came the anguished cry of the Apron Man echoing across the rain-slick grounds. And then suddenly, without warning, Mrs. McCormick, Katherine, the Ice Queen, was weeping. It began with a sharp insuck of breath, as if someone had pricked her with a pin, and then the ice melted and in the next moment she was sobbing her heart out.

She tried to hide her face beneath the brim of her hat as she bent to fumble through her purse for a handkerchief, but O'Kane saw that face naked and transformed, crumpled like a flower, and he saw the pain blossom in those rich insulated eyes. It was a revelation to him: she was human, after all, and more than that, she was female, intensely female, and never more female than in that moment. Her shoulders shook, her breath came in gasps, and even as her mother reached out to comfort her, O'Kane felt something give inside him. He wanted to get up and take charge, wanted to touch her, take her by the hand, but all he could do, roasting in the chair as the flames snapped and the sobs caught in her throat and the doctor wrung his hands, was murmur, "There, there," over and over, like an idiot.

And then she looked up, the fire catching the sheen of her eyes and illuminating her wet face till it glowed like the face of some tortured saint amongst the cannibals. When she spoke, after a long, rending moment, her voice was soft and small, so small you could barely hear it. "And you meant to stick by your injunction then?"

This caught Hamilton by surprise. He groped behind him for the edge of the desk, sat himself down for half an instant and jumped up again as if it had been electrified. "What injunction? What do you mean?"

In the tiniest, most miserable voice: "No visitors."

Hamilton drew himself up and let out such a deep rattling sorrowful breath it sounded as if he'd turned his lungs inside out. His eyes jumped and jumped again. "I'm sorry," he said.

"Not even his wife?"

But the doctor was already swiveling his head back and forth on his shoulders like a human metronome, and O'Kane, welded to the chair in awestruck silence, could see where he was beginning to develop the jowls that would be his badge of high seriousness in the future. The man was a master negotiator, and he knew when to give and when to stand firm. "Not even his wife," he said.

•   •   •

Long after Hamilton had disappeared and Nick and Pat Thompson begged off on the grounds of marital concord, O'Kane sat over his beer and a plate of cold baked beans, hard-boiled eggs, salt herring and crackers with Martin, the third and youngest of the Thompson brothers. It was past nine o'clock and the barroom was raging with light and noise against the cold rain and lifeless streets beyond. O'Kane picked up an egg, feeling half-boiled himself, what with the sainted whiskey and the good cleansing Boston brew percolating through his veins, and he began to peel it as if it were the very precious and frangible skull of an infant—or a monkey. Mart, though his eyes were glazed and his hair sticking straight up from his parting like the ruff of a grouse, watched with a kind of rapt fascination, as if he'd never seen anything like it before. He was big-headed and big-shouldered, like his brothers, but he was young yet—just twenty—and from the ribcage down he faded away to nothing. O'Kane carefully arranged the fragments of eggshell on the bare wood of the table, one at a time, then bit the denuded egg in two and washed it down with a swig of beer.

"Guess I ought to be going," Mart sighed. "If I'm ever going to get up for work tomorrow."

O'Kane said, "Yeah, I know what you mean," but it was a matter of form. He didn't feel like leaving, not yet. He felt like . . . finishing his egg, to get something on his stomach, and then having another beer. No more whiskey, though: he'd had enough. That much he understood.

Rosaleen would be expecting him. Or no: she'd been expecting him for three hours and more now, and she would be laying for him like an assassin, furious, burnished to a white-hot cutting edge, her voice gone off into another, higher, shriller register, the accusatory register, the vituperative and guilt-making register. She would call him a drunk, a social climber, a puppet of the McCormicks, and she would mock his tweeds and howl anathema to California.

"One more?" O'Kane said.

Someone at the bar behind him—he didn't bother to turn round and see who—shouted out, "You damned fool, if I'd've known you were going to salt the damn thing instead of smoking it or even jerking it, for crying out loud, I would've give the whole damn carcass to the orphanage."

Mart seemed to take an unnaturally long time in answering. His eyes were small and seemed even smaller in proportion to that outsized head, and as O'Kane gazed hopefully into them, already picturing the yellow sizzle of a final tasteless and dilatory beer, they were no more than distant grayish specks, planetary bodies faintly revealed in the universe of that big numb face, and receding fast. Mart shrugged. Reached down to scratch his calf. "I don't see why not," he said finally, and his enunciation could have been clearer, a whole lot clearer. "Okay," he said. "Sure. One more."

These were the dregs of their celebratory party: the half-filled glasses, the cold beans and herring, the shouts and smells of the crapulous strangers hemming them in on every side, the dead rinsed-out April night and the rain drooling down the windows—and above all, the lingering boozy glimmer of the golden fraternity of California. They would be leaving in two weeks by special car—a car called the *Mayflower*, customized by the Pullman Company with locks on the doors and restraints on the windows, and was O'Kane the only one who saw the pure and lucent beauty of that resonant name? It was an omen, that's what it was. They were pilgrims, leaving Plymouth Rock and North Boston and Waverley behind for the paradise in the west, for the hibiscus, the jasmine, the tangerines and oranges and the dates that rained down from the palms like a reward just for being alive.

They'd never have to buy another scuttle of coal for as long as they lived. And overcoats—they could throw away their overcoats and the moth-eaten mufflers and mittens that went with them. And if that wasn't enough, their McLean salaries were to be doubled the minute they stepped aboard that train with Mr. McCormick. That would mean forty dollars a week for O'Kane, and he just hoped the grapefruit ranchers, cowboys, oil barons, hidalgos and señoritas of Santa Barbara would leave him something to spend it on. If he let himself drift a minute he could feel that forty dollars in his pocket already, two tens and a twenty, or maybe four tens or eight fives. Forty slips of green-backed paper, a whole groaning sack of silver coins. He felt like he'd won the lottery.

But then he thought of Rosaleen again—saw her as vividly as if she were standing there before him, gouging him with her eyes, her jaws clamped in rage and resentment, going to fat at nineteen and always demanding more, more, more from him, as if he were the original cornucopia—or one of the McCormicks himself. She was the kind to kick up a fuss when he went out after work, even if it was only for a glass or two, even if it was only on a Saturday, because she was like a child, like an infant, always afraid of missing out on something—but give her a taste of it and she drank like a brewer's horse. Sure. And there was no way in the world she was going to leave her own mum and da and her saintly brothers and traipse halfway around the globe with the likes of him and he must be as crazy as his idiots and morons to think she'd so much as budge because good Christ in heaven Waverley was enough of a trial as it was. That's what she'd told him, time and again, *California*, and she spat all four syllables in his face like the stones of some sour inedible fruit, *I'd as soon go to hell and back.*

Something clenched in his stomach, his holy whiskey burning away down there in a sea of beer and immolating the hard white albumen of the egg as if it were paper put to fire, and he wondered briefly if he was going to be sick. He fought it down, swiveled round in his seat and shouted "Waiter!" in the direction of the bar, but with no one specific in mind. The mob there was just a blur, nothing more. "Waiter! Two more over here!"

Dr. Hamilton had bought the first two rounds, like a sport, like a creature of flesh and blood and a friend of the working man, and it must have been five-thirty or six at the time, still light beyond the windows, though with the rain and gloom you could hardly distinguish day from night. O'Kane would never have described the doctor as a convivial man, or even a cheerful one—he was too much the worrier, the stickler for detail, too much the scientist—but tonight he was nothing short of giddy, for him at least, offering up a crusty joke or two and making a toast to "the healing sun and gentle zephyrs of California." He was flushed to the roots of his beard with pride and pleasure—he was was going to have his apes and California too, and he was going to be known from here on out as personal psychiatrist to Stanley Robert Mc-Cormick, of *the* Chicago McCormicks. Of course, he would be overseen by one of the most exacting men in the field, Dr. Adolph Meyer, but Dr. Meyer was going to be three thousand miles away in his warren at the Pathological Institute of New York—a very long three thousand miles.

They all stood to shake hands with the doctor when he left (after an hour or so, during which he'd sipped at a single stale beer like somebody's maiden aunt out celebrating a third-place citation at the flower show), and everybody felt fine. And then Nick bought a round of whiskies, and O'Kane found himself narrating the events of the morning's meeting for the table at large. The Thompsons were hungry for the details—this concerned their lives and careers too, and the lives of their families—and they leaned in to crowd the space of the little table with their massed heads and lumpen arms and the crude architecture of their shoulders. They hadn't been invited to the meeting and O'Kane had, because O'Kane was head nurse and Dr. Hamilton's right-hand man and they weren't, even though both Nick and Pat were older than he and had more years in at McLean. Neither seemed resentful—or at least they didn't show it—but still O'Kane felt compelled to give them the fullest accounting he could, with dramatic shadings and embellishments, of course. He was Irish and he loved an audience.

He told them how he'd worked himself into a sweat just trying to get there on time, nervous and unsure of himself, how he'd charged across the wet lawn with the Greek and the Apron Man hooting at his back and dashed by Miss Ianucci's desk without stopping—and he gave them a moment to consider the picture of Miss Ianucci sitting there with her mobile legs and the spill of her uncorseted front in that taut shirtwaist—and then he was describing Mrs. McCormick and what she was wearing and how the old lady, Mrs. Dexter, had grilled him. All that was fine, all that he enjoyed. But when he came to the part about Mrs. McCormick's—Katherine's—breaking down, he couldn't do justice do it, couldn't even begin to. "She was like a child," he said, trying to shape the scene with his hands, "a little lost child. She broke down and cried right there in Hamilton's office, and there was nothing her mother or anybody else could do. It was so . . . I felt like crying myself."

"Yeah, sure," Nick said. He spoke in a measured growl, like a chained dog, the smoke of the cigarette squinting his eyes till they were no more than slashes in the blank wall of his face. "And I guess that's supposed to prove she's human then, just like us peasants."

Pat sniggered. Mart's eyes flitted round the table. There was a crash in the vicinity of the bar, followed by a curse and a thin spatter of applause. Nick just sat there, huge and squinting, watching O'Kane.

All of a sudden O'Kane felt the anger coming up in him—what did they know, they hadn't been there, none of them—and before he could stop to think he was defending her, the Ice Queen herself. "You can be as hard-nosed as you want about it, Nick, and I felt the same way myself, I did—until this morning. And you know what made her break down? It was Dr. Hamilton. 'No visitors,' he said, 'not even his wife,' and that's what got to her. She loves her husband, no matter how crazy he is, and she wants to be with him—it's as simple as that. And I don't care what you say."

They were quiet a moment, pulling at their cigarettes and solemnly rearranging the glasses on the table, all three watching him out of identical eyes. Then Pat, reflectively: "They say she's in it for the money. Her husband committed, and all those McCormick millions just there for the taking."

"And she's legally entitled to it." Nick was massaging the stub of his cigarette in the ashtray. His head floated up like a balloon, bobbing over the table on the taut cord of his neck. "So long as the McCormicks don't buy her off or get the marriage annulled. She's his wife, and that's the long and short of it. But all that aside—and I think Eddie's gone sweet on her, is that it, huh, Eddie?" He leaned back, folded his arms across his chest and gave his brothers a leer. "Who's going to give Rosaleen the bad news—you, Pattie? How about you, Mart?"

They all three guffawed and slapped the table and dug their fingers in their ears, while O'Kane put on a sheepish grin and ducked his head, all part of the ritual. But he was raging inside: they didn't understand, they weren't there, they didn't *see* her.

"But as I was saying," Nick went on, and the smoke and alcohol had roughened his voice till it wasn't much more than a croak, "all that aside, Dr. Hamilton was right, absolutely and unconditionally—you can't let Mr. McCormick have any visitors, and *especially* not the wife. Or the mother or sister either—or any woman, for that matter. Not after what he did to that little nurse from Rhode Island, what was her name—Florabelle? Christabel? Something like that"

"Arabella," O'Kane said. "Arabella Doane."

Nick just shook his head, and no one was laughing now. They looked down the long tunnels of their beers, stretched their legs under the table, stared vacantly round the room as if seeing it for the first time. Mart suppressed a belch, patting his lips gently with the back of his hand. "That was a crime," Nick said finally, "a real crime. And frankly, it makes me wonder what I'm doing going all the way out to California for a man like that."

O'Kane had nothing to say to this. He was thinking about Arabella Doane. She was a shadow in a back corner of his mind, a cat you pick up to stroke and then put down again when it stops purring. He remembered her hair—amazing hair, the exact color of ripe peaches—

and the locket she wore with a miniature of Florence Nightingale, the Lady of the Lamp, inside. O'Kane knew about that locket because he'd played with it where it dangled between her breasts, and he knew the acid-sweet taste of her mouth like an apple split in two, and the strange wild scent of her when she was aroused. That was before Mr. Stanley McCormick got to her—and how he managed it was a mystery to all of them. But he got to her, all right, and if it wasn't for the fact that she broke away long enough to scream there would have been hell to pay, real hell, the kind that involved the police and maybe even the mortician. . . . Now she was back in Rhode Island, with her mother, but the look of her that day, the way her eyes had melted away to nothing and the color had gone out of her so you could see every lash and hair on her head like brushstrokes in oil, came to him in infinite sadness.

Up at the bar, two drunks in working clothes had begun to harmonize on a doleful faltering version of "In the Sweet By and By," their heads down low to the polished mahogany counter, and O'Kane felt so depressed in that moment it was as if a mountain had collapsed on him. He was making a mistake, he was sure of it, the whole thing was wrong, absolutely and irreparably, and California was no dream but a nightmare, a sandpit, a trap. A man like that. Arabella Doane, Katherine Dexter McCormick. *In the sweet by and by*, the drunks sang, joined now by a chorus of ragged whiskey-choked voices that mocked the promise of the refrain, *We shall meet on that beautiful shore.*

But then Pat gave his brother a shove and said, "The man's disturbed, Nick—you can't blame him for that. He needs help, is all, like the rest of them."

"That's right," O'Kane heard himself saying, and the moment had passed. What had happened to Arabella Doane was regrettable— horrible, unconscionable—but they were on a mission now, and the mission was called Mr. Stanley McCormick. He was going to get well— they were going to make him well—and when he was well he was going to reward them and then they'd have their orange groves and their bungalows and all the rest. That was it, that was what it was all about.

Suddenly, and maybe it was the whiskey—sure it was, of course it was—he found himself in the grip of a strange pounding exhilaration that was like a rocket going off inside him, and he could barely contain himself. He wanted to get up and dance, lead a parade, roll over Niagara Falls in a barrel. "Come on," he said, "cheer up, Nick. This is supposed to be a celebration, isn't it?" And in the next moment, the blood pounding in his ears from the rapid ascent, he was on his feet and roaring, "Who'll drink with me?" and the Thompsons were rising from their chairs like statues come to life and they were all banging their mugs together in a percussion of joy. "To California!" he shouted, and his voice leapt an octave to drown out the funereal maunderings of the drunks at the bar. "To California!"

But now it was just O'Kane, Mart and the herring. The vocalists were long gone, and Nick and Pat and Dr. Hamilton too. The crackers were stale, the eggs like wood pulp. And here was the last beer, served up on a wet cork tray, just like the first one. He lifted it to his lips, but it didn't smell right—it smelled like vinegar, like must, like the warm yellow fluid in the chimp's glass—and he set it down untasted before pushing himself up from the table, bidding farewell to the ghost of Mart's fading eyes and making his way to the door, where somebody conveniently shoved his hat and overcoat into his face. And then he was on the street, five blocks from home, and the wind picked up the rain and poured it down his collar.

It wasn't so late—9:30 by his watch—but no one was out, not even the last lonely man in town, and the streets were silent but for the incessant hiss of the rain. The storefronts were a wall of nothing, holes punched in the night, and the trees clawed at the dim globes of the streetlights. His head ached. The suit grabbed at him under the arms, and the cuffs of his trousers were already wet through again, and he could barely drag his feet for the weight of them. At the first corner he stopped to turn his face to the sky and smell the night, but there was nothing to smell except the wet cobbles and the cold, if the cold has a smell. He stood there a long moment, solitary in the dark, until he was sure his collar was ruined and his suit shrunk beyond repair, and then he turned and headed home to his wife.

2.

E V E

The first woman Stanley McCormick ever saw — really saw, in the way
that Adam saw Eve — was his sister, Mary Virginia. Stanley was nine at
the time, a skinny, precocious, secretive boy with skittish eyes and a
burrowing instinct. He used to like to get underneath things — beds, set-
tees, ramparts he would construct of pillows in the drawing room or
folding chairs in the lofty cavern of the ballroom. These were his secret
places, his lairs and hideouts, where he could evade his brother Harold,
dodge the piano teacher and elude the governess, his sisters and
whichever starchy long-nosed missionary-of-the-day had been invited
to breakfast, tea or supper. But most of all, when he was hidden and secure, a bag of hard candy to hand, an adventure by Jules Verne or
James Fenimore Cooper propped up on his chest and the lamp softly
glowing, he could escape his mother. She was the one, the one whose
love could pulverize rock and draw all the planets out of their orbits to
come crashing down and obliterate him in his bed, she was the one he
most wanted to escape — and most wanted to be with.

It was May of 1884, just after his father died. The house was in mourning—the city of Chicago was in mourning, the nation, the whole vast roofless world—and Stanley didn't know what to do with himself. No one had ever died before, not in his experience, and what upset him more than the death itself was that he didn't know what was expected of him, other than to look sorrowful. Should he beat his breast, throw himself down the stairs, carry on like Mary Virginia? People patted him on the head, bent down to whisper things in his ear and peer into his startled eyes. Did they expect him to cry, was that it? Or was he supposed to bear up like a man?

His mother was no help. She never stopped moving, not even to sit down, her face battered with grief till it looked like a piece of luggage dragged from port to port, and everywhere she went she was exiled from him—from *him*, Stanley, her last and youngest child, her baby— by a phalanx of mourners. He wanted to be earnest, wanted to be good, wanted to grieve properly, acquit himself well, please her, but whenever he looked up for approval, all he saw was hair and ears and the backs of heads. The heads converged on her, supported on shoulders like moving walls, there was a sudden blossoming of black armbands, and at the level of his eyes he could see nothing but hands that vanished and reappeared like some conjurer's trick, big-knuckled veiny hands glittering with jewelry and clutching the drinks and sandwiches the servants scurried to provide through the din of grieving. He was there, startled, in kneepants and a collar that was too tight, trying to avoid the crash. He'd never realized death could be so loud.

And it got louder. Telegrams arrived nonstop, newspapers ran headlines and front-page eulogies. The employees of the McCormick Reaper Works sent over a replica of the reaper composed of five thousand flawless gardenias, with the main wheel symbolically broken, and four hundred workers shuffled in a solemn double line past the catafalque. Presidents, premiers, sultans, grand viziers, emperors and beglerbegs sent their condolences. Cyrus Hall McCormick, inventor of the reaper, multimillionaire, recipient of the Cross of the French Legion of Honor, cranky, old, bullheaded, unloving, rheumatic, wheezy and tyrannical, was dead at seventy-five. Dead, and lying there in the drawing room in his coffin, as pale as a toad preserved in a jar of formaldehyde.

When it came time to pay his last respects, Stanley was led into the drawing room by his big brother, Cyrus Jr. Cyrus Jr. was then a bearded

young man of twenty-five who suddenly found himself in control of a
business that grossed seventy-five million dollars a year and whom
everybody said looked just like Papa. Stanley couldn't see the resemblance. His father was an old man, the oldest person of either sex he'd
ever seen, sixty-five when Stanley was born, seventy by the time Stanley began to understand who he was, and finally, in the end, a fleshless,
soulless artifact as ancient and unfathomable as a fossilized dinosaur
egg. Stanley liked dinosaurs—he liked to dream about the rending teeth
of the big carnivorous ones and the armor they all wore to protect
themselves, even the slowest and smallest—but he didn't like his father.
Or hadn't liked him.

And as he approached the coffin, Cyrus's hand huge and soft in the
feeble grip of his own and burning like a furnace, like a steam engine,
like molten rock, he felt nothing but guilt. Not sorrow, not loss, but
guilt. People looked at him and saw a grieving son, but what they didn't
know was that when his mother had convened the family nightly to
pray for his father's recovery, Stanley had bowed his head and pleaded
with God to take the old Reaper King away forever. And God had listened, because Stanley didn't love his progenitor and provider the way
a son should—he feared him, feared and loathed him and shrank away
from his booming wheeze and his twisted shellacked hands and the
smell of something gone dead and rotten that seeped like poison from
his flaring old hair-choked nostrils. It was a terrible thing not to love
your father, a sin that reverberated through all the chasms of hell and
howled in the very ears of the Devil himself. Stanley was a patricide, an
ingrate, a worm. And he was only nine years old.

But there it was, the casket, huge, big as a boat and polished till you
could see your face in it, and not just in the brass or gold or whatever it
was, but in the wood too. It was elevated on a dais in the center of that
familiar room with its old French furniture and wainscoted walls and
the vaulted ceiling painted to mimic a summer sky replete with cottony
clouds and birds on the wing, and that made it seem even bigger. This
was the ship that would take the Reaper King on his final voyage, down
to a place where it was always dark and wet and where the insects
would burrow into his flesh and lay their eggs to hatch . . . and then to
heaven, because Stanley's father was a good man who'd served humanity and God too and fed the multitudes, just as Christ had—Stanley
knew that and would never deny it. He knew it because his mother had

told him so. Told him again and again till he'd grown up with a whole litany of his father's goodness to hold up against the living picture of the crabbed bitter old immitigable figure sunk into the wheelchair in the upper hallway.

Stanley's legs were leaden, his feet stuck to the floor. There must have been two hundred people there, friends, relatives, strangers, packed in shoulder-to-shoulder, and he couldn't look into their faces, couldn't even lift his head. He watched his feet, studying the sheen of his high-button shoes as they stuck and pulled free of the carpet, stuck and pulled free, step by step, closer and closer. The drinks and sandwiches were gone now, but the whole house smelled of them still, and this room especially. It smelled like a kitchen, reeking of canapés, smoked sausage, fish eggs and something else, something indefinable—perfume, he guessed it was. But not the sort of perfume ladies wore—something deeper, harsher, more intense and astringent. He was thinking about that, about what kind of perfume that might be and how the undertaker and his silent gliding palm-rubbing assistants just might happen to know, when all at once Cyrus Jr. squeezed his hand, a sudden violent pressure, and Stanley looked up to see the bright stony rail of the casket right there in front of him and his dead father's nose projecting above it like some etiolated mushroom springing up out of the ground after a storm. He felt dizzy, as if he'd been etherized, and his legs almost failed him—they didn't seem to have any bone left in them, weren't even attached to his hips anymore—and then his mother was there, rising up from beside the coffin to wrap him in her arms.

She'd been kneeling in the shadows like some sort of supplicant, like the maharajah's widow who throws herself on the funeral pyre, and he saw that his sister Anita was there too, eighteen and bereft, her wide baleful face like a picked-over field, and Missy Hammond, the governess, with the swollen hump of her disfigurement and the little red-flecked clots of her eyes staring up at him in misery. And Harold—Harold was kneeling beside them, his shoulders bunched and his hands clasped before him, Harold, his confidant and playmate, only two years older than Stanley and a virtuoso of sinuosity who only wanted to throw a ball and tackle and be tackled till he was indistinguishable from the sod itself, and here he was transformed into a professional mourner, as hollow and cringing as one of the undertaker's assistants. It was a shock: Harold had loved their father, really loved him, and Stanley hadn't. The shame burned into him, and he buried his face in his mother's dress.

And then, somehow, he found himself up on the dais with his mother, staring down at the unhinged face of his dreams. There he was, his father, monstrous in death, as big as any giant or ogre, stretched out on his back as if he were sleeping, his eyes closed, his beard thrust up in a gray spume that shrouded his throat and chin and the new tie they were going to bury him in . . . but he wasn't sleeping, he was dead, and there was a rigidity to his fresh-shaven cheeks and a depth to the pits and trenches beneath his eyes that all the mortician's powder in the world couldn't conceal. Stanley tried his best to look sad, aggrieved, troubled and heartsore, his mother right there beside him, clergymen fluttering on the periphery like a flock of crows, aunts, uncles and per-fect strangers mewling and weeping and dabbing at their eyes, but he only managed to look the way he felt: scared. He wanted to bolt, break away from his mother and all her insuperable power to hold him there, and run before they saw the truth in his eyes, before the rotting stiff perfumed corpse of his father lurched upright in the casket and roared out his perfidy. And he might have, he might have broken for the door and shamed them all, if it wasn't for Mary Virginia.

All this time she'd been waiting in the wings, weeping and gnashing her teeth, a prisoner of grief, but now, finally, her moment had come. Stanley wasn't aware of it. He was only aware of himself, slouching on the dais with all those people looking at him and wanting only to run, hide, burrow, hating his mother for holding him there and the mourners for invading his house and his father for dying and for having been alive in the first place. He was vaguely aware that someone was missing, someone vital, but he wasn't thinking and he didn't care and he only wanted to die himself, die on the spot and get it over with—until he heard his sister's first shattering cry. Everything changed in that mo-ment. Suddenly he was outside of himself, floating high over the room with the painted birds and watching his big sister annihilate the whole sorry long-faced crowd with the violence of her grief.

She came hurtling in from the hallway in a black shift that was like an undergarment, her arms naked, her feet bare, her hair kinked and wild and beating at her face like a flail, and all on the crest of that first rising shriek. Everyone in the room, even Mama the all-powerful, was frozen in place — or no, not frozen but melted down like silica and then quick-cooled to the fragile inanimacy of glass. But that first heart-seizing shriek was nothing more than a preface, an overture, a promise of what was to come. The next cry, protracted and operatic, crescendo-ing in a series of gut-wrenching whoops that sounded as if some animal were being eviscerated and eaten alive, scoured the walls and the ceil-ing and polished those glass faces and glassy eyes till nothing existed but Mary Virginia McCormick, the fount and apotheosis of grief.

Unimpeded, all but unrecognizable, her mouth open in a rictus of screaming and her limbs jerking and twitching with the exaltation of some uncontainable force, she darted across the rug and through the pall of smoked sausage and embalmer's perfume, past the mourners and undertaker's assistants and the members of her own family, vaulted the rail and plunged into the coffin as if she were diving into a swimming pool. "It's me!" she cried, thrashing at what was left of the Reaper King till it seemed to Stanley's stricken eyes that the corpse had come to life in a hideous rehearsal of his worst fears. No one moved. No one breathed. "Papa," she sobbed, "it's me, Mary Virginia," and her hands were right there, right in the thick of it, wrapped tight round the rigid throat and reanimated beard. "Don't you recognize me?"

It was a shame, everyone agreed, because Mary Virginia was the beauty of the family, a roll of the genetic dice that comes round only once in a generation. And she was as talented as she was pretty, good with languages and clever at drawing, an accomplished pianist who played with the subtlety and compassion of a woman twice her age and all the courage and ferocity of a man. She was twenty-three and unmar-ried at the time of her father's death, though there had been no lack of suitors, her physical attractions enhanced as they were by the allure of her father's fortune. In the two years since her coming out, there had been three offers for her hand. Her mother — Nettie Fowler Mc-Cormick, a real force in Chicago society and a matchmaker nonpareil — had convoked a family council on each of the three occasions, and each time, though the aspirants were well connected and had money of their own, Papa had to take them aside and gravely decline on his daughter's behalf. And that was a shame, a real shame. But the McCormicks were scrupulous to the point of rigidity, and they felt they had no choice but to let the young men in question understand just what they were letting themselves in for.

The sad truth was that Mary Virginia was sick, sick in a way that didn't show, not right away and not on the surface. Hers was a sickness that seemed to deepen as she grew into it, stretching and elongating to accommodate her like the skin of an anaconda. Ever since her thirteenth birthday she'd become increasingly distant, detached from the world of people, things and obligations, as if some essential thread had been cut in her mind. There were times when she didn't seem to recognize her parents, the governess, her own sisters and brothers. She wouldn't eat. Wouldn't talk. For hours at a time she crouched over her bruised knees, praying frantically, hysterically, chanting the name of God the Father until it was like a curse. Other times she couldn't seem to catch her breath, dashing from room to room in a panic, blue in the face, choking for air when there was air all around her. And then she couldn't sleep, sometimes for days, for weeks, and it would terrify Nettie to creep into her room at two or three in the morning and see her lying there rigid, staring into the crown of some private universe, awake but no more conscious of her mother than if she were blind and deaf.

At fifteen she came to life again, resurrected, hyperkinetic, throwing sparks from her fingers and laughing openmouthed at the great ongoing joke of the world, her every motion arrested and then accelerated and accelerated again till she rushed aimlessly from one room to another in a spastic herky-jerky trot that was like a cruel parody of poor Missy's affliction. Where before she'd been without affect, wiped clean of emotion, now suddenly she became as passionate as a lover with Nettie, her own mother, clinging frantically to her at bedtime, protracting a goodnight kiss till it was a torture. She walked in her sleep, talked gibberish, scared off her schoolmates. And then, just after her sixteenth birthday, she began to mutilate herself.

It was one of the nurses, a French girl by the name of Marie Lherbette, who first reported it. Nettie was in the drawing room nestled in a Louis XVI chair across from an eager, well-fed young man whose passage to China she had agreed to pay on behalf of the Presbyterian Missionary Society. On the low table between them stood a tray of finger sandwiches and a pot of tea draped in a cozy crocheted by her grandmother in the early days of the century. The young man was making a complicated point about the Asiatic mind and the woeful lack of a Christianizing influence in so ancient but corrupt a culture, when Marie Lherbette knocked and entered the room with a low bow.

"Yes?" Nettie said. "What is it, Marie?"

The nurse looked down at her feet. She was twenty, pretty enough in her own way, and dutiful, but to Nettie's mind too much imbued with, well, Frenchness, to be entirely trustworthy. "If madame please, may I have a word in private?"

"Now? Can't you see that I'm occupied?"

"There is"—the nurse searched for the word—"gravity in what I must tell you."

Gravity? Nettie took one look at the nurse's face and then rose and excused herself to the young man. A moment later she was following the nurse up the stairs to the children's rooms. "What is it?" she demanded. "Is it Anita? Mary Virginia?"

"Miss Mary Virginia," the nurse whispered over her shoulder, hurrying up the stairs and down the hall with quick nervous thrusts of her feet. Nettie struggled to keep up, her skirts tugging at her knees and clinging obstinately to her ankles, the carpet hissing beneath her, the furniture turned to stone. And then they were through the door and into her daughter's room, and Nettie saw Mary Virginia stretched out on the bed in her insomniac's trance, naked but for a pair of socks, saw the perfect bloody handprints on the flowered wallpaper and the long glistening runnels that trailed away from her private place and down her inner thighs as if some animal had been at her.

They took her to the McLean Hospital in Waverley, Massachusetts, where she was prodded, pinched, weighed, measured, auscultated, analyzed and interrogated by the biggest men in the field of psychiatry the McCormick money could attract—which is to say, all of them. Unfortunately, none of the experts could agree. One felt her problem was neurasthenia, another, delusional insanity, and yet another, dementia praecox. They wanted to keep her for observation—and for her own protection. She hadn't bloodied herself again, except for two barely noticeable puncture marks she'd worked into her right underarm with a pen nib, but during the trip from Chicago in the private Pullman car, she'd begun to hold passionate conversations with phantoms out of thin air, and twice she'd attempted to throw herself from the train. Fortunately, Cyrus Jr. was there to restrain her, but Nettie was crucified with the burden of it.

Six weeks, the doctors said. At least. And so, reduced nearly to prostration herself, what with Mary Virginia's collapse, Papa's illness and her little ones pining for her in Chicago, Nettie decided to rent a house in Waverley and send for Harold and Stanley. It was one of Stanley's earliest memories. Missy Hammond and their French nurse, Marie, were going to take him and Harold on a vacation trip for six whole weeks—and did he know how long six weeks were? And how many days were in a week? And what the first letter of the alphabet was? Yes. And they were going to go on the choo-choo train all the way across the great state of Illinois, through Indiana—could he say *Indiana?*—and Pennsylvania and New York to Massachusetts, where Mama and Big Sister were. Big Sister was sick, very sick, but she would be better soon and then they would all come home.

Stanley was two at the time, Harold five. Of the trip, he recalled a sensation of intense, blinding greenness, a sea of green beyond the moving windows, vast and oceanic, a world bigger than comprehension would allow. And of the house in Waverley he remembered nothing, except that the sun was there to illuminate this new, expansive and undifferentiated world of green, and that the deep grass beyond the edge of the yard was a place where snakes lived. His mama told him about them, lean hard whiplike things with the false glitter of a present wrapped for Christmas, little hidden gifts of poison and death that he must never touch. That was what he remembered of that trip to Massachusetts in the summer of '77, that and his big sister. Who was sick.

Mary Virginia improved at McLean. There was no miraculous cure, certainly not the sort of cure Nettie was expecting, demanding, hounding the doctors for day and night, but at least the imaginary conversations ceased and there were no more bloody stigmata on the walls. They all went home together, back to the brownstone mansion on Rush Street, with the ballroom that could accommodate two hundred and the steam-heated stable for the horses and the goat and cow (the Reaper King liked his milk fresh) and the pony Anita would get for *her* sixteenth birthday five years later. Mary Virginia grew older and prettier, but she had to withdraw from the Misses Kirklands' Academy before graduation because Miss Nevelson, her Latin teacher, had a detachable head and kept putting it on backward and Mary Virginia couldn't abide that—it was just the sort of thing she'd always hated—and so Nettie had arranged for a private tutor at home. There was a year of tenuous peace, and then, at eighteen, Mary Virginia broke down again, victim of amorphous fears, and she had to be hospitalized—this time for six months.

A relatively smooth period followed, a time during which she haunted the rooms of the house at all hours of the night like some lost and wandering soul—but placid, thankfully—and then gradually, as in the unfolding of some natural event, she grew more excitable, and in her excitement, she turned to the piano. Suddenly she was up at dawn, hammering away at the keys with a fury that would have paralyzed a Chopin or even a Liszt, thundering and banging till her fingers were blunted and there was blood on the keys, using her elbows, her chin, even her teeth, and she went on for hours, sometimes seven or eight hours at a stretch, and nothing could distract her or dissuade her. Nettie wouldn't have objected if only she'd play nicely, play properly, play some discernible tune. But no, her playing was an atonal orgy, sense-less, barbaric, animalistic—it was disturbing, that's what it was, and *she* was disturbed, her daughter was disturbed, and Nettie meant to put an end to it.

One night, as Mary Virginia lay tranced in her room, Nettie had the piano removed and taken to her brother-in-law's place on East Erie Street, on permanent loan. If she never heard another note of piano mu-sic as long as she lived, Nettie would account herself blessed. As for Mary Virginia, she woke at dawn as usual, went to the place in the par-lor where the piano had been, and without a word fell to her knees and began to pray. She prayed through the morning and afternoon and into the evening, through that night and into the next morning and the night and morning after that, her prayers stentorian, jangling, beating at the hallowed air of the McCormick sanctuary like the outraged hammers of fifty-six ivory keys.

She prayed herself into the hospital that time, but she was back at home and more or less placidly tranced as her twenty-first birthday ap-proached. Nettie was against a coming-out party, but the Reaper King insisted. What would people think? That Cyrus Hall McCormick's el-dest daughter was mad? That he had no confidence in her? That her life was over before it had begun? Nonsense. She would have a coming-out party like any other girl of her age and class, and furthermore, it would be conceived and conducted on the grandest McCormick scale, a scale calculated to leave the Armours, Swifts and Pullmans in the dust. Was that clear?

It was. And in the grip of a February cold snap Nettie opened the house to six hundred and fifty guests, who were served champagne and oysters by an army of servants, followed by a formal dinner for fifty in the library and dancing till twelve in the third-floor ballroom. Mary Virginia, cool as the waxing moon in a white crepe gown and three-button French gloves, stood calmly—some said lethargically—in the receiving line, along with her parents, Cyrus Jr., and six white-clad alumnae of the Misses Kirklands' Academy, and smiled at each of the six hundred fifty guests.

"Good evening," she said to them, to each of them, individually, her voice disconnected from her body and her glorious, shining face, "my name is Mary Virginia McCormick and I am very pleased that you could come on the occasion of my entrance into society." There were no prayers, no screams, no conversations with imaginary auditors, and the whole thing went off without a hitch, but for a very tricky half hour during which Johnnie Hand, the bandmaster, had acceded to the guest of honor's request to sit in at the piano. Mary Virginia bent over the keys with a frown of concentration as the guests, band members and servants put on their about-to-be-charmed faces, and then launched into something that at first bore the faintest passing resemblance to a Chopin polonaise, but which quickly degenerated into the jangling, horrid, obscene cacophony her mother knew so well. The polite smiles dissolved from one face after another, the bandmaster looked stricken, and Mrs. Eulalia Titus, of Prairie Avenue, had to be assisted to the ladies' room after one of her spells came up on her.

Nettie tried to end it with applause after the first minute or so, and the audience took it up dutifully, enthusiastically, and for a moment Mary Virginia's efforts were drowned out by a tidal wave of applause, but when the clapping subsided, she was still at it. Head bent over the keyboard, elbows flailing, all thumbs and knuckles and flashing wrists, she tortured the instrument with variations no civilized ear had ever conceived of. At the five-minute mark, Nettie tried again, crying "Bravo!" and beating her hands together so forcefully she thought she'd dislocated both her wrists. And again the audience took it up, thankfully, beseechingly, crying "Bravo!" as if sounding a retreat. But Mary Virginia played on, played on till the ballroom was empty and Cyrus Jr. and one of his Princeton classmates had to take her by the wrists and pry her fingers away from the last thunderous chord that reverberated through the room like the end of a barrage.

Yes. And now she was mourning for her father.

Initially—for the first few seconds, anyway—Stanley was all right. No one was paying any attention to him—they were all looking at Mary Virginia, his big sister, the savior rushing in at the last minute to cow them all and rescue her little brother, and he soared, he really soared . . . but when she went right by him and threw herself on that cold dead thing that used to be their papa, Stanley plummeted from the ceiling like a clay pigeon. This was his big sister, the angel in human form who used to take Harold and him on outings to the park, the furnace of affection who bundled him up on wintry afternoons for skating and hot chocolate on the lake and whispered in his ear till he shivered and pampered him when he caught cold, and she was ignoring him. She hadn't come for him—she didn't even see him.

Someone screamed. There was a rush for the coffin, Mama's face lit with the sudden hellfire of her fury, Harold gaping in bewilderment and Missy and Anita biting down on their knuckles as if they were beef ribs or chicken wings, and Stanley made himself invisible. As soon as his mother let go of his hand, he was gone, vanished in the midst of the confusion, chairs rumbling, people crying out, all those oversized bodies in furious concerted movement. He didn't stay to see his big brother and his uncles Leander and William wrest Big Sister away from his dead father, didn't see the look of savagery and puzzlement on her face, didn't see her toss and bite and kick till the flimsy rag of her shift pulled up over her hips to expose the scored and naked flesh beneath it. No: he ran straight downstairs to the oak wardrobe in the linen closet and burrowed.

Later, much later—it must have been past midnight—he ventured out into the hallway. He'd missed supper and Mama hadn't come for him, which meant she was suffering with one of her headaches and mewed up like a prisoner in her room. He'd heard Marie calling for him, and then later Missy and Anita, but he'd just burrowed deeper among the towels and bedthings. He didn't need them—he didn't need his big sister or his mother or anybody—and even if he did, he couldn't have done a thing about it. Once he climbed into the big bottom drawer of that wardrobe and inched it closed by applying his right shoulder to the rough unfinished surface of the plank above, he was powerless. There was something inside him gnawing its way out, something he'd swallowed, something alive, and it wouldn't let him catch his breath or move his arms and legs or even lift his head to see where it was slashing through the skin of his belly with its claws and teeth and filling that hermetic space with a beard that wouldn't stop growing till there was no room left in the box and no air either. For Stanley, a good boy, a bright boy, a pleasing and normal boy, it was the beginning of terror. From now on, there would be no place to hide.

The evening became the night, and all that while Stanley lay there rigid, listening to the enveloping sounds of the house, all the noise of the comings and goings and the clatter of silverware and crystal and the murmurous voices of the servants in the hall. He fought down his hunger, denying himself, shriving himself, lying there as still as the corpse of his father in the drawing room below. Finally, though, it was a need of the living that drove him out of his box: he had to pee.

By the time he crept from the wardrobe and stuck his head out the door to make sure no one was about, he had to go so badly he was squeezing himself, squeezing his peepee, though Mama wouldn't let him call it that anymore. It wasn't a penis either, not in Mama's vocabulary. No: it was just a dirty thing little boys had attached to them for a dirty purpose and he wasn't ever to touch it except to make pee, did he understand that? He didn't understand, but every time she told him he nodded his head, looked down at the floor and let his eyes lead the retreat.

The hallway was deserted. Someone had left a light burning at the far end of it, outside the room they still called the nursery, and there was another light on in the bathroom across the hall. There wasn't a sound anywhere. The mourners had taken their big blunt shoes and their furs and jewelry and their long condoling faces and gone home, and everyone else had turned in for the night—there was a funeral to attend in the morning, after all. Stanley squeezed himself. Two miniature goads stabbed at him down there, on either side, just above the groin. He held his breath a moment, listening, and then he darted across the hall to the bathroom, swinging the door shut behind him. He was peeing—relieving himself, and yes, it was a relief, the only relief he'd had all day—when he glanced up at the mirror and saw that someone was easing open the door behind him.

"I'm in here," he sang out, turning away instinctively to shield himself. There was no answer but the faintest metallic grating of the hinges, the door swinging inexorably open, the noise of his urine in the porcelain bowl a sudden embarrassment, a steady boiling pent-up stream he was helpless to stop. He shot a nervous glance over his shoulder, expecting Harold. "Just a minute!" he cried, but it was too late.

It wasn't Harold standing there in the doorway, but Mary Virginia, in her black shift and bare feet. She looked puzzled, as if she'd never seen a bathroom—or Stanley—before.

As for Stanley, he tried to force his penis back into his pants before he was finished and got hot pee all down the front of himself. *Dirty, dirty, dirty,* he could hear his mother saying it already. His face flushed. The blood thundered in his ears. He backed away from the toilet.

For a long moment, Mary Virginia stood there rocking to and fro on feet that were so white they seemed to glow against the checkered tiles. "Stanley the elf," she said finally, and her voice wasn't right. Her words were slurred and slow, as if she had something in her mouth. "The little hobgoblin," she said. "The boy who can snap his fingers and disappear."

Stanley watched her feet move across the floor, fascinated by the way her toes gripped and released the tiles. "Don't be afraid," she said, and she reached out to tousle his hair, "they've sedated me, that's all. For my peace of mind. So I can rest."

Stanley tried to smile. His pants were wet and uncomfortable, and his underpants too, already binding in the crotch, and he was hungry and tired, exhausted from the strain and terror that had crept up on him as he lay in that drawer all through the day and into the night.

Mary Virginia—Big Sister—gave him a wan smile in return, and then, just as casually as if he wasn't there at all, she hiked up her shift and sat on the toilet. She looked off into space and he heard the fierce hissing sound of her pee as he turned away to wash up—*Always wash up,* his mother told him, *always.* He was confused. His face was hot. He wanted his mother.

But then Mary Virginia began to laugh, a high hoarse chuckling laugh that startled him and made him turn round again despite himself. "Stanley the moper," she said. "You're always so mopey, Stanley — what's the matter? Is it Mama?" And then: "I'll bet you've never seen a woman pee before, have you?"

Stanley shook his head. His sister's legs were white, whiter than her feet, and the shift was hiked up over her knees.

"Women sit down when they pee, did you know that? Because we don't have a little peepee like boys do — women are different." She rose awkwardly, as if she couldn't catch her balance, and muttered something he didn't catch. Then she said, "Would you like to see?"

He didn't know what to do. He just stood there at the sink, frozen in place, and watched his big sister pull the shift up over her head until she was white all over. Hugely white. White as a statue. And he saw her breasts, heavy and white under the glow of the gaslamp, and her navel, and the place where her penis should have been and there was only hair, blond hair, instead. "You see?" she said, the words thick in her mouth, and he thought for a minute she was eating candy, caramel candy, and she was going to give him some — she was only teasing him, that's what this was all about.

But there was no candy, he knew that, and he wanted only to run, run for the drawer in the wardrobe that would never give him a moment's comfort again, run to his mother, run to Harold, Missy, Anita, anyone — but he didn't. He stood there at the sink and stared at the white glowing naked body of his sister, his big sister who was very beautiful and very sick, until she bent for the shift and covered herself again in the featureless black of her mourning.

After that, after the funeral and the letters of condolence and the black crepe, Mary Virginia went away. Stanley couldn't place the time exactly — it could have been a week after the funeral, two weeks, a month — but Mama saw to the arrangements, and Big Sister was gone. He never told anyone about that night in the bathroom, not even Harold, but it stayed with him long after the funeral, a deep festering pocket of shame. Girls were different from boys and women from men, everyone knew that, but now Stanley, alone among his friends and schoolmates, knew how and why they were different, and it was a knowledge he hadn't asked for, a knowledge that complicated his dreams and made him shy away from his mother, Anita, Missy and all the other females who crowded into his life. He looked into their faces, looked at their hair, their skirts, their feet, and knew how white they were underneath their clothes, the palest bleached-out belly-of-a-frog sort of white, with breasts that hung there like the stumps of something missing and that scar between their legs where there should have been flesh. It was an excoriating vision, a waking nightmare, more than any nine-year-old boy could be expected to carry with him for long, and it took all that spring and a summer in the Adirondacks before it finally began to fade.

Mary Virginia visited Rush Street only once a year from then on, always in the company of her doctor, a small thin-lipped woman with the figure of a man and great wide bulging eyes that so fascinated the boys they couldn't look at her without giggling. These visits were brief—two or three days at a time that had Mama and Anita so wrought up and fearful you would have thought Mary Virginia was an anarchist with a ticking bomb, but in fact she was as docile as a cow and nearly as fat. She made her last visit to Chicago in 1892, for the Christmas holidays, descending on the house in a storm of servants, white-clad nurses and luggage. Stanley was no longer a boy. He'd begun his freshman year at Princeton that fall, involved with a thousand things and arduously growing into the six-foot-four-inch frame that left him towering over his classmates, and he hadn't given a thought to his crazy big sister in months—she was gone, out of sight, an embarrassment to him and the family. But when he saw her that Christmas coming down the stairs like a somnambulist or sitting beside her mannish little doctor at the dinner table, he was shocked at the change in her. His big sister the beauty had been transformed into a clinging overweight spinster who would burst into tears if you stopped talking to her even for a minute.

She kept to her room mostly, and with the whirl of festivities, the parties, presents, songs and toasts, Stanley saw little of her. In fact, over the course of the three days she spent with them, he was alone with her only once—after lunch on the last day, when she suddenly looped her arm in his and asked him to take her out for a turn round the garden. It was raw and drizzling and her skirts would be ruined, but both Mama and the bug-eyed doctor gave him a look, and he went.

Stanley wasn't good at small talk, but he chattered away at the swollen moon of her face, afraid to stop for fear of setting her off, and they went round the yard twice before she said a word. They were passing through the denuded arbor for the second time when all of a sudden she tugged violently at his arm and pulled herself close to him, face to face, as if they were dancing a minuet. She was trying to tell him something, but she stuttered now and drawled out her words till they were whole private symphonies of meaning—utterly unintelligible, even to her doctor. The drizzle beaded her lashes and brows and glistened on her hat. It was cold. He looked into her eyes and they were floodplains of madness. "St-Stanley," she said, making an effort. "Little brother—"

She was puffy and white, soft as dough, and he knew how white she was underneath—saw it in a flash, the whole thing coming back to him in that instant—and while his mad hopeless fat-faced sister clutched at his arms and breathed in his face he felt himself growing hard in a sudden shock of shame and desire. And hate—hate too. What was she doing to him? What did she want from him? Couldn't she just leave him alone? He tried to push her away but she held on, drawing him down till their faces were inches apart, her lips cracked and flushed with blood, her tongue moving against the roof of her mouth like some amphibious thing crawling up out of the mud. "St-Stanley," she stuttered, fighting to get the words out through the tight weave of her sickness. "You-you're my favorite, you are, you know why?"

He didn't know why. His groin was throbbing. He was a member of the Guitar and Mandolin Club and the tennis team and he had a term paper to write on the poetry of Robert Herrick and in two days he'd be back on the train to New Jersey. There was a dog barking somewhere. He could smell beef and gravy on her breath.

"Because you . . . because you're just like me."

3.

PSYCHOPATHIA SEXUALIS

It was their second day out of Boston on the New York Central Line, and Massachusetts was already behind them—and half of New York too. O'Kane studied the timetable and let the names of the stops whisper in his head: Albany, Schenectady, Herkimer, Utica, Syracuse. To him, these were exotic ports of call, every one of them, places he'd heard about for years but never thought he'd see—the cities whose names sat so lightly on the tongues of the drummers and other worldly types he encountered while shoveling up beans and egg salad at the lunch counter or sipping a whiskey in the hotel bar, all the while trying his level best not to seem as ignorant, circumscribed and provincial as he was. He'd got down at Albany and walked to the end of the platform and back, just so he could say he'd been there, but he really didn't get much of a thrill out of it—the whole time he was afraid the train would suddenly lurch out of the station and leave him palpitating in the dust. And what was there to see, anyway? Tracks. Refuse. A dead pigeon with feet as rigid as window poles and half a dozen lumps of petrified human waste.

Schenectady, Utica and the rest he watched from the window, but he wanted to be awake and alert and ready to jump down when they pulled into Buffalo, where McKinley had breathed his last, and he wanted to see the Canadian border when they crossed over into Ontario for the run down to Detroit. His mother had given him a new Kodak to record the trip for her and he'd dutifully snapped away at the picturesque and the quotidian alike—the meandering stream, the lone horse in the field, the back end of a barn in need of paint—but it was Buffalo he meant to capture and preserve. That and Canada. And the West, of course.

Nick and Pat were at the far end of the car in a pair of red plush chairs, playing cards and smoking five-cent cigars, looking like nabobs on their way out to inspect the tea plantations. Dr. Hamilton was in his compartment, frowning over a leatherbound book that featured pen-and-ink drawings of apes in their natural habitat, and Mart was in the forward compartment, sitting with Mr. McCormick. And since Mr. McCormick was calm—catatonic, actually, his legs crooked at the knee, his eyes locked on the ceiling and his head frozen in the air six inches from the pillow—there was nothing for O'Kane to do but stare out the window and wait for his turn to relieve Mart at Mr. McCormick's bedside. He gazed out beyond the flickering ghost of his own reflection and into the neutral wash of the evening and saw the same scrim of trees, hills and creeks he'd been seeing for the last day and a half, scenery served up like something on a tray, too much scenery, a long unbroken visual glut. A town hurtled by like a hallucination, two streets, clothes on a line, a dog sniffing at something in a muddy yard. Then trees. The yawning gape of a farm. More trees.

O'Kane pushed himself up and stretched. In the back of his mind was an inchoate notion of letting himself out of the car and wending his way up through the train to the diner, where he envisioned the Negro waiter pouring him a cup of black coffee and maybe serving up something sweet on the side, some vanilla ice cream with maybe a bit of that dry Canton ginger sprinkled on it or some Bent's Biscuits or even a bite of cake. The *Mayflower* was the last in a train of fourteen cars, plus locomotive and tender, and because Dr. Hamilton felt it was too dangerous to risk bringing a cook along, they were taking all their meals in the dining car—as if Mr. McCormick could do anybody any harm in his present condition. Hamilton wouldn't even allow a porter to come in and tidy up, and that was one more thing the nurses had to do, though O'Kane could hardly complain since he was the worst offender when it came to generating a private little midden of newspaper, used crockery and the like or forgetting where he'd dropped his socks and trousers in the cramped compartment he shared with Mart. But the food was good, the best he'd ever had, six courses for dinner with consommé to start and a selection of cheeses before the dessert and coffee, real first-class and no limit to the luxury of it. Of course, it ought to have been, for what the McCormicks were paying. Nick had told him they'd had to buy twenty first-class tickets all the way from Boston to Santa Barbara just for the privilege of hooking up a private car.

But he was tired. And he did think he would take an amble and stretch his legs if nobody needed him, and maybe he'd have more than one cup of coffee—he definitely meant to be awake for Buffalo. He folded his hands behind his head, arched his back and stretched again. He hadn't slept well the past two nights—last night because of the excitement of finally being underway, the rails beating time with his racing heart till he began to think he was part of a drum corps, rat-tat-tat and high-stepping it down the dusty road all the way to Cali-forn-eye-ay. The night before that he was with Rosaleen, their last night together under the roof of the cute little walkup on Chestnut Street that had somehow managed to become a stone round his neck, a big hollowed-out stone full of furniture and baby things and pots and pans and doilies cinched tight round his windpipe and the water rising fast. But it was their last night and she was sweet and wet and pulled him to her with a fierceness that made his blood rise again and again till they were at it all night long. They'd forgotten their differences and made up beforehand and they'd had a nice dinner she fixed of lamb chops and new potatoes with the mint jelly he liked, the baby hot and soft in his lap and sleeping away like a little saint. *Who're you going to choose,* and he'd put it to her point-blank, *your husband or your father?* And she'd given him that melting coy down-arching big-eyed look and said, *You, Eddie, you,* and that was it. She was going to come out in a month or so, with Nick and Pat's wives and little ones, courtesy of the McCormicks—once everything was settled. And that was all right. He guessed.

The train reared under his feet and he was a kid on skis again, coming down the big hill out back of the glue factory, and then he caught his balance and called out to Nick, "Think I'll stretch my legs and maybe get a cup of coffee—anybody want anything?"

Nick was in a mood. He didn't like traveling. He'd traveled once all the way from Washington, D.C., to Boston, for his father's funeral—and it wasn't in any private car, either, as he'd reminded them a hundred times already—and by the time he got there his father was six feet deep in the ground and his mother's heart was permanently broken—and then *she* went and died three months later. And if it wasn't for Pat and Mart and his looking out for them to get ahead in life, he wouldn't be traveling now. He never even bothered to turn his head, and O'Kane had to repeat himself before Pat finally looked up from his cards and said, "No, no thanks, Eddie—nothing for me."

O'Kane stood there a moment, the car rolling and bucking under his feet, the chandeliers swaying to some phantom breeze and the scenery racing along on both sides as if it would never catch up—which it wouldn't, of course, because they were leaving it all behind, everything, and a whole lot more to come—and then he decided he'd better look in on Mart and the doctor and see if they wanted anything. He'd learned to take smaller steps than usual, adjusting to the movement of the car, but he was awkward on his feet and he wound up shuffling down the long tongue of red carpet like a drunk on his way to bed. He slammed off the wall just outside the doctor's compartment, but the door was closed and there was no sound from within, so he continued on past till he got to the last compartment on the left, Mr. McCormick's, and stuck his head inside the door.

Mart was sitting there beside the bed, the gaslamp glowing, a book spread open in his lap. The book was one of Mr. McCormick's—a fat handsome volume called *The Sea Wolf*, one of two dozen or so pressed on them by Mrs. McCormick just before they left Boston. She'd appeared on the platform fifteen minutes after they'd carried her husband aboard and got him settled in his compartment, and O'Kane was the one she collared, though Pat and Mart were right there beside him in a welter of baggage and porters and the two coffin-sized steamer trunks marked HAMILTON they had to wrestle aboard. "Mr. O'Kane," she called, hurrying up the platform in a dress the color of Catawba grapes, her little weasel-faced chauffeur at her side.

O'Kane was struck dumb. He hadn't laid eyes on her since that morning at McLean, and here she was, calling out his name in a public place, her face warm and animated, her ankles chopping at her skirts and showing off the dark ribbed stockings and buckled pumps as if there were nothing more natural in the world. She glided effortlessly through the crush of people, and he was surprised to see how tall she was, taller than he'd remembered—five-eight or five-nine even, and that was subtracting an inch for the heels. O'Kane's smile was slow-growing, stealthy almost, and before he could compose himself she was standing right there before him in her wide-brimmed hat and the clocked veil and her Catawba-colored gloves. He was an idiot. An oaf. He didn't say hello. He said "Yes?" instead, as if he were a clerk in a shoe store.

The chauffeur gave him a look. O'Kane had disliked him on sight the first time they'd met—or been thrust into one another's company. He was a little man, even smaller than he'd first appeared, especially in contrast to Mrs. McCormick—Katherine, that is. He was wearing one of those monkey caps, and his arms were laden with brown-paper parcels.

"I was afraid we'd miss you," she breathed, aspirating each syllable to show that she really had been hurrying. She was flushed—or was it his imagination? And if it was, why would he want her to be flushed? It was nothing to him. Her eyes locked on his and he tried not to flinch. "I was with my mother all the way out in Brookline and we just rushed the whole way . . . but it was—is my husband all right? Is he comfortable?"

"Oh, yes," O'Kane assured her, "we carried him in not fifteen minutes ago and we've got Nick right there locked in the compartment with him, but of course he's blocked still and not really all that aware of his surroundings. . . ."

She had nothing to say to this. Though she hadn't been allowed to see him, she must have known perfectly well the sort of state her husband was in. O'Kane had seen it before, too many times to count. With this sort of catatonia a patient would seize up to the point where he wouldn't walk or eat and he became totally mute, as if he'd never acquired the power of speech. Sometimes he would freeze in a single attitude like a living sculpture, and then, without warning, break loose in all sorts of violent contortions, as if all that pent-up energy and fear and fury had suddenly burst like a blister inside him. For the past month they'd been force-feeding Mr. McCormick, the tube down his throat, the mush in the tube, and either he or Nick or one of the other nurses working the patient's throat to make sure he was swallowing and not asphyxiating on his food. There was a young girl of eighteen at the Boston Lunatic Asylum who died that way, the food all fouled up in the passage to her lungs, and O'Kane remembered one old man scalded to death when they lowered his rigid form into a bath nobody had bothered to check and he was so far gone he never flinched or cried out or anything.

She looked down at her feet and then raised her head and looked past O'Kane to where Pat and Mart were struggling to hoist one of the doctor's trunks up into the car. "I've brought some things for him," she said, and that was the signal for the chauffeur to disburden himself, unceremoniously dumping the packages in O'Kane's arms. There were six of them, and they couldn't have been heavier if they were stuffed with gold bullion. "Books, mostly," she said, "but I've included two boxes of the chocolates he likes, the foil-wrapped ones from Schrafft's, and some stationery in case he—well, if he should feel up to writing. And I do expect that if my husband hasn't improved enough to read to himself, then certainly you and the other nurses will sit by him and read aloud. You can't imagine the difference it would make."

O'Kane wasn't much of a reader himself, and he doubted that even the second coming of Christ and all his trumpeting angels, enacted live in the railway car, would have had much effect on Mr. McCormick in his present condition. But she was paying the bills, and O'Kane was on his way to California. "Of course, we'll be happy to read to him," he said, trying on his smile of depthless sincerity, the one he'd used on every woman and girl who'd ever crossed his path till Rosaleen caught up with him. "You can rest assured on that score."

But now, rocking gently in the moving doorway and staring down at the insensate form of his employer and the broad bristling plane of the back of Mart's head nodding over the open book, he saw that if anything, poor Mr. McCormick would have to dream his own books in his poor blocked hallucinatory mind. "Hey, Mart," he said, "I'm going down for a cup of coffee and maybe a bite of something—you want anything?"

Mart swung round in his seat and gave him a faraway look, the spread wings of the book taking flight across his lap. All three of the Thompson brothers had been born with enormous heads, like bulldogs—and it was a wonder their mother survived any of them—yet it didn't seem to affect them like some of the hydrocephalics you saw on the ward. No one would mistake any of the brothers for a genius, but they got on well enough—especially Nick—and Pat and Mart would lay down their lives for you. Mart wasn't too good with sums, and simple division was beyond him, but he was a reader, and aside from the fact that there was too much space between his eyebrows and his hairline and he had to have his hats specially made, you'd never know he was any different from anybody else. Besides, when you came right down to it, it didn't exactly take a Thomas Edison to pin a delusional paranoic to the floor or usher a bunch of halfwits out into the yard for a little exercise.

"Good book?" O'Kane asked.

"Huh?" Mart scratched the back of his head, blunt fingers digging in luxuriously and fanning white to the white scalp beneath. "Oh, yeah, sure. It's a sea story."

O'Kane tried again. "You want a cup of coffee from the diner?"

Mart had to think about it. He let the flecks of his eyes settle on O'Kane as the train shook itself down the length of its couplings and thundered over a rough patch of the roadway, reminding them that, appearances to the contrary, they weren't in a house, hotel or saloon but hurtling through the fall of night at speeds faster than any human being was meant to travel.

The book suddenly snapped shut like a set of jaws and sailed across the compartment; O'Kane had to brace himself against the doorframe to keep from pitching forward into Mart's lap. Catching himself, he glanced down instinctively at Mr. McCormick, but his employer just lay there undisturbed and unchanged, riding out the rough patch like lint on a blanket, his eyes moist and unblinking, a thin stream of drool leaking from the corner of his mouth and radiating across one cheek. He wore the strangest expression, halfway between mild surprise and unholy terror, as if he'd misplaced something trivial—an umbrella, his checkbook—but in that instant realized it was buried beneath a pile of rotting corpses. His hair was combed and precisely parted and he was dressed in the suit and tie and stiff formal collar the McCormicks insisted upon for his daytime attire, as if they expected him to spring out of bed at any moment, shake it off and go back to the office.

"Black," Mart said finally. "Two lumps. You going to relieve me soon?"

Still braced in the doorway as the train picked up speed on a straightaway and the wheels settled into a smooth placatory drone,

O'Kane fished out his watch. "I've still got an hour or so," he said. "What I think I'm going to do is sit awhile in the diner or maybe the club car, just for the change of scenery. . . ."

There was no response. Mart just stared at him.

"Mart, it's a joke—change of scenery?" O'Kane gestured at the windows and the shadowy blur beyond. Still nothing. He shrugged and gave it up. "Anyway, give me twenty or thirty minutes and I'll be back with your coffee, okay?"

The train lurched again, a sudden violent jolt that rocked the car like a rowboat, and the book slid back across the floor as if attached to a string. Distracted, Mart never said yea or nay—he merely reached down to pluck up the book and thumb through the pages till he found his place. Then he swung his legs round, adjusted himself in his seat and cleared his throat. "Now, you remember this part of the story, Mr. McCormick," he said, speaking to a spot on the wall just above the pillow and the frozen drained grimacing mask of their employer's face. "The shark bit off Mugridge's foot and Humphrey realized he knew who the lady was." There was no reaction from Mr. McCormick, and as O'Kane turned to leave he could hear Mart begin to read in a soft, hesitant voice: " 'Among the most vivid memories of my life are those of the events on the *Ghost* which occurred during the forty hours succeeding the discovery of my love for Maud Brewster . . . ' "

O'Kane made his way back to the head of the car, his internal gyroscope adjusting to the little leaps and feints of the wheels, thinking he might just stop in the parlor car for the added stimulant of a whiskey or two before he had his coffee. Booze was nothing to him, though it had ruined his father—and his father before him—and he could take it or leave it. Tonight, though, he felt he would take it, and the more he thought about it the more he could taste the premonitory bite of it at the back of his throat and feel the tidal surge of the blood as it carried little whiskey messages to the brain. He was wearing the new suit he'd ordered from Sears, Roebuck even before he ruined the Donegal tweed—both the Mrs. McCormicks insisted that all of Mr. McCormick's attendants be dressed as proper gentlemen at all times because Mr. McCormick was a gentleman and accustomed to the society of gentlemen—and he stopped a moment to admire his reflection in the barred glass of the doorway. He was looking uncommonly good tonight, he thought, in his Hecht & Co. fancy black-and-blue-plaid worsted with the sheeny black bow tie and brand-new collar—like a swell, like a man who had his money in oranges or Goleta oil. And the suit had only cost him thirteen-fifty at that, though the outlay had exhausted his savings and got Rosaleen screeching and flying around the apartment like some hag on a broom.

At any rate, he'd just turned his key in the lock when he became aware of a sudden sharp hiss behind him, as if someone had let the air out of a balloon, and even as he glanced over his shoulder to see the apparent figure of Mart sailing through the air in defiance of gravity, he didn't yet appreciate what was happening. It wasn't until Mr. McCormick burst through the doorway half a second later that O'Kane made the connection, seeing and understanding wedded in the space of a single heartbeat: Mr. McCormick was loose. Unblocked, untangled, unfrozen. And loose. O'Kane made the connection, but he made a fatal error too. Caught up in the engine of the moment, Mart lying there in a heap against the paneling like an old rug and Nick and Pat already springing up from their cards to intercept their employer and benefactor as he raged down the length of the carpet in a milling frenzy of limbs and feet and fists, O'Kane surged forward and forgot all about the key.

He was a big man, Mr. McCormick, no doubt about it, thirty-three years old and in his prime, with a gangling reach and the muscle to qualify it, and when the fit was on him he was a match for any man, maybe even the great John L. himself. He never hesitated. Jaws clenched, eyes sunk back into the cavity of his head till they were no human eyes at all, he came on without a word, and Nick, shouting "No, no, Mr. McCormick, no, no!" flung himself at his right side while Pat went for the left.

Their efforts were in vain. Nick missed his hold and went sprawling into a low mahogany table in an explosion of crystal, and Pat, who'd managed to lock his arms around Mr. McCormick's neck and shoulder, took half a dozen sharp jabs to the gut and fell away from him like a wet overcoat. Mr. McCormick wouldn't listen to reason. Mr. McCormick was in the grip of his demons, and his demons were howling for bloody sacrifice. There was no sense in cautioning him, no sense in wasting breath on mere words, and so O'Kane just lowered his shoulder and came at him down the full length of the car in a linebacker's rush. Unfortunately, Mr. McCormick was in motion too, having kicked Pat free of his left foot, and the two met head-on in the center of the car.

They met, of that much O'Kane was certain, but things were a bit hazy beyond that. Something sharp and bony, some whirling appendage, calcareous and hard, came into contact with the ridge of bone over his left eye and for a moment he wasn't sure where he was — or even who he was. Mr. McCormick, on the other hand, wasn't even winded and had somehow managed to stay on his feet, knees and elbows slashing, a sort of long drawn-out whinny coming from deep inside him, goatish and stupid. "Ooooooouuuuuuut!" he seemed to be saying. "Ooooooouuuuuu-uut!" And then O'Kane was on his knees, Pat and Nick scrabbling behind him, the doctor aroused and livid and shouting out unintelligible commands, and Mr. McCormick was at the door and the door had a key in it and the key was turning under the concerted pressure of Mr. Mc-Cormick's long, dexterous and beautifully manicured fingers.

O'Kane saw that key and thought his heart would explode. What was he doing? What had he been thinking? That was his key in the lock and Dr. Hamilton would find that out soon enough and give him the dressing down of his life, maybe even sack him for dereliction of duty and yet another violation of the three p's (Never allow a patient access to the keys, never!). Even as he sprang desperately forward, O'Kane could see the orange groves and the jasmine-hung patios and wistful señoritas dissolving like a mirage. Sprinting through the car for all he was worth, Nick and Pat at his heels, he could only watch in horror as Mr. McCormick tore open the door and flung himself headlong into the vestibule, already grabbing for the door to the next car . . . and what sort of car was it? A sleeper. A Pullman sleeper with murals, chandeliers, plush green seats that converted to berths — and women. Women were in that car.

"Stop him!" Nick roared. "He's got a key!"

But it was too late to stop him. He was already in the adjoining car, his angular frame thrashing from side to side, already reduced to a pair of oscillating shoulders rapidly diminishing down the long tube of the aisle. By the time O'Kane reached the door of the sleeper, Mr. Mc-Cormick was at the far end of it, startled faces gaping pale in his wake, an elderly gentleman sprawled in the middle of the carpet like a swatted fly, the train screeling down the tracks and the whole darkling world violent with the rush of motion. O'Kane was the fastest man in his high school class, a natural athlete, and he poured it on, vaulting the old man, brushing back passengers, porters and conductors alike, but still Mr. McCormick kept his lead, wheezing and bucking his head and throwing out his long legs like stilts. He reached the head of the car, jerked open the door, and disappeared into the next car up the line.

What went through O'Kane's head in those frenetic moments was probably little different from what was going on in his employer's convoluted brain, a whirling instinctual process that supersedes thought and allows the limbic system to take over: it was as simple as chase and flee. O'Kane was pugnacious, smart, tough in the way of the man who could survive anything, anywhere, anytime, and he was determined to have his way. And Stanley? Stanley was like a rubber band twisted back on itself till it was half its normal length and then suddenly released, he was a cork shot from the bottle, a bullet looking for the wall to stop it.

O'Kane finally caught up with him in the dining car, but only because Mr. McCormick had been distracted by a passenger seated at one of the tables, a passenger who had the misfortune to be of the gender that was both his nemesis and his obsession: a woman. He'd led the chase through three cars, bobbing and weaving in his maniacal slope-shouldered gait, apparently looking to run right on up through the length of the train, over the tender and across the nose of the locomotive to perch on the cowcatcher and trap insects in his teeth all the way to California. But there was a young woman seated in the diner, facing the rear of the train and having a genteel, softly lit evening meal with an older woman, who might have been her mother or a traveling companion, and O'Kane watched in horror as Mr. McCormick pulled up short, snapped his head back like a horse tasting the bit, and in the same motion skewed to the left and fell on her. Or no, he didn't fall—he dove, dove right on top of her. Plates skittered to the floor, food flew, the elder woman let out a howl that could have stripped the varnish from the walls.

"Mr. McCormick!" O'Kane heard himself cry out like some schoolyard monitor, and then he was on him, grabbing at the taller man's pumping shoulders, trying to peel him away from his victim like a strip of masking tape and make everything right again, and all the while the lady gasping and fighting under all that inexplicable weight and Mr. McCormick tearing at her clothes. He'd managed to partially expose himself, rip the bodice of her dress and crumple her hat like a wad of furniture stuffing by the time O'Kane was able to force his right arm up behind his back and apply some persuasive pressure to it. "This isn't right, Mr. McCormick," he kept saying, "you know it isn't," and he kept saying it, over and over, as if it were a prayer, but it had no effect. One-armed, thrashing to and fro like something hauled up out of the sea in a dripping net, Mr. McCormick kept at it, working his left hand into the lady's most vulnerable spot, and—this was what mortified O'Kane the most—taking advantage of the proximity to extend the pale tether of his tongue and lick the base of her throat as if it were an ice in a cone. "Stop it!" O'Kane boomed, tightening his grip and jerking back with everything he had, and still it wasn't enough.

That was when Nick arrived. In the midst of the pandemonium, the flailing and the shrieking and the useless remonstrances, plates over-turned and the roast Long Island spring duck in the elder woman's lap, Nick brought his vast head and big right fist in over O'Kane's shoulder and struck their employer a blow to the base of the skull that made him go limp on the spot. Together they hauled him off the distraught young woman and hustled him back down the aisle like an empty suit of clothes, leaving the apologies, excuses, explanations and reparations to Hamilton, Pat and a very pale and rumpled Mart, who were just then making their way through the door at the rear of the car.

The doctor's color was high. The spectacles flashed from the cord at his throat and his eyes were spinning like billiard balls after a clean break. "Sheet restraints," was all he could say, looking from the slack form of the patient to O'Kane, Nick and the devastation beyond. The lights flickered, the train rocked. A dozen anxious faces stared up at them from plates of beef Wellington, Delmonico steak and roast squab. "And don't you even *think* about loosening them until we reach California."

Now it was night. The train licked over the rails with a mournful, sub-dued clatter, barreling through the featureless void for Buffalo and points west. The lamps had been turned down and the car was dark but for a funnel of light in the far corner, where Mart, a puff of cotton gauze decorating the flaring arch of his forehead, shuffled through the motions of a game of solitaire. Nick and Pat had retired to their com-partment, from which a steady tremolo of contrapuntal snores could be heard against the perpetual dull rumble of the train's buffeting. Mr. Mc-Cormick was in his compartment at the rear of the car, awake and rigid as a board, wrapped in a web of sheets dampened and twisted until they were like tourniquets and watched over by no one, at least not at the moment. O'Kane had relieved Mart and it was his job to sit with the pa-tient through the night, reading aloud from Jack London or Dickens or Laphroig's *Natural History of California* till the windows became translucent with the dawn, but O'Kane wasn't at his post. No, he was sitting opposite Dr. Hamilton in the latter's cramped compartment, listening to a lecture on the nature of responsibility, vigilance and the three p's.

"There really is no earthly excuse for having left that key in the lock," Hamilton was saying, his voice never rising above its customary whisper despite his obvious agitation. The presidential spectacles threw daggers of light round the little box of a room. He fidgeted with his hands and tugged spasmodically at his beard. O'Kane shifted in his seat. To his reckoning, this was the twelfth time the issue of culpability had come up, and now, as on each of the previous eleven occasions, O'Kane pursed his lips, bowed his head and gave Hamilton the look his mother called "the choirboy on his deathbed."

"We've got to understand, each and every one of us, what a danger Mr. McCormick is in his present condition, not only to others but to himself," the doctor went on. "Did you see what he did to that young woman in the space of something like thirty seconds? Shocking. And believe me, I've seen the whole range of psychosexual behavior."

There wasn't much O'Kane could say to this. He was waiting to be dismissed, waiting to do his penance at the patient's bedside and get it over with, let life go on and the dawn break and Buffalo appear on the horizon like some luminous dream. And he was waiting for something else too, something Hamilton couldn't guess at and would never suspect: he was waiting for the doctor to retire so he could slip up to the parlor car and have a couple whiskies to steady his nerves and ease the tedium of the coming hours—if he hadn't actually needed them before, he needed them now.

But the doctor wasn't finished yet. He was going to make O'Kane squirm, make him appreciate the hierarchy of the McCormick medical team and what he expected of his underlings, because he wouldn't tolerate another lapse in security like the one tonight, even if it meant instituting certain personnel changes, and he hoped O'Kane caught his meaning. "I don't have to emphasize," he said, pulling at his beard with one hand and fumbling around for his pipe with the other, "how much Mr. McCormick's health and welfare means to all of us, to me and Mrs. Hamilton, to you and your wife and your co-workers and their wives. This is the opportunity of a lifetime, and I will not have any unprofessional behavior or personal shoddiness jeopardize it."

O'Kane watched the doctor's hands tremble as he tamped the tobacco in the bowl of his big curved flugelhorn of a pipe and lit it. He'd
never seen him so worked up and he didn't like it, didn't like it at all. He
didn't like being lectured to either. And while he might have looked
composed and contrite, all the while he was seething, thinking he could
just reach out and snap the doctor's reedy stalk of a neck like a match-
stick and never have to listen to another word.

Hamilton shook out the match and looked up from his pipe. "What
I mean is, I'm afraid we're going to lose him if he gets free again."

"Lose him? You don't think he's suicidal, do you?"

"Pfffft!" The doctor waved an impatient hand and turned away in
disgust, pulling vigorously at his pipe. The smoke rose in angry plumes.
He wouldn't dignify the question with a response.

O'Kane was irritated. "I may not have the clinical experience you
do, or the education either, but believe me I've seen more cases of dementia praecox than you could—"

"Schizophrenia," the doctor corrected. "Kraepelin's configuration—
literally, 'early insanity'—isn't half so useful as Dr. Jung's."

The smell of incinerated tobacco filled the compartment till there was
no other odor in the world. Smoke wreathed the lamp, settled on the
pages of the ape book spread open on the bed beside the doctor's flank,
drew a curtain over the room. "Think of it this way," Hamilton went on,
lecturing out of habit now, " 'schizo,' a splitting, and 'phrenia,' of the
mind. A schizophrenic, like Mr. McCormick and his sister before him,
has been split down the middle by his illness, withdrawing from our
reality into a subsidiary reality of his own making, a sort of waking nightmare beyond anything you or I could imagine, *Edward*." The way he pronounced the name was a goad in itself, a slap in the face. I'm in charge
here, he was saying, and you're an ignoramus. "And if you don't believe
these patients are eminently capable of doing anything they can to escape
that nightmare, including inflicting violence on themselves—extreme violence—then you're a good deal less observant than I give you credit for."

"Yes, yes, all right—schizophrenic, then. It's all the same to me."
O'Kane was hot, angry, humiliated by this whole idiotic scene. He'd left
the key in the lock. He was wrong. He admitted it. But Hamilton just
wouldn't let it go. "Call it what you will," O'Kane said, and he couldn't
help raising his voice, "I've seen them so blocked they've had to have
their fingers pried away from the toilet seat, and while you're home in

bed in the middle of the night I'm the one who has to hose them down after they've smeared themselves with their own, their own—"

"I'm not questioning your experience, Edward—after all, I hired you, didn't I? I'm just trying to acquaint you with some of the special considerations of this case. The greatest threat to Mr. McCormick is himself, and if you want to live in California and tramp through those orange groves you're always talking about, you're going to have to be on your toes twenty-four hours a day. We can't have a repetition of what happened here this evening, we just can't. And we won't. If it wasn't for the serendipity of the young woman's being there, as callous as that may sound, I don't doubt for a minute that he would have thrown open the last door in the last car and kept on going out into the night—and by the way, did you see how much she resembled Katherine?"

"Who?"

"The young woman—what was her name?"

"Brownlee," O'Kane said. "Fredericka Brownlee. She's from Cincinnati," he added, not because it was relevant but because he loved the sound of it: *Cincinnati.* "I found out she's on her way home from Albany, where her mother and her were visiting—I think it was her mother's aunt." The reference to Katherine had taken him by surprise—he hadn't seen the resemblance and he hated to admit that Hamilton was right, not now, not tonight, but maybe there was something there after all. She was younger than Mrs. McCormick—twenty-two or twenty-three maybe—and not really in her league at all, but there was something in her eyes and the set of her mouth and the way she threw back her shoulders and stared straight into you as if she were challenging you to anything from a game of chess to the hundred-yard dash, and that was like Katherine, he supposed. They were both part of that class of women used to getting their own way, the ones who wanted the vote and wanted to wear pants and smoke and turn everything upside down—and had the money to do it.

Hamilton had made him come along when they paid Miss Brownlee a visit, checkbook open wide, after they'd got Mr. McCormick secured and she'd had an opportunity to change clothes and treat the two minor abrasions on her left cheek where Mr. McCormick had ground her face into the fabric of the seat. It was an awkward meeting, for obvious reasons, but Dr. Hamilton was at his smiling, genial, smooth-talking, manipulative best, and O'Kane, after having given each of the porters a dollar and a five-spot to the old gentleman who'd been trampled, didn't have to do much more than look sympathetic and work up a rueful grin when the occasion demanded it. Mrs. Brownlee, her features pinched with outrage, said she was incapable of believing that even the most depraved monster would attack an innocent child absolutely without warning or provocation and in a public place no less and that in her estimation this wasn't a matter for apology or even remuneration but the sort of thing the police and the courts of law ought to take up, not to mention the authorities of the New York Central Line who'd allowed this person to be brought aboard in the first place.

Hamilton purred and simpered and pursed his lips, squeezing out apologies and mitigations in short whispery bursts while the elder lady scorched him with every sort of threat known to mankind, short of surbate and crucifixion, and Miss Brownlee stared down at her clasped hands and then at the black gliding window before finally settling her eyes on O'Kane. She'd been badly frightened, physically injured, subjected to a humiliating and vicious assault, but now she was bored — or so it seemed to him — profoundly bored, and she just wanted to forget the whole business. And she was looking into O'Kane's eyes to see if he was bored too, and there was something complicitous in that look, something challenging, flirtatious even.

O'Kane stared back at her, saying nothing, letting the doctor carry the weight of the negotiations — five hundred dollars was the figure they finally settled on, and it was only because Mrs. Brownlee was willing to make an exception for the McCormick name and agree to hush the thing up and abjure all mention of courts and lawyers — and he couldn't help seeing her as she was half an hour earlier, bleeding and impotent, Mr. McCormick on top of her and her face twisted with fear, and that gave him a strange sensation. He'd rescued her and should have felt charitable and pure, should have remembered Arabella Doane, but he didn't — he wanted to see her nude, nude and spread out like dessert on the thin rolling mat of his berth. There was a thread of crusted blood just under the slash of her cheekbone and a blemish at the corner of her mouth, the flawless bone-white complexion tarnished and discolored, and he looked at that blemish and felt lewd and wanton, felt the way he did when Rosaleen rolled over in bed and put her face in his beneath the curtain of her hair and just breathed on him till he awoke in the dark with a jolt of excitement. It wasn't right, it wasn't admirable, but there it was.

"You really think she looks like Mrs. McCormick?" O'Kane said after a moment.

The doctor hadn't responded to his comment regarding the Brownlees' itinerary, apparently finding the destinations of Cincinnati and Albany considerably less exotic than O'Kane did. Pipe dangling from between clenched teeth, he shifted his buttocks and took up the ape book with both hands, glancing at O'Kane as if surprised to see him there still. "I would have thought it was obvious," he murmured, his eyes flipping in a weary, mechanical way. The lecture was over. He looked sleepy, already disengaging himself, thinking now only of his pajamas, his toothbrush and his apes. "Not that this girl has the hundredth part of Katherine's charm and sophistication," he sighed, fighting back a yawn, "but physically, I think there's no question—"

For the past fifteen minutes O'Kane had wanted nothing more than to escape this miserable little box of a room, his ears burning, the foretaste of whiskey teasing his tongue and dilating his throat, but now he lingered, puzzled. "So what you're saying is of all the women on the train he could have, well, assaulted—he chose her purposely? Given that the fit was on him, of course."

The doctor's eyes were dead behind his spectacles. He yawned again and bunched his shoulders against a sudden dip of the rails. "Yes. That's right. He might have attacked any woman—or he might have thrown himself under the wheels, as I said . . . but he chose her."

"But why? Why would he want to attack a woman that reminded him of his own wife?"

The question hung there a moment, the noise of the train clattering in to fill the void; deep down, O'Kane already knew the answer.

Hamilton sighed. He rocked on the edge of his bed, spewing smoke and wearing a faint thin-lipped smile. *"Psychopathia Sexualis,"* he said.

O'Kane couldn't be sure he'd heard him, what with the sacerdotal rasp of the Latin and the uncontainable rushing silence that magnified every nick and fracture of the rails till it roared in his ears. "I'm sorry," he said. "What did you say?"

But instead of repeating himself, Hamilton set down the pipe and bent over to slide a suitcase from beneath the bed. He unlatched it and threw back the lid and O'Kane saw that it was filled with books. The doctor fumbled through them a moment and fished out a thick volume bound in leather the color of dried blood. "Krafft-Ebing," he grunted, dropping the book in O'Kane's lap. "Here, Edward—educate yourself."

The night rolled on toward morning. Buffalo came and went. O'Kane, fortified by three quick whiskies and as many beer chasers, sat by the glow of the gaslamp and studied the wooden form of his employer. Mr. McCormick was blocked again, frozen and immobilized and no more harm or trouble than a gargoyle or bookend, but he was in a more restful position now, held in place by the sheets like an Egyptian mummy that would fall to pieces if it weren't for its wrappings. It was sad, though, as sad as anything O'Kane had seen at the lunatic asylum in Boston or in his two years at McLean. Mr. McCormick was a fine figure of a man, really, as handsome as any stage actor or politician—if you could get past the bughouse look in his eyes, that is—and here he was, in the prime of his life and with all his wealth and education and a wife like Katherine, reduced to this. He was no better than an animal. Worse. At least an animal knew enough to keep itself clean.

O'Kane watched his employer's face for signs of life—the clamped lips, inflexible jaw, the nose like a steel rod grafted to his face and the pale blue gaze of the eyes focused on nothing—and wondered what he was thinking or if he was thinking at all. Did he know he was traveling? Did he know he was going to California? Did he know about oranges and lemons and the kind of money a man could make? But then what did he want with money? He had all the money any hundred men could ever want, and look at all the good it did him.

For the past hour O'Kane had been reading, but he wasn't reading aloud and he wasn't reading *The Sea Wolf* either. No, the book spread open in his lap was the one Dr. Hamilton had given him, and it took his breath away. It was nothing short of an encyclopedia of sexual perversion—and never mind the title and degrees attached to the author or the resolutely clinical tone. A parade of sexual cannibals, pederasts, satyrs, urine drinkers and child molesters the likes of which no human fancy could have invented marched across the page, rank upon rank, each filthy obsession leading to a yet filthier one. It was scandalous, is what it was, though all the climactic moments were rendered in Latin to mask the shock of it, and O'Kane had to rely on context, a vivid imagination and his early training as an altar boy to piece it out.

He'd been deep into a section called "Lust Murder (Lust Potentiated as Cruelty, Murderous Lust Extending to Anthropophagy),'' the alcohol working in his brain like a chemical massage, totally unconscious of where he was or what he was doing, when Mr. McCormick suddenly made a noise deep in his throat. It was a croak or groan, the sort of deep regurgitant sound a dog makes when it's working up a puddle of vomit. But then, just as abruptly as it arose, the noise ceased, and Mr. McCormick never moved a muscle the whole time, his eyes still fixed and his head frozen over the pillow like the high dive at the city pool that never got any closer to the water.

Suddenly he groaned again and his lips parted. "Uh-uh-uh-uh-uh," he said.

"Mr. McCormick? Are you all right?" O'Kane reached out a hand to touch his shoulder and reassure him.

This gave rise to a vibrato ratcheting, like a door opening on unoiled hinges: "Eh-eh-eh-eh-eh."

"It's all right. I'm here with you. It's me, O'Kane. Lie still now—you need your rest."

"Eh-eh-eh-eh-eh."

The eyes hadn't moved, not even to blink. The teeth were clenched tight and the ratcheting, creaking, back-of-the-throat rasp seemed to be forcing itself right through the bone and enamel. "There, there," O'Kane murmured. "Would you like me to read to you, is that it?" And he was leaning forward to set down Krafft-Ebing and pick up Jack London, when he caught himself. Sea stories were such a bore—all those spars and jibs and tortured cockney accents. He hated sea stories. He'd always hated them. It was then that an idea came to him, a wonderful golden perverse inspiration. What the hell, he thought, the whiskey barreling through his veins on its admirable journey to his brain and his tongue and the fingertips that turned the pages. *Educate yourself, Edward.*

"Let's see," he said, leafing through the big volume in his lap, " 'Koprolagnia, Hair Despoilers, Mutilation of Corpses,' ah, here we are. Oh, you'll like this, Mr. McCormick. You'll really like this." And then, in the precise, well-modulated voice the nuns had dredged out of him fifteen years earlier, he began to read aloud as the train beat through the night and his audience of one lay rigid and enthralled: " 'Case 29, the Girl-Cutter of Augsburg.' "

4.

FALSE, PETTY, CHILDISH AND SMUG

All her life Katherine Dexter had been disappointed in men. Men had failed her in more ways than she could count—some actively and with malice aforethought, others passively, through no fault of their own. They'd let her down when she most needed them, broken her heart, stood in her way, barred the door and thrown up the barricades. She didn't like to generalize, but if she did she would find the average man to be false, petty, childish and smug, an overgrown playground bully distended by nature and lack of exercise until he fitted his misshapen suits and the ridiculous bathing costume he donned to show off his ape-like limbs at the beach. He was unreliable, loud, demanding, clannish, he defended his prerogatives like a Scottish chieftain, and he expected the whole world to bow down to him and fetch him his pipe and news-paper and coffee brewed just the way he liked it, with cream and sugar and the faintest hint of chicory. And why? Because men were the patri-archs and providers of the earth and obeisance was their due, and that was the way of things, ordained by God, Himself a male.

She let out a sigh. She was tired, cranky, disoriented, her nose had begun to run and she could feel a headache coming on. She'd wrapped up her affairs on the East Coast in a sustained frenzy of list-making, shopping and packing, her mother more a hindrance than a help, and she'd been stuck on the train for six days on top of that. And now here she was, seated on the divan in the reception room of her suite at the Potter Hotel in palmy Santa Barbara, with an invigorating view of the brown-sugar beach and the naked glaring belly of the ocean, in the process of being disappointed all over again.

The men in question this time were Cyrus Bentley, a beaky glabrous little functionary of the McCormicks who never seemed to stop talking, even to pause for breath, as if it were some sort of trick, like fire breathing or sword swallowing, and his accomplice, Dr. Henry B. Favill. Dr. Favill was a tall, elegant and icily imposing man who was inordinately proud of his dog-eating Indian ancestors, unhappy in marriage and stuffed to the eyeballs with McCormick money. They were the family attorney and physician, respectively, solid men in their late forties, universally admired and petted and accustomed to getting their own way. The theme of their little gathering was Stanley. Stanley had provided the context for all previous relations between these two gentlemen and Katherine, and they always took care on these occasions to refer to him by his Christian name and never "Mr. McCormick," "your husband" or even "the patient," by way of asserting previous claims. They'd been looking after the family's legal and medical interests since she was a girl at Miss Hershey's School in Boston, and they made it clear, in no uncertain terms, that she was the interloper here.

Katherine was thirty-two, a newlywed who might as well have been a widow. Stanley was beyond her now, locked away in the prison of his excoriated mind, but she was hopeful of a cure, always hopeful, and she wasn't about to be cowed by anyone. She swooped in low over the plate of fresh orange and pineapple slices that lay like a gauntlet on the low table between them and cut Bentley off in the middle of an unpunctuated sentence. "So what you're saying, in crude terms, is that you want to buy me off—is that it?"

Bentley had been leaning forward in his seat and idly rubbing at the place on his right calf where the garter was cutting into his flesh, but now he jerked upright like one of those mechanical bell-ringers carved into a village clock in the Tyrol. Before she'd finished he was sputtering and blustering for all he was worth. "Not at all, not at all," he was saying, and he just had to spring up and pace round the room, protesting and expostulating and waving his hands like flags of truce. "It was just that the family thought that under the circumstances it would be more convenient for you if perhaps the marriage were terminated—or annulled, we could arrange that, no problem there—and of course the first thing we thought of was your comfort and accommodation, and please forgive me if I feel obliged, through my legal training, to attach a specific sum to such considerations. . . ."

She wasn't going to let them get to her, no matter how exhausted she was or how much her head ached and her nose dripped. And she wasn't going to be talked down to like one of the empty-headed heiresses and overfed widows they'd grown sleek on, and she knew the type, weak as watered milk, running round in a dither till the big strong lawyer and the big strong doctor took charge of all their little trials and tribulations. "What about my marriage vows?" she said, making sure to enunciate each word even as she pressed the handkerchief to her recalcitrant nose. "In sickness and in health, Mr. Bentley. What do you say to that?"

There was a silence. For once, Bentley had nothing to say—at least not immediately. She looked beyond him, out the open window to the veranda and the sea and the strange brown-girded islands across the channel. "My husband needs me," she said, "now more than ever. Did that ever occur to you?"

This was Favill's cue. He uncrossed his legs and planted his big feet firmly on the carpet, as if he were getting ready to spring at her. "But that's just the point, Katherine. He doesn't need you, not according to Dr. Meyer—or your own Dr. Hamilton either. Women upset him. They disturb him. And if it wasn't for . . . ," he trailed off suggestively, watching her out of eyes the color of chopped liver.

"For what?" Suddenly her blood was up. It had been a long, frustrating day, the culmination of a frustrating week, month, year. She'd been obliged to breakfast that morning with her mother-in-law and Stanley's sane sister, Anita, and the atmosphere had been so acidic that everything tasted like grapefruit and vinegar, and then she'd spent the forenoon with the new chauffeur grinding along an endless labyrinth of dusty roads in one of the two Packard motorcars the McCormicks insisted on Stanley's having, trying to find the celebrated Montecito hot springs, where even now her mother was soaking her arthritic joints while Katherine was left alone here to fend off the McCormick hounds. "Go ahead," she demanded, "say it: if it wasn't for me he wouldn't be like this. Isn't that what you mean?"

Favill never took his eyes off her. He never so much as blinked. He didn't give a damn for her and her Dexter heritage that went back to the founding of the Colonies and six centuries in England before that or the fact that she had her own fortune and could buy and sell any ten Indian chiefs—all he cared about was the McCormicks, parvenus one generation removed from the backwoods of Virginia, people who couldn't even have licked her father's boots. "More or less," he said.

"No reason to be uncivil, Henry," Bentley clucked, circling round them like the referee at a boxing match. He put his hands on the back of the chair in which he'd been sitting a moment before and leaned forward with an air of false intimacy, a lawyer right down to his socks. "No reason at all," he said, addressing Katherine now. "But if you'll forgive me, we have reason to believe that—how shall I say this?—that given Stanley's mental and physical condition during the period of your connubial relations, the marriage was never, well—" He threw his hands in the air, like a Puritan at a peep show. "You've been trained in the sciences, Katherine. I think you know what I mean, from a biological standpoint, if not a legal one."

So that was what this was all about.

She felt very tired all of a sudden, tired and defeated. The bastards. The unfeeling, unthinking, meretricious, sheet-sniffing bastards. They'd gone snooping after every last shameful shred of bile and gossip, interrogating chambermaids and butlers, extracting testimony from her mother-in-law and Stanley's sisters and brothers and the team of psychiatrists they'd had swarming all over him since his breakdown, and they thought they had something on her, thought they could shame and bully her and beat her down. But they were wrong. She wouldn't crack, she wouldn't. She sat there like a pillar, though she hurt all the way through to the marrow and a hundred nights came back to her in a shattering rush and the look on Stanley's face and his fright and rage and the unyielding impregnable fortress of his outraged flesh and impacted mind. She sat there and fought the itch in the back of her throat and the seepage in her sinuses. They wouldn't dare talk to her like this

if her mother were here. Or her father. But her mother was soaking her
bones in a hot tin tub of mineral water in the middle of a dusty eucalyptus grove somewhere in the hills, and her father was eighteen years
dead, another disappointment.

All right, she decided, if that was the way they wanted it, that was
the way it would be. She stood. Rose so quickly that Favill had to
spring from the chair like a bouncing ball to avoid being stranded there.
Bentley looked deeply pained—or perhaps it was just constipation.
"Did you—?" he began, exchanging a look with Favill. "Or rather, do
you need some time to consider our proposal, because we're perfectly
willing, that is, we, I—"

Still she said nothing. She just stood there, her heart pounding, the
hat clamped to her head like a war bonnet, staring them to shame. "I
won't bother showing you the door," she said finally, and she couldn't
control the edge in her voice. "And you tell the McCormicks there's no
price in blood or money or all the kings' ransoms in the world that could
ever sway me, not one iota. I'll be married to Stanley when you're all in
your graves, and he's going to get well, he is, do you hear me? Do you?"

The next disappointment was Hamilton. Though he'd been tiptoeing
around her, doing his whispery, smooth-talking, eye-flipping best to
avoid putting her out in any way, shambling and shuffling and all but
kissing the ground she walked on, he'd yet to relent on the one issue
that mattered most: allowing her access to her husband. If she could
only see Stanley, even for an hour, she knew she could help bring him
out of it. The very sight of her would spark him, it would have to—for
all anybody knew, he might think she'd deserted him. And even if his
response was, well, difficult, at least it would be something, at least he'd
know she was there still and that somebody besides his lantern-jawed
nurses cared about him. Stanley had been at Riven Rock for just over a
month now—and she'd given Hamilton that month, willingly, though
she could hardly sleep for worry and felt like one of the walking dead
dragging herself around the corridors of her mother's house on
Commonwealth Avenue and she hadn't been to the theater or the symphony or even out to dinner—and now she wanted to exercise her
rights and prerogatives as a wife, and not coincidentally as the pa-
troness who signed the doctor's checks and underwrote his ape colony.

She'd waited long enough, she'd been patient, she'd listened to every excuse in the book and a whole codicil more. The time had come. Tonight—and she was determined in this—she would see Stanley.

But first, as the sun settled in to slather the sea and baste the pale walls and exotic trees till everything seemed to glow and drip with a thick oleaginous light, Katherine went in to draw a bath and cleanse herself of Bentley and Favill and the lingering taint of the McCormicks. She knew they resented her, her mother-in-law in particular, as stifling and selfish a woman as ever walked the earth, but it was a shock to realize how deeply they must have despised her to unleash the dogs and set them on her without a second thought—and on her first day in Santa Barbara, no less. That hurt. On top of her headaches and her cold and everything else. She wasn't looking for acceptance—she couldn't have cared less about the McCormicks and their pathetic little circle—or even warmth, but civility, that much she expected. What did they think she was, some passing whim of Stanley's? Another McCormick conquest—or purchase? Did they think they were the only ones pacing the floor at all hours of the night and so keyed up they couldn't even keep a piece of toast on their stomach? She'd been there with him when he broke down. She'd seen the eyes recoil in his head, watched him punish the walls and the furniture and all the dumb objects that fell across his path. She was the one who'd had to listen to his ravings and lock the door of her bedroom and hide in the closet till she thought she was going to suffocate, she was the one who'd run from the house as if it was on fire. And where were the McCormicks then?

Standing there in the hotel bathroom, listening to the water thunder into the big porcelain tub while the brainless sun pressed at the windows and some alien bird croaked from the cover of the palms as if it were half dead and hoping something would come along and finish it off, she felt like crying all over again. She'd never felt so sick and miserable in her life, not even when they'd denied her admission to MIT and made her crawl on her belly through four years of basic science classes the boys had got in high school as a matter of course. It wasn't right. It wasn't fair. It wasn't even decent. Favill she could understand—at least he was a real man, long-boned, big-shouldered, with an Ottawa chief's blood in his veins and the power to crush his adversaries in a fair fight, but Bentley, Bentley was a worm, a creeping spineless thing that made its living in the gut of something greater, or at least larger. She had no respect for either of them, but even less for Bentley, if that was possible. He wasn't even a man.

She studied her image in the mirror, staring into her own eyes till the moment passed. It was a trick she'd learned as a girl, a way of focusing her anger when they tried to beat her down, and they always tried to beat her down—boys, men, insinuating lawyers, smug administrators and hypocritical teachers alike. She remembered the chess club she'd organized at school in Chicago before her father died and they moved to Boston. It was a good school, the finest the city had to offer, catering to the children of the moneyed class and with no expense spared for teachers, books and facilities, but to Katherine's mind the best thing about it was that the sexes weren't segregated. Boys and girls sat side by side in the classroom, given equal access to the best that was known and thought in the world and encouraged to compete as equals. And when Katherine started up the club, her teacher, Mr. Gregson, an extremely old young man with a wispy two-pointed beard and the faraway look of a high-wire artist, encouraged her. At first. But she soon played herself out of competition with the other girls, who were only marginally interested in the game to begin with, and into the realm of the boys. And the boys played as if this game of war were war in fact and never mind that the queen was the power behind the throne and the king a poor crippled one-hop-at-a-time beggar hardly more fit or able than a pawn, *he* was the object of the game and they all knew it. The club lasted two and a half weeks and Katherine took on all comers, the line of boys waiting to be the first of their fraternity to beat the girl sometimes four and five deep. But then all of a sudden Mr. Gregson discovered an obscure prohibition against board games buried deep in the school code, and the club was disbanded.

Steam rose. The water hissed and rumbled. She felt the cool of the tiles beneath her feet and the faintest touch of the steam against her skin, and it calmed her. She bent over the sink and shook out her hair. Loose and unpinned, it was an avalanche of hair, uncontainable, the hair of a wildwoman, an Amazon, and she threw back her head and teased it with her stiff fingers till it was wilder still. She wiped a palm across the glass and stood back for a better look. She saw a naked young woman with flaring eyes and aboriginal hair, strung tight as a bow with the calisthenics she sweated through each and every morning of her life, as fierce and hard and pure as any athlete, though the whole world saw her as nothing more than an ornament, another empty head for the milliner to decorate, one more useless mouth for chattering about the weather and plucking hors d'oeuvres from the tip of a toothpick. But she wasn't just another socialite, she was Katherine Dexter McCormick, and she was inflexible, She wouldn't break—she wouldn't even bend. She'd fought her way through the Institute against an all-male faculty and a ninety-nine-percent-male student body that howled in unison over the idea of a female in the sciences, and she would fight her way through this too. The McCormicks. They were poor, primitive people. Not worth another thought.

She pulled open the door. "Louisa!" she called, poking her head into the hall while the steam wrapped its fingers round her ankles and the water uncoiled from the faucet with a roar.

The maid came running. A brisk skinny girl from a pious family in Brookline who must have thought California the anteroom to heaven judging from the look on her face, she scurried across the room with a stack of towels three feet thick. Katherine took the towels from her, and she didn't attempt to cover her nakedness, not at all. Louisa looked away.

"Lay out my blue skirt—the crepon—and the ve..et waist. And my pearls—the choker, that is." She paused, the towels clutched to her, the sun across the room now, in flood, the steam escaping in wisps. "What's the matter with you? Louisa?"

The girl looked up and away again. "Ma'am?"

"You don't have to be shy with me. Surely you've seen a woman's body before—or maybe you haven't. Louisa?"

Again the look, whipped and defeated, as if the human body were an offense, and suddenly Katherine was thinking of a girl she knew in Switzerland when she was sixteen—Liselle, of the square hands and muscular tongue, the first tongue besides her own Katherine had ever held in her mouth. "Ma'am?" the maid repeated, and still she wouldn't look, suddenly fascinated by something on the floor just to the left of where Katherine was standing.

"Nothing," Katherine said, "it's nothing. That'll be all."

At five that evening, the sun still looming unnaturally over the shrubbery and the hidden bird tirelessly reiterating its grief, the car came for

Katherine and her mother. Katherine wasn't ready yet, though she'd
had all afternoon to prepare herself, and when the front desk called to
say that the chauffeur had arrived, she was seated at the vanity, pinning
her hair up in a severe coil and clamping her black velvetta hat over
it like a lid. Her nose had stopped running—and she wondered vaguely
if she wasn't allergic to some indigenous California pollen—but her
headache was with her still, lingering just behind the orbits of her eyes
like a low-rumbling thundercloud ready to burst at any minute. More
than anything, she felt like going to bed.

Her mother, on the other hand, was jaunty and energetic, having
poached herself for three hours and more in the gently effervescing waters of the spa, and every time Katherine glanced up from the mirror
she saw her bustling round behind her in a new hat, a hat that to
Katherine's mind had been better left in its box. Permanently. And then
buried in a time capsule as an artifact of the civilization that had been
blindly building toward this millinery apotheosis since the time of the
Babylonians. The hat—a Gainesboro in turquoise and black with so
many feathers protruding at odd angles you would have thought a pair
of mallards was mating atop her mother's head—was all wrong.
Josephine was dressed in black, her shade of choice since widowhood
had overtaken her eighteen years ago, and while Katherine had no
quarrel with her mother's injecting a little color into her apparel, this
wasn't the time for it. Or the place. Who could guess what Stanley
would be like—or what his reaction to such a hat would be? And
Katherine couldn't help recalling the time, just three weeks into their
honeymoon, when he'd flown into a rage and demolished seventeen of
her mother's most cherished hats, and half of them purchased in Paris.

But she was having enough trouble with her own outfit, which
she'd changed a dozen times now, to worry about her mother's. She'd
finally settled on a dove-gray suit of Venetian wool, though the climate
was a bit warm for it, over a high-collared silk shirtwaist in plain white.
She didn't want to wear anything provocative, given Stanley's excit-
ability, but then there was no need to look like a matron either, and
she'd spent a good part of the afternoon crossing and recrossing the
strip of carpet between the mirror and the closet, trying on this combi-
nation or that and quizzing her mother and Louisa until she was satisfied. Stanley had always liked her in gray, or at least she thought she

remembered him claiming he did, and she hoped there would be something there, some spark of recollection that would help bring him back to the world.

Outside the window, the palms rattled oppressively in a sudden breeze off the ocean, and the irritating bird, whatever it was, discovered an excruciating new pitch for its deathsquawk—*raw, raw, raw*—and when her mother stumped across the room for the hundredth time in her ridiculous hat, Katherine wanted to scream. She was a bundle of nerves, and why wouldn't she be? Fighting off the McCormicks and their dogs, traveling better than three thousand miles over one set of jolting rails after another till every muscle in her body felt as if it had been beaten with a whisk, her whole life thrown into turmoil by Stanley's wild-eyed tantrums and the catatonia that turned him into a living statue. She hadn't seen him in over six months now, and she felt as tentative and expectant as she had on her wedding night.

She was still fussing in the mirror—her hair wasn't right, and she wasn't sure about the hat either—when the front desk rang a second time to remind them that their driver was in the lobby. "Come on, dear," Josephine urged, suddenly looming in the mirror behind her, "we mustn't keep poor Stanley waiting—that is, if we do actually get to see him this time." Exasperated, Katherine rose from the stool and fumbled for her wrap and her purse and the chocolates and magazines she meant to bring for Stanley, and her mother, hovering at her elbow, began a soliloquy on the theme of disappointment and all the little false alarms they'd had in Waverley and how she couldn't stand to see her daughter moping around and looking so absolutely heartbroken all the time and how they shouldn't get their hopes up too high because there was no telling how poor Stanley was adjusting to his new surroundings, if one was able to speak of his adjusting at all.

Poor Stanley. That was how her mother had always referred to him, even before his breakdown, even when he was as handsome and fit and well-spoken as any man who'd ever stepped across the threshold of the high narrow-shouldered house on Commonwealth Avenue, as if she could detect the fragility at the core of him like a diviner descrying water in the bones of the earth. "I don't know, mother," Katherine said, turning to her as the maid held the door for them, "I really don't know. But Dr. Hamilton promised in his last letter . . . that is, he didn't actually promise, but he was optimistic that the change would do Stanley good, not to mention finally being settled in a healthful climate, and I really don't see any reason—"

"Just as I suspected," Josephine said, striding briskly through the door and out into the resplendent halls of the Potter Hotel, her skirts crepitating, the wings of her hat flapping in the breeze she generated. "Don't say I didn't warn you."

And then they were in the car, arranging veils, leathers and various rugs to keep the dust off, while the chauffeur, a tense little man with a bristling sunburned neck and a pair of sunburned ears that stood straight out from his head, wrestled the steering wheel and fought the gear lever with brisk angry jerks of his shoulders. Katherine and her mother were perched in back of him on the leather banquette seat, as exposed to the elements as they would have been in a buggy, and after the first mile or so, when they turned from the wide boulevard that ran parallel to the beach in order to circumvent an inlet called "The Salt Pond," Josephine began to complain. "I don't see how anyone could ever get used to these rattling machines," she shouted over the stuttering roar of the motor. "The smell of them—and the noise. Give me a nice quiet brougham and an even-tempered mare any day."

"Yes, mother," Katherine replied through her gauze veil, "and I suppose horses don't smell at all—or scatter manure across every road from here to Maine and back." She was beginning to enjoy herself for the first time since she'd arrived, her headache receding, her nose drying up, and the air new-made from the sea and pregnant with the scent of a million flowers, citrus blossoms, *Pittosporum undulatum*, jasmine. The place wasn't really so bad at all—she'd pictured the Wild West, men in serapes and drooping mustaches, women in mantillas, an utter void—but the Potter had surprised her (it really was a first-class hotel, the equal of anything you'd find in the East), as had the charming adobes and grand Italian villas she glimpsed through the stands of eucalyptus. There was a surprising air of culture and civility about the place, and there was no denying its natural beauty, with its sea vistas and the dark stain of its mountains against an infinite cloudless sky. It was like a tropical Newport, a conflation of the Riviera and Palm Beach. Or better yet, the Land of the Lotos Eaters, "In which it seemed always afternoon."

For once, she thought, the McCormicks had been right. (And oh, how they'd campaigned to bring Stanley west, Nettie crouching nightly over the idea like some beast with its kill, dragging it up and down the length of the drawing room in her clamped and unyielding jaws while Bentley and Favill beat the sacrificial drums and sister Anita wailed the ritual lament.) Now that she was here, now that she was actually in the car and on her way to Riven Rock, the sun leaping through the trees ahead of her and the scented breeze kissing the veil to her lips, Katherine could feel the rightness of it. This was what Stanley needed. This was it. This was the place that would make him well.

"I just don't understand this craze for motoring," her mother observed in a casual shriek. "It's so — oh, I don't know — debilitating. And I don't doubt for a minute that all that *driving* contributed to poor Stanley's decline." The car lurched to the left to avoid a wagon rut, righted itself, and then immediately pounded over a section of road that was like a cheese grater. "I know I'll be a nervous case myself if I have to do much more of this — and to think he did it *willingly*, as some sort of *hobby* — "

This was a rather galling reference to Stanley's passion for motorcars — a passion Katherine had never shared, but which she felt compelled to defend out of wifely loyalty. "That's perfectly absurd, mother, and you know it. If anything," she shouted, "driving calmed him."

Stanley had been one of the first in the country to have an automobile, as people were calling them now, and he always insisted on driving himself, the chauffeur accompanying him solely as a hedge against mechanical emergencies. In fact — and her mother knew it as well as she did — if it weren't for motoring, she and Stanley might never have met. Almost five years ago now, in the summer of her final year at the Institute, she'd gone to a resort in Beverly with a group of mostly young people — Betty Johnston and her brother Morris, Pamela Huff, the Tretonnes — to sleep late, swim and ride and play tennis and forget all about the circulatory systems of reptiles and the thesis looming over her head. They were playing croquet on the main lawn one afternoon when Stanley suddenly appeared, striding over the hill and through the cluster of wickets in goggles and a greatcoat so thick with dust he looked as if he'd been dipped in flour preparatory to some cannibal feast. And what was he doing there to miraculously recognize her from the dancing class they'd attended together at the age of thirteen and twelve respectively all those years ago in Chicago and to charm her with that sweet recollection and a hundred other things? He was motoring. Across country. Or at least that part of it that lay between the Adirondacks and Boston.

Katherine couldn't help but smile at the memory, but then, as the chauffeur guided them back along the route they'd taken to the hot springs and into the umbrageous environs of Montecito, she began to wonder why her mother had brought up Stanley's driving—was it only to provoke her? To widen the gulf between her and her husband? To weigh in on the side of annulment, divorce, a settlement? She stole a glance at her mother's flapping form, the mad hat, the streaming veil and the smug ghostly expression, and she knew.

"Mother?"

"Yes, dear?" her mother screamed.

"You haven't been talking to Mr. Bentley, have you? Or Mr. Favill, maybe?"

No response. The engine whined and chewed away at itself; a pair of ugly glittering birds heaved up and out of the roadway, leaving a long wet pounded strip of meat behind them. "Turkey vultures," Katherine whispered to herself, "*Cathartes aura*," and it was automatic with her to classify everything that moved. She peered at her mother's face through the clinging wraith of the veil and felt her heart sink. The headache was back. Her sinuses were in flood. She felt betrayed. "Have you?" she cried into the wind.

"I'm sorry," her mother shouted, leaning forward and cupping her hands to her mouth, "I didn't hear you. Dear."

"Yes, you did," Katherine shouted back. "You met with them, didn't you? Didn't you?"

But all her mother would say, as the chauffeur jerked his shoulders and the car twitched and shimmied and plunged into one pothole after another, was, "Very pleasant gentlemen, both of them."

After that, they drove on in silence, the dusty roads of Santa Barbara giving way to the dusty cartpaths of Montecito, "the Millionaires' Eden," as the newspapers had it, the place where robber barons, industrialists and breakfast food magnates alike came to escape the snow and potter around their grandiose estates in a botanical delirium of banana trees, limes, kumquats and alligator pears. Katherine was predisposed to hate the place—Why did the McCormicks always have to pull the strings? What was so bad about Waverley and Massachusetts? Had no one ever gotten well there? — and now, her mood spoiled again, she settled in to loathe it in earnest. There was beauty everywhere she looked, intense, physical, immediate, but her eyes were veiled and it was a cloying beauty, destructive and hateful, the sort of beauty that masked the snake and the scorpion — and the McCormicks. Even when the chauffeur turned off Hot Springs and onto Riven Rock Road and they passed through the main gate and the big stone fairy castle of a house stood before her, the house of the Beast bristling with roses, Stanley's house, she made herself feel nothing.

Then the engine coughed and died with a final tubercular wheeze, and the silence washed over them like a benediction. Josephine was the first to free herself of her veil, which she'd pinned jauntily to the towering precipice of her hat. Leaning over the side of the car to shake out the dust and kick the rug from her legs in the same motion, she observed drily that the house was a bit ostentatious, wasn't it?

It was. Of course it was. What else would you expect of the McCormicks? Katherine unpinned her own veil and patted her hair back in place while the little chauffeur — Roscoe something-or-other — scrambled out to help her down. But she wasn't ready yet — she would take her own good time — and she sat there a moment gazing up at the windows opaque with sun and wondering if Stanley were behind one of them, if he were gazing out at her even then. The thought made her self-conscious, and her hands fluttered involuntarily to her hair again.

The history of the house, as she knew it, was as sad as anything she could conceive of. Her mother-in-law had built it as a refuge for Mary Virginia in the late nineties, a private sanatorium with one patient — out of sight, out of mind — and they couldn't have picked a spot farther from Chicago society unless they'd gone up to the Alaska Territory or put her on a boat for the Solomon Islands. It was a place where Mary Virginia could be alone with her doctor, her nurses, the scullery maids, cooks and washerwomen and the horde of Sicilian gardeners who'd transformed the property from a sleepy orange grove with a clapboard farmhouse plunked down in the middle of it to a proper estate with proper grounds that wouldn't have been out of place in Grosse Pointe or Scarsdale. Nettie had hired the Boston architectural firm of Shepley, Rutan and Coolidge to design the house — two stories, in the style of the Spanish missions, with rounded arches and a tower at one end—and she'd got a noted botanist, Dr. Francisco Franceschi, to oversee the landscaping, with its 150 specimens of daphnes imported from Japan, the nine-hole golf course and all the rest. And that was sad. Because the McCormicks felt if they sank enough money into the place they could salve their consciences, breathe easy, close the chapter on their sad mad daughter and sister.

But it got even sadder than that, because Stanley was here then, sweet-tempered, vigorous, witty, a twenty-one-year-old Princeton grad with a sweet shy smile and eyes that fastened on you till you felt there was no one else alive in the world. He'd come with his mother to give her support and help with the arrangements. But simply to help wasn't enough for Stanley—he was a perfectionist, a zealot, mad for detail. He met daily with Dr. Franceschi, quizzed the stone masons and arborists, pored over the plans with the young architect Shepley, Rutan and Coolidge had hired to oversee construction, moving a wall here, adding a nook or courtyard there, and a window, always a window. He was the one who'd suggested moving the patient's quarters from the ground floor to the second story—for the views—and he'd designed the rooms himself, right down to the molding of the windows and doorframes and the tiles in the bath.

That was what hit her now, the irony of it, and that was saddest of all: poor Stanley had been designing his own prison and he never knew it. No one did. He had all the promise in the world—member of half a dozen clubs at college, editor of the school paper, chairman of the Casino committee, tennis prodigy, scholar, painter, athlete, poet, the McCormick wealth at his fingertips and every possibility alive to him— and when Mary Virginia was moved to Arkansas to be with her new doctor, no one suspected that Riven Rock would be anything other than a happy place, a winter resort, one of half a dozen McCormick homes scattered round the country. But Stanley still had promise. He did. Bucketloads of it. He was a young man yet and he had plenty of time to get on with his life and do something in the world—if he could just get well again. That was the first step. That was what mattered, and all the lawyers and doctors and quibbling McCormicks in the world didn't have a thing to do with it.

Katherine still hadn't moved. The sun melted into the windows, the sky yawned, the stillness was absolute. Her mother was down on the pavement now, feathers everywhere, a whole aviary's worth, gazing up at her with the clear-eyed, analytic look Katherine remembered from her girlhood and the odd case of tonsillitis or indigestion it was meant to ferret out. The chauffeur, so wiry and intense behind the wheel, seemed to have died on his feet as he stood there poised to help her down from the floating step of the Packard. "Katherine?" Josephine was saying. "Are you all right?"

"I'm fine," she heard herself say.

"Because if you're not," Josephine went on, "we don't have to do this at all, not today, not when you're still so worn out and exhausted from your trip —"

Then she was on her feet, towering above them, moving forward to descend from the car while the windows exploded with light and the chauffeur's clawlike hand suddenly appeared on the periphery to offer support, and she watched her own tight-laced foot as it hovered in the air over the terra incognita of her husband's private asylum. "I told you I'm all right," she said, and there it was again, that hint of asperity and exasperation, " — didn't I?"

Her mother shut up then, clamping her lips together and setting her jaw in her best imitation of pique, too giddy with California and her mineral soak to harbor any real resentment and too concerned about the delicacy of "the Stanley situation," as she'd begun to call it, to push any further. In silence, trailed by the chauffeur and walking as stiffly as two strangers looking for their seats at the opera, Katherine and her mother went up the walk, mounted the great stone slabs of the front steps and rang the bell. O'Kane appeared at the door even before the tympanic echoes of the bell had died away in a series of dull reverberations that seemed to take refuge in the huge clay pots that stood on either side of the entrance. He looked startled. Looked as if he'd been expecting someone else altogether. Or no one at all. "Good evening," he managed to sputter, holding the door for them and trying his best to compose his face around a smile.

"Good evening," Katherine returned, but brusquely, in the way of getting it over with, and she didn't acknowledge his smile with one of her own—she was too wrought up for smiling, too sad and angry and pessimistic, and O'Kane's awkwardness irritated her. What did it mean? That they hadn't been expected? But that was absurd—someone had to have dispatched the car, and at breakfast her mother-in-law had gone on ad nauseam about the charms of Riven Rock and how much everyone was looking forward to her seeing and approving of it. Or was it Hamilton? Was he going to flip his eyes and tell her that Stanley had taken a turn for the worse and she couldn't see him, her own husband, in his own house, after waiting day by miserable day through six nightmarish months and traveling all this bone-rattling, sinus-pounding, headache-forging way?

"Oh, Mr. O'Kane," her mother shrieked behind her, "so nice to see you again—and how are you finding California? Missing your wife, I'll bet? Hm? Yes?"

Katherine wanted to strangle her. She wanted to wheel round on her and shout, "Shut up, mother, just shut up!" and even before she had a chance to see what crimes against taste Stanley's own small-town philistine of a mother had committed with regard to the furnishings, she found herself snapping at O'Kane. "Where's my husband?" she demanded, striding into the room with half a mind to begin trying doors at random.

O'Kane slammed the front door on the chauffeur and sprinted to her even as Nick Thompson rose from a chair at the foot of the stairs to intercept her. "Is he upstairs, is that it?" she demanded of the blunted eyes and napiform head of the elder Thompson. There seemed to be pottery everywhere, shelves of it—urns, bowls, vases, cups—and all of it a dull earthen brown. The place was hideous—it looked like a Spanish bordello, like a bullring, and she had a sudden urge to smash every last clay pot and Andalusian gewgaw in a frenzy of noise and dust and shattering because she knew in that moment they were going to stop her from going up those stairs, saw it in their eyes and the way they slung their shoulders at her and braced themselves as if she were one of the madwomen they'd kept locked away at McLean in a shit-bespattered cell.

She had her foot on the first step when O'Kane caught up with her—and he wouldn't dare touch her, he wouldn't dare—leaping three steps in a bound and turning to face her from the higher stair, his arms spread in expostulation, the big man, the cheat, the deceiver, disappointment made flesh. "Mrs. McCormick, no," he said, "please. Dr. Hamilton said—"

"Step aside," she said.

"Mrs. McCormick," pleading, his stricken face and meaty hands, and now Nick was there beside him, her mother tugging at her arm from behind, "I'm sorry, very sorry, but Dr. Hamilton said your husband can't have any visitors just now — yet, I mean — and especially not *women*, because of what happened on the train, that is, the incident — "

"What incident?" She felt her heart stop. "What are you talking about?"

She saw O'Kane exchange a glance with Nick Thompson, and then Nick, with his big head and bloat of muscle, said that she'd better talk to the doctor and O'Kane agreed, his head bobbing up and down on the fulcrum of his chin, and her mother said, Yes, that would be best, in the sort of voice she used on the cats when they scratched the furniture.

Katherine's pulse was like a Chinese rocket. Drums were pounding in her head. It was all she could do to keep from screaming. "All right, then," she said, shaking off her mother's hand and struggling to keep her voice steady, "I'll talk to the doctor. Where is he?"

Another look passed between the two men on the stairs. "He's outside," O'Kane said after a moment.

"Outside?" Katherine was astonished. She'd come all this way and Hamilton wasn't even here to greet her? "What's he doing, taking the air?"

"No," Nick began, tugging at the knot of his tie with one blocky forefinger and wincing under the constraint, "he's out there with the — "

"The apes," O'Kane interjected. "Or monkeys. You see, this sea captain — from Mindanao — he was here no more than an hour ago with the first of the two monkeys — hominoids, that is — in a wicker cage. He heard Dr. Hamilton was looking for hominoids and he got a ride out here with Baldessare Dimucci, the manure man, and, uh, the monkeys — hominoids — were overheated or chilled or something and Dr. Hamilton had to see to them right away, because if he didn't, well, he was afraid they'd — "

Katherine raised her voice then — she couldn't help herself. It wasn't right to show any emotion with the help — it just brought you down to their level, and she'd known that all her life — but she just couldn't restrain herself, not here, not now. "Enough!" she cried. "I don't give two figs for the manure man and his monkeys — I want to see my husband. And if I can't see him, I want to know why. Now, will you lead me to

Dr. Hamilton this instant or am I going to have to terminate the employment of every last person on these grounds and start all over
again?"

Sixty seconds later, after having determined that her mother would
rather stay behind and "have a nice chat with Mr. Thompson," Katherine was back outside, following O'Kane through the garden at the rear
of the house. If she weren't in such a state she might have appreciated
what Dr. Franceschi had accomplished with his bold arrangements of
daphnes and rock roses, the flood of gazanias, long-necked birds of
paradise, nasturtiums the size of saucers, but appreciation would have
to wait. She saw nothing but an undifferentiated mass of vegetation and
the back of O'Kane's head, where the soft blond hair of his nape joined
in a V and descended into the white band of his collar. The path took
them through the garden and into an open field of golden, waist-high
grass, from the depths of which two piebald cows looked up at them
stupidly, and finally into the dense shade of a stand of live oak.

"Dr. Hamilton?" O'Kane called, and there was an odd note to his
voice, a note of warning, as if to intimate that he wasn't alone. He
slowed his pace, edging forward into the shadows, Katherine right behind him. It was warm. She could feel the perspiration on her brow, at
the hairline, just under the brim of her hat.

"Edward?" The doctor's voice came from somewhere off to the
right, arising disembodied from the twisted maze of snaking limbs and
overarching branches. "Are they here already?" the voice called. "Because if they are, you're going to have to stall them a minute while I —"

"I've got Mrs. McCormick with me," O'Kane shouted, and in that
instant the doctor appeared, materializing out of the gloom where two
massive gray trunks intersected like crossed swords not thirty feet away.
He was in his shirtsleeves, his collar was unfastened and there seemed to
be something in his hair, some foreign matter, dander or fluff or something — or was it straw? "Katherine!" he cried, scurrying across the
cracked yellow earth in dusty shoes and a pair of trousers that looked as
if they'd been used to clean out the stables. "How good to see you!"

She allowed him to take her hand while he writhed and groveled
and disparaged himself for the state of his clothes and hair and most of
all for not having been there to greet her in person, but it was all the
fault — a chuckle here, nervous and high-pitched — of the hominoids,

the anthropoids, the monkeys, because didn't she see that they'd gotten very lucky indeed with Captain Piroscz and she had to have a look at them, just a look, because they were so, so *engaging*—

At this juncture there was a long trailing inhuman shriek from the clump of vegetation just ahead, and the wizened frowning face of a little fur-covered homunculus peered out at them from a frame of cupped leaves. "Oh, there you are, you little devil," Hamilton chided, and he inched forward with his left arm crooked at the elbow and held out stiffly before him, as if he were inviting the thing to dance. "Come on," he crooned, "come to Papa."

The monkey—Katherine recognized it from her lab work as a rhesus—merely stared at the doctor out of its saucer eyes. It was a spectacularly unattractive specimen, the color of mustard left out to dry overnight on the edge of a knife, its fur patchy and worn and its skin maculated with open sores and dark matted scabs. There seemed to be something wrong with one of its front paws and its eyes weren't quite right—there was some sort of film or web over the cornea. When Hamilton got within five feet of it, coaxing and making kissing noises with his lips, it let out another howl and vanished into the canopy overhead.

The doctor dropped his arm to his side and let out a little laugh. "I'm sorry, Katherine," he said, and she could see that he wasn't sorry at all, "sorry to have to put you through this—they're just feeling their oats, that's all. And perhaps I shouldn't have released them, but they were looking so pathetic in that cramped bamboo cage and you just knew they hadn't so much as stretched their limbs the whole way across the Pacific, probably not since they'd been captured in the jungles of the Orient . . . besides which, this is where I've decided to construct the apery and I do intend to give them as much freedom as possible." There was a pause, as if he were thinking about something else altogether, and then he clapped his hands suddenly and wrung them as if they were wet. "Well," he said. "And so how are you?"

Katherine was about to say that she wasn't feeling well at all, that she was worn out from worry and travel and not a little irritated and that she was stunned and disconcerted to find the doctor's henchmen daring to interfere with her seeing her husband and that furthermore she demanded to know just where she stood, but she never got the

chance. Because at that moment, as the doctor slouched there in disar-
ray and O'Kane shuffled his feet in the dirt and the declining sun cop-
pered the branches of the trees, the monkey suddenly plopped down
from above and landed squarely on Hamilton's head, digging its fingers
into his scalp and hissing like a cornered cat. But that wasn't all: in the
next instant it was joined by another, which came sailing out of thin air
to adhere, caterpillar-like, to the doctor's shoulder. "Screeee-screeee!"
they jeered, boxing furiously at one another with leathery fists while the
doctor's pince-nez flew in one direction and his collar in the other. And
then, just as suddenly as they'd appeared, they were gone again,
hurtling through the branches like phantoms.

Katherine couldn't help herself. She was furious, maddened, out for
blood, but at the sight of the punctilious little doctor's utter helplessness
in the face of such primitive energy, she had to laugh. To his credit, the
doctor laughed too. And O'Kane, the bruiser, who'd gone absolutely
pale at the sight of the tiny hominoids that couldn't have weighed a
twentieth of what he did, joined in, albeit belatedly and with a laugh
that trailed off into a whinny.

"They just won't listen to reason," Hamilton snorted, facetious and
gay, the pince-nez dangling jauntily from his throat, his collar crushed
underfoot. The monkeys rode high in the treetops, chittering and
screeching. O'Kane shuffled his feet. Katherine pressed a handkerchief
to her face, suppressed a sneeze. "Ha!" Hamilton exclaimed, "I know
the type, don't think I don't," and he let out an extraneous laugh. "The
devils, the very devils—they're even worse than my patients."

That was when my gaiety went out of the air, as thoroughly as if it
had been sucked into a vacuum. Katherine's face was burning. Now,
suddenly, she felt nothing but outrage. "I want to see my husband," she
said, and her voice was small and cold.

Hamilton frowned. He was hateful, ridiculous, a smear of monkey
urine on his sleeve, lint in his hair—he was a man and he was going to
deny her. "I've been meaning to write you," he said.

5.

GIOVANNELLA DIMUCCI

O'Kane had been dreaming of Rosaleen—or someone like her, a silvery succubus of feathery lips and needful flesh hovering just out of reach— when he was awakened, as he was every morning, by the strangled croaking wheeze of Sal Oliveirio's bedraggled rooster. This was succeeded by the lowing of cows and a garbled disquisition in Italian featuring three or four voices, and then, after a bit, by a smell of woodsmoke and the potent aroma of coffee and eggs sizzling in the pan. He didn't get up right away—he wasn't on duty till eight this morning—but lay there staring at the ceiling and the thin veneer of light on the windows, hoping to fall back into the dream. He had a hard-on—it seemed he always had a hard-on lately, day and night, and that was because he was living the life of a monk in his cell—and he stroked himself with a slow yearning rhythm, thinking of Rosaleen, the girl on the train, Katherine, until the moment of release came and he could lie still again.

But he couldn't get back to sleep, and that was annoying because sleep was a refuge from boredom and he was bored, he had to admit it—itchy and restless and bored. It was the middle of July and he'd been in California for seven weeks now, living in a ground-floor room in the servants' quarters of the big stone house, while the servants — wops, mostly, but there were a couple of Spaniards or Mexicans mixed in — crowded into the cottages out back. Mart was in the room next to him, but Nick and Pat had moved into town when their families came out to join them — and Rosaleen was supposed to have come with them, two weeks ago now, but O'Kane had put her off. He told her it was because he hadn't been able to find a decent place for her and the baby, and that was the truth — he hadn't. Of course, he'd been into town exactly four times since he'd arrived, and when he was there — at night, in the company of Mart and Roscoe LaSource, the chauffeur — he wasn't looking for apartments.

He felt bad about that, and he missed his son — and Rosaleen too, and maybe even his parents and Uncle Billy and his sisters into the bargain — but he wanted to experience California on his own, wanted to suck everything he could out of this otherworldly place where lizards licked over the rocks and the flowers were like trees and the ocean stretched all the way to China. It was just what he'd imagined, only so much richer and more complex, as if what he'd pictured California to be was just the first page in a whole encyclopedia of imaginings. There were ferns twenty feet tall, trees that shed bark instead of leaves, palms as thin as lampposts, and flowers, flowers everywhere — the whole world was flowers. It was drier than he would have guessed — it hadn't rained a drop in the whole time he'd been here, if you discounted the mist that settled on everything and made a lingering dream of the mornings — and he'd never realized that Riven Rock and all these grand estates were going to be so far from town, five miles at least. Maybe he ought to buy a bicycle — or sprout a pair of wings. Christ, as it was he felt as much a prisoner as poor Mr. McCormick, and that was what he missed most — the saloons, the shops, the pavement, streetlights, civilization.

He'd never lived in the country before, never awakened to roosters and cows, never spent so much time with foreigners — Italians, that is. They were everywhere, shambling along the dirt lanes in baggy pants and sweat-stained shirts, hewing stones, trimming hedges, hoeing up weeds in the orchards, not to mention slapping the hind end of every cow and goat in the county six times a day and pounding the laundry in big tubs out in the courtyard or creeping through the house with mops and brooms and a look of greasy resignation. But they were all right, the Italians. Most of them spoke English, or at least a version of it he and Mart could untangle, and he sat most nights on a rock in the middle of the orange grove with Sal and Baldy and some of the others, passing a jug of red wine or a jar of that liquid fire they called grappa. And their women weren't half bad, the young ones especially. They were more the bucolic type than Miss Ianucci maybe, but one or two of them really managed to get his attention.

And the oranges. They were right there hanging from the trees, no different from apples or peaches back East, and not a day passed when he didn't get up in the morning and saunter out in the perfumed air and pick himself two or even three of them and shuck the peels while he walked, the sun in his face, hummingbirds hanging over the flowers like bits of colored foil suspended in the air and the mountains standing up in front of him all wrapped in mist like an oil painting.

But still, he couldn't help thinking of Rosaleen as he heaved himself out of bed, slapped some water on his face and swept his hair back with the comb while he studied his chin in the mirror and debated whether he could get by without a shave. Maybe he should send for her—the McCormicks were paying for it. Then he could get a place downtown, on one of those streets up by the old Mission with all the shade trees, and he'd be close to the saloons and the lunch counters and the Chinese laundry, and he'd get it steady every night and never have to wake up to the damn chickens and feel so lonely and cored out. That's what he was thinking as he stood at the mirror knotting his tie and beginning to entertain notions of breakfast, Sam Wah's flapjacks and three eggs cooked in butter with a slab of fried ham and the fresh-baked bread he could already smell, when he happened to glance down at the letter on the bureau. It was from Rosaleen and it had come two days ago, and though he'd read it through six times already, in his present frame of mind he couldn't resist idly picking it up. And once it was in his hand, he almost involuntarily unfolded it and smoothed it out on the cool marble surface:

Dear Eddie:

The son is shinning I bot a new pair of short pance for Eddie Juner thank you for the money. He is so cut & I want you every nite so much to stick your thing in me I'm like a starving woman

with someboddy cooking bakon in the air so pleese Eddie send for
the tikets becoz Mildred Thompson and Ernestine and the boys all
left tow weeks ago & I miss you

Yours in Love & Lust,
Rosaleen

He could hear her voice and see her in a jerky series of poses,
mainly sexual, that was as flickery and fleeting as one of Edison's motion pictures, and that softened him. But then he took another look at
the looping backward scrawl of her cursive and the spelling that never
got past the third-grade level and wondered what had ever possessed
him to marry her. When she told him she was pregnant back in September, the two of them walking home hand-in-hand from Brophy's Bar &
Grill, the sky full of stars and her lips swollen like sponges and so sweet
he might have been licking the lid of a jar of honey, he should have run
and never looked back, should have bolted for Alaska, Siberia, any-
place. But he didn't. He married her. Stood at the altar and swore before God and Father Daugherty to live with her for the rest of his life.
Yes. But she was in Waverley, returned to the bosom of her family, back
with her father and mother and her fat-faced semimoronic brothers,
and he was here, in California, without a care in the world. And how
could you argue with that?

Mart was in the dining room, hunched over his plate and chewing
with a mindless stolidity, when O'Kane came in for breakfast. The doctor and Mrs. Hamilton weren't up yet. They were staying in one of the
guest rooms in the east wing, with their squally little baby, until they
could find a suitable house in the neighborhood. The servants were fed
in the servants' hall, to the rear of the house, and Mr. McCormick was
fed by his nurses, through a tube, at nine o'clock on the dot. So on this
particular morning, with the palest whitest ghostliest sun suspended in
an ether of mist that washed away the background till the whole house
might have been a ship at sea, it was just Mart and O'Kane at breakfast. "Top of the morning to you, Mart," O'Kane crowed, tipping back
the cover of the serving tray while the housemaid, a sexless spinster in
her forties by the name of Elsie Reardon, fluttered around him with a
pitcher of fresh-squeezed orange juice in one hand and a gleaming silver coffee urn in the other.

Mart grunted a reply. He'd washed his hair, which he combed

forward to soften the great gleaming lump of his forehead, and the hair, dangling wetly, had the effect of a bit of packing material pasted atop a lightbulb. There was egg on his chin.

"I don't know how you stand it," O'Kane sighed, sinking into the chair across from him. "I mean, being a bachelor out here in the middle of nowhere when your brothers are at home getting theirs every night and even Dr. Hamilton's got his wife with him . . . and the wops, they're out there in those cottages screwing like dogs. I can't stand it. I'm going crazy here."

Mart looked interested. He set down his fork, dabbed at his chin with the napkin. Elsie poured coffee with a scandalized face, then stumped out of the room. "What about Rose?"

O'Kane shrugged. "I'm talking about now, today, tonight. I'm used to having it, you know? Of course, look who I'm talking to—you probably never had a good screw in your life, am I right?"

Mart protested, but weakly, and O'Kane saw the truth hit home.

"It's like this ham"—and he held up the pink slab of it on the tines of his fork, crisp from the pan and iridescent with smoke-cured grease. "If Elsie didn't give you any tomorrow, you wouldn't think much of it. But if two days went by, three, a week—you know what I mean? And sex—well, that's a real bodily necessity, just like food and water and moving your bowels—"

"And whiskey," Mart put in with a sly smile. "Don't forget whiskey."

O'Kane grinned back. "What do you say we talk Roscoe into going into town tonight?"

And then it was the morning routine. Say goodnight to Nick and Pat, who were just coming off their shift, and hello to Mr. McCormick, bent up double like a pretzel in his bed; then it was strip off Mr. Mc-Cormick's nightgown and swab up the mess he'd left on the sheets, pack the whole business up for the laundress and give Mr. McCormick his shower bath, and all the while O'Kane thinking about Robert Ogilvie, director of the Peachtree Asylum in Stone Mountain, Georgia, who suspended all his catatonics on a rack in a big metal tub, day and night, and just changed the water when it got mucked up. No stains, no smells, no laundry—just a plug and a faucet. Now that was progress.

"He's not looking real good this morning," O'Kane observed when they first walked into the room and stood over the fouled bed and saw the position Mr. McCormick had got himself into.

Mart was oblivious. He merely bobbed his big head with the hair dried round it in a fringe and stared down at their employer as if he were a piece of furniture. "I've seen him worse."

Sometime during the night Mr. McCormick had hunched himself up like a fetus in the womb, and he'd managed to lock one foot behind the other in a way that looked uncomfortable, painful even—the sort of thing you'd expect from a swami or contortionist. He was breathing hard, his ribs heaving as if he'd just come back from a ten-mile run, and his eyes were open and staring and his hands locked together in an un-breakable clasp, but he didn't respond to them at all. They had no choice but to lift him out of bed as he was, a hand each under his armpit and buttock, and haul him over to the shower bath where the water would take some of the crust off him and they could get at the rest of it with a bar of Palm Olive soap and the scrub brushes, and it wasn't any different from any other day, but for the pose he was in. Still and all, it was a strange sensation to have to drag a man around like that, a grown naked man worth nobody knew how many millions and as lifeless as a side of beef hanging from a meathook. Only his eyes were alive, and they didn't register much—the quickest jump to the needles of water in the shower bath or the light bulging at the windows and then back to nothing.

It was eerie. Unsettling. No matter how often O'Kane experienced it or how many patients he'd seen like this—and he'd bathed them one after another at the Boston Lunatic Asylum, twenty at a time, hosing them down afterward like hogs in a pen—it still affected him. How could anybody live like that? Be like that? And what did it take for the mechanism to break down, for the normal to become abnormal, for a man like Mr. McCormick, who had everything and more, to lose even the faculty of knowing it?

"I wish he'd come out of it, Mart," he said after they'd set him down on his side under the spray of the shower bath. "Even if he got violent again—anything."

"Are you kidding?" Mart rubbed the spot over his left eye where their employer had slugged him on the train. Steam rose from the floor. Water hissed against the tiles. Mr. McCormick, his skin glistening and

the hair a dark skullcap pressed to his temples and creeping up the back
of his neck, began to grunt softly.

"Think about it, Mart—he's Stanley McCormick, one of the richest
men in the world, and he doesn't even know it. I mean, I've been so
blind drunk I didn't know where I was and I've slept in an alley once
and one time I woke up on the beach with a bunch of crabs scuttling all
over me, but I knew right away I was Eddie O'Kane."

Mart didn't seem to grasp the point. He just stared down at the
hunched-up shape on the naked tiles and began to shake his head. "I
wish he'd stay like this forever, nice and quiet." And then he lowered his
voice, because you could never tell what Mr. McCormick was thinking
or what he might retain. "If he gets well he won't need us anymore,
that's for sure—and then where would we be?"

At nine, after they'd massaged Mr. McCormick's muscles to loosen
him up a bit and got his feet untangled, Mart pried open the patient's
jaws with a wooden dowel and O'Kane jammed the feeding tube between his teeth. (And Mr. McCormick had good strong teeth, but
they'd gone yellow because he wasn't able to keep them up.) The tube
consisted of a hollowed-out piece of bamboo a headhunter might have
used to blow darts through and an ordinary kitchen funnel, and for
breakfast Mr. McCormick was having the same thing they'd had—ham,
eggs, toast and coffee—but it had been painstakingly reduced to a thick
black gruel by Sam Wah, the Chinese cook. While O'Kane was thus
employed, hovering over the gaping mouth of his patient like some
flightless bird with its unfathomable chick, waiting out the tedious drip
of the mash, repetitively wiping the patient's mouth and chin and pinching his nostrils to encourage the swallowing reflex, he couldn't help reflecting on the lack of progress Mr. McCormick had made over the
course of the past two months.

He hadn't always been like this. When he first came to McLean two
years back, he'd just broken down and the prognosis was good. He was
very disturbed, of course, particularly the first couple of days, lashing
out at anybody who came within three feet of him and raving to beat
the band about all sorts of things—Jack London, his father, dentists,
the Reaper Company and women, especially women, shouting out
"cunt" and "slit" and "whore" till the walls rang and his face was as
bleached out as a ream of white bond paper scattered in the snow—but
after a week in the sheet restraints he came around. He was calm sud-

denly, reasonable, a dignified gentleman who dressed himself in the morning without any tics or other nonsense and went around chatting and joking with the other patients and their relatives till people began to take him for one of the doctors. And Mr. McCormick, loving a joke, played along, dispensing advice, walking down the corridors arm-in-arm with the disappointed parent, the cousin from Bayonne, the somber sibling and the grim-faced husband, and he was fine with the women too, the soul of courtesy and with the softest, most genteel and solicitous voice O'Kane had ever heard.

Within a week he'd singled out O'Kane—called him "Eddie" and asked for him especially—and together they took long walks on the sanatorium grounds, played golf, croquet, shuffleboard and chess. He insisted there was nothing wrong with him—just nerves and overwork, that was all—and he spoke and dressed so beautifully and had such a smile on his face for everybody, O'Kane almost came to believe him. In the evenings he would hold the ward spellbound with tales of his travels—and he'd been everywhere, all the capitals of Europe, Egypt, way out to Albuquerque, Carson City and San Francisco—and he charmed everybody, doctors, nurses and patients, with his jokes. He was forever joking—not practical jokes, nothing malicious or unbalanced, as you found with so many of the other patients, nothing like that at all. Nothing off-color either. And while the jokes themselves might have been old in his mother's time ("What did the breeze say to the windowscreen?"; " 'Don't mind me, I'm just passing through' "), he took such obvious delight in them, his face opening up with that gift of a smile he had and his eyes crinkled to slits, they were irresistible, even when you'd heard them ten times already.

Everyone was optimistic. Everyone was pleased. Nerves, that's all it was. But then one morning, after an extended visit from his wife, he wouldn't get out of bed. The smile was gone, the jokes dead and buried. He wouldn't talk, wouldn't eat, wouldn't use the toilet or clean himself. Dr. Hamilton, Dr. Cowles and Dr. Meyer all tried to reason with him, talking till their throats went dry, pleading, remonstrating, cajoling and threatening—they even brought the august Dr. Emil Kraepelin all the way from Munich to try his hand—but Mr. McCormick just seemed to sink deeper into himself, like a man mired to his chin in quicksand and not a thing in the world anybody could do about it. It wasn't long after that that he attacked Nurse Doane—Arabella—and had to go back to the sheet restraints.

The hope was that California would bring him around, but as far as O'Kane could see it was an exercise in futility. At least so far. Mr. Mc-Cormick was as blocked now as he'd ever been, so deeply buried beneath his layers of phobias and hallucinations he didn't even recognize his nurses. And no one seemed to care—he'd been delivered to Riven Rock trussed up like a prize turkey and with no more consciousness than a fat feathered bird and that was the end of it, out of sight, out of mind. No one except Mrs. McCormick, that is. Katherine. She'd stayed on the whole time, long after Mr. McCormick's mother and sister and Mr. Harold McCormick had left, coming out to the estate every morning without fail, probing Hamilton and the nurses, quizzing the maids, the butler and even the cook with his deracinated English. *What did my husband have for breakfast? Is he eating? How's his color?* O'Kane had twice seen her creeping round the shrubbery with a pair of opera glasses in the hope of catching a glimpse of her husband when he was wheeled out on the sunporch. But Nick and Pat had lost all interest, treating their employer as if he were just another drooler on the violent ward, Mart didn't seem to trouble himself much one way or the other, and Hamilton was so busy with his apes and finding a house and mollifying his wife over the move from Massachusetts, he'd barely had time to stick his head in the door lately.

And where did that leave O'Kane? Out here in the wings of Paradise with a bunch of wops and an ache in his groin that was like a fever, waiting for the day when Mr. McCormick would get well again and reward his diligence and loyalty, the day when his own oranges would hang heavy on the limbs and he could finally, at long last, take center stage and let the drama of his own life begin.

In the afternoon he was sitting at the desk in the upper hallway, just inside the barred door to Mr. McCormick's quarters, playing solitaire and flipping open his watch every thirty seconds to personally record the testudineous advance of time, when Dr. Hamilton came stutter-stepping up the stairs, all out of breath. "Edward," he cried, "Edward, you've got to see this!"

O'Kane looked up from the cards, glad of the distraction. He gave a glance to Mart and the bundled form of Mr. McCormick in the center of the bed behind him and then got up to unlock the door, ever mindful of the three p's. "What is it?" he asked, turning the keys in their locks. "Another hominoid?"

In the light of the hallway, illumined by the tireless California sun streaming in through the upper windows, the doctor's head seemed to glow. He was showing a lot of scalp lately, pale striations against the dun slick of his hair, and O'Kane saw with a shock that his hairline had begun to recede—and when had that started? His face too—the lines seemed to have deepened and there was something else, something altogether queer about him . . . but of course, he'd shaved his beard. "You shaved your beard," O'Kane heard himself saying.

The doctor waved him off, as if it wasn't worth mentioning—but it was, because that beard was his psychiatric badge, the very twin of the beard that sprouted from the face of Dr. Freud. How could he practice psychiatry without a beard? It was unthinkable. "The wife never cared for it," Hamilton explained, breathing hard from his exertion, "and besides, with the hominoids it was becoming a liability—Mary was afraid it would attract fleas. Or worse. But enough of the beard—I've got something to show you, Edward, something truly astounding, the best find yet. Come on, come on: what are you waiting for?"

And then they were down the stairs, through the kitchen and out the back door, heading toward the hominoid laboratory, the doctor so worked up it was all he could do to keep from breaking into a trot. O'Kane could hear the screeching and caterwauling of the monkeys long before they hit the path that wound in under the oaks, and he could smell them too—a ripe festering flyblown reek of hominoid sweat and vomit and the killing stench of monkey fur clotted with excrement. And he could call them monkeys now, outside Hamilton's hearing anyway, because that's what they were: nine rhesus monkeys and a pair of olive baboons. Apes, as it turned out, weren't so easy to come by. The doctor had made application to every exotic animal dealer, circus and zoo up and down the coast, hoping for chimps, but there were none to be had.

He found monkeys, though, and there were more coming. After the first two ratlike little things died with blood leaching out their ears and anuses, the doctor got lucky and was able to purchase nine more at a single stroke from one of the local millionaires, an eccentric who had a whole menagerie running wild on his property, ostriches, kangaroos, boa constrictors, impala and dik-dik, and he'd tracked down the baboons in a decrepit zoo in Muchas Vacas, Mexico, where a few pesos went a long way. O'Kane was just happy he didn't have to look after the things—and they hadn't been there two weeks when Hamilton began hinting around, but in the end he wound up hiring two scrawny little brown men, one wop and one Mexican, to construct the cages and hose the reeking piles of crap out of them every morning.

Monkeys didn't have a whole lot of appeal for O'Kane—they reminded him too much of the droolers and shit-flingers he'd been wedded to for the past seven years, and that was an era he wanted to put behind him, permanently. He was head nurse to Stanley McCormick now, and before long he'd be an orange rancher or an oil man, strutting around the lobby of the Potter Hotel in a Panama hat while his own motorcar stood out front at the curb. Of course, as long as he was under the thumb of Hamilton he'd at least have to feign interest in hominoids, but he really didn't see the point—a whole wagonload of monkeys wouldn't cure what ailed Mr. McCormick. And as far as he could tell, Katherine wasn't much for hominoids either, though she was willing to go along in the hope that Hamilton's experiments would lead to a cure for her husband, and she spent a good part of each visit out there under the trees listening to Hamilton go on about hominoid micturition, auto-eroticism and frequency of copulation. The doctor had given the monkeys names like Maud, Gertie and Jocko, and the way he talked about them you'd have thought he'd personally fathered them all. ("Jocko achieved coitus with Bridget six times yesterday, and twice with Gertie," he would say, or, "The minute I let Jimmy into Maud's cage she assumed the sexually submissive posture and exposed her genitalia.") To O'Kane's way of thinking, the whole business was a bit, well, excessive. Not to mention dirty-minded.

But there was Hamilton, standing between the grinning wop and the grinning spic, ready to flick a filthy checkered tablecloth off what looked to be a cage behind him. He was beaming like a magician. The monkeys screeched and stank. Sunlight filtered softly through the trees. "Ready, Edward? Voilà!"

The tablecloth fluttered to the ground and the cage stood revealed. Inside was a pale orange aggregation of limbs and hair that looked like nothing so much as a heap of palm husks until it began to stir. O'Kane saw two liquid eyes, nostrils like gouges in a rubber tire, the naked simian face. "Jesus, Mary and Joseph," he said, "what is it?"

"Orang-utan," the doctor pronounced. "Literally, 'man of the forest.' His name is Julius, and he comes to us all the way from Borneo, courtesy of one of Captain Piroscz's colleagues, Benjamin Butler, of the *Siam*." The doctor's grin ate up his face. "Our first ape."

O'Kane took a step back when Hamilton reached down to unlatch the mesh door of the cage. He was thinking of the one-eyed chimp in Donnelly's and the way it had taken hold of Frank Leary's hand—and wasn't that a fine thing for an ape to do?

"It's all right," the doctor reassured him, "he's quite tame. A former pet. Come on, Julius," he cooed, his voice sweetened to the hypnotic whisper he used on his ravers and lunatics, "come on out now." A pair of oranges, held seductively aloft, was the inducement.

"Are you sure—?" O'Kane began.

"Oh, yes, there's nothing to worry about," Hamilton said over his shoulder. "They've had him on shipboard since he was a baby and they all loved him, the whole crew, and they hated to give him up, but of course now that he's full-grown it became too dangerous, what with the rigging and pots of hot tar and whatnot. . . . Come on, that's a boy."

Soundlessly, the shabby orange creature unfolded itself from the cage, crouching over its bristling arms like a giant spider. O'Kane took another step back and the two keepers exchanged a nervous glance— the thing was nearly as big as they were, and it certainly outweighed them. And, of course, like all the rest of the hominoids, it stank like a boatload of drowned men.

Julius didn't seem much interested in the oranges, but he folded them into the slot in the middle of his plastic face as if they were horse pills and shambled through the dust to where the monkeys and baboons were affixed to the doors of the cages and shrieking themselves breathless. He exchanged various fluids with them, his face drooping and impassive even as they clawed at the mesh and bared their teeth, then sat in the dirt sniffing luxuriously at his fingers and toes before lazily hoisting himself into the nearest tree like a big dangling bug, where he promptly fell asleep. Or died. It was hard to tell which—he was so utterly inanimate and featureless, it was as if someone had tossed a wad of wet carpeting up into the crotch of the tree.

O'Kane could feel Hamilton's eyes on him. "Well?" the doctor demanded. "What do you think? Magnificent, isn't he?"

The two keepers had moved off into the big central enclosure
Hamilton had designed as a communal area where his hominoids could
"interact," as he called it, busying themselves with setting up the apparatus for one or another of the doctor's arcane experiments. The monkeys, locked up in their individual cages, watched them with shining
eyes. They knew what the doctor's experiments meant: eating, fighting
and fucking, and not necessarily in that order. O'Kane was at a loss for
words.

"You don't look terribly enthusiastic, Edward," Hamilton observed,
the beardless jaw paler than the rest of his face, like the etiolated flesh
beneath a bandage. His eyes did a quick flip.

"No, it's not that—I was wondering if you can get more, uh, hominoids like this orange one. It must be pretty rare. I have to admit I've
never seen anything like it."

"Oh, it is, it is. But apes are what we want, Edward. The *Macacus
rhesus* is a splendid experimental subject, and we're fortunate to have
them, the baboons too, but the apes are our nearest cousins and the
more of them we can get, the more thorough—and relevant—my studies will be. Don't you see that?"

O'Kane was working the toe of his shoe in the friable yellow dirt,
creating a pattern of concentric circles, each one swallowing up the
next. He wanted a drink. He wanted a woman. He wanted to be downtown, with Mart and Roscoe LaSource, his elbows propped up on a
polished mahogany bar and a dish of salt peanuts within easy reach.
"Listen, Dr. Hamilton," head down, still working his shoe in the dirt,
"there's something I've been wondering about, and I don't mean to
sound disrespectful or to question your methods in any way, but I can't
really see how all this is supposed to help Mr. McCormick. What I
mean is, the monkeys are out here going through their paces and he's in
there twisted up like a strand of wire, and I may be wrong, but I don't
see him getting any better."

The doctor let his eyes flip once, twice, and O'Kane was reminded
of a bullfrog trying to swallow something stuck in its craw. There was a
long silence, the monkeys chittering softly in anticipation of their release into the larger pen, the breeze shifting ever so subtly to concentrate their odor. O'Kane wondered if he'd gone too far.

"First of all, Edward," Hamilton said finally, his eyes looming up amphibiously from beneath the gleaming surface of his spectacles, "I want to say how pleased I am to see that you're taking an active interest in Mr. McCormick's condition. As I've said, he is the key to everything we do here, and we can never lose sight of that fact. Dr. Kraepelin may have pronounced him incurable, but both Dr. Meyer and I disagree with that diagnosis—there's no reason why he shouldn't experience if not a complete cure then at least an amelioration of his symptoms and a gradual reintegration into society."

There was a sudden crash from the direction of the big cage, followed by a duet of Mexican and Italian curses—*puta/ puttana, puta/ puttana*—and O'Kane glanced up to see the keepers fumbling with a gaily painted wooden structure the size of a piano. He recognized it as the clapboard chute the doctor had designed to test his monkeys' mental adroitness: there were four exit panels, and the monkeys had to remember which one was unlocked and led to the reward of a banana. In the same instant Hamilton jerked his head angrily round, his voice igniting with fury: "Be careful with that, you incompetent idiots! If you so much as chip the paint I'll dock your wages, believe me, I will!" and then he broke into Italian—or maybe it was Mexican. The veins stood out in his throat and his face took on the color of the plum tomatoes the wops were growing out back of the cottages. O'Kane was impressed.

He must have raved at them in their own language for a good minute or more, and then he turned back to O'Kane as if nothing had happened, the coolest man in the world, his voice reduced to its habitual mesmeric whisper. "Certainly Mr. McCormick's case is a difficult one, Edward, and I can assure you it disturbs me no end to see him as thoroughly blocked as he is now, but that's all the more reason to take extraordinary measures, to go where no man has gone before in an attempt to uncover the psychological underpinnings of infrahuman behavior—sexual behavior, that is—so that we can apply them to our own species, and, specifically, to Mr. McCormick, whose generosity has made all this possible to begin with."

But how long was it going to take? That's what O'Kane wanted to know. Six months? A year? Two years? Three? "But just last fall I was playing golf with him," he heard himself saying, "and now he can't even talk. And you're telling me a bunch of monkeys or hominoids or whatever you want to call them mounting each other six times a day is going to get him up out of that bed?"

Again, a silence. The doctor patted down his pockets till he produced his pipe, tobacco and a match. He took his time lighting the pipe, watching O'Kane all the while. He was in control here and he wouldn't be rushed. Or provoked. "I'm telling you, *Edward*," he said, emphasizing the name in that irritating way he had, "that as Charcot, Breuer and Chrobak all observed, and Dr. Freud's brilliant *Drei Abhandlungen sur Sexualtheorie* reaffirms, all nervous disorders have a genital component at root. Do you doubt for a moment that Mr. McCormick's problem is sexual? You saw how he attacked that woman on the train and that female nurse at McLean, what was her name?"

"Arabella Doane," O'Kane said mechanically.

"Sex is the root and cause of every human activity, Edward, from getting up in the morning and going to work to conquering nations, inventing the lightbulb, buying a new coat, putting meat on the table and looking at every woman that passes by as a potential mate. Sex is the be-all and end-all, our raison d'être, the life force that will not be denied." The doctor had moved a step closer. O'Kane could see the dark bristles like flecks of pepper on his chin. "We are animals, Edward, never forget it—and animals, these hominoids that don't seem to impress you all that much, will one day reveal our deepest secrets to us." As if on cue, one of the monkeys began to howl in orgasmic ecstasy. The doctor's eyes were blazing. "Our sexual secrets," he added with a failing hiss of breath.

It was just then, just as the very words passed the doctor's lips, that O'Kane happened to glance up and see Giovannella Dimucci crossing the path behind them in a brilliant swath of sunlight. She was wearing a pair of clogs and he could see her bare ankles thrusting out from beneath the hem of her skirt, the bright trailing flag of her hair, her breasts shuddering against the fabric of her blouse and her hands moving at her sides with rhythmic grace as she disappeared round the bend. O'Kane looked back at the doctor, at the monkeys clinging to their cages in lust and hope and at the big orange lump in the crotch of the tree. He wiped a hand across his face, as if to erase it all. He was sweating, and he was conscious of a corresponding dryness in his throat, the parched ache of the saint in the desert.

"Well," he said with a sigh, as if he could barely tear himself away, "it's a fine ape you've got there, doctor, and I thank you for taking the time to show it to me and explain everything — I feel better now, I do — but I've got to be getting back . . . Mart'll be wondering where I am. So. Well. Good-bye."

Giovannella Dimucci was the daughter of Baldessare Dimucci, who hauled manure from Crawford's Dairy Farm in a creaking horse cart for sale to orange growers and wealthy widows with flower beds and half-acre lawns. She was seventeen, strong in the shoulders, eager and quick to please, and she'd been working in the kitchen for the past week while the regular maid, a hunched little wart of a woman by the name of Mrs. Fioccola, recuperated from the birth of the latest of twelve children, all of them girls. O'Kane caught up to her as she was ascending the back steps, an empty slops bucket in her hand. "Giovannella," he called, and he watched her turn and recognize him with a smile that spread from her lips to her eyes.

"Eddie," she said, and it was his turn to smile now. "What a surprise to see you this time of day." She set down the bucket and let her smile bloom. There was movement behind the screen door — Sam Wah at the stove, his back to them, and one of the other maids, O'Kane couldn't tell which, at the sink with a pile of dishes. From around the corner, by the garage, came the sounds of Roscoe tinkering with the cars, an engine alternately roaring and wheezing, and the faint, sweet smell of gasoline. Still smiling, a busy finger between her lips, Giovannella let her voice drop: "Aren't you supposed to be with Mr. McCormick now? Or did you change shifts?"

O'Kane moved toward her, as if in a trance, and sat right down at her feet on the lower step. He could smell the perfume of her body, soap on her hands, the sour vinegary odor of the slops bucket. "Yes, yes, I am" — a wink, squinting up the length of her and into the sun framing her head and shoulders and the dark cameo of her face — "you really know my schedule, don't you?"

No blush, but the smile faltering for just an instant before it came back again. She glanced over her shoulder at the silhouette of Sam Wah, then tugged at her skirts and sat lightly beside him. "Sure I do. I know everybody's schedule — even Mr. McCormick's."

"Smart girl," he said.

"Yes, I'm a smart girl." The trace of an accent. She was nine years old when her father emigrated from Marsala and she was as American as anybody, as Rosaleen even, but darker, a whole lot darker, darker than any Irishman ever dreamed possible. Rosaleen's skin was china-white, chalky, lunar, so pale the blue veins stood out in her ankles and wrists and between her breasts; Giovannella's was like Darjeeling tea steeped in the pot and dipped into a cup of scalded milk, one drop at a time. He was in love with that skin. He wanted to lick her fingers, her hands, her feet.

"He's a very dangerous man," O'Kane said to distract himself.

"Who?"

"Mr. McCormick."

The sun, the flowers, the soft gabble of the chickens, the roar of the motor. Giovannella lifted her eyebrows.

"He's what they call a sex maniac—you know what that is?"

She didn't. Or at least she pretended she didn't.

"He needs—well, he has physical needs all the time, for women, you understand? He gets violent. And if he's not satisfied, he'll lash out if he has the opportunity and attack a woman, any woman—even his wife."

Her face had turned somber and he wondered if he'd gone too far, if he'd shocked her, but then the mask dissolved and she leaned in close, her hand on his elbow. "Sounds like the average man to me."

Suddenly O'Kane was on fire. It was as if an incendiary bomb had gone off inside him, three alarms and call out the village companies too. "Listen," he said, "you know I really like you, you're a real kidder, but it's such a grinding bore here, isn't it? What I mean is, I think I can get Roscoe to take us into town tonight in one of the Packards, that is, if you want to come . . . with me, I mean . . . together."

She looked over her shoulder again, as if someone might be listening. Her head bobbed low and her eyes took on a sly secretive look. Her father would never let her go, O'Kane knew that, though Baldy never suspected O'Kane was a married man. It was just the way the Italians were when it came to their women—especially their daughters. They were wary of every male between the ages of eleven and eighty, unless he was a priest, and no matter how drunk they were on their Bardolino and grappa they always had one eye open, watching, waiting, ready to pounce. He was sure she was going to say no, sure she was going to plead her father's prohibition and her mother's lumbago and the crying need to look after her ragged shoeless little brothers and sisters and keep the fire going under the big pot of pasta e fagioli, but she surprised him. Compressing her lips and sucking in her breath, her eyes leaping round the yard to fasten finally on his, she whispered, "What time?"

O'Kane was drunk when he got in the car, drunk when he instructed Roscoe to pull over on a dark lane by the olive mill while Mart fidgeted in the front seat and Giovannella, dressed all in white, darted barefoot out of a gap in the oleanders and climbed into the leather seat beside him with her shoes in her hand and smelling of garlic and basil and melted butter till it made his mouth water, and he was drunk as Roscoe fought the gears and Mart looked straight ahead and Giovannella fit herself in under his arm and nuzzled the side of his face.

They had a high time of it in town, all four of them going into a lunchroom and having fried potatoes and egg sandwiches with ketchup, which sobered O'Kane enough to allow him to concentrate on the way Giovannella sipped sarsaparilla from a straw, and then they went on to Cody Menhoff's restaurant and saloon, where O'Kane restoked his fires with whiskey and beer till he practically attacked her on a bench out front of the Potter Hotel. And the thing was, she didn't seem to mind, giving as good as she got, and by the time she hopped down from the car again and disappeared in the gap in the oleanders like a sweet apparition, it was past midnight and O'Kane was in love.

By the end of the week she'd let him do everything, out under the stars by Hot Springs Creek where they lay naked for hours on a quilt his grandmother had pieced together by candlelight back in Killarney. He was careful to withdraw before he came, but she was reckless and passionate, thrashing beneath him and clinging to his shoulders and groin with a ferocity that made it almost impossible to tear himself away, and in that moment when he felt the uncontainable rush coming up in him it was like a wrestling match, like war, like the birth and death and resurrection of something as terrible as it was beautiful. But he was stronger, and he prevailed. He'd got one girl knocked up already and he was damned if he was going to knock up another one.

Giovannella sat up quaking in the rinsed-out light of the moon and sobbed over his spilled seed, touching her fingers to the glistening puddle on the taut brown drum of her abdomen and then sucking the tips of them till her lips glistened too. "Eddie," she sobbed, over and over, "don't you love me? Don't you want to give me a baby? Eddie, it's a sin, a mortal sin, and you don't love me, I know it, you don't." He'd whisper nonsense to her, promise her anything, then she'd quiet down for a minute and he'd take a long drink from the jug of wine and hand the jug to her and she'd take a drink, her breasts trembling and swinging free with the movement of her arms and he'd put his hands out to steady them and press his mouth to hers to kiss away the sobs and before long they were at it again, locked together like adversaries, like lovers.

He couldn't get enough of her. All day, every day, he felt her touch, the whole world gone tactile, electricity surging through him, his clothes chafing, the blankets on his bed itching and binding like so many hair shirts. He wanted to be naked. He wanted to be with her, wanted to touch her, taste her, run his fingers through her hair, over her breasts, into the wet silk of her cleft. He didn't write to Rosaleen. He didn't open her letters. She was dead and buried and so was Eddie Junior, a mistake, a mysterious excrescence that had grown up out of nothing, a mound of yeast, a toadstool, a cancer, this thing that emerged from a quick hot struggle with heavy clothes on a cold night in a cold barn. *"Giovannella,"* he said to himself, whispering her name even as he lowered Mr. McCormick into the shower bath or listened to the doctor go on about his monkeys or sat at breakfast with poor simple Mart and discussed the weather. *"Giovannella,"* he breathed, *"Giovanella Dimucci."*

A month went by. And then there came a night when he went into town with Mart and Roscoe and no thought for her. He was drunk, very drunk, and he went swimming off West Beach in his clothes and ruined his shoes and a good pair of trousers. He woke at four A.M. with a spike driven through his head, as parched as a desert nomad, and somehow she was there, in his room, perched atop him with her legs splayed and her hands balled up, muttering to herself. "You son of a bitch!" she cried the minute he opened his eyes in the gloom, the hard little nuggets of her fists raining down on his chin, his ears, his mouth, in a buffeting fury that was like a storm at sea. He tried to shush her, afraid Mart would hear from the adjoining room, or worse, Hamilton from the far side of the house, and he held up his forearms to deflect her blows, but he was too weak and too sick and her fists hit home again and again. He writhed, bucked his hips, tried to roll out from under her, cursing now, outraged and violated, the taste of his own blood on his lips, but she made a vise of her thighs and the drink sapped him until finally he could only cradle his head in his arms and wait her out.

How long it went on he couldn't tell, but when she was done sobbing and punching and flaying his forearms with her teeth and nails, she leaned forward till her face was in his and he could feel the harsh fury of her breathing on the naked surface of his eyes, his lips, his cheekbones. Her breath was metallic. Acidic. It wilted him where he lay. "I would kill myself for you," she hissed, "kill my parents, my sisters and brothers, kill the whole world." And then she was gone. Through the window, out into the night, and back to the shuck mattress she shared with her sisters Marta and Marietta in the dark seething fastness of the Dimucci household.

They made it up the next day and he loved her over and over again, in every way he could dream or devise, and she clawed at his back and begged him to be a man, a husband, and stay inside her till he gave her a baby, but he wouldn't and they fought over that. Sated, panting, slick with sweat, they lay side by side on the quilt beneath the trees, silent as enemies, until she sat up and dressed herself and left without a word. Then he made himself scarce for a couple of days and he didn't see her. He took the precaution of putting a lock on the window, and he felt bad about it, but he couldn't have Dr. Hamilton catch her climbing into his room. Or Katherine—what if she found out? He went into town to Nick's place to celebrate Ernestine's birthday and drank enough beer to float a ship and never once whispered Giovannella's name to himself. She wasn't around in the daytime anymore—Mrs. Fioccola was back in the kitchen now and Giovannella had no business at Riven Rock—and her only recourse was to come lurking round at night and throw pebbles at the windowpanes. The pebbles came like hail. The window rattled furiously in its iron frame. Dogs barked in the night, and twice the servants came frothing out of their cottages and chased phantoms round the courtyard. And how did O'Kane feel? He felt irritated. He didn't need this. She was like a madwoman, like a harpy, and all he'd wanted was a girl, all he'd wanted was innocence, softness, the gentle yielding of love.

A week went by, and O'Kane took to walking into town at night, five miles there and five miles back, avoiding the Italians who gathered after supper on the big rock in the orchard with their checkers and squeezebox and grappa; he sat up till one and two in the morning with

Nick and Pat and the softly snoring husk of their employer, shun-
ning his room till he was so shot through with exhaustion he could shun
it no longer. To his relief, there were no more pebbles, no more alarums
in the night. Giovannella was gone. It was over. And he was just trying to adjust to the sad reality of that fact, feeling a little wistful and
blue, when on a clear flower-spangled Saturday morning, Baldessare
Dimucci and his eldest son, Pietro, trundled up the long stone drive in
their manure cart and parked in front of the garage. Elsie Reardon
came to get him. "There's two men want to see you, Eddie," she said,
peering in through the bars to Mr. McCormick's quarters. "Two wops."

When Hamilton summoned him to the library that evening after his
shift, O'Kane didn't think anything of it—usually the doctor wanted to
compare notes on Mr. McCormick's progress, or lack of it, either that
or talk his ear off about Julius's bowel movements or Gertie and how
many times she'd been mounted by Jocko while Mutt looked on. But as
soon as he stepped into the room and saw Mrs. McCormick and her
mother sitting there like hanging judges and the doctor drawing a face
about half a mile long, he knew he was in for it. Even before Katherine
said, "Good evening, Mr. O'Kane, please take a seat," in her iciest voice
and the mother flashed him a quick fading smile out of habit and the
doctor cleared his throat ostentatiously and let the light glare off his
spectacles so you couldn't see his eyes flipping, O'Kane was thinking of
how to explain away the little contretemps in the courtyard, dredging
up mitigating circumstances and constructing an unassailable wall of
half-truths, plausible fictions and unvarnished lies.

Over the years, in his relations with women—and those relations
had been extensive, prodigious even—he'd learned that it was always
best to deny everything. And so he'd attempted to do with Dimucci
père and fils, but the Dimuccis, choleric and quick to act, the end product of centuries of blood feuds and immutable codes of peasant honor,
would have none of it. "Eddie," the old man cried out so that every
blessed soul within a thousand yards could hear him, "you ruin-a my
daughter Giovannella and now you got marry," while the son, five-foot-
nothing and with a face like a fox caught in a leg snare, glared violence
and hate. They wouldn't listen to reason. O'Kane tried to tell them they
weren't in Sicily anymore, that this was a free country and that Giovan-

nella was a grown woman and as guilty as he—guiltier, for the way she
strutted around the kitchen and pouted her lips over every little thing
and let her breasts hang loose like ripe fruit in a sack—but when he got
to the part about ripe fruit Pietro came for him and, regrettably, he had
to pin him to the wall of the house like a butterfly on a mounting board.

He felt bad about that. He was no monster. He didn't want to hurt
anybody. In all the time he'd been with Rosaleen he'd only slipped from
the straight and narrow two times, not counting Giovannella, and then
only when she was so big with the baby she couldn't satisfy him—or
wouldn't. She refused to use her mouth or even her hand, and she was
downright peevish about it, as if he'd asked her to shoot the pope or sell
her soul to the devil or something. And both times, sure enough, some
Judas betrayed him—he suspected it was her oldest brother, Liam,
who always had his nose in somebody's business, or her schoolfriend,
Irene Norman, who worked at Bisby's Lunchroom and chewed over
every piece of gossip in town three times a day—and Rosaleen had
raised holy hell, as if she needed anything to set her off. He denied
everything. Told her whoever was filling her head with all that crap was
a small, mean-spirited person who wasn't worth giving a thought to, but
Rosaleen screeched her lungs raw all the same and dented every pot
and pan in the house. "Admit it!" she demanded, screaming. "Admit it,"
she whispered after a night of lying awake beside him and sobbing, "admit it and I'll forgive you," but he knew better than that, knew he'd
hear about Eulalie Tucker and Bartholemew Pierson's wife Lizzie every
minute of every hour of every day of his life if he breathed a word.

But now, in the library, surrounded by the rich and many-hued
spines of the hundreds of beautiful leatherbound books Katherine had
stocked on the teakwood shelves in the past weeks against the day of
her husband's recovery, he felt at a loss. How much did they know?
How much did it matter? Was he their nigger slave, to be whipped and
reprimanded and hounded over every little detail of his private life?
That was what he was thinking as he took his seat and tried to look at
Katherine without blinking or staring down at his shoes. There was a
moment of excruciating silence, during which he heard the call of a
monkey echoing forlornly over the grounds. "Yes?" he said finally, taking the initiative. "Can I be of help?"

Katherine stiffened. She was dressed in velvet, in the royal shade of
maroon Monsignor O'Rourke used to don for Lent and Advent, with a

matching hat and plume of aigrettes. Her posture, as always, was flawless, knees and feet pressed together and neatly aligned, her back held
so rigidly it was concave, her chin thrust forward and her lips clamped
tight. "You certainly can," she said, and her eyes gave him no respite.
"Perhaps, Mr. O'Kane, you could offer an explanation of this incident—
or rather, this affair—with the peasant girl."

He tried to hold her eyes, tried to project innocence, humility, a
ready willingness to do all he could to clear up what was at worst a
simple misunderstanding, but he couldn't. Her eyes were like whistling
bullets, explosions in the dark. He looked to the mother, but she was off
in a dream of her own, and then to Hamilton, but he was mimicking
Katherine. "Well," he said, trying on his winningest smile, the one his
mother claimed could restart the hearts of the dead, raising his eyes to
meet hers and grinning, grinning, "it's all innocence is what it is, a
school-girl crush, that's all. You see, the girl in question was filling in
here temporarily in the kitchen while Mrs.—"

Katherine cut him off. She took that rigid coatrack of her perfect
back and perfect shoulders and leaned so far forward he thought she
was going to splinter and crack. "You do understand, Mr. O'Kane, that
I am in charge here now?" she said, and he was quick to note the edge
of impatience in her voice.

This was no time for improvisation—she was the conductor and he
was the orchestra. "Yes, ma'am," he said, and meant it. In the past months
she'd redecorated the house, removing the gloomy Spanish paintings,
heavy black furniture and pottery to the attic above the garage and re-
placing it with seascapes and western scenes, modern chairs and sofas
with square edges and low backs, draperies that gave back the light and
made the place look less like a West Coast version of McLean and more
like the home of an important and consummately sane man with just the
slightest, most temporary indisposition. She'd hired a new head gardener,
a landscape architect and half a dozen new wops and Mexicans. And
though the McCormicks still owned the house and Mr. McCormick paid
a monthly rental back to his mother, all decisions, no matter how trivial,
went through Katherine. She was in charge. There was no doubt about it.

"Good," she said, "because I want you to keep that in mind when
you hear what I'm about to say."

O'Kane glanced round the room. The doctor shifted uneasily in his
chair; the old lady smiled faintly.

"I've spoken with the parties involved, Mr. O'Kane—in Italian, so as to be absolutely certain of the facts—and I find your behavior reprehensible. You've trifled with this young girl's affections, Mr. O'Kane, and worse, you've taken advantage of her. Ruined her, as they say. Do you think a female is just an object, Mr. O'Kane, a bit of flesh put on this earth to satisfy your lusts? Is that what you think?"

O'Kane's head was bowed, but he was fuming. He didn't give a damn who she was, she had no right—he was no slave—he was free to— "No," he said.

There was a pause. The lights glinted on the spines of the books, the crystal on the sideboard. The old lady, Katherine's mother, seemed to be humming to herself.

"Now Dr. Hamilton tells me you're an excellent nurse," Katherine went on, her voice strung tight, "and I know personally how devoted you are to my husband, but believe me, if it weren't for that I'd dismiss you on the spot. Do you understand me?"

"Yes," he said, and he was croaking, croaking like a frog, like something you'd step on and squash.

"Because as long as you work for Mr. McCormick you are his representative in the community and you will conduct yourself as befits his unimpeachable moral standards or you will find yourself looking for employment elsewhere. Not to mention the fact, which is perhaps the saddest feature of this whole affair, that you are a married man. You've taken holy vows, Mr. O'Kane, before God and man, and there is no earthly excuse for abjuring them. You disappoint me, you really do."

O'Kane had nothing to say. The bitch. The meddling snooty Back Bay bitch. How dare she dress him down like some schoolboy? How dare she? But he kept quiet because of the orange trees and Mr. McCormick and the best chance he had. He'd show her. Someday. Someday he would.

"There's one more thing," she said, relaxing finally into the embrace of the chair, though her feet remained nailed to the floor. "I've purchased two second-class tickets in your wife's name. I will expect her here by the end of next week."

6.

THE HARNESS

The second woman Stanley McCormick ever saw in a natural state was a French streetwalker by the name of Mireille Sancerre who wore undergarments of such an intense shade of red she was like a field of poppies suddenly revealed beneath the muted lights of her room. "Do you like maybe to watch?" she asked coyly as he lay paralyzed on her patchouli-scented sheets and saw the flaccid silky things fall from her to expose the whiteness at the center of her, the whiteness he expected and dreaded and lusted for. He was twenty years old, four months out of Princeton and a neophyte in the art studios of Monsieur Julien on the rue de Clichy in Montmartre. His brother Harold, who'd graduated with him in June, had just married Edith Rockefeller, and his mother, feeling Stanley's loss, had taken him on a tour of Italy and the antiquities of Europe as a way of distracting him. They got along beautifully, Stanley and his mother, savoring the chance to be alone together after the separation of college, but they quarreled over Stanley's plan to stay on in Paris for a few months and study sketching. To Nettie's mind, the most corrupt and iniquitous city in Europe was hardly the place for her youngest child to take up residence on his own for the first time in his life, while Stanley argued that Paris was the cynosure and sine qua non of the art world and protested that he might never have such an opportunity again.

"Mother," he cried, his face working and his eyes like mad hornets buzzing round his head as he stalked back and forth across the gilded expanse of their suite at the Elysée Palace Hotel, "it's the chance of a lifetime, my one opportunity to study with a French master before I go home to Chicago and step back into the harness. I'm only twenty. I'll be at the Reaper Works until I die."

Nettie, enthroned in her chair, lips drawn tight: "No."

"But mother, *why?* Haven't I been good? Haven't I done well at college and made you proud? Better than Harold—a hundred times better. I'm just asking for this one little thing."

"No."

"Please?"

"No. And that's final. You know perfectly well the temptations a young man of high character would be assaulted with daily in a city like this, a place I've always felt was full of foreigners of the very lowest repute, what with their obscene and sacrilegious views and their mocking attitude toward the moral and reflective life, and don't you think for a minute I haven't seen these pig-eyed Frenchmen smirking at us behind our backs. . . . And what of your health? Have you thought about that? Who's going to nurse you if that Egyptian fever comes back again— you're still frail from that, you know, and your color is nothing short of ghastly. Hm? I don't hear you, Stanley."

He had no answer to that, though he felt his color was fine, a little blanched and pallid, perhaps, but nothing out of the ordinary. He'd been pacing and now he stopped in front of the sitting room mirror and saw a face he barely recognized, staring eyes and collapsed cheeks, a gauntness that frightened him—he did need to gain back some of the weight he'd lost in his bout with typhus, he admitted it, but where better to do it than in the gustatory capital of the world?

"And your nervous condition—what about that?" his mother persisted. "No, I couldn't leave you here, never—I'd be prostrate with worry the whole way back. You wouldn't want that, would you?"

No, Stanley wouldn't want that, and he knew all about the severity of her heart condition and how much she needed him and how it would absolutely rend her to be without him even for a day, let alone two months or more, especially now, of all times, when Harold and Anita were gone and she had to go back to that big empty house all by herself and be alone with the servants, but for the first time in his life he stood up to her. For two weeks he gave her no peace, not a minute's worth, imploring, importuning, beating his breast, brooding and glowering and slamming doors till even the servants were in a state, and finally, against her better judgment, she relented. She found him a suite of very suitable rooms with a Mrs. Adela van Pele, a pious Presbyterian lady in her late middle age from Muncie, Indiana, who ran an irreproachable establishment in Buttes-Chaumont while her husband, the celebrated evangelist Mies van Pele, converted headhunters along the Rajang River in Borneo, and she had a long talk with Monsieur Julien, who assured her that her son would sketch only the most suitable subjects — that is, still lifes and landscapes, as opposed to anything even remotely corporeal. Satisfied, but weeping and tearing at her hair nonetheless, Nettie took passage home — alone. And it was on the very night of his mother's departure — on the way back from seeing her off, in fact — that Stanley, the blood singing in his ears, encountered Mireille Sancerre.

Or rather, she encountered him. He was walking down an unfamiliar street near the Gare du Nord at the time, wondering what to do first, and not paying a bit of attention to his surroundings. Should he go out for a meal at any restaurant that struck his fancy, and no one there to debate or belittle his choice? Or have a drink at a café and watch the people stroll by? Or he could go to a show, one of the titillating ones he'd heard so much about at college, or even, if he could work up the nerve, find a little shop where he could purchase a deck of those playing cards with the pictures on the reverse and steal silently back to his rooms to examine them at his leisure before Mrs. van Pele could get hold of him and coax him into singing hymns till bedtime.

Of course, just as keenly as he was tempted, he was struggling with his impure desires, thinking of how pious Mrs. van Pele really was, and what good company, and how generous it was of her to praise his voice, when Mireille Sancerre bumped into him. But this was no ordinary bump, the sort of casual contact one might encounter between acts at the opera or at a gallery or museum — it was a head-on collision, with plenty of meat and bone behind it. One minute Stanley was loping down the street in a daze, and in the next he was entangled, arm-in-arm and breast-to-breast, with a young woman, a female, whose entire repertoire of scents exploded in his nostrils while her huge quivering eyes seemed to burst up out of the depths of her face like buoys pinned beneath the waves and suddenly released. "Oh, monsieur, pardon!" she gasped. "Des milliers de pardons!"

And then, he never understood how, she convinced him in a matter of seconds to throw over every principle he'd ever held sacred and every last drop of the ethical and religious training he'd imbibed since birth, and come with her to her apartment. There were no introductions through mutual acquaintances, no recitations of the poetry of Elizabeth Barrett Browning or exchanging of coats of arms, no preliminaries of any kind. Within a hundred and eighty seconds of their encounter, Stanley found himself walking off down the street with this magnificent glossy thing on his arm, this little painted *poupée*, going he knew not where but prepared to kill anyone who might stand in his way.

"And so," she said again as the red sheaves fell away from her like the petals of a stripped flower to show all that chilling nullity beneath and the severed breasts and the black bull's-eye of hair right in the middle of the canvas, "do you like maybe to watch?" and in that moment her index and middle fingers disappeared inside of her like a magician's trick, right there in the center of that black bull's-eye, and he said no, the voice caught like a burr in his throat, no, he didn't want to watch, he couldn't watch, he was feeling faint and his blood was rushing like the famous cataract where all the brides and grooms of America went to celebrate their honeymoon and would she please, could she please, turn out the light. . . .

In the morning, he didn't know where he was — or at first, even who he was. He was a creature of nature, that was all, a pulsating nexus of undifferentiated sensations, and he had eyes, apparently, that opened and saw, and ears that registered the sounds filtering up from the street, and a groin that lived entirely on its own. He saw that he was in a cheap room, cheaply decorated, empty wine bottles on the dresser, discolored plates soaking in a tub on the floor, eggs in a basket, apples, a border of faded crepe tracing the perimeter of the ceiling, female clothes in a heap. For a long while he just lay there staring, and he was outside himself, he was, because there was some dark place inside him that knew what he had done and reveled in it and wanted to snuff it up and snuff up more of it, and he refused to let that dark place see the light.

Finally, after the sun had invaded the curtains to illuminate the foot
of the bed and trace a series of parallelograms across the floor, he sat
up. He was alone. He'd known he was alone from the moment he'd
opened his eyes and begun to absorb sensation like a sponge, but he
hadn't wanted to admit it because to admit it would be the first step in
recalling the name Mireille Sancerre. But now he was up and now he
recalled that name—it was on his lips like a fatal kiss—and everything
he'd done came hurtling at him in a shriek of accusation. He wasn't
wearing any clothes. He was naked. He was naked in a strange
woman's bed—Mireille Sancerre's bed. Slowly, with the dread and re-
luctance of the fear that verges on hysteria, he let his fingers creep
across his abdomen and touch the hair between his legs, caked and
crusted hair, laminated with the juices of Venus, and then, in a panic of
hate and renunciation, to his penis.

His penis. It was there, whole and alive, and it began to grow in his
hand until he pictured it like some terrible uncontainable thing out of a
fairy tale, the beanstalk that would sprout right up through the roof and
up into the reaches of the sky, and he snatched his hand away. Oh, what
had he done, what had he done? He was venal. Doomed. Condemned
to hell and perdition. He wished he was back in college again, back safe
in his rooms with his books and pennants and his leather harness—the
one he'd fashioned for himself when he first discovered the sin of self-
pollution. He was only a sophomore then, but that was the start of it—
and this, this was the end, all of life dirtier and progressively dirtier and
every one of us an animal rooting in it. The first time he'd ever awakened with the wet evidence of his depravity on the sheets he'd gone
right out to the nearest saddlery and brought himself a bridle and a set
of leather-working tools. Ignoring his classes, he worked furiously at
the thing, working through trial and error and with every particle of his
perfectionist's zeal, until, by suppertime, it was done. Two cuffs for his
hands and two for his ankles, joined by the knotted strips of the short-
ened reins, and he wore it every night, his harness, so that he would
never—could never—touch himself while he slept and dreamed or
woke in the groggy sensual limbo of dawn. And how he wished he had
that harness now. . . .

But it was too late. Of course it was. The damage was done, he'd
given way to his bestial instincts and he'd ruined a woman, ruined
Mireille Sancerre, and there was only one thing to do: marry her. For

the sake of his soul and hers. Yes, of course. The only thing to do. The realization gave him new life, and all at once he was up out of the bed and fumbling for his clothes—but what time was it? He couldn't seem to find his watch or his stickpin, the one his mother had given him on graduating Princeton, the one with the three winking sapphires she said were no match for his eyes . . . and then, as he pulled on his trousers and his jacket and felt through all his pockets, he was amazed, in the way of a man staggering out of a train wreck, to find that his wallet was gone too. But of course, he understood in an instant that Mireille Sancerre had taken his things, as a down payment on the mortgage of her ruination, and she had every right to them, every right to everything he owned. . . . After all, she was the one, the only one: she was his wife.

Stanley stayed on in her room through the hobbled morning and the decrepit afternoon, afraid to show his face on the street, the corruption festering in his flagitious eyes and sensual mouth, and though he was so thirsty he could have crawled a mile for a single drop of water and so gutted with hunger he was like a mad howling carnivore in the jungle, he never moved from the bed. Sometime in the late afternoon he found himself back in the wardrobe in the linen closet on the day before his father's funeral and there was a rasping harsh voice excoriating him there, a disembodied voice that raked the flesh from his bones, and he couldn't have moved if he'd wanted to. The sun shifted, paled, died. At long last, when it was dark, fully dark, he came back to that bed in Mireille Sancerre's cheap room that smelled of fermenting vegetables and scraps of rotting meat, and he saw his chance. In an instant he was on his feet and leaping at the door he'd been staring at all day, the door that gave onto a gloomy sweat-stinking stairwell, and before he could think he was charging down the stairs, oblivious to the startled faces on the landings and the cries at his back, down the stairs and into the street. He stumbled then and fell, a searing nugget of pain in his left palm and his knee too, but he picked himself up, found his legs and ran, ran till he could run no more.

Two weeks later, Harold stopped by Mrs. van Pele's to look him up. He brought Edith with him—they were honeymooning in Europe and had just arrived on the Continent after a week's stay in London—and Edith balanced herself like a buttercup on the cushions of Mrs. van Pele's best chair with a glass of Mrs. van Pele's best sherry on her knee

while Harold went up to fetch Stanley down from his rooms. Unfortunately, Stanley wasn't fetchable—at least not at first. Harold found him
in bed, lying atop the bedclothes on his side with his wrists and ankles
drawn up awkwardly behind him; his face was turned to the wall and
he didn't look up when his brother entered the room.

"Stanley!" Harold boomed, and he was an effervescing bubble of
enthusiasm, filled to bursting, a twenty-two-year-old millionaire intoxi-
cated with his new bride and his travels and his unshakeable alliance
with the Rockefellers. "Wake up," he cried, "Harold's here! Come on,
little brother, get up out of that bed and let's drink some champagne and
celebrate!"

But Stanley didn't get up out of bed—he barely lifted his eyes. As
Harold looked on, stupefied, Stanley's shoulders began to heave, his
visible eye clouded over and he began weeping, his breath coming in a
series of harsh protracted gasps that seemed to suck all the air out of the
room.

"What is it, Stanley?" Harold said, the enthusiasm erased from his
voice. "Are you still sick? Is it that Egyptian thing?"

A long moment, the gasps fighting for control. "Worse," Stanley
croaked, "a thousand times worse. I've lost my immortal soul."

It took nearly an hour to extract the story from him, Stanley hesitant and euphemistic, his shame burning in his eyes as he talked on and
on about repentance, atonement and eternal damnation, and twice during that time Harold descended to the parlor to commiserate with his
bride, whom he would divorce twenty-six years later for the ambitious
operatic fleshpot, Ganna Walska, and twice sent down for scalding
cups of tea. Stanley told him how he'd been searching for the unfortunate girl for two weeks now and had even gone to the trouble of hiring
a private detective to track her down, but with no success. He'd been in
too much of a state over the enormity of his crime to have paid any attention to the street or even the neighborhood where he'd awakened on
that fateful morning, and though he'd haunted the alleys and byways
around the Gare du Nord every night since, he'd been unable to locate
her. He didn't know her address, her place of business, her connections,
and yet he was determined to do the right thing by her—determined, in
short, to marry her.

When Harold had heard him out, the room stifling, his wife impatient and petulant and the landlady wearing the mask of a tragedian as

she tiptoed through the door with the tea things, he felt nothing but relief. Only Stanley could be so hopelessly naive, he thought, Stanley
the holy, Stanley the sheltered, and he didn't want to laugh at that
naïveté—this was a delicate situation, he knew that—but in the end he
couldn't help himself. "Is that it?" he said. "Is that all of it?" And then
he laughed. Guffawed. Let out with a howl his wife could hear downstairs as she fretted and grimaced and swore she'd get him back for this.

"Stanley, Stanley, Stanley," he said finally, and the laughter rolled
off him in sheets, like a disturbance of the weather, and there was no
stopping it. "Don't you see? She's a prostitute, a *putain*, a whore. She's
had you and a thousand other men. She's no purer than Beelzebub—
and she's gone and fleeced you on top of it. Why do you think she disappeared? Because your sapphire stickpin and your gold watch and the
hundred-franc notes in your wallet bought her a six months' holiday in
a very comfortable hotel in Marseille or Saint-Tropez or some such
place."

Stanley was sitting up now, staring into the dark waters of his
teacup like a suicide brooding over the Seine. His voice was dead in his
throat. "I've got to marry her."

"Don't be absurd."

Those swollen suffering eyes, the eyes of the anchorite and the mad
suffering saint: Stanley was staring at him now. Fixedly. "Easy for you
to say—you're a respectable man. You're married. You're clean."

· Harold was on his feet, all patience lost, striding to and fro with the
shell of an empty teacup in his hand. It was getting late, Edith was furious and Stanley, gloomy deluded Stanley, was spoiling his good time.
He gave it one more try, pulling up short right in front of him, right at
his very feet. "She's a slut, Stanley, a professional. You don't owe her
anything, not money or redemption—if I were you, I'd be worrying
about disease, not marriage. It's crazy. Mad. Irresponsible." Suddenly
he was shouting. "You don't marry a whore!"

"She's not a whore."

"She is."

"She's not. You don't even know her."

"Why did she let you have her then? Why did she take you home?
Huh? Why do think she makes her offices in the street?"

Stanley was silent a long while, and they looked at each other in
mutual disgust, each wondering how he could possibly be related to the

other. From below came the faint unremitting buzz of Mrs. van Pele's banalities as she bored Edith into an upright grave. Finally, just as Harold felt he could take it no longer, on the very brink of slamming his way out of the room and to hell with his little brother and his saintly scruples, Stanley spoke up. "What am I going to tell Mother?" he said.

After that, Stanley never strayed from the straight and narrow. He came home directly after his lessons with Monsieur Julien, and to help fill his evenings when he wasn't praying with Mrs. van Pele or entertaining her with his clarion renditions of "Macedonia" and "Surely Goodness and Mercy Will Follow Me All the Days of My Life," he took vocal lessons with the renowned tenor, Antonio Sbriglia. There was no thought of playing cards, obscene or otherwise, no desire to frequent cafés or even restaurants, no further mention of marriage to Mireille Sancerre or anyone else. He polished his modest skills under Monsieur Julien's tutelage, producing a series of charcoal studies of the Pont-Neuf at every hour of the day, from the savage tranquillity of dawn to the miasmic melancholy of the swallow-hung evening, and he became expert at reproducing Cézanne's apples. He was genuinely offended by the excesses of Toulouse-Lautrec and Degas, and though Monsieur Julien urged him to begin a study of the human form, he steadfastly refused. Two months to the day after his mother departed for the United States, he was on the boat home.

For the next six years, Stanley lived with his mother in the family fortress at 675 Rush Street, fixed in the mise-en-scène of his childhood like a stamp in a philatelist's album. He had his own room now, of course, with a view of the gardens and a private bath, but the nursery where he'd spent the better part of his life remained unchanged and the halls were a stew of recollected odors, from the sharp stab of the camphor ointment his father used to rub on his ankles and knees to assuage the ravages of his rheumatism to the ghostly echo of Mary Virginia's French perfume and the lingering dark must of a long-dead beagle by the name of Digger. He worked full-time at the Reaper Works, of which Cyrus Jr. was president and Harold vice president, juggling his schedule to accommodate his course load at Northwestern, where he was studying contract law. Officially, he was comptroller of the company, but Nettie was grooming him to oversee the legal department as well, thus consolidating all the McCormicks' vital interests in the hands of her sons, after the model of the Medicis.

As for social life, Stanley was limited to two friends from Princeton—one of whom lived in New York and made infrequent trips to the Midwest—and the companions his mother chose for him from among the duller and more complacent scions of Chicago's most rigorous and devout mercantile families. After a few failed experiments, she decided against including young ladies in her dinner and card parties, concluding that Stanley, whose health was still delicate, wasn't at all ready for the emotional strains of courtship and marriage, just as she herself wasn't ready to give him up, not yet anyway. Certainly he would be married one day, that was an absolute, but he was too young yet, too shy, too much in need of his mother's guidance.

In the spring of his second year at home, when the Parisian debacle had begun to fade from his memory (though the face of Mireille Sancerre would flower in his mind at the most inconvenient times, as when he was taking his final exam in Contracts or ordering half a dozen shirts from the wilting young brunette at Twombley's), he agreed to accompany his mother to Santa Barbara, to see to the arrangements for Mary Virginia's house there. The spring semester had just ended, and with his brother's collusion he was able to take a six-week leave from the Reaper Works. It was decided that somebody had to see mother through the ordeal of getting Mary Virginia settled once and for all, and since Anita had her young son to look after, and Cyrus Jr. and Harold were both too wrapped up in the business to take off just then (a very difficult time, what with the cutthroat competition from Deering, Warder, Bushnell and Glessner and a battle raging over entry into the markets in India and French Indochina), Stanley was elected.

He didn't mind. Not at all. Though he took pains to conceal it, he wasn't really feeling himself—hadn't been for some time. It was his nerves, that and a certain intensification of his little compulsive habits, like washing his hands over and over till the skin was raw, or adding a column of figures fifteen or twenty times because each time he was afraid he'd made a mistake and each time confirmed that he hadn't but might have if he weren't so vigilant, or avoiding the letter R in his files because it was an evil letter, one that growled in his ears with unintelligible accusations and fierce trilling criticisms. He'd been working too hard. Putting too much pressure on himself to perform at the top of his law school class and do the sort of job his mother expected of him at the Reaper Works. Let Cyrus and Harold stay behind—he was glad of the change. So glad he found himself whistling as he packed his bags, the very ones he'd brought back from France, and though he did get a bit bogged down over the question of what to bring and what to leave behind—he drew up long tapering lists on scraps of paper, bits of cardboard, anything that came to hand, and then promptly lost them—he did finally manage to get everything he needed into three steamer trunks and an array of suitcases and handbags so overstuffed they nearly prostrated a team of porters at the station. And on the morning they left, the sun so brilliant everything seemed lit from within, he felt like a subterranean released from the deepest pit.

The first day out, he did nothing but sit at the window with an unopened book in his lap. The country soothed his eyes and he watched the Chicago sun draw away west into Missouri and go to war with the clouds. He slept well and ate well (his mother had brought along a skeleton crew of servants, including the Norwegian cook), and by the third day he was so relaxed he began to feel restive. That was when Nettie suggested he take a look at the plans for Mary Virginia's house, to see what he thought, because she was wondering herself about the music room, whether it should be in the east or west wing, depending on the sunlight and Mary Virginia's inclination to play piano in the morning or evening, and if it would really matter all that much because of the plethora of sunshine in California anyway. What did he think?

Stanley took up the blueprints like a man snatching a life jacket off the rail of a sinking ship. He spread them out on the table and studied them for hours, oblivious to everything, his mother, the servants, the yellow plains of Texas and the distant dusty cowboys on their distant dusty mounts. With a T square and a handful of freshly sharpened pencils, he began a detailed series of modifications, moving walls, drawing elevations where none had been provided, even sketching in shrubbery and the odd shadowy figure of Mary Virginia seated at the piano or strolling across the patio.

What did he think of the plans? That they were all wrong, that they were an insult, a product of nescient minds and ill-conceived notions. What did he think? That Shepley, Rutan and Coolidge should be dismissed for incompetence, that any fool off the street could have come up with a more practical and pleasing design and that the architects' man in Santa Barbara had damned well better bring his drawing board along. But all he said to his mother was, "If it's all right with you, I'd like to suggest some changes. . . ."

They wound up staying nearly four months, taking rooms at the Arlington (the Potter, with its sea views, six hundred rooms and twenty-one thousand dollars' worth of custom-made china plate, wouldn't be completed until 1903), and in that time Stanley altered every least detail of the original plans, from the height of the doorways to the type of molding to be used in the servants' quarters. And he altered them daily, sometimes hourly, obsessed, fixated, stuck in a perfect groove of concentration. Inevitably, this caused some friction with the people who'd been engaged to do the actual building—Shepley, Rutan and Coolidge's architect quit within the month, as did the builder, and the architect's replacement, sent all the way from Boston, didn't last out the week. Stanley wasn't fazed. Nor was Nettie. She had faith in her son, and she was heartened to see him so concerned for his poor sister's welfare, pouring all his Fowler intensity into his blueprints and his beautiful orthogonal drawings and the elevations with their darling little puffs of shrubbery and people moving about the rooms—and it *was* the Fowler coming out in him, the perfect image of her own father, which wasn't to deny the McCormicks anything, not at all, but she knew her boy. And the way he went after those architects and builders and even the Sicilian stonemasons—nothing escaped him. And if he was indecisive, well, that was a Fowler trait too, and it only meant that he was passionately involved, putting himself to the test over and over again, questioning everything.

In the way of these things, construction didn't begin in earnest until Nettie and Stanley returned to Chicago, when the most equanimous of the architects was able to move forward expeditiously and no questions asked. Stanley fell back into his former way of life—the courses in Torts and Accounting, the big open office high above the floor of the Reaper Works where the tyrannical *R* lurked amongst the files, dinner with his mother and whatever Chester, Grover or Cornelius she deemed suitable for him that evening—and he forgot all about Mary Virginia, the house of her confinement, California. But he did leave his mark on the place, not only in the elaborate schema of alterations that became the house itself, but in the most essential way of all: he named it.

When Nettie acquired the property it was known simply as "the Stafford place," after the man from whom she'd purchased it, O. A.

Stafford, who'd had it from Colonel Greenberry W. Williams, who had in turn purchased it from José Lugo and Antonio Gonzales, *dueños* of the original Mexican land grant. People had begun referring to the property, which still featured Stafford's two-story frame house, his orange and olive groves and his succulent garden, as "the McCormick place." To Stanley's mind, this clearly wouldn't do. I. G. Waterman, who owned the adjoining estate, called his place "Mira Vista," and the Goulds, out on Olive Mill Road, had "La Favorita." Then there was "Piranhurst," "Riso Rivo," "The Terraces," "Cuesta Linda," "Arcady." If Mary Virginia's house and grounds were going to be in any way reflective of her class and status, someone would have to come up with a suitable name, and while Cyrus, Harold and Anita went unwittingly about their business in Chicago and his mother spent more and more time sitting in the hotel gardens, Stanley began to fret over it. In fact, during the last month of his stay, the innominacy of the place became as much an obsession to him as the shoddy plans, and he stayed up late into the night sifting through Spanish and Italian dictionaries and poring over maps of Tuscany, Estremadura and Andalusia for inspiration.

And then, one afternoon in the final week of their California sojourn, it came to him. He was walking over the grounds with his mother and Dr. Franceschi, the landscape expert, elaborating his feelings regarding caryatids, statuary in general and the function of fountains in a coordinated environment of the artificial and the natural, when they emerged from a rough path into a meadow strewn with oaks all canted in one direction. The trees stood silhouetted against the mountains, heavy with sun, their branches thrust out like the arms of a party of skaters simultaneously losing their balance. It was October, the season of evaporative clarity, the sky receding all the way back to the hinges of the darkness beyond. Butterflies hung palely over the tall yellow grass. Birds called from the branches.

"What curious trees, Dr. Franceschi," Nettie said, shielding her eyes from the sun, "all leaning like that, as if someone had come along and tipped them."

Dr. Franceschi was a thin wisp of a man in his fifties, vegetally bearded, with quick hands and the dry darting eyes of the lizards that scurried underfoot and licked over the rocks. "It's the prevailing winds that do it," he said in a voice as breathy as a solo flute, "shearing down from the mountains. They call them sundowners—the winds, that is."

"What about that one over there?" Stanley said, pointing to a tree that defied the pattern, its trunk vertical and its branches as evenly spaced as the tines of a fork. It was a hundred yards off, but he could see that there was a band of rock round the base of it, a petrified collar that seemed to hold it rigid.

"Oh, that, yes: I'd been meaning to show you that particular tree. It's quite a local curiosity."

And then they were crossing the open field, Nettie compact and busty, the jaunty horticulturist bouncing up off his toes like a balletomane, Stanley loping easily along with the great sweeping strides that made locomotion seem a form of gliding. As they drew closer, Stanley saw that the massive slab of sandstone girding the tree was split in two, and that the tree seemed to be growing up out of the cleft. "Very curious," Dr. Franceschi was saying, "one of those anomalies of nature— you see, there was a time some years ago when an acorn fell from that tree there"—pointing—"or that one maybe, who knows, and found a pocket of sustenance atop this blasted lump of stone, and you couldn't find a less promising environment, believe me—"

But they were there now and Stanley had his amazed hands on the rock itself, a massive thing, chest-high, big as a hearse, rough to the touch and lingeringly warm with the radiation of the sun. It was the very stuff of the earth's bones, solid rock, impenetrable, impermeable, the symbol of everything that endures, and here it was split in two, riven like a yard of cheap cloth, and by a thing so small and insidious as an acorn. . . .

riven rock . . .

that was the place where he was now and no one had to tell him that or whisper over him like he was a corpse already and with the reek of illicit sex on their fingers like eddie had on his because eddie was down among the women he could hear and smell and feel in their tight-legged female immanence out in the yard and giggling in the cottages tiptoeing through the kitchen and oh mr. mccormick can never should never and will never know a thing about it a man like him that can't control his unnatural urges and i heard about a man like that once from my cousin nancy cooper in sacramento hung like a barnyard animal and he had a woman a negress that would come to him on foot six miles one way just so she could feel him in her and if you believe nancy and i do it was just too much for her and she died underneath him of an excess of pleasure and apoplexy and he went right out and got himself another negress just like her only bigger . . .

but let them whisper let them stand over him and say their prayers for the dead—"Think about it, Mart, he's Stanley McCormick, one of the richest men in the world, and he doesn't even know it"*—and violate his every orifice with their tubes and their hoses and lay him on his side in the shower bath that was like the chinese water torture and what did they think he was eddie and mart and dr. gilbert van tassel monkeyman hamilton that they could rape him like that no covering no place to hide naked as a rat and why didn't they just leave him alone all of them his mother and katherine and cyrus the president and harold the vice president and anita too with her big swollen suety tits and her insinuating hands like he was some sort of pet or something some sort of baby . . .*

but it was his nerves and he was blocked that was all just a temporary condition not a thing like mary virginia his crazy bughouse sister with her white nightmare of a naked body and he would be up and about and better any day now just like at mclean the first time but no he wouldn't no he wouldn't because what they didn't understand and appreciate not a one of them especially katherine who only wanted to climb atop him and make his penis disappear inside her like mireille sancerre's fingers and wouldn't give him any peace not a second not a minute not an hour and she was lurking around somewhere even now he knew all about it with her binoculars and her sorrowful pitying face all drawn-up like a lemon-squeezer's poor stanley poor poor stanley what they didn't understand was that he couldn't move a muscle to save his life because the Judges wouldn't allow it they howled and shrieked in execration if he so much as shifted his tongue when sex-stinking eddie forced that tube down his throat the Judges who wouldn't let him move and cried out his sins from every corner of the room sloth and depravity and sexual deviation and comptrollership not the presidency or even the vice presidency and corruption in his heart and impotence with his wife and deceit of his mother the Judges shouting him down with their lips writhing like a spadeful of earthworms through the black gnarled ape's beards that covered their mouths and their screaming wet cunts . . .

but all night he lay there and all day it was tuesday wasn't it always tuesday and tuesday again and tuesday till all the months fell away like leaves from the trees and the years too and he prayed to the Judges to release him to commute his sentence time off for good behavior if only he could keep himself from sinning if only he could get back in the harness just once more just one more time . . .

7.

STANLEY OF THE APES

When Rosaleen stepped down off the train, thinner and paler than he'd remembered, with the Irish bloom caught in her cheeks and her eyes like tidal pools filling and draining and filling again and little Eddie all grown up in her arms, O'Kane was helpless: he felt the surging oceanic tug of her—he couldn't resist it, didn't want to—and plunged in like a deep-sea diver. "Rose!" he called, spreading his arms for her, and he wanted to kiss her right there in public, wanted to have her on the platform, in the ferns, and how could he possibly wait till he got her back to the fresh-painted apartment on Micheltorena Street with the garden and birdbath out back and the big high-gunwaled boat of a bed Ernestine Thompson had helped him pick out? He was trembling. He was in love.

She didn't say a word. Just held him, the surprising strength of her arms, the baby alive between them like a living sacrament, golden hair and a navy blue sailor's suit, cooing and burbling and giving out a smell of new-made flesh, his flesh, Eddie O'Kane's.

"You look beautiful, Rose," he murmured, still attached to her but

drawing back now for a quick glance of appraisal, "never more beautiful, even on the night I met you at Alice Dundee's." He was feeling sentimental, filled to the eyes with soggy emotion, like when they sang the
old songs at Donnelly's, and he wanted to say more, wanted to whisper
intimacies into the soft white shell of her ear and smell the shampoo in
the curling wisps of hair that had fallen loose there, but he caught the
eye of a sour-looking man in evening clothes and bit his tongue. This
wasn't the place.

People were moving past them on the platform, society types, the
rich come to soak themselves in the hot springs and suck up all the fat
rich things the hotels had to offer, and all at once he felt self-conscious.
An old lady with a matching pair of spoiled little apricot-colored dogs
stopped to gape at them as if they were a couple of spaghetti twisters
just off the boat and he was embarrassed, he was, and he just wanted to
get this over with, get past the awkwardness and take her home.

And then, without warning, she began to cry and he felt his teeth
clench. She gasped out his name—"Eddie! Oh, Eddie!"—and it was a
war cry, an accusation, a spear thrust right through him and pulled out
again. He let go of her and she looked off into the distance, biting her
lip, before wearily lifting her free arm to dab at her eyes with the sleeve
of her dress, a new dress, pale ocher, the color of the last leaf left on the
elm tree at the very end of the fall, blanched and twisting in the wind.

"Four months, Eddie," she said, trailing off in a series of truncated
sobs that were like hiccoughs, *erp, erp, erp*. Her eyes incinerated him. She
snatched in a breath. "My father cursed you every day, but I knew you
wouldn't desert me, Eddie, I knew it." And all at once she was thrusting
the baby at him like a hastily wrapped gift, the child that used to be a
baby, with his forcemeat legs and the look caught between fright and
wonder as if he didn't recognize his own father even and where was the
reward in that? O'Kane couldn't take him, not yet, and held up his
hands to show how inadequate they were.

"Look how big he's gotten," she demanded in a high strained chirp
of a voice, "did you ever think he'd be so big?" This was succeeded by a
whole lexicon of baby talk as she bobbed her tearful angry hopeful face
up and down like a toy on a string and touched her nose to Eddie Jr.'s
and let him dangle finally from one gloved hand until his feet touched
the pavement in his scuffed white doll's shoes and he stood there grinning and triumphant.

" 'Oose 'ittle man is he, huh? Huh?" Rosaleen cooed and the people flitted by and the cars pulled up at the curb and O'Kane stood erect in the glow of the late afternoon sun, at a loss, his hands hanging limp at his sides, half a wondering smile on his face.

Roscoe was waiting for them at the far end of the platform, the car at their disposal, courtesy of Katherine and Dr. Hamilton, who'd given O'Kane the afternoon off. Roscoe squared his chauffeur's cap on his head, very formal, very impressive, and gave O'Kane a hand with the luggage while Rosaleen and the baby settled themselves in the rear seat, and then they were off, up the gradual incline that was State Street and into the trembling blue lap of the mountains that hung over the town like a pall of smoke. "Such a grand car," Rosaleen purred, but she wasn't smiling, not yet, "and you know it's my first ride ever, don't you?" He stole a peek at her under the inflexible arch of her hat, his brown colleen, his wife, and kissed the corner of her mouth as tenderly as he knew how until she turned to him and kissed him back, just a peck, with lips as cold as the stones of the sea.

She was pleased with the apartment, he could see that, though she fussed around the place for half an hour, saying things like "Oh, Eddie, you call this a sofa, and those *curtains*, and what an unusual bed—is that lacquer on it or what?" and quietly disparaging the view, as if there were another ocean and another set of islands he could have presented her with, but it was for form's sake, for the sake of establishing their roles, or reestablishing them, she in the house and he at Riven Rock earning a handsome wage as an essential cog in the McCormick machine. Through it all, the baby was a saint, nothing less. He crawled around the front room a bit, putting things in his mouth and pulling them out again all glistening with drool, and then he fell into a sleep that was like a coma, not so much as a snort or whimper out of him. By then the sun was almost gone, the sitting room walls lit like the inside of a peach, everything rosy, everything fine—but for the one thing, the most important thing.

Rosaleen was in the kitchen, poking her head in the cabinets, inspecting the icebox. She'd seen everything twice already and O'Kane was beginning to think she was avoiding him. It had been four months. She was hurt and angry, and she had a right to be. He stood at the window, awkward in the silence, handsome Eddie O'Kane with the three o'clock luck in his eye and never at a loss for words, and here he didn't know what to say, how to begin it—with an apology, an excuse, a plea? Or maybe he should just move into her and touch her, this exciting stranger hovering over the kitchen sink. "Are you hungry?" he finally asked.

She drifted into the room then, slow and insouciant, and gave him the full benefit of her eyes. "I'm famished, Eddie," she said, and her voice had the same effect on him as that first sure sip of whiskey on a night when the barroom is lit like the reaches of heaven and nothing is impossible, "famished," she said. "For you."

And so it went, Eddie O'Kane and the bliss of domesticity. Elsie Reardon moved into the room he vacated in the servants' quarters and Roscoe came for him every morning at 7:30 after dropping off Nick and Pat. Mart wasn't too pleased, having to spend the first hour of his day sitting alone with Mr. McCormick in that interval when the shifts changed, and maybe he was a little jealous too, used to having O'Kane to himself and hungering after his own bride and his own life but so shy and tongue-tied he'd die in his tracks if a girl so much as looked at him. Katherine and her mother packed up and went back east at the end of October, Dr. Hamilton procured another dozen monkeys from God knew where, and Julius, the big orange ape, lacking any other apes to mount, sniff and soak with urine at the doctor's pleasure, was given the run of the place, appearing as if by legerdemain on the roof of the garage one minute and in the kitchen the next, his feet drawn up under him on a three-legged stool and a perspiring glass of milk clamped firmly in his spidery hand. And at home, in the three-room apartment they rented from a retired munitions salesman by the name of Rowlings who lived upstairs and watched every move they made, Rosaleen, who was no housekeeper at all, tried her best to move the piles of rubbish from one corner of the place to another and spent a good hour every evening immolating a piece of meat on the new Acme Sterling Steel Range in the kitchen.

Before long it was winter, iceless and snowless, sunshine pouring down like liquid gold, hissing rains that stood the earth on its head and rattled the boulders in Hot Springs Creek like the teeth of a boxer's jaw and every leaf of every tree green as the Garden of Eden. O'Kane sent his mother pictures of the palms and the winter flowers and she wrote him that nobody in the neighborhood could believe it, weather like that, and what a bitter winter it was at home, his cousin Kevin down with a lung disorder and the doctors baffled and Uncle Billy suffering with the ague, but she was fine, if you discounted the sciatica that was like the devil's own pitchfork thrust into her every fifteen seconds, night and day, and his father, knock on wood, was as strong as the day he retired from the ring, preserved as he was in alcohol like a fish in a jar, and not so much as a sniffle. O'Kane had no complaints about the weather — he didn't miss the snow a bit, not even at Christmas — but as the days wore on, Rosaleen began to get under his skin.

The apartment was too small, for one thing, though it had seemed plenty big enough the day he'd rented it, and the baby was always underfoot, walking now, into everything, howling all night like a cat skinned alive and filling his diapers like the very genius of shit. His favorite trick was picking through the trash, which Rose never emptied, and whenever he was quiet for more than five minutes at a time you'd be sure to find him crouching behind the sofa with a half-gnawed bone or an orange gone white with mold. And that was a funny thing, the oranges. When O'Kane was a boy, they were five cents each, the price of a beer, and he saw them at Christmas only, and only then if he was lucky. And now he was drowning in them, oranges like an avalanche, a nickel a basket, and he didn't even like the flavor of them anymore, too cloying, almost poisonously sweet, and with all that juice running down your chin and gumming up your fingers.

But Rosaleen. She was so insipid, stupid as a clam, nattering on about sewing and patterns and what was prettier the blue or the yellow till sometimes he wanted to jump up from the table and choke the breath out of her. And her housekeeping — or lack of it. She was as filthy and disorganized as her whey-faced mother and her tuberous brothers, dirty Irish, shanty Irish, not fit to kiss the hem of his mother's dress and you never saw so much as a speck of dust in the O'Kane household, no matter how poor they might have been. She was putting on weight again too, and that drove him to distraction, because every time he looked at her, the fat settling into her hips and thighs and ballooning her breasts till she could barely straighten up, he was sure she'd gone and got pregnant again. And that he couldn't abide. Not at his age, not when he had his whole life ahead of him still. Maybe it wasn't right, but the way he felt, the burden of just one kid more would put him in the asylum himself—they'd have to chain him to Mr. McCormick and they could rave at each other and piss their pants side by side. Well, and not to put too fine a point on it, as his father would say, it was inevitable that he began to stray, just a bit, from the nest.

First it was two nights a week, Friday and Saturday, and who could blame him for that? And he did take Rose with him now and again, when they could get the girl from down the street to mind little Eddie, and he had to spoil his own evening and watch her get drunk as a sow and listen to the incessant nagging whine of her voice every time he lifted a glass to his lips—"Eddie, don't you think that's enough now," and "Let's go home, Eddie, I'm bored," and "How can you stand this place?" The two nights stretched to three and then four and he began to run with some of the boys at Cody Menhoff's. Sometimes, just for the hell of it, they'd have a shot and a beer at every place in town and then all pile into a car and drive up over San Marcos Pass and all the way out to Mattei's Tavern in Los Olivos and he wouldn't come home till three in the morning, stinking, absolutely stinking. That took the smile off Rose's face, all right. She'd pounce on him like a harpy and their wars would rage all over the apartment and out onto the front porch, furniture flying, the baby squalling, Old Man Rowlings punctuating every shout and cry with an outraged thump from above.

Spring began in February and lasted through the end of May and it was a glorious time, the vegetable world in riot, every breeze a bargeload of spices. Saturday afternoons he'd take Rosaleen and Eddie Jr. to the park or hop the streetcar down to the beach, where he'd lie flat on the sand with a beer propped on his chest and stare up into the sky while his face and limbs turned brown as a wop's. The Ice Queen—Katherine—returned in May and she never said a word to him about Rosaleen or Eddie Jr., just hello and good-bye and how did my husband look and what did he eat today, stiff as ever, winter on two feet, and she took her lawyers with her down to the Santa Barbara Municipal Courthouse and had her husband declared incompetent.

O'Kane first heard about it one night when he couldn't get home after work—Roscoe was running Mrs. McCormick across town to some fancy-dress party and wouldn't be back till late. The last thing he wanted was to stick around the place, and Rosaleen was sure to give him hell over it, the meal ruined and she slaving over the stove since three and all the rest of it, but he had no choice unless he wanted to walk—and he didn't. He was able to cajole a plate of home fries and ham out of the Chink cook—and he would have killed for a beer or even a glass of wine, but there was nothing in the house and Sal and the rest of the McCormick wops had been pretty cool to him ever since the Dimucci business—so he took the plate and a glass of buttermilk up-stairs to see if maybe Nick wanted to play a couple of hands of poker to while away the time.

Nick was sitting behind the barred door to the upstairs parlor with a newspaper spread out on the footstool before him, and Pat was lean-ing back in a chair just outside the open door to Mr. McCormick's bed-room. "Can't get home to the hearth," O'Kane said, setting down his plate so he could dig out his keys and swing open the heavy iron door, "so I figured I'd stop round and see what the night nurses are up to. Anybody for a hand of poker?"

Nick didn't think so. Not right then, anyway. Pat stirred himself, glanced over his shoulder at Mr. McCormick, who was apparently asleep, though you could hardly tell because he'd been so blocked and lifeless lately, and said that yeah, he might play a hand or two.

"By the way," Nick said in a casual rumble, "did you see this in the paper?"

O'Kane had started across the room, thinking to set plate and glass down on the sideboard while he pulled out the card table, and he stopped now, arrested in mid-stride. "What?"

"This. Right here."

O'Kane stood there like an altar boy with the collection plate held out stiffly before him, except it was ham and potatoes on the plate and not a heap of pocket-worried coins, and he was no altar boy, not any-more. He looked over Nick's shoulder to where Nick's thick stump of a finger was pointing, and there it was, the cold truth about the Ice Queen, in 6-point type:

M'CORMICK GUARDIANSHIP TO WIFE

Mrs. Katherine Dexter McCormick, wife of Stanley Robert Mc-Cormick of Riven Rock in Montecito, petitioned today in Superior Court to have her husband declared an incompetent person. Mr. McCormick, youngest son of the late Cyrus Hall McCormick, in-ventor of the mechanical reaper, has suffered from mental illness since shortly after his marriage to Mrs. McCormick in 1904. The

Honorable Baily M. Melchior, Superior Court Judge, appointed
Mrs. McCormick, along with Henry B. Favill and Cyrus Bentley,
both of Chicago, as joint guardians.

"So what do you think of your poor heartbroken wife now, Eddie—
'She loves him and she wants to be with him,' isn't that what you said?"
Nick was squinting up at him from eyes set deep in the big calabash of
his head. He was running a finger along the lapel of his jacket and
smirking as if he'd just won a bet at long odds. From across the room,
Pat let out with a strangled little bark of a laugh.

O'Kane shrugged. "There's no love lost between her and me," he
said, and he was thinking of the lecture her Imperial Highness had
given him on trifling with a girl's affections, as if she would have the
vaguest notion of what went on between a man and a woman, and that
still rankled, because no woman was going to tell him what to do, especially when it came to his own private affairs. "I'm in this for Mr. Mc-
Cormick's sake, and I wouldn't walk across the street for her, if you
want to know the truth."

"That comes as a surprise to me," Nick rumbled, still with that
mocking tone, his eyes glistening, cat and mouse. "You were the one
had the crush on her—and not so long ago at that. Am I right, Pat?"

The plate was going cold in his hand. Outside, beyond the windows, the sky was darkening. It was getting late, and he knew Rosaleen
would be working herself up, pans burning on the stove, garbage up to
her ankles, the baby squatting behind the couch with some scrap of of-
fal in his mouth and she taking a hard angry pull at the bottle she kept
hidden away in back of the icebox where nobody would think to look.
He thought of ringing up Old Man Rowlings and having him give her a
message, but then why bother? She'd be riding her broom by now anyway. He gave Pat a look and then turned back to Nick with another
shrug. "Let's just say my eyes have been opened."

Nick was turned halfway round in his chair, neckless and massive,
his shoulders looking as if they'd been inflated with a pneumatic pump.
"Right from the start I told you she was a gold digger, didn't I?"

"I'm not going to defend her, not anymore, but I still think you're
wrong. If I'm not mistaken, she's got her own millions that her father
left her—and that château in Switzerland and all the rest of it. So what
does she need with his money?"

"Hah. You hear that, Pat? 'What does she need with his money?' Come on, Eddie, wake up. Did you ever in your life meet anybody thought they had enough money? You get that rich, you only want to get richer."

O'Kane still hadn't set the plate down—or the buttermilk either. He was beginning to feel like a waiter. And he was hungry too, but there was something here that needed to be settled—or at least thrashed out.

"And I'll tell you another thing," Nick said, and he dug a pre-rolled cigarette out of his breast pocket and stuck it between his lips, "this right here"—tapping the newspaper—"really opens things up for your Mrs. Katherine McCormick."

"What do you mean?"

The flare of the match, a whiff of sulphur. "Don't you get it? He's incompetent and she's got hold of the will she had him make out the day after they got married—the one that leaves everything to her?—and now she can traipse all over the country and do whatever she damn well pleases in any kind of society, because when they ask her 'So where's your husband?' she just dabs at her eyes and says, 'The poor man's locked away at Riven Rock with his nurses—and he's mad as a loon.' "

Pat let out another laugh. He'd come awake now, setting all four legs of the chair down on the floor and hunching forward, elbows propped up on the buttress of his thighs. "So you think she'd be seeing other men then? Secretly, I mean?"

"Call a spade a spade, why don't you, Patrick." Nick let the smoke spew out of his nostrils, a blue haze settling in his lap and then rising, deflected, to irradiate his blunt features and the vast shining dome of his forehead. "You mean whoring around, don't you?"

"It's not right to talk about her like that and you know it," O'Kane heard himself say, and immediately regretted it. Here he was, defending her again.

"Not right?" Nick echoed. "Why not? You think just because she's a millionaire's wife she's any better than you? You think she doesn't itch between her legs like any other woman?"

It was a stimulating proposition, the Ice Queen in heat, but O'Kane never had the opportunity to pursue it. Because just then there was a movement in the room behind Pat, and when he looked up Mr. Mc-Cormick was standing in the doorway.

At first no one moved, and they might have been at the very last scene of a play, just before the lights go down. A long slow moment breathed by, the smallest sounds of the house magnified till every creak and rustle was like a scream. And then, very slowly and deliberately, O'Kane crossed to the sideboard and set down the plate and beside it the glass, freeing up his hands—just in case. "Mr. McCormick!" he cried, his voice animated with pleasure and surprise, as if he were greeting an old friend on the street, and he exchanged a glance with Pat, careful to make no sudden moves. "Good evening, sir. How are you feeling?"

Nick had folded up the newspaper, and though he hadn't got to his feet, you could see he was ready to spring if need be; Pat, inches from Mr. McCormick and all but impotent in the grip of the chair, looked up with quickened eyes. This was the first time Mr. McCormick had been out of bed in two weeks or more, and the first time in memory he'd got up without any prompting. He'd been violent on the last occasion, veering from a state of utter immobility to the frenzy of released energy that was like a balloon puffed and puffed till it exploded, and it had taken both O'Kane and Mart to subdue him. But now he merely stood there in his crisp blue pajamas, stooped and hunched over to the right where the muscles of his leg had gone slack from disuse. He didn't seem to have registered the question.

"You must be feeling better," O'Kane prompted. It was vital to engage him in conversation, the first step—he was waking up, coming out of it, coming back to the real world after his long sojourn in the other one.

Mr. McCormick looked right at him, no bugs, no demons, no eyes crawling up the walls. "I . . . I . . . is it lunchtime yet? I was wondering about lunch. . . ." And then: "I've been sleeping, haven't I?"

For all his experience and all the cynicism it bred, O'Kane was exhilarated, on fire: Mr. McCormick was talking! Not only talking, but making sense—or nearly—and he wasn't lashing out, wasn't cursing and spitting and attacking his nurses as if they were the devil's minions. He was hungry, that was all, just like anybody else. In a flash O'Kane saw ahead to the weeks and months to come, the feeding tube discarded, Mr. McCormick dressing himself, using the toilet, joking again, Mr. McCormick reaching into his breast pocket, pulling out his checkbook, *Let's see about that acreage you were interested in, Eddie . . .*

"Hello, Mr. McCormick," Nick offered from his chair in the corner of the room, and Pat, his face hung like a painting at the level of Mr. McCormick's waist, echoed the greeting.

"My wife," Mr. McCormick said, and it was as if they didn't exist, his eyes focused on some point in the distance, through the walls and across the grounds and all the way out to that fancy-dress party on Arrellaga Street. He shuffled into the room, unsteady on his feet, skating on gravel, his arms leaping to steady himself. "Katherine," he said, and the name seemed to surprise him, as if he hadn't spoken it, as if the syllables had somehow separated themselves from the air and spontaneously combined. He shuffled his feet. Started forward. Thought better of it. Stopped. Finally, moving with the wincing deliberation of a man walking across a bed of hot coals, he made the center of the room, his shoulders violently quaking. "Mother," he said, and he was looking straight into O'Kane's eyes now, "I must have fallen asleep. . . ."

"Mr. McCormick!" O'Kane had no choice but to raise his voice, calling out to someone drowning at sea, the waves crashing, the rocks drawing nearer, and he couldn't let him go under again, he couldn't. "Mr. McCormick, *sir.* Good *evening!* Don't you want something to *eat?* Look, look here," gesturing to the plate on the sideboard and waving him on like a traffic cop, "don't you see what we've fixed you for dinner? Good *ham,* it's delicious. Here, try a bite—you like *ham,* you know you do."

And there he was, pale as water, standing suddenly at the sideboard in his pajamas, barefooted, long-armed, slumped to one side like a poorly staked sapling, and he was eating, forcing the congealed lumps of potato into his mouth, his jaws working, eyes lit with accomplishment, normalcy, the first step. . . .

But it wasn't to be.

The three of them watched in silence as he ate, jamming the food into his mouth with both hands, gulping and gnashing, licking his fingers and wiping his palms on the breast of his pajamas, and that was fine, a small miracle, until the demons took him and he swung violently round on them with O'Kane's fork clutched in his hand. Now he was hunted, brought to bay like an animal, the old fever in his eyes. "My wife!" he shouted, "I want my wife! Do you hear me?! Do you?!"

O'Kane's voice was a long swallow of syrup, the most reasonable and soothing voice in the world. "Mr. McCormick, it's me, Eddie O'Kane. And look, your friends Nick and Pat too. Your wife isn't here—you know that. You've been asleep, that's all. Dreaming. And here's your luncheon, nice, just the way you like it."

Mr. McCormick took a spastic slice at the air, wielding the fork like a dagger. His bare toes gripped the floor. He shifted his weight from foot to foot. "You," he sputtered. "They, they—Katherine. I want to fu-fuck her, I do, and you bring her here right now. D-do you hear me? Do you?"

How much of the conversation had he overheard? O'Kane was thinking about that as he signaled Pat with his eyes and began to inch forward, careful to keep his weight on the balls of his feet. *You think she doesn't itch between her legs like any other woman?*

And then, just before he hurled the fork at O'Kane's face, smashed the plate and glass and tore the sideboard out from the wall preparatory to upending it on Pat's shins, Mr. McCormick dropped his voice and lulled them for just the fleetingest instant. "I want to fu-fuck her," he breathed, bowing his head, and he might have been a boy telling his mother what he wanted for his birthday—then, only then, did he explode.

The fork took a divot out of O'Kane's cheek, just below his right eye, and he could hear it rattling across the floor behind him as Pat sprang forward and Mr. McCormick, shaky on his feet but with the astonishing dexterity of the deranged and otherworldly, upended the sideboard and danced clear. There was a keening in the air now, a razor-edged hysterical singsong chant, "No, no, stay away, stay away," Mr. McCormick backing into the corner in a wrestler's crouch, O'Kane and Nick going in low to pull his legs out from under him.

It was a brief but savage struggle that twice saw Mr. McCormick break free and rush the barred door as if he could dart right on through it, but there was no key in the lock this time and they finally ran him to the ground in his bathroom, where he tried to hold the door against the combined weight of the three of them. The shame of it all was Nick. Nick lost his temper. Cursing, his eyes dark streaks in the livid pulp of his face, he was the first through the bathroom door, and he ignored all the rules—open hands only, no blows, use your legs and shoulders and try only to restrain the patient, not subdue him—standing back from Mr. McCormick and letting his fists fall like mallets, the thump of flesh on flesh, not the face, never the face, hitting their employer and benefactor repeatedly in the chest and abdomen until he went down on the tile floor. But that wasn't enough for Nick—he was possessed, mindless, as crazed as Katzakis or the Apron Man or Gunderson, the big Swede with the rolled dough for arms who killed and decapitated his wife and daughter and held six men at bay for over three hours till finally they had to chloroform him. Nick wouldn't stop. He kept pounding Mr. Mc-Cormick over and over again, though Mr. McCormick was bundled up on the floor with his hands over his head, crying "No, no, no!"

"Nick!" O'Kane roared, snatching at the heavy arms as they rose and fell, and he felt it coming up in him himself, the uncontainable hormonal rush that makes every one of us a potential maniac. Before he knew what was happening he'd jerked Nick to his feet, spun him around and driven his fist into the soft dollop of flesh in the center of that shining sphere of an overcooked face.

"Eddie!" Pat was shouting, "Nick!" bodies everywhere, the footing treacherous, Mr. McCormick hunched up in the fetal position on the cold hard tiles but with one eye open, one glistening mad eye on the madness churning above him, Nick coming back at him now, at O'Kane, squaring off, shouting, "You son of a bitch I'll kill you!" and the fury of their voice magnified in that confined space till the bathroom echoed like some private chamber of hell.

All that was bad enough—the abuse of Mr. McCormick when he was defenseless and just coming out of his haze; the fight with Nick that dredged up all the mistrust and rancor that must have lain brooding between them like a copperhead with somebody's foot on its tail, though he never suspected and never would have admitted it if he had; the grim prospect of the championship bout awaiting him when he finally did get home to Rosaleen—but for O'Kane, on that unlucky night, it was just the beginning.

No sooner had Pat separated him and Nick than he turned and stalked out of the apartment, his knuckles raw, Nick raving at his back, Mr. McCormick all but comatose on the floor. "Go on, get out of here, you stinking son of a bitch!" Nick bellowed. "I don't know what the fuck you're doing here anyhow—you're on the day shift, jackass!" He went right on down the stairs and out the front door without a word to anybody, and then he was walking up the drive, engulfed by the night. The lights faded at his back and the darkness closed in on him, a smell

of tidal flats on the air, the cold underbelly of the fog catching and tearing and spilling its guts in the treetops. He didn't think about it twice:
he just started walking.

Five miles. His feet were blistered—he wasn't used to this anymore—
he was bleeding from the cut under his eye where the fork had gouged
him, and his upper lip was split and swollen. He raged against Nick the
whole way, Nick who was thirty-four years old and resented O'Kane
because O'Kane was younger, smarter, better looking, because O'Kane
was head nurse and he wasn't. Well, fuck him. O'Kane had blackened
one of his eyes for him and done some damage that wasn't so obvious
maybe, but he would feel it tomorrow, that was for sure. He walked on,
the anger tapering off inside him as the fog came down and the chill of
the night took hold of him—and he was getting soft, as addicted to the
sun as a lizard on a rock, and what would Boston be like now? Two cars
went by, but they were going in the wrong direction. And then, to cap
things off, he got to the foot of State Street five minutes after the last
streetcar had left.

What he needed was a drink. Or two. But for some unfathomable
reason—birth, death, the end of the universe and all things available to
man—Cody Menhoff's was closed at 9:45 P.M. on a Thursday night in
the middle of May with grown men expiring for the want of a drink,
and he stood there dumbfounded at the locked door, licking the
crusted-over scab on his lip, till he heard a shout from across the street.
"Hey, partner," someone called to him, "you looking for a drink?"

He wound up in a saloon in Spanishtown, the seething hovel of
mud-brick houses and ramshackle chicken coops where all the Mexicans and Chinks who worked the hotels lived and where you could always find a drink and a whore—not that he was looking for the latter,
not especially. What he found himself doing was drinking dirty brown
liquid out of a dirty brown cup with a character in a peaked cap and
military mustaches who could have been Porfirio Díaz himself for all
O'Kane knew. But he didn't care. He had no prejudices—spics, wops,
Chinks, Krauts, Micks, it was all the same to him. Set up another round
and let's chase it with a couple of those Mexican beers that smell like
wet pussy and taste like they were strained through the crotch of somebody's union suit. Yeah, that's right, that's the one. *Slainte!* How you say
it? *Salud.* Okay, *salud!*

He was there an hour maybe, long enough to forget his split lip and the pain radiating from a place just above his left temple where Nick had twice caught him with a right hand that felt as if it had been launched from a cannon, and then he thought he might want to see some American faces for a while and wandered up the street to a place he'd been to once or twice before. It was festive inside. Full of life. He saw a raft of women's hats, pinned-up hair, men in shirtsleeves. The player piano was going and some drunk, a guy he thought he might have recognized from Menhoff's, was singing along and running his hands over the keys in pantomime:

They heeded not his dying prayer
They buried him there on the lone prairie
In a little box just six by three
And his bones now rot on the lone prairie

He had a terrific voice, the drunk, very plaintive and evocative, and O'Kane asked him if he knew "Carrick Fergus" and he did but there was no roll for it so they had to settle for "The Streets of New York," which they ran through twice, O'Kane harmonizing, and then "Alexander's Ragtime Band." That made them thirsty, so they sat at a table and O'Kane ordered whiskey for them both and never mind the chaser, and he was just settling in and feeling expansive, telling the drunk—whose name was Joe something—about Mr. McCormick and how he'd finally woken up like Sleeping Beauty and how he, O'Kane, came to have this gash in his cheek and the split lip and aggravated temple, when he looked up and saw Giovannella Dimucci sitting across the room in the dining area with a man who had his arm around her shoulder and was leaning in to whisper something in her ear. But Giovannella wasn't looking at the man she was with. She was staring across the room. At O'Kane.

Who can say what a man feels at a time like that? What miswired connections suddenly fuse, what deadened paths and arterial causeways come roaring to life all in an instant? O'Kane pushed himself up from the chair without so much as a word to Joe something, who was in the middle of a disconnected monologue revolving around the loss of his hat, his wallet and his left shoe, and propelled himself across the crowded room in a kind of trance. His hips were tight, as compact as pistons, he could feel the heavy musculature of his legs grip and relax and grip again with each stride as he swung his shoulders out and back in a rhythmic autonomous strut, his heart beating strong and sure, everything in the sharpest focus. He wasn't looking at Giovannella or the man with her, or not at his face anyway—his eyes were locked on the arm that insinuated so many things, the arm he wanted to break in six places. It would have been no use pointing out to him that it was Giovannella's absolute and unfettered right to go where and with whom she pleased and that it was nobody's business but her own as to when and how that unwitting arm had come to drape itself so casually across her shoulder, no use at all. The die was cast. Words were useless.

O'Kane walked right up to the table and tore the arm off Giovannella's shoulder as he might have stripped a dead limb from a tree and found to his consternation that the arm was attached elsewhere. There was a question of sinew, bone, cartilage, and the initially startled and then outraged flaxen-haired and beefy farmboy in a pair of pale blue washed-out overalls who formed the trunk of this particular tree. "You can't do that," O'Kane said, meaning a whole range of things, and when the arm spontaneously tried to reassert itself he slapped it away and showed the farmboy the bloody divot under his eye and the aggravated temple and the lip that had gone yellow with pus, and the farmboy desisted. And still without looking at her, without so much as giving her a glance, O'Kane reached out unerringly and hoisted Giovannella to her feet. "We're getting out of here," he said, and he was fixing his lunatic glare on the farmboy's evil-eyed companion in the event he wanted his arm wrenched out of the socket too. And then, as if Giovannella might have harbored any doubt as to his meaning or intentions, he lowered his voice to a primal growl and gave the statement a sense of urgency: "Right now."

She wasn't happy. She fought him every step of the way, through the maze of tables, into the foyer and out the door into the deserted street. No one challenged him—they barely looked up from their beers—and just let the farmboy and his evil-eyed companion come after him, just let them. He dragged her half a block before she broke away from him, shifted her weight like a professional boxer and hit him with everything she had, and right where it was tenderest, right where Mr. McCormick's fork had opened up his flesh, so that it felt now, for the briefest sharpest instant, as if his whole face were slipping off the bone like a rubber mask. "You bastard!" she screamed.

"Me?" He was outraged, stung to bitterness and enmity at the sheer unreasonableness of her response. Was she crazy? Was that it? "You were the one sitting in a dive like that with some jerk's arm around you like some common —"

She hit him again and was rearing back to unleash a complementary blow with the sharp little bundle of knuckles that was her left fist, when he caught her arm at the wrist. Quick as a bolt, she came back at him with the other hand, but he caught that one too. And he wasn't thinking, not at all, but somewhere inside him he registered the sensation of holding fast to those two frail and quick-blooded wrists that were like birds, sparrows snatched out of the air and imprisoned in the grip of his unconquerable hands, and it was electric. It surged through him, and there was no power on earth that could stop him now. "Like some common whore," he said.

She spat at him. Kicked out with jackknifing knees. Cursed him in Italian first and then in English. It didn't matter. Not at all. Because he was supreme and he had hold of her wrists and he wasn't letting go, not right then, maybe not ever.

He led her down the street in an awkward dance, both of them shuffling sideways, till he found a place thick with trees at the far northern verge of the Potter Hotel grounds, and there was never any question of the outcome. For all the power of her charm and her black persuasive eyes and her body that was flawless and young and without stint of constraint, he was more charming and more persuasive — and more powerful. She had to understand that, and finally, after he'd been rough with her, maybe too rough with her, she did. She clung to him beneath the night-blooming bushes in the dark of the starless night, her skin naked to his, and sobbed for him, sobbed so hard he thought she would break in half, and then, only then, did he let go and feel the warmth infuse him as if his blood had been drained, and whiskey, hot burning Irish from the sainted shores, substituted in its place. They lay there through the slow-rolling hours and they talked in low voices and kissed and let the fog come down like the breath of something so big and overwhelming they could never have conceived of it, and this time, when he pulled her to him, he didn't have to force her.

Ah, yes. Yes. But all idylls have to end, as well he knew, and all too often they end with clamminess and insect bites and an ache in the head. They end with the break of day, a prick of the fog turned to driz-

zle, the painful rasping of some misplaced bird. Giovannella looked at
him out of the eyes of a bride and he knew he was in way over his head.
"I promise," he told her, "I swear," and he bundled her in his arms,
turned inside out with guilt and regret and fear and self-loathing—and
yet, at the same time, he was swelling to the point of bursting with
something else altogether, something that felt dangerously like . . . well,
love.

Head throbbing, his suit a mess, his face worse, he went into the hotel, while Giovannella waited shivering in the woods, and telephoned
Roscoe. Roscoe was just getting up, just getting ready to have his
breakfast in the kitchen of the big house while Sam Wah jabbered at
him in Chink-English and Nick and Pat drank black coffee and prepared for the end of their shift and the ride home, after which he
planned to pick up O'Kane in front of the apartment on Micheltorena.
O'Kane talked him out of that. O'Kane called in his markers, reminding
Roscoe of all he'd done for him over the course of the past months and
of the brotherhood of their barroom binges in the days before Rosaleen
arrived, and Roscoe agreed to forego breakfast and slip down to the
Potter Hotel to take Giovannella out Olive Mill Road to the place
where the gap showed in the oleanders—and take O'Kane to work.

How he made it through that day O'Kane would never know.

He cleaned himself up as best he could in the bathroom he'd formerly shared with Mart and that Mart now shared with Elsie Reardon,
avoiding Pat—and Nick—altogether. Roscoe was mum. They didn't
even know O'Kane was there, had no reason to suspect he wasn't at
home awaiting his morning ride and his daily regimen of laving and
force-feeding Mr. McCormick (daily, that is, but for Saturday afternoons and Sundays, when Dr. Hamilton sat with their employer and
benefactor and the door remained shut except to admit a pair of wops
with mops). Mart had heard his brothers' version of the previous
night's events, but he didn't seem eager to leap to judgment—as ready,
in his bigheaded, dilatory way, to lay blame at Nick's door as at
O'Kane's. And O'Kane spent most of the day reprising his own version
aloud, hoping to get Mart in his camp, water thicker than blood and all
that, and trying to erase the memory of Giovannella and how unutter-
ably stupid he'd been to stir that kettle up again, love or no love. What
he refused to think of or even admit to the murky periphery of his consciousness for the smallest splinter of a second, was the problem that

made all others seem as insignificant as the exact phrasing of the legend that would one day appear on his tombstone: Rosaleen.

He telephoned her at eight that morning and poured a heavy gelatin of lies into the mouthpiece, telling her of the way the car had broken down so completely they couldn't even get it to roll if they pushed it and how Mr. McCormick had come to life in a sudden frenzy and beaten him about the head and face and she should see his lip and how finally he was forced to spend a forlorn and monastic night sharing a bed with Mart who of course snored the whole time. Rosaleen was silent on the other end of the line and he could picture her in Old Man Rowlings's cramped parlor, Old Man Rowlings fuming somewhere in the background, Rosaleen chewing her lip in that way she had, her eyes teeming in her head, one slow foot perched on the bridge of the other. "I'll be home tonight after work," he said. "Okay?"

Her voice rolled back to him like the big black ball in the bowling alley, uncertain, untrue, and yet clattering all the same: "Yeah, Eddie. Okay."

And then it was evening. And then he went home.

She was waiting for him at the front door, Eddie Jr. propped up on her hip like a shield, and he thought of the heavy leathern shield Cuchulain used to wield and all the fierce blood of their warrior ancestors seething in Rosaleen's veins, and she was holding a broom too—a broom she didn't even know the proper use of—to complete the picture. He opened the gate and came up the walk and though his head ached still and his lip stung and the side of his face throbbed and he was as beaten-down and exhausted as he'd ever been in his life, he knew there was something wrong with that picture, something radically wrong, and he was immediately on his guard. "Hello, honey," he called, and the greeting had a hollow ring to it, desperate and false. She said nothing in response, but her lip curled back from her teeth and he saw that she was making an effort to restrain it, whatever it was, till he was in the house and the door was shut behind him.

"Liar," she snarled as he brushed past her and into the ashpit of the parlor.

How did she know?

What did she know?

His brain, dormant with exhaustion, churned to sudden life—there was nothing for him now but to face his accuser and parry every fresh accusation with a fresh lie. "What?" he said, all innocence. "What are you talking about?"

Her face was twisted, the face of one of the doctor's hominoids suffering through an experiment, all hate and murder and bloodlust. "You were downtown at Huff's last night, drunk as a pig. Zinnia Linnear saw you."

"She needs glasses."

"Don't lie to me, you son of a fucking bitch."

"I swear it, I spent the night at Riven Rock. Look. Look at my face, why don't you? Huh? You see that? Mr. McCormick did that to me and I spent the night like a choirboy in Mart's bed with Mart snoring like a sawmill, I swear to God—"

She wasn't mollified, not in the least—she had something else, he knew it, something she was holding in reserve, roll out the caissons and let it fly. The baby, riding her hip, reached out to him. "Da-da," he said. "Da-da."

"You were with a woman," she said, and her voice was pitched low, the first premonitory rumble of the inchoate storm. "A dago."

He tried to avoid her, duck away, hide, tried to change the subject, clear the air, give her a chance to calm herself and absorb the thick palliative of his lies, but she wouldn't have it. Everywhere he turned, she was there, the baby her shield, her voice the high agitated hoot of a seabird: "Who was she? Huh? Some whore you found under a rock? Did you lay her? Did you?" He went into the bedroom to change his shirt, a man who'd been at work for two solid days and sweating under the arms with the strain of providing for his family and could he expect a moment's peace in his own home, the home he worked twelve hours a day to pay for? No. No, he couldn't. She was there in the bedroom, hooting, and when he pushed himself up to escape to the kitchen and reach behind the icebox for the solace of the all-but-empty bottle she kept sequestered there and he was never to know of in all its shame and hypocrisy, he lifted it to his lips to a barrage of hoots—"Who was she? Who?"—until finally he could take it no more, and no man could, not if he was blind, deaf and paralyzed.

He didn't mean to get violent. He didn't want to. He hadn't planned on it. It made him feel bad. But it was just like the time in Waverley, her face a puffed-up ball presenting itself to him over and over again, and he a spiker at the net, and yet it was different too, radically different, because the baby was there, attached to her hip and yowling as if he'd been orphaned already. He loved that baby and he didn't want to hurt it—*him*, Eddie Jr., his son—and he loved Rosaleen too, he did, but she kept coming at him, the white moon of her face, the big stitched ball, and when finally he did hit it, that surging swollen sphere of a hateful twisted little interrogatory wife's face, when his patience was exhausted, when Job's patience would have been exhausted, when all the popes and martyrs would have rattled their holy desiccated bones and screamed for murder, it was more a matter of reflex than anything else. Once, he hit her once, once only. And he made sure, in the way of a thoughtful man putting down a horse or a favorite dog, to hit her hard enough and squarely enough to prevent even the remotest possibility of a rebound.

That was in May, when Mr. McCormick was declared incompetent and Giovannella began showing up at Riven Rock again at all hours of the day and night, and Rosaleen, the smallest crook stamped into the bridge of her nose like a question mark turned back on itself and her eyes rimmed in black like a night raider's, packed her bags and took the baby with his bruised thigh and walked out the door to the streetcar and took the streetcar to the train, but for O'Kane the events came so fast and furious he could hardly be sure of the year, let alone the month. And how was Rosaleen? everyone wanted to know, especially people like Elsie Reardon. And the baby? They were fine, O'Kane insisted, and he relied on memory to supply the fresh details about little Eddie's puerile raptures and adorable doings, but he ached inside, ached till he had to get drunk most nights of the week and cry himself to sleep in the calmed waters of the big wooden ark of a bed he'd bought to float and sustain his bliss, and for a month he was bereft, and for a month he fabricated and prevaricated and spun his complex weave of wishful thinking and feathery invention before admitting to all and sundry that Rosaleen had gone home to Massachusetts to nurse her ailing mother. And father. And her brother with the bone cancer and the sixteen children.

All that hurt. And it should never have happened. He knew who to blame—himself, of course, a man who just wasn't ready yet for the yoke of marriage and family. And Katherine. Mrs. McCormick. The Ice

Queen. If she hadn't stuck her nose in where it didn't belong none of this would have happened. He could have gotten Giovannella—or whoever—out of his system and waited till the time was right, until he was ready, really ready, and then maybe things would have been different.

Once the month was out, he settled up with Old Man Rowlings and took a room in a boardinghouse not far from the train station and within easy walking distance of Menhoff's, O'Reilly's and the hole-in-the-wall bars of Spanishtown. The furniture he sold off to whoever wanted it, and wouldn't you know that Zinnia Linnear, like some sort of veiny blue vulture, was first in line for the oversized bed, the bureau and the set of mostly chipped secondhand china. There were fireworks off Stearns Wharf that Fourth of July and what must have been three hundred boats, each with a kerosene lantern, spread across the glowing water like the stars come down from the sky. O'Kane remembered that Fourth of July in particular, not simply for the concatenation of un-lucky events leading up to it, but because Giovannella was there with him at the end of the wharf, her wide glowing uncandled face lit again and again by the trailing streamers of red, white and blue.

It was sometime around then—July, maybe August—that Mr. Mc-Cormick came back to life again. He got up out of bed one morning and stepped into the shower bath like any other man, ordered up his break-fast and asked for the newspaper. O'Kane was stunned, and even Mart, who was slow to register surprise (or any other emotion, for that mat-ter), seemed impressed. In fact, the two of them just stood there speech-less as Mr. McCormick, dressed in his pajamas and robe, seated himself at the table in the upper parlor and buttered his toast with the brisk assiduous movements of a man sitting down to breakfast before leaving for the office. It was an entirely normal scene, prosaic even, if you dis-count the fact that he had to use a spoon to butter his toast, Dr. Hamil-ton having proscribed all sharp-edged implements in the aftermath of the fork incident. When Mr. McCormick finished spooning up his eggs, nice as you please, patted his lips delicately with the napkin, stretched and took the newspaper, O'Kane sent Mart for Dr. Hamilton—the doc-tor had to see this.

Hamilton came on the run, dashing through the entrance hall and taking the steps two at a time, and he was still breathing in short muted gasps as he smoothed back his hair and straightened his tie on the landing outside the barred door to the upper parlor. He tried his best to achieve a casual saunter, as if he'd just happened by, but he couldn't seem to control his feet, skipping through every third step or so as he crossed the room. O'Kane watched him slowly circle the patient, eyes flipping behind the lenses of his pince-nez, lips silently moving as if rehearsing a speech; Mr. McCormick, absorbed in the paper, which he held up rigidly only inches from his face, didn't seem to notice him. And then, very tentatively, as if afraid of breaking the spell, Hamilton tried to draw Mr. McCormick into conversation. "Good morning, Mr. Mc-Cormick," he said in his customary whisper, "you're looking well."

There was no response.

"Well," the doctor said, rubbing his hands together in a brisk, businesslike way and moving into the periphery of Mr. McCormick's vision, quite close to him now, "it certainly is a glorious sunshiny day, isn't it?"

Still no response.

"And to see you looking so well on such a glorious day—that gives us all pleasure, doesn't it, Edward? Martin? And sir, Mr. McCormick, I can only presume you're feeling better?" A pause. "Am I right?"

Very slowly, as if he were an actor in a farce parting the curtains to reveal the painted smile on his face, Mr. McCormick lowered the newspaper to uncover first his hairline, then his brow, his eyes, his nose, and finally, with a flourish, the broad radiant beaming dimple-cheeked grin spread wide across the lower part of his face. Mr. McCormick was grinning, grinning to beat the band, and you could see the light in his eyes as they came into focus and settled warmly on the reciprocally grinning visage of Dr. Hamilton. "And who might you be?" he asked in the most gratuitous and amenable tones.

The doctor couldn't help himself. He let his eyes have their way three times in rapid succession—blip, blip, blip—worked his shoulders as if to shrug off some invisible beast clinging to his jacket and hissing in his ear, and said, "Why, Mr. McCormick, it's me, Dr. Hamilton, Gilbert—your physician." He spread his arms. "And look, your old friends, Edward O'Kane and Martin Thompson. But how are you feeling?"

The grin held. O'Kane was grinning too now—and so was Mart. All four of them were stretching their facial muscles to the limit, goodwill abounding, and you would have thought they'd just heard the best joke in the world. "What is this place?" Mr. McCormick asked then, and no trace of hesitation in his voice, no stuttering or verbigeration at all.

Dr. Hamilton turned to O'Kane and Mart as if this were the drollest thing he'd ever heard, then came back to Mr. McCormick, all the while rubbing his hands and flipping his eyes in a paroxysm of nervous energy—and grinning, grinning as if it were the conventional way of wearing a face. "Why, it's Riven Rock, Mr. McCormick—in California. The place you designed for your sister, Mary Virginia—surely you remember that. Such a beautiful place. And so comfortable. Did you encounter any particular difficulties in the design?"

"I—I—" and now the old hesitation, the scattered eyes, at once lost and receding, but still the grin held. "I—I don't recall . . . but I—I must have been ill, isn't that, that right?"

Hamilton, trying for gravity, the grin banished: "Yes, that's right, Mr. McCormick, you've been ill. But look at you now, alert and aglow with health and happiness. . . . Do you recall your illness, its nature, anything at all about it?"

Mr. McCormick turned to O'Kane then and winked an eye—actually winked, like an old crony in a bar. "Yes," he said, and the grin widened still further. "A c-cold, wasn't it?"

The change lasted three days. Mr. McCormick got himself up each morning, shower-bathed (and sometimes for as long as two hours at a time), took his breakfast, read the paper. He conversed, joked even. And though he was very tired, exhausted from his long travail, he was able to move about without too much difficulty, favoring the right leg and walking with a tottering deliberation, as if he were on a tightrope over a howling precipice. He needed help in dressing still, easily frustrated—baffled, even—over the proper way to slip into a shirt or jacket and repeatedly trying to slide both feet into a single pantleg. But still, everyone was heartened, O'Kane especially. Mr. McCormick was coming out of it. Finally. At long last.

As it turned out, though—and this was sad, hopes raised and hopes dashed—O'Kane was merely indulging in a bit of wishful thinking. Those three days of lucidity, those three days of dramatic and visible improvement, of the lifting of the veil, of release, only adumbrated Mr. McCormick's worst crisis since his breakdown. No one could have foreseen it. Not even Dr. Hamilton, who fired off a telegram to Kath-

erine, now back in Boston, trumpeting the news of the change in her
husband's condition. Or she, who wired him back the minute she received it: HE WAS EATING? STOP DRESSING HIMSELF? STOP READING THE
NEWSPAPER? STOP COULD SHE SEE HIM? STOP NOW? Optimistic, all his
diagnostic sails flapping in a fresh breeze of hope and speculation—but
cautious, ever cautious—the doctor wired her back to say: NOT YET
STOP.

And a good thing too. Because what happened during O'Kane's
shift on the fourth day after Mr. McCormick awakened from the dead
came as a shock, to put it mildly. O'Kane had never seen anything like
it, and he thought he'd seen everything. No one was to blame, at least,
and that came as a relief to all concerned, but if he were to scratch deep
enough in the sediment of culpability, O'Kane could have named a
candidate—Katherine, Katherine yet again. She meant well, he would
never deny that, but because she meant well—and because she was a
snooping imperious castrating bitch of a woman the likes of which he
could never have imagined even in his worst nightmare—she couldn't
help sticking her nose in where it didn't belong.

The problem this time was with the window in Mr. McCormick's
bathroom. Katherine couldn't leave it alone. After she'd finished with
the first floor of the house, consigning the McCormick furniture, pictures and pottery to the garage and remaking the place in her own
image—when it was all done, from paint to draperies to rugs—she began to fixate on the second floor, the floor she'd never seen, the floor
from which she was interdicted on Dr. Hamilton's strictest orders. She
studied it constantly—or at least the outer walls and windows and the
tiled expanse of the sunporch—watching for a glimpse of her husband
through a pair of opera glasses. Inevitably she found something to dis-
please her, and in this case it was the bathroom window.

The bars disturbed her. They made the place look too much like a
fortress—or an asylum. She consulted with Hamilton and then brought
in a young architect and a crew of Italians who removed the perfectly
serviceable standard one-inch-thick iron bars while Mr. McCormick
lay tranced in his bedroom and replaced them with steel louvers. The
louvers had been designed to ensure that a fully grown man of Mr. Mc-
Cormick's height and weight couldn't work his arm through any of the
apertures and make contact with the glass beyond it—and of course,
they'd been constructed to a standard of strength and durability that

would prevent their being bent or mutilated in any way that might afford Mr. McCormick an avenue of escape. What the architect hadn't taken into account was the ingenuity of Mr. McCormick—or his strength. Especially when the fit was on him.

It was late on that fourth day, toward the end of O'Kane and Martin's shift, and the evening was settling in round the house, birds calling, the sun hanging on a string, the islands in bold relief against the twin mirrors of sea and sky. Mart was in the parlor, working on a crossword puzzle by way of improving his vocabulary, and Mr. McCormick had retired for a nap before dinner. O'Kane was seated in a chair across the room from Mart, his feet propped up on the windowsill, gazing into space. He was thinking about his room and the bland indigestible cud of grease and overcooked vegetable matter his landlady was likely to serve up for dinner—and his first drink, and Giovannella—when he heard the unmistakable sound of glass shattering and falling like heavy rain to the pavement below.

He didn't stop to wonder or think, vaulting out of the chair like a high-jumper and hurtling across the floor to Mr. McCormick's bedroom, which he found empty, and then to the bathroom, which he found locked. Or not locked, exactly—there was no lock—but obstructed. Mr. McCormick seemed to have jammed something—something substantial—up under the doorknob. O'Kane twisted the knob and applied his shoulder to the unyielding slab of the door, all the while tasting panic in the back of his throat, a harsh taste, precipitate and unforgiving. Mart was right behind him, thank God, and in the next instant there were two of them battering at the door, Mart standing back five paces and then flinging himself at the insensate oak with the singlemindedness of a steer in a chute. Once, twice, three times, and finally the door gave, splintering off its hinges and lurching forward into a barricade of furniture with a dull echoing thump. And where had the furniture come from? From the stripped and ransacked bedroom behind them. While they were lulled to distraction in the soothing plenitude of the late afternoon, decoding their crossword puzzles and gazing idly out the window, Mr. McCormick had silently dismantled his room and built a bulwark against the door to cover his escape.

Oh, yes: his escape. That was what this was all about—the barricaded door, the shattered glass, the imploded peace of the lazy languorous late afternoon in Paradise—as O'Kane was to discover in the next moment. He scrambled up over the plane of the door, which was canted now at a forty-five-degree angle, just in time to see Mr. Mc-Cormick vanish through a ragged gap in the louvers that looked as if an artillery shell had passed through it but was in fact created by Mr. Mc-Cormick himself, using main strength, ingenuity, and a four-inch-thick length of cherrywood that had formerly served as a table leg. O'Kane cried out, his mind a seething stew of featureless thoughts, the three p's tumbled together with Dr. Hamilton's lectures on the train, Katherine's denunciatory fury and the stark crazed pulse-pounding phrase "suicidal tendencies," and he rushed to the window and thrust his head through the gap in horror, expecting anything, expecting the worst. What he saw was Mr. McCormick, eyes sunk deep in the mask of his face, fierce with concentration, clambering down the drainpipe with all the agility of a, well, of a *hominoid.*

By the time O'Kane reached the ground floor, burst through the front door and tore round the corner of the house, Mr. McCormick had vanished. *Why,* he was thinking, *why does this always have to happen on my shift?* and then he was in motion, frantic, irrepressible, charging round the courtyard and shouting out for Roscoe, the gardeners, the household help and any stray Italians who might have been dicing garlic or nodding over a glass of wine in their tumbledown cottages, dogs barking, chickens flying, the whole place a hurricane of fear and alarm. "Mr. McCormick's loose!" he bellowed, and here came Mart and Roscoe and a host of sweating dark men gripping hoes and hedge clippers. "Lock your women indoors," he cried, "and all of you men fan out over the property—and if you find him, don't try to approach him, just stand clear and send for me or Dr. Hamilton."

They were systematically beating the bushes, describing an ever-widening circle around the house under O'Kane's command, when Dr. Hamilton appeared on the run, flashing through the trees from the direction of the apery in a white lab coat stippled with the various leavings of his monkeys and baboons, not to mention Julius the orangutan. He slashed through the kitchen garden, across the courtyard and right on up to O'Kane, who was searching the bushes around the daphne bed to the west of the house. "My God," the doctor gasped, out of breath, his eyes whirling, and he repeated it over and over again, wheezing for breath, "my God, my God, my God."

"He can't have gone far," O'Kane said, "his legs won't carry him. He's not in condition."

The doctor just stood there, a sharp wedge of the declining sun isolating the right side of his face, the tic replicating itself in his cheek now and at the corner of his mouth. "How?" he sputtered. "Who was—? When did—?"

"No more than ten minutes. We almost had him—he pried open the new louvers with a stick of wood."

"Shit." The doctor let out a string of curses, every trace of the therapeutic whisper gone out of his voice. "What's the nearest estate—Mira Vista, isn't it? Who's there now—are there any women?" His face was a small thing, flushed and bloated beneath the tan he'd acquired in the company of his hominoids, his hair wet through with sweat, and sweat descending in a probing and tentative way from his temples to trace the clenched lines of his jaw. "We've got to warn them. Notify the police. Call out the bloodhounds."

"But he can't have gone far—and he's got almost ninety acres of his own to run around on . . . but I was just concerned, if, well, there's any possibility of what we discussed before, if he might try to—"

"You idiot," the doctor shouted, and there was no vestige of control left in him, "you unutterable moron. What do you think? Why do you suppose we keep him locked up? He could be lying dead under any one of these damned bushes even now, and here we are standing around jawing about it. Action, that's what we need, not a bunch of lame-brained questions and what-ifs. We've got to, got to—" and then he broke off abruptly and darted away in the direction of the garage.

Night fell, and still no sign of Mr. McCormick. On regaining his senses, Hamilton decided against involving the police for fear of possible repercussions, but all the neighbors within a one-mile radius were warned and all available men, including the Dimuccis, were called out to help with the search. The number of flashlights was limited—two from the house and one from Roscoe's trove in the garage—and the laborers went poking through the brush with lanterns and torches held aloft, despite the risk of fire. Roscoe had gone for Nick and Pat and they joined the search too, but O'Kane, smarting from the way Hamilton had assailed him and still carrying a lingering grudge against Nick, went off on his own with one of the flashlights.

It was the dry season, the tall grass of the fields parched till it turned from gold to white, the frogs thick along the two creeks that merged on the property, clamorous in their numbers, filling the darkness with the liquid pulse of their froggy loves and wars. O'Kane followed Hot Springs Creek south to where it joined with Cold Stream and then traced that back north along the Indian ceremonial grounds the estate had swallowed up, thinking that Mr. McCormick might have been attracted to the water or the thick growth of reeds and scrub oak that shadowed the banks—he could have crouched there for a week and no one would have found him, and certainly not in the dark. The beam of the flashlight—a gadget O'Kane had never even seen till he came to Riven Rock—picked out the odd branch or boulder, flattening it to two-dimensionality as though it were pasted to the wall of darkness, and O'Kane stumbled among the rocks of the streambed, blinded by the light. He kept his balance the first few times, but then a rock skittered out from under his feet and he pitched forward into the waterborne rubble, cradling the flashlight to his chest and skinning both knees in the process. He lay there recumbent a moment, thinking of rattlesnakes, evil-eyed and explosive, and gave up the streambed for the cultivated paths.

He saw the flickering lights in the distance, heard the occasional shout—in English and Italian both—but he ignored them. Searching alone, weary now, tired of the whole business, he made his way back toward the main house, skirting the lawns and plodding mechanically through the Clover Garden, past the hothouses and the looming blocky rear wall of the garage till he was close enough to the apes to smell them. The hominoids, that is—the monkeys and baboons that were unlucky enough to provide the grist for Hamilton's theoretical mill. O'Kane had observed enough of the doctor's experiments by now to form an opinion, and his opinion was that they were bunk. Aside from running the monkeys through the big wooden box with the gates in it, all Hamilton and his seedy-looking assistants seemed to do was make the monkeys fuck one another—or anything else that came to hand. Once, O'Kane had seen the wop lead a stray dog into the communal cage, and sure enough, the monkeys came chittering down from their perches and one after another fucked the dog. They threw a coyote into the cage. The monkeys fucked that. They tossed an eight-foot-long bullsnake into the cage. The monkeys fucked it and then killed it and ate it.

As far as O'Kane could see, the only thing Hamilton had established was that a monkey will fuck anything, and how that was supposed to be applied to Mr. McCormick and all the rest of the suffering schizophrenics of the world, he couldn't even pretend to guess.

But he was drawn toward them now, almost irresistibly, the potent reek of the close air beneath the trees, the susurrus of their nocturnal movements, a sound like a distant breeze combing through a glade lush with ferns. The sound calmed him, and for a minute he forgot about Mr. McCormick and forgave the monkeys their stink. And then, all in an instant, he came fully alert.

The monkeys had begun to hiss and chitter the way they did in daylight, the noise sailing out to him and rushing back to roost again in the darkness ahead. He quickened his pace, shining the beam off the great twisted branches of the oaks and then catching the wire mesh of the big central cage that rose up into the crown of the trees. There was movement at the top of the cage, and there shouldn't have been, all the monkeys put to rest in their individual cages at nightfall, but they were noisier now, much noisier—the gentle rustling of a moment ago become the jangling rattle of steel padlocks and cage doors straining against their latches—and he could see the tiny bodies flailing themselves to and fro behind the mesh. The light shot round in his unsteady hand, a root grabbed for his foot, and he was trying to understand, to fathom what was happening, when suddenly every hominoid in the place was screeching loud enough to raise the holy dead.

What was it? There, high in the branches of the central cage, the movement again. He stepped closer, the screeching, the stench, struggling to steady the light, and then, as if in a sudden vision, it became clear to him. These were no monkeys in the branches—they were too big, much too big. These were no monkeys, but apes, the rutilant naked one, white as any ghost, and the shaggy hunkering split-faced one, and their hands moving each at the place where the other's legs intersected, two hands flashing in that obscene light until O'Kane, who now truly had seen everything, flicked it off.

Mercifully.

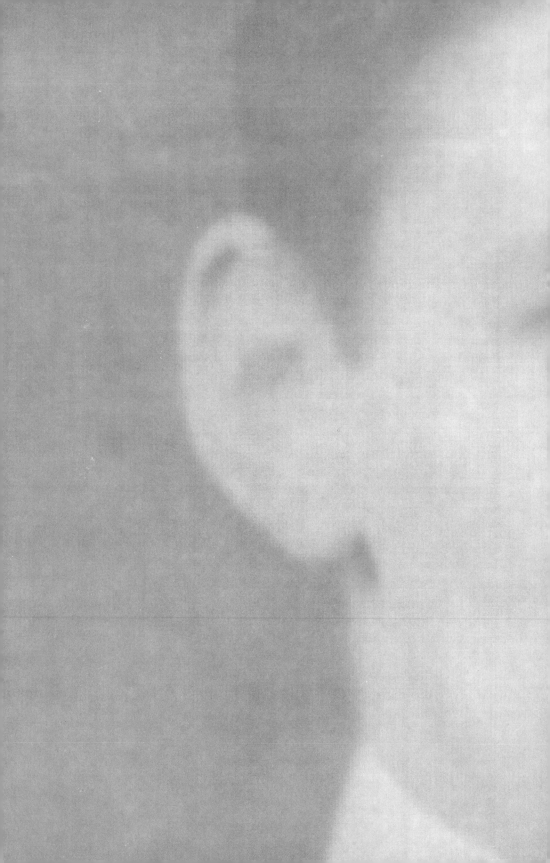

PART II

Dr. Brush's Time

1.

LOVE IS LOYAL,
HOPE IS GONE

The headline, set there for all the world to see in bold 30-point type, hit Katherine like a slap in the face. Her cheeks reddened. She felt the water come to her eyes, and her heart was suddenly beating at her ribs like a caged bird: LOVE IS LOYAL, HOPE IS GONE. And it got worse, much worse: SOCIETY FAVORITE CLINGS TO DEMENTED HUSBAND: HE'S ENSCONCED IN MANSION AT MONTECITO; WIFE COMES TO VISIT BUT CANNOT SEE HIM. She looked up at Carrie, whose face showed nothing, and then at her maid, Louisa, who looked as if she'd swallowed a live rat, and then finally at her hostess, Mrs. Lavinia Littlejohn, who'd just handed her the paper, already folded back to page 19. Mrs. Littlejohn was wearing that vacant smile Katherine's mother seemed to be afflicted with more and more these days, as if smiling for a woman of her generation were some sort of twitch or tic. "I, um, thought you'd want to see it, dear," Mrs. Littlejohn said, and the smile wavered a moment, uncertain of itself, and then came back stronger than ever.

Katherine held herself absolutely rigid, staring down at the newsprint in her lap until the letters began to shift and meld, and then, in her embarrassment, she looked up to survey the room again. Louisa was just vanishing through the door to the front parlor, where a dozen women were striding energetically to and fro, putting the finishing touches to banners and placards and chatting softly among themselves in the way of troops going into battle. Mrs. Littlejohn was still watching her, still smiling her autonomous maternal smile, and Carrie—Carrie Chapman Catt, Katherine's special friend and comrade-in-arms—was studiously looking out the window. "I don't know what to say," Katherine murmured, "it's so . . . humiliating to have my privacy violated like this. I feel like I've been raped."

Carrie looked her full in the face. She pursed her lips and made a tsking sound. "After two years in the Movement, I should think you'd be used to it—you've seen what they've written about me. But take the paper in the other room and find yourself a quiet nook—read it. All the way through. Really, there's nothing but praise for you in there. And don't let the headlines upset you—they're made to be intentionally insipid and tasteless. That's how they sell newspapers."

Yes, but she'd wanted to keep the Dexter name out of it—and Stanley's too. And her own deepest hopes and pains, her marriage, her suffering—how dare they? How dare they print a word about her private life? They could howl "No to Petticoat Rule" all they wanted—that was part of the privilege of living in a democracy, no matter how wrongheaded it was—but there were certain things that had to be held sacrosanct.

"Go on," Carrie urged, maternal herself now, Mrs. Littlejohn clucking away in harmony, every doily on every table aglow with solicitude, "read it. It makes you out to be a saint, Kat, it does—and it's publicity, good publicity that people can't help linking with our cause."

Katherine couldn't believe what she was hearing. Carrie Chapman Catt, the woman she admired above all others, admired to the point of worship even, she who had founded the National Woman Suffrage Association and demanded of her amenable second husband (now amenably deceased) four months of absolute freedom a year and the money to campaign for the vote in the manner to which she was accustomed, was willing to offer her up to the canaille for mere *publicity*. Katherine was stung. And in that moment she didn't know what was worse, her dirty laundry aired in public by a bunch of ink-stained hacks or her idol's cold streak of realpolitik. She set her jaw. Stood. And without a word to either woman stalked out of the room and up the stairs to the bedroom Mrs. Littlejohn had provided for her and Carrie during their campaign amongst the Fourth of July revelers on Nantasket Beach.

The house was near Hull and it looked out on Hingham Bay, the bay that gave onto the serious ocean, the true ocean, the cold somber Atlantic, and there were no palms here, no zephyrs, no parrots or monkeys or orange trees or anything else that smacked of frivolity or sensuality. Katherine settled into an armchair by the window and read through the article as if she were gulping water after three sets of tennis:

> It is not a case of lovers separated in death, but rather a separation in life, to overcome which if it were possible millions would be no barrier. In this case it is not a hero but a heroine who furnishes the lesson in constancy, and her most intimate acquaintances, those of the smartest set in New York, in Boston and Chicago, bow to her with admiration that is born of respect.
>
> The heroine is the beautiful, intellectual and highly-accomplished Mrs. Katherine Dexter McCormick, the young wife of Stanley McCormick, whose father was the brains behind the gigantic harvester corporation, an institution whose wealth no one could accurately estimate.
>
> Stanley McCormick is insane, suffering from a form of dementia. He lives in California, where a mansion in the exclusive city of Montecito, which is populated by a colony of retired millionaires, is maintained for him.

The letters fled like ants across the page, accumulated into big black staring words with heads and pincers and then sentences that bit and stung and made her flesh crawl, *beautiful, intellectual, highly-accomplished, insane:* how dare they? How dare they? And then, farther on down the page, all wounds became one wound:

> Dr. Hamilton does not allow her to see her husband, much less converse with him. And yet, nothing daunted, Mrs. McCormick goes to Montecito in December of each year and spends the Yuletide season near the man she loves.

Stanley McCormick does not know that his wife visits in the vicinity. This his wife knows and though she would give her life to be of benefit to him she sadly turns from the sanatorium and soothes herself with solitary walks on the grounds.

The mansion is surrounded by a garden that is beautiful to behold. It has been referred to as a veritable Garden of Eden with its tropical foliage, palms, long winding driveways and miniature forests. In this garden Mrs. McCormick forgets as she roams, listening to the song birds, viewing with keen interest a small menagerie maintained by Dr. Hamilton in which many specimens of the monkey tribe predominate. There is a scientific reason for this menagerie, but this is known only to scientists.

She wanted to tear the paper to pieces and fling it from her, but she didn't, she couldn't, and though she tried not to think of Stanley—her Stanley, nobody's but hers, not his mother's or his sisters' or his brothers', not anymore—though she'd thrown herself body and soul into the suffrage movement as a way of forgetting, here it was all over again, all her private pain, and served up to titillate the great unwashed in their linoleum kitchens. What would her mother think? And her father—he must be turning over in his grave.

Hope is gone, indeed. How would they know? They'd snooped and prodded and poked around enough to hear word of the hominoid colony, and yet they couldn't begin to fathom its purpose or the hope it represented. This was obscene. Irresponsible. Yellow journalism at its worst. And whom had they been talking to? Hamilton, certainly. Some of the staff—O'Kane? Nick? She remembered giving an interview herself, one of dozens connected with her work for Carrie and NAWSA, but she never dreamed they'd pry into her personal life as if she were an Evelyn Nesbit or Sarah Bernhardt or some such person. And they were wrong—hope was very much alive, even if it was dampened by the steady drizzle of the years. She hadn't seen Stanley face to face in more than five years now, since he was at McLean, and he'd gotten so much worse before his recent improvement, what with his escape through the louvers and his descent all the way back into the darkness, so far back it was as if he'd been entombed all this time, but there was hope, there was. His nurses had taught him to walk again and to eat and he was lucid sometimes now, or so they told her . . . and science, science was

making leaps all the time, what with glandular research and psycho-
therapy, with Freud, Jung, Adler. There was hope, abundant hope, and
she would never give way to despair — and why didn't they print that?

She'd been sitting there for some minutes, the paper in her lap, the
bay beyond the windows scoured by tight bands of cloud that were like
steel springs coiling and uncoiling over the steely plane of the water, the
voices of the women in the parlor below drifting up to her in snatches.
And then she looked down at the story again, the story about her, the
beautiful and intellectual Katherine Dexter McCormick, and settled on
the last paragraph, the one that canonized her:

> One of Mrs. McCormick's friends the other day said:
> "Such a character as that woman possesses is an object lesson
> for the world. It would seem to me that she is living over a volcano
> and would be the most unhappy woman in the world. I know of
> her unstinted popularity in the leading social sets of the East, how
> easy it would be for her to forsake her afflicted husband and live
> the natural life, but she consecrated herself to Mr. McCormick and
> if she does not get her reward in this life, she surely will in the
> next."

Despite herself, despite the demon of publicity and her anger and disappointment and the silent vow she was even now making never to
speak with the press again, she couldn't help feeling a flush of gratifica-
tion over those lines set in print so cheap it came off on your gloves —
because, after all, they were true.

It was quarter to four when Carrie and Mrs. Littlejohn came for
her, and neither of them made reference to the newspaper article — that
was in the past, already forgotten, the smallest pebble in the road to
equality. "Everyone's ready," Carrie said, striding briskly across the
room to snatch her hat from the bureau in a flurry of animated elbows
and flashing hatpins, "though the day is rotten in the extreme, could
even rain, and I wonder just how many bathers will be out there on the
strand and if the whole thing isn't just going to be another grand waste
of time."

Katherine was already on her feet, grabbing up her purse and para-
sol and smoothing down her dress as if girding for battle — and it was a
kind of battle, the antisuffragists as nasty as any mob, and they were

sure to be there, jeering and catcalling, their faces twisted and ugly and shot through with hate. They were drunk too, half of them, tobacco stains on their shirts and their fingers smeared with grease and nicotine and every sort of filth, yammering like animals, big testosterone-addled beasts out of some Darwinian nightmare. They were afraid of the vote. Afraid of Temperance. Afraid, incredibly, of women. "And the local authorities?" she asked, slipping in beside Carrie to arrange her hat in the mirror. "The sheriff or whoever? Are they still threatening to deny us our right to speak?"

Carrie turned away from the mirror to give her a look. "What do you think?"

"So what will we do?"

"What else? Defy them."

They were met on the boardwalk by the Norfolk County sheriff and two of his deputies. The sheriff was ancient, just barely alive from the look of him, and the deputies were huge with an excess of feeding, twin butterballs squeezed into the iron maidens of their distended duff-colored uniforms. "You'll need a permit to hold a rally here," the sheriff wheezed, wearily lifting his watery old turtle's gaze from the stony impediment of Carrie's face and easing it down on the minefield of Katherine's. Behind Katherine were fourteen women waving the purple, white and gold banners of the Movement and brandishing placards that read HOW LONG MUST WOMEN WAIT FOR LIBERTY? NO TAXATION WITHOUT REPRESENTATION and, the stiffest goad of all, DON'T TREAD ON US!

"We have no such permit," Carrie responded, her voice ringing out as if she were shouting through a megaphone, heads turning, a crowd already gathering, children on the run, "as you well know, since your cronies at the courthouse have denied us one, but we have certain inalienable rights guaranteed us under the First Amendment of the United States Constitution—the rights of free speech and peaceable assembly— and we intend to exercise them."

"Not in Norfolk County, you won't," the old sheriff rasped, clamping his jaws shut like a trap.

"Go back to your kitchen, grandmaw!" a voice jeered, and there they were, the unshaven potbellied Fourth of July patriots gathered round their beery smirks, but there were women in the swelling crowd too, women with uplifted eyes and proud faces, women who needed to hear the news. All of a sudden Katherine felt as if she were going to explode, and she couldn't keep it in, not here, not now, not in the face of this mindless barbarism, this naysaying and mockery. She whirled round to face the hecklers, and they were thirty or forty strong already, as if they'd been waiting all morning for this, for a little blood sport to ease the tedium of sucking on the bottle between shoving matches and filling each other's ears with their filthy stories and crude jokes, and how could they dare presume to address Carrie Chapman Catt like that, *grandma* indeed. Suddenly she was shouting at the biggest and stupidest-looking behemoth in the crowd, and no matter if he'd opened his mouth or not. "And you go back to the saloon where you belong, you common drunkard," she cried, feeling the blood rise in her like a geyser. "It's tosspots like you who ought to be banned from voting, not good decent sober women!"

That brought the storm down, all right—not the literal one, the one festering in the clouds and rumbling offshore in a tightly woven reticle of lightning—but the hurricane of testicular howls that was only awaiting an excuse to explode in all its wrath. Curses—the very vilest— rained down on them, faces nagged, an overripe tomato appeared out of nowhere to spread its reeking pulp all over the front of Katherine's dress. Through it all, Carrie's voice rang out: "To the water, ladies! If they won't let us speak on the soil of Norfolk County, then we'll bring our message home from the sea!"

Someone started the chant—"Forward, out of error,/Leave behind the night,/Forward through the darkness,/Forward into light!"—and then they were marching, down the length of the boardwalk and out onto the sand, their heels sinking away from them, shouts, jeers and laughter in their ears, and they didn't stop marching until they were in the surf, sixteen strong and now seventeen and eighteen, the waves beating at them like some hostile force, their dresses ruined, shoes destroyed, and still they chanted while the sheriff blustered and wheezed and tried to head them off and the bullies pelted them with rotten vegetables, scraps of flotsam and seawrack, anything that came to hand.

The wind picked up and the waves pounded at them. Carrie spoke, and she was as full of fire as Katherine had ever seen her, and no, the women of America were not waiting, they were not asking, they were demanding their rights and they were demanding them now. And then Katherine spoke, the clean salt smell of the spume driving down the sour reek of the tomato pinned to her breast like a scarlet letter, and she wouldn't wipe it away, wouldn't give them the satisfaction. She spoke extempore and afterward she couldn't remember what she'd said, but she remembered the feeling of it, the intensity and exhilaration of doing battle, of thrusting her words like bayonets into the very heart of the crowd that gathered on the shore to hear them.

"Go back to your husband!" some idiot shouted just before the storm broke—the literal one, with all its fierce lashing of wind and rain and even hail, the one that emptied the beach till she was preaching to the dumb sand and the oblivious gulls and the sisters who'd linked hands with her. *My husband,* she thought, and they were singing the "Marseillaise" there in the wind and the rain and the surf, singing "For All the Saints," *my husband might as well not even exist.*

Afterward, when they'd staggered out of the surf and darted barefoot up the beach like so many schoolgirls at a picnic interrupted by a shower, they were giddy and heedless, the laughter running through them like a spark firing the engine of their exhilaration over and over again, and the pulse of it kept them giggling and grinning and thrusting their ecstatic faces at one another as the chauffeurs squeezed them dripping and shivering into Mrs. Littlejohn's twin Pierce Arrow sedans, a Cadillac touring car and a Chalmers Six loaned for the day by an invalid neighbor of Mrs. Littlejohn who was highly sympathetic to the cause. And of the two women who'd spontaneously joined them in the surf, one—Delia Bumpus, proprietress of a rooming house in Quincy— came along for the celebratory ride back to Mrs. Littlejohn's, a bona fide convert. She was a robust woman, huge above her stockings, and her laugh was contagious as they piled out of the cars and gathered round the fire in the drawing room in a flurry of tea things, blankets, towels and warm terry robes provided by a whole army of servants. "I thought you were all crazy," she roared, lifting her skirts to the fire, "and I was right!"

Everyone laughed at that and ten voices flew into the breach, shrill with excitement. "Did you see the look on that sheriff's face when Carrie read him the riot act?"

"My God, yes!"

"I thought he was going to die of a stroke right there—"

"He must have been seventy."

"Seventy? He was a hundred if he was a day—"

"What? You didn't recognize him? Methuselah's grandfather?"

Laughter and applause.

"Let me tell you, if he was the only unregenerate male standing between us and the vote I would blow him over myself, just like this—*poof!*"

More laughter, percolating round the delicate china cups of beef tea and orange pekoe blend. The fire leapt and snapped, women sank into armchairs in a sisterhood of splayed limbs and neatly balanced cups and saucers, a faint scent of woodsmoke charged the air and everything seemed laminated with the intensity of a waking dream, the cut flowers glowing with an aniline light, the oil paintings hanging above their heads like halos, and as the kitchen staff piled a table high with cold cuts, toast points and caviar, plums and raspberries from the orchard, the storm beat deliciously at the windows and shook the floorboards beneath their feet. Katherine, the hair hanging wet in her face as she rubbed at it with a towel that smelled like sunshine on the grass, felt like a girl again—she might have been in the gymnasium at Miss Hershey's School after calisthenics, the sweet aching odor of girls' sweat in the air, hard-earned sweat, sweat that was the equal of any boy's or man's. She was glowing, melting. She was made of india rubber, molasses, pure maple syrup settling into a mold.

"Yes, yes, yes!" came a shriek from Maybelle Harrison, wife of the textile manufacturer, caught with a piece of toast arrested halfway to her parted lips. She was standing in front of the fire, tall as any Amazon, her hair wrapped in a great white terrycloth turban. "The crowning moment for me was during Katherine's speech, and a stirring speech it was, Katherine, really first-rate"—cheers and applause—"because that was when Maude Park suddenly disappeared beneath one of these enormous breakers and came up spouting like a porpoise—"

They were sisters, all of them, Maybelle Harrison cheek by jowl with Lettie Strang, governess to Mrs. Littlejohn's granddaughters, Jane Roessing exchanging pleasantries with Delia Bumpus, late of the boardinghouse, and not a thought of class or social position. This was the spirit of the Movement, the spirit of women without men, the spirit of Lysistrata and Sappho, the very scene Katherine had dreamed of when she'd joined the nascent women's club at MIT, striding through the door and into the embrace of three trembling doelike creatures as bewildered and uncertain as she and yet no less determined. She stretched luxuriously and cradled the hot cup in her hands, rain tapping at the windows, the flow of laughter and conversation ebbing and flooding round her, and thought, This is the way the world should be.

But it wasn't, and no one knew that better than she.

There was no sanctuary, no enchanted castle, no safe haven full of fine things and exulting women, not unless you built it yourself. And you didn't build it yourself, you couldn't, not when you were fourteen and as dependent on your father as he was on his capricious God in His capricious heavens. Because that was how old she was, fourteen, when the world of men came crashing down on her, pillars, buttresses, scaffolding and all.

It was in the spring, a month or so after the chess club fiasco, and the carriage had just brought her home from school (there was no reason to stay late anymore, and Mr. Gregson couldn't seem to look her in the face no matter what she did to please him, as if she were the one in the wrong). Her mother was out—at a tea someplace, or maybe it was a charity function—and her brother Samuel was away at Harvard. The house was unnaturally quiet, the servants in the kitchen, the cats asleep in the window. She was reading—*Middlemarch*, and she remembered the book to this day—puzzling over Dorothea Brooke and her thirst for learning that was so all-consuming as to allow her to throw herself away on a crabbed sexless old mummy like Casaubon, when there was a thump in the front hallway, as if someone had thrown open the door and tossed a sack of meal on the carpet. The cats raised their heads. Katherine set down her book. And there is was again, louder now, more distinct, as if a second sack had been flung against the wall and then rebounded off the first. Curious more than anything—all she could think of was her mother and a pair of shopboys with a new purchase that was too bulky to bring up the back stairway—she eased into her slippers and went to the door to investigate.

It wasn't her mother. There were no shopboys, no sacks of meal, no china cabinets or ottomans wrapped in brown paper. When she pulled open the door to the hallway she saw her father there, leaning into the wall and clenching his teeth in a grimace of almost maniacal concentration, as if he were trying to push his way through the wainscoting; behind him, the outer door stood open to the soft haze of the sun and the branches of the budding trees along the street. "Father?" she said, more puzzled than alarmed—she'd never in her life known him to come home from the office before six. "Are you all right?"

He turned his face from the wall then and fastened his eyes on her, and it was the strangest thing but she couldn't hear anything in that moment, not the noise of the traffic in the street or the shouts of the children on the lawn next door—it was as if she'd gone deaf. But then a single noise began to intrude on her consciousness, the harsh abrasive grinding of his teeth, bone on bone, as loud suddenly as the rumble of a gristmill. She started toward him, no time for thought or wonder or even fear, her arms outstretched to receive him, bundle him, protect him, and all at once the wall heaved and threw him out into the center of the hallway on legs that had gone dead, and he was lurching past her in a blind stagger, already reaching out with his useless hands for the door to the library.

This was her father, Wirt Dexter, one of the great jurisprudential minds of his time, son of the founder of Dexter, Michigan, grandson of John Adams's secretary of the treasury, fifty-nine years old and never sick a day in his life, Daddy, Papa, Pater, the man around whom Katherine had molded her existence like a barnacle attached to a piling sunk deep in the seabed. He was fearless, unwavering, a defender of unpopular causes, the wide-shouldered softly smiling man who would tenderly cut up her meat with a few magical strokes when she was too little to chew and who sat up with her and a storybook when she couldn't sleep. And now, drained of color, unable to speak, his teeth grinding like two stones and his legs locked at the knee, he staggered right past her as if she'd never existed.

How he managed to twist that door handle and slip inside the door and lock it against her, she would never know, but it was one of the bravest things she'd ever seen, an act of will so monumental it awed her to this day even as the hurt of it rose like bile in her throat. The door slammed. She found her voice. "Father!" she cried, pounding at the door. "Daddy, Daddy!"

"Go away!" he growled, "damn you, get away!" And then she heard him on the carpet, thrashing across the floor like a dog shot between the shoulders, the lamp crashing over and the servants there in the hallway with their frightened faces, Mrs. Muldoon and Nora and Olga, and no hope in all the world because he was dying, dying behind that locked door so as to spare her, his daughter, his Katherine.

They buried him, and a month later her mother informed her they'd be leaving Chicago as soon as she could make the arrangements. And where were they going? To Boston, to be near Samuel, who was the hope of the family now. And he was, Samuel, a great hope, a great man ab ovo, his father in miniature, hard-working, right-thinking, serious, magnetic, older and wiser at twenty-one than most men at thirty or even forty, as sure of his career in the public weal as any Dexter before him. Katherine was bereft. She didn't know what to do. She was four-teen years old. She went to Boston with her mother — a provincial place, pinched and fastidious, choked in the stranglehold of society — and clung to the pillar of her handsome and accomplished older brother while the tide rose and the sea rushed in. And that was all right, the best she could do, until one afternoon four years later Samuel developed a sudden fever, broke out in a purple rash that made him look as if he'd been pounded all over with a hammer, and died before morning.

"Katherine? Are you with us?"

She looked up from her tea and the room was there in all its solidity and permanence, the smell of wet hair, women's hair, and of cake and woodsmoke and beef broth, and she was back in the present and flash-ing Jane Roessing a triumphal smile. "Just tired," she said. "Or not tired exactly — more the way I feel after a long walk in the woods. Re-laxed. Calm. And yet exhilarated too."

"Wordsworthian?"

Katherine laughed. "Sure, emotion recollected in tranquility and all that. But I feel more like Lucy Stone or Alice Paul at the moment." She slid over on the sofa and patted the cushion beside her.

Jane folded her skirts under her and sat lightly in the spot indi-cated. She was from Philadelphia, about Katherine's age, and had mar-ried a man considerably older, a manufacturer of some sort who'd been a champion of women's rights — when he died, eight years ago, he left her everything. Ever since, she'd put all her energy and resources into the Movement, traveling around the country and helping to organize local chapters, and in the spring she'd been in Washington with Inez Milholland for the great protest march. They had dozens of friends in common, but for one reason or another Katherine had never met her till the previous evening at Mrs. Littlejohn's dinner reception. She'd liked her right away. Jane was a dynamo, one of those bustling energetic women who seem to be so much taller than they actually are, always alert, always amused, bobbing and weaving through Mrs. Littlejohn's parlor under a mass of rust-colored hair that stood up buoyantly from her scalp no matter the pressure of hat, comb or pin. Her eyes were the faintest palest most delicate shade of green, like a Song dynasty vase, and she always managed to look self-possessed and wise—not in the way of accumulated wisdom, not necessarily, but in the way of the prankster, the class clown, the girl with the sharpest tongue in school.

"Carrie showed me the newspaper piece," she said, reaching for her hair with both hands as if to gather it all in, section by section, as if she were winnowing a bush for berries. "It was really quite touching, I thought—the parts about you, I mean." She paused. Let her green gaze sweep the room and then come back again. "You must have suffered."

Katherine bowed her head. It was the first expression of sympathy she'd heard in years and it made her want to weep aloud, beat her breast, lay her head in the lap of the woman beside her and sob till all the hurt and antipathy of the McCormicks and their minions was drained from her, all the fierceness of the struggle with Stanley and his keepers and the burden of Riven Rock, the desolation of being a wife without a husband, forever the odd one out at this gathering or that. (*Mrs. McCormick*, they called her, *Mrs. McCormick, shall I hail a cab for you?* and what a joke that was.) She couldn't respond. She tried, but nothing came out.

Jane was sitting right beside her now and she could smell the exotic rich dampness of the roots of her hair and feel the warmth of the thigh pressed to hers and somehow Jane's arm was resting on her shoulder and Jane was rocking her, ever so gently, till all she could think of was the skiff she'd had as a girl on Lake Michigan and the softest of breezes that would come all the way from Minnesota or Canada just to set it atremble, just to rock her.

"Listen," Jane murmured, turning her face to her, and all the other women in that room might as well have been on another planet for all Katherine was aware of them, "I know what you're going through, I do. When Fred died I was only twenty-five, with no children and both my parents gone, and his family treated me like some sort of criminal, like I was the one who'd given him heart disease and no matter that he was nearly sixty and had had two heart attacks already. To them I was an outsider and nothing more, and when the will was read that room was like a pot boiling over, and if looks could kill—"

Jane gave her a final pat, shifted away from her and bent forward to dig through her purse. Katherine was stunned. It was as if this woman beside her had read her deepest thoughts, as if they'd inherited the same set of unfeeling moneygrubbing in-laws, as if . . . but that was enough. Her husband was alive still, and there would come a day when he recovered and they were perfectly happy, like any other couple.

"Sorry to get so maudlin." Jane had straightened up and eased back into the chair and she held something now in her hand, something that glittered in the light of the fire. It was a cigarette case, Katherine saw, silver, with Jane's initials—J.B.R.—inlaid in gold across the facing. "Do you smoke?" Jane asked in the most casual voice in the world.

"Smoke?" Katherine had barely recovered herself. "You must be joking."

"No, not at all," and Katherine watched the unfolding ritual with fascination, the neatly sprung case, the tamped cigarette, the flare of the match and finally the long slow inhalation that drew tight the flesh of Jane's throat as if she were taking in the very breath of life itself. "How is it," Jane began, the blue vapor escaping her lips and nostrils in pale wisps, its odor sweet and harsh at the same time, like the smell of leaves burning in the gutter, "how is it that men can smoke in public and women can't?"

"Well," and Katherine looked round to see that every woman in the room was making an effort not to stare, "it's just not done, not in our set anyway. Maybe among seamstresses and such—"

Jane lifted her eyebrows. "And in Paris?"

"That's entirely different."

"Oh?" And there was that sly look, the look of the girl who circumvented all the rules and sent clever notes up and down the aisles when the teacher's back was turned. "You know"—exhaling again—"I think the thing that most irritates me about the whole little dominion of men and their precious vote and their property rights and all the rest is how illogical it is, how smug and self-serving, using our sex against us—'Oh, it's not ladylike to smoke.' Well, is it ladylike to vote, wear trousers, mount a bicycle? Is it ladylike to pay property taxes like any other citizen and stand by at election time and watch some illiterate from Ballyshannon step up to the ballot box—or worse, sell his vote for two shots of rye whiskey? Hm?"

The buzz of conversation had died momentarily in the wake of

Jane's putting fire to that little tube of compacted leaves and bringing it to her lips, but now it started up again, a whole clamor of voices.

"Look, it's clearing," someone observed.

"Oh, is it?"

"Yes, look over there, out over the water."

"Just in time for fireworks—we will have fireworks, won't we, Lavinia?"

Katherine tried to compose herself. Why was she so upset? She'd been in the presence of woman smokers more times than she could count—in Paris, Geneva, Vienna. "I couldn't agree more," she said finally, focusing on those mocking green eyes, "but the vote is one thing—even the issue of trousers or bicycles or the ridiculous practice of riding sidesaddle—and yet a personal habit that many, male *and* female, might find objectionable—"

"Have you ever tried one?"

Was she blushing? Thirty-eight years old and blushing like a schoolgirl? She was remembering those summers in Switzerland, at Prangins, and Lisette. "Well, to tell the truth," and suddenly she was giggling, "yes, yes I have."

Without a word, Jane snapped open the silver case and held it out to her, and Katherine accepted it, chose a cigarette and leaned forward for the flare of the match and the first harsh-sweet insuck of smoke. She inhaled. Looked into Jane's eyes. And almost immediately she coughed, smoke everywhere, spewing from her like a chimney, and she coughed and coughed again. And then they were both giggling and fanning and ducking their heads against a roil of smoke, Jane adding hers to the mix, a whole tornado of smoke, a Vesuvius, and some of the others were crowding round the sofa, their eyes bright with the triumph of the day and the sense of recklessness that came with it, of knocking down the barriers, throwing open the floodgates and no turning back. "May I have one?" Carrie asked, and they all laughed at that, but then Carrie did take one, the ritual reenacted, the silver case and the white orderly row of cigarettes, the two women's heads coming together as one over the gift of the sacramental fire, and Maybelle Harrison had one and pretty soon everybody in the room was coughing and laughing and laughing and coughing.

It was then that the first rocket went off at the end of the Littlejohn pier, a flash of light against the silhouette of a quick hunched-over skeleton of a man who might have been the gardener or the chauffeur or the rumored Mr. Littlejohn himself. Up it went, trailing sparks, to burst in a bloom of fire over the churning somber waters as everyone rushed to the window and applauded. "You know," Jane said, catching Katherine by the elbow as the next rocket hurtled straight up into the air with a crash of artificial thunder, "it's really not as bad as you might think."

Katherine was puzzled. "What?"

The smirk, the eyes, the beautiful unconquerable snaking tendrils of hair. "Being widowed so young."

And then another rocket went up, and another.

In December, Katherine returned to California. It had been a busy year—hectic—what with the women's parade in March, the summer's rallies, the International Woman Suffrage Alliance meeting in Budapest (which Carrie had asked her to chair), and she hadn't been to Riven Rock since last year at this time, for Christmas. She felt bad about that, awful really, and there were nights when she awoke in her anonymous hotel room in Washington or Cleveland or San Francisco, not even sure of what city she was in, and she could have sworn she heard Stanley's voice calling out to her. She wasn't one to neglect her duties. And as long as Stanley was alive, he was her duty, her first duty, in sickness and in health.

And he'd improved, he had, in this year of 1913, in a way the annual reports Hamilton prepared for the guardians and the court couldn't begin to do justice to. The reports were always so terse—"There occurred some mental clearness, then delirious excitement, after which he became dull"—no more than a line or two to justify a whole year in a man's life. But she wrote Stanley once a week, unfailingly, no matter where she was or how pressing the demands on her time, and he'd been able to write back on several occasions—and that alone told her more than any sterile report. Of course, his penmanship was still a bit convoluted, little curlicues and all sorts of baroque decorations adorning his consonants and what appeared to be miniature faces peering out from the confines of his vowels, and his subjects—the weather, the garden, the food—were rather more limited than she'd care to see, but at least he was writ-

ing. He was taking his meals at table now too, and though he was re-
stricted to a single spoon, he was eating with some sense of decorum, or
so Hamilton had informed her in his most recent letter, and he was taking an interest in the newspaper, sometimes even reading it aloud to his
nurses. The sinking of the *Titanic* the previous year had especially excited his imagination and for some months after the tragedy all he could
apparently talk of was the death of John Jacob Astor after he'd so gal-
lantly secured his young wife in the last remaining lifeboat.

On her first day back, she took the car out to Riven Rock as soon as
she'd breakfasted. She was alone this time, her mother unable to join
her for another two weeks yet ("I've got a hundred loose ends to tie up
here, Katherine, for heaven's sake, presents to buy yet for your uncle,
the servants, all the Moores and Mrs. Belknap too, and I just don't
know when I'll ever get my head above water even for a minute—").
She tried to keep her feelings under control as the car came up the long
winding drive under the canopy of overarching branches, thinking of
Stanley, poor sweet misunderstood Stanley, and knowing there was still
no chance at all of getting to see him, even for a minute—it was too disturbing for him, Hamilton said. Far too disturbing. After Stanley's
near-disastrous escape, all women had been banished from the house,
even the maids, who'd been replaced by a rotating team of local men,
including two Chinese Sam Wah had recruited as sous-chef and dishwasher respectively. Dr. Hamilton felt it too dangerous to have any
woman in the house, both for them and Stanley, even if he never saw
them. The knowledge that they were there was enough to set him off,
the faintest echo of a feminine voice, even a scent—and yes, victims of
mental disorders did have extraordinary sensory perceptions, keen as
an animal's in some cases. Or so the doctor claimed.

In any case, Katherine entered that womanless fortress at nine A.M.
on a day as soft as a hand on your cheek, the third of December and it
might as well have been June. She was met at the door by Torkelson,
the new butler, a man who seemed utterly undistinguished, as bland
and unprepossessing as a sentient doormat, and then she was in the library with Mr. O'Kane, the first woman to enter that room since she'd
left it a year ago. Dr. Hamilton, she was promised, would arrive shortly
from his house on lower Hot Springs Road—she hadn't been expected
quite so early.

"So, Mr. O'Kane," she said, glancing round to take inventory of the room with an eye to further improvements, and already she was shuffling through a stack of papers left out on the secretary for her. "And how have you been?"

"Oh, I've been well, ma'am," he replied, "very well indeed," and when she glanced up he looked down at his shoes. He was certainly a good-looking man, what with his rugged build and fair hair, the way he held himself, and now that he was into his thirties—or was he twenty-nine?—he had a finish about him that was very pleasing. And he was bright too, for a nurse, but of course that was part of the problem with this whole unfortunate situation—bright and presentable as he might have been, he was no sort of companion for her husband, who was a gentleman and used to the company and stimulus of other gentlemen. Dr. Hamilton was acceptable, to a degree—at least he was educated—but the Thompsons, good-hearted and well-meaning through they were, couldn't have been Stanley's mental equals when he was six. And how could he hope to improve if this was the only company he kept?

"I'm very gratified to hear that," she said, leaning into the corner of the desk now and working through the papers a second time—bills, receipts, a report from Mr. Stribling on the various improvement projects going forward on the grounds. "And how's your wife?"

A silence. She looked up.

"Still back in Massachusetts, ma'am—nursing her sick mother. And father. And her brother, poor man, who's got cancer of the brain."

Katherine pursed her lips and then couldn't suppress a cold little smile. "That's a lot of nursing."

"It is, yes."

"Four years' worth, by my count."

O'Kane said nothing. Outside the sun was brightening in gradual increments, like a gas lamp slowly screwed up till the room was filled with light.

"And your son?" Katherine asked.

"I haven't seen him, devoting all my time to Mr. McCormick, as I'm sure you're aware, but I'm told he's doing well, a regular little tiger, he is."

"Oh?" Katherine was irritated. The man was a womanizer, a Lothario, as insensitive to a woman's thoughts and feelings as he might have been to a trained seal's, thinking of one thing only, as if sexual attraction were the end rather than the beginning of a relationship, and it was shameful the way he'd deserted his wife and child and then had the gall to lie about it. Nursing her mother, indeed.

O'Kane was standing at the door, waiting to be dismissed. He hadn't moved an inch since she'd entered the room. "Well, Mrs. McCormick, I'll tell you," he said, looking up now to engage her eyes, bold as brass, "to be truthful, sometimes you enter a matrimonial state with the best of intentions all round, and things just don't seem to work out." He paused. "You know what I mean?"

That stung—and she was in no mood—and she might have said something she would later regret, was right on the verge of it, when there was a rap at the door and they both turned, expecting Hamilton. The door pushed slowly open, and it wasn't the doctor standing there in the doorway, not at all—it was Julius, the big orange ape. Katherine was so surprised she let out a gasp, and in the next moment she was laughing, as much at herself as at this gangling pouchy hunched-over thing shuffling into the room like an animated bedspread. Julius. She'd forgotten all about him.

He crossed the room on his knuckles, skittering lightly over the carpet without seeming to touch it, using his feet less for locomotion than as a sort of rudder. Ignoring O'Kane, he came straight to Katherine, gazing up at her out of eyes the color of sunlit mud and tugging gently at her skirts with one long leathery hand. He made a soft cooing or grunting sound and announced his presence olfactorily as well, bringing with him his own little pocket of redolence. He stood nearly five feet tall, weighed one hundred eighty pounds and had an armspan of seven and a half feet, and if he'd wanted to he could have traversed Montecito without ever touching ground, relying on brachiation alone. And right now he had hold of her hand and was sniffing it as if it were the rarest of treasures, a look of simian transport on his face.

"He's a nasty stinking smelly beast," O'Kane observed, "and I for one wouldn't be giving him the run of the place, that's for sure—but then it's not for me to say, is it?"

Katherine paid him no mind. Julius was amusing, he was delightful, and now he was kissing her hand like some country swain, a tickle of whiskers, the warmth of his lips, and she was thinking how much she liked animals, dogs, cats, horses, apes, even snakes and bats and such, the whole reason she'd gone into biology in the first place. And when was the last time she'd had a pet?

"Julius!" she cried, utterly charmed, "you're tickling me!" And then she looked at O'Kane, trying to keep a straight face. "Dr. Hamilton writes that my husband and Julius are quite inseparable—"

O'Kane winced as if he'd bitten down on something rotten. He shuffled his feet and addressed a point just over her left shoulder. "That's Dr. Hamilton's doing, not mine, and as I say, I don't think it's a healthy or even a decent thing—"

"But why? He seems quite tame. And if he helps my husband show an interest in things, if he stimulates him in any way, that's got to be positive. Surely you wouldn't object to a dog or a cat or some more conventional pet, would you, Mr. O'Kane? And an ape is so much more intelligent—"

Julius dropped her hand and mounted the swivel chair in a single fluid motion, spinning once, all the way round, and then, as if resisting the temptation to twirl himself as a child would, he tucked his legs under the desk and made a pretense of looking through the papers, for all the world like some jowly potbellied old banker at his desk.

O'Kane seemed on edge, and she remembered the day Hamilton had got his first two rhesus monkeys from the ship's captain and the look on O'Kane's face when they came flying out of the trees. He was afraid, that was all, frightened of a creature as placid and harmless as poor Julius—but of course, being typically male, he would never admit it. Even now, she noticed, he kept his distance—and you didn't see Julius going up to kiss *his* hand. "No," he said, "it's not that," and he was fumbling for his words. "A pet would be fine, and I've seen improvement in patients of all types with a little dog, for instance, but . . . Julius is . . . he seems to be a bad influence on Mr. McCormick—"

"A bad influence?"

"He—well, Mr. McCormick sometimes apes Julius's behavior, if you'll forgive the expression, and not the other way round."

Katherine lifted her eyebrows. Julius was playing with the paperweight, a glass ball the size of a fist, balancing it on the tip of his flattened nose and then inserting it in his mouth like some petrified fruit.

"I mean, for instance, when we take Mr. McCormick for a drive in one of the cars, to calm him, you know, and provide the stimulus of a change of scene, Julius always comes along, and if Julius, say, presses his face to the glass, well then so does Mr. McCormick, and it's just not—"

"Dignified?"

"Yes, that's what I mean—it's not dignified."

Julius had cocked his head and begun to make a series of muted lip-smacking noises and soft disembodied cooings that sounded like a ventriloquist's rendition of a flock of doves taking sudden flight, and he fixed his eyes apprehensively on the door, which stood open still. Katherine turned to look, and so did O'Kane. She heard footsteps in the hall then and in the next moment Dr. Hamilton appeared in the doorway, spectacles flashing and a wide welcoming grin on his face, but when she turned round again, Julius had vanished.

Over the course of the next two weeks, Katherine made the trip out to the estate every day, seeing to the multifarious issues, large and small, that had accumulated in her absence, and every day, at three, she secreted herself in the bushes on the knoll to the west of the house and watched as O'Kane and Mart led Stanley out onto the sunporch for a bit of air and exercise. She felt faintly ridiculous about the whole business— a woman of her age and position crouching in the shrubbery like a bird-watcher or a Peeping Susan—and depressed too, the misery of her situation brought home to her every time a wasp settled on her hat or the voices of the gardeners rose from below. What was she doing? What was wrong with her? Other women went to the theater on their husband's arm, chatted with him over meals, felt his solid presence in bed beside them, had children and grandchildren and a house full of warmth, and the closest she could get to Stanley was through a pair of ground lenses magnified to a power of 460 feet at 1,000 yards.

But there he was now, wandering round the sunporch like a refugee, dragging his right leg behind him and hunching his shoulders as if carrying some great weight there. She twisted the focus on the binoculars and was struck anew by how old Stanley looked—he would be forty next year, and you wouldn't have guessed he was a day under fifty. And how thin. Certainly some of that was attributable to the long period during which he'd had to be tube-fed and the tasteless mush he'd been forced to consume, but now that he was eating on his own she would have thought he'd put some weight back on. Of course, it was difficult to tell at this distance, but it seemed he'd got some of his color back, and that was something anyway. And the look in his eyes—it was so much more like the old Stanley, the Stanley she'd fallen in love with, the man who had such an irresistible presence, so forceful and passionate, and yet shy and vulnerable too.

There—that look—that was how she remembered him, that was it exactly. He was saying something to O'Kane, waving his arms in his excitement, his eyes tightly focused, marshaling arguments, making his point. All in an instant he'd come to life, as if some hidden key had been turned inside him. That was how he was that first year, the year when he'd swept her off her feet, the year when she went to bed each night whispering "Stanley Robert McCormick" over and over, like a prayer, until she fell into the chasm of sleep.

He'd come to Beverly like an apparition, like a winged god sent to combat the twin forces of boredom and Butler Ames, who'd been pursuing her so singlemindedly over the course of the past month you would have thought he'd forfeit his inheritance if he wasn't married by the fifteenth of September. It was a gay party, and she welcomed that because it was the antithesis of her life at the Institute and the senior paper ("Fatigue of the Cardiac Muscles in Reptiles") she'd be returning to in all too short a time, but it was frivolous too, and after the first week, deadly dull. Every day was a lithograph of the one before. There was tennis in the morning, swimming and rowing in the afternoon, déjeuner sur l'herbe, croquet, word games, dancing and music in the evening, and Butler Ames straining to be witty the whole time, quoting the same tired lines from Swinburne or Wilde night after night while Pamela Huff and Betty Johnston and Ambler and Patricia Tretonne sat there and grinned as if they'd never heard them before. It was a rest, yes, but there was a whole seething world out there, a world of child labor, disenfranchised women, tenements and factories, and there wasn't a person in that whole resort, from the overfed guests to the women who scrubbed the floors and the men who boiled up the lobsters, who'd ever even heard of Ida Tarbell, Jacob Riis or Frank Norris. Except Stanley. And when he glided across that sunlit lawn with his great loping strides, leather helmet and goggles dangling from one bright scissoring hand, she was ready for him.

They were out in front of the hotel, the whole party, drinking champagne from an iced bucket and playing an endlessly dilatory game of croquet, and they looked up as one at the solemn figure cutting across the lawn on his way from the stable where he'd garaged his motorcar.

"Good God, what was *that?*" Ambler Tretonne cried after Stanley had passed from hearing. Ambler was thirty-two, with a broad bland face and puckered lips that gave him the look of one of those fishes that puffs itself up when it's hauled from the water, and he stood a full three inches shorter than Katherine. When he'd married Patricia five years earlier, his father's paper mills came into happy conjunction with her father's chain of daily newspapers.

"An intrepid motorist, no doubt," Butler Ames returned, hanging over a bright varnished ball and lifting his witty face to the group. "Back from a hard day of scaring cows out of their hoofs."

And Katherine? She didn't recognize him, not then, not at first, but how could she? She was twelve when she'd seen Stanley last, a child, and now she was twenty-eight years old, fully grown and mature, the only graduate of Miss Hershey's School who wasn't married, widowed or dead.

But Stanley recognized her. He entered the dining room at 7:00 P.M. sharp, dressed in evening clothes, his face tanned and teeth flashing, a head taller than anyone in the room, and when he looked up from the menu he caught her eye where she was sitting in the far corner with Butler Ames and the rest, and every time she glanced up after that his pale blue eyes were fixed on her. After dinner, when everyone under the age of seventy had retired to the ballroom for ices, dessert, drinks and dancing, he tracked her down with the aid of Morris Johnston, Betty's brother. She'd just danced a rag with Bulter Ames and was catching her breath, a little giddy with the glass of wine he'd persuaded her to take, when something in Butler's face made her look up.

Morris was standing there with this hulking tall man, a man matched to her own height, which Butler Ames, at five foot six, most emphatically was not, and the man—Stanley—was smiling a secret, mysterious sort of smile, as if he'd just solved an intricate puzzle. "I know you," he said, even before Morris made the introductions. "Didn't you used to live in Chicago?"

Stanley joined their party, and though Butler Ames blustered, cajoled and wisecracked without pause as the band played on, took a breather and played on again, it was as if he didn't exist except as a minor irritation on the periphery of her consciousness, like an insect,

Culex pipiens pipiens. She was lost in reminiscence, transported all the way back to her girlhood in Chicago, when her father was alive, and her brother, and there was nothing at all the matter with the world that a good grade on an exam or a few dancing lessons wouldn't cure. Stanley's mind was astonishing. He remembered every detail of those lessons, right down to the names and addresses of nearly all the boys and half the girls, and he remembered the day Monsieur LaBonte had paired them all off according to height, the day they'd first met.

"My God," she said, "that was sixteen years ago. Can you believe it?"

"It snowed that afternoon," he said. "Six inches."

"I'm amazed at your memory, I really am."

He smiled, that was all, and here was the shy Stanley revealed, self-deprecating, self-effacing, never one to advertise himself. He might have said, "Yes, and I graduated with honors from Princeton and now I run the Reaper Works along with my brothers," or "I have every reason to remember—how could I forget *you?*" That was the line Butler Ames would have taken. Or any of the other heavy-breathing young bachelors who seemed to close in on her like a swarm of gnats whenever she left her books and went out into society. But Stanley was different. With Stanley there was no pretense, no pressure, no aggression. And he listened, he listened to her rather than himself, and the more they talked the more she felt the tug of memory pulling her down link by link into a shifting pool of nostalgia, her father's face there before her, the lake at twilight, Prairie Avenue piled high with drifts, a big gray carthorse collapsing in its traces while her father tried to hurry her past.

Before long, she and Stanley were huddled by themselves, the width of the table between them and the rest of the party, all of whom, excluded from reminiscences of the LaBonte Dancing Academy, Bumpy Swift and George Pullman, picked up the general conversation and carried it elsewhere. "And what do you make of the Beaneaters this season?" she heard Morris ask at one point, and Butler's answer, "Give me the American League any day." And then, out of nowhere, "Have you read Debs's *Unionism and Socialism*?" Stanley asked, and the rest of the night fell away into some hidden crevice in the smooth continuum of time. When she looked up again, the band had vanished, the ballroom was empty and all the others had gone off to bed.

That was how Stanley courted her—with socialism, unionism, progressivism, reform—instead of flowers and banter and meaningful glances. He sought her out first thing in the morning, even before she'd had a chance to come down to breakfast, and he launched into a polemic against inherited wealth, greedy capitalists like his father who took the means of production to themselves and robbed the workers of their labor, spoke of Saint-Simon, Fourier, Owen and Marx as if he'd known them personally, and yes, he'd broken down in tears over *How the Other Half Lives* and hoped one day to convert the new International Harvester Company to a fully cooperative enterprise, as he'd done with his ranch in New Mexico. They played tennis together, swam, he took her boating, and all the while they debated the issues of the day until she felt as if some great shining light were opening up inside her.

By the third day, she couldn't help telegraphing her mother to tell her about him, about Stanley Robert McCormick, heir to the Mc-Cormick fortune, a tall physical man from Chicago who wasn't afraid of the intellectual side of things, right-thinking, sweetly shy, worth all the Butler Ameses of the world put together. And her mother, who'd been nagging her for the past six months to think of what she was going to do when she graduated MIT next year at the age of twenty-nine, already old for marriage and the very last hope of the Dexter line, telegraphed back within the hour: MAKE ME A HAPPY WOMAN.

But that was all a long time ago, an Ice Age ago, and now the best she could do was watch her handsome husband through a pair of binoculars like a field biologist studying the habits of some rare creature in the wild—that, and make sure he had every comfort, every material thing money could buy to ease his trials, and the best treatment available to bring about his cure. And even if she couldn't be with him for Christmas, she was determined to scour every shop and every catalogue and bury him in an avalanche of presents so that his doctor, handing each one over, would announce, like a benediction, This one's from Katherine.

And she was doing just that one morning after her mother arrived, directing O'Kane and LaSource to carry in great towering armloads of foil-wrapped gifts and arrange them under the tree in Stanley's quarters, when Julius suddenly appeared out of nowhere to clamber through the open door and into the back seat of the car. Her first thought was to shoo him away—it was two days before Christmas and she was anxious to get back to the hotel and relax with her mother over a cup of eggnog and a concert of Christmas carols in the courtyard where poinsettias grew up out of the ground in a red blaze that mocked the pitiful hothouse plants they had to make do with in Boston—but then she looked at him there, one leg folded over the other, his eyes lit with expectation, and changed her mind. Suddenly she was whimsical. The beautiful and intellectual Katherine Dexter McCormick, hard-nosed suffragist, brilliant organizer, manager of all Stanley's properties and her own too, the woman who never let herself go, looked at that strange pleading hunched-up figure of male dejection sunk into the leather seat and felt silly, lighthearted, girlish. It was Christmas. Julius was in the car. What a lark it would be to show him off to everyone in the hotel. After all, if you could have tropical palms, birds of paradise and poinsettias in December, you could have a tropical ape too. Maybe she'd even see if she could find him a Father Christmas outfit—and a fluffy white beard.

She had to open the windows, not so much as to allow Julius to snake out a long-fingered hand and snatch at the roadside vegetation or the odd bicyclist, but enough to dissipate the very intense and peculiar odor he carried with him. For the most part he behaved himself, cooing softly, licking the windows with a dark spatulate tongue, surprising her fingers with his own—he liked to hold hands, like a child—and she fell into a reverie as the trees slid by and the sun spread a blanket of warmth over the interior of the car. She was thinking about Hamilton and the hope he'd held out to her—Stanley had improved, he'd definitely turned the corner, and he, the doctor, was full of optimism for the future, perhaps even to the extent of allowing her a Christmas visit next year, if not sooner—but she was puzzling too over something he'd said just yesterday.

It was the middle of the afternoon and she'd just started up the hill with her binoculars when he scurried out the back door of the house and fell into step with her. "About this new man coming in after the New Year," he began, "I just wanted to say—"

"What new man?"

"Do you mean to say Dr. Meyer hasn't apprised you of the situation?"

"Why no—he hasn't said a word."

"Oh, well, in that case, well, you know how much I appreciate what you've done for me here and I'll always be grateful for it—in terms of the hominoid colony, I mean—but my researches have gone about as far as they can, I think, and they've been enormously successful and enlightening and I really do feel I can write them up and make a significant contribution to our knowledge of human sexuality. . . . Well, what I'm trying to say is that the new man is a fellow who's been working quite closely with Dr. Meyer at the Pathological Institute, an excellent man by the name of Brush, Dr. Nathaniel Brush—"

"But Gilbert, you're not thinking of leaving us, are you? With my husband improving so? It would, it would be a blow to him, to us all—"

But Hamilton, turning away so she couldn't see the telltale quirk of his eyes, evaded the question. "He'll be working with me for a while, to get him acquainted with Mr. McCormick and our day-to-day operations here, all under the direction of Dr. Meyer, of course, and really, I have the utmost confidence in Nat Brush, I do—"

She came out of her reverie when Julius suddenly presented her with a hat, a lady's hat, replete with pins and feathers and a small but unmistakable quantity of well-tended brunette hair, torn out by the roots. One minute she was gazing out the window, brooding over Hamilton's evasiveness, and the next she was staring down at the unfamiliar hat in her lap. It took her a moment, and then suddenly she was craning her neck to peer out the back window and pounding on the glass partition all in the same motion. Roscoe brought the car smartly around—it was new, one of the matching pair of Pierce Arrow sedans she'd ordered for Stanley in the wake of her weekend at Lavinia Littlejohn's—and they backtracked to where they found a hatless and irate young woman stopped astride her bicycle in front of a clump of cabbage palm. Katherine got out of the car, the hat held out before her in offering, mortified, absolutely mortified, and she was apologizing even before she'd crossed the road.

The young woman, a pale welt of anger stamped between her eyes, began cursing her in Italian, and she was pretty, very pretty and young, a girl really, and where had she seen her before?

"Scusi, scusi," Katherine was saying in a hush, spreading her hands wide in extenuation. "I'm so sorry, I feel terrible. You see, it was"—and she gestured at the car—"it was our pet, Julius. He's an ape, you see, and I know I shouldn't have had the window open, but—"

"I don't want nothing from you," the girl spat, glaring, and she snatched her hat back and furiously jammed it down over her ears, the bicycle all the while clutched between her legs.

"I—really, can I offer you something, for the inconvenience? The price of a new hat? A lift to town, perhaps?"

The girl made a rude gesture, thumb under chin, and brushed at the air with flapping hands, as if scattering insects. "Get away from me, lady," she snarled, and then repeated herself: "I don't want nothing from you." She shoved forward in an angry, unsteady glide, her feet pounding at the pedals, and then she was gone.

That should have been Katherine's warning right there, and if she'd been thinking she would have turned round and gone straight back to the house to divest herself of one very importunate ape, but she wasn't thinking, and she didn't go back. "You naughty boy," she scolded, shaking a finger at him as she climbed back into the car, and he looked so contrite, burying his face in his hands and hunching his shoulders in submission, that she hesitated. He cowered there in the corner of the seat, emitting a series of soft high-pitched sounds that might have been the whimpers of a baby fussing in a distant room, and Katherine marveled at how human and tractable he really was: he'd been naughty, and he was sorry for it. She leaned forward and tapped on the glass to get Roscoe's attention. "Drive on," she commanded.

It was a mistake. Oh, Julius was a model ape for the rest of the drive, holding hands with her and peering out the window with a docile, almost studious look, but when the car pulled up in front of the Potter, with its promenading guests, snapping pennants and all-around bustle of activity, he began to show signs of excitement. In particular, he kept swelling and deflating the naked leathery sacks of his jowls as if they were bellows or a set of bagpipes, and his eyes began to race round in their sockets. As the doorman approached, he was banging the crown of his bald head against the window, over and over, till the car had begun to rock with the motion.

"Now, Julius, take my hand and behave yourself," Katherine said, as the door pulled back and Roscoe helped her down onto the pavement. Uncoiled, Julius sprang down in a sudden flash of bright orange fur, and all eyes were on them. People stopped in mid-stride. A pair of bicyclists skidded to a halt. The doorman gaped. But Katherine, smiling serenely, held tight to Julius's hand and ambled up the walk as if noth-

ing at all were out of the ordinary, and that was part of the joke, of
course it was, to stroll right on into the hotel lobby as if she were on the
arm of her husband. And it was all right, faces breaking out in surprise
and delight after the initial shock, Katherine soaring, humming a
Christmas tune to herself—"God Rest Ye Merry Gentlemen"—until
they reached the revolving glass doors.

She was able to lead Julius in, breaking her grip on his hand just as
the transparent compartments separated them, but then Julius balked.
Perhaps it was the novelty of the situation, the oddness of inhabiting
that little glassed-in wedge of space, or maybe it was fear and bewilderment, but Julius suddenly put on the brakes and stopped the door fast.
Katherine was trapped, as were an elderly woman she recognized from
the breakfast room and a man in a bowler hat and corkscrew mustache
who seemed to have skinned his nose on the panel in front of him. They
looked first to her, and then to Julius, who stood there resolute, his
massive arms locked against the glass on either side in all their rippling
splendor. "Julius!" she cried, her voice magnified in that vitreous cubicle till it screamed in her own ears, "now you stop that this instant!"
And she leaned forward with all her weight, the old lady and the
bowler-hatted gentleman taking her cue and simultaneously flinging
themselves against the glass walls in front of them.

The door wouldn't budge, not a fraction of an inch. But the fifth
partition was open to the lobby, and one of the bellhops, a powerfully
built young man, stepped into the breach, and with a mighty effort, coordinated with the renewed impetus of Katherine and her fellow
hostages, succeeded in moving the doors just enough to trap himself as
well. Julius lifted his upper lip and grinned at her like a horse. He
licked the glass. Cooed. But nothing would move him. And no matter
how furiously the young bellhop and the man with the skinned nose ex-
erted themselves, the door remained fixed in position, as immovable as
if it had been welded to the floor.

A crowd gathered. Someone called the fire department. Katherine
had never been more embarrassed in her life, both men and the old lady
looking daggers at her, the rest of the pullulating world, from floor-
sweeps to *jeunesse dorée*, studying her as if she were a sideshow attraction, elbows nudging ribs, smirks spreading across faces, silent quips
exchanged by bug-eyed strangers in the walled-off vacuum of the
lobby. She took it for half an hour—half an hour at least—the firemen

there with their useless pry bars, Julius the equal of all comers, and then she broke down, and she didn't care who was watching or where her dignity had fled.

"Julius!" she screamed, pounding at the glass like a madwoman, "you stop this now! You stop it!" She sobbed. She raged. She backed up and kicked savagely at that grinning intransigent unreasoning glassed-in hominoidal face till she broke a heel and fell reeling to the little wedge of tiled floor beneath her.

Julius did a strange thing then. He dropped his arms, just for an instant, just long enough to part the fringe of orange hair concealing his genitalia and expose himself, right there, inches from her face, the long dark organ in its nest, the meaty bald testicles, the maleness at the center of his being, and then, before anyone could act, he shot out both hands again to catch the glass on either side of him and hold it fast in his indomitable grip.

2.

FOR THE MAIN AND
SIMPLE REASON

It was in 1916, in the spring, that Dr. Brush took over for Dr. Hamilton. O'Kane remembered the day not only for what it represented to Mr. McCormick and the whole enterprise of Riven Rock—a changing of the guard, no less, and this far along—but for the heavy fog that lay over the place late into the day, and no chance of clearing. It was a transformative fog, thick and surreal, and it closed everything in like the backdrop to a bad dream so that he half expected to see ghosts and goblins materializing from the gloom along with Rosaleen and his father and the walleyed kid who'd rubbed his nose in the dirt when he was six and afraid of everything.

He was sitting with Mart and Mr. McCormick in the upper parlor, just after lunch—and Mr. McCormick had eaten very nicely, thank you, allowing the napkin to be tucked into his collar without a fuss and using his spoon with a wonderful adroitness on the peas, potatoes and meat loaf—when there was a sound of footsteps on the stairs and they all three glanced up in unison to see a huge puffing seabeast of a man laboring up the steps under the weight of the cigar clenched between his teeth. O'Kane's first impulse was to laugh out loud, but he restrained himself. It was too much, it really was—the man was a dead ringer for William Howard Taft, right down to the pinniped mustache and the fifty-six-inch waistline. And after Hamilton, with his Rooseveltian spectacles, O'Kane was beginning to see a pattern developing here—he supposed the next one, if there was a next one, would look like Wilson, all joint and bone and sour schoolmastery lips. Was this some sort of private joke Dr. Meyer was pulling on them—Dr. Adolph Meyer, that is, who looked just exactly like what he was, a Kraut headshrinker with a gray-streaked headshrinker's beard and a sense of humor buried so deep not even the Second Coming could have exhumed it?

"Mr. McCormick, I presume?" the fat man called when he'd reached the landing and stood poised outside the barred door like a traveling salesman unsure of the neighborhood. He was trying for a genial smile, but the cigar wedged in the corner of his mouth distended it into a sort of flesh-straining grimace. "And Mr. O'Kane? And that would be Mr. Tompkins, yes?"

"Thompson," Mart returned in a voice dead and buried while Mr. McCormick blinked in bewilderment from his place at the table—he wasn't used to new people, not at all—and O'Kane got up from his chair to unlock the door and admit the new psychiatrist. Rising from the chair, moving through the desolate space of that penitentiary of a room, the most familiar room in the world, a place he knew as well as any prisoner knew his cell, he couldn't help feeling something like hope surging through him—or maybe it was only caffeine, from Sam Wah's black and potent Chinese tea. But who was to say that this man standing so mountainously at the door wasn't the miracle worker who would transform Mr. McCormick from a disturbed schizophrenic sex maniac incapable of tying his own shoes into a kindhearted and grateful millionaire ready to reward those who'd stood by him in his time of need?

"We were expecting you earlier," O'Kane said, by way of making conversation until he could insert the three separate keys into the three separate locks and let the swollen savior in so they could shake hands and get off to a proper start.

"Yes," Dr. Brush rasped, chewing around his cigar, "and I expect Gilbert'll be up in arms over it, but I'm late, you see, for the main and simple reason that this damnable fog made it damned near impossible to find the door of the hotel, let alone give the damned driver a chance of finding the damned road out here—and where in hell are we, anyway? Good God, talk about the hinterlands—"

Actually, he'd been scheduled to take over more than two years earlier, and Hamilton had prepared O'Kane and the Thompsons and everybody else for the passing of the baton, but word had it that Katherine had opened her checkbook and said, "How can I persuade you to stay on, Dr. Hamilton?" And Hamilton, who'd already written up his monkey experiments for some high-flown scientific journal and was anxious to get back and circulating in the world of sexual psychopathology, where new advances were being made almost daily, had, so Nick said, demanded on the spot that she double his salary and provide him with the use of a new car. "Done," Katherine said, and wrote out a check. And so, Dr. Brush was late. Not just by a couple of hours, but by two years and more.

There was an awkward moment after the door had been shut and treble-locked behind him, when Brush began advancing hugely on Mr. McCormick and throwing out a grab bag of hearty greetings and mindless pleasantries, wholly unconscious of the telltale signs that Mr. McCormick was feeling threatened and on the verge of erupting into some sort of violent episode, but O'Kane caught the big man by the elbow and steered him toward an armchair on the far side of the room. "Wouldn't you be more comfortable over here, doctor?" he said so that everyone could hear him. And then, sotto voce, "You've got to give Mr. McCormick his space, at least until the two of you are better acquainted— he's very particular about that. You see, he's not sitting there alone—his judges are there with him, wigs, robes, gavels and all, though you and I can't see them."

The big man looked perplexed. He must have been forty or so, though it was hard to tell considering the amount of flesh he carried, especially in the face—every line and wrinkle was erased in the general swell of fatty tissue, giving him the look of a very well fed and pampered baby. "Well, I just—" he began, looking down at O'Kane's hand clamped round his arm and then allowing himself to be led, like some great floating zeppelin, to the chair. "I just felt"—and now he looked again to Mr. McCormick, who was doing his shrinking man routine, hunching his shoulders and declining into the chair so that soon only his head would be visible above the tablecloth—"that we should meet, and as soon as possible, Mr. McCormick, sir, for the main and simple reason that we'll be spending so much valuable time together in the coming weeks and months, and while I, er, should really have waited for a proper introduction from that good friend of yours, Dr. Hamilton, I just thought, er, for the main and simple reason—"

Mr. McCormick spoke then, and with no impediment. "Dr. Hamilton is no friend of mine."

Brush was on it like a hound. "Oh? And why do you say that, sir? I'm told he's been your very good friend over the course of many years now and that he's very much concerned for your welfare, as indeed Mr. O'Kane and Mr. Tompkins are, and I myself."

No reply from Mr. McCormick, whose chin now rested at the level of the table. O'Kane could read the look in Mr. McCormick's eyes, and it wasn't auspicious, not at all. "Well, then, Dr. Brush," he interjected, clapping his hands and rubbing them together vigorously, "why don't you let me show you around a bit, at least until Dr. Hamilton arrives?"

While Mart entertained Mr. McCormick with some hoary card tricks Mr. McCormick had already seen half a million times, O'Kane led the psychiatrist into the bedroom. "There isn't much to see here, really," he apologized, indicating the brass bed bolted to the floor in the center of the room. Everything else, right down to the pictures on the walls and the nails that held them, had been removed. There were no curtains, no lights. Here and there along the walls you could make out a faded patch where a piece of furniture had once stood.

"Rather spartan, isn't it?" the doctor observed, swinging his tempestuous frame to the left and poking his head into the bathroom, which contained only toilet, sink and shower bath, and the infamous window, of course, now louverless and with the neat grid of iron bars neatly restored.

"We did have a rug," O'Kane said, "a Persian carpet, really quite the thing. But we found that Mr. McCormick was eating it."

"Eating it?"

"At night, when no one was watching. Somehow he managed to get a section of it unraveled with just his fingers alone, and then he'd pull out strands of it and swallow them. We found the evidence in his stools. Of course, the rest of the stuff, the furniture and pictures and all that, well, he destroyed most of it himself the last time he escaped."

And then they were back in the upper parlor, standing around awkwardly, awaiting Dr. Hamilton, who'd spent two hours that morning awaiting the fog-delayed Dr. Brush. By this time, Mr. McCormick had retreated to the sofa, where he was reading aloud to himself in a cacophonic clash of words and syllables: " 'TARzan is NOT an APE. He is NOT LIKE his peoPLE. HIS WAYS are NOT their ways, and SO TARzan is going BACK to the LAIR of his OWN KIND. . . .' "

O'Kane was just about to suggest that they take a tour of the lower floor and then perhaps look round for Dr. Hamilton, who was most likely out in the oak forest overseeing the dismantling of his hominoid colony, when Dr. Brush abruptly swerved away from him and loomed up on Mr. McCormick, cigar smoke trailing behind him as if it were the exhaust of his internal engine. "How marvelous, Mr. McCormick," he boomed, "you read so beautifully, and I can't tell you how therapeutic I find it myself to read good literature aloud, for the main and simple —"

But Dr. Brush never had a chance to round off his homily, because at that moment Mr. McCormick slammed the book shut and hurled it at him end over end, prefatory to leaping out of the sofa and tackling the doctor round the knees. The flying book glanced off the side of Brush's head and he was able to take a single hasty step back before Mr. Mc-Cormick hit him and he found himself swimming through the air with an improvised backstroke before crashing down on one of the end tables, which he unfortunately obliterated. O'Kane was there in an instant, and the usual madness ensued, he tugging at one end of Mr. McCormick's wire-taut body and Mart at the other, but Brush, for all his size, proved remarkably agile. Without ever losing his masticular grip on the big tan perfecto, he was able to fling Mr. McCormick off, squirm round and pin him massively to the floor beneath all three hundred twenty-seven pounds.

Mr. McCormick writhed. He cursed, scratched, bit, but Dr. Brush simply shifted his weight as the crisis demanded, not even breathing hard, until finally Mr. McCormick was subdued. "Ha!" Brush laughed after a bit, O'Kane and Mart standing there stupefied, their hands hanging uselessly at their sides. "Trick I learned at the Eastern Lunatic Hospital. Always works. The patient, you see, after a while he feels like he's a little bird nestled inside the egg, not even a hatchling yet, and calm, so calm, for the main and simple reason that I represent the mother bird, a nurturing force that cannot be denied, for the main and simple —"

"Just a minute, Dr. Brush — I don't mean to interrupt, but I think, well, I'm afraid you're hurting Mr. McCormick," O'Kane put in, alarmed by the coloration of his employer's face, which had gone from a deep Guinea-wine red to the palest blood-drained shade of white.

The big doctor was unconcerned. He squared the cigar in his mouth, shifted his haunches. "Oh, no, no, that's just the thing, don't you see — a little compression. It's what they all need."

Afterward, when apologies had been made all around and Mr. Mc-Cormick, very contrite, was put to bed for his afternoon nap, O'Kane felt it politic to escort Dr. Brush out onto the fog-shrouded grounds in search of Dr. Hamilton. "Can't see a damned thing," Brush complained, moving cautiously forward as O'Kane, familiar with the terrain, led the way. "Afraid of barking a damned shin. Or worse. You sure he's out here?" And then, in a stentorian voice: "Gilbert? Gilbert Hamilton! Are you there?"

The trees stood ghostly, ribbed in white like so many masts hung with tattered sails. The leaves were damp underfoot. Nothing moved, and there was no sound, not even of birds. O'Kane felt his way, and he didn't even have the stench of the hominoids to guide him. All but two of the baboons and monkeys had been sold off to private collectors or donated to zoos, and Hamilton was packing up his notes and equipment and shipping it back east to his mentor, a small monkey-obsessed scholar by the name of Yerkes who'd spent some time at Riven Rock a year ago. As for Julius, he'd been removed from the premises after the Potter Hotel incident and sold for a song to a traveling circus — on Katherine's orders.

There was a smell of burning in the air, and of something else too, something rank, and before long they could hear the crackling of a fire, and then they saw the flames, a moiling interwoven ball of them, up ahead at the edge of the oak grove. Two figures, in silhouette, slipped back and forth in front of the fire, feeding the flames with scraps of tim-ber. As they drew closer, the big doctor tramping heavily behind him and cursing steadily under his breath, O'Kane recognized Hamilton's gnomelike assistants, and he called out to the shorter of them, the Mexi-can. "Hey, Isidro, you seen Dr. Hamilton?" And then, showing off one of the handy phrases he'd picked up amongst the denizens of Spanish-town: "El Doctor Hamilton, dondy estis?"

They were at the edge of the fire now and O'Kane saw that the two men were burning up the dismantled cages, wire and all. Paint sizzled and peeled. Wood split. Fingers of flame poked up through the mesh, weaving an intricate pattern, leaping high to drive back the fog even as the smoke settled in to replace it. The heat was intense, a hundred stoves stoked to capacity, and they had to step back away from it; O'Kane looked at the two scurrying men and hoped they knew what they were doing—a blaze like this could get out of hand and bring the whole place down, orchards, cottages, Pierce Arrows and Mr. Mc-Cormick too. Isidro, the Mexican, paused with an armload of rubbish to consider the question of Hamilton's whereabouts, then nodded his head toward the place beneath the trees where the cages had stood even this morning.

They found Dr. Hamilton fussing around a pile of odds and ends he meant to keep, the chute with the doors at the end of it, a couple of the smaller cages, a pegboard he'd used to gauge the monkeys' intelligence. "Gil!" Dr. Brush boomed, bobbing through the fog to seize Hamilton's hand. "I'm late, I know it, but it was for the main and simple reason of this damned fog, and I hope you'll forgive me, but I'm here now and I've met everybody and I'm raring to go."

"Nat," Hamilton said, shaking with one hand and adjusting his spectacles with the other. "Yes, well, the weather's been unusual. Sorry for the inconvenience."

"Pah!" Brush returned, waving a big flipperlike hand. "No inconvenience to me, for the main and simple reason that I'm here to stay. California. God bless it. But what's this—leftover monkeys?"

He was pointing to a small cage set atop the psychological chute. In it, O'Kane saw, were the two remaining hominoids, a pair of rhesus monkeys the doctor called Jack and Jill. They were runts, even for monkeys, and though they'd been displaced and seen all their companions exiled and their home of the last several years demolished, they still had the spirit to fuck—which is what they were doing at the moment, black lips drawn back in erotic transport, the cage swaying rhythmically to the persistent in-and-out motion of the monkey on top, presumably Jack, but you never could tell. That much O'Kane had learned about hominoids.

Hamilton seemed a bit fuzzy. "Yes," he said, gazing down on them, "the last two. Jack and Jill. I'd had half a mind to take them with me, but now I'm not so sure. The zoo down in Los Angeles is filled up with them—rhesus, that is—and I can't seem to get rid of them in any case."

The big doctor huffed a few times. His cigar had gone out, but he still clutched it with his teeth as if it were the last link of a breathing tube and he a sponge diver wending his way along the bottom of the sea. "Why not set 'em free? Let 'em go. Liberate 'em. For the main and simple reason that they're sentient creatures, just like you and me, and it's a cruelty to keep them caged up like that, and the climate here'll support 'em, I don't doubt that, for the main and simple—"

"Yes, I've thought of that," Hamilton said. "Haven't I, Edward?"

O'Kane hadn't the faintest idea what Hamilton had or hadn't thought of, but he nodded his head anyway.

"Well?" Brush demanded. "And so?"

Hamilton took his time, the fog settling in, the fire of demolition snapping and roaring off in the distance. He looked down at the copulating monkeys. "If there's one thing I've learned after all these years of study," he sighed, "it's that they're nothing but dirty stinking little uncontrollable beasts. Set them free?" He looked up. "They don't deserve it."

It was about that time that Giovannella came to O'Kane with the news that she was pregnant. She wasn't Giovannella Dimucci anymore, but Giovannella Capolupo, married, at her father's insistence, to a little hunched-over wop with a single black eyebrow drawn like a visor across the top third of his head. Guido, his name was, Guido Capolupo. He had a shoemaker's shop in a back alley in Spanishtown, with a cramped little cell of an apartment above it, which was convenient for O'Kane, who was then living at a boardinghouse not five minutes away.

Giovannella, sleek and beautiful, with her eyes like chocolate candies and her feet primly crossed at the ankles, sat waiting for him in the parlor under the watchful eye of the landlady, Mrs. Fitzmaurice. It was a Saturday afternoon, 2:00 P.M., and he'd just come back from his half-day shift at Riven Rock and collapsed into his bed like a jellyfish, utterly drained after a long night of celebrating somebody's birthday at Menhoff's, he couldn't remember whose. He closed his eyes. And in the very next instant there was an impatient rapping at the door and who was it? Mrs. Fitzmaurice. And what did she want? There was a young lady downstairs for him.

"Giov," he crooned, crossing the carpet and taking her hand, feeling better already, and he couldn't kiss her there in public, though he wanted to, and he couldn't read her chocolate-candy eyes either. "What do you say?"

"I'm pregnant."

At first it didn't register on him. The sun was fat in the windows and outside the streets were placid and inviting, all the long Saturday afternoon stretching languidly before him. Since he was up, he was thinking of maybe suggesting a stroll up to Menhoff's, for a little hair of the dog. He blinked. Tried on a smile.

Giovannella was beaming suddenly. "I thought you'd be mad, Eddie, but I'm so happy." She gave his hand a squeeze, though Mrs. Fitzmaurice, studiously watering her geraniums at the far window, was watching like a moral executioner, ready to pounce at any hint of impropriety.

O'Kane wasn't following. "Mad? About what?"

"You're the father, Eddie," her voice soft as a heartbeat. "Didn't you hear me? I'm pregnant."

In the next moment he had her out the door and they were stalking up the street, pedestrians trying not to stare, the streetcar clanking by, a roadster parked at the curb, a sedan beyond, an old Reo beyond that. His blood was surging, and it wasn't all bad. He *was* angry, of course he was angry, but there was a crazy exhilaration to it too. Sure the kid would be his—her husband, Guido, looked to be about a hundred and twelve years old though she insisted he was only thirty-six, and how could she have relations with a guy who looked like that, even if he was her husband? Of course the kid was his—unless she'd been fooling around with somebody else, and if she fooled around with him why wouldn't she fool around with somebody else? But no, it had to be his, and it would come out with fair hair and sea-green eyes, he just knew it, and Baldy Dimucci and this Guido would hit the roof. There'd be a vendetta. Sicilian assassins. They'd crawl through the ground-floor window at night, brutally dispatching Mrs. Fitzmaurice and old Walter Hogan, who spent half his life snoring in a chair by the front door, and then come up the stairs and cut his own miserable throat.

Someone honked a bicycle horn. The greengrocer—Wilson—came out from behind a display of muskmelons and threw a pan of water in the gutter. "You'll have to get rid of it," O'Kane said.

Giovannella stopped dead in her tracks, Giovannella the fury, Giovannella the lunatic. The candy melted out of her eyes. "What did you say?" she demanded. "I think my hearing must not be so good."

The fat-ankled woman from the Goux Winery waddled past them with three kids in tow. A man with a panting dog almost ran into them. People were everywhere, swells ambling up the street from the Potter, women shopping for groceries, kids darting in and out of alleyways with balls and hoops. "Not here, Giov," he said, and he wanted to take her by the arm and steer her someplace, someplace quiet and out of the way, but he couldn't do that, because she wasn't Giovannella Dimucci anymore—she was Giovannella Capolupo and he had no right to touch her. In public, anyway.

Suddenly she lurched away from him, her face twisted and ugly, and broke into a clumsy trot, fighting the weight of her skirts. He gave it a minute, inconspicuous Eddie O'Kane, just another guy out for a Saturday-afternoon stroll, and then made his way up the street after her. By the time he got going, she was already a block ahead of him, still kicking out her skirts in an awkward trot, her head bobbing like a toy on a spring, people stopping to turn and stare after her. O'Kane quickened his pace, but not so much as to attract attention.

He caught up with her in front of Diehl's Grocery, a place that catered to the carriage trade of Montecito—O'Mara smoked hams from Ireland in the window, jars of curry and chutney from India, pears in crème de menthe, the sort of place that had no business with O'Kane or he with it. But there was a line of limousines parked out front, one of them Mr. McCormick's, which meant that Roscoe was around somewhere, and Sam Wah stalking the aisles inside, inspecting ginger root from Canton and curls of candied melon from Cambodia. Giovannella was standing at the window, her back to the street, staring at a perfectly stacked pyramid of tangerines. He saw her face reflected in the glass, her lips puffed with emotion, eyes like open wounds, and felt something give inside him. "Giovannella," he said, "listen to me—can't we talk?"

In the smallest voice: "I don't want to talk to you, Eddie."

Sam Wah's face suddenly loomed up in the window, caught between two pink-and-brown hams, and Sam smiled a gap-toothed smile and O'Kane waved, and then, whether the whole world was watching or not, he took Giovannella by the elbow and led her down the alley and into the next street over. They walked in silence, out of the commercial district and into a residential area, neat houses with deep-set porches and roses climbing up trellises. They found a place to sit on the knee-high roots of a big Moreton Bay fig tree that spread out over an empty lot like ten trees all grafted together. There was no one around. He took her hand and she gave him a sidelong look that seemed to have some conciliation in it, but with Giovannella you never could tell. Sometimes when she looked her softest she was about to explode, and when she exploded she could do anything, throw herself in front of a streetcar, jump off a building, rake your eyes out.

"I'm sorry," he said. "I didn't mean that, what I said back there on the street."

"Eddie," she said, surrender, forgiveness and reproach all in two syllables and one tone, and she took hold of him with a strength and intensity that was intoxicating and terrifying at the same time and kissed him, forcing her tongue into his mouth, again and again, crushing him, tearing at him, till finally he had to put his hands on her shoulders and come up for air.

"I'm not going to have my son raised by some wop shoemaker, that's all," he said.

That only made her hold on tighter. She was a woman drowning in the surf and he the lifeguard sent to rescue her, her nails like claws, every muscle straining to drag him down, and she wouldn't let go, wouldn't let him get his face clear, no neutral zone here, no calling for time out, her lips his lips, her nose his, her eyes and her breath. "Oh, yeah?" she said, and her voice was dangerous. "And what about the son you already have—who's raising him? Huh? You tell me. Who's raising him, Eddie?"

Rosaleen was raising him, and if she had some man in her life, he didn't know about it. He sent her money, when he remembered, and she sent him silence in return. No letters, no photographs, no nothing. But if he pictured her, and he did once in awhile, lingering over a beer when nobody was around, a mournful tune playing on the victrola, he pictured her alone and waiting, a photo of handsome Eddie O'Kane on the wall above her bed.

"That's none of your business," he said.

A breeze came up and scoured the ground, scraps of paper suddenly pasted to the roots of the tree, branches groaning overhead. Still she clung to him, her breath hot in his face, the smell of her skin, soap, perfume. "You're my husband, Eddie," she whispered, "you're the one. Be a man. Take me away someplace, San Francisco, Los Angeles. Or back home to Boston, I don't care, I'll go anywhere with you."

"This is my home. Mr. McCormick —"

"*Mr. McCormick.* Don't tell me about Mr. McCormick." She pushed away from him, her eyes dilated and huge, hair falling loose at her nape and whipping round her shoulders. "It's only a job, Eddie — you can get a job anywhere, a big strong man like you, an American born here and with an education too. Where's your three o'clock luck you're always telling me about? Trust it. Trust me."

But the curtain had fallen in his mind. The play was over. "You'll have to get rid of it."

"Never."

"I'll arrange it. I'll ask around. He — whatever his name is — he'll never have to know. Nobody will."

Suddenly, and he didn't know quite how it happened, they were boxing. Or she was boxing and he was just trying to fend off her blows. They struggled to their knees, then their feet. She swung at him, just like Rosaleen. "I hate you," she sputtered, gasping, swinging, her voice dead calm between one ratcheting breath and the next. "It's murder you're talking about, you son . . . of a bitch, murder of an . . . innocent soul . . . How can you even . . . think of it, and you a . . . Catholic?"

She stopped swinging then and stood there rigid, but he kept his hands up, just in case. He glanced round to see if anybody was watching, but the lot was deserted. Her eyes were wet. She made a noise deep in her throat and he thought she was going to start crying on him, but she snapped back her head in a sudden fierce motion and spat down the front of his shirt, a glistening ball of Italian sputum that hung there like a jewel on a string. "Don't you have any feelings at all?" she demanded, and still she wasn't shouting. "You stinker," she hissed. "You pig. Don't you have a heart?"

Well, he did. He did have a heart, but he wasn't going to start a war with all of Sicily and he sure as hell wasn't going to have somebody named Guido Capolupo raising his own flesh and blood, and so as soon as Giovannella had turned her back on him and fled across the lot in her stiff-legged skirt-hampered trot, he went up to Menhoff's to see what he could do about it. He figured he would have a beer and a whiskey to ease the throbbing in his head and the sourness of his gut—though he didn't need the stuff, not really, not like his old man—and maybe make some discreet inquiries, that was all.

Menhoff's was pretty lively that afternoon, and that helped him get over his initial shock, glad-handing people, putting on a face—he even shot a couple games of pool. But for all that he was in another world, aching all the way down from his grinding molars to the marrow of his bones, and why use chalk on the cue when he could powder it with the dust of his own teeth? He'd been planning a picnic at the beach with a girl he'd met at a party the week before, but he knew he couldn't go through with it now, and he rang her up and begged off in a blizzard of promises and lies. Giovannella was right—abortion was a dirty business, as foul a sin as there was. And he was a Catholic still, though he didn't go to Mass anymore, except for Christmas and Easter, and he believed God was watching him and judging him and holding him in contempt even as he sat there at the bar and lifted a beer to his lips. But what was the alternative? He tried to picture himself in San Francisco, a place he knew only from postcards, Giovannella swelling up till her navel was extruded and her tits were like balloons and her legs lost their shape, and what then? Living in sin. A baby that was a bastard in the eyes of the church and society too. And then another baby. And another.

He'd been with Mr. McCormick eight years now, longer than he'd been at the Boston Asylum and McLean put together, and he was making good money, and putting some of it in the bank against the day he struck out on his own, and whether it was in oranges or oil or even one of these new service businesses sprung up in the wake of the automobile, he didn't know anymore. But he wasn't about to leave Mr. McCormick. It was a question of loyalty—he wanted to see him improve, he did; in a way he'd staked his life on it—and even with Hamilton leaving and this new man, Brush, coming in, he knew he was going to be at Riven Rock for a good long while yet. But Giovannella. Giovannella, Giovannella, Giovannella. He could just let it go, turn his back on her and let the shoemaker raise a little O'Kane like one of those hapless sparrows the cowbird preys on, shoving its egg right in on top of the nest and nobody the wiser. He could. But it would hurt, and he'd already had enough hurt from Rosaleen and Eddie Jr.

He was on his second round—or was it his third?—when Dolores Isringhausen walked in. She was with another woman, both of them in furs, cloche hats, bobbed hair and skirts crawling up their calves, and a whole noisy mob of people shouldering in behind them. She was from New York, Dolores, married to a rich man off playing boy scout on the Italian front, and she ran with a fast crowd. Nobody in Santa Barbara had ever seen anything like her. She smoked, drank Jack Rose cocktails and drove her own car, a little Maxwell runabout with all-white tires she'd had shipped out from the East. O'Kane was fascinated by her. He'd sat with her a couple of times with one group or another and he loved the knowing look on her face and her glassy cold eyes and the way the dress clung to her hips, always something silky and tactile and never the stiff penitential weeds half the women in town dragged themselves around in, as if they were traipsing from one funeral to another. And she didn't seem to have any objection to saloons, either.

"Hello, Eddie," she said, coming right up to him at the end of the bar, the other woman trailing behind her with a pasted-on smile and an empty greeting for this one or that. "You're looking glum. What's the matter? It's Saturday. The night beckons."

As if to prove her wrong—about the glumness, that is—he flashed her a smile, all teeth, the smile of a caveman just back from clubbing a mastodon and laying it at the feet of his cavewoman inamorata, and he shifted his shoulders inside his jacket to show her what he had there. His eyes fastened on hers. "I was just waiting for you to come in and brighten the day."

Her eyes were the strangest color—purple, he guessed you'd call them—and he saw that she was wearing some sort of theatrical makeup on her upper lids to bring them out. She didn't respond to his overture, not directly. Ducking her head, she fished a cigarette holder out of a black bead reticule and gave him a look. "Why don't you come sit with us," she said, nodding toward the restaurant in back, where Cody Menhoff himself was scurrying around setting up a table for her. "You can light my cigarette for me." And then she was sweeping across the room, the other woman right behind her and the rest of the group converging on the table with its clean white cloth and a platter of sandwiches and a

Jack Rose cocktail in a tall-stemmed glass set right in the center of it like a tribute.

There were four men in her party (all jerks, and O'Kane could have whipped any two of them with one hand tied behind his back) and three women made up to look like Parisian streetwalkers, or what O'Kane supposed Parisian streetwalkers would look like. He wouldn't know. Not actually. Unlike these swells, with their thin-lipped smiles and their cigarette holders and racquet club drawl, he'd never been to Paris. Or to New York, for that matter.

Dolores and her friend of the vapid smile made the party nine, and O'Kane brought it to ten. She made a place for him right beside her and as the conversation veered from the War to skirt lengths to gossip about people O'Kane didn't know, she leaned in close and gave him the full benefit of her eyes and her husky timbreless voice: "How about that light you promised me?"

O'Kane put a match to her cigarette and the whole table lit up, smoke everywhere, glasses already empty and the waiter bringing another round, and every one of them drinking a Jack Rose cocktail (1½ oz. apple brandy, juice of ½ lime, 1 tsp. grenadine; shake with ice and strain into a cocktail glass).

"What's the matter, Eddie," Dolores purred, lifting her chin to exhale, her lips contracted in a little pout, "don't you smoke?"

He shrugged. Smiled. Let his eyes climb right out of his head and into hers. "Once in a while I like a cigar with a glass of whiskey, usually late at night. I'm not one for cigarettes, though, not generally."

"Oh, you'll like these. Here, try one."

And then she was touching the glowing tip of her cigarette to the one he'd plucked from her monogrammed case and he was as close to her as he'd been to Giovannella an hour ago, only this was different, this was nice, the beginning of the dance instead of the end. "Swell," he said, exhaling. "Very smooth."

She looked at him. "They ought to be. They came all the way from Turkey."

They talked through the afternoon and into the evening, and she drank Jack Rose cocktails as if they were no more potent than lamb's milk and smoked up all the cigarettes in her case. And what did they talk about? Life. Santa Barbara. Mr. McCormick. Her husband. Italy. The War. Music. Did he like music? He did, and when they went out

front arm-in-arm to climb into her car and drive out to Mattei's for supper and the rest of the party be damned, he pressed her up against the
hood and sang to her in the soft lilting tenor that was another legacy of
his father:

You shall have rings on your fingers
And bells on your toes,
Elephants to ride upon
My little Irish rose.

She let him kiss her then, a lingering oneiric kiss that gave him time
to adjust to her—she was taller than Giovannella, leaner, her lips taut as
rope—and then they were in the car and breathing hard, both of them.
"That was beautiful, Eddie—the song, I mean," she murmured, her
voice husky and low, "and the kiss too, that was nice," and then she put
the car in gear and it was the first time in his life he'd been in an automobile and a woman driving, and he told her his ma had taught him the
song, back East, back in Boston, where he was born.

"And the kiss?"

He took hold of her hand. She was playing a game he liked better
than any he could of. "It was a hundred girls taught me that, but none
as pretty as you."

It was still light out, and as the car climbed smoothly up through
the San Marcos Pass and snaked down into the farmland of the Santa
Ynez Valley, O'Kane gazed out on the world and saw it in all its lam-
bent immanence, caught there for him as if on a motion picture screen,
only in color, living color. Every bush along the roadway was on fire
with blossoms, the trees arching up and away from the windscreen of
the car in a wash of leaves and each a different shade of green, the
mountains cut into sections like towering blocks of maple sugar pressed
in a mold, enough maple sugar to sweeten all the tea in China. He was
glowing with the whiskey and the anticipation of what was coming, a
sure thing, the deserted wife and the husband off sitting around a
campfire in one of those places you read about in the newspaper, and he
sank back in the seat and listened to the engine, gazing out into all that
spread of the natural earth, and didn't he see the face of God there, God
the all-forgiving, and His Son the redeemer?

Sure he did. And this wasn't a fierce and recriminating God who would rear back and hurl bolts of lightning and cause the earth to erupt and point the infinite finger of damnation at a child-murdering adulterer hurrying on his way to indulge yet another sin of the flesh . . . no, no, not at all. The Lord was smiling, a smile broad as a river, tall as any tree, and that smile made O'Kane feel as if a lamp had been lit inside him. Everything would work out, he was sure of it. Of course, he was stewed to the gills, and that might have had something to do with this sudden manifestation of the Deity and the feeling of benevolence and well-being that had stolen over him in the space of a breath . . . but still, there it was, and as he sat there molded into the seat beside Dolores Isringhausen with the whiskey in his veins and the slanting sun warm against the swell of his jaw, he thought maybe he'd died and gone on to his reward after all.

It was early the next morning, after they'd made love twice on the satin sheets in her bedroom, and the slow quiet cigarette-punctuated murmur of their conversation had fallen away to nothing, that he thought of Giovannella again. Dolores lay on her back beside him, sprawled like a doll thrown from a cliff, her breasts fanned out on the fulcrum of her rib cage, her legs splayed. She was smoking, the cigarette standing erect between her lips, jetting a stream of smoke straight up into the air, and he was idly stroking the hair between her legs, as relaxed as a dead man except for the accelerating spark of Giovannella in his head.

"Dolores?" he said into the silence of the room.

"Hm?"

"Do you know any doctors? Personally, I mean."

And though when the sun came up it was Sunday, the Lord's day, and all the faithful were trotting in and out of the churches whether they were Catholics or Protestants or Egyptian dog worshipers, O'Kane was on his way to Giovannella's with the stiff white slip of paper on which Dolores Isringhausen had written a name and address in her looping graceful boarding-school hand, and when he got there he waited round the corner till the shoemaker went out to do whatever it is shoemakers do on Sundays. Then he looked over his shoulder, swallowed his pounding heart, and mounted the swaybacked stairs on the outside of the building.

Giovannella looked startled. Not hopeful, not angry, just startled. "You can't come here today, Eddie. Guido, he only went out for a walk—he could be back any minute."

"To hell with Guido," he said, and he was in the apartment, pulling the door closed behind him. And what was the first thing he saw, nailed to the wall in the vestibule in all His crucified agony? Sure: Christ, staring him in the face.

"Eddie. You got to go. You can't—"

"I brought you this," he said, holding the slip of paper out to her.

There was nothing in her face. He watched her eyes drop, her lips part, and there, just the tip of her tongue. She was no reader. "Cy . . . rose? . . . Brown," piecing it out, "one-two, one-two Cha . . . pala. M, period, D, period." She looked up. "M.D.? What does that mean?"

"Doctor," he said, and he shifted on the balls of his feet, feeling sick and evil, "M.D. means doctor. Don't you know anything?"

Comprehension started at the corners of her mouth and worked its way up through the clamped muscles of her jaw to her eyes, and they weren't loving and kind eyes, not this morning, not any more. She let out a curse, something in Italian, and though he couldn't appreciate the nuances, he got the gist of it. "You son of a bitch," she said. "You big cocky son of a bitch. What makes you sure it's your baby, huh?"

"Because you told me. Because you came to me. Guido can't make you feel a thing, isn't that what you told me? That he's only this big?"

"He's a better man than you."

"The hell he is."

"He is. And didn't you ever think I might have just said that for you, to make you feel like a big man, huh? Because I did, I did, you son of a bitch. I lied. I lied to you, Eddie. Guido's hung like a horse—how do you like that? And you'll never hurt my baby—*my* baby, not yours. Never!"

It was Rosaleen all over again, and he had half a moment to wonder about the shifting magnetic poles of love, from Venus to Mars and no middle ground, no place to regroup and sound the retreat, and when she came at him with the ice pick that had been lying so quietly atop the icebox all this time he was only trying to protect himself, and both of them watched with the kind of astonishment reserved for the magician in the cape as the shining steel rivet passed right on through his open palm and out the other side as if there was no such thing as flesh and no such thing as blood.

.   .   .

"You'll have to forgive me if I don't shake," O'Kane said, nodding a greeting to Dr. Brush at the door and holding up his bandaged right hand in extenuation, Mart right behind him, the string orchestra already playing something light as air and the big new room beyond all lit up and festive. "Ah, and this must be Mrs. Brush," he said, feeling convivial, ready to break into song, tell jokes, quaff a beer or a cup or two of punch laced with gin. He was about to say he'd heard a lot about her, but then he realized he'd heard nothing, not a word. She could have been a Fiji Island cannibal with a bone through her nose for all he'd heard about her, but here she was, standing right beside her husband at the door, a pinched, rawboned woman with a squared-off beak of a nose and two staring black eyes no bigger than a crow's.

She reached for his bandaged hand and then drew back as if she'd burned herself on a hot stove, but immediately reached for it again, and then once more, before O'Kane finally offered his left hand and tucked the bandaged one discreetly behind his back. But the sequel was even stranger, because she went through the same routine all over again, reaching out for his good hand and then drawing back once, twice, three times, and when he looked into her face for an answer she greeted him with a whole battery of facial tics and distortions — enough to make the gone-but-not-forgotten Hamilton look like an amateur. She said something in a loud squawk of a voice, twitching and shaking and jerking her head up and down all the while, before Dr. Brush intervened.

"Gladys, yes," he boomed, swinging tumultuously round in the entrance hall and slamming the door behind them. "These are the two men I told you about, Edward O'Kane — we call him Eddie — and Martin Tompkins, er, Thompson. That's it, dear, yes, go ahead and say hello — "

Mart, thick-headed and slow to grapple toward judgment or even awareness, gave Mrs. Brush a bewildered look and reached for her hand, which she immediately snatched away and hid behind her back. Mart looked to O'Kane, and O'Kane's eyes told him everything he needed to know: the psychiatrist's wife was a nutcase.

And what was she wearing? Something plain and old-fashioned, drab as a horse blanket, and hanging right down to the floor, as if this were the nineteen-oughts still. But she was smiling, or at least that seemed to be a smile flashing through the frenetic semaphore of tics, twitches and grimaces, and that was enough for O'Kane. He smiled back, offered her his arm, which she took after another whole rigama-

role of back and forth and back and forth again, and led her up the six
steps and into the big room full of familiar and not-so-familiar faces.

The celebration was both in honor of Dr. Brush's taking over the
reins and to christen the new theater building, built so that Mr. Mc-
Cormick could have a comfortable place in which to view moving pictures, concerts and plays. It was a grand building, the size of any three
houses a normal family would occupy, dominated by the vast two-
story-high theater, with offices for Dr. Brush and the estate manager to
either side and a bedroom for Mr. McCormick tucked in back in the
event he should tire while watching a picture. Everyone felt he needed
more stimulation—Drs. Meyer, Hamilton and Brush, Katherine, even
the Chicago McCormicks—and the theater house was designed to
serve the purpose. It was a short walk from the main house—no more
than four or five hundred feet—and the landscape architects had put
sprinklers high up in the trees along the path so that Mr. McCormick
could hear the soothing murmur of a gentle rainfall as he strolled to and
from the building in fair weather, and there was stimulation for you:
rain on command. Nor had they overlooked security: all the windows
were protected, inside the double panes of glass, with a graceful cast-
iron filigree in a handsome diamond pattern, and the doors to each of
the rooms were fitted with triple locks, and for each lock a separate key.

It was amazing, it really was, and yet O'Kane couldn't help thinking
of the poor simple lunatics at the Boston Asylum, all herded into a cage
to have the crusted shit blasted off them with high-pressure hoses. But
then they weren't Mr. McCormick, were they? And Mr. McCormick,
being a gentleman, was used to gentle things, and O'Kane, being his
nurse, applauded anything they could do for him, especially when
money was no object. Stimulation? Give him all the stimulation he
could stand, just so long as it didn't overexcite him and push him all the
way back down the long tunnel of tube-feeding and diapers.

But everybody in the neighborhood was gathered here now, for
drinks and frivolity and the showing of a new Bronco Billy picture from
Santa Barbara's own Flying A Studios, and as O'Kane stepped into the
room with the frantically grinning Mrs. Brush beside him, he felt as
pleased as he had on Christmas Day as a boy. Nick's wife had put up
decorations, streamers and such, there was a big spread on a table in
the corner and a bar set up and a guy in a tuxedo standing behind it.
And balloons, balloons all over the place. The orchestra had been play-

ing an air when he first came to the door, cheerful and fluty, but now they shifted into something you could feel in the soles of your feet and a couple of people got up to dance. He handed Mrs. Brush over to a big glowing bald man who suddenly loomed up on his right—Dr. Ogilvie, Mr. McCormick's nominal dentist—and headed for the bar.

He ordered a highball and while the bartender was fixing it he glanced over his shoulder to see Katherine standing there not ten feet away, and she laughing at something the woman next to her was saying. She looked good, damned good, all in green and with a little green hat perched up on top of her hair like a bird's nest. He wasn't going to talk to her, of course, unless it was strictly necessary, and he turned back to the bar before she could catch him looking. That was when Dr. Brush and Mart elbowed their way in, the doctor flushed and hearty and lecturing Mart about the main and simple reason of something or other. "Eddie!" he cried, and a big arm looped itself over O'Kane's shoulder, an arm heavy as a python, and O'Kane could smell liquor on the doctor's breath. "They treating you all right?"

"Sure. Yeah." O'Kane lifted the glass to his lips, whiskey fumes probing at his nostrils, and made believe he was diving for pearls.

"You fellows are all right," Brush boomed, and he was squeezing Mart under his other arm, squeezing the two of them as if they were prize hams. "But listen. Eddie. I really want to tell you, for the main and simple reason, well, Gladys thinks you're a prince. And so do I."

O'Kane looked at Mart. Mart was clutching a drink, looking big-headed and dazed. It must have been something for him, going from his monk's cell in the back of the big house to all this.

"Listen. Between us. Because we're friends and, er, fellow employees of Mr. McCormick, you may have noticed that my wife's a little, what should we say—excitable? Not to worry. She was a patient once. Of mine, that is. Brilliant woman, one of the sharpest minds I've ever known—"

O'Kane, uncomfortable under the doctor's grip, gazed out across the room to where Mrs. Brush stood with the dentist, putting her face through all its permutations and showing her teeth like a rabbit at the end of every sequence. She didn't look all that brilliant. In fact, she looked suspiciously like some of the loonies he'd known at McLean.

"Tourette's syndrome," the doctor was saying. "It's not a form of insanity, not at all, just a weakness. A moral weakness, really. And we're working on it, we are. You see, her mind races ahead of her body just like an automobile stuck in neutral and the accelerator to the floor, causes her all sorts of embarrassment for the main and simple reason that she refuses to control it . . . but really, she's no crazier than you or I, not underneath, and I, er, I appreciate the way you gave her your arm there, Eddie, it was white of you."

It was then that Dolores Isringhausen walked in with her friend of the vacuous smile and two men with penciled-in mustaches and their hair all slicked down with grease. Or she didn't walk exactly—she sashayed, rolling her corsetless hips from side to side like a belly dancer, and she managed to make every woman in the place, even Katherine, look like yesterday's news. In three years, every woman in America would look like her—or try to—all natural lines, legs and boyish figure, with the peeled-acorn hat and eye makeup, but for now she had the stage all to herself, she and her friend, that is. O'Kane was electrified— he hadn't expected this—and two emotions simultaneously flooded his system with glandular secretions that made him feel as twitchy as Mrs. Brush: lust and jealousy. Who were those men, and one of them with his hand on her elbow?

In the next moment he was crossing the crowded room, all of Montecito there in their jewels and furs and cravats and nobody worried about the presumptive host of the party locked away in his room in the big house with the iron bars on the windows, not in the least, and it was no small wonder that he himself had been invited. Of course, he'd already seen the picture that afternoon with Mart and Mr. McCormick, but still he had to admit it was decent of Katherine—and Brush, he supposed—to include the nurses in a gathering like this. There were millionaires and tycoons here tonight and he was brushing shoulders with them, and not as somebody's bootlick or bottle washer either—he was off-duty, a guest like anybody else. That was something, and he knew it and savored it, and he promised himself he'd be on his best behavior, smiling Eddie O'Kane, quick with a handshake and a witty aside.

He caught up to Dolores at the buffet table, which was all piled up with good things from Diehl's Grocery and two of Diehl's best men in monkey suits back there to serve it up. She already had a Jack Rose cocktail in her hand with the long black velvet glove clinging to it like a second skin, and she was laughing at something one of the mustachioed little weasels was saying, her head thrown back, her pulsing white kissable throat exposed for anyone to see. It had been three days since he'd gotten to know her in the way that counted most, the way you could keep score by, and he hadn't seen or heard from her since—he didn't know her phone number and he didn't have a car to drive out to her place and nose around. But that was all right. It wasn't love or anything like that he was feeling, but just a good healthy appetite for second helpings, and he didn't want to seem overeager. Casual, that was the way he was, smooth as silk.

Still, when he saw the way she was laughing and the guy's hand touching hers to drive home the joke—and what was so funny?—he couldn't help bristling, though he knew he shouldn't and that this wasn't the place for it and that he had no more right to her than any half-dozen other men, and her husband not the least of them. "Dolores," he said, in a throat-clearing sort of way, "I see you made it to our little gathering."

She turned a face to him that was like a mask. His hand was throbbing. Was she going to cut him, was that it? The company too rich for him? Good enough for her in bed but not here amongst all these swells and capitalists? "Eddie," she said, the voice caught low in her throat, no inflection at all, "how nice to see you again."

He started in on a little speech about Mr. McCormick, how he was indisposed and what a shame it was he couldn't attend his own party, playing off the status of being Mr. McCormick's intimate and puffing himself up as if he were the host and all this his, when the mustachioed character cut him off. "You're a friend of Stanley's?" the man said. "I knew him at Princeton."

"Well, I—" O'Kane stammered, and he felt himself sinking fast, over his head, out of his depth, and what was he thinking?

Dolores saved him. "My God, Eddie," she gasped into the breach, "what did you do to your hand?"

He held it up gratefully, a white swath of bandage that was the sudden cynosure of the whole party, and invented an elaborate story about protecting Mr. McCormick from a deranged avocado rancher who objected to their crossing his property on one of their drives, brandishing it in the other man's face as if challenging him to offer the slightest contradiction. And he felt good all of a sudden, not giving half a damn what the other guy thought or who he was or how much money he had: Dolores was on his side, which meant that she wanted her second helpings too. And from him, handsome Eddie O'Kane, and not this penciled-in little twerp in the fancy-dress suit.

"What a shame," she said, "about your hand, I mean." And then she introduced the man in the mustache: "This is my brother-in-law, Jim — Tom's brother. He's visiting at the house for the week, and he's just back from Italy, where he saw Tom — "

And then the talk veered off into news of the War in Europe and all the American volunteers over there and how the U.S. was sure to be drawn into it before long, and O'Kane, bored with the whole subject, excused himself and went back to refresh his drink, figuring Dolores could come to him when she was ready. He found Mart still there, dissecting the Red Sox with an older gentleman whose jowls hung down on either side of his nose like hot water bags. "That Ruth's a hell of a pitcher," the old man was saying, lifting a glass to his lips, "and if Leonard and Mays hold up I don't doubt for a minute we'll be back in the World Series again this year."

"But we've got no hitting," Mart said. "It's like a bunch of women out there, what I read anyway."

"Well, you're a bit off the beaten path out here, son, but you're right there. We've got enough, though — and this fellow Gardner at third's a good man, really capital. . . ."

O'Kane, fresh drink in hand, drifted away again, not even deigning to glance at Dolores now — he was as sure of her as he'd ever been of any girl or woman in his life — and hoping Katherine would leave early so he could loosen up a bit. But just a bit, he reminded himself, and he could hear his mother's voice in his head: *Use your manners, Eddie, and your nice smile, and that head God put on your shoulders, and you'll go as far in life as you want to.* He thought maybe he'd circulate a little, meet some people. Who knows — maybe he could pick up some tips on growing oranges or finding a piece of property with one of these oil wells on it or oil under the ground anyway, and how did anybody know it was there in the first place?

That was when the orchestra went Hawaiian, stiff old Mr. Eldred putting down his violin and picking up a ukulele that was like a toy and strumming away as if he were born in Honolulu. It was a surprise, and everybody cried out and clapped their hands as "Song of the Islands" somehow arose from his rhythmically thrashing right hand and the rest of the orchestra came tiptoeing in behind him. O'Kane had been standing amid a group of regular-looking fellows who were heatedly debating the merits of a business that dealt in millimeters and centimeters of something or other, thinking he would wait for the appropriate moment to butt in and ask their opinion of the land offerings in Goleta, but as one they turned to the orchestra and began clapping in time to the ukulele.

He couldn't really understand this Hawaiian craze—the music, to his ears, was as bland as boiled rice, nothing like the syncopated jolt of ragtime or jazz, which is what they ought to have had here and why couldn't Eldred pick up a trumpet if he was going to pick up anything? No, the only good thing about Hawaii was the hula as danced by a half-naked brown-skinned girl in a grass skirt, and he'd seen a pretty stimulating exhibition of that one night at a sideshow in Los Angeles with Mart and Roscoe, who'd happened to borrow one of the Pierce automobiles for the evening and no one the wiser. "See the gen-u-wine article straight from the Islands!" the barker had shouted. "The gen-u-wine Hawaiian hula danced without the aid of human feet!" That had been something and well worth the dime it had cost him.

But this, this was a farce. Inevitably, a whole chain of half-stewed men and big-bottomed women would get up and start swaying obscenely across the floor, making fools of themselves and stopping the conversation—the useful and potentially useful conversation—dead in its tracks. And sure enough, there they were already, and Eldred launching into "On the Beach at Waikiki" now, O'Kane ordering another drink and looking on skeptically from behind the screen of Mart's head, the old Red Sox fan right up there in front of the orchestra wagging his jowls like one of those big-humped cows from India. O'Kane didn't care. He was enjoying himself anyway, a break from the routine, and the Ice Queen would tire of all this and go on back to her hotel soon, he was sure of it, and then he could fend off the little guys in the mustaches and let Dolores Isringhausen take him home in her car and do anything she wanted with him.

That was an inviting prospect, and he leaned back on the bar and let the booze settle into his veins, his eyes drifting languidly over the crowd, and no, he wasn't going to look at Dolores, not yet, or Katherine either. His bones were melting, his legs were dead and he was feeling all right and better than all right, when suddenly a massive shimmering sphere of flesh welled up in his peripheral vision and a big adhesive hand took hold of his wrist and was jerking him in the direction of the band. It was Brush. Dr. Brush. He was wearing a grass skirt and one of those flower necklaces over a bare blubbery chest and he had Mrs. Brush trailing from one hand and O'Kane from the other and there was no yielding to the onward rush of that tumultuous moving mountain of flesh. "Kamehameha!" Brush shouted, wriggling his hips. "Yakahula, hickydula!"

O'Kane felt his face go red. He was fighting like a fish at the end of a line and he saw Dolores's face haunting the crowd and her sudden satiric smile and he was bumping into somebody—the dentist, wasn't it?—and a drink spilled and then another. He finally broke the doctor's grip and pulled up short in the middle of the whirling mob, everyone laughing, screaming with hilarity, and Brush hurtling onward in all his volatile-bosomed glory till he was right in front of the orchestra and every eye in the house was on him.

Eldred strummed till his hand looked as if it was going to fall off, the orchestra caught fire and Dr. Brush shook and shimmied and drove all his floating appendages in every conceivable direction while his poor oscillating wife tried to keep up with him through the whole panoply of her jerks and twitches. And that was the moment of revelation for O'Kane, his hopes as feeble suddenly as a dying man's: Brush was no savior or miracle worker and there was no way in the world he would ever even scratch the surface of Mr. McCormick's illness—for the main and simple reason that he was a congenital idiot himself.

3.

THE ART OF WOOING

When Stanley McCormick strode across the croquet lawn at the Beverly Farms Resort Hotel in Beverly, Massachusetts, on that still, sunstruck afternoon in the summer of 1903 and Katherine Dexter glanced up and saw him for the first time in her adult life, he really wasn't himself. He'd been driving all day, driving hard, driving as if a whole gibbering horde of demons was on his tail with their talons drawn and their black leathery wings beating him about the head and shrieking doom in his ears. Something had seized him at breakfast that morning, an agitation, a jolt of the nerves that was like a switch thrown inside him, his whole being and private interior self taking off in a sudden frenzy like a spooked horse or a runaway automobile. That was why he'd had to leave his chauffeur behind when they stopped for gasoline at a feed store in Medford and the man never knew it till he came out from behind the shed where he was relieving himself to see the car hurtling up the road (nothing personal and Stanley wished him well, he did, but when the switch was thrown there was nothing he could do about it), Stanley driving on himself in the Mercedes roadster that was exactly like the one John Jacob Astor had entered in the New York-to-Buffalo endurance run two years earlier, ramming along down roads that were no better than cartpaths in a tornado of dust, flying chickens and furiously yapping dogs. He didn't stop at all till he got to Danvers, the throttle open wide all the way, the engine screaming, and he breathless with the adrenaline rush of beating along at speeds in excess of twenty miles an hour.

At Danvers he got down, shaking so hard he was afraid his legs wouldn't hold him upright, and already there was a crowd gathering, farmers in overalls and their red-faced wives, children on whirling legs, the man who sold insurance and the bank clerk just released to his lunch hour. Stanley tried to manage a smile, and he knew he must have been a sight, six foot four and looking like a man from Mars in his goggles and leather cap and the sweat-drenched greatcoat all furred with dust, feathers and moribund insects, but his facial muscles didn't seem to want to cooperate. He lifted a feeble hand in greeting or warning or capitulation, he didn't know what or which, and staggered into the restaurant next to the barber shop with the sign in the window that said HAIRCUT & SHAVE TWO BITS.

Inside it was cool and dark, walls paneled in pine, a scent of sweet pine sap at war with the cooking smells, boiled wienerwurst, fried onions, beef gravy, lard vaporizing in the pan. Stanley couldn't see a thing at first, dazed from the drive and the sun and the flywheel spinning round unchecked somewhere in the middle of his chest, under his sternum, and it wasn't his heart, it was something else, the switch thrown, the throttle on full, everything rushing, rushing. And what did he want? A sandwich, that was all. And something to drink. Soda water. A Coca-Cola. Root beer. But why was it so dark in here? It took him a moment, racing and whirling, though he was standing stock-still two feet inside the door, every face turned to him, to realize he was still wearing his goggles. And further, that his goggles were encrusted with a filthy opaque scrim of road dirt and insect parts, making night of day and sorrow of joy and creating fear where there was nothing to fear. He lifted the goggles and pushed them back up atop his head.

And saw . . . a waitress. Standing right there in front of him with her womanly shape and her fine and interesting closely gathered womanly features—and her eyes, her eyes with a question in them. "Will you be having luncheon today, sir?" she was saying, and everybody in the place, at the counter and seated at the dark-wood tables, was hanging on the answer.

Stanley: "Yes. Yes, I'd like that. Luncheon, yes."

The Waitress: "Can I show you to a table?"

Stanley: "Yes. Certainly. Of course. That's just what I need. A table." But he didn't move.

The Waitress: "Maybe you'd like to clean up first, in the lavatory?"

Stanley: "Excuse me?"

The Waitress (movement at the door now, the crowd drawn to the roadster beginning to disperse and filter into the restaurant for a glass of water and some soda crackers and a good long look at this dusty apparition in the long trailing coat): "I said, maybe you'd like to clean up? The lavatory's in back there, down the hall, first door to your left."

And then Stanley was moving again, the flywheel spinning, down the hall, through the door and into the lavatory, sink and toilet and last year's calendar on the wall. He stripped off the leather cap and goggles all in one motion, shrugged off the coat and found a hook for it on the back of the door. He stood over the toilet and relieved himself, throwing back his head to look up into the pigeon-haunted opacity of the skylight, chicken wire set in the glass for reinforcement. The noise of his urine against the porcelain was the most mundane sound in the world, a trickle and splash that took him back to the camp in the Adirondacks, he and Harold making water against the rocks like Iroquois raiders and Mama never knowing a thing about it. He saw the granite promontories, slabs of gray weathered rock layered like the skin of an onion, the fir trees stark against the iron water, and his fish, the gleaming iridescent thing he'd pulled from the secret depths and the guide saying it was the biggest lake trout he'd ever seen and Stanley should be proud—and he was proud.

He was winding down. The switch clicked off. It was all right, just nerves, that was all. He ran the water in the sink and that was good too, the sound of it, the smell of that lavatory, and then he looked into the mirror and there was nothing there. No one. No person. No Stanley Robert McCormick, son of Cyrus Hall McCormick, inventor of the mechanical reaper. Just the wall behind him and the stall with the toilet. It was a trick, that was it, a trick mirror, the back wall painted there to scale and sealed behind a pane of translucent glass. He lifted his hand to the glass and touched it, and that was strange and frightening, be-

cause he could feel it, hard and real, but he couldn't see his hand reflected there.

The switch. It was off still, shut firmly and decisively off somewhere back there in the Adirondacks and the belly of that fish, that
trout, but there was a finger on it now and the finger was itching to flick
it on again, to start the cycle all over and the racing and the fear that
was nameless and formless but no less terrifying for all that. He turned
abruptly from the mirror and forced his head down till he could take in
one thing at a time and build the world back to normalcy like a child
with a set of wooden blocks, one block atop the other till a castle
fortress rose from the center of the rug in the ballroom, towers, battle-
ments and all. His shoes, he was staring at his shoes. They were not
black. They were brown, but the brown was dust, road dust, and the
road dust was there because he'd been motoring across country—and
he'd been motoring for his nerves, to settle them, to relax and massage
them like overused muscles. What had Dr. Favill advised? A break
from the Harvester Company, a vacation. "Why not something brac-
ing?" he'd asked in all his rhetorical fervor. "A walking tour of the Heb-
rides? The Swiss Alps?" All right. And there were the cuffs of his
trousers, sure, and the skirts of his jacket, his shirt front, and this, this
was his tie, dangling loose.

He was ready. Ready for anything. And he swung back precipitately on the mirror, steeled and ready, and it was the biggest mistake
he'd ever made, the switch thrown right back on again and no stopping
it now: he was there, he was there in the mirror, all right, his hands and
his class ring and his suit and the shoulders it concealed, but instead of
his head, Stanley Robert McCormick son of Cyrus Hall McCormick in-
ventor of the mechanical reaper's head, there was the head of a dog. His
eyes were the dog's eyes and the dog was him. That shrank him. That
sent him down. A dog? Why a dog? He'd always liked dogs—he
thought of Digger the beagle while looking at the dog in the mirror—
but this was an ugly dog, a rutting stinking lusting un-Christian unre-
deemed whoremongering woman-ruining boxer dog, with a staved-in
face and a tongue that hung down like a limp red phallus all smeared
with the jism that was its drool. . . .

He was out again in the hallway, the lavatory door sighing closed
behind him, a murmur of voices and the sounds and smells of cooking
out there before him, and his feet carried him there, wanting some-

thing—a sandwich and a root beer—but did they serve dogs? There, out of the hallway now and standing rigid by the coatrack and every shining face and every furtive eye turned to him, and . . .

The Waitress (again): "Are you ready for your table now, sir? Sir?"

Stanley: "I'm . . . I don't think I'm . . . I can't . . . I-I don't think I'm hungry anymore—"

The Waitress (blanching, pinching, shrinking): "That's fine, absolutely. It happens to me all the time, one minute I'm wanting a slice of pie just as if I could die for it—lemon meringue's my favorite—and the next minute I feel like I just got done eating a cow and I couldn't hold another bite. . . . Well. You take care now."

The switch was on and it got him back through the door and into the street and past the crowd of gapers and auto fanciers and barefoot kids out of school for the summer, and then he was on the road again, driving fast, hell-bent for leather, boxer dogs, winged things and womanly waitresses all left panting in his wake.

What helped him that day, as paradoxical as it may seem, was a flat tire. Flats were as common as rain in those days, when roads were unpaved, tires scarce and garages, mechanics and gasoline stations nonexistent, and every motorist routinely carried a jack and tire iron, an air pump, tire patches and spare inner tubes, in addition to as much surplus fuel and oil as he could find room for. So too Stanley. Usually he would get out and stretch his legs while the chauffeur repaired the tire and remounted the wheel, but on this occasion the chauffeur was back in Medford and the road, as far as he could see in either direction, was empty. And clearly, the car just wasn't going to go much farther with a punctured tire and blown inner tube.

Stanley climbed down from the car. It was the last day of August, lazy, hot and still, not a breath of breeze, solid white clouds bunched like fists along the horizon. He could smell the grass, acres of it, an infinity of grass, grass and weeds and rank shoddy stands of sumac against a complex of trees so thick and variegated he might have been in the Amazon instead of Massachusetts. Tiger moths floated up out of the roadside weeds, grasshoppers impaled themselves on spears of light, cows looked on stupidly from the fields. Without thinking twice he sloughed off his coat and jacket, peeled back his goggles, and bent to the cool substantial handle of the car jack, and the switch had already shut off, so dead and null and detached from the place inside him where it had been wired it was as if it had never existed, as if he hadn't raced and trembled and seen a dog staring back at him in the lavatory mirror at the restaurant where he'd tried to eat and couldn't. All memory of it was gone, vanished, erased. He was a man at the side of a country road, stopped somewhere between a town and a village, changing a tire.

He got his hands black, and the grit of the road worked itself into the knees of his trousers. There were grease smears on his shirt. Sweat dripped from the tip of his nose and puddled in the dust. And he burned, his face reddened till it looked as if he'd been slapped to consciousness, faded, and been slapped again. But he did it. He changed the tire, without help, thanks or advice from anybody, and as he mounted the running board and slipped back behind the wheel, he felt as if he could do anything, brave any danger, as tough and intrepid as Sitka Charley, the Malemute Kid, Jack London himself.

The mood carried him to Beverly, got him down out of the car to ask about local accommodations and purchase fuel at the general store, and it swept him right across that vibrant glowing greensward of a croquet lawn and into the field of Katherine Dexter's keen sciential vision. He bathed, changed, combed his hair and trimmed his mustache in the mirror, and there he was, reproduced just like anybody else, and he even went so far as to wink at his own image in the glass. And then he went down to dinner, and he'd never been so hungry in his life.

The dining room was lively, full of vacationers bending to their soup and chops amid a subdued clatter of silverware and a crepitating hum of conversation that was soothing and reassuring at the same time, and after standing in the vestibule a moment, Stanley allowed the maître d' to show him to a table. When the waiter appeared, Stanley thought he might have a glass of wine for the stimulus—he was feeling exhilarated from his feat of driving and the adventure of the tire, and he wanted to prolong the sensation. He gazed out idly over the crowd of diners, the animated faces, the busy elbows, the pleasure everyone seemed to be taking in the smallest things, and he didn't notice Katherine, not at first, and he was thinking how pleasant it was to be sitting in that dining room way up north of Boston, roving free and with no one to account to, like a knight errant, if knights had automobiles. Then the wine arrived, chilled, in a bucket of ice, and the waiter presented him with the menu.

He began with the ox joints consommé, followed by cucumber spears, olives and the boiled halibut with egg sauce and Parisienne potatoes. He chose the boiled leg of mutton with caper sauce for his meat course, with apple fritters, boiled onions, new green peas and the tomato salad au mayonnaise. For dessert, he began with the bread pudding in cognac sauce, then sampled the Roquefort and Edam cheeses with fruit and biscuit, and he was lingering over his café noir when he happened to glance up and catch the eye of a young woman seated all the way across the room from him in the midst of a gay-looking young group.

Or he didn't catch her eye, not exactly—she seemed to have caught his. She was staring at him, and she never flinched or turned away when he looked up and saw that she was staring. Normally he wouldn't have made a thing of it—if anything, he would have shied away and pretended to study the configuration of his cuticles for the next half hour—but he'd never felt so good and the wine was sparkling in his veins and invading his eyes and inhabiting his smile, and there was something about her that was maddeningly familiar, almost as if he knew her. . . . And after all he'd been through that day, well, he couldn't help himself. When one of the men in her party got up from the table and crossed the room to the lavatory, Stanley rose inconspicuously and made his way to the lavatory too. Avoiding the mirrors, he watched as the man emerged from one of the stalls and washed up at the sink, and then he cleared his throat, introduced himself and asked if he might not have an introduction to the young lady in blue?

The man was Morris Johnston. He was of average height and build, he dressed in an average way, and his hair and eye color were resolutely average as well—that is, he was neither stout nor thin, not showy but no stick-in-the-mud either, and his coloring was mouse brown. "Oh, you mean Katherine?" he said, not at all taken aback.

"Yes," Stanley managed, tugging at his collar, which suddenly felt like a garrote round his throat, "Katherine," and he was trying out the name. "I think I know her. What's her family name?"

Morris flashed a smile. "Dexter," he said. "Katherine Dexter. But you're not from Boston, are you?"

It all came back to him then, from the look of Monsieur LaBonte's tortured mustaches to the smell of the wax on the polished floorboards of his studio and the feel of that twelve-year-old girl in his arms, all wing and bone and tentative shuffling feet, the girl who was Katherine Dexter, now grown and mature and sitting in the next room, dressed in blue. "No," he said, remembering the moistness of her palms in that overheated room, the proximity of their bodies, the quality of her laugh on a certain winter day when the temperature plummeted and the snow dropped softly from the sky like the plucked feathers of some rare celestial creature, "I used to know her in Chicago."

He was shy, Stanley, furtive still, the boy who burrowed, but there was something about Katherine that made him want to open up, turn himself inside out like a glove or a sock, to hide nothing, to spill it all, fears, dreams, hopes, predilections, theories, fixations. They reminisced about Chicago, and when they'd gone round for the second time and remembered everything twice and exhausted the roster of mutual acquaintances and experiences, he saw the light fading in her eyes—she was tired? bored? sated with Monsieur LaBonte and Prairie Avenue and Bumpy Swift?—and he felt a terrible tension rising in him. He had to hold her there, he had to, even if it meant reaching out to touch her wrist where it lay so casually, so nakedly perfect on the table before him, touch it and seize it and pull her to him, though he knew he could never do that, even if he'd sat beside her every night for a thousand years. But if she left him, if she got up from the table, if she danced with Morris Johnston or yawned and put a hand to her mouth and excused herself to turn in for the night or even to use the ladies' room, he would die. His mouth was full of ashes, his heart was pounding, and even as she leaned toward this other one, this Butler Ames, a whisper on her lips, he felt the voice tighten in his throat and heard himself blurting, "Have you read Debs's *Unionism and Socialism*?"

It was the key, the first principle, the beginning. And so much was engendered there, the broken wall, the burning roof and tower, because the key fit and the key turned, and from that moment on he wooed her with the sweetest phrases from the driest texts, with reform, the uplifting of the poor, the redistribution of wealth and the seizing of the means of production for the good and glory of the common man.

In the morning, at first light, he was outside her door, rapping. He needed to talk to her, but he didn't want to disturb her, didn't want to spoil her sleep or upset her schedule—they'd been up past one, after all—and so he rapped gently. Very gently. So gently he could barely detect the sound himself. There was no response and he knew he should leave it at that, but he needed to talk to her—he'd been up all night with the need of it—and he rapped harder. And when that got no reaction he began to thump the door with the heel of his hand, louder and progressively louder, until finally he forgot himself altogether and he was boxing with that mute stubborn unreasoning slab of wood, left/right, left/right, and he set up such a racket that the janitor came running with his mop and an old woman in a cap poked her head out of the next door up the hall and chastised him with a look that wilted him on the spot. "Shhhhh!" she hissed. "Get away from there now. Are you crazy?"

He ducked away, shamefaced, and let his shoulders sag beneath the weight of his criminality, but ten minutes later he was back at Katherine's door again, rapping. This time, the instant his knuckles made contact with the wood, her muffled voice rose wearily from some buried niche of her room: "Who is it?"

"It's me, Stanley. I've got to talk to you."

"Who?"

"Stanley. From last night?"

A pause. "Oh, Stanley." Another pause. "Yes. All right. Just let me get dressed."

"That's fine," he said, raising his voice so she could hear him through all that rigid cellulose and the vacant space of her sitting room, "because I wanted to tell you what I've done with my ranch in New Mexico—that's where I've spent the better part of the past two years, you know, roughing it like a cowboy in all that fine air and dramatic scenery, you should see it, you really should—but what I wanted to tell you is that I've organized the ranch as a cooperative concern where we all share equally in the profits, from the meanest hand to the one-legged Mexican cook, every one of us equal under the western sun, and you might not know that I'm the one who instituted the profit-sharing scheme at the Harvester Company, against my brothers' objections, and I set aside the money for the McCormick Factory Workers' Club too—"

And then the door opened and there she was, Katherine, the sweetest compression of a smile, her eyes searching his, and she was dressed in her tennis whites, a racquet dangling casually from her hand. "Do you play?" she asked.

"I — well — yes — I — well, in college, at Princeton, that is — "

"Singles?"

"Sure."

"You don't mind playing before breakfast, now? Because if you do, don't be afraid to tell me." She was smiling up at him as if he'd just bought her all of Asia and laid the deed at her feet. "You'll play then?"

"Sure."

But this was a conundrum, a real conundrum. It weighed on him as he hurried back to his room to change into his tennis things while she waited just outside the door, and he was still worrying it as he won service on a spin of the racquet and took his position behind the baseline. He'd never played tennis with a woman before and he didn't know the etiquette involved: he didn't want to overpower her — that wouldn't be gentlemanly, not at all — and yet he didn't want her to think he was playing down to her either. And so he tried to moderate his serve accordingly, putting the first one right in the center of the box at what must have been half the usual velocity, and with a very nice straightforward bounce to it. She surprised him by driving it directly back at him, and the surprise showed: his return was a bit tardy and he slapped the ball impotently into the net. She was glowing, beautiful, her hair pulled back in a tight chignon beneath the straw boater that was cinched under her chin with a strip of white muslin. "Love-fifteen," she chirped.

"I'm sorry," he called, "I'm afraid I'm a bit rusty, I've been so busy lately with the Harvester business and the ranch and a thousand and one other things I just haven't had time to, to — "

The ball was in the air, rising above the arc of his racquet as if it had a life of its own, and he served again, this time with a bit more muscle, and again she drove it right back, a wicked slashing shot into the far corner he just managed to return with a flailing backhand, and he felt a momentary thrill of satisfaction over that effort until she caught the ball at the net and put it away with a stroke as efficient as it was elegant. He admired that, he really did, a woman so athletic and fit, so nimble — she was like an Olympian, like Diana the huntress with her bow, only in this case the bow was a tennis racquet, and as he bent to retrieve the ball he congratulated himself on his evenhandedness and restraint, though of course he would have to assert himself before long, etiquette or no. "Love-thirty," she called.

By the fourth game he was down three games to one and sweating so copiously you would have thought he'd been in for a swim with his clothes on. Katherine, on the other hand, was barely ruffled, as neat and composed as she'd been when she emerged from her room an hour ago. She was a master, it seemed, at putting the ball just out of his reach and whipping him from one end of the court to the other with a whole grab bag of trick shots, lobs, aggressive net play and stinging ground strokes. He began to strain, hammering his serves as if the object of the game was to put the ball right through the turf and bury it three feet deep in the ground, and of course, the harder he tried the wilder his shots became. He double-faulted, then double-faulted again. By the end of the first set, which she won, six games to one, he was panting just like a—well, a dog.

"Are you all right?" she asked. She was standing at the net, preparing to switch sides. There wasn't a mark on her, not so much as a single bead of sweat, though it was a muggy morning, the temperature eighty already—at least.

"Oh, no, no—I—it's just—well, I do admire the way you play. You're really quite good."

She gave him a mysterious smile, but she didn't say a word.

Later, over breakfast on the patio, he sank into his chair and swatted gnats while she told him all about her career at the Institute, the circulatory systems of snakes and toads and her hopes for the emancipation of women. And how did he feel about it? Did he believe women should have the vote?

Well of course he did—he was right-thinking and progressive, wasn't he? And he told her so, but he didn't really elaborate, because he was exhausted, for one thing—all that motor travel, his frayed nerves, up all night, three sets of tennis—and because he was fixated at that moment on the way Katherine's lips parted and closed and parted again to reveal her even white teeth and the animated pink tip of her tongue as she spoke, her eyes flashing, her knuckles drilling the table in declamatory fervor. He realized then, in that gnat-haunted moment with the sugary scent of new-mown grass on the air and his melon getting warm and his eggs cold, that he wanted to kiss those lips, touch that tongue with his own, and more, much more: he wanted her, all of her, right down to and including the problematic whiteness at the center of her. Katherine, he wanted Katherine. He wanted to marry her, that's what he wanted, and the knowledge of it came to him in a moment of epiphany that made him shudder with the intensity of his longing and the nakedness of his need.

"Are you catching a chill?" she asked, scrutinizing him with her ice-blue gaze.

"No," he said.

"And you're not eating—don't tell me you're not hungry after all that exercise?"

This was the time to tell her how he felt, this was the time for sweet talk, for lovers' banter, the time to say, How can mere food hope to sustain me when I have the vision of you to feast on?, but he didn't tell her that, he couldn't, and he fiddled with his fork a minute before lifting his eyes to hers. "When the masses have enough on their plates," he said, "when the tenements have been torn down and good decent housing erected in their stead and on every table a leg of lamb and mint jelly, then I'll eat."

Two days later, Katherine was gone. Her vacation was over, the new semester beginning, her thesis beckoning. Before she left, she gave him a blue bow tie and a box of maple sugar candy molded in the shapes of squirrels, rabbits and Scotch terriers, and he gave her a copy of the Debs pamphlet and a first edition of Frank Norris's The Pit. He'd begged her to stay, prostrating himself at her feet, all wrought-up with speeches about conditions in the textile mills, settlement houses and the immigrant poor, but he never mentioned love—it wasn't in his power—and she had to go, he understood that. Still, he was devastated, and no sooner had she boarded the train than he was off for Boston in the Mercedes. He packed hurriedly, with none of the indecision that had plagued him in recent years, and he brought Morris Johnston along with him, both as a sympathetic ear he could fill with praises of Katherine and as a buffer against any subversive lavatory mirrors that might spring up like windmills in his path.

On arriving, he took rooms at a hotel near Katherine's mother's place on Commonwealth Avenue and began his siege. He sent flowers daily, whole greenhouses full, and he called each evening on the stroke of seven, his palms sweating, heart thumping, eyes crawling in his head.

The maid greeted him with a sentimental smile, and Mrs. Dexter, Katherine's mother, beamed and prattled and plied him with an endless array of sweetmeats, sandwiches, fruits, nuts and beverages, while he sat awkwardly in the parlor and thought of Katherine dressing in the empyreal realms above him. And did Mr. McCormick appreciate how clever her daughter was? Mrs. Dexter wanted to know. She'd tried to discourage her with this scientific business from the beginning, heaven knew, because science just wasn't a lady's provenance, or hadn't been, until Katherine came along to tackle it with her keen intellect and persevering nature, but now she had to admit that her daughter couldn't have made her prouder, and would he like another chocolate?

And Katherine. She was receptive, very sweet and encouraging, a paragon, especially during his first few visits, and that made him soar with a kind of elation he'd never known, but by the end of the week she'd begun to beg off on account of her studies and he found himself spending more and more time with Mrs. Dexter, a teacup balanced on one knee and a plate of sandwiches on the other. She had to study, of course she did—she was a brainy intellectual young woman and she'd been working eight years for this—but still it threw him into a panic. What if she were using her studies as an excuse, a way to get rid of him early so she could slip out at nine or ten and flit around with Butler Ames, whom he'd already encountered twice on her very doorstep? He was beside himself. He couldn't eat. Couldn't sleep. And he didn't dare look in the mirror.

But on Friday she consented to go to dinner and the theater with him, and he took her and her mother to dine at his hotel and then to a very amusing production of *The Importance of Being Earnest*. At least Stanley found it amusing, and Katherine seemed to enjoy herself too, laughing in all the right places, but he worried that it might be too frivolous for her, not enough concerned with the pressing issues of the day, and when they got back to her place he started in on Debs again, by way of compensation. "Do you know what Debs says?" he began as Mrs. Dexter made a discreet exit and the maid set down a plate of poppy seed cakes and vanished.

Katherine sat across from him, in an armchair. Outside, it was raining, the streets shining with it, the sound of the horses' hoofs magnified in the steadily leaking night air. You could hear them—clop, clop,

clop — and that was all, but for the hiss of the rain and the ticking of the clock on the mantelpiece. "No," she sighed, tucking her feet up under her skirts and settling into the chair. "I don't really know."

" 'The few who own the machines do not use them,' " Stanley quoted, leaning forward with a sage look. " 'The many who use them do not own them.' You see? Simple, direct, brilliant. And of course the result is the sort of inequity you and I see and abhor every day but that the rest of the world seems to turn its back on. He wants national laws to protect workers against accidents on the job, unemployment and old age insurance programs, public works for the unemployed — and until workers take over the means of production, a decrease in the work hours as production increases — "

She didn't seem to be listening. She was stirring a cup of tea with a demitasse spoon, her eyes unfocused and vague.

"He says," Stanley went on, "he says — "

"Stanley?"

"I — um — yes?"

"Please don't take this the wrong way, but while I admire your commitment to the progressive causes, I really do, don't you ever stop to wonder why you seem, well, so obsessed with them?"

"Me? Obsessed?"

She laughed then, and he didn't know whether to laugh with her or to bristle because she might have meant it as a barb, the tiniest dart that would tear his flesh open, a wound that would grow wider and wider till there was room enough for all the Butler Ameses of the world to march right on through him. His face was blank. He reached for a poppy seed cake and got it halfway to his mouth before he thought better of it and set it back carefully on the plate.

"Could it be a defensive reaction, do you think? I mean, because you and I have so much in contrast to the poor?"

"Well — I — yes. Yes, of course. My father, you see, he's the one. He wouldn't allow a union in his shop, the Haymarket Riots, all that, and it's not right, it's not. My father — " he said, and he found he couldn't quite organize his thoughts beyond that, because his head was suddenly filled with the image of that cranky imperious old man with his jabbing rapier of a beard, filling the halls of the house with his roars and his bile and his unloving fierce stifling presence. "My father — " he repeated.

Katherine's voice was very soft, so soft he had to strain to hear it over the noise of the rain, the plodding horses, the ticking of the clock that rose suddenly in volume till it was like a whole symphony of clocks all beating time in unison, tearing away at the hours, the minutes, the seconds he had left before she got up and dismissed him. "I know it must be hard," she said, "but you have to put it behind you. And as admirable as progressive reform may be, there are other things in life—music, painting, all the arts—and when a man and woman are alone together, when they're as intimate as you and I are now, don't you think there are more appropriate things to talk about?"

"Well, yes," he said, but he didn't have a clue.

Another sigh. "Oh, Stanley, I don't know about you. You're very sweet, but really, you do have a lot to learn about the art of wooing." And then she stood and the maid was there and the evening was over.

He was back the next day, undeterred, ready to hire Cyrano to rehearse his speeches for him, anything, but he couldn't seem to get socialism out of his head. In the afternoon, he took Katherine and Mrs. Dexter to the art museum, and he was able to talk knowledgeably about Titian, Tintoretto and the Dutch masters and fill them in on his experiences as a pupil of Monsieur Julien in Paris, but inevitably he found the conversation veering back toward social welfare and reform, because what was art after all but a plaything of the rich? Katherine couldn't dine with him that evening—she was busy preparing for the following day's classes—and he brooded over a long tasteless repast, which he interrupted three times to wire his mother on the subject of Katherine and her perfection, her intellect, her beauty, and his mother wired back almost immediately: WORRIED SICK STOP HAVEN'T HEARD FROM YOU IN A WEEK STOP VERY INCONSIDERATE STOP KATHERINE WHO? STOP YOUR LOVING MOTHER.

Then—and he couldn't help himself; he felt he'd explode like an overbaked potato if he had to look at those pallid hotel-room walls another second—he took a stroll past Katherine's house. A stroll, that was all. A constitutional. For his health. He had no thought of snooping, no thought of encountering Butler Ames or his ilk on the doorstep or catching Katherine slipping into a coach in her dinner clothes, nothing of the kind. It was raining again. He'd forgotten his umbrella and his silk hat was like a lead weight bearing down on the crown of his head and the shoulders of his overcoat were soaked through by the time he'd made his eighth circuit of Katherine's block. And when he became conscious of that, the wetness beginning to seep through now, he just happened, by the purest coincidence, to be passing by the front entrance of Mrs. Dexter's neat and prim narrow-shouldered stone house at 393 Commonwealth Avenue.

Katherine had made it very clear that she couldn't see him, and he respected that, he did, but he couldn't seem to prevent himself from mounting the steps and pressing the buzzer anyway. All sorts of things went through his head in the interval between pressing the buzzer and the maid's appearance—visions of Butler Ames, with his blowfish eyes and prissy little hands, making love to Katherine over a box of chocolates, Katherine husbanded with nineteen faceless suitors, Katherine out dancing at that very moment and not lucubrating over a stack of scientific texts shot through with diagrams of the internal anatomy of lizards, turtles and snakes—but there was the maid with her mawkish smile, and the entrance hall, and Mrs. Dexter rushing to greet him as if she hadn't seen him in six months rather than six hours.

His reward for braving the elements was a tête-à-tête with Mrs. Dexter that stretched past eleven o'clock (and wasn't it just five after eight when he arrived?), a gallon and a half of scalding tea and the ever-present platter of poppy seed cakes and sandwiches, which were soggy now and looking a bit frayed around the edges. Mrs. Dexter said things like, "You know, I'm afraid Katherine's had so many gentlemen calling on her lately that she's going to have to hold a lottery if she ever wants to get married"; and, "That Butler Ames is a darling, a perfect darling, don't you think so?"; and, "Did I ever tell you the time Katherine saw her first Angora goat—she was three at the time, or was it four?" Ever polite, Stanley sat there stiff as a post and made the occasional supportive noise in the back of his throat, but otherwise he didn't have much to say—about progressivism, Butler Ames or anything else.

Finally, at half-past eleven, Katherine crept into the room in a pair of carpet slippers and her mother jumped up as if she'd been bitten and promptly disappeared. "Stanley," Katherine said, extending her hand, which he rose to take in his, and then she clucked at him as if he were a naughty child or a puppy that's just peed on the carpet. "Didn't I tell you I couldn't see you tonight?" she scolded, wagging a finger at him, and he would have felt miserable, abject, run through with a rusty sword of rejection and humiliation, but for the fact that she was smiling.

Now. Now's the time, he told himself. "I—well—I just happened to be in the neighborhood and I thought—"

They were still standing, hovering awkwardly over the tea table and the platter of soggy sandwiches. She arched her eyebrows. "Just happened?"

He laughed—a braying nervous peal of a laugh—and she joined him, her whole face lit up, and then somehow they were both seated on the sofa, side by side. "All right," he said, "I admit it, I just couldn't—well—you know what I mean, I couldn't stay away—from you, that is."

And what did she say? "Oh, Stanley"—or something like that. But she was smiling still, showing her teeth and her gums, and there was no mistaking the light in her eyes: she was glad he'd come. That made him bold, reckless, made him stew in the moment till he was a pot boiling over and there was no need for Debs now, his eyes on hers, hands clenching and unclenching in his lap as if they were feeling for a grip on a slick precipice, the taste of stale tea coming up in his throat. "Listen, Katherine," he said, "I've been meaning to, to say something to you, I mean, I've been thinking about it all day, and I—I—"

That smile. She leaned forward to toy with one of the sandwiches, then lifted it to her lips and took a bite, carving a neat semicircle out of the center of it. "Yes?"

"Well, let me, let me put it this way. What if there was a man, a young man, of good family and with good intentions, but not worthy of consideration in the eyes of a woman, well, a hypothetical woman sort of, well, like yourself . . . and he really, but he hadn't done anything in his life, he was nothing, a worthless shell of a hypothetical man not fit to kiss the hem of this hypothetical woman's skirt, but he, he—"

She'd begun to see what he was driving at, or fumbling toward, and she tried to compose her face, but it wasn't working—she looked like nothing so much as a woman hurtling toward a crash in a runaway carriage, the smile gone, the sandwich arrested in mid-air, something like shock and fright in her eyes, but Stanley was committed, he was driving forward and there was no stopping him. "Stanley," she said, her voice lost somewhere deep in her throat, "Stanley, it's late—"

He wouldn't listen, didn't hear her. "You see, this man, this hypothetical man, is so far beneath her he would never presume to even entertain the faintest hope in the world that she would, she might, well . . . marry him, I suppose, but if he asked her, this hypothetical but utterly worthless man who hasn't accomplished a thing in his whole life, would she — would you — I mean, knowing the circumstances —"

There was a furrow between her eyebrows, and why had he never noticed that before? She didn't look apprehensive now so much as puzzled — or pained. "Stanley, are you asking me what I think you are?"

He took a deep breath. His heart was thumping like a drum. "I just, well, I wanted your opinion, because I value it, I really do —"

"Are you asking me —?"

He couldn't look her in the eye. All the drums of the Mohawks were pounding in his ears. *Thumpa-thumpa-thumpa-thumpa-thump.* "Yes."

"But we've just met — you don't know anything about me. You're joking, aren't you? Tell me this is a joke, Stanley, tell me —"

The rain, the clock, the hoofs, the drums. He looked up, as sorrowful as any whipped dog. "No," he said, "it's no joke."

4.

ONE SLIT'S ENOUGH

As it turned out, Dr. Brush wasn't a man to rock the boat, even if it was in his power to do so, which it wasn't. O'Kane liked him well enough — he was hearty, quick with a laugh, a big physical man who relished his food and drink and didn't go around acting as if he was better than everybody else in the world who didn't happen to be a millionaire or a psychiatrist — but he didn't respect him in the way he'd respected Dr. Hamilton. For all his dallying with his monkeys and all his airs and the stiff formality of him, at least Hamilton was a first-rate psychiatrist, one of the best men in the country, and Mr. McCormick had improved under his care, even if it was by fits and starts. Not that Brush didn't have top-notch credentials, in addition to being handpicked by Dr. Meyer, but he was just too, well, clownish to make anything of himself in the long run, and that boded ill for Mr. McCormick. Hamilton had gotten what he wanted out of Riven Rock and then made himself scarce; Brush seemed content to bob like a great quivering buoy on the ebbing tide of that particular psychological backwater.

Oh, he started out energetically enough, eager to make a good impression like any other man in a new position, especially one who knows he's going to be held accountable to the Ice Queen on the one hand and to Dr. Meyer, the world's most humorless man, on the other. Basically, he adhered to Dr. Hamilton's regimen, which accorded strict hours for Mr. McCormick's activities, from the time he woke to the length of his shower bath and the hour he retired in the evening, but, being the new man in charge, he couldn't help tinkering with one or two small things here and there. In the beginning, that is. Only in the beginning.

The first thing he did, and to O'Kane's mind this was a mistake, most definitely a mistake, was to attempt to apply the talking cure to Mr. McCormick. In those days—and this was in the summer and fall of 1916—the talking cure was considered little more than a novelty, a sort of glorified parlor game for the rich and idle, like dream analysis or hypnosis, and few psychiatrists had taken the lead of Dr. Freud in applying it to their severely disturbed patients. Like most people, O'Kane was deeply skeptical—how could you talk a raving lunatic out of drinking his own urine or stabbing his invalid grandmother a hundred times with a cocktail fork?—and Dr. Hamilton, though he subscribed to Freud's theories and was ready to lecture O'Kane and the Thompsons at the drop of a hat on such absurdities as infantile sexuality and mother lust, never applied the talking cure to Mr. McCormick. Better he felt, to keep the patient to a strict regimen, with a good healthy diet and sufficient exercise and intellectual stimulation, and let nature take its course. But Brush was new to the job, and he wanted to assert himself.

Both O'Kane and Martin were present for the first session. It was a sunny morning, glorious really, the early fog dissipated, the summer at its height, and Mr. McCormick was taking the air on the sunporch after breakfast. The porch—or patio, actually—adjoined the upper parlor and was walled around to a height of eight feet, with barred windows at eye level and wicker furniture bolted to the concrete beneath the Italian tiles and arranged in a little cluster in the middle of the floor. The door to the sun porch was always kept locked when not in use and the furniture had been situated with an eye to preventing Mr. McCormick's getting close enough to one of the walls to be able to boost himself over. It was a two-story drop to the shrubbery below, and even for a man of Mr. McCormick's agility, that could well prove fatal.

Mr. McCormick had eaten well that morning—two eggs with several strips of bacon, an English muffin and a bowl of cornflakes with sugar and cream—and he seemed to be in an especially good mood, anticipating a new moving picture Roscoe had brought up from Hollywood the previous evening. It was a Lillian Gish picture, and Mr. McCormick, who wasn't allowed to see women in the flesh, really savored the opportunity to see them come to life on the flat shining screen in the theater house. More than once he'd had to be restrained from exposing his sex organ at the sight of Pearl White hanging from a cliff or Mary Pickford lifting her skirt to step down from the running board of an automobile, but the doctors felt nonetheless that the mental stimulation provided by the movies far outweighed any small unpleasantness that might arise from their depiction of females—in distress or otherwise. O'Kane wasn't so sure. He was the one who had to get up in the middle of the film with the light flickering and Mr. McCormick breathing spasmodically and force Mr. McCormick's member back into his pants, and that had to be humiliating for Mr. McCormick—and it certainly was no joy for O'Kane either. No, seeing women like that, all made-up and batting their eyes at the camera and showing off their cleavage and the rest of it, must have just frustrated the poor man all the more. Anybody would go crazy in his situation, and half the time O'Kane wondered if they shouldn't just go out and hire a prostitute once a month and let Mr. McCormick—properly restrained, of course—release his natural urges like any other man, but then that wasn't being psychological, was it?

At any rate, Dr. Brush showed up that morning just after O'Kane and Mart had taken Mr. McCormick out onto the sunporch, and he was determined to give the talking cure a try. "Mr. McCormick," he cried, lumbering through the door and booming a greeting in his lusty big hail-fellow voice, "and how are you this fine morning?"

Mr. McCormick was seated in one of the wicker chairs, his feet up on the wicker settee, hands clasped behind his neck, staring up into the cloudless sky. He was dressed, as usual, as if he were on his way to his office at the Reaper Works, in a gray summer suit, vest, formal collar and tie. He didn't respond to the greeting, nor acknowledge the doctor's presence in any way.

Undeterred, Dr. Brush strode hugely across the tiles and stationed himself just behind Mr. McCormick, leaning forward to maneuver his great sweating dirigible of a face into Mr. McCormick's line of sight.

"And so," Dr. Brush boomed, "aren't you the lucky one to have such fine weather here all the year round? It must be especially gratifying in the winter, for the main and simple reason of defeating the ice and snow, but can you imagine how they're all sweltering in that humidity back East . . . and here, it's as pleasant as can be. What do you think it is, Mr. McCormick—seventy? Seventy-two, maybe? Huh?"

No response.

"Yes, sir," the doctor concluded with a stagey sigh, "you're a lucky man."

Mr. McCormick spoke then for the first time since he'd been led out onto the porch. He still had his head thrust back and he was viewing Dr. Brush upside down, which must have been a bit peculiar, though it didn't seem to faze him much. "Lucky?" he said, and his voice was barely a croak. "I'm-I'm no luckier than a dog."

"A dog?" And now the doctor was in a state of high excitement, dodging round the patio with little feints of his too-small feet and finally squeezing himself into the chair opposite Mr. McCormick. "And why do you say that, sir? A dog? Really. How extraordinary."

Mart, who was leaning against the wall just to the left of the door, cracked his knuckles audibly. O'Kane had been pacing back and forth in the shade at the far end of the patio, and he stopped now and found himself a good spot at the intersection of two walls and leaned back to listen. Mr. McCormick, still staring up into the sky, said nothing.

"A dog?" Brush repeated. "Did I hear you correctly, Mr. Mc-Cormick? You did say 'a dog,' didn't you?"

Still nothing.

"Well, if you did, and I'm quite sure there's nothing wrong with my hearing—or maybe there is, ha! and I'd better have it tested—well, and if you did say 'a dog' I'd be very interested to hear just why you should feel that way, for the main and simple reason that it's such an extraordinary position to take, and I'm sure both Mr. Thompson and Mr. O'Kane would like to hear your reasoning too. Wouldn't you, fellows?"

Mart grunted, and it was hard to say whether it was an affirmative or negative grunt.

O'Kane ducked his head. "Yeah," he said, "sure."

"Do you hear that, Mr. McCormick? All your friends would like to know just how you feel on the subject. Yes? Mr. McCormick?"

And yet still nothing. O'Kane wondered if Mr. McCormick had

even heard the question, or if he'd already shut his mind down, as impervious as a rodent buried deep in its burrow. At least he wasn't violent. Or not yet, anyway.

The doctor pulled a cigar from his inside pocket and took a moment in lighting it. He drew on it, expelled a plume of smoke and gave the patient a canny look, which was unfortunately lost on Mr. McCormick, who continued to gaze into the sky as if he were Percival Lowell looking for signs of life on Mars. "Perhaps you feel caged-in here, is that it, Mr. McCormick?" the doctor began. "Is that what you're saying—that you'd like more liberty? Because we can arrange that—more drives, more walks outside the estate, if that's what you want. Is that it? Is that what you mean?"

After a silence that must have lasted five or six minutes, Dr. Brush changed his tack. "Tell me about your father, Mr. McCormick," he said, leaning forward now and addressing Mr. McCormick's long pale throat and the underside of his chin. "He was a great man, I'm told. . . . Did you love him very much?"

A gull coasted overhead. It was very still. Somewhere down below, off in the direction of the cottages, someone was singing in Italian, a monotonous drone that swung back and forth on itself like a pendulum.

"Did you . . . did you ever feel that you disliked him? Or harbored any resentment toward him? Perhaps he disciplined you as a boy or even spanked you—did that ever occur?"

O'Kane became conscious of the movement of the sun, the sharp angle of the shadow beside him creeping inexorably nearer. He tried to make out the words to the song, though he couldn't understand them anyway, and he tried not to think of Giovannella. Mr. McCormick, who had a genius for rigidity—he would have made the ideal sculptor's model—never moved a hair. He didn't even seem to be breathing.

"Well," the doctor said after a bit, and he got massively to his feet, puffing at the cigar, and began to pace back and forth, counting off the tiles, "well and so." He stalked round back of Mr. McCormick again and again forced his face into Mr. McCormick's line of vision. "And your mother," he said, "what is she like?"

The second thing the doctor tried was by way of effecting certain small refinements in the daily schedule, for the sake of efficiency. He started with Mr. McCormick's shower bath. "Eddie," he said, taking O'Kane aside just after his shift had ended one evening, "you know, I've been thinking about Mr. McCormick's day and how he goes about using his resources, for the main and simple reason that I think we could inject a bit more efficiency into the scheme of things. Shake him up, you know? It's the same old thing, day in and day out. You'd think the man'd be bored to death by now."

O'Kane, who had remained head nurse despite the change of regime and had seen his salary increased by five dollars a week since Brush took over, felt it prudent to act concerned, though he saw nothing at all wrong with the schedule as it stood. It wasn't the schedule that was holding Mr. McCormick back, and it wasn't the lack of intellectual stimulation either—it was the lack of women. Get him laid a few times and see what happened—he couldn't be any worse for it than he was now. He gave Brush a saintly look. "What did you have in mind?"

"Well, I was looking at this item here, the shower bath," the doctor said. They were standing at the doorway to the upper parlor; Mr. Mc-Cormick had been put to bed and Nick and Pat had just begun their shift. " 'Seven to eight A.M.: shower bath.' Now doesn't that seem a bit excessive? Even in the interest of proper hygiene? Why, I spend no more than five minutes under the shower myself, and ha! you'll have to admit there's a good deal more of me to wash than there is of Mr. McCormick. What I'm thinking is, couldn't we cut that time back— gradually, I mean—till he takes a normal shower bath of five or ten minutes, and then we can apply the savings in time to his improvement and cure—"

O'Kane shrugged. "Well, sure, I suppose. But Mr. McCormick is very adamant about his shower bath, it's one of his pet obsessions, and it may be very difficult to—"

"Ach," the doctor waved a hand in his face, "leave that to me— obsessions are my stock in trade."

And so, the following morning, once O'Kane and Mart had ushered Mr. McCormick into the shower bath, Dr. Brush appeared, barefooted and mountainous in a long trailing rain slicker the size of a two-man tent. "Good morning, good morning!" he boomed, the raw shout of his voice reverberating in the small cubicle of the shower bath till it was like a hundred voices. "Don't mind me, Mr. McCormick," he called, his pale fleshy toes gripping the wet tiles, water already streaming from the hem of the rain slicker, "I'm just here to observe your bathing in the interest of efficiency, for the main and simple—but just think of me as one of your efficiency experts you manufacturing men are forever introducing into your operations to cut corners and increase production. . . . Go ahead, now, don't let me interfere—"

Mr. McCormick was seated naked on the floor beneath one of the three showerheads, rubbing furiously at his chest with a fresh bar of Palm Olive soap. He looked alarmed at first, and even made as if to cover his privates, but then seemed to think better of it, and turning away from the doctor, he continued lathering his chest.

"Now I thought," the doctor went on, steam rising, the water splashing against the walls and leaping up to spatter his legs, "that we might begin today by limiting our bathing to perhaps, oh, how does fifteen minutes sound to you, Mr. McCormick? You see, and I'm sure you'll agree, that's a more than reasonable length of time to thoroughly cleanse ourselves, for the main and simple reason that the human body can only hold so much dirt, especially when one bathes daily, don't you think?"

O'Kane stood in the bathroom doorway, his usual station, where he could observe Mr. McCormick at his bath and yet not intrude too much on him, and Mart was in the parlor, preparing the table for Mr. McCormick's breakfast. While the shower stall was quite large—there was room enough for three people at least—O'Kane couldn't help feeling the doctor was taking an unnecessary risk. There was no telling how Mr. McCormick might construe this invasion of his privacy, efficiency or no, and if he were to get violent, there was always the possibility of a nasty fall, what with the slick tiles and steady flow of water. He didn't like the situation, not one bit, and he gloomily envisioned himself charging into the fray and ruining yet another suit.

But Mr. McCormick surprised him. He didn't seem particularly agitated—or not that O'Kane could see. He merely kept the white slope of his back to the intruder and soaped himself all the more vigorously as the doctor went on jabbering away and the water fell in a cascade of steely bright pins. This went on for some time, until at a signal from Brush, O'Kane called to Mart and Mart went below to cut off the water supply.

A moment later, the shower ran dry. Mr. McCormick darted a wild glance over his shoulder at the doctor and then at O'Kane—Here it comes, O'Kane thought, tensing himself—but Mr. McCormick did nothing more than shift his haunches on the wet tiles so that he could reach up and try the controls. He twisted the knobs several times and then, in a sort of crabwalk, moved first to his left and then to his right to try the controls of the other two spigots. He was a long time about it, and when he was finally satisfied that the water had been cut off, he found the exact spot where he'd been situated before the interruption and continued soaping himself as if nothing were the matter.

Dr. Brush, for his part, was saying things like "All right, now, Mr. McCormick, very good, and I suppose we'll just have to move on, won't we?" and "Now, isn't that an improvement? Honestly now?" He stood there optimistically over the slumped form of their employer, his toes grasping the floor like fingers, the yellow slicker dripping, the short hairs at his nape curling up like duck's feathers with the moisture. But Mr. McCormick wasn't heeding him. In fact, Mr. McCormick was expressing his displeasure with the whole business by applying the dwindling bar of Palm Olive as if it were a cat o' nine tails, and when it was gone, he reached for another.

"Well, then," Dr. Brush confided to O'Kane later that day, "it's a contest of wills, and we'll just see how far the patient is prepared to go before he sees the wisdom of employing himself more efficiently."

The next morning, the doctor was back, only this time there was but one bar of soap in the dish and the shower was curtailed after ten minutes. Again, Dr. Brush made all sorts of optimistic assertions about time and energy saving and the value of discipline, but Mr. McCormick never wavered from his routine. He soaped himself for a full hour after the shower was stopped and appeared for breakfast with greenish white streaks of Palm Olive decorating his cheeks and brow, as if he were an Indian chieftain painted for war. And then the next day after that, the shower was cut to five minutes and only powdered soap was provided, but still Mr. McCormick persisted, as O'Kane knew he would. When the water was stopped, Mr. McCormick rubbed himself all over with the powdered soap till it dissolved in a yellowish scum and hardened like varnish all over his body.

The climax came on the fourth day.

Dr. Brush ordered that no soap be provided, and he appeared as usual, jocular and energetic, reasoning with Mr. McCormick as if he were a child — or at the very least one of the aments at the Lunatic Hospital. "Now can't you see," he said, his voice flattened and distorted by the pounding of the water till the water was cut off by signal five minutes later, "that you're being unreasonable, Mr. McCormick—or no, not unreasonable, but inefficient? Think if we were running the Reaper Works on this sort of schedule, eh? Now, of course, your soap will be restored to you as soon as you, well, begin to, that is, for the main and simple—"

Mr. McCormick bathed without soap and he didn't seem to miss it, not on the surface anyway, but he sat there under the dry shower for a good hour and a half, and when he got up he reached for his towel, though he was long since dry himself. No matter. He took up that towel like a penitent's scourge and whipped it back and forth across his body till the skin was so chafed it began to bleed and he had to be dissuaded by force. The next morning he never even bothered to turn the shower on, but simply took up the towel as if he were already wet and rubbed himself furiously in all the chafed places till they began to bleed again, and it was only after a struggle that took the combined force of O'Kane, Mart and Dr. Brush to overcome him, that he desisted.

And so it went for a week, till Mr. McCormick was a walking scab from head to toe and Dr. Brush finally gave up his vision of efficiency. In fact, he gave up any notion of interfering with Mr. McCormick at all, either through adjusting his schedule or drawing him into therapeutic conversation, and after that, for the year or so before he was called away to military duty among the shell-shocked veterans of the Western Front, he really seemed content to just—float along.

Well, that was all right with O'Kane: he had his own problems. As the fall of 1916 bled into the winter of 1917 and the War drew closer, his skirmishes with Rosaleen and Giovannella seemed to intensify till he was in full retreat, capable of nothing more than a feeble rearguard action. At least with Rosaleen the battles were fought through the U.S. Postal Service and at a distance of three thousand and some-odd miles. He hadn't heard from her in two years, and then suddenly she was dunning him for money, letters raining down on him in a windswept storm of demands, complaints and threats. And what did she want? She wanted shoes for Eddie Jr., who was the "spiting immidge of his father" and going to be nine soon, and a new Sunday suit for him too, so he'd look his best for her wedding to Homer Quammen, and did he remember Homer? And by the way, she was filing papers for divorce and she felt he owed her something for that too, and he shouldn't think for a minute that her remarrying would in any way lift his obligation to support Eddie Jr., especially since Homer was as "pore as a church moose."

He sent her the money, forty dollars in all, though he resented it because he was putting away every spare nickel against a land deal Dolores Isringhausen's brother-in-law was letting him in on, and he never heard a word of thanks or good-bye or anything else. The letters stopped coming though, so he assumed she'd got the money, and by the time he did finally hear from her he'd forgotten all about it. It was in December, sometime around Christmas—he remembered it was the holiday season because Katherine was back in town, piling the upper parlor hip-deep in presents and wreaths and strings of popcorn and such and generally raising hell with Brush and Stribling, the estate manager—and he'd just got back from his shift with a thought to wheedling a sandwich out of Mrs. Fitzmaurice and then going out for a drink at Menhoff's, when he noticed a smudged white envelope laid out on the table in the entry hall for him. He recognized Rosaleen's cramped subhuman scrawl across the face of it—Edw. O'Kane, Esq., C/O Mrs. Morris Fitzmaurice, 196 State Street, Santa Barbara, California—and tucked it in his breast pocket.

Later, sitting at a table at Menhoff's, he was searching his pockets for a light to offer the girl from the Five & Dime when he discovered it there. He lit the girl's cigarette—her name was Daisy and she had a pair of breasts on her that made him want to faint away and die for the love of them—and then he excused himself to go to the men's, where he stood over the urinal and tore the letter open, killing two birds with one stone. Inside, there was a photograph and nothing more, not even a line. He held it up to the light with his free hand. The photo was blurred and obscure, as if the whole world had shifted in the interval between the click of the shutter and the fixing of the image, and it showed a wisp of a kid in short pants, new shoes and a jacket and tie, smiling bravely against a backdrop of naked trees and a hedge all stripped of its leaves. O'Kane looked closer. Squinted. Maneuvered the slick surface to catch the light. And saw the face of his son there shining out of the gloom, Eddie Jr., his own flesh and blood, and he would have known that face anywhere.

Sure. Sure he would.

He stood at the urinal till he lost track of time, just staring into the shining face of that picture, and he felt as bad as he'd ever felt, bad and worthless and of no more account than a vagrant bum in an alley. His son was growing up without him. His mother and father didn't even know their own grandson, his sisters didn't know their nephew. Nobody knew him, nobody but Rosaleen—and Homer Quammen. God, how that hurt. She might as well have sent him a bomb in the mail, raked him with shrapnel, flayed his flesh. He thought he was going to cry, he really thought he was going to break down and cry for the first time since he was a kid himself, the sour smell of piss in his nostrils, mold in the drains, the air so heavy and brown it was like mustard gas rolling in over the trenches, but then he heard the ripple and thump of the piano from the front room and came back to himself. Daisy was out there waiting for him, Daisy with all her petals on display and ripe for the picking.

All right. So. He shook himself, buttoned up, flushed. And then, and it was almost as if he were suffering from some sort of tic himself like poor Mrs. Brush, he felt his right hand contract and the picture was crumpled and lying there in the urinal alongside the scrawled-over envelope. He never got another one. And he never heard another word about divorce either.

With Giovannella it was different. And worse. A whole lot worse. She'd defied him, of course, and after she pulled the slick red spike out of his palm and they stopped right there to consider the phenomenon of his blood sprouting and flowering in that white pocket where just an instant before there'd been no blood at all, she never said a word, not I'm sorry or Forgive me or Did I hurt you? No, she just tore up the slip of paper with Dolores Isringhausen's doctor's name on it and threw it in his face, and he was clutching his hand and cursing by then, cursing her with every bit of filth he could think of, and Jesus in Heaven his hand hurt. "Whore!" he shouted. "Bitch!" You fucking Guinea bitch!" But her body was rigid and her face was iron and she clutched that gleaming spike of steel in her white-knuckled fist till he was sure she meant to drive it right on through his heart, and he backed out the door and went on down the rickety stairs, cursing in a steady automatic way and wondering where he could find a doctor himself—and on Sunday no less.

She wouldn't see him after that. And he wanted her, wanted her as badly as he'd ever wanted anything in his life, and not to wrangle and fight over husbands or babies or San Francisco or anything else, but to love her, strip her naked, splay her out on the bed and crush her in his arms and love her till there was no breath left in her. But she spurned him. He crept up to the apartment above the shoe repair shop and she shut the door in his face; he waylaid her in the street when she went out to the market and she walked right by him as if she'd never laid eyes on him before in her life. When he grabbed for her elbow—"Please, Giovannella," and he was begging, "just listen to me, just for a minute"— she snatched it away, stalking up the street with her quick chopping strides and her shoulders so stiff and compacted they might have been bound up with wire.

But what really tortured him was watching her grow bigger, day by day, week by week. Every Sunday afternoon she strolled up and down the street on the arm of Guido, the amazing Italian dwarf who couldn't have weighed more than a hundred and five pounds with his boots on, and she made sure to pass right by the front window of the rooming house and all the saloons of Spanishtown—and Cody Menhoff's too, just for good measure. At first you couldn't tell, nobody could, because the baby was the size of a skinned rat and it wasn't a baby at all, it wasn't even human, but by the end of June she was showing and by mid-July she looked as if she were smuggling melons under her skirt. He would follow her sometimes, half-drunk and feuding with himself, and he would watch as people stopped to congratulate her, the men smiling paternally, the women reaching out to pat the swollen talisman of her belly, and all the while Guido the shoemaker grinning and flushed with his simpleminded pride. O'Kane felt left out. He felt evil. He felt angry.

The baby was born at the end of October. O'Kane heard of it through Baldy Dimucci, who was passing around cigars as if he were the proud father himself, and no hard feelings over what had happened eight years ago—and more recently too. Or were there? The old man had sought him out as he came down to lunch in the kitchen of the big house one sun-kissed afternoon just before Halloween. O'Kane had seen the truck in the drive that morning (no more donkey carts for Baldy: he'd prospered, owner of a thriving nursery business now and a new Ford truck too) and had wondered about it, but he didn't make the connection with Giovannella and the baby till Baldy came through the kitchen door, unsteady on his feet and reeking of red wine and cigar smoke. "Hey, Eddie," he said, while Sam Wah scowled over the stove and O'Kane spooned up soup, "you hear the good-a news?"

"Good news? No, what is it?"

Baldy advanced on him, his face crazy with furrows, eyes lit with wine, a big garlic-eating grin. "Giovannella," he said, and he wasn't as drunk as he let on, "Giovannella and-a my son the law, they have their baby."

O'Kane just blinked. He didn't ask what sex it was or if its hair was blond and one of its green Irish eyes imprinted with a lucky hazel clock, because he already knew, and the knowledge made him feel sick and dizzy, as if the ground had dipped beneath him. So he didn't say anything, didn't offer congratulations or best wishes to the new mother — he just blinked.

"Here," Baldy said, standing over him in his best suit of clothes and the wine stains on his shirt, "have a cigar."

O'Kane went straight to her apartment after work, but he didn't dare go up because there was a whole red-wine-spilling, accordion-playing, pasta-boiling wop hullabaloo going on up there and people all over the stairs, boisterous and laughing out loud. And when he did manage to sneak up two days later, the door was answered not by Giovannella but by a big square monument of a woman who shared a nose and eyes with her and nothing more. This was the mother, and no mistaking it. She said something in Italian and he tried to see past her into the familiar room, but she filled the whole picture all by herself and she knitted her black eyebrows and repeated whatever it was she'd said on pulling open the door and finding him there on the landing with his mouth hanging open. "Giovannella," he said, the only word of Italian he knew, but the woman didn't look to be all that impressed. One trembling blue-veined maternal hand went to the cross at her throat, as if to ward off some creeping evil, while the other gripped the edge of the door to bar his way, and in the instant before she slammed the door in his face with a violence that rocked the whole rotten stairway right down to its rotten supports, he heard the baby cry out, a single searing screech that resounded in his ears like an indictment.

The day he finally did get a look at Giovannella's baby — his son, another son, and he a stranger to both of them — was the day Dolores Isringhausen came back from New York to open up her villa for the winter. It was a Saturday, and when he got off his shift there was a note

waiting for him in the front hall at Mrs. Fitzmaurice's. The envelope
was a pale violet color, scented with her perfume, and all it said on the
front was "Eddie." He tore it open right there, standing in the hallway
and old Walter Hogan watching him out of bloodshot eyes. "Got in last
night," he read, "and I'm already bored. Call me." She hadn't even bothered to sign her name.

He called her and her voice purred inside him till it felt as if all his
nerve endings had sprouted fine little hairs, and he pictured her as he'd
last seen her, in a Japanese robe with nothing underneath. "It's Eddie,"
he'd said, and she came right back at him with that cat-clawing whisper: "What took you so long?" They made a date for supper, and he
kicked himself for not having a car to squire her around in. He didn't
like her driving—it was wrong somehow. It made him feel funny, as if
he was half a man or a cripple or something, and he didn't want anyone
to see him sitting there like a dope in the passenger's seat and a woman
behind the wheel. The thing was, he didn't need a car, not with Roscoe
ferrying him to and from Riven Rock six days a week and everything in
downtown Santa Barbara an easy walk or a seven-cent streetcar ride.
He was saving his money, because he didn't intend to be a nurse forever, and a car was just a drain, when you figured up the cost of gasoline, tires, repairs, and how many times had he seen Roscoe up to his
ears in grease? But tonight he could sure use one—anything, even a Tin
Lizzie that'd crank your arm off—just to pull up in Dolores's drive and
toot the horn a couple of times, and he felt cheap and low and thought
he ought to stroll up to Menhoff's to raise his spirits a bit.

That was when he spotted Giovannella. She was across the street in
front of the greengrocer's, bending over to inspect the tomatoes, and
beside her, in a perambulator the color of a bat's wing, was the baby.
Guido was nowhere in sight. O'Kane looked both ways and back over
his shoulder to make sure no one was watching, then crossed the street
and slipped up behind her, just another face in the crowd, and he was
actually squeezing the fruit like a discerning housewife when he peered
into the perambulator and saw the miniature features puckered like a
sinkhole in the ground, eyes shut fast, a frilly blue bonnet pulled down
over invisible eyebrows. But the skin—the fat clenched hands, the sinking face—was the color of Giovannella's, Giovannella's purely, without
adulteration, cinnamon on toast, Sicilian clay. Or dirt. Sicilian dirt.

Giovannella was aware of him now, looking up from her tomatoes while Wilson, the big-armed greengrocer, weighed them for her in a silver shovel-scoop of a scale, staring at him out of her stygian eyes. Her lips curled ever so slightly at the corners. "He's beautiful, my baby, isn't he, Eddie?"

O'Kane looked to Wilson, and Wilson knew, everybody knew. Except maybe Guido. "Yeah," he said, "sure," and he felt numb all over, as if he'd been to the dentist and breathed deep of the gas till his mind fled away.

Oh, and her smile was rich now, her lips spread wide, teeth gleaming white in the sun. "You know what we decided to name him, Eddie? Huh?"

He didn't have a clue. He looked to Wilson again and Wilson looked away.

" 'Guido,' Eddie. We named him 'Guido.' After his father."

And what did he feel then? Relieved? Thankful? Glad he hadn't fathered another child to be raised a stranger to him? No. He felt betrayed. He felt rage. He felt jealousy, hot and electric, like a wire run right on up through him from his cock to his brain and the current on full. Wilson disappeared behind his melons and Guinea squash. A woman in a felt hat faded from black to gray bent over the radishes and then moved away down the aisle and into the cool depths of the shop. He looked hard at Giovannella. "What are you saying?"

The baby might as well have been carved of wood—it was there, in the carriage, sunk into itself. Giovannella tucked the brown paper sack of tomatoes under one arm and gave him a savage look. "You're a big man, huh, Eddie? Always so cocksure—isn't that right? The ladies' man. The big stud." She bit her lip, shot a glance around to see if anybody was watching. He was confused, adrift on a heavy sea, the sun throwing shadows across the street and the pavement glowing as if it was wet with rain. What did she want from him? What was the problem?

And then, as if he'd been awaiting his moment in the center of the stage, the baby woke up and flashed open his eyes—and there it was, for all the world to see, the green of Dingle Bay and three o'clock in the afternoon.

Well, and that ruined the day for him, put a real kibosh on it, sent him into a funk that only whiskey could hope to salve. Of course, the moment the kid opened his eyes she whisked him away, the wheels of the perambulator spinning like a locomotive's and the first feeble waking cry magnified into an infantile squall of rage, but by then she was at the corner and hustling down De la Guerra Street until the stony white columns of the First Security Bank swallowed her up. He didn't follow her. Let her go, he thought, let her play her games, and wouldn't she have made a sterling assistant to Savonarola, the hot iron glowing in her hand? The bitch. Oh, the bitch.

His hand shook under the weight of the first whiskey, and he sat at a table in the corner, stared out the window and watched the pigeons rise up from the street and settle back down again till he knew every one of them as an individual, knew its strut and color, knew the cocks from the hens and the old from the young. There they were, fecund and flapping, like some mindless feathered symbol of his own feckless life, leaping up instinctively as each car passed and then pouring back down again in its wake, oblivious, strutting, pecking, fucking. He was thinking about Giovannella and Rosaleen and Eddie Jr. and little Guido— *Guido*, for Christ's sake—and wondering where he'd gone wrong. Or how. He was no biologist, like Katherine, but he knew that if the male of the species—namely, Eddie O'Kane—sticks his thing in the female enough times, no matter the time of month or the precautions taken, eventually she's going to swell up and keep on swelling till there's another yabbering little brat in the world.

But he caught himself right there. This was no ordinary brat, this was no black-eyed little shoemaker's son, this was Guido O'Kane, his son, and he had to take responsibility for him. But how? Slip Giovannella money each month and play the Dutch uncle? Catch the shoemaker in an alley some night and make her a widow and then go ahead and marry her, which is what he should have done in the first place? But then—and there was an icy nagging voice in the back of his mind, the voice of the Ice Queen reading him the riot act in the downstairs parlor—he was already married, wasn't he?

All this was going through his head when the little two-seat Maxwell with its trim white tires and expressive brakes pulled up to the curb and sent the pigeons into a paroxysm of flight. He could see Dolores Isringhausen sitting at the wheel, her pearl gloves, the way she cocked her head back and the glassy cold look of her eyes. She didn't get out of the car. She didn't come in. Just tapped the horn as if she were summoning some lackey, some black buck to slip into the manor house and service her while the master's away, and what did she think he was? He didn't move a muscle. Raising the glass to his lips, he took a long slow sip, as if he had all the time in the world, eyes locked on hers all the while. He wanted to gesture to her to come in, but he didn't, and when she tapped the horn again, her features drawn in irritation, he got up, crossed the barroom and went to her.

"What was that about?" she said, glancing up as he climbed in beside her. "Didn't you see me? You were looking right at me."

She didn't wait for an answer, the car lurching forward with a crunch of the tires, and by the time he got settled they were charging down State toward the ocean, the blue skin of the sky joined to the blue skin of the sea by a thin gray seam of mist that blotted the islands from view. She had the top up, for discretion's sake, and she drove too fast, dodging round a market wagon and a double-parked car, nipping in behind the trolley and shooting through the intersections as if there was no other car on the road. "I saw you," he said, and he could feel the weight lifting off him, just a hair, "and it was good to see you, damn good. . . . I just needed a minute to feast my eyes on you and think how lucky I am. Or how lucky I'm going to be."

"What's the matter," she said, bunching her lips in a moue, "all your girlfriends on strike?" She leaned into him for a kiss, but she never took her eyes off the road. They rattled over the streetcar tracks and in and out of a pair of potholes that nearly put his skull through the canvas roof, and then she swung left on Cabrillo, heading away from town. "You still seeing the little Italian slut, the one with the dirty eyes? You know, the breeder?"

"Nah," he lied, "there's nobody right now." And he gave her his smile, their faces so close, the car jolting, the smell of her. "I've been saving myself for you."

By way of response, she produced a flask from beneath the seat, took a drink and handed it to him. "Then I guess I can expect a pretty hot time," she said finally, giving him a sidelong glance, her smile tight around lips wet with gin, and like any other actor taking his cue, he reached out and laid a hand on her thigh.

They didn't stop at a roadhouse, lunchroom or restaurant, but went straight up Hot Springs Road and into the hills of Montecito in a hurricane of dust and flying leaves that didn't abate till she swung into the tree-lined drive of the villa and glided up to the garage. She killed the engine and he wondered if he should go round and open the door for her, but she didn't seem to care one way or the other, and in the next moment they climbed separately out of the car and headed up the walk in front of the house. The place was deserted, no servants or gardeners or washerwomen, no eyes to see or ears to hear, and she took him by the hand and led him straight up to the bedroom. He knew what to do then, and as the afternoon stretched into the evening and the sun crept across the floor through the French doors flung open wide on a garden of ten-foot ferns, he used his tongue and his fingers and his hard Irish prick to extract all the pleasure from her he could, and it was like breaking for the goal with the ball tucked under his arm, like swinging for the fence, one more empty feat and nothing more. He didn't love her. He loved Giovannella. And he thought about that and how odd it was as he thrust himself into Dolores Isringhausen with a kind of desperation he couldn't admit and the sun moved and the woman beneath him locked her hips to his and he felt the weight slip back down again, hopeless and immovable, till it all but crushed him.

He must have fallen asleep, because when the phone rang in the next room it jolted him up off the sheets and she had to put a hand on his chest to calm him. He watched as she got up to answer it, her legs and buttocks snatching at the light, and not a sag or ripple anywhere on her. How old was she, anyway—thirty-five? Forty? He'd never asked. But he could see she'd never had any children—or if she had, it was a long time ago. He took a drink from the flask and watched a humming-bird hovering over the trumpet vine with its pink cunt-shaped flowers and listened to her whispering into the receiver. And who was that she was talking to—tomorrow's lay?

She came back into the room in a susurrus of motion, hips rolling in an easy glide, and straddled the white hill of his knee. He waited till she'd reached over to the night table for a cigarette and held a match to it, and then he said, "So your husband—he isn't back from the War yet, is he?"

"Who, Tom?" She twitched her hips and rubbed herself there, on his knee, and he could feel the warmth and wetness of her. "He's never coming back—he's having too much fun pulling the trigger on all the whores of Asiago."

"Does he know about you? I mean, that you're—"

"What? Unfaithful? Is that the word you're looking for?"

He watched her eyes for a signal, but they were as glassy and distant as ever. She merely shrugged and shifted her thighs to accommodate the angle of his knee. "Yeah," he said, "I guess."

"What do you think?"

What did he think? He was a little shocked, that was all, to think
how loose her morals were—and her husband's too. He wouldn't put up
with that sort of thing, not if he were over in Italy fighting the Huns or
the Austrians or whoever they were. He didn't say anything, but she
was watching him, working herself against his shin now, the tight little
smile, the bobbed hair, the gently swaying breasts.

"Better I should lock myself in a nunnery till the great warrior
comes home?"

No. Or yes. But he'd leapt ahead of her already, and he realized he
didn't give a damn for her or her husband or what they did with their
respective groins—he was thinking about that half-Italian baby in the
perambulator and the pale wondering face in the crumpled-up photograph. "You mind if I ask you something?"

She gave him a look he couldn't gauge and he felt her body tense,
though she shrugged and said, "Sure, go ahead," and let the smoke seep
out of her nostrils in two ascending coils.

"I was wondering—you never had any kids, did you? Children, I
mean?"

"Me?" She laughed. "Can you picture me as a mother? Come on,
Eddie."

"But how—?"

"Ah," she said, twisting round to snub out the cigarette in the hammered brass ashtray on the night table, "I see where this is going. She
had the baby, didn't she, your little peasant girl?"

He couldn't meet her eyes. "Yes."

"And it's yours?"

"Yes."

And then she laughed again, and the laugh irritated him, made him
feel that spark of anger that always seemed to go straight to his hands.
"You think it's funny?"

In answer, she collapsed on him, pinning his face to the pillow and
forcing a kiss that was like a bite, and then she rolled off him and lay
sprawled on her back beside him. "I do," she said. "And it is funny, because you're like a baby yourself, like you were just born and still kick-

ing. Sure, give me that look, go ahead, but to answer your question, I use a Mensigna pessary, Eddie," and she reached between her legs to show him.

And now he *was* shocked, and maybe a little frightened too. She held the thing up where he could see it, a black rubber tube all slick with her juices—and his. It was unholy, that's what it was, a murder weapon, a mortal sin you could see and feel and hold in your own two hands.

"It comes in fourteen sizes," she said, enjoying the moment and the look on his face. "The only problem is," and she was coy now, coy and already moving into him, "you have to go to Holland to get one."

The rains that winter seemed unusually heavy, one February storm alone dropping eight inches in a single day over the sodden town and its sandbagged saloons, lunchrooms, barbershops, corner groceries and cigar stores and converting lower State Street into a chute full of roiling mud that inundated all the first-floor shops and dwellings. The dark sucking river that rode atop the mud washed a whole flotilla of cars out to sea while the incoming waves cannonaded the harbor and drove half the boats moored there up against the shore until there was nothing left but splinters. The sky was a torn sheet, gone gray with use and flapping on the line.

O'Kane enjoyed it, at least at first. He missed weather, real weather, the nor'easters that roared in off Boston Harbor on a blast of wind, the thunderstorms that ignited the summer sky and dropped the temperature twenty degrees in the snap of two fingers, but after he ruined a new pair of boots beyond repairing and had to drink at a Chink place in Spanishtown for a week because Menhoff's had six inches of mud all over the floor and creeping up the legs of the chairs, he began to feel afflicted. The rain kept coming, and everyone felt the burden of it, even Mr. McCormick, who announced he'd go mad if he didn't see some sunshine soon. It was a trial, a real trial, but the rains made the spring all the sweeter, and by March you'd never think a drop had ever fallen or would ever again.

Dolores Isringhausen went back to New York the morning after St. Patrick's Day (which she didn't spend with O'Kane), Giovannella began to soften toward him and even let him in once or twice when Guido wasn't looking to admire the baby up close, but no kissing and no touching, and Mr. McCormick improved to the point where he was more or less rational at least fifty percent of the time—and this despite Dr. Brush's retreat from active intervention to a strictly custodial role. Or maybe because of it. Just leave the man alone, that was O'Kane's philosophy, and if he wanted a two-hour shower bath, let him have it. Why not? It wasn't as if he had a train to catch.

And then it was June, and Dr. Brush, all three hundred and twenty-seven pounds of him, was called up to serve his country behind the lines with the American Expeditionary Forces in Europe. He left his wife with a cousin (hers) on Anapamu Street, had a long talk with Mr. McCormick about duty and patriotism and the conduct of the War, and headed out on the train, the only member of the McCormick medical team to be called to active duty. They stationed him in England, and O'Kane pictured him tucking away an English breakfast with two pots of tea and then sitting around under the elms with a bunch of spooked one-legged vets and asking if their fathers had spanked them.

As it turned out, Brush would be gone just over two years, and though he wasn't accomplishing a damn thing as far as O'Kane could see, except maybe by accident, the McCormicks—and Katherine— insisted on a replacement, the best money could buy. Or rent. Dr. Meyer came all the way out himself and brought the interim man with him, a Dr. August Hoch, who'd succeeded him as head of the Pathological Institute in New York. Dr. Hoch was a Kraut—all the headshrinkers were Krauts, it seemed, except Hamilton and Brush, and that was all right with O'Kane, since they'd invented headshrinking in the first place. It was just that there was a lot of anti-German sentiment in the country around that time, and understandably so, and it didn't make it any easier bellying up to the bar at Menhoff's when everybody in town knew you had a Kraut over you. In fact, he'd had to wipe the floor one night with a guy in a lunchroom who called Dolores Isring-hausen a Hun to her face, and the irony of it was she wasn't even German—her maiden name was Mayhew.

But Dr. Hoch was all right. He was a keen-eyed old duffer with gray chin whiskers and a thin white scar that carved a wicked arc from just beneath his left eye to the back hinge of his jaw. O'Kane was there the day Meyer and Hoch walked in on Mr. McCormick, who'd just re-turned from his morning exercise—a tortuous and many-branching stroll to the Indian grounds and back. Mr. McCormick was off in the corner, holding a private conference with his judges, and Dr. Meyer, whom Mr. McCormick knew well from his semiannual visits, went right up to him and said he had somebody he'd like him to meet. "Or perhaps," he added, his accent thick as sludge, "you will already know him, yes?"

Mr. McCormick left off with his judges and turned slowly round, his eyes passing mechanically from Dr. Meyer's black-bearded face to Dr. Hoch's gray-bearded one. He seemed to recognize Dr. Meyer, and that was all well and good, but Hoch was obviously a puzzle. There was something in his eyes—a spark of recognition? fear? bewilderment?— but O'Kane couldn't read it.

"To refresh your memory, maybe," Dr. Meyer went on, rocking back on his heels as if he were about to perform some acrobatic feat, "you will recall that Dr. Hoch examined you in nineteen hundred and seven, when you were a guest at McLean, but perhaps you forget because then you are not so well as you are now?"

Dr. Hoch came forward, a shambling sort of man in a shapeless gray suit who'd let his mustache and chin whiskers go so long without trimming that they hung down to his collar and completely obscured his throat. The scar shone in the morning light like a trail of dried spittle or the glistening track a slug leaves on the pavement, silvery and ever so faintly luminescent. "How do you do, Mr. McCormick," he said with a little bow, and he didn't extend his hand until Mr. McCormick automatically reached out his own. "It is a great pleasure to see you once again, yes?" and his accent was thicker than Meyer's.

Mr. McCormick held onto Dr. Hoch's hand a long while—so long, in fact, O'Kane began to think he'd have to move in and break the grip—and twice he raised his free hand as if to touch the doctor's scar, but then dropped it again to his side. "Yes," Dr. Hoch said finally, "and I see perhaps that you are interested in my scar?"

Mr. McCormick let go of the doctor's hand then, and he fluttered round a bit, stamping his feet and wringing his hands as if they were wet before stuffing them awkwardly into his trouser pockets. He loomed over the doctor, who couldn't have been more than five-four or five-five. It seemed as if he were about to say something, but he bit his tongue and just stared at the side of the doctor's face, watching in fascination as Hoch traced the line of his scar with a blunt fingertip.

"This," Hoch said, "this is what we call in Germany a dueling scar. From my student days. You see, it was thought to be a cosmetic attraction to the ladies, a sign of virility or a badge of honor perhaps, but of course that was all foolishness then, the vanity of the young, and I do not know if students of today in the university they still have this — what do you say, 'rite'? — anymore." And then he said something in rapid-fire German to Meyer, who rattled something back.

"Ah. So. Herr Doktor Meyer informs me that this habit is no longer so much practiced as formerly." He gazed up at Mr. McCormick, like some wood gnome confronting a giant — and Mr. McCormick was a giant, despite the stoop that rounded his shoulders and at times bent him over double, depending on the degree of punishment his imaginary judges were inflicting on him. "Would you like to touch it?" the doctor said, his eyes glinting.

And Mr. McCormick, who didn't favor physical intimacy and had never touched anyone except in anger in all the time O'Kane had known him, reached up tentatively to explore the side of Dr. Hoch's face with two tremulous fingers. He traced the crescent of the scar over and over, very gently, so gently he might have been petting a cat. It was all very strange, Mr. McCormick stroking, the doctor submitting, the room so silent you would have thought they were all locked away in an Egyptian tomb, and then Mr. McCormick looked as if he wanted to say something, his lips moving before any sound came out. "So, it — it," he stammered, withdrawing his hand and tucking it away in his pocket, "it is possible after all."

"Possible?" Dr. Hoch just stood there, inches from their stooped-over and trembling employer, looking up steadily into his eyes. Dr. Meyer shot a glance at O'Kane, but O'Kane was dumbfounded. This was something new, this touching, and it would have to play itself out.

"To-to be a man," Mr. McCormick said, and then sang out one of his nonsense phrases, "one slit, one slit, one slit."

"Yes, yes it is," Dr. Hoch said, his face a web of lines that bunched and gathered around that one terrific silvery slash, and he didn't ask about mothers or fathers or boom out platitudes — he just waited.

"With a razor, I mean." Mr. McCormick had straightened up now and he looked round the room as if seeing it in a new light. "When, when Eddie and Mart shave me, it's a, it's a dangerous thing, to be cut like that, but it can, you can — "

The little doctor was nodding. "That's right," he said.

"I mean, what I mean is . . . if I was cut there"—and he reached out to touch the scar again—"it would, just, heal, and then I w-would have a scar too." He rocked back on his feet. "But here," he said, drawing a finger across his throat, "here it's very . . . dangerous. And here," pointing down, "you're not, not a man anymore."

"But Mr. McCormick," O'Kane broke in, "you know we always use a safety razor, you know that—"

Hoch looked at Meyer. Meyer looked at Hoch. Mr. McCormick drew himself up till his shoulders were squared and he was the very model of proper posture. He waited till he was sure he had O'Kane's attention, and the doctors' too, and then spoke in a clear strong uninflected voice, "Yes, Eddie, I know."

Well. O'Kane was impressed—all that over a scar—but he thought nothing more of it as the summer faded into autumn and the War news dominated every conversation and Giovannella warmed and melted and gave way to him again, stealing out on Saturday afternoons to linger with him on a mattress in the garage out back of Pat's house while the baby shook his rattle and pumped his legs and arms in the air. Meanwhile, the bearer of the scar, Dr. Hoch, was very patient with Mr. McCormick—none of this talking cure business—sitting with him throughout the day and into the night, putting in longer hours than O'Kane or Mart or anybody on the estate. Mostly he would just sit there with him, rumpled and avuncular, reading out an interesting bit from a book or magazine now and again, walking Mr. McCormick to and from the theater building and accompanying him on his walks. Sometimes the two of them would sit for hours and not say a word, and other times Mr. McCormick would be positively verbose, going on and on about the reaper—"the Wonder of the Reaper," he called it, after some book about his father—and his two brothers and the crying need for social welfare and reform in this cold unforgiving world.

They talked of the War too, and that was a bit odd, from O'Kane's point of view anyway, because here were the American millionaire and the prototypical Hun sitting cheek by jowl, but they never came to blows over it or even raised their voices, not that O'Kane could recall. War news trickled through to them all winter, often several days late, through the Los Angeles, Chicago and Santa Barbara papers, and the papers brought news of Katherine too. She was in Washington throughout that year—1918—and the next, where she'd been hand-picked by the president himself to sit on the National Defense Women's Committee, doing all sorts of things to prosecute the War, from putting women to work to selling Liberty Bonds and dreaming up those patriotic posters you saw everywhere. Every month or so she'd send Mr. McCormick detailed maps of the Western Front, showing the battle lines and trenches. He would pore over them for hours, commenting on places he'd visited on his honeymoon and sketching in all sorts of antic figures to represent armies, gun emplacements, and naval, horse and even air squadrons.

For a while there, especially through the summer and fall of 1918, the War became one of his pet obsessions, and he drew not only Dr. Hoch into it, but O'Kane himself. When the armies advanced or retreated he painstakingly erased his figures and symbols and moved the lines forward and backward and drew them in all over again. He analyzed the offensive at Amiens over and over, and he'd never been more lucid or articulate, not since his golfing days at McLean, and when the papers announced the American victory at St. Mihiel in September, he paraded around the upper parlor for hours, shaking his fists and uncannily imitating the whistle and crash of a bombardment while the rumpled little doctor sat on and watched with his scarred impassive face.

Katherine returned in December for the holidays, and that was when the business of the scar came up again. She was late in getting to California because of her duties with the Defense Committee, arriving just two days before Christmas. She seemed tired, worn about the edges, and as she stood in the theater building under a monumental wreath of holly and mistletoe handing out Christmas bonuses to the employees, she looked old. Or older. O'Kane watched her, always the lady, always perfect, always carved of the clearest coldest ice, and tried to tot up her age—she would have been, what, forty-one? Or forty-two? Well, for the first time it had begun to show—nothing extreme; she was hardly a hag yet—but there it was. Her clothes were as rich as ever, but they were yesterday's fashions, the heavy drapery of the suffragette and the matron, nothing at all like the skimpy satiny look of Dolores Isringhausen or the walking light that was Giovannella. She was getting old, but so was everybody else, even lucky Eddie O'Kane, who was going to be thirty-six come March. And he felt it most keenly when he came up to her and she took his hand and gave him his envelope and a smile that didn't mean a thing, not yea or nay, and he almost wished she'd come round cracking the whip again so they could all go back and start over, drenched in hope.

Anyway, the next day, the day before Christmas, she came to the house early in a flurry of presents and fruitcakes and rang up her husband from downstairs, to chat with him and extend her Christmas greetings. O'Kane was playing dominoes with Mart when the phone rang and the doctor got up to answer it. "It's for you, Mr. McCormick," he said, and his eyes were moist and wide. "It's your wife."

It took Mr. McCormick a minute to get up the steam and cross the room to where the doctor stood holding the telephone out to him, and when he did start across the floor he regressed into his two-steps-forward-one-step-back mode, hunching his shoulders and dragging down his face, his right leg suddenly dead and trailing behind him in a kind of wounded tango. When he finally did get to the phone, lift the receiver to his ear and bend to the mouthpiece, he didn't seem to have much to say other than a moist gulping swallow of a hello. She seemed to be doing all the talking. At least at first.

Dr. Hoch settled into an armchair at a discreet distance, and O'Kane and Mart went on with their game, but all three were listening, of course they were—if not for therapeutic reasons, then for curiosity's sake; that, and to poke a hole, however small, in the tight fabric of their boredom.

Five minutes into the conversation, Mr. McCormick's voice suddenly came up in a froglike croak. "Did you see Dr. Hoch's scar?"

There was a silence while she responded, and if O'Kane strained to hear over the crackle of the fire and the ambient sounds of the house, he could just make out the faintest whisper on the other end of the line, and it was funny—she could have been halfway around the world for all the faintness of her voice, but here she was right downstairs. That must have been odd for Mr. McCormick, because he knew where she was as well as anybody. But then he was used to it, O'Kane figured. Sure. And what a thing to get used to—to have to get used to—like the prisoner in solitary who falls in love with the mouse that shares his cell or the galley slave who comes to like the feel of the oar in his hand.

But now Mr. McCormick was saying something about cuts—his singsong chant, "one slit, one slit, one slit" creeping into it. "I can be cut too," he said. "Sh-shaving. In my throat. Ever think of that?"

She was saying something, the tiniest whisper of a mechanical squawk. The fire snapped. Mart stretched and something popped in his shoulders.

"You're in Washington!" Mr. McCormick suddenly shouted. "With me-men! You're in Washington all alone, ar-aren't you? I know you are, I know, and do you kn-know what Sc-Scobble did to his wife, or— or almost did, because she was, was UNFAITHFUL?" And he roared out this last so that the doctor jumped and O'Kane had to fight himself to keep from getting up and pacing round the room.

She said something back, trying to calm him, Now, Stanley, you know better—

"Do you know?" he roared.

Silence on the other end. Apparently she didn't.

And then, in a voice as calm as it was clear and unobstructed, he was quoting, quoting a poem:

> *Scobble for whoredom whips his wife and cries*
> *He'll slit her nose; but blubbering she replies,*
> *"Good sir, make no more cuts i' th' outward skin,*
> *One slit's enough to let adultery in."*

He stood there poised over the phone a long moment, and whether Katherine was making any reply to this or not, O'Kane never knew, but he felt his heart turn over and his eyes were burning as if he'd got caustic soda in them. He hadn't given it much thought, Mr. McCormick locked away here in his tower and she out there in the world, but of course she was unfaithful to him, how could she not be, Ice Queen or no? It had been twelve years at least. And how could any woman go without it as long as that?

THE MATCH

OF THE YEAR

When Katherine refused him, all but laughing in his face on that rainy thick-bodied September night with the horses clopping stupidly through the streets and the clock thundering doom in his ears, Stanley got to his feet, made a curt bow and bolted for the door, deaf to her calls and pleas. "Stanley, what are you doing?" she cried, springing up in alarm. "I was just . . . I thought we were—" she protested, hurrying after him, but he never hesitated, not even to retrieve his hat and coat, flinging himself down the stairs and out into the rain. "Stanley!" she called, her voice echoing down the stairway and out the open door. "Be reasonable! You've got to give me time!"

He never even heard her. He was running, the hair hanging wet in his face, his collar askew and his shirtfront soaked through to the skin, and he ran all the way back to the hotel, arms pumping, elbows flailing, eyes flashing white. Pedestrians fell away from him beneath the bonnets of their umbrellas like so many wilted toadstools, carriages swerved to avoid him as he slashed across the street, dogs barked at his heels. "Watch where you're going," someone growled and a police officer shouted out to him, but he paid no heed. He never felt the cobblestones beneath his feet or the raindrops on his face, didn't smell the wet richness of the old stones or the barnyard ferment of the horse dung in the gutters, didn't notice the way the night gathered around the streetlights as if to smother them.

She'd laughed at him. Refused even to take him seriously. Made a joke of the whole thing. But then why wouldn't she? He was a fool, ungainly, stupid, the least likely suitor in the world, not half the man Butler Ames was. What had he been thinking? A woman like Katherine could have her pick of all the men in the world, and why would he ever think she'd stoop to consider someone like him?

The clerk at the front desk gave him a startled look when he burst through the door in his wild-eyed, rain-soaked, hatless frenzy. "Are you all right, sir?" he asked, practically shouting, and the bellhop rounded the corner at a dead run. "Have you been injured? Should I call a doctor?"

"The bill," Stanley wheezed, and what had become of his voice? He pounded his breastbone with an urgent fist. "I want to, to settle up."

"Sir?" the clerk said, making a question of it, and then he took a closer look at Stanley's eyes and collar and the water dripping from his nose and chin, and changed his tone. "Yes, sir," he said, all servility and unctuous concern. "I have it right here. Mr. McCormick, isn't it?"

"I'll be wanting my motorcar brought round."

Again the clerk lapsed into amazement. He flashed a nervous look at the bellhop. "Sir?"

"My automobile. From the stables out back. I'll need it brought round, at, at once."

"But sir, it's nearly midnight and our motor man has gone off duty — I'm afraid no one here can operate the machine, sir, and besides, don't you know it's raining?"

Stanley was extracting bills from his wallet and laying them out in a neat row on the marble countertop. "Never mind," he said, "I'll fetch it myself. And please, just put this toward the bill, and, and keep the change."

"What about your luggage, sir?" The clerk was shouting at his retreating form, but Stanley never looked back.

The Mercedes wasn't equipped with a top, but that didn't faze Stanley. He draped a rug over his knees, wrapped himself in a tan duster, settled his saturated scalp beneath a wide-crowned felt hat and started off down the dark street in a roar of backfiring cylinders and ratcheting gears. The rain drove down in silver sheets and beat off the dash and the seats till there was a regular stream flowing between his feet and out over the running board. His hat collapsed and his goggles steamed up. The wind cut through him. And once he left the city, heading for the Adirondacks and his mother, the blackness closed over him and the thin stream of illumination from the headlamps was all but swallowed up in it. He couldn't see a thing.

Still, he kept going. He was in shock, so hurt and mortified he felt like a burnt-out cinder, immolated in shame, and he had no other thought than to make it home as quickly as he could. He hurtled through the night, spooking foxes, skunks and opossums and striking terror in the breast of every slumbering horse and stertorous cow within earshot, and through it all he was picturing the yellow pine camp on Saranac Lake with its six-foot-high fireplace and overstuffed couches and a hundred rustic nooks and niches where he could burrow deep and lick his festering wounds.

Katherine had rejected him. That was the fact of his life. It was his sorrow and his burden and it wet him through and hurled wind in his teeth and basted him in mud. Inevitably, though, as the night wore on and the car rocked and lurched its way through the storm, the thunder of the elements and the even, unbroken whine of the engine began to soothe him. Sure. He was making good time, conquering the night, alone and adventuring, and he got as far as Westborough before he took a wrong turn, blew out both front tires simultaneously and sank to the axles in an evil-smelling plastic mud that sucked the boots from his feet the minute he abandoned the car.

There were no lights anywhere. But he labored on, barefooted, and the night was hallucination enough for him. He followed one road to another and on to the next till it was dawn and still raining and a farmhouse loomed up out of the gloom like an island at sea. The farmer obliged him by taking him back into town—which he'd somehow managed to circumvent by a good five miles during his nocturnal ramblings—and then wishing him the very best of everything as he stood shivering and shoeless on the platform at the Westborough train station. He caught the first train to Albany and hired a man and a coach to take him up to Saranac as he huddled sleepless on the cold leather seat, Katherine's face slipping in and out of his consciousness and a whole host of unattributed voices chanting in his ears till he had to put his hands up and force them shut.

Naturally, he caught cold.

And his mother, brisk and censorious, orbited his bed day and night as if all the doctors and serving girls on earth had been carried off by the plague. She forced beef broth on him every fifteen minutes, deluged him with syrups and tonics, scalded him with mentholated vapors and hot water bottles. "It all comes of womanizing," she scolded, wiping his nose with a camphor-scented handkerchief.

"Womanizing? I wasn't—"

"Well, what do you call it then? Certainly not courting in any sense of the word as I know it, not with a young woman your own mother has never laid eyes on in her life."

"But I just met her—"

"And another thing—I've been asking around this past week and I'm told that your Miss Katherine Dexter is a cold fish if there ever was one, the sort of spoiled young woman who wouldn't even give a proper tip to her own mother's maid. She's entirely scientific, is what I hear, practically an atheist, like this odious Englishman with his descent of man and his monkeys and all the rest of it, and she had no more idea of worshiping the Lord than a naked aborigine."

Stanley breathed vapors and swallowed broth, watching the leaves shrivel and fall outside his window and listening to the lake slap mournfully at the shingle, and every day he wrote Katherine a letter, sometimes as long as twenty or thirty pages, and every day he had one of the servants take it down to the post office. He didn't have an opportunity to gaze in the mirror much—his mother insisted he stay in bed—but as he lay there brooding he began to see how ridiculous he must look in Katherine's eyes. He felt he had to explain himself to her, and the beginning of any credible explanation had to take into account his shortcomings—if he wanted to be honest with her. And he did want to be honest. He had to be. Because this was no mere flirtation or passing fancy—this was the whole world and everything in it.

One of his shorter letters, which ran to fifteen pages, painstakingly indited in an unrestrained flood tide of tottering consonants and tail-lashing vowels, began like this, without date or salutation:

I know you know I am as useless as a stone in your path, and no one is more conscious of that than I, a man who has never accomplished a thing in all his twenty-nine years, a blot on society, a parasite who never earns a cent by the sweat of his brow but feeds off the poor and oppressed in the name of "Capitalism." I have no talent for anything, I've never cultivated my mind, I'm consumed by degrading thoughts all the day long and half the nights, too, and live in a putrid scum of sin. I cannot blame you for refusing me. In fact, I applaud you and urge you to prefer Butler Ames or any other man over me, because I esteem you above all women and want only the best for you. Life to me is as dull as the grave and I live only to beg and pray for your happiness. You are all and everything to me and I hope you will believe me when I tell you I am not fit to lick the dirt from your shoes, if any dirt would ever adhere to them, which I doubt . . .

He realized he'd gone a bit overboard, but then once he fixated on something he just couldn't seem to let it go, and his letters became more and more slavish and self-denigrating until even Fu Manchu would have seemed wholesome compared to the Stanley Stanley exposed.

Katherine's replies were brief and never alluded to his letters, not in the slightest. She wrote of the weather, her mother's latest contretemps with a milliner or maître d', the gustatory habits of the checkered garter snake. She didn't specifically prohibit him from visiting (though she reminded him of how deeply absorbed she was in her studies), and so he saw his opportunity and took the train for Boston as soon as his mother let him out of bed. The first time—in early October—he stayed on for a week, and then, at the end of November, for two weeks more. He was rewarded for his perseverance by Mrs. Dexter—"Please, Stanley, call me Josephine"—who sat with him in the parlor every night through both of his visits, regaling him with reminiscences of her youth as he worked his way dutifully through the soggy fish-paste sandwiches and poppy seed cakes and pot after pot of undrinkable tea. But it was worth it, because Katherine seemed genuinely pleased to see him, shining like a seal and flush with her accumulation of knowledge, and when she could squeeze a social hour or two into her schedule, she permitted him to take her out to the theater or a concert.

At Christmas, she came to Chicago to stay with a girlfriend while her mother was in Europe, and Stanley was elated. He and Nettie had retreated to Rush Street when the weather turned bitter in the Adirondacks, and though he hadn't felt up to going back to work yet he'd begun sketching again and had done half a dozen portraits of Katherine in a brown wash over chalk and brown ink—all from a single photograph she'd given him. Of course, he was no good as an artist and had no right to attempt a portrait of her—it would take a Pintoricchio or a Cellini to do justice to her—but still he thought he'd managed to capture something she might find interesting and he'd been wrestling with the idea of another visit to Boston to present her with one of the sketches. Or maybe two of them. Or all six. He could barely restrain himself, bombarding her with flowers and telegrams, sick with the thought that Butler Ames or some other oily competitor was getting the jump on him and yet not wanting to seem overeager, when he got her letter informing him that she was coming to Chicago on the nineteenth to visit Nona Martin, of the upholstering Martins, and he melted away in a sizzle of anticipation like a pat of butter in a hot pan.

When the train arrived, Stanley was waiting at the station with his chauffeur and his new car, a Packard equipped with a tonneau cover for the passenger seat. He was standing there like a sentinel when she stepped down from the train, his arms laden with flowers, three boxes of candy and the most recent of the portraits, wrapped in brown paper. The train was fifteen minutes late and he'd been practicing his smile so long his gums had dried out and somehow managed to stick to the inner lining of his mouth, so he had a bit of trouble with the speech he'd rehearsed. "Katherine," he cried, taking her hand in an awkward fumble of flowers and candy while the chauffeur negotiated the transfer of her luggage from the porter, "I can't begin to tell you how much this means to me, your coming here to Chicago—your visit, I mean—because this is the high point of my miserable, foul, utterly worthless existence, and I, I—"

She was wearing a fur coat and the smell of the body-heated air caught in its grip was intoxicating. She lifted the veil of her hat to reveal a smile and two glad and glowing eyes. "Stanley!" she exclaimed. "What a surprise! It's so thoughtful of you to come meet me, but you didn't have to go out of your way, really you didn't." And then she let out a kind of squeal and fell into the arms of a girl in a fox coat with hair the color of old rope and Stanley felt as if he'd been rejected all over again. But no, this was Nona Martin and she was pleased to meet him—Katherine had told her so much about him—and pleased too to accept a ride in his motorcar.

Stanley was lit up like a bonfire, electrified—*Katherine has told me so much about you*—as he squeezed in beside the girls, struggling all the while with the framed sketch in its heavy brown wrapping. Katherine was right there, right there beside him, and he could smell her perfume and the sweet mint of her breath. "For you," he said, handing her the portrait in a confusion of wrists and elbows and the constricting bulk of coats and mufflers and gloves, "I—I hope you won't be, well, I hope you—I mean, I, uh, I took the liberty of drawing, uh, *you—*"

She smiled her secret thin-lipped smile, tore away the paper and held the portrait high up to the light as the car banged away over the streets like a roller coaster and all three of them had to hold onto their hats. "It's beautiful," she said, and she turned the smile on him now and showed him her teeth, the teeth he loved, and the other girl came into the picture suddenly, her wide grinning seraphic face looming over Katherine's shoulder, and she was cooing praise too. And Stanley? Well, it was winter in Chicago, the sun weak as milk, the wind howling, ice everywhere, but it was high summer inside of him and all the boats beating across the lake in full sail.

Even then, though, even as he sailed through the streets on the fresh breeze that was Katherine, the heavy seas were building. His mother wasn't going to let him go without a fight, and when Katherine and Miss Martin came to dinner two nights later, the storm broke in all its fury. Nettie had insisted on a formal eight-course dinner and a guest list of eighteen, including Favill and Bentley and their wives, Cyrus Jr. and his wife, Missy Hammond, Anita (who'd been a widow going on eight years now) and an assortment of dried-up female religious fa-natics in their sixties and seventies who hadn't found anything pleasant to say to anyone since the Battle of Bull Run. She sat at the head of the table, while Cyrus took up the honorary position at the far end, and she seated Katherine across from Stanley and as close to herself as she could bear—that is, with a buffer of one crabbed Presbyterian mummy on her immediate right and another on her left.

The soup had barely touched the table when she cleared her throat to get Katherine's attention and said, in a voice that was meant to carry all the way down to Cyrus's end of the table, "And so, Miss Dexter, perhaps, as a scientist, you'd like to give us your opinion of Mr. Charles Darwin and his perversion of everything God tells us in the Bible?"

Katherine looked into Stanley's eyes a moment and he could see the steel there, case-hardened and inflexible, before she turned to his mother, looking past Mrs. Tuggle, the mummy on her right. "My training has been in the sciences, yes, Mrs. McCormick, and I do tend to take a scientific view of phenomena beyond our ken, but I must remind you that Darwin's theories are only that: theories."

There was a silence. Every conversation had died. Anita was staring, Cyrus Jr. fussing with his shirt studs. Favill smirked. The mummies faintly nodded their wizened heads.

"And what is that supposed to mean?" Nettie had knitted her hands in front of her, as if she were praying for strength. "Do you believe in all this sacrilegious bunk or don't you?"

Katherine sighed. Lifted the water glass to her lips, took a sip and then set it down again, in perfect control. "Since you ask, Mrs. McCormick, I have to say that I do believe in Darwin's theories as to the origin of our species through evolution. I find his arguments utterly convincing."

Stanley was about to say something, anything, a comment on the weather or the soup or the way the electric lights were holding up, just to throw his mother off the scent, but she was too quick for him.

"And this Negro music the young seem so eager to dance to, this 'Maple Leaf Rag' and all the rest of it, I suppose you find this sort of thing proper, do you?"

"I'm afraid I don't have much time for dancing, Mrs. McCormick," Katherine said, and she glanced up and down the length of the table before coming back to her again. "I'm very busy with my studies."

"Yes," Nettie said, all but spitting it out, "so I'm told. Snakes, isn't it?"

The following afternoon, in a bleak cold rinsed-out light that made the whole city look as if it had been sunk to the bottom of Lake Michigan, Stanley and his mother escorted Katherine to Harold's place in the landau—Nettie wouldn't dream of setting foot in a motorcar—and had a tense lunch with Harold and Edith. The verbal sparring resumed over fricasseed chicken, boiled onions, beef tongue and ice cream, and continued through the farewells and out into the carriage. Stanley was at a loss. He should have been ebullient, irrepressible, kicking up his heels and shouting hosannas, because here were the two people he cared most about in the world, together at last, but instead he felt as if he'd gone into battle, a bewildered infantryman caught between opposing generals. "And your family, Katherine? I hear your father has passed on," Nettie said, "and your mother never entertains," and Katherine came back with, "Tell me about your other daughter, the older one — Mary Virginia?"

They'd just turned into Rush Street when Nettie suddenly rapped at the window and ordered the carriage to a stop. Perplexed, the driver climbed down and came to the window. "Ma'am?" he said, showing his teeth in a nervous little grin.

"Where are you taking us?"

"Home, ma'am. Six-seventy-five Rush Street."

"Rush Street? Have you lost you senses? We have a guest with us, and she needs to be transported all the way back out to Astor Street, to the Martin residence."

"But Mother," Stanley was saying, "I told Stevens to drop you first, since we're so close — I mean, there's no need for you to — "

"Drop *me*? Whatever are you talking about? *We've* invited Miss Dexter, and *we* shall see her home. Really, Stanley, I'm surprised at you — where are your manners?"

"No, I, well — I was going to, well, see Miss Dexter home myself, after I, after we — "

"Nonsense."

Katherine held her peace. Stevens stood there in the cold, the horses stamping and shuddering, the wind sending a fusillade of leaves and papers down the street in a sudden blast. Stanley was seated between the two women, and he didn't dare look at Katherine, not on this battleground, not now. "I was only thinking of you, Mother, what with your heart condition and knowing how hard it is on your legs and the circulation to your, well, your feet, to, to sit cooped up like this, and I just, well, I just thought you'd be more comfortable at home."

He watched his mother's face tighten a notch and then suddenly let go, like an overwound spring. "All right," she sighed, and now she was the invalid, the dying matriarch (who would, paradoxically, live another eighteen years in perfect health), too sick and enervated to fight. "It's very thoughtful of you, Stanley. Drive on, Stevens," she ordered in a diminished voice. And she was patient, biting her tongue until they'd

arrived and Stanley was helping her up the walk and into the vestibule
of the house while Katherine sat wrapped in her furs in the coach and
watched her own breath crystallize in the stinging air. Then, just as the
door shut behind them and Stanley was helping her off with her coat,
his mother murmured, "Yes, Stanley, you're right—and you're such a
dear to think of your poor old mother. Obviously, Stevens can see Miss
Dexter home on his own and there's no need at all for us to bother, with
the weather so bitter—and that wind. It could even snow, that's what
they're saying."

"But, but"—Stanley was holding his mother's coat out away from
him as if it were the pelt of some animal he'd just bludgeoned and
skinned—"I wanted to, that is I intended to take Katherine, I mean,
Miss Dexter—to see her, I mean, home, that is—"

His mother turned a trembling face to him and took hold of his arm.
"I won't hear of it."

"But no, no, you don't understand. Katherine's waiting for me."

"Nonsense. You're staying right here. You'll catch your death out in
that wind, and besides, it's not proper you being all alone with her like
that without a chaperone. Oh, maybe these modern girls think nothing
of it, but believe you me, I, for one, won't stand for it."

Before he could think, Stanley had jerked his arm away. The blood
was in his face, and he could hear the tick of the steam radiators and the
faint sound of carolers off down the street somewhere. "I'm going," he
said, "and don't try to stop me."

His mother's eyes boiled. Her face was like the third act of a
tragedy. She swung an imaginary sword and cleaved the head from his
body. "What," she said, "you defy me?"

Stanley clenched his jaw. "Yes."

And then they were struggling, actually wrestling at the doorway in
plain sight of Katherine, his mother clutching at his arm as if she were
drowning amid the crashing waves she herself had summoned up, and
Stanley tore his arm away again, and he didn't want to hurt her, not
physically or emotionally, but when he broke loose she collapsed to the
floor with a sob that sucked all the air out of him. It was the moment of
truth. The moment he'd been awaiting for thirty years. He drew himself
up, squared his shoulders and cinched the muffler tight against his
throat. "I'm going now," he said.

Katherine was waiting for him. Her eyes never left him as he emerged from the house, strode up the walk and climbed back into the carriage. He felt heroic, felt he could do anything—climb the Himalayas, beat back invading hordes, mush dogs across the frozen tundra. "Katherine," he said, and she rustled beside him, her face turned to his, the carriage moving now and the rest of the afternoon and the city and everything in it left to them and them alone, "Katherine, I just wanted to, to—"

"Yes?" Her voice was lush and murmurous, floating up to meet his out of the depths of the gently swaying compartment. A fading watery light flickered at the windows. Stanley dreamed he was in a submarine, rising up and up, insulated from everything.

"Well, to tell you—"

"Yes?"

"About Debs, Debs and what he said in the paper the other—the other, well, day. It was the most significant thing I've—" but he couldn't go on. Not really. Not anymore.

In February, in Boston, they became secretly engaged. Stanley had come down by train and set himself up with rooms at the Copley Plaza just after Groundhog Day. After a week of hemming and hawing and discoursing on Jack London's childhood, labor unions, black lung disease and the will he'd executed leaving all his moneys and possessions to be divided equally among the 14,000 McCormick workers, he put another hypothetical proposal to her and she amazed and exalted him by accepting. But only on the condition that they keep the engagement confidential till the end of the term, because the papers were sure to take it up—BOSTON SOCIALITE TO WED M'CORMICK HEIR—and it would just be too much of a distraction in light of her thesis and exams. They had a celebratory dinner with Josephine, who swore to keep their secret and delivered a breathless monologue on the cruciality—*Was that a word?* of preserving the Dexter line, not to mention the Moores and McCormicks—*And who were his mother's people?*—and how she hoped Katherine wouldn't stop at four or five children, what with the threat of disease in the world today, and did Stanley know how they'd lost Katherine's brother, the sweetest boy there ever was?

He did. And he hung his head and pulled mournfully at his cuffs and offered Josephine his handkerchief, but he was soaring, absolutely, no dogs in the mirror now. Katherine loved him. Incredibly. Improbably. Beyond all doubt or reason. He mooned at her across the table through the soup and fish courses and kept on mooning and beaming and winking till the dessert was in crumbs and the coffee cups drained, and after she'd pecked a goodnight kiss to the hollow of his right cheek, he phoned up an old friend from Princeton and went out to drink champagne into the small hours of the morning.

The next afternoon he was back at Katherine's door, pale and shaking, his head stuffed full of gauze and his eyes aching in their sockets. No one was home and the maid wouldn't let him in, so he sat on the stoop in a daze and watched a skin of ice thicken over a puddle in the street until Katherine came home and found him there. "I can't let you do this," he said, rising from the cold stone in a delirium of shame and self-abnegation.

She was in her furs and a scarf, the brim of her hat faintly rustling in a wind that came up the street from the Bay. "Do what?" she said. "What are you talking about?" Her smile faded. "And what are you doing out here in this weather — do you want to catch your death?"

Slouching, miserable, crapulous, chilled to the bone, his veins plugged with suet and his fingertips dead to all sensation, he could only croak out the words: "Marry me."

She puzzled a minute, her bag and books clutched tight in her arms, her eyes working, her hat brim fluttering, and then she decided he was joking. "Marry you?" she echoed, talking through a grin. "Are you asking me again? Or is that the imperative form of the verb?"

"No, I . . . I didn't mean that. I mean, I can't let you do this to yourself, throw your life away, on, on someone like me."

She tried to make light of it, tried to slip her arm through his and lead him up the stairs, but he broke away, his face working. "Stanley?" she said. And then: "It's all right now. Calm down. Come on, let's discuss it inside where it's warm."

"No." He stood there shivering, fitfully clenching and unclenching his hands. There was ice in his mustache where his breath had condensed and frozen. "I don't deserve you. I'm no good. I've never — I won't ever . . . Didn't you read my letters?"

The wind picked up. Two men in overcoats with bowlers clamped manually to their heads went by on the opposite side of the street. Katherine looked uncertain all of a sudden. "I have a confession to make," she said, ducking her head and pulling at the fingers of her gloves. "I'm afraid I didn't read them, not all of them. They were beautifully written, I don't mean that . . . it's just that they were so, I don't know, depressing. Can you forgive me?"

Stanley was thunderstruck. He forgot everything, forgot where he was and what he was doing and why he'd come. "You didn't read them?"

In the smallest voice: "No."

A long moment passed, both of them shivering, a couple in a silver-gray victoria giving them a queer look as they trundled past in a clatter of wheels, hoofs and bells. From down the street came the voices of children at play, shrill with excitement. "Well, you should read them," Stanley said, his face drawn and white. "Maybe then you'd . . . you'd change your mind."

She was firm, Katherine, unshakable and tough, and now she did loop her arm through his. "I'll never change my mind," she said. "Here"—all business now—"help me with my things, will you, please?" She handed him her books before he could protest and tugged him toward the door.

He tucked the books firmly under his arm and allowed himself to be led up the steps, where Katherine let her handbag dangle from her wrist and rang the bell rather than fumble for her key. "The letters," he said, and they weren't finished with the subject yet. "They—they're nothing, they barely scratch the surface. You don't know. You can't know. You see, I'm"—he turned his head sharply away from her—"I'm a sexual degenerate."

"Stanley, really," she said, and the maid's footsteps were audible now, echoing down the hallway like gunshots. "You have to calm yourself—it can't be as bad as all that."

He tried to pull away, but she held fast to him. "It *is*," he cried in a kind of whinny, his frozen breath spilling from him like some vital essence. "And I have to tell you this, I have to," the maid at the door now, the tumbler clicking in the lock. "In all honesty, I can't—what I mean is, Katherine, you don't understand. I'm, I'm"—and he dropped his voice to a ragged chuffing whisper—"I'm a *masturbator*."

"Good afternoon, madame," the maid said, pulling back the door. "And sir."

Katherine's face showed nothing. "Good afternoon, Bridget," she said, ducking out from under the woolen scarf with a graceful flick of her neck and reaching up to unpin her hat in the vestibule with its mahogany-framed mirror, Tiffany lamp and Nottingham curtains. Stanley was staring down at the rug. "Bring us some tea in the parlor, would you?" she said, addressing the maid. "And some biscuits."

"Oh, I can't—" Stanley said, still studying the pattern of the rug, "I really, I have to go, I—"

"We need to talk, Stanley." There was no arguing with the the tone of Katherine's voice. She made an impatient gesture. "Come, give Bridget your coat and we'll sit by the fire—you must be chilled through."

Again he let himself be led, slumped over and shuffling, a man of sixty, eighty, a hundred, his face transfigured with pain and mortification. She helped him to the couch and sat beside him. They listened in silence as the clock chimed the half hour—four-thirty, and starting to get dark. Stanley shifted uneasily in his seat. "I'm so dirty," he groaned.

"You're not. Not at all."

"I'm not suited for marriage. I've done filthy things."

She seized his hand, and she was as wrought-up as he was, but it wasn't his revelation that disturbed her—certainly masturbation wasn't a nice habit, not the sort of thing you'd discuss over dinner or cards, but she was a biologist, after all, and she took it in stride—no, it was the idea of it that got to her, the mechanics of the act itself. She kept picturing Stanley, alone in his room and touching himself and maybe even thinking of her while he was doing it, and that sent a thrill through her. She could see him, stripped to his socks, his long strong legs, the pale hair of his thighs and chest and abdomen, Stanley, her fiancé, her man. She loved him. She wanted him. She wanted to be there in that bedroom with him.

He was inexperienced, like her, she was sure of it. And that was the beauty of the whole thing. Here he was, a big towering physical specimen of a male, and yet so docile and sweet, hers to lead and shape and build into something extraordinary, a father like her father. And there was no chance of that with Butler Ames and the rest—they were smirking and wise, overgrown fraternity boys who tried women on for size, like hats, and went to prostitutes with no more thought or concern than they went to the barber or the tailor. But Stanley, Stanley was malleable, unformed, innocent still—and that was why everything depended on getting him away from his mother, that crippling combative stultifying monster of a woman who'd made him into a pet and all but emasculated him in the process. He needed to get free, that was all, and then he could grow.

Katherine squeezed his hand as the maid clattered into the room with the tea things. "It's nothing to worry about," she said. "Really. It's your nerves, that's all."

The room was warm, secure, wrapped up in its particularity, suspended in time. Katherine waited till the maid had set down the things and left. "It doesn't matter what you've done," she whispered, and she wanted to kiss the side of his face, the bulge of his jaw, the place at the corner of his right eye where a lock of hair dangled like a thread of the richest tapestry, "because you have me now."

In June, their engagement was officially announced, and the papers in Boston, New York, Washington and Chicago all ran stories trumpeting their wealth, family connections and accomplishments, and a dozen smaller papers, including the *Princeton Tiger*, printed prominent notices. Stanley was described as "the Harvester Heir" in most of these accounts, a "motoring enthusiast" and "amateur artist," and Katherine was, simply, "the Boston socialite and scientific graduate of the Massachusetts Institute of Technology." The *Boston Post* decreed their engagement "a betrothal of the highest expectation and promise" and the *Transcript* was moved to pronounce it "the match of the year."

Josephine was in her glory, fielding telegrams, canvassing caterers, bakers and florists and prattling her way across the Back Bay through one parlor after another. Nettie was less pleased. Her letters—separate letters—to Stanley and Katherine seemed to accept the betrothal as a fait accompli, but she made no bones about her disapproval of the match, especially in her letter to Katherine, in which she questioned her future daughter-in-law's morals, education (there was too much of it), taste in millinery and footwear, dietary habits, religiosity and commitment to her last and most precious child. The word "love" never came up. As for Stanley, he seemed to be in permanent transit between Chicago and Boston, his nerves on edge, obsessing over the smallest details—"What sort of rice should we provide for the guests to shower us with, arborio or Texas long-grain?"—and every once in a while, dashing into the men's room at the station or coming through the doors

at the Copley Plaza, he began to think he was seeing that dog again in
the glass. But he tried to brush it off—not to worry, the smallest of
things—and instead concentrated on collecting all the announcements
from the various newspapers and mounting them on red construction
paper as a memento for Katherine. They set a date in the fall, the bride's
favorite season.

It was then, just when everything seemed to be going forward and
all the major hurdles had been leapt, that things began to break down.
Suddenly Stanley was having palpitations—he couldn't seem to stop jittering, bouncing up off his feet, shaking out his fingers till they rattled
like castanets, twisting his neck and gyrating his head in response to
some frenetic inner rhythm—and all he could talk about was Mary Virginia. Mary Virginia and his genitals, that is.

He came bobbing and jittering into the house on Commonwealth
Avenue early one morning two weeks or so after the engagement had
been announced, his eyes fluttering, his face in flux, talking so fast no
one could understand him. He frightened the maid, upset the cook and
chased Josephine's cat all the way up into the rafters of the attic in an
excess of zeal. Katherine, who'd been dressing in her room, came out
into the hall to see what the commotion was, and she watched Stanley
dart past her up the stairs in pursuit of the cat, never even giving her a
glance. When she caught up with him on the steps to the attic, he couldn't
seem to explain himself—he was afflicted with logorrhea, the words
tripping over one another and piling up end to end, and he was going
on and on about something she couldn't quite catch, aside from the frequent repetition of his sister's name. She'd never seen him like this—his
eyes bugging out, his hair a mess, every cell and fiber of him rushing
hell-bent down the tracks like a runaway freight train—and she was
frightened. She managed to get him outside, out in the sunshine and
fresh air, to try to walk it out of him, whatever it was.

They walked the length of Commonwealth Avenue, from the Public
Garden to Hereford Square and back—or actually, it was more of a jog
than a walk, Stanley setting an accelerated, stiff-kneed pace and
Katherine clinging to his arm and struggling to keep up. The whole
while Stanley kept shaking and trembling and running on about Mary
Virginia and her illness and some sort of mysterious "whiteness," as if
she were lost in a blizzard somewhere instead of quietly ensconced with
her nurse and doctor on a grand and faultless estate in Arkansas. It

wasn't till they'd passed the house for the second time, Stanley wet through with perspiration and the neighbors giving them looks that ranged from shock to alarm to amusement, that Katherine began to discern what he was driving at.

Leaping along, straining to look up into his face, her breathing labored and her mood beginning to fray, she managed to gasp out a little speech. "There's no mental illness in my family, Stanley," she wheezed on an insuck of breath. "On my mother's or my father's side, so the chances are very remote that our children will suffer, if that's what's worrying you, and it is, isn't it?"

"She's sick," he said, never breaking stride. "Very sick."

"Yes," she gasped, "I know, and it's right of you to bring it up now that we're going to be married, but I really don't—can't we stop here, just for a minute?"

It was as if she'd waved a flag in front of him or given a sudden jerk at a leash—he stopped as abruptly as he'd started, his feet jammed together, one arm clasped in hers, sweat standing out on his brow and his hat soaked under the brim in a dark expanding crescent. "It's not just that," he said, and he was talking not to her but to the ground beneath their feet. "It's my genitals."

"Your *what?*" They were stopped on the walk in front of a yard full of roses. Bees dug into the blossoms. The perfume of the flowers wafted out into the street. Everything had such an air of calm and normalcy— except Stanley. Stanley was making faces and staring down at his shoes. And that wouldn't have been so bad except that two smart young women suddenly emerged from the yard under a trellis of white and yellow roses and gave them a long look before brusquely stepping around them.

"My genitals," Stanley repeated.

Katherine studied him a moment, his nostrils like two holes drilled in his head, his eyes locked on the ground and every other part of him jerking into motion and relaxing again in a long continuous shudder. She waited till the women were out of earshot. "Yes," she said. "All right. What about them?"

"I—well—I—what I mean is, maybe they've been . . . damaged."

"Damaged?"

"From, you know, from my *habits*—"

She was a patient woman. And she loved him. But this wasn't the sort of romance she'd dreamed about, this wasn't being swept off her feet and wooed with tender intimacies and anticipatory pleasures—this was psychodrama, this was crazy. It was hot and she was perspiring and she'd meant to go out with her mother and look at some lace for her trousseau, and now here she was making a spectacle of herself in the middle of the street and Stanley carrying on over nothing—yet again. She was fed up. The furrow she was unaware of crept into the gap between her eyebrows. "If you're so worried," she said, "then why don't you go see a doctor," and she turned and stalked off down the street without him.

He called her from his hotel later in the day to tell her he was taking her advice and catching the next train to Chicago to see a specialist and that he'd return at the end of the week and she shouldn't worry. But by nightfall he was back on her doorstep, Bridget in hysterics, her mother's face drawn up tight in a knot, and Stanley acting as oddly as he had that morning—or even more oddly. He'd boarded the train and gone as far as New London, he said, still talking as if a howling mob were at his heels and this was the last speech of his life, but then he'd got to thinking about their situation and had changed trains and come back because there were a few things that just couldn't wait a week—or even another day.

She looked at him a long moment. "What things?" she asked, ushering him into the parlor and closing the door behind them.

He seemed confused, agitated, his movements jerky and clonic. He knocked over a vase of gladioli, water spreading a dark stain across the tabletop, and didn't even seem to notice. "Things," he said darkly. "Vital things."

She watched the water fan out, seeking the lowest point, and begin a slow, steady drip onto the carpet. She'd made a date with Betty Johnston to go visiting that evening and she was already impatient and exasperated. "You'll have to be more specific, I'm afraid," she said. "If I don't know what these vague 'things' are, how can you expect me to discuss them with you?"

He kept shuddering and twitching, shifting his weight from one foot to the other like a tightrope walker. "About us," he said. "About our, about my—"

"Genitals?" she offered.

He averted his face. "You shouldn't say that."

"Say what? Isn't that what this is all about? Your genitals? Not to mention hypochondria. Correct me if I'm mistaken, but isn't that the subject under discussion? Didn't you just leave this morning to go to a specialist and clear up the suspense?" Suddenly she felt very tired. The whole thing seemed hopeless, as if she'd been wrapped up in a blanket and pitched headfirst into the dark river that was Stanley, and no coming up for air. "Listen, Stanley," she said, and she could hear the rustle of skirts in the hallway, her mother and Bridget listening at the door and fidgeting with their sleeves and buttons, "you've got to get a grip on yourself. You're acting *crazy*, don't you realize that?"

He stopped his quivering then, automatically and without hesitation, and for the first time he seemed to notice the overturned vase and the dripping water, and when he bent for it she assumed he was going to set it upright, to rectify the problem and make amends. But when he lifted it from the table—heavy leaded crystal with a sharp crenellated edge—and kept lifting it till it was cocked behind his ear like a football, she couldn't help opening her mouth and letting out a tightly wound shriek of fear and outrage even as the mirror behind her dissolved in a flood of silvered glass.

Her mother, the claws of disappointment raking her face, agreed that yes, it might be for the better if she were to go to Europe for a while to think things over. But it wasn't the end of the world—everyone had second thoughts, "even your own mother, and look what a saint your father turned out to be." It was normal—entirely normal—and nothing to cry over. So she should dry up her tears and pack her things and think of it as the vacation she so rightfully deserved after all those grinding hours she'd put in at the Institute. That's right. Go ahead now. And hush.

The next morning, while Stanley was on his way to Chicago to consult his specialist about the arcana of his body and mind, Katherine directed Bridget and the two younger maids to begin packing her things for an indefinite stay at Prangins. She'd made up her mind—it was the only thing to do—and yet why did she feel so sick and miserable? She couldn't sleep. Couldn't eat breakfast or lunch. She ached and creaked like a ship at sea, converting dry handkerchiefs to wet ones, her eyes and nose running in spate, and she spent the afternoon in bed with a headache. The maids tiptoed by the door and the clothing whispered in the hallway, the hatboxes, the steamer trunks, all these particles of her life in sudden motion. She lay there through the long afternoon, watching the curtains trace the sun, and she'd never felt so desolated in her life, not since her father and brother left this earth.

But there was no sense in crying—Stanley was too much for her, too big a reclamation project, she could see that now, and everything he was, the vision she had of him, lay shattered on the parlor floor. She had to get away, she knew that, but it wasn't going to be easy. Because even while she grieved and fought to steel herself against him and the kind of life she'd hoped for, she kept thinking of him in the grip of his mother, of Nettie, the vampire who would drain him till he was a withered doddering white-haired husk of himself sitting at the foot of her deathbed and the dust gathering like snow. Katherine couldn't let her do that to Stanley—no man deserved such a fate—and what's more, she couldn't just walk off and leave the playing field to Nettie. She was a Dexter, and the Dexters never quit on anything.

Suddenly she was up and scattering the maids, bending over the trunks and suitcases and unpacking in a raw fury of motion, each dress and skirt and shirtwaist returned to its hanger a lightening of the load, but that was no good either, and before long she found herself slowing and slowing until the process began to reverse itself and she was packing all over again. And why? Because she was going to Switzerland, to Geneva, to Prangins, and she was going to stay there until all this was sorted out and she could look at herself in the mirror and say that nothing in the world could compare to being Mrs. Stanley Robert McCormick. And if she couldn't? If she honestly couldn't? Well, there was always Butler Ames—or the Butler Ames who would come after him.

The shadows were lengthening on the wall and the house had fallen into a bottomless well of silence when Bridget stuck her head in the door. Did madame need assistance? Katherine looked up. There were dresses everywhere, an avalanche of them, hats, coats, scarves, shoes. "Yes," she said, "yes," and by nightfall order reigned, everything packed, filed and arranged and her passage booked on a steamer leaving for Cherbourg three days hence.

How Stanley got wind of it, she would never know. But as the gangplank was drawn up and the anchor weighed and her mother and the servants standing solemnly amongst the crowd and waving handkerchiefs in a slow sad sweep, he suddenly appeared, a foot taller than anyone on the quay, a giant among men, hurtling through the crowd on the full tilt of his manic energy. She was hanging over the rail with a thousand other passengers, a handkerchief pressed tragically to her face and one white-gloved hand waving, waving, already bound over to the smell of the sea, coal smoke, dead fish and third-class cookery. And there he was, Stanley, Stanley Robert McCormick, standing tall in the June sun, shouting up to her amidst the pandemonium of voices and engines and the two irrevocable blasts of the ship's horn.

"Katherine!" he was shouting, and she could see his face and its diminished features as if from a cliff or the edge of a cloud, and somehow, even from that height, she could hear his voice piercing through the din as clearly as if he were standing beside her. "It's all right," he cried, waving something above his head, a sheet of paper, some sort of certificate, the boat drawing massively back now till it seemed as if it was the dock that was moving and she was stuck fast. "I can have"—and here the ship's horn intervened, the rumbling metallic basso obliterating all thought and comprehension and Stanley's voice trailing off into the faintest persistent whine of desperation and hope—"I can have *children!*"

6.

OF DEATH AND

BEGONIAS

O'Kane was eating a steak at Menhoff's on a wind-scoured November night when news of the Armistice came over the telegraph — belatedly, because the wires had been down since morning. The wind had kept people in, but there were a few couples having dinner under the aegis of Cody's chaste white candles and the usual crowd out in the barroom swallowing pickled eggs and gnawing pretzels while their beers sizzled yellow and their shots of whiskey and bourbon stood erect beside them like good soldiers. Nothing short of the apocalypse would have kept that crowd from exercising their elbows, and O'Kane meant to join them after a while, but for the moment he was enjoying his steak and his French-cut potatoes and his first piquant glass of beer while the wind buffeted the windows and made the place feel snug as a ship's cabin.

He was reading a bit in the paper about the completion of Las Tejas, a new Montecito palace modeled after the Casino of the sixteenth-century Villa Farnese in Viterbo, Italy, when Cody Menhoff himself came bursting out of the kitchen in a white apron singing, "The War's over! The War's over!" Actually, the dishwasher was the first to hear of it, beating a procession of shopowners, drummers and tomato-faced drunks by a matter of minutes. He'd been out back dumping a load of trash when he heard a hoot and looked up to see a pack of boys hurtling down the alley in a scramble of legs and white-capped knees, a flag flapping behind them like wash on a line. "What's the news?" he shouted, though he'd already guessed, and one of the boys stopped banging two trashcan lids together long enough to tell him that the Huns had made it official. He'd relayed the news to Cody, and Cody, a big Dutchman with a face like a butterchurn, roared through the place and set up drinks on the house for all comers.

Before long there was a string of cars going up and down the street honking their horns, and the front room began to fill up, wind or no wind—and this wasn't just a capricious breeze, this was a sundowner, the dried-out breath of the season that came tearing down out of the mountains in a regular cyclone, bane to all hats and shake roofs and the brittle rasping fronds of the palm trees. But there was no wind inside Menhoff's, except what the crowd was generating itself. People were cheering and making toasts and speeches and then somebody sat down at the piano and struck up the National Anthem and everybody sang along in a bibulous roar, and when they'd gone through it three times they sang "God Bless America," "Yankee Doodle" and "The Stars and Stripes Forever." It was heady and glorious, and though O'Kane had planned on limiting himself to two shots only (things had been slipping away from him lately and he was trying to curb himself) there was no stopping him after that. He got into the spirit of things, slapping backs, crowing out jokes and limericks, dancing an improvised jig with Mart, who'd turned up just past nine with Roscoe and a glowing high-crowned face of victory. By ten O'Kane was off in a corner, singing the old sad songs in a fractured moan of a voice, and when Roscoe came for him the next morning he had to vomit twice before he could get his suit on and go out to see how Mr. McCormick was receiving the news.

The celebration lasted a good six weeks, right on through Christmas. You could step into any place in town, from the lowest saloon with the pitted brass rail and the sawdust on the floor to Menhoff's and the dining room at the Potter, and there'd always be somebody there to raise a glass to the Armistice. And then it was Christmas, and you had to have a nip of the holiday cheer or you weren't properly alive, and a week after that the New Year floated in on a sea of dago wine and a raft of nasty rumors about the Drys and Prohibition and the women's vote, not to mention the influenza epidemic, and O'Kane told himself he'd taper off as soon as the deal went through with Jim Isringhausen for the orange grove he'd been saving for all his adult life—or most of it, anyway—because he'd have to celebrate that and no two ways about it.

He never missed a single day's work—only a drunk and an alcoholic boozer would fall down on his responsibilities like that—but he would go out to Riven Rock at eight A.M. with the fumes of his morning booster on his breath and practically beg Sam Wah to scramble him up a couple of eggs to settle his stomach. It was a bad time, his head always aching, the colors rinsed out of everything so that all the stage props of the paradise outside the door seemed faded and shabby, and he began to worry about winding up like his father, that flaming, bellicose, ham-fisted lump of humanity sunk permanently into the daybed and unable to keep a job for more than two weeks at a time. He had to cut back, he really did. And throughout the winter he promised himself he would. Soon.

Mr. McCormick seemed to continue his gradual improvement during this period, though the news of the Armistice hit him hard on two accounts. For one, he could no longer follow the offensives and mark up his maps and bury his nose in five or six different newspapers each day, and that left a widening gap in his life, though Dr. Hoch tried to interest him in any number of things, from growing orchids and learning the clarinet to lawn bowling and crossword puzzles. The second thing was his wife. Now that the War was over and women on their way to getting the vote, there was no excuse for Katherine to be away from him for so long a time. She hadn't been to Riven Rock since the previous Christmas, when he'd accused her in so many words of adultery, though she sent him weekly letters and packages of books, clothes, candies and new recordings for his Victrola. That was all right as far as it went. And Mr. McCormick appreciated it, but his wife was out there in the world and he wasn't, and the idea of it was a source of constant agitation, a low flame flickering under a pot and the water inside simmering to a boil.

O'Kane was in the upper parlor with Mr. McCormick, Mart and Dr. Hoch one day three weeks after the Armistice, when a letter from Katherine arrived with the morning mail. It had been a dull morning,

Hoch unusually silent and Mr. McCormick fretting round and haunting the rooms like a caged animal, and even the movie had failed to materialize because Roscoe had a touch of the grippe and hadn't been able to make the trip into Hollywood the previous evening, and there was nothing new from Flying A, just four years ago the biggest studio in the world and now about to fold up its wings and die. The winds were still blowing, tumbleweeds rocketing down out of nowhere and accumulating against the back door and every windowsill decorated with a ruler-perfect line of pale tan dust, and that made the atmosphere all the more oppressive. O'Kane's head was throbbing and his throat so dry it felt like a hole gouged out of the floor of Death Valley, but still he made an effort to engage Mr. McCormick in conversation and even began a much-interrupted game of chess with him. And Dr. Hoch, recognizing Mr. McCormick's restlessness as a symptom of something worse to come, ordered the sprinklers in the trees to be turned on, but instead of the usual anodynic whisper of falling water there was nothing but a kind of distant blast as of a firehose hitting a wall and the occasional tremor of the windowpanes as the wind attempted to make the glass permeable.

All three of them—O'Kane, Mart and Dr. Hoch—watched as Mr. McCormick accepted the mail from the butler through the iron grid of the door and dropped into an easy chair to read through it. The first two letters apparently didn't interest him, and after examining the return addresses and sniffing at the place where the envelopes had been sealed, he let them fall carelessly to the floor. But the third one was the charm, and after examining the writing on the face of the envelope for a long moment, he slit it open with a forefinger and settled down to read in a voice that was meant to be private but which kept breaking loose in various growls and squeals and a high scolding falsetto that seemed like another person's voice altogether. Mr. McCormick was some time over the letter, bits and pieces emerging into intelligibility now and then as his voice rose from a whisper to a shout and fell off again: *Jane Roessing's house—seven degrees above zero—you remember Milbourne—dog died—new hat—Mother down with influenza.*

There was a silence when he'd finished, and into the silence Dr. Hoch projected a question: "Any news?"

Mr. McCormick looked up blankly. "It's from K-Katherine."

The doctor, owlish and quizzical: "Oh?"

"She—she won't be coming till the night before, or the day, that is, the day before Christmas. Too busy, she says. War business, you know, mopping up. The—the suffrage movement. She's in Washington."

"Ah, what a shame," Dr. Hoch said, but his heart wasn't in it. He hadn't been feeling well himself lately, and he looked it, pale and shrunk into his collar, his face wrinkled and sectioned like a piece of fruit left out to dry in the sun. There was pain in his eyes, a cloudy scrim of it, and the dullness of resignation. He'd confided to O'Kane that he'd taken the job at Riven Rock for health reasons—the Pathological Institute had become too much for him, and the climate here, amongst the celebrated Santa Barbara spas, was bound to do him good. But it wasn't doing him much good as far as O'Kane could see—his beard had gone from gray to white inside of a year and the only thing you saw in his face was the scar, which seemed to grow more intense and luminous as the rest of his flesh shrank away from it. Amazingly, he was two years *younger* than Meyer, but anyone would have taken him for Meyer's father. Or grandfather even. And another thing—he wasn't a Kraut, but a Swiss, and so was Meyer, though they both talked Kraut, and he'd explained to O'Kane that German was the language of his part of Switzerland, near Basel, and that some Swiss spoke French and others Italian. O'Kane had just shaken his head: every day you learn something new.

Mr. McCormick was still sunk into the easy chair, Katherine's letter draped across his chest, his legs splayed and his eyes sucked back into his head. He'd been agitated all morning, and now he was looking unhinged, every sort of disturbing emotion playing across his face. O'Kane braced himself.

"A shame," Hoch repeated, "but at least you can look forward maybe to speak with her on the phone just at Christmas and then you will share the intimacy of her voice, no?"

"She's a bitch!" Mr. McCormick snapped, leaping out of the chair with a wild recoil of legs and arms, and he rushed up to the doctor and stood trembling over him as he tore the letter to pieces and let the pieces rain down on the doctor's white, bowed head. "I hate her!" he raged. "I want to kill her!"

"Yes, yes, well," Dr. Hoch murmured, never moving a muscle, "we all have our disappointments, but I'm sure you will feel very much different when she is here in this house and you are speaking with her on the telephone apparatus. But now, well" — and he clapped his hands together feebly — "I'm not feeling so very good as I might and I was thinking maybe we all go for a ride, what do you think, Mr. McCormick? All of us together — Mr. O'Kane, Mr. Thompson, you and me? For the change of scenery, yes? What do you say?"

Mr. McCormick's face changed in that instant. He looked to O'Kane and Mart and then back to the doctor with an enthusiast's grin. He liked his ride, but in Dr. Brush's time — and now Hoch's — the rides were few and far between, because they were dangerous and a whole lot of bother for everyone concerned. Mr. McCormick, of course, had to be watched every second, wedged between O'Kane on the one side and Mart on the other, while the doctor, be it Hamilton, Brush or Hoch, was obliged to sit up front with Roscoe.

"Yes," Mr. McCormick said, grinning wide round his decaying teeth — he hated dentists with an unreasoning passion and put up such a fight the doctors had all but given up on having his teeth treated — "yes, I think I'd like that. I'd like that very much. For a, a change, sure. I'll order Roscoe to bring one of the cars round. And we can take a lunch in paper sacks — can't we?"

Mr. McCormick always took a while getting himself from one place to another — it was one of his quirks — and both O'Kane and Mart had to help him choose the proper hat, gloves and overcoat and reassure him that he looked fine, absolutely fine and splendid, and that the weather outside wasn't really anything to concern himself over. "It's not like we're in Waverley anymore," O'Kane joked, and then he and Mart had him at the barred door to his quarters, and the keys turning in the locks.

There was no trouble, not on the stairs anyway, and Mr. McCormick, who'd just last month turned forty-four in a big fraternal celebration in the theater building, was looking every bit the lord of the manor with the hair silvering at his temples and a slate-colored felt hat that brought out the keenness of his eyes. He stood up straight for a change, with his shoulders squared and his head held high, and he didn't drag his right foot or stop in the middle of the stairway and back up two steps for every one he went down — one of his favorite tricks. No, he was the soul of propriety until Torkelson, the butler, opened the front door for him, and then he was off, slipping out of O'Kane's grip like a Houdini and darting right past Roscoe and the waiting car.

This was nothing new. Probably half the time he got out of the house for his walks or the trip over to the theater building for a concert or movie, he'd break into a run and O'Kane and Mart would have to run along with him, as if they all three were training for the marathon. Dr. Hamilton had felt that the running would do Mr. McCormick "a world of good" and that the staff should give him his head, so long as he didn't break for the bushes or attempt to leave the property. Brush didn't seem to care much one way or the other, and Hoch, in his Kraut—or Swiss—enthusiasm for physical suffering, concurred with Hamilton's feelings on the subject. And so Mr. McCormick ran, and O'Kane ran with him—which at least had the unforeseen benefit of burning the whiskey out of his pores.

On this morning, though, Mr. McCormick got the jump on both him and Mart, and by the time they got around the car he was streaking up the drive, at least fifty yards ahead of them. "Wait up, Mr. Mc-Cormick!" O'Kane shouted, his temples already feeling as if they were about to explode. "What about our drive?"

If Mr. McCormick heard him, he gave no sign. He just kept on, running in a flat-out sprint, running as if all his judges and demons were flocking after him, and he didn't head for the main gate but instead surprised O'Kane by lurching to his left, plunging deeper into the property. The road that way led to the stone garage that was set back away from the house in a grove of trees, and then it branched off to the west toward Ashley Road and the far side of the property. O'Kane chugged along, Mart at his side. "The son of a bitch," he cursed. "Why today of all days? My head feels as big as a balloon."

Mart, whose head *was* as big as a balloon, just grunted, trotting along in his dogged, top-heavy way. "He's heading toward the Ashley gate," he observed in a wheezing pant, and O'Kane looked up to see their employer wheeling again to his left and disappearing up the long snaking drive that bisected the estate. And that got his heart pounding, because that was where the nearest house was, Mira Vista, and there were women there now, imperious pampered overfed society women— women like Katherine.

O'Kane gave it all he had, but he wasn't worth much that morning, and he would have been the first to admit it. Sam Wah's salvatory eggs were coming up in his throat like a plug, like something evil he was giving birth to, and his legs had begun to go numb from the hip sockets down when he became aware of a rumble and squeal at his back and turned to watch Roscoe motor on by in a farting blast of fumes, Dr. Hoch wired into the seat beside him with his beard flapping in the breeze through the open window. O'Kane kept going, though Mart had fallen by the wayside. He followed the dwindling rear panel of the big Pierce car until the gate appeared down a stretch of concrete road all hemmed in by trees and the car began to get larger again. A moment later he was there, choking for breath, feeling just exactly like the victim of an Indian uprising with six or seven arrows neatly stitched into his lungs, his groin and his liver.

Roscoe was still at the wheel, pale and washed out from his bout of the grippe, but Dr. Hoch was standing there at the open gate with Mr. McCormick, and Mr. McCormick didn't even seem to be sweating. "What the—" O'Kane panted, flinging himself against the hood of the car for support. "What—?"

"Oh, Eddie," Mr. McCormick said, his eyes gone away to hide in his head again. "Hi. I was just—I thought—well, we should go out this gate today, so I-I came to open it, because we should see the begonias, the new begonias—"

O'Kane was stunned. He was obliterated. He had maybe nine breaths more to draw on this earth and then it was over. "Begonias?" he wheezed.

Mr. McCormick gestured for him to turn round and look behind him. Bewildered, O'Kane slowly pivoted and gazed back down the road that fled away into the distance and to the moving stain that was Martin Thompson limping there at the far end of it. And sure enough, there they were, a whole fresh-planted double row of them on either side of the pavement and stretching all the way back to Mart and beyond: begonias.

And then Christmas fell on them from the realms of space, the earth twisting round the sky and Aldebaran bright and persistent in the eastern sky, the season festive, the stuffed goose, the songs and drinks. Marshall Fields' in Chicago sent out a decorated Christmas tree and foil-wrapped presents for the whole staff (which now numbered fourteen in the household and forty-seven on the grounds), along with the usual baubles and candies and tan-shelled Georgia pecans, and baskets of prime California navels that had traveled from the San Fernando Valley to Chicago and back to California again. Outside, on the front lawn, the big Monterey pine, as wide around at the base as two men fully outstretched till their fingertips met on either side, was festooned with multicolored lights and set ablaze in the night. O'Kane sent his mother a sweater of virgin wool and a porcelain reproduction of the State of California flag for his father, and he sent Eddie, Jr. a jackknife care of his mother and not Rosaleen, who couldn't be trusted with anything you didn't tie round her neck with a note attached to it. And he found a filigreed bracelet in fourteen-carat white gold for Giovannella, who refused it on the grounds that Guido would want to know where it came from. "I'll wear it only for you, Eddie," she said. "When we're alone. In bed."

Katherine came and went in her customary storm of gifts, complaints and commands, but not before O'Kane had the opportunity to listen in on her annual conversation with her husband—this time from her end of the line. It was the day before Christmas and she'd just arrived, late as usual, and that hurt Mr. McCormick to the quick and she didn't even seem to notice. The windows were smeared with rain, it had been dark for an hour or so, and O'Kane was drunk, drunk on the job, and God help him if the Ice Queen were to pin him down with one of her endless interrogations and catch a whiff of it on his breath. He shouldn't have been drinking, and he knew it, but it was Christmas and Sam Wah was brewing a wicked pungent rum punch with raisins and slivers of orange peel floating round the top of it and half the people on the estate were slipping in and out the back door stewed to the gills. And besides, he was depressed. It was his tenth Christmas in California, ten years of nursing and drinking and getting nowhere. He wasn't rich yet or even close to it, he didn't own an orange grove or an avocado ranch, his one son was an alien to him all the way across the country in Boston and the other one was named Guido—and why not get drunk?

Anyway, he was sneaking out of the kitchen and through the back hall to the central stairway after quaffing his sixth murderous cup of hot Chinese Christmas punch, when he heard Katherine's voice and froze. It wasn't as if he was surprised to see her—they'd all been tiptoeing around and looking over their shoulders since early that morning, even Hoch—but he was half hoping she wouldn't come at all. She didn't bring anybody a lick of happiness—just the opposite—and it was his opinion, shared by Nick, Pat and Mart, that Mr. McCormick would have been better off without her. The way he'd paced and fretted and worked away at himself with the soap that morning was just pathetic, as if he was afraid she could smell him over the line. He was so excited he hadn't been able to eat his breakfast and pushed everything but the soup away at lunch, and he barely noticed the little gifts the employees had given him — Ernestine Thompson had knitted him a scarf from her and Nick, Mart gave him a pencil sharpener, and O'Kane, in a symbolic gesture, presented him with a keychain inscribed with the legend WHEN ALL THE DOORS OPEN TO YOU. They were nothing more than tokens really, but in past years Mr. McCormick had made a big deal over them.

"What do you mean by that?" Katherine's voice rose in anger. Edging out into the entrance hall, O'Kane could see movement in the library beyond. It was Katherine, and her back was to him. She held the telephone in one stiff ice-sculpted hand, tilting her head forward to speak into the mouthpiece. Torkelson was stationed just outside the door like a cigar-store Indian, his face wiped clean of all interest or emotion, a butler to the core. He was staring right at O'Kane, but he never even blinked.

"I will not be talked to in that tone of voice, Stanley, I just won't. . . . What did you say? Do you want me to hang this phone up right now? Do you? . . . All right, now that's better. Yes, I do love you, you know that — "

O'Kane watched her shoulders, the movement of her wrist as she manipulated the receiver, the light gathered in her hair. He knew he should hightail it up the stairs before she turned and spotted him, but he didn't. He was caught there, fascinated, like a boy in the woods watching the processes of nature unfold around him. There were birds in the trees, toads at his feet, snakes in the grass.

"Now Stanley — no, absolutely not. How many times do we have to go through this? I haven't seen or heard of Butler Ames in God, ten years and more, and no, I haven't been to dinner with Secretary Baker. . . . I resent the implication, Stanley, and if you're going to — no, absolutely not. Newton Baker is a friend, an old friend of the family, and as Secretary of War under President Wilson he naturally came to instruct us from time to time, and we — "

There was a silence and Katherine shifted her weight from one foot to the other and turned her profile to the open door. Her face was pale and blanched, but she was wearing makeup and red lipstick and she looked dramatic in the lamplight, like a stage actress awaiting her cue. She was listening, and O'Kane could imagine the sort of disjointed and accusatory speech Mr. McCormick must have been delivering on the other end of the line, and he watched as she held the receiver out away from her ear and tried to compose herself.

"Don't you say a word abut Jane Roessing—she's a saint, do you hear me? . . . That's absolutely disgusting, Stanley, and I'm warning you, I am—really, I just don't believe what I'm hearing. Everything is me, me, me—but did you ever stop to think what *I'm* going through?

"No, I'm not trying to upset you, I just want you to understand my position, to think for one minute what it must be like for me to have to go out in society without you on my arm, with no man at all, always the odd one out—

"Yes, I know you're trying to get well. No. No, now I won't listen to this, and you leave Jane out of it, she's been a—I have nothing to hide. Yes, she is here. She's come to keep me company at the hotel, and I promise you I won't neglect you. I'll be here every day for the next two weeks, and you just tell me what you need and I'll—"

O'Kane made his move then, trying to slip up the stairs while she was distracted, but even as he took the first tentative step he watched her face change—"No," she thundered, "damn you, no; I've never . . . Jane is just a *friend*"—as she swung round to slam the receiver down on its hook and let the full furious weight of her gaze settle on him. He snapped his head round—he hadn't seen her, didn't even know she was back, he was just a nurse doing his duty—and he felt his legs attack the stairs in a series of quick powerful thrusts. And it almost worked, almost, because he was halfway up the staircase and the iron grid of the upper parlor door in sight when her voice, strained and distinctly unladylike, caught up with him. "Mr. O'Kane," she called. "Mr. O'Kane, will you come here a minute, please?"

Slouching, hands thrust deep in his pockets, O'Kane descended the stairs, crossed the entrance hall and passed within six inches of Torkelson where he stood pasted to the wall outside the library door (he could see the pores in the man's face opening up like the craters of the moon and the fleshless nub of his butler's nose, and he swore to himself if Torkelson so much as lifted his lip in anything even vaguely resembling a smirk he was going to slug him, if not now, then later). Torkelson never moved. He drifted away on O'Kane's periphery and then O'Kane was in the library, conscious of the peculiar odor of the books—calfskin and dust, the astringent ink and neutral paper—and of something else too, something unexpected: cigarette smoke. Katherine was brilliant, glaring, incinerated in light. She gave him a curt nod, stepped round him and called out, "You can go now, Torkelson," before pulling the door shut.

O'Kane's senses were dulled. He felt as if he were wading through hip-deep water. He stood there stupidly, all the saturated neurons of his brain shutting down one by one, until he finally noticed that he and Katherine weren't alone. There was another woman present, a redhead in a holly-green dress short enough to show off her legs from the knees down—very good legs, in fact, and O'Kane couldn't help noticing. She was sitting in a wing chair against a wall of books and smoking a cigarette in an ivory holder.

"It's good to see you again, Mr. O'Kane," Katherine said, turning back to him, but she didn't smile and she didn't hold out her hand. She nodded brusquely to her companion. "Mr. O'Kane, Mrs. Roessing. Jane, Mr. O'Kane."

O'Kane gave them each a tight little grin, the sort of grin the hyena might give the lion while backing away from a carcass on the ancestral plains. He was feeling woozy. Sam Wah must have poured half a gallon of rum into that punch—and God knew what else.

"Have a seat, Mr. O'Kane," Katherine said, and she was pacing back and forth now.

He did as he was told, lowering himself gingerly to the very edge of the wing chair opposite Mrs. Roessing.

"I just wanted to tell you that I'm back," Katherine said, "and that I plan to be here for the next two weeks, seeing to estate matters, and that Jane—Mrs. Roessing—will be assisting me. Then I've got to get back to Washington and don't know when I'll return. Now: how is my husband—in your opinion? Any change?"

"He's more or less the same."

"And what does that mean? No improvement at all?"

O'Kane was ready to tell her what she wanted to hear, that her husband was advancing like a star pupil, making a nimble run at sanity, needing only time and money and the ministrations of girls, women and bearded hags to make him whole again, but the alcohol tripped him up. "A little," he shrugged. "We've let him have a carpet in the upper parlor again, and he's been very good about it. And he's been running quite a bit—for his exercise."

"Running?" She paused in mid-step, her eyes slicing into him.

"Yes. He seems to want to run lately—when we accompany him on his daily walk, Mart and me, that is. And we took him for a drive a few weeks back, and he seemed to enjoy it."

"And that's it? That's the extent of his improvement as you see it—running? Well let me tell you, I've just got off the phone with him and he seems as confused as ever—or more so. And irritating"—this for the redhead, with a nod and a martyred look. "Stanley *can* be irritating."

"With all due respect, Mrs."—he almost slipped and called her Katherine—"Mrs. McCormick, and I'm no doctor, but I do feel your presence excites him and he's not himself, not at all—"

Another look for Mrs. Roessing. "Yes, that's what every male doctor and every male nurse has been telling me for twelve years and more now."

Katherine surprised him then—shocked him, actually. Suddenly she had a cigarette in her hand, as if she'd conjured it out of thin air, and she crossed the room to Mrs. Roessing and asked her for a light in a low hum that said all sorts of things to him. He watched in silence as the two women bent their heads together and Katherine lit her cigarette from the smoldering tip of Mrs. Roessing's.

"And Dr. Hoch," Katherine said, exhaling. "His health, I mean—he's holding up? Spending time each day with my husband?"

O'Kane looked from one woman to the other. He hadn't even heard the question. Katherine was smoking. He'd never dreamed—not her. She might have been Queen of the Ice Queens, but she was a lady, a lady above all—and ladies didn't smoke. But then he'd suspected all along that this sort of thing went hand-in-hand with marching in the streets and emancipation and all the rest of it. Radicals, that's what they were. Pants wearers. She-men.

"Mr. O'Kane?"

"Hm?"

Katherine's face was like an ax. It chopped at him in the screaming light. "You haven't been drinking, have you?"

He tried to put on one of his faces, Eddie O'Kane of the silver tongue, one of the world's great liars. "Noooo," he protested. "I, just—I haven't been feeling well, that's all."

That brought the redhead to her feet, those fine legs flexing, the holly-green dress in a frenzy of motion. The two exchanged a look. "You haven't been running a fever, have you?" It was Mrs. Roessing talking now, and she had one of those elemental voices that gets inside you to the point where you want to confess to anything. "A kind of grippe of the lower stomach? Runs?"

O'Kane was confused. His face was hot. Both women loomed over him. "I—no. No, it's not that, it's, uh—my head. My head aches, that's all. Just a bit, the tiniest bit."

"The chauffeur—Roscoe—he was ill, wasn't he?"

O'Kane nodded.

"The grippe?"

"That's right."

Katherine spoke up again now, and her face was so pale you would have thought she'd been embalmed. "And my husband? He, he hasn't been sick—?"

And that was how O'Kane, drunk on Chinese Christmas punch and caught between two fraught and ashen women, learned that the Spanish influenza, which was to kill twice as many people worldwide as the War itself, had arrived in Santa Barbara.

One of the first to go was Mrs. Goux, the thick-ankled woman from the winery who trundled up and down the street each morning with an air of invincibility, trailing children and parcels and one very dirty white dog. She left behind a distraught husband and a grief-addled brood of seven, all of them howling from the upstairs windows that gave onto State Street across from Mrs. Fitzmaurice's, and that was depressing enough, but before anybody could catch their breath the husband and four of the children died writhing in their blankets with temperatures of a hundred and a six. Then it was Wilson, the greengrocer, a man in his thirties with the shoulders of a fullback and great meaty biceps who'd never been sick a day in his life. He told his wife he was feeling a little dyspeptic the day after Christmas and she chalked it up to overindulgence, plain and simple, and wouldn't hear a word of the hysteria boil-

ing up around her—not until he died two days later, that is. Their eldest
son came down with it next—he couldn't have been more than twelve
or thirteen—and Wilson's brother Chas, who ran the ice company, and
Chas's wife, and they were all three of them dead and laid out by the
New Year.

O'Kane was spooked. He walked by Wilson's and the shutters were
down and a black wreath hanging on the door, and from the front door at
Mrs. Fitzmaurice's he could see the sheet of paper taped to the window
of the winery: CLOSED UNTIL FURTHER NOTICE. The streets were deserted. Menhoff's was like a tomb. And Fetzer's Drugstore sold out of
gauze masks in fifteen minutes. But how did you catch the 'flu in the first
place? From other people. And how did they catch it? From other people. And the first one, the very first case—how did he catch it? Mart was
of the opinion that it was a judgment of God, "because of the War and
all," and Nick said it was demobilization that was spreading it. Mrs. Fitzmaurice put it down to uncleanliness, and no use discussing it further—
you didn't see anybody in her house coming down with it, did you?
O'Kane took a pint of whiskey up to his room each night and lay on the
bed and brooded, and when New Year's Eve rolled around he went out
and celebrated with a crowd that was so scared they had to drain every
bottle in sight just to reassure themselves.

At Riven Rock, they were relatively lucky. Only Mart and one of
Sam Wah's kitchen boys—a moonfaced kid known only as Wing—came
down sick. Mart was laid up for a week and a half in the back room at his
brother Pat's house, and Pat's wife Mildred wrapped him in cold towels
to bring down the fever and poured hot chicken broth down his throat
when he broke out in shivers. Wing died. That was a terrible thing—he
was just a boy, Wing, with a quick smile, a thin trailing braid of hair like
Paul Revere's in the old lithographs and not a word of English—and it
hit everybody hard, but none harder than Katherine. Not on Wing's
account—she didn't even know him except as a name in the accounts-
payable column in the weekly pay ledger—but on Mr. McCormick's.
The infection was in the house, not out in the fields or festering in the
gutters and saloons, but right here at Riven Rock. It had struck Mart
and Wing. It could strike her husband.

The thought seemed to galvanize her. She postponed her return to
Washington for the duration of the epidemic, and for the first week,
when the fear was fresh and new, she burst through the doors at Riven

Rock each morning at eight, Mrs. Roessing, two maids and Dr. Ur-vater, one of the local sawbones, in tow. All of them were wearing gauze masks — "The 'flu is spread pneumonically," she kept saying, "as much or more than by direct contact" — and she insisted that the whole staff, including a champing and furious Sam Wah, wear masks as well. And while Dr. Urvater depressed Mr. McCormick's tongue and looked into his ears and chatted amicably with Dr. Hoch about cheeses and leder-hosen and such, Katherine swept through the lower rooms in a flurry of servants and a powerfully salubrious odor of disinfectant. Every sur-face was wiped down with a solution of bleach or carbolic acid, and the doorknobs, bannisters, telephones and light switches were swabbed hourly. She was a scientist. She was an Ice Queen. And the 'flu had bet-ter take notice.

For his part, O'Kane did as he was told. He wore a gauze mask, looked suitably grave and made a show of turning doorknobs with a bleach-soaked cloth in hand, but the minute Katherine left for the day or he ascended the stairs and entered Mr. McCormick's sanctum, he peeled off the mask and tucked it in his pocket. He'd never seen any-thing like this epidemic — every time you turned around you heard about somebody else dropping down dead — and it scared him, it did, but to his mind Katherine was taking things a bit far. He had no fears for himself — he had his father's constitution and nothing could touch him, unless it came out of a bottle, and there was no degree of luck in the world that could save you from that — but he was afraid for Mr. Mc-Cormick, even if he did think the masks and disinfectant were just a lot of female hysteria. The rest of the staff shared his fears, though nobody wanted to talk about it. Mr. McCormick might have been crazy as a bedbug, but he was the rock and foundation of the place, and if he fell, how many would fall with him?

Their employer and benefactor seemed fine, though — hale and hearty and in the peak of health. On doctor's orders (and Katherine's, working behind the scenes) he wasn't allowed out for his walks or even to go to the theater building until all this blew over, and that made him a touch irritable. He took to wearing his gauze mask atop his head, like a child's party hat, and he toyed with Dr. Urvater over the tongue depres-sor and the thermometer, clamping down like a bulldog and refusing to let go until Dr. Hoch pushed himself up from the couch and intervened. Every day he talked with Katherine on the phone, she in the downstairs parlor with her carbolic acid and he a floor above her, and that seemed to have an exciting effect on him, but as far as O'Kane could see he didn't develop so much as a sniffle, let alone the 'flu.

"I think she's going way overboard," Nick said one morning as he and O'Kane were waiting for Mr. McCormick to finish up his shower bath. He was filling in for Mart on the day shift, while Pat sat alone with Mr. McCormick through the nights. "Rubbing down the god-damned doorknobs, for Christ's sake. But better too much too soon than too little too late, that's my motto."

"I know what you mean," O'Kane said, standing at the door to the shower room, just out of reach of the spray. Mr. McCormick was crouched naked over the wet tiles, meticulously soaping his toes, and O'Kane was reflecting on how he'd spent more of his adult life looking at Mr. McCormick in the nude than at any woman, and that included Giovannella and his long-lost wife. "We'd be in hot water if anything happened to him. I'll be all right once I get in on this citrus ranch I was telling you about—Jim Isringhausen's only looking to line up a couple more investors—but if I wasn't working here, I don't know what I'd do. I'd hate to have to go back to mopping up shit and blood on the violent ward."

"Amen." Nick let out a sigh. He was leaning back against the tile wall, droplets of condensation forming on his eyebrows and the fine pickets of hair that stood guard above the dome of his forehead. He was blocky and big, still muscular but running to fat in his haunches and around the middle because all he and Pat ever did was sit by Mr. Mc-Cormick's bed all through the night and then sleep when everybody else was up and about. And he wasn't getting any younger. "Yeah, I'd be in a fix if anything happened to Mr. McCormick, and so would Pat and Mart. Of course, not everybody would be so bad off if he went and kicked the bucket."

"What do you mean?"

"Well," he said, a sly look creeping across his face, "*her*, for instance. You know: your sweetheart."

"Katherine?"

He nodded, watching for a reaction. "Makes you wonder why she's playing Florence Nightingale around here, doesn't it? If he was to go, she'd be the one to get everything, the houses and the cars and more millions than you could count. And no more crazy husband."

Nick had a point, but it only confirmed what O'Kane had maintained all along—Katherine really cared about her husband's welfare,
and it wasn't just an act, say what you would about her. And he wondered about that and what it meant, especially when he thought about
Dolores Isringhausen and how she treated her husband—or Rosaleen,
or even Giovannella and her little shoemaker. Women were conniving
and false, and he'd always believed that—all of them, except his mother,
that is, and maybe the Virgin Mary. And every marriage was a war for
dominance—who loved who and who loved who the most—a war in
which women always had the upper hand, always scheming, always
waiting for the chance to stab you in the back. But not Katherine. Not
the Ice Queen. She had her husband right where she wanted him—in a
gilded cage—and no sick canary ever got better care.

"By the way," Nick said, and Mr. McCormick had begun to sing to
himself now, a tuneless low-pitched moan that could have been anything from a highbrow symphony to "Row, Row, Row Your Boat," "did
you hear about the wop shoemaker? You know, the one with the little
wife, you, uh—" and he let his hands round out the phrase.

"What about him?"

"You didn't hear?"

"No, what?"

"He's dead. Two, three days ago. Ernestine told me because she went
to get her boots resoled and there's a wreath on the door of the place and
all these Guineas beating their breasts and hollering in the street. It's a
shame, it really is, and I don't think any of us are safe anymore—not till
this thing burns itself out or it gets all of us, every last one, and then we
won't have nothing to worry about, will we?"

O'Kane had Roscoe drop him off in front of Capolupo's Shoe Repair as
soon as he got off his shift, but the place was closed and shuttered and
there was no answer at the door to the apartment above. He rattled the
doorknob a few times, pounded halfheartedly at the windowframe, and
then, for lack of a better plan, sat down to wait. He'd worked overtime
to help cover for Mart, and it was late—quarter past nine—and he
couldn't imagine where Giovannella would be, unless they hadn't
buried the shoemaker yet and there was some sort of Guinea wake going on someplace. He leaned back, wishing he'd thought to pick up a

pint of something or even a bottle of wine, and pulled the collar of his jacket round his throat. It was cold, cold for Santa Barbara anyway, probably down in the mid-forties. He listened to the night, the sick bleat of a boat horn carrying across the water from the harbor, the ticking rattle of a car's exhaust, a cat or maybe a rat discovering something of interest in the alley below, and all the while he thought about Giovannella and what he would say to her. And just thinking about her and how she'd be free now to come to him anytime, day or night, and no excuses or explanations for anybody, was enough to spark all sorts of erotic scenarios in his head, and he saw her climbing atop him, her lips puffed with pleasure, nipples hard and dark against her dark skin, it's like riding a horse, Eddie, come on, horsie, come on—

He couldn't marry her, of course, and she knew that—it would be bigamy, even though she was trotting around town with his green-eyed son in a pair of kneepants and you'd have to be blind not to know it was his son and nobody else's—but for half an hour or so he thought how it might be to take up housekeeping with her somewhere far enough away so nobody would know the difference. They could get a place in Carpenteria, seven miles to the south and right on the ocean, with that sweet breeze fanning the palms and everything so small and quiet, and just claim they were man and wife, and who was going to dispute it? But then he'd have to get a car, and renting a house—that would be something, like moving in with Rosaleen and Old Man Rowlings all over again, the baby squalling, shit strewn from one end of the place to the other . . .

At ten-thirty, chilled through and thoroughly disgusted with himself—and with Giovannella and even Guido for having the bad grace to die off and stir the pot like this—O'Kane pushed himself up and went back along the hushed and empty streets to Mrs. Fitzmaurice's. The place was dark, but for the light in the entrance hall, and he let himself in with exaggerated caution, wondering vaguely if there was anything left in the emergency bottle he kept on the floor behind the bureau— and he was picturing it, actualizing that amber bottle in his mind— when he saw that there was a package for him on the table in the hall.

It was small, no bigger than a pack of cigarettes, and with a slight heft to it, more than paper would carry anyway. Dirty white tape was double- and triple-wrapped around the outside of it and he could see the imprint of a thumb under a loop of tape and a few stray hairs

trapped beside it in the film of glue. He recognized the handwriting immediately: Rosaleen's. For a moment he hesitated, turning the thing
over in his hand. This couldn't be what it felt like—a gift, a belated
Christmas gift, maybe from Eddie Jr.—no, it couldn't be. If Rosaleen
had anything to do with it, it was going to be the sort of thing he'd be
better off looking at tomorrow, in the light of day, when Giovannella
wasn't so much in his mind.

He shifted the package from one hand to the other, looking off
down the length of the dark parlor with its spidery plants and dim furniture and the rugs that had been beaten to within an inch of their lives.
What the hell, he thought, and he sat in the stiff chair in the hallway
and tore the thing open. The tape slipped away from his fingers, the paper fell to the floor. And now he was even more bewildered than he'd
been a moment ago: here was the jackknife he'd sent to Eddie Jr., come
right back to his hand like a boomerang. But wait, there was more, a
message, a note curled up like a dead leaf inside the husk of tape and
wrapping paper and inscribed in the smudged semiliterate scrawl that
spoke so eloquently of Rosaleen's innermost being:

Deere Eddie:
I cannot live a lie anymore. I never wrote you in sept. but the
spannish flue hit here and our son died of it. He was burried in the
St. Columbanus cemetary and I never told your mother or anybody heres the Jack nife back he would of loved it.

Yours, etc
Rosaleen

He didn't have a chance to react, because at that moment somebody
began tapping insistently at the window set in the front door. (And how
was he supposed to react anyway—fall to his knees, tear his hair out,
bemoan his fate to the heavens? The sad truth was that he'd never
known his son. A stranger had died someplace, that was all, and so
what if he had Eddie O'Kane's eyes and his walk and the look of him
when he smiled or brooded or skinned his knee and came running to his
mother with the tears wet on his face? So what?)

The tapping grew louder—*chink-chink-chink-chink*—and he dropped
the letter and drifted stupidly toward the door. There was a face
pressed to the glass in the dark of the night, the image of his own won-

dering face superimposed over it. It took him a minute, because he was thinking of ghosts, of the disinterred spirits of little deserted bare-legged boys dead of the epidemic 'flu and come back to haunt him, and then he realized who it was tapping with a coin at the brittle glass and not a thought to Mrs. Fitzmaurice sleeping the wakeful sleep of the eternally vigilant at the end of the hall: it was Giovannella.

She was saying something, mouthing the words behind the glass to the accompaniment of a series of frantic gestures. She had to see him — she wanted to — did he know?

He opened the door and there she was, brushing past him and into the hallway with her broad beautiful face and her eyes that knew every-thing about him, and Guido, little Guido, his only surviving son, thrown over her shoulder like something she'd picked up at the market, like so many pounds of pork roast or beef brisket. As soon as he'd closed the door she whirled round on him and clutched at his neck with her free hand, crushing her mouth to his, and it was theatrical and wild and it brought his attention into the sharpest of focus. "He's dead," she hissed, throwing back her head to look him in the eye. "He's dead of the 'flu."

He put a finger to his lips. Mrs. Fitzmaurice would be pricking up her ears, past ten o'clock at night and a strange woman in the house, Mrs. Fitzmaurice, who was raging and furious and sexless as a boot. "Shhhh!" he warned, half-expecting to see the landlady stationed be-hind him in her declamatory nightgown that fell to the floor and be-yond. "I know."

She pressed into him again, held him tight, little Guido sandwiched between them, the heat of her and her odor like no other woman's, cloves, garlic, vanilla, onions frying to sweetness in the pan. "I'm scared, Eddie," she whispered. "Guido . . . I . . . I nursed him, and he died burning up with the fever and so sad and pathetic he couldn't open his mouth to say a word to me or even the priest, no last words, no nothing . . . and the smell of him — it was horrible, like he was all eaten up inside and nothing left of him but shit." She was trembling, a vein pulsing at the base of her throat, the hair fallen loose under the brim of her hat and slicing into her eyes. "I'm afraid I might've . . . or little Guido, Eddie, our son. They say you can catch it just by walking past somebody on the street, and you have to understand, Eddie, I nursed him, I nursed Guido."

Her eyes were two revolving pits, two trenches draining everything out of her face, and she wouldn't let go of him. He was scared too. First Eddie Jr. and now this—what if she did catch it? What if she died, like Wilson and Mrs. Goux and Wing? What then? He looked over his shoulder, down the hallway to Mrs. Fitzmaurice's door, everything soft and indistinct in the dim light of the lamp. "You're young and strong," he heard himself saying. "If you get it, you'll shake it off. Like Mart. Did I tell you about Mart?"

"I'm a widow, Eddie," she said.

He nodded. She was a widow. Widowhood. Viduity. That was the state she was in, a sorry state, twenty-eight years old and bereft, and with a son to raise.

"We can be together now."

He nodded again, but he didn't know why. He wanted to tell her about Eddie Jr., about the regret that was ripening inside him till it was about to turn black and become something else, something rotten and despairing, something cold, something hard. He wanted to tell her, but he couldn't. And he tried to pull away from her—just to breathe—but she wouldn't let go.

"Did you hear what I said?"

Looking down, looking at her feet in a pair of dusty old high-buttoned shoes some customer must have left behind at the shop: "I heard. But listen, let's go outside and talk so Mrs. Fitzmaurice—"

"I don't want to go outside. I want to be here. With you. Look," she said, backing off a step and stripping the child away from her shoulder so he could see the fat infantile face staring sleepily into his own, "your son, Eddie. He's your son and you're my husband. Don't you under-stand? I'm a widow. Don't you know what that means?"

"I'm married," he said. "You know that."

He watched the lines gather in her forehead while her eyes nar-rowed and her mouth drew itself tight. "I spit on your marriage," she said, swinging wildly away from him, and he was afraid she was going to knock over one of the darkened lamps, afraid she was going to wake the house, stir up Mrs. Fitzmaurice, turn everything in his life upside down.

He told her to shut up, to shut the fuck up.

She told him to go to hell.

And who was that now? Somebody at the head of the stairs—was it

Maloney?—and an angry voice looping down at them like a lariat. "Keep it down, will ya? People are tryin' to sleep up here."

"Come on," he whispered, "let's talk about it outside."

"No. Right here. Right now."

He rolled his eyes. He was tired. He was angry. He was disappointed. "What do you want from me? You want me to move you into a new brick house tonight, with new curtains and furniture brand-new from the store with the paper wrapping still on it? Is that what you want?"

She stood there immovable, black widow's weeds, the black veil caught like drift on the crown of her hat, the child fat and imperturbable and staring at him out of his own eyes.

"Come on," he coaxed, "let's go over to Pat's and talk things out where we can be comfortable, and we can, you know. . . . I want you," he said.

"I want you too, Eddie." And she moved into him and pulled his head down to hers and kissed him again, a fierce furious sting of a kiss, all the madness and irrationality of her concentrated in the wet heat of her mouth and lips and tongue, and he knew it would be all right, all right for both of them, if he could just take her up to his room and make love to her, ravish her, fuck her.

She pulled away and gave him a long analytic look, as if she were seeing him from a new perspective, all distance and shadow. The muscles at the corners of her mouth flexed in the faintest of smiles.

"What?" he said. "What is it?"

"I'm pregnant."

Well, and it was déjà vu, wasn't it? Simple arithmetic: one child subtracted, one child added. All he could say was, "Not again?"

She nodded. Saturated him with her eyes. Behind her, blighting both walls of the narrow hallway, were the dim greasy slabs of the oil paintings Mrs. Fitzmaurice had rendered herself, kittens and puppies frolicking in an unrecognizable world of bludgeoning brushstrokes and colliding colors. She shifted the child from one shoulder to the other.

"Jesus," he said, and it was a curse, harsh and harshly aspirated.

Her voice fell off the edge and disappeared: "I want you to take care of me."

This was his moment, this was the hour of his redemption, the time to cash in his three o'clock luck though it was past eleven at night, and he could have taken her in his arms and whispered, Yes, yes, of course I will, but instead he gave her a sick smile and said, "Whose baby is it?"

"Whose—?" The question seemed to stagger her, and suddenly the weight of the child on her shoulder, little Guido Capolupo O'Kane, seemed insupportable, and she began fumbling behind her as if for some place to set him down. It took her a minute, but then she came back to herself, straightening up, arching her back so that her breasts thrust out and her chin lifted six inches out of her collar. "Guido's," she said, "it's Guido's," and then she found the doorknob and let in the night for just an instant before the door clicked shut behind her.

And handsome Eddie O'Kane, who'd failed every test put to him, and wasn't rich and wasn't free and had to bow and scrape to Mrs. Katherine Dexter McCormick and her demented husband and chase after every skirt that came down the street? What did he need? That was easy. Simple. Simplest thing in the world.

He needed a drink.

7.

_____

P R A N G I N S

The Dexter château stood on a hill just outside Geneva, at Prangins, in the village of Nyon. It was a turreted stone structure of some twenty rooms surrounded by orchards and formal gardens and with a great lolling tongue of lawn that stretched all the way down to the shore of the lake, where Josephine kept a pair of rowboats and a forty-foot ketch. No one knew exactly how old the place was, but portions of it were said to date from the time of the Crusades, after which it was built up and fortified by successive generations of noble and not so noble men. Voltaire had once lived there, and in 1815 it was acquired by Napoleon's brother, Joseph Bonaparte, who made use of a secret tunnel in the cellar to slip off into the night when his existence became a liability to too many people. The property was surrounded by a formidable wall and high, arching iron gates, and when Katherine broke off her engagement to Stanley, she fled across the Atlantic and closed the gates behind her.

She needed time to think. Time to settle her own nerves, and never mind Stanley's—he'd meant to hit her with that vase, he had, right up until the last minute. He could have scarred her for life, killed her—and for what? What had she done to deserve it? She'd lost her patience maybe and she'd been short with him, but only because he was so obsessive and gloomy, making mountains of molehills all the time, afraid of her touch, afraid of what was happening between them, afraid of love. All that she could understand and forgive, but violence was inexcusable, unthinkable, and the truly awful thing was what it said about Stanley in his darkest soul.

The first day at Prangins all she did was sleep, and when Madame Fleury, the housekeeper, poked her stricken face in the door inquiring if madame wanted anything to eat, Katherine told her to go away. At dusk, she thought she ought to get up, but she didn't—she just lay there, sunk into the pillows, holding herself very still. She watched the darkness congeal in the corners and fan out over the floor, and then she was asleep again, the night a void, black and silent, no wind, not a murmur from the lake. In the morning, she woke to the sound of birds and the shifting light playing off the water, the floating aqueous light of her girlhood when she would spend half the day rowing out into the lake till she was beyond the sight of shore, and for the first thirty seconds she didn't think of Stanley. She was at Prangins, behind the walls, behind the gate, secure and safe and with nothing to do but read and walk and row and all the time in the world to do it, and what was so bad about that? Suddenly she was hungry, and she realized she hadn't eaten since she'd got off the train from Paris, her stomach in turmoil, in revolt, but growling now in the most placable and ordinary way. She rang for the housekeeper and had breakfast sent up, a good Swiss breakfast of fresh eggs and cheeses and wafer-thin slices of Black Forest ham with rolls hot from the oven and fresh cream for her coffee, and she ate it all in a kind of dream, sitting at the window and gazing out over the lake.

She forced herself to get dressed and to greet the servants, most of whom she hadn't seen in nearly a year, and then she went down to the lake and took one of the rowboats out. There was a breeze with a scent of snow blowing off the mountains, but the sun was warm and she relished the feel of the oars in her hands, the spume, the rocking of the boat, each stroke taking her farther from all the complexities of her life, from Stanley and wedding gowns and arborio rice by the bushel—and the specter of babies, that too. What had he shouted over the clamor of the crowd and the mindless blast of the ship's horn? *I can have children!*

That was sweet. It was. And she did want a baby, not only for Stanley's sake and her mother's and to honor the memory of her father and all the Dexters before him, but for the most personal and selfish of reasons: it was her privilege and her will. As a woman. As an independent woman of independent means. For twenty-nine years she'd developed her mind and body, and to what end? To make her choice, her own free choice, without regard to convention or expectation or the demands of the world of men, to be married or not to be married, to have a child or not, to study the biological sciences at the Institute or scale Mount Everest, and she'd chosen Stanley, nobody else. Strapping, shy, artistic Stanley, athletic Stanley, manly Stanley. He was her biological destiny, her husband, her mate, and they would come together in the dark and he would impregnate her — that was the way it was supposed to be, that was what she'd wanted. She thought about that, tugging at the oars and feeling her blood quicken, savoring the flex and release of the muscles in her shoulders and back, and pictured herself in a white nightdress in a field of white flowers, pregnant and glowing like the Madonna of the Rose Bush. It was frightening, beyond her control — beautiful and heady and frightening.

But Stanley was in Chicago, where he belonged and where he had to stay until he got a grip on himself. She'd been gentle with him — he had to understand that she needed to get away by herself, and though the engagement was officially broken, the ring returned and the caterers and the florists and their minions called off, there was hope still, if he would only give her time. Gentle, but firm. She didn't tell him when she was leaving or where she meant to go, but only that he shouldn't attempt to follow her, no matter what. He had to respect that. And if he did, and if he improved his outlook and settled his nerves and she had a chance to calm herself too, then maybe, just maybe, there was hope for them yet.

By noon — or what she took to be noon from the position of the sun stuck in the clouds overhead — she was hungry again, and that was a good sign. She didn't have anything with her, not so much as an apple or pear, and she let herself drift a while, cradled by the waves, the smell of the wind and the water playing on her senses till the hunger was a physical ache, and then she made for an inn on the Geneva shore and sat in a vast dining room and had lunch over a newspaper and a pot of tea while a punctilious waiter with drooping mustaches fussed over her.

She had the soup, a salad, roast duck with potatoes and vegetable, and she lingered over dessert, reading a paragraph at a time from the paper spread out before her and then lifting her head to gaze out on the lake in reverie. When finally she climbed back into the rowboat with the aid of an overly solicitous concierge and the frowning waiter (Wouldn't madame prefer a taxi? One of the boys could return the boat in the morning—"Cela ne pose pas de problème"), the sky had closed up like a fist and a light drizzle hung suspended in the air. She thanked them for their concern, but really, she said, she'd prefer the exercise. Clucking and protesting, the concierge held an umbrella out over her head as she settled herself on the thwart, and then watched in disbelief as she shoved off nimbly and swung the bow around into the vague drifting belly of the mist. The visibility was poor, and she might have been in real danger, but she stuck close to shore and rowed until she was no longer aware she was rowing, until there was nothing left in the universe but her arms and the boat and the lake.

Two weeks passed. She saw no one. She swam, walked, rowed, read French novels, helped the cook plan the menu and even took up the needlepoint her mother had abandoned the previous fall, and she wasn't bored, not yet, but getting healthier and steadier and calmer as each day fell into the next. She was sitting at breakfast one morning, absorbed in a Maupassant tale—the one about the plump little courtesan and the coach full of hypocrites—when Madame Fleury informed her that there was a man at the gate inquiring after her.

"A man?"

"Oui, Madame. He says he knows you. He won't go away."

And what was this, a little spark? Hope, fear, anger: it couldn't be. "Did he give you his card? A name?"

The housekeeper was a plain, angular woman in her forties, an adept at driving all expression from her face and suppressing any hint of emotion in her voice; the house could be in flames and she would knock quietly at the door to ask if madame would be needing anything. Her mouth tightened just perceptibly round her words: "He refused, madame. But we haven't opened the gate, and Jean Claude is keeping an eye on him."

Katherine set down her teacup. Her heart was pounding. "Well, is he from the village then? Is he a tradesman, a gentleman, a goatherd?"

The housekeeper gave a shrug, and it was a Gallic shrug, respectful

only to the degree that was necessary, while managing at the same time
to convey not only impatience but a deep disillusionment with the question. She pursed her lips. "Jean Claude says he has a motorcar."

And then she was up from the table, no time to think, no time to
manage her hair or grab a hat or worry about what she was wearing,
and down the stone steps and out into the circular drive, the gravel
skewing awkwardly beneath her feet, all the way to the gate, breathless,
sure it was a false alarm, some Oxford boy on his Grand Tour come to
inquire about the history and architecture of the place, a motoring enthusiast experiencing mechanical difficulties, a friend of her mother's,
some busybody from the village . . . but she was wrong. Because it was
Stanley, Stanley standing there at the gate like some apparition exhaled
from the earth and given form in that instant. His hands were gripping
the bars on either side of him as if to hold him upright, his shoulders
were slumped, his head bowed penitentially.

"Stanley!" she called, trying not to run, aiming for poise and composure, but after a moment she couldn't feel her feet at all and she was
running despite herself. He was frozen, welded to the bars—he didn't
move, wouldn't lift his head or raise his eyes. Jean Claude, the gate-
keeper, gave her an odd look, and he seemed ready to rush forward and
prevent whatever it was that was about to happen.

She was there, at the gate, her hands clutching his, and she was
looking up into his flat suffering face through the iron grid. She uttered
his name again, "Stanley," and then she didn't know what to say and
still he wouldn't look at her, his head hanging, shoulders bunched, the
hair in his eyes, utterly abject, the whipping boy come back for his punishment. Everything stopped then, the earth impaled on its axis, the sun
caught in its track, the breezes stilled, Jean Claude's face the face of a
photograph, until finally it came to her and she knew what to say, and it
was almost as if she were speaking with her mother's voice or Miss
Hershey's from all those years ago when she sat in the schoolroom and
learned French, deportment and the finer points of etiquette with the
other wide-eyed and nubile Back Bay girls: "How nice of you to come."

The wedding was in September, and because it took place in Europe
and because it was cursorily announced and precipitately arranged, the
American newspapers had a field day with it: SECRET M'CORMICK

NUPTIALS; SOCIALITE WEDS M'CORMICK HEIR IN SWISS RETREAT; M'CORMICK-DEXTER WEDDING SHROUDED IN SECRECY. Actually, there were two ceremonies—a civil ceremony before a magistrate in Geneva and a private celebration at Prangins presided over by a French cleric of indeterminate affiliation whom Nettie suspected of being a Unitarian or even a Universalist. She'd booked passage as soon as Stanley had wired her that a date had been set, and she campaigned from the beginning for a church wedding there in the very birthplace of Presbyterianism—anything else would have been sacrilege, anything else would have cut her to the quick, torn her heart out and trampled on it—but it was Katherine's wedding, Katherine's château, and Katherine had hegemony over Stanley now, and no matter how fiercely Nettie fought, right up until the nasal clod of a Frenchman pronounced them man and wife, she was doomed to failure. Stanley had made his choice, his leap, and it was like leaping from one forbidding precipice to another, and there was nothing she could do about it.

She made an uneasy peace with Josephine, who at least conducted herself like a lady and showed a remarkable degree of taste in the charm of the statuary and gardens at Prangins, but Nettie would never forgive her daughter, the scientist, the unholy little snit who'd stolen away her last and youngest, and even as the Frenchman was intoning, "Je vous déclare maintenant mari et femme," she stood behind Stanley hissing, "Godless, Godless." And thank the Lord she'd brought Cyrus Jr. along to sustain her or she might have fainted dead away right there (neither Anita nor Harold would dignify the proceedings with their presence, and that was what it amounted to, though Anita had her child to look after and in Harold's case, well, someone had to stay behind and keep an eye on the business). She did cry though, as mothers are wont to do on such occasions, but her tears were of an entirely different order from Josephine's, who whimpered like a deprived three-year-old throughout the course of both ceremonies, if you could call them that— no, her tears were tears of rage and hate. If she could have struck Katherine dead right where she stood in her Gaston gown with its pearls and lace and the ridiculous puffed pancake of a hat she wore high up off the crown of her head so that she was nearly as tall as Stanley when you added it all up, heels, hat, chignon and veil, she would have, so help her God, she would have.

And how did the bride feel? For her part, Katherine was satisfied.

Or more than satisfied — she was ebullient, triumphant, the battle over and the citadel taken, and she was gracious in victory. And in love too, having leapt the same chasm as Stanley, and there was no more anxiety, no more fear of the free fall and crash: he was her husband and she was his wife. She was content. Without reservations. As sure as she'd ever been of anything in her life. And what had made it all right and chased away her last remaining doubts was Stanley himself, prostrate before her on that early summer morning outside the château gates.

He was so contrite and pitiable, pale as a corpse, two weeks' worth of sleepless nights staring out of his eyes, every fiber of him yearning for her. He couldn't defend himself or explain how he'd gotten there or why or what his presence portended for them both — he was overwhelmed by his feelings, that was it, as simple as that. He loved her. He couldn't live without her. And she didn't have to hear him say it or read it in a perfumed letter because she could see it in his eyes and his face and the way he held himself in a kind of hopeless and penitential despair: she'd warned him not to come and he'd disobeyed her. That melted her, that melted her right there, and she brought him in and fed him bonbons and madeleines and she showed him round the place, all twenty rooms, riding up off the balls of her feet as if she were lighter than air and barely able to keep herself tethered, and then they were out on the lake and rowing, and she knew there was nothing more she needed in all the world than to have Stanley at her side.

Yes, and now they were married, and there wasn't anything anybody could do about it, not Nettie or her odious little rat of a lawyer — Foville or Favril or whatever his name was — or the walking broomstick that was Cyrus, so stiff and formal and tripping over his boarding school manners, as tactless as a shoe-shine boy. But what did that matter to her? She hadn't married the McCormick family, she'd married Stanley, and now the rest of her life was about to begin. She waited, breathless, a little flushed with the champagne she'd drunk, while the party broke up and her mother ushered the guests out into the reception hall and Stanley stood grinning and pale beside her. All the guests were going into Geneva for the night, and Josephine too — "I want you to have the place to yourself, sweet," she'd said, "just you and Stanley and the servants" — and in the morning they'd embark on their honeymoon, first to Paris for a month, to shop and stroll through the galleries, to visit Cartier & Fils and Tervisier & Dautant, and it would be one grand party, even if Nettie insisted on coming along—and Josephine. And she laughed to herself, a private trilling little chime of a bride's laugh, wondering if two mothers on one honeymoon would somehow manage to cancel each other out.

She took Stanley's hand in hers as the guests—there were only fifty or so, the most intimate group—began to make their exit. It was eight-thirty P.M. on September 15, 1904, and the day hung in tatters over the lake while the hall rang with laughter and good wishes and the intoxication of all that had happened and all that was to come. Stanley's fingers were entwined in hers. Her peignoir—ivory silk with a border of Belgian lace the color of vanilla ice cream, Stanley's favorite—was laid out on the big canopied bed in the Bonaparte suite upstairs. "Good night," she said to one guest after another, "good night, and thank you so much," while Stanley stood erect beside her, his right arm extended, shaking hands, grinning like a child, a lover, a Hindu ecstatic, his every word measured and apportioned and the current of anticipation almost sizzling in his fingertips. She could feel it. She could.

And then there was the whole adventure of going to bed, the dismissal of the servants, the separate dressing rooms and baths, the shy smiles, the endearments, the bed itself. Katherine took her time, brushing out her hair, sick with joy, a twenty-nine-year-old virgin at the moment of release. She rubbed lotion into her face and hands, dabbed perfume behind her ears, and when she laid her dressing gown beside the wedding dress on the loveseat and stepped out of her undergarments, she felt a thrill go through her that was like nothing she'd ever experienced, a chill and a fever at the same time, the blood exploding in her veins like gunpowder. And then the nightgown. She lifted her arms, short of breath all of a sudden, and let the silk run down her like water. Twenty minutes had passed since she'd squeezed Stanley's arm and pecked a kiss to his cheek at the door to his dressing room. The hour was at hand.

She slipped into the bedroom on naked feet, the warm sheath of silk gathering at her breasts and hips and flowing gently across her abdomen. Two candles were burning ceremonially on either side of the bed—her mother's idea—and there were flowers everywhere, a whole jungle of them, the air thick as wax with their scent. She could hardly breathe for excitement, and was that Stanley? There, beneath the covers—that shadow on the bed? No, it wasn't, and her fingers told her what her eyes hadn't been able to: the bed was empty. The room was empty. And Stanley's door was shut. "Stanley?" she called, and when she got no answer she tried again, a little louder this time, and she realized she could scream at the top of her lungs if she wanted to and there was nobody to hear her, not even the servants. That made her feel strange. It made her feel bold, randy, made her feel like a wife. "Stanley?"

Not a sound.

She tried the handle of his door: it was locked. She tapped at the door and called again. "Stanley?"

This time, from deep in the room beyond, there came a muffled reply, a grunt of acknowledgment so strained and distant it might have been coming from Bonaparte's secret tunnel in the bowels of the house. "I'm ready," she said, her lips pressed to the door. "I'm ready for you."

Another grunt, nearer this time, and the sounds of movement, followed by a profound and brooding silence. And what was the matter? It took her a moment, and then a smile came to her lips. He was shy, that was all, shy as a maiden, and wasn't that sweet? She didn't want a Butler Ames or a Casaubon to initiate her into the pleasures of married life, she wanted this, she wanted Stanley, a neophyte like herself who would go slowly and allow her to discover the delights of Eros in mutual exploration, in partnership, in marriage, and no cast of lovers and whores and lusty widows looking over her shoulder. All right. She would give him time. "I'll be waiting for you in bed," she whispered. "Should I put out the candles?"

And now his voice, right there, on the other side of the door: "No, it's—yes, yes, do that and I'll be—I'll be just a minute, some things I have to, yes, of course—"

She drifted back to the bed, her respiration easing from a gallop to a canter, and leaned forward to cup her hand behind first one candle and then the other, puffing darkness into the room. The sheets welcomed her, the night gentle, stars framed in the window that looked out over the lake, and she'd pulled open the curtains for that at least, sidereal light, compass points to steer by. She fanned out her hair on the pillow and lay there on her back, waiting. What did she think of? Everything. Everything that had happened to her in her entire life, and she saw every face, every incident, heard every word replayed, and the stars shifted, and still Stanley's door remained closed. How much time had passed? Had she fallen asleep? She got out of bed, the carpet a continent beneath her feet and now the cold stone sea of the floor, and she was at the door again and no whisper from her lips this time, nothing, not a word. The handle turned with a click under the pressure of her fingers and she swung open the door.

Stanley's face, pale as the moon, stared up at her in alarm from the secretary in the far corner of the room. He was seated before it in a stiff-backed chair, hunched over the leaf on his elbows amid a confusion of papers, envelopes, pens and pencils. He didn't attempt a smile.

"Stanley, what in the world are you doing?" she said in a kind of amazement that verged on stupefaction, and why did she feel so naked and vulnerable suddenly, the negligee clinging to her in all the wrong places and her husband's startled eyes just beginning to grapple with the image of her? She noticed the clock then, up on the mantelpiece, an ancient block of carved wood and Swiss works that marked the hour with a dull rasp instead of a chime. She was further amazed. "It's nearly four in the morning," she said, and there was exasperation in her tone, wifely impatience, disbelief, shock even.

"I, well," he began, and she saw that he was still in his tuxedo and tails, the top hat sprawled casually on the desk beside him, "—you know, work, correspondence, that sort of thing. I am still, well, *comptroller* of the Harvester Company, though you'd never think it, and I—well, and there're the thank-you notes, because so many people have—and Harold, I needed to write Harold and tell him about the day, about us, I mean."

She was dumbstruck. "But Stanley, darling, this is our wedding night. . . ."

The light of the lamp, which he'd propped up on the near corner of the desk, split his face in two. He turned away from her to scribble something on the sheet of paper before him and he was stiff and bristling, the pen gouging at the paper till the nib gave way and he reached irritably for another. It took her a moment to realize he wasn't going to respond.

"Darling, Stanley," she said, "can't it wait? At least till morning?" And she crossed the room to him and laid a hand on his shoulder. He made no movement, not even a twitch, but kept on writing till he thought to shield the paper with his hand. "Stanley, come on now, be reasonable," she said, her voice soft and murmurous, and she ruffled the hair at the back of his neck.

He turned his face to her now, both hands nested over the paper on the desk so that she couldn't see what he was writing, and what was this—secrets? Secrets on their wedding night? "I, I—" he began and trailed off. He seemed half asleep, drugged, mesmerized.

She let her hand roam over his shoulders. "Come on," she murmured, "it's time to come to bed. With me. With me, Stanley."

"Yes," he said, staring up at her out of a fixed and wary eye, "yes—I—I know that, and I want to, I do, but you see, if you just give me a minute, that's all I need, a minute more, just to finish up, I'll, well, that is—"

What could she say? She was stunned and hurt. This was her wedding night, this was what she'd been looking forward to all her life, wasn't it? What was wrong? Was it her? Was he rejecting her? Having second thoughts? She'd known he was shy, certainly, and that was one of the traits that endeared him to her, but this went beyond the bounds of any modesty or reticence she could possibly conceive of—he hadn't even undressed yet. It was as if he had no intention of it, as if this night, of all nights in their lives, wasn't consecrated, as if she hadn't been waiting for him in the next room through all the lingering unfathomable hours. And then it came to her in a slow seep of understanding as she stood there rubbing his clenched shoulders and he averted his face and screened the letter from her: he was afraid of her. Afraid of his own wife. Afraid of the sheets, the bed, the complicated mechanics of love. He was suffering, she could see that, suffering for love of her, and it softened her.

"All right," she said finally, bending forward to brush the crown of his head with a kiss, wondering what to say, how to phrase it, how far she dared go, "but I don't see how you can be thinking of business and correspondence at a time like this."

He wouldn't look at her. She felt him stiffen under the touch of her hand where it lingered on his shoulder.

"All right," she sighed, "if you must, if your business means that much to you, but promise me you'll come to bed in a minute, won't you? Just a minute?" She brought her face close to his, the light of the lamp harsh and radiant, but he turned his head away and delivered his extorted promise to the tabletop.

"Yes," he said. "I promise."

●   ●   ●

In the morning she changed the bed herself, before the chambermaid had a chance to poke her nose in the door—no bloody sheets to display here, no flag of virginity, not even the good clean wholesome impress of two bodies lying entwined as one. She bundled up the sheets and stuffed them into the fireplace atop a pyre of pine kindling and split oak, where they made a quick and furious blaze before settling into ropy clots of ash. Stanley had fallen asleep at the desk and he was sleeping still when she awoke at eight to a heavy fuliginous light that spread like a stain over the lake until the sky was as dark as it had been just before dawn, when she'd first awakened. By nine, it was raining.

Katherine lay there prostrate on the stripped mattress, gazing out through the bed curtains at the water lashing the windows, afraid to move. She was hungry, famished—she'd hardly eaten a thing the day before for sheer excitement—but she was also afraid to ring for breakfast because then everybody would know, all servants notorious for their gossip and none more so than the frenchified Swiss, who always moved about the place as if they were on loan from an empress and missed absolutely nothing. But what to do? Her mother would arrive soon enough, every possible question in her eyes, and then Stanley's mother would follow, just in time for a light luncheon before the whole rampant entourage entrained for Paris and the Elysée Palace Hotel.

Finally, as the clock in the next room struck ten with the faintest repeated rasp, she tiptoed to the door and peered in. Stanley was asleep still, head down, elbows splayed, a basket full of crumpled paper at his feet. He was snoring, a wheeze and stertor that animated the papers scattered round him, and she realized she hadn't heard the sound of a man snoring since her father died—he used to fall asleep in the library after dinner, the newspaper slipping from his lap, a cup of hot malted milk cooling on the table beside him. She found the scene oddly touching, Stanley snoring there at the open secretary, his cheek pressed to the leaf while his lips fluttered and the long lashes of his eyelids meshed like a doll's, but she had to wake him all the same—it wouldn't do for the servants to find him like this.

She thought of shaking him and calling his name in a protracted whisper—"Stanley, Stanley, wake up"—as she expected she would on ten thousand mornings to come, but when she was actually in the room, actually approaching his splayed and sleeping form, she couldn't bring herself to do it. And why not? Because he would be embarrassed, mortified, caught in a lie, and she didn't want to see the look on his face, the pain and bewilderment in his eyes and the shame—she didn't want to be the one to remind him of the futile negligee and the lonely bed. So she took the easy way out—she retreated to the door and slammed it three times in succession before darting out of the bedroom, into the hall, and down the stairs to breakfast.

Eyebrows were raised. The servants crept around the halls like undertakers, Madame Fleury choking on her own suspended breath, her eyes oozing and doleful. And where, they wondered, was the master of the house, the king and patriarch and deflowerer of virgins? Sleeping late. He wasn't to be disturbed. And of course this revelation was in itself cause for eyebrows to be raised still further. Katherine ignored them. She ordered breakfast, watched the rain, and ate, one small bite at a time.

Stanley appeared at noon, looking confused. He'd bathed and changed into a charcoal gray suit with a stiff formal collar and tie. Katherine, already dressed in the outfit she would wear to Paris on the train, was in the parlor, seated at the window with a book she was pretending to read. "Ah, well," Stanley said, poking his head in the door like a child playing a prank, "so there you, well, are. I just, well—" and then he was in the room, tall and solemn, his shoulders thrown back and something—a neatly folded slip of paper—making its way from one hand to the other and back again. He rocked on his heels. Smacked his lips. Opened his mouth to say something, but couldn't quite seem to close it around the words he wanted.

"Good morning," Katherine said. "Or should I say, 'Good afternoon'?"

He didn't seem to know how to respond. He merely stood there, just inside the door, watching her out of hooded eyes.

"Did you sleep well?" She didn't want to be acerbic, didn't want to provoke him, but she couldn't seen to help herself. She was angry. She was. And humiliated too.

"I—well—I, I'm sorry, I, you know—work . . . and then, before I knew it—" and he threw his hands in the air in a gesture of helplessness, the neatly folded slip of paper going along for the ride.

Katherine felt the blood rush to her face. He was just standing there like a block of wood, like an oaf, his hands dangling, a fleck of shaving cream stuck to the underside of his chin. "Well?" she demanded. "Don't I deserve a kiss?"—and she wanted to add, "at least," but held back.

Suddenly he was in motion, striding across the great cavernous stone room with its faded tapestries and the wall of long narrow windows giving onto the gray void of the lake, and he didn't look tender, not at all—he looked determined, dutiful, martial almost. He bent to her stiffly as she raised her chin and compressed her lips, and stiffly, he kissed her—on the cheek, no less. She rose from the chair to take him in her arms, but he backed off a step, every mortal ounce of him working and twitching, and what was this? He was thrusting the paper at her, a crisply folded sheet of stationery with the McCormick monogram embossed in the corner.

"Katherine," he said, "I wanted—last night, I—here," forcing the paper into her hand, his smile high and tight, feasting on her with his eyes. "Go ahead," he said. "Open it. Read it."

She unfolded the paper and held it up to the light, standing there beside him on the morning after her wedding night with the rain beating at the windows and the servants lurking in the halls. It was a will. Four lines, signed and dated, and nothing more.

> I, Stanley Robert McCormick, being of sound mind and body, do hereby consign all my monies, assets and real property, in toto, to my wife, Katherine Dexter McCormick, in the event of my death.

She didn't know what to say. It was so unexpected, so odd—and so morbid too. Was this what he'd been writing? Was this what he'd hidden from her the night before? "Stanley," she murmured, and she couldn't seem to find her voice, "you didn't have to do this—there's plenty of time to think of such things, years and years . . ."

He was beaming, all his teeth on display and his eyes lit like hundred-watt bulbs. "It's a surprise," he said. "That's what I—last night—it wasn't business, not all of it, you see, because—because I was, well, I was thinking of you—"

And now she didn't have to say anything, and neither did he. She wrapped her arms around him, pressed herself to him, one flesh, and lifted her face to his and found his lips. And they were like that, in that very pose, the first real kiss of their married life and every sentimental emotion charging through them, through them both, when Katherine's mother swept in the door, all feathers and perfume and brisk commanding energy, and Stanley's mother right behind her. "And will you look at this," Josephine crowed, "look at the lovebirds!"

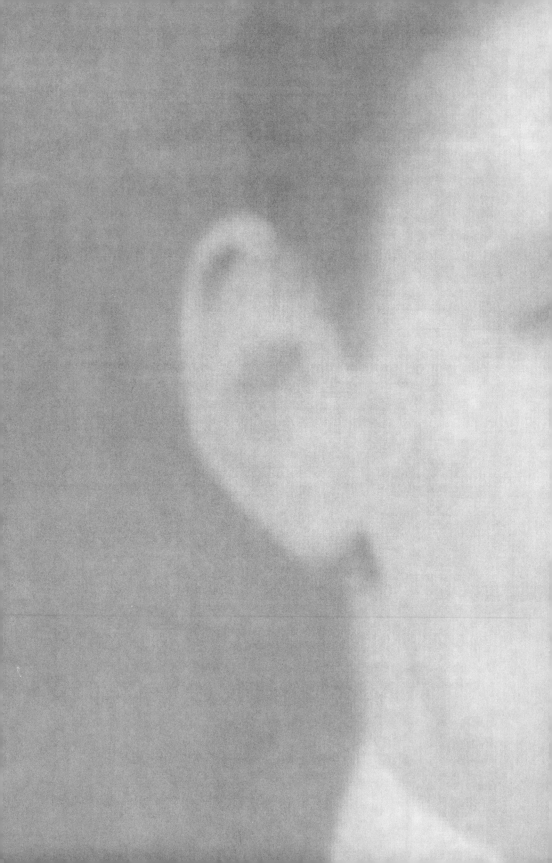

PART III

Dr. Kempf's Time

1.

___

BENIGN STUPORS

O'Kane was sprawled on a circular patch of lawn in the middle of the daphne garden, along with Mart and Mr. McCormick, and all three of them were lathered in sweat and breathing hard. Mr. McCormick had been especially frisky on his walk that morning, leading them on a chase from one end of the grounds to the other, elbows pumping and nostrils flared, his eyes fixed on some invisible lure in the distance. Up they went, all the way to the top of the estate with its inhuman rise in elevation and vertiginous views of the Channel, and then they turned round and charged back down again, Mr. McCormick leading the way with his lunatic strides, feinting this way and that, till they'd circled the house three times and finally come to rest here, among the daphnes. Mart was lying prone on a stone bench near the fountain, inanimate but for his tortured breathing, and Mr. McCormick himself was stretched out on the lawn and staring up into the granular sky, his jacket balled up beneath his head to serve as a pillow. It was absolutely still, not a breeze, not a sound. The sun all but crushed them with its weight.

"A shame about Hoch," O'Kane said after a while, just to say something.

Mart grunted. Mr. McCormick stared up into the sky.

"I liked him, you know what I mean, Mart? He wasn't so excitable as Hamilton or Brush, if that's the word I'm looking for. And Mr. Mc-Cormick really came to like him too, didn't you, Mr. McCormick?"

O'Kane hadn't expected a response—he and Mart spent half their lives talking right through their employer and benefactor—but Mr. Mc-Cormick surprised him. He shifted his head to get a closer look at O'Kane, his eyes shrinking into focus. "Dr. Hoch?" he echoed, his voice high-pitched and unstable. "Wh-what happened to him?"

"You remember, Mr. McCormick—it was just yesterday, yesterday morning. Dr. Brush gave us the news."

There was a pause. A reflective look stole over Mr. McCormick's features. After a while he said, "No, I don't remember."

"Sure you do. You were very upset at the time—and I don't blame you. All of us were upset."

Dr. Brush had returned from the War a month ago, in August, just in time to take the baton from Hoch, who was fading fast. If anything, the rigors of the Western Front had left the good doctor fatter and heartier than ever, and with a raft of platitudes and a whole shipload of for-the-main-and-simple-reasons he'd explained to Mr. McCormick that Dr. Hoch had passed on early that morning of congestive heart failure—a weakness that ran in his family. But Mr. McCormick shouldn't feel too badly, he said, because Dr. Hoch was an elderly man who'd lived a full and rich life and made innumerable contributions to the field of psychiatry, including the manuscript of a new book—*Benign Stupors*—which he'd been able to complete before his heart gave out.

Mr. McCormick was sitting over his breakfast at the time, fastidiously dissecting two fried eggs and a thick pink slab of ham with a soup spoon, the only implement available to him. "How elderly?" he asked without looking up.

"Hm? What?" The question had caught Brush by surprise.

"Dr. Hoch," Mr. McCormick said in the small probing voice of the rhetorician, "how-how elderly was he?"

Brush produced a stub of cigar from somewhere and jammed it in his mouth. "Hoch?" he repeated. "Oh, I don't know—in his sixties, anyhow."

"Fifty-one," Mr. McCormick corrected, still without looking up. "And do you know how old I am, Dr. Brush?" He didn't wait for an answer. "I'll be forty-five in November. Am I an elderly man too?"

"Why, of course not, Mr. McCormick—Stanley," Brush boomed, all his flesh in motion as he shimmied round the room on his too-small feet, "you're a young man still, in the flush of health and vigor, for the main and simple—"

Mr. McCormick had waited until the breakfast dishes had been cleared and he'd got dressed and made his way to the theater building before he gave vent to his feelings on the subject. In a roaring stentorian voice that drowned out the hypnotic *tick-tick-tick* of Roscoe's projector and nullified the antics of Charlie Chaplin and Marie Dressler, he announced: "I don't want to die!"

Brush's voice leapt out of the darkness: "You're not going to die, Mr. McCormick."

"I am!"

There was movement now, O'Kane and Mart positioning themselves, Brush rising mountainously from his folding seat in a swirl of shadow. Up on the screen, Charlie Chaplin spun round and booted a policeman in the rear, and O'Kane laughed aloud despite himself. "Now, now," Brush was saying, looming over the slouched form of their employer, "you're a healthy mean, Mr. McCormick, in the peak of health, and you know it. Why, you've got the best of everything here, the most salubrious possible environment—"

Mr. McCormick's voice, pinched thin as wire: "He's a stinking rotting corpse, with—with things coming out of his eyes, because that's— that's the part they eat first, the eyes, and you *know* it!"

"I know no such thing, for the main and simple reason that that is just too morbid a thought for me to hold." Brush was waving his arms now in the flickering light, the lower half of the Little Tramp's face appearing fitfully on his shoulder as if in some ghostly manifestation. "Think of him in heaven, in the arms of God—"

"God's a fraud," Mr. McCormick spat, wrenching his neck angrily round. "And so are you."

And then there was the inevitable roughhousing, the collapse of the chairs, the curses, shouts and whimpers, the fumbling for the light switch and Dr. Brush's intimate presentation of his persuasive and salvatory flesh to the recumbent form of their employer and benefactor.

Understandably, O'Kane didn't want to push the subject now—he was burned right down to the wick after that footrace round the property and up that damned hill, and he'd had enough exercise for the day, thank you. "Well, anyway, at least we've got Dr. Brush back," he said, lamely. "And he's all right. I guess."

Mr. McCormick didn't seem to have an opinion on the subject. He just stared up into the sky as if he might find Dr. Hoch up there somewhere, seated on the edge of a cloud. And Mart—Mart was no help. His arms dangled over the sides of the bench and his breathing slowed till he began to snore. O'Kane lay there a while, hands cradling his head, enjoying the silence and the glory of the day, until he began thinking about the one thing that sustained him lately—booze, or more specifically, the pint bottle of bourbon whiskey he'd sequestered in the reservoir of Mr. McCormick's toilet. It was past noon and there was no reason they should be lying in the grass when they could be inside making themselves presentable for lunch—and other activities. He saw himself slipping into the bathroom as Mr. McCormick spooned up his meat loaf and gravy, saw the bottle all striped with water and felt the cork twist out of the neck of it and the swallowing reflex of his throat that was the nearest thing he had to an orgasm lately, since he'd sworn off women, anyway. "Well, and so," he said with as much cheer as he could muster as he pushed his weary parched self up off the grass, "what do you say, gentlemen—time for lunch?"

And that would have been all right, because Mart woke with a start and Mr. McCormick found his legs and began mechanically brushing off his jacket preparatory to slipping it back on—if it weren't for the gopher, that is. O'Kane didn't even know what it was at first. A little thing, like a rat, only pale and yellowish almost to the color of a butternut squash, and it suddenly popped its head out of a hole in the ground and tore twice round the patch of lawn before vanishing down a second hole like water down a drain. Mr. McCormick was dumbstruck. At first. And then he got excited. "Did you see that?" he said. "Did you? Did you see it?" And by now he was down on his hands and knees, probing into the thing's lair with his right hand and forcing his arm in up to the elbow. "What is it?" he kept saying.

"Beats me," O'Kane said with a shrug. "A weasel?"

Mart came over and stood there looking at the hole and Mr. Mc-

Cormick ruining his cuffs and the sleeve of his jacket. "That's no weasel," he said. "Are you nuts or something? A weasel's long and skinny."

"So what is it then?" O'Kane demanded. He didn't really give a good goddamn one way or the other, but he hated for Mart to show him up.

Mart scratched his head. "A groundhog," he said, but he didn't sound too sure of himself.

By this point, Mr. McCormick had got his whole arm in the burrow, right up to his shoulder and he was scooping out dirt with his bare hand. "It's in there, I know it is," he said, and then he got to his feet and collapsed that portion of the burrow he'd already excavated, falling once again to his knees and thrusting his arm into the new opening. He looked up, perplexed. "It's—it's going for the daphnes," he said.

"Nothing to worry about, Mr. McCormick," O'Kane assured him, sensing an episode coming on, "I'll get the head gardener to take care of it right after lunch. And say, speaking of lunch," pulling his watch out with a flourish, "if we hurry we'll be just in time."

Mr. McCormick ignored him. He was digging furiously now, with both hands, crouched over the expanding burrow like a fox terrier. Already his nails were ruined and you could see the blood like a tattered ribbon moving beneath the scrim of filth on his right hand. Mr. McCormick was distracted. He was obsessed. He was being sick and pathological. O'Kane didn't want any violence, not now, not today—all he wanted to do was go back to the house for lunch and a drink sneaked in the toilet—but he would have to intervene, and soon, he could see that. He signaled to Mart, but Mart wasn't paying any attention—Mart was standing over Mr. McCormick's shoulder and peering down into the excavation, saying, "I think it goes this way, yeah, that's right, through the flowerbed and then maybe under those bushes over there—"

O'Kane took him by the arm. "Maybe Dr. Brush will know what it is," he said in a falsely hearty voice. "Mart, why don't you go get Dr. Brush?" And then he tightened his grip and dropped his voice, adding, for Mart's benefit only, "Right now. Right this minute. You understand me?"

When Mart returned ten minutes later with a wheezing, puffing and blustering Dr. Brush in tow, Mr. McCormick had already excavated a looping twenty-foot furrow through the daphne bed and back into the lawn, where he was working furiously with a stick he'd found beneath the oleander bushes (the very bushes O'Kane had been repeatedly warned to keep him away from, as their flowers, leaves and branches were all highly toxic). "Mr. McCormick," Brush bellowed, even as he was fighting to catch his breath, "what is this? You're ruining the flower beds! And the beautiful lawn Mr. Stribling has worked so hard on."

Mr. McCormick never even glanced up. It was his estate and he could dig the whole place down to China if he wanted to. "It's—it's a— a—a groundhog," he said. "It lives here. Under the grass."

"Yes, yes," Brush said, bending over him now, "I have no doubt of that, but what's it to you, Mr. McCormick, really? I'm sure the creature isn't doing any harm, and if it is, well, we have the excellent Mr. Stribling and his professional gardeners to see to it. Now come on, come out of there and let's get cleaned up and have some lunch. Doesn't that sound like a good idea?"

"No," Mr. McCormick said, digging, and the dirt was flying furiously in the direction of the doctor so that Brush had to back up to avoid having his cuffs filled with it. "No. I want this, this thing. I want to k-kill it. It's destroying the, the flowers, don't you see?"

There was no use arguing with him, not when he was like this, and nobody really wanted to get down there in the dirt and restrain him, not after the free-for-all in the theater house yesterday, so Dr. Brush did the politic thing and sent Mart to fetch Stribling.

Stribling was a standoffish sort of fellow for a gardener—or landscape architect, as he liked to call himself—and on the few occasions O'Kane had run into him, usually while jogging from one end of the estate to the other behind Mr. McCormick's bobbing and weaving form, the man had been brusque and uncommunicative. He was in touch with Katherine by post and while he did submit all major plans to her for approval, he pretty much had free rein to continue the work of his predecessor, a famous wop whose name O'Kane could never remember, and he always had his team of laborers, truck drivers and manure spreaders under the gun. If they weren't shoveling silt out of the reservoir or constructing a water tower, they were building stone bridges over the creeks and repairing and extending the roads, not to mention clipping every leaf of every shrub like a horde of overzealous barbers. It took no more than five minutes and Stribling was there, another man in tow — a gaunt tall Irishman with a wandering eye — the kind of man O'Kane's mother would have called a long drink of water. If O'Kane recalled correctly the man's name was O'Hara, or maybe O'Mara — the day laborers came and went like the weather and there was no way to keep track of them, not unless they turned up at one of the saloons, that is. Both Stribling and the Irishman had shovels slung over their shoulders.

"Ah, there you are, Mr. Stribling," Brush hollered, "and I see you've brought one of your, uh, associates along too, and all the better. You see, we have a problem, for the main and simple reason that some sort of groundhog has got under the lawn here and Mr. McCormick is very concerned about it, isn't that right, Mr. McCormick?"

The dirt flew. Mr. McCormick said nothing.

Stribling and his man stepped up to examine the trench through the flower bed, the ravaged lawn, the uprooted oleanders. "It's a gopher," Stribling said matter-of-factly, and he was so burned by the sun you would have thought he was a spaghetti twister himself. He laid a finger alongside his nose and gave Mr. McCormick a look. "We'll get him, don't you worry," he said. "But here, Mr. McCormick, you don't have to do that now — a trap's the thing, that's what we need."

The Irishman, his nose peeling and his eye wandering, began to shovel dirt back into the hole, but Mr. McCormick would have none of it. "Step away from there," he said, glaring up at the man, and dug all the more furiously, every stitch of clothing on him ruined beyond washing or repair. The knees of his trousers glistened with compacted mud, his collar was a sop, his tie a rag.

"It's past one, Mr. McCormick," Brush remonstrated, " — you know you'll miss lunch now if you don't hurry, and we've got to allow time to clean up."

O'Kane put in his two cents then: "That's right, Mr. McCormick. Lunch."

For the next hour, as the sun roved overhead and they shifted from one foot to another, the five of them stood there watching Mr. McCormick at his work. He'd made his way through the oleanders and across the gravel walkway beyond and into another flower bed, this one of impatiens, fragile gawky things that drooped and fell over if you looked at them twice, and all the while Stribling saying things like "It's no use, Mr.

McCormick, he's got a burrow a hundred yards across at least" and "There's literally scores of the things out there and even if you get this one another one'll move right back in—trapping's the thing, I tell you."

Finally, and they were well into the third hour by now, Mr. Mc-Cormick got up from the convoluted trench he'd managed to gouge out of the earth with his two bare hands and a stick of oleander, and looked Stribling in the face, no more than two feet from him. Bleeding in half a dozen places, his hair hanging in his eyes, their employer was all but unrecognizable behind a film of sweat and filth. "And what am I paying you for?" he suddenly snapped, pushing up against Stribling with his chest thrust out and spitting the words in his face. And then, trembling and gritting his teeth, he jerked his head round on the Irishman. "And you?" he said. "What am I paying you for? To stand around and, and watch? Dig, I tell you!" he shouted, his voice rheumy and dangerous all of a sudden. "Dig! Dig or you'll—you'll be looking for another j-job! Both of you!"

Stribling gave Brush a sour look, but turned away from Mr. Mc-Cormick without a word and leaned into his shovel, and so did the Irishman. Dr. Brush, who'd kept up a steady stream of bluster and re-monstrance for the better part of this ongoing charade, suddenly started in on a new tack, assuring Mr. McCormick that the task was in good hands now and that that was all the more reason to head back to the house and clean up—yes, and see what Sam Wah could put to-gether for a late lunch. Because Mr. McCormick must be hungry after all that prodigious exercise, just the sort of thing to build an appetite, for the main and simple reason that the body needed fuel, didn't it?

But Mr. McCormick merely stood there, filthy and bleeding, watch-ing the men dig. Stribling kept his head down, and he dug steadily, but O'Kane could see that he was concentrating on the doomed flower bed, trying to cut his losses and confine the scope of the excavation. It was past three and both Stribling and his assistant were up to their hips in a trench you could have flooded and rowed a boat across when Mr. Mc-Cormick folded his arms and said, "That's it. That's enough."

They all looked up hopefully, all five of them, Stribling and the Irishman in a sweat, Brush all blustered out, Mart half comatose and O'Kane bored to tears and desperate for a drink.

"You can bury him now," Mr. McCormick said.

They all looked at one another. It was O'Kane who finally spoke up. "Who—the gopher?"

Mr. McCormick slowly shook his head and looked up at the sky. "Dr. H-Hoch," he said.

When the year turned—'19 into '20, that is—O'Kane's worst fears about the Katherines of the world were confirmed. Riding in on the skirts of Petticoat Rule, the Drys and the Bible-thumpers got the Volstead Act passed, prohibiting "the manufacture, sale or transportation of intoxicating liquors," and before women even got their vote (a proposition about which O'Kane was dubious to begin with) he was denied his God-given right to drink himself into a stupor—even in the privacy of his own antiseptic room. January 18, 1920: that was the day of infamy. The day of doom. The day every last shred of joy went out of his life. He watched in shock and disbelief as the saloons of Spanishtown boarded up their doors and the Women's Christian Temperance Union paraded through the streets, pouring out good whiskey in the gutter. Menhoff's was still open, but only as a restaurant, and Cody would serve you a beer with your steak if you were foolish enough to ask for one—near beer, .5 percent alcohol, less than you'd find in a can of sauerkraut.

Oh, O'Kane had stocked up, of course, stashing six cases of beer and two of rye whiskey under his bed and secreting the odd bottle of bourbon in his wardrobe and ten pints of sloe gin in the steamer trunk he kept in Mrs. Fitzmaurice's attic—he even buried half a dozen jugs of wine just inside the front gate at Riven Rock—but he was bereft without the conviviality of the saloons. So what if he'd spent half his adult life considering various positions on God, immortality and Ford transmissions as expressed by one drunken halfwit or another? What else was there to do? He tried reading. He bought himself a Victrola. Rain beat at the windows and every day brought news of some fool going blind and deaf drinking antifreeze or rubbing alcohol—and how about that fireman in Pennsylvania who bought up all the lilac hair tonic in town and drowned in a sea of his own vomit? O'Kane went steadily through his stock, mostly alone, but sometimes in the company of Mart or Pat or one of the lost souls who used to inhabit the front room at

Menhoff's, and as the bottles turned up empty, he felt like a condemned man marking off the days until his execution.

Into this vale of tears stepped Jim Isringhausen.

Jim came out in February to open up his brother's place and make his move on one thousand acres of prime flat well-watered citrus land in Goleta, four miles to the north of Santa Barbara. Demand was up since the War ended and people back East were just going crazy for oranges, lemons, tangerines, limes, grapefruits, kumquats, you name it, and what they were getting from Florida was a drop in the bucket compared to what California could produce. Now was the time to get in on it before every used car salesman and soda jerk with a hundred bucks in his pocket got wind of it, not to mention the big conglomerates. And he came to O'Kane first, because O'Kane had been with him from the beginning on this, and he'd been patient, sitting on his hands for two years now while Jim consolidated his holdings and lined up investors, and Jim appreciated that, he did.

He told O'Kane all this on their way out to inspect the property on a day of biblical splendor, the sea leaping, the mountains chiseled, the sun hanging in the blue-veined sky like a big Valencia orange. Jim was looking good. He was wearing a checked sport jacket and white duck trousers, spats over his shoes, and his hair was frozen to his head with French pomade and his mustache so neat and refined it was barely there. The car was new, a yellow Mercer roadster with blood-red wire wheels and a fold-down canvas top. The wind was in their faces. Everything flashed and winked in the brilliant California light. Jim Isringhausen passed O'Kane a silver flask and O'Kane drank deep of ambrosia—Scotch whiskey, the real stuff, smoke and peat and the very baaing of the sheep all in one swallow, whiskey like you couldn't find anymore and maybe never would again.

"So what did you say you've got to put up," Jim said, gently disengaging the flask from O'Kane's reluctant fingers and putting it to his own lips, "—three thousand?"

The wind beat at O'Kane's hair, the sun warmed his face. He squinted his eyes and felt the hope come up in him again, a breath of it, anyway. "Just about. Twenty-nine and something."

Jim turned to him with the flask. He had the look of a priest on his face, all sympathy and concern. "That's not your whole life savings, is it? Because I wouldn't want to put you under any strain here—I mean, this is as close to a sure thing as you'll find on this green earth, but nothing's a hundred percent, you know that, don't you?"

O'Kane shrugged. He lifted the flask to his lips, casual as a million-aire. "No," he lied, "I've got some put away still."

He was no idiot. He knew what Jim was saying: there was risk in-volved. But there was risk involved in anything, in walking across the street, gulping your food, looking into a woman's eyes on a Saturday night. This was his chance, and he was going to take it — all he needed to see was a row of orange trees, and he was in.

"All right," Jim said, "call it three then — if you can round it off between now and next Tuesday, which is when we close the deal. At two hundred an acre, we need to raise twenty thousand dollars down against the bank loan and another thousand in reserve to hire a bunch of wops to water the trees and pick the fruit. Three'll get you thirty shares, at a hundred per. Sound good, pardner?"

"Sure," O'Kane said.

Jim put both hands on the wheel as they swept too fast into a turn banked the wrong way; the wind sheared at them, there was a delicious jolt and Jim downshifted and hit the gas on the straightaway that sud-denly opened up before them. "By the way," he said, "Dolores sends her love."

O'Kane chewed over this bit of information as the flask came back to his hand and they swung off the pavement and onto a snaking dirt road that bloomed with dust and insects and flying bits of chaff. *Dolores sends her love.* Well, fine — O'Kane hadn't seen or heard from her in two years, not since her husband came back from the War. He'd asked Jim about that, trying to sound casual, and Jim had told him they were over in Europe, reconstructing a villa someplace in Italy — not that it mat-tered two figs to O'Kane one way or the other. Women were a thing of the past for him. He'd given up. After Rosaleen and poor Eddie Jr. — and Giovannella.

He hadn't seen her either, the widow Capolupo. He heard she'd moved back in with her parents, pregnant with a dead man's baby — or so she claimed. And he hadn't heard whether she'd given birth to a wop or half a wop, and he just didn't care, not anymore. If he could make his fortune here, in oranges, and get out from under the McCormicks and set himself up someplace — in San Francisco maybe, or Los Angeles — well then he might just possibly think about finding some young girl of twenty with some grace and style about her and settle into his forties with something to show for his life. But right now he didn't need the complications. Or the heartache either.

The car swung round a bend and all at once they were in the groves, running along between rows of orange trees, glossy copper-green leaves and the oranges hanging fat and sweet in every one, as if this were Christmas, endless Christmas, and every tree decorated just for them. Jim pulled over at the end of one of the long tapering rows, where the trees suddenly gave out and the open fields began, yellow mustard up to your armpits and some kind of hairy blue flowers strug-gling through the weeds and a riot of every possible thing reaching up out of the dirt—everything but oranges, that is. "Well," Jim said, throwing out his arms, "what do you think?"

O'Kane looked over his shoulder at the ranks of unassailable trees, and then out into the field. Jim's white trousers were stained with flecks of yellowish mud. There were gopher mounds everywhere, and at least now O'Kane knew what they were. "I don't know," he said. "What am I supposed to think?"

"I guess it's kind of hard to picture," Jim said, wading out into the undergrowth, "but once we get this cleared out of here and give these trees some attention—"

"What trees? You mean"—a gesture for the grove behind them—"those aren't the trees right there?"

Jim Isringhausen was bent over something in the deep grass. "Here, look," he said.

O'Kane saw a sapling no thicker than his finger, four feet tall maybe, with a puff of vegetation at the top of it. And then he saw the others, the smallest stunted flags of copper-green leaves poking out here and there from the morass of weeds. "That's an orange tree?" he said, and even as he said it he understood how elusive a thing a man's fortune could be.

Jim Isringhausen had straightened up, holding his hands out in front of him as he rubbed the dirt from them. "Yep," he said, "that's it. And before you know it these little beauties'll be producing like their big sisters behind you."

O'Kane just stared at the place Jim had cleared in the weeds and the leafy stalk of nothing stuck in the middle of it like an arrow shot down out of the sky. Then he looked over his shoulder again, at the deep-green wash of leaves and the oranges hanging uncountable in the interlocking grid of branches that went on as far as he could see. "It's going to take a while," he said finally.

Jim didn't deny it. "Yeah," he said, working his heel against the running board to dislodge a clot of mud from his gleaming tan shoe. "But not as long as you think."

After that, things began to go downhill, a long steady slide that was so gradual O'Kane wasn't even aware of it, not at first. It was as if everything in his ken—Mr. McCormick, Dr. Brush, Riven Rock, Mrs. Fitzmaurice, the hoarded whiskey and beer and Mart and Pat and the accrued weight of all those saved and salvaged dollars—was on an incline and the top end of it tipping up higher and higher every day. O'Kane gave Jim Isringhausen his life's savings—and talked Mart into putting up a hundred and some odd dollars too, to round off the investment at an even three thousand. He'd stood in that overgrown field and looked at those sorry twigs and saw the whole thing unfold, the gophers ravaging the roots, the well run dry, Jim Isringhausen back in New York enthroned in some townhouse like J. Pierpont Morgan, the weeds dead and parched and fallen away to the faintest skeletons of what they were and the orange trees as barren and dead under the summer sun as the grainy yellow dirt itself. But he didn't care. It was a chance, that was all. The worst chance, maybe, but he was tired of waiting, cored out with it, exhausted, worn down, reckless and mad and seething with self-hate and the blackest kind of fatalistic despair: throw a nickel in the ocean and see if it makes a splash.

He drank beer with the whiskey and when that ran out he drank the bourbon. He was sick in the mornings and his throat was dry through the afternoons, his sinuses clogged, his head throbbing. He drank the sloe gin and it tasted like some sort of liquefied tooth powder, and then he dug up the wine and drank that. There were bootleggers in town now, weasel-faced desperadoes who drove up from Mexico with tequila and mescal and Pedro Domecq brandy, but it was eight dollars a bottle, nine, ten, and what the local entrepreneurs were making out in the canyons was a quarter the price, even if it was just about undrinkable. What they called whiskey was grain alcohol diluted with tap water, colored with caramel and flavored with prune juice, and "Scotch" was all of the above with a dose of creosote added for taste and texture. It was like drinking strychnine, battery acid, toilet cleanser, but it did the trick, and O'Kane resorted to it, a loyal customer, a daily customer, a customer whose hands shook as he tried to unfold the money and slip it into the palm of Bill McCandless from Lompoc or Charley Water-house from Carpinteria or Farmer Caty from God knew where. They ran the stills—they made the shit—and handsome Eddie O'Kane took it back to his room and drank it. Oh, once in a while he'd go up to Men-hoff's and order a hamburger sandwich and a ginger ale and sit there drinking ginger ale after ginger ale till the bottle in his back pocket was empty and somebody had to help him out the door, but mainly he just went to his room and stared at the walls.

And what walls they were. Mrs. Fitzmaurice had interred them be-neath a thick fibrous covering of the cheapest grade of wallpaper ap-plied with liberal quantities of glue over what must have been plaster, also liberally applied. These were not sheer walls, not by any means— they plunged, leapt, bulged, threw up a cordillera here, sank into the depths of a laguna there. The wallpaper pattern was meant to represent some sort of tubular flower, endlessly repeated in blue, violet and char-treuse, and if O'Kane stared at it long enough, the flowers first became bells, then sausages, and finally, if he'd had enough Lompoc swill, sev-ered heads, elongated in the most horrible and unnatural way. There wasn't much furniture to obstruct his view—a washstand, bed, ward-robe, chair and table—but that was all right with O'Kane. He had the opportunity to contemplate furniture all day long at Riven Rock, room after room of it, the finest money could buy. He didn't need to bring it home with him—and he didn't need the encumbrance either. Posses-sions were for the rich, and he wasn't rich and never would be—not un-less Jim Isringhausen pulled off some sort of miracle.

Mrs. Fitzmaurice had graced his room with her chef d'oeuvre, an ambitious four-foot-long-by-two-foot-high canvas that daringly inter-mixed puppies and kittens both in what seemed at first glance to be a demonic battle over the remains of a disemboweled kitten, but on closer inspection proved to be an innocent tug-of-war over a ball of yarn. This inspirational piece had pride of place on the wall over the bed, where O'Kane had to twist his neck to study it while lying there drinking and listening to the only record he had (a distant, hissingly ethereal rendi-tion of "Semper Fidelis" that sounded as if it had been recorded in the locker room at Notre Dame). One wall was broken up by a window, another by the door; the third was an uninterrupted medley of bell-like and sausagelike flowers. His fellow boarders—there were eight of them, all in various stages of unhope and decay—strenuously avoided him, except at meals, when a certain degree of contact and even conversation was inevitable, but he began skipping meals and avoiding them in the hallways even before they had a chance to avoid him.

So it went, through the winter, into the spring and the parched, citrus-wilting summer. O'Kane began to miss the odd day at work when the ersatz whiskey or Scotch or "Genuine Holland Genever" was especially bad and hit him so hard even the fillings of his teeth ached, and he didn't like to do that, miss work, and he knew it was the beginning of the end of everything he'd ever struggled and hoped for, but he just couldn't seem to muster the energy to care. And no one else seemed to care either. Brush was on the way out, even a blind man could see that. He'd stopped putting in regular hours altogether, and half the time when he did show up it was no more than a hello and good-bye for Mr. McCormick before he puffed and blustered his way out to the theater house and buried himself in his office. Mart was as thickheaded as ever, oblivious to everything, and Nick and Pat were putting on weight till they looked like twin bulldogs, asleep on their feet. And Katherine, the presiding genius of the place, was nowhere to be seen. She was a name in a newspaper clipping, Mrs. Stanley McCormick, running around the country with a bunch of birth control fanatics and blood-sucking feminists—now that women had got the vote and voted down drinking, they wanted to do away with babies too. And sure, why not—let the stork fly down out of heaven with them so women could spend all their free time smoking and griping and wearing pants.

There was a real decline in the upkeep of the place, too—so much so that even O'Kane noticed it through the scrim of his alcoholic haze. Torkelson was gone, lured away by one of the nonschizophrenic local millionaires, and the new man, ponderous, slow-moving, with a phony English accent and the ridiculous name of Butters, let the household staff get away with murder. There was dust everywhere, great roiling clouds of it rising from every chair you sat in, Mr. McCormick's shirts were haphazardly laundered and indifferently ironed, the male house-maids spent half the day lolling around the kitchen with their feet up and you never saw a broom or feather duster in action anymore, let alone a mop. Outside, it was even worse. Stribling had given notice the day after the gopher incident and for lack of a better alternative, Brush had put the skinny Irishman in charge (O'Mara his name was, not O'Hara, he was from Poughkeepsie, New York, and he didn't know a cactus from a coconut), and everything went to hell in a handbasket. There were Italians asleep under the bushes in broad daylight, gophers eating their way through the gardens and plowing up the lawns, whole flower beds gone dead for lack of care, and no one seemed to notice, least of all Mr. McCormick—he just went on talking to his judges, reading aloud in half a dozen voices and veering off across the estate at a mad canter every time somebody opened the door and let him out.

It was late that fall, on a day of slanting sun and scouring winds that tossed the trees and twisted themselves around puffs of yellow dust, that O'Kane, drunk on the job, broached the subject of his orange-grove investment with his employer. Mart was asleep on the sofa. Dr. Brush was in his office. There wasn't a sound anywhere in the house but for the gasp and sigh of the wind. "Mr. McCormick," O'Kane said, setting down the book he'd been staring at for the past half hour without effect, "I'd be curious to know your opinion on something—an investment I've made with Jim Isringhausen. In citrus."

"Who?" Mr. McCormick was moving round the table, hopping lightly from one foot to the other, arranging the chairs and table settings for lunch, a thing he particularly liked to do. Some days he'd spend as much as an hour or more positioning and repositioning the chairs, shifting plates, spoons, cups and saucers a quarter inch to the left or right, worrying over the napkins in their rings, endlessly rearranging the cut flowers in the vase in the center of the table. It was one of his rituals, one of the more innocuous ones, and all the doctors had encouraged him in it, even Brush—at least he was doing something.

"Jim Isringhausen," O'Kane repeated. "He says he used to know you at Princeton."

Mr. McCormick had the look of a wading bird standing there over the table, some lean beaky thing studying to spear a frog or a minnow and gulp it down whole. His eyes went briefly to O'Kane's and then fell away again. "Never heard of him," he said, realigning spoon and plate on the doctor's side of the table, and then he said something under his breath to one of his judges. This wasn't unusual, particularly at mealtimes, and O'Kane thought nothing of it. Often Mr. McCormick would set extra places at the table, and when Dr. Brush questioned him about it, he would explain that they were reserved for the judges. Today there were only four places — for Mart, O'Kane, Dr. Brush and their host — so it was safe to assume that the judges had already eaten.

"Sure you have," O'Kane heard himself say, a faint tocsin ringing somewhere in the back of his fuddled brain, " — Princeton, '96. He was your classmate."

Mr. McCormick commenced hopping from foot to foot again; this was another of his rituals, and it meant that the floor was on fire. When the floor wasn't on fire it was made of glue, a very efficacious and un-yielding glue, and he had to strain to lift his feet. But now he was hopping, and because he was hopping, he was too absorbed to respond to O'Kane's assertions.

"He lives in New York," O'Kane went on, and he was beginning to feel just the tiniest bit desperate now, marshaling his facts till the weight of them would give him the reassurance he was looking for. "He has something to do with the stock exchange, I think. And his brother, you know his brother — or you know of him. He has that grand big place out on Sycamore Canyon Road, the one we pass by on our drives sometimes?"

When Mr. McCormick still didn't answer, O'Kane, who was feeling very strange and out of sorts, as if he had a fever coming on — or a hangover and fever combined — sat brooding a moment, trying to recol-lect just what he did know about Jim Isringhausen, aside from the fact that his sister-in-law was a terrific lay. Not much. Not much at all. He worried it over a bit, then tried a new tack. "Mr. McCormick, when you were . . . well, before you came to Riven Rock, before you were mar-ried, I mean, I was just wondering how you felt about investing in real estate — in general, I mean."

Mr. McCormick had hopped himself across the room to the win-dow, where he stood holding a spoon up to the light, periodically breathing on it and then buffing it on his shirttail. He gave O'Kane a blank look.

"Your properties. Your ranch in New Mexico. All those buildings in Chicago. Your house in Massachusetts."

This was a real stumper, and it seemed to take Mr. McCormick back a ways. O'Kane wasn't really expecting an answer at this point, and he didn't know what he was after anyway — sure Mr. McCormick was rich and grand, but he'd inherited his money and he was mad as a loon, and what did that make O'Kane for seeking advice of him?

Mr. McCormick hopped back to the table, left foot, right foot, left, left, right, and replaced the spoon. He stood fretting over the arrangement a moment and then turned a bloodless face to O'Kane. "My, my wife m-manages all my p-property. I don't, I don't"—long pause—"I don't concern myself with that anymore."

What had he expected? The voice of the oracle? Sound financial advice? A loan? O'Kane sank deeper into his chair. Everything in the room seemed to be in motion, every atom bucking up against the next till the furniture and walls were frantic with activity, and he knew he needed a drink. He lurched to his feet, shook Mart awake and ducked into the toilet, where he lifted the ceramic lid of the reservoir and fished out a pint bottle of whatever it was Charley Waterhouse had sold him a case of the night before. O'Kane had decanted a quart of the stuff into two pint bottles for ease of transport and concealment, and now, visions of orange groves dying in his head, he raised the cool glass aperture to his puckered lips and kissed it long and hard, letting the fever flare up again till he didn't know whether he was going to vomit or pass out—or both.

When he came back into the room, Mr. McCormick was remonstrating with somebody in the high querulous tone that meant he was about to have an episode, but it wasn't Mart he was addressing. Mart was out again, slumped in a chair and snoring softly. No, Mr. McCormick was pleading with his judges—"I didn't mean it—I didn't want to—I never—I'm ashamed, I am!"—and O'Kane prepared himself for the worst. But this time, the worst was far worse than he could ever have imagined, because just before the walls started moving and the ceiling came alive with flickering eyes and snouts and a scramble of fur, the judges appeared in stiff congress over their plates, bearded and stern, three of them, three bearded scowling merciless men, and all their six merciless eyes fastened on him, smiling Eddie O'Kane, only he didn't have any smile for this occasion, because he was in uncharted waters now and going down fast.

All right. Sure. So he laid off for a while. He wouldn't go near the stuff, not if you stabbed him with a sharp stick and drove him into a cage and forced it down his throat. Of course, it was just that swill, that was the problem, the impurities and such—he was lucky he wasn't blinded or rendered impotent or insane. He hadn't really seen the judges—it was just the booze, the bad stuff, a bad batch. But he laid off all the same and he got to work every day, and though his guts were full of hot magma and he couldn't shit to save his life and his head was like an eggshell in a vise and his legs so heavy he could hardly stand up, he began, very gradually, to experience the world as it really was, without a crutch, without a filter.

The first thing he noticed, shivering and sweating at the same time as he vomited in the toilet at the end of the hall and fucking Maloney who he was going to kill and dismember and maybe boil and eat banging on the door in his boorish inconsideration and impatience, was that he'd begun to get his sense of smell back. It was amazing: he lived in a world of odors. Piss suddenly reeked under his shoes. His socks were vaporous, his underwear yeasty. The hallway outside his door smelled as if somebody had died in it just prior to being immured in the walls. He could smell Mrs. Fitzmaurice's facial unguent from where he lay in bed, all the way down the stairs and around the corner and through the door to her sad and solitary widow's room. And he could smell her sadness too, the smell of disuse, old flesh, a body mewed up and wasted. There was a car parked out front and it had gasoline in the tank and he could smell the gasoline. And food: onions, lard, beef, canned beans, some sort of spice—what was it? Basil? Yes, basil. He hadn't smelled basil in years—hadn't smelled anything for that matter—and it brought tears to his eyes.

Next thing he knew, he had an appetite.

First the smell, and then the hunger. He started getting up for breakfast, sitting around the table at Mrs. Fitzmaurice's with his fellow boarders, flapjacks like stones, porridge like stones before they petrify, syrup like squeezed stones, but he ate it, ate it all and cleaned his plate with a sop of bread. At ten-thirty every morning, instead of taking a booze break, he ambled down to the kitchen and sweet-talked Sam Wah into frying him a beefsteak or a piece of liver with onions, and at lunchtime he sat there across from Mr. McCormick in the very lap of one of the judges and buttered up his bread and dug into his soup as if he hadn't eaten in a week. He took dinner at Menhoff's because he was too late getting home for Mrs. Fitzmaurice, and she'd never charged him, except for Saturdays and Sundays, and when he drank a bottle of ginger ale he studied the label with a wistful smile: "Reminding you of the Eighteenth Amendment and the Volstead Act, the contents of this bottle is sold to you on the understanding that it will not be used or mixed with alcoholic liquor."

His suits, which had hung slack on him, began to fit again. He took pains with his hair and his teeth and made sure he washed under the arms every morning, and a month later, after swearing off Charley Waterhouse, Bill McCandless, and even Cody Menhoff, who was now selling a finer class of homemade gin under the table and the county sheriff looking the other way, O'Kane found he'd recovered something else too: his libido. He woke each morning with a tire iron between his legs, and when he strolled down the block to wait for Roscoe to pick him up he leered at every female between the ages of twelve and sixty and tipped his hat so many times he wore out the brim. He needed a woman. And he thought of little else through the rest of that week and into the next, the terrible quandary of where to find one burning in his brain every time he dropped the needle on his Sousa record, unlocked the barred door to the upstairs parlor or set off cross-country with Mart and Mr. McCormick on one of their mad runs. Listening to those faint trumpets, tubas and sousaphones, jogging along behind Mr. Mc-Cormick, he turned the problem over in his mind: women, the sort of women he was seeking, were gathered thick as pigeons over cocktails in the speakeasies that had sprung up around town, but to get to them he'd have to drink a cocktail too, and one cocktail would lead to another till he was past caring and lost his appetite and his sense of smell and began to see Mr. McCormick's judges sitting there before him in all their undeniable corporeality.

It was in this state, goatish and disgruntled but alive to every sensory current of the world, that O'Kane came up the stairs at Riven Rock one morning to find Mr. McCormick extended as far as he could reach through the bars of the upper parlor door with both his hands locked round the throat of Sam Wah, the cook. Sam's face was an ugly color, bloated and dark as a bruise, and though his hands were in turn clamped to Mr. McCormick's wrists, he was barely struggling, his feet half-lifted from the floor, his eyes beginning to film over. And Mart? Where was he? Unconscious on the floor behind Mr. McCormick, a glistening bright carnation of blood blooming out of the corner of his mouth.

O'Kane lost no time—he was up the stairs in a trice, methodically attacking Mr. McCormick's forearms, not a word exchanged between them, nothing but grunts and curses and the fierce hissing insuck of breath, until Mr. McCormick released the cook and the cook fell to the floor like a sack of old clothes. But Mr. McCormick wasn't done yet, not by any means. As soon as O'Kane forced his hands away, Mr. McCormick seized O'Kane by both arms and drew him violently up against the rack of the bars, and while that struggle went on, Sam Wah rose shakily to his feet, massaged his throat with an angry trembling hand and launched into a high-pitched litany of Chinese complaint. O'Kane finally got a purchase on Mr. McCormick and they paused, locked in a stalemate, each gripping the other's arms through the inflexible iron bars.

"You no like, I no cook!" Sam Wah shouted, dancing round the landing and shaking his fist. "Mistah Cormah, you got no right!"

O'Kane, casting a quick glance beyond his employer's seething face, saw the breakfast things scattered across the room behind him, and gathered that Mr. McCormick had objected to the way the cook had prepared his eggs.

"You got no right take my neck like this, Mistah Cormah!" Sam Wah was livid. He stripped the apron from his chest, balled it up and flung it on the floor beside the toque that had fallen there at some earlier stage of the altercation. "Mistah Cormah, I got tell you, after fo'teen year, I quit!"

His grip rigid in O'Kane's, Mr. McCormick just stood there on the other side of the bars, and he never even blinked, never said a word, but his jaw was set and there was something in his eyes that said he would never let go, the bruised defiance of a very spoiled little rich boy who would die before he would admit he was wrong.

The upshot of all this was a revolution in the culinary life of Riven Rock. Brush, who really didn't want to be bothered, consulted with Butters and the nurses and whoever else would listen to him, and discovered that male cooks were few and far between — not to mention the male kitchen help Sam Wah took with him when he departed. As a stopgap, they promoted a Mexican gardener who claimed to have been a cook at a restaurant in Veracruz before the revolution. He lasted three days, during which the house was filled with strange and disquieting odors. Every meal he prepared seemed to consist of some sort of glutinous bean and rice paste wrapped in a thin bread-like substance no one could identify, and all of it so everlastingly and excoriatingly hot it was like pouring flaming kerosene down your throat. Mr. McCormick became very disturbed and spent the whole of every morning shut away in his toilet, trousers down around his ankles, folding and refolding his toilet paper while he awaited the next intestinal emergency.

Next they tried a fleshless sun-blasted old man who used to run a chuckwagon for sheepherders in the Goleta foothills, but all he knew how to cook was mutton, and after a week of that—boiled, fried, fricasseed, roasted and baked in a clay pit till it was mummified—they took to calling in orders at Diehl's Grocery, three meals a day. Finally, deeply frustrated and in high dudgeon, Dr. Brush took O'Kane aside one afternoon and asked him what he thought of hiring a woman—just to do the cooking and the kitchen work.

"A woman?" O'Kane repeated, as if they were speaking of some alien species, and he was thinking of Elsie Reardon and the other female maids they'd had in the early days. It seemed so long ago. So long it was as if the prohibition against women had been written in stone and brought down from the mountaintop.

"Yes," Brush shouted, and he was impatient with all this, resentful of having to act as estate manager and majordomo of the house as well, when it was clearly his duty as a trained psychiatrist to devote himself to higher things, for the main and simple reason that that was what he'd been trained and hired to do. He gave O'Kane an exasperated look. "Mr. McCormick has been, well, calmer lately," he said, "aside of course from the unfortunate incident with the cook, that is, and if we give strict orders that the woman is not to leave the kitchen under any circumstances and keep a sharp and vigilant eye on the patient, well, I don't see any reason why we can't, well, employ a female here. It's clear we can't go on like this."

O'Kane watched him a moment, trying to gauge the extent of the doctor's agitation, and then he shrugged. "Sure," he said. "Why not?"

And so it was that he came into the house the next morning to a smell of sauces and spices and fresh baked bread so intoxicating he thought he would faint with the anticipation of it, real food—Italian, it smelled like—and not the unvarying and nameless crud Mrs. Fitzmaurice served up at the boardinghouse. He let himself in upstairs and carefully locked the door behind him, a woman in the house again and this no time to be lax or forgetful, and found Mart reading to Mr. McCormick out of a book of Shakespeare's plays. They both looked tranquil and they both turned their heads to smile at him as he swung away from the door and came into the room. "Good morning, Mart, Mr. McCormick," he said, and he could feel it himself, a change come over them, a charm, the benediction of food.

"M-morning, Eddie," Mr. McCormick said in a high cheery voice. Mart, whose busted lip had healed nicely by this time, looked up from the book and grunted out a greeting.

"Smells good," O'Kane said, and the odor, redolent of sausage, garlic and pomodoros, had risen from the kitchen to invest the upper floor.

"Yeah," Mart said, wagging his big head and grinning. They all three of them involuntarily swallowed.

"So who's the new cook?" O'Kane asked, sliding in beside Mart on the sofa.

Mart glanced at Mr. McCormick; Mr. McCormick's eyes glistened. He had a look on his face, something new—nobody had to tell him there was a woman downstairs. "I don't know," Mart said. "Some widow, I think. A wop."

O'Kane lifted his eyebrows. Something was wrong here, and he felt it all the way down in his gut where all of that spaghetti and ravioli and lasagna was destined to go. It couldn't be. There were a thousand widows in the country, war widows, old ladies in black shuffling along the sidewalks, women whose husbands had died at sea, in auto wrecks and train derailments, of heart failure and cancer, and sure they had to support themselves, even if they were old and feeble. Still, he found himself getting to his feet and looking round the room in a daze. "Will you excuse me, Mr. McCormick?" he said. "I just need to go downstairs a minute—I forgot something."

And then he was on the staircase, the sweet rising odor of marinara sauce and fresh-baked bread stronger and stronger as he made his way down the steps, into the servants' hall and through the swinging doors to the kitchen. Steam rose round him, parting in wisps and wraiths with the stimulus of the fanning doors, all the burners of the stove were on high and the hot liquid bubbling and hissing in the big cast-iron pots, and there was a figure there, a familiar figure, a figure he knew as well as any on earth, a bit fuller maybe, a shade older, but it was her and no denying it: *Giovannella*.

"Hiya, Eddie," she said, turning a cold unsmiling face to him, indifferent as the wind, "long time, no see."

2.

___

LA LUNE DE MIEL

The day after their wedding Stanley and Katherine went on to Paris along with their mothers and servants and six hundred pounds of luggage, and the honeymoon began in earnest. Unfortunately, Stanley seemed to experience some difficulty in putting his affairs in order and finding the ideal spot in his steamer trunk for his socks, handkerchiefs and underwear, and they missed their train and were late getting in. It was a disappointment for Katherine, who'd been looking forward to an evening on the town, not simply for her own sake, but for Stanley's — she was hoping the change of scene would distract him so he wouldn't be so preoccupied when finally, inevitably, at the shining climax of the evening, they found themselves in bed together. But it wasn't to be.

Everyone had been packed and waiting, the servants solicitous, the bags stowed away, the carriage out front in the circular drive, and Stanley nowhere to be found. It was raining still, and the raw wet earth of the flower beds gave off a dank odor of the sifting and winowing of the centuries. Earthworms — *Lumbricus terretris* — sprawled across the walk, and how many of those blind blameless creatures had Katherine dissected under the direction of one bearded professor or another? She'd been out to the carriage twice already to see to things, stepping carefully round the pale bleached corpses of the worms, and now she stood in the vestibule with her mother, adjusting her hat in a rising storm of excitement, eager to be on her way, to begin the adventure, to leave the stone towers and the placid lake behind and get on with her life as Mrs. Stanley McCormick. Nettie was already settled in the carriage and Jean Claude was stationed at the door with a black spreading umbrella, awaiting their pleasure. "Whatever can be keeping Stanley?" her mother wondered aloud, craning her neck to catch a glimpse of the clock in the hall behind them.

Katherine smoothed her gloves, peered through the windows at the rain melting into the pavement and plucking relentlessly at the black canvas top of the carriage, and then laid a hand on her mother's arm. "You go ahead, mother," she said. "I'll go up and see what's keeping him—we won't be a minute."

She found Stanley in his room, pacing back and forth between an open trunk and two eviscerated suitcases. He had something bundled in his arms, some sort of garment—longjohns—and there were notebooks, pens, sketch pads, socks, ties and shaving things arranged on the bed in neat little piles, a novel he'd left out to read on the train, his tennis racket and bathing costume. "Stanley, darling," she said, standing there at the door in her hat and coat, "what are you doing? Don't you know everyone's waiting? We'll miss the train."

His color was high and a lock of his hair had fallen loose. "I—well, it's my underwear, you see, because I can't just go off on a day with weather like this and not think about it, especially the temperature differential in Paris and what it'll be like on the train, and so I just, well, I needed time to sort things out and decide—"

"Your underwear?" She was stunned. "Stanley, the train is leaving in forty-five minutes. If we don't go right this instant we're going to miss it. This is no time to worry about underwear."

"No, no, no," he said, gesturing, the limp garments draped over both arms, "you don't understand. You see, I order my longjohns specially from Dunhill & Porter in London, and they come in eight gradations of weight so as to meet every possible contingency, from, from, well *snow* to the sunshiniest day in August, when, of course, one wouldn't want to suffocate—" and he let out a strange hollow yelp of a laugh. "Don't you see?" he said, bending now to the steamer trunk and patiently folding the garments in his arms. She could see that he was laughing still, chuckling to himself and shaking his head. "She wants me to freeze — " he said, addressing the depths of the trunk, " — my own w-wife."

She crossed the room to him, murmuring, "Here, let me help," but he stiffened and turned away from her. "Stanley," she said, "please. It's not cold at all — it must be fifty-five or sixty degrees out there — and they're sure to be having Indian summer weather in Paris this time of year. . . ."

He paid her no mind, but kept folding and unfolding his underwear and carrying it from one bag to another, and no sooner did he settle on a place for it than he pulled it back out and started the whole process all over again.

"We're going to miss the train," she said. "Stanley. Are you listening to me? *We're going to miss the train.*"

His eyes went suddenly to hers and there was a pleading look in them, a look that both begged for help and rejected it at the same time. "I can't," he said. "I'm, I'm not ready. I can't."

Her mother's voice came up the stairwell then, tremulous and interrogatory: "Katherine?"

"Leave it," Katherine urged. "Leave it for the servants to send on. We'll buy you new things as soon as we get in, better things, Parisian things, and all this will be on the next train if you need it. Come on," she said, taking him by the arm, "come on, Stanley, we've got to go."

He wasn't violent, he wasn't rough, he wasn't pettish or peevish, but he was immovable all the same. He looked down at her from his height, looked at her hand urgent on his arm, and said, simply, "No." Then he pulled away from her and crossed the room to his suitcase, trailing the vacant legs of his longjohns behind him like pennants.

Suddenly she was angry. "Stanley!" she snapped, and she couldn't help herself, honeymoon or no honeymoon. She stamped her foot; her voice shot up a register. "You stop this now!" she shouted, and here she was, shrill as a fishwife on the second day of her marriage, but her patience was at an end and the train was rolling into the station and she wanted to go, to go now, and no more frittering or vacillating or neurotic displays.

She was about to stalk across the room and take his arm again when she started at a sound behind her and turned around, expecting her mother. It wasn't her mother. It was Stanley's mother, Nettie, the ogre herself, the rain beaded on her hat and caught in a fine sparkling mist on the collar of her fur coat. Her jaw was wet and her mouth barely moved as she spoke. "I'll handle this," she said.

Nettie did finally get Stanley moving—how, Katherine would never know—and they both emerged from the room within half an hour, the suitcases and trunk neatly packed and secured and standing watch at the door, Nettie on Stanley's left arm, his coat draped over his right, but still they missed the first train and the evening was ruined as far as Katherine was concerned. There was some satisfaction in finally getting under way, sitting there in the intimacy of their compartment with her erect and proper husband at her side, even if she did have to share him with his mother and hers, but it wasn't what she'd hoped for. They made small talk, gazed out the window at the dark French countryside and the flitting lights, dined pleasantly enough, but all the while Stanley seemed tense and wooden, nodding his head automatically at any remark addressed to him, his hand—the hand she held in hers—as stiff as a marionette's. And if he was wooden, if he was a puppet, then who was pulling the strings? Katherine gazed at Nettie's tight self-satisfied smile as the train shot smoothly through the night and they talked in small voices of French painting, escargot, people they'd known in Chicago and the unsuitability of birds as pets, and she felt as depressed and deflated as she'd ever felt in her life.

When they finally arrived, Stanley was visibly drained. The whole business of the wedding and the move out of his hotel to Prangins for a night and then out of Prangins for Paris must have wrought havoc on his nerves. He was emotionally delicate, Katherine knew that, and she appreciated that in him—he was sensitive, artistic, retiring, as kind and thoughtful as any man in the world, the sort of husband women dream of. But the exhaustion was written on his face for anybody to see and when finally they were shown to their suite at the Elysée Palace, he merely wished her good night, ducked into his room and shut the door firmly behind him. She stood there a moment in the center of the salon, exhausted herself, thinking she should go to him, if only to pet and comfort him, but then she heard the sudden sharp rasp of the latch falling into place on the inside of the door and she sank into the nearest chair and cried till she was all cried out.

In the morning, Stanley was his old self, smiling and relaxed, and Katherine felt renewed too—they'd both been tired, that was all. They breakfasted in their room, treating each other with the exaggerated tenderness of a couple celebrating their golden wedding anniversary, and everything seemed right, the way she'd pictured it, gentle and soothing and intimate. Until Nettie showed up, that is. She burst in on them at nine, wanting to know if Stanley had taken his fish-oil capsule and if they were still planning to tour the Musée du Jeu-de-Paume or the Louvre. Immediately, Stanley's mood changed. A moment before he'd been gay and communicative, slathering his toast with butter and reminiscing about how he and Harold used to play at Indians when they were boys and steal out into the yard to eat their toast dry beneath the shrubbery, and now suddenly the words died in his throat. No, he admitted, he hadn't taken his fish-oil capsule, but he had it right here somewhere, and he would, and yes, they were planning on the Louvre, but he needed time to finish, well, his breakfast, and he hoped his mother wouldn't be too disappointed if they left at ten?

If Stanley's mother was going, then it was only right that Josephine should go too, and Katherine tried to make the best of it, chatting with her mother and snuggling beside Stanley in the carriage on the way over. But as they strolled through the galleries, Stanley quietly commenting on one painting or another, he unconsciously took his mother's arm, and Katherine and Josephine were left to bring up the rear. Then there was lunch. Nettie had invited some horrid missionary's wife who apparently ran a boardinghouse where Stanley had stayed while under the tutelage of Monsieur Julien. Her name was Mrs. van Pele, a dumpy, opinionated, undistinguished woman in her sixties, and Stanley nearly jumped out of his skin when she entered the room. He shot up from the table so precipitously he nearly knocked it over, his face flushing, and if it weren't for the potted palm behind him he might have fled the restaurant altogether. "Adela," Nettie chirped, trying to cover Stanley's confusion while the waiter looked on suspiciously and Katherine and Josephine gaped in bewilderment, "how nice of you to come. You know Stanley, of course, and this is his wife, Katherine, and her mother, Mrs. Josephine Dexter."

Stanley didn't offer his hand, nor did he bend forward to accept Mrs. van Pele's; he just stood there, his face crimson, staring down at his feet and clenching his fists. "So nice to see you again, Stanley," Mrs.

van Pele said, settling into a chair with the assistance of the maître d', "and congratulations. I wish you all the best."

"I'm so ashamed," Stanley murmured, raising his head to address the entire table, the maître d' and the waiter as well. "I don't—I, well, I've never told anybody, I'm so ashamed, but I was impure and violated my mother's wishes and your hospitality too—"

"Nonsense," Nettie said, and her voice cracked like a whip. "Sit down, Stanley. You've nothing to be ashamed of."

A silence fell over the table as Stanley slowly sank back into his seat. The tinkling of silverware and the buzz of voices became audible all of a sudden. Katherine was bewildered. She tried to take her husband's hand, but he pulled away from her.

"Utter nonsense and rubbish," Nettie said after a moment, as if for clarification. "You've just been married, Stanley. You have responsibilities now—you're not a boy anymore."

The waiter had retreated a few steps, wincing and sucking at his teeth, and Mrs. van Pele and Josephine began talking simultaneously, when Stanley stood again. "Excuse me," he murmured, pushing back the chair, "I need to, well, freshen up—that is, I mean, I'll be right back."

"Sit *down*, Stanley," Nettie said, peering up from beneath the armature of her hat.

Stanley didn't listen. His face was heavy, his shoulders slumped. He looked round the table as if he didn't recognize anyone there and then strode directly across the room, up the three steps to the entrace and out the door and into the street, and he never looked back.

Katherine didn't know what to do. She looked at her mother, at the missionary's wife, and then finally at Nettie: her husband, for some reason fathomable only to him, had just deserted her in a public place. On the third day of their honeymoon, no less. She was stunned. "Where could he possibly—?" she heard herself say.

Nettie said nothing.

"He's probably just gone out for some air, dear," Josephine said, and then she glanced over her shoulder and made a face. "It is a bit stuffy in here."

Mrs. van Pele agreed. Wholeheartedly.

And now suddenly Nettie was on her feet, a short brisk square-shouldered woman of sixty-nine who looked several years younger, dressed in the latest fashions from the Parisian couturiers and as used to the prerogatives of command as any mere Napoleon or Kaiser. Her hat alone—a massive construction of felt, feathers and velvetta—could have inspired awe in any officer corps. "Adela, Josephine," she said, "would you excuse me for just a moment—I'm sure Stanley's quite all right; if anything it's just the excitement of seeing you again, Adela, so soon after the drama of the wedding, and I see now that perhaps we shouldn't have surprised him—but I do need a moment to speak privately with Katherine." She gestured for Katherine to rise and follow her. "You'll come with me into the next room, please? It'll only take a minute."

Puzzled, Katherine rose from the table and followed Nettie's brisk martial form through the main dining area and into the ladies' salon, where Nettie settled herself in a plush chair in front of an oval mirror in a gilt frame and directed Katherine to the chair beside her. There were two other women present, at the far end of the room, conversing in low tones. Katherine sank into the chair with an air of impatience—she was beginning to feel distinctly irritated, and who was this woman to think she could command her too?

"I'll get right to the point," Nettie said, drawing her mouth tight and staring into Katherine's eyes. "I don't pretend to know what's upset Stanley this afternoon, but I will say this"—she paused—"*change* has been very difficult for him. He's the best boy in the world, fine and bright and loving, but he suffers from a nervous condition. It's his extreme sensitivity, that's all, his artistic side coming out, but of course we've had him examined by a number of specialists because of his older sister, Mary Virginia. You see, Mary Virginia has been diagnosed as—"

Katherine cut her off. "Yes, I know. She suffers from dementia praecox. Stanley told me. Ages ago. But I really don't see how that should affect him in any way."

"Exactly. But he *is* delicate emotionally, and for some years now he's had bouts of nervous prostration, and I thought I'd better just tell you what you're in for, since you were so anxious to come between him and his family. He doesn't need coddling, not at all, but he does need understanding, and he does have his moods."

Katherine watched herself in the mirror, her face pale and eyes alert, the slightest movement of her hands and forearms duplicated as she smoothed the skirt over her knees. "I'm perfectly well aware of that," she said, and her tone couldn't have been colder or more final.

Nettie leaned forward, all the combative lines round her mouth and eyes drawn into fierce alignment. "I don't know if you appreciate what I'm saying: we're afraid his condition could worsen. We hope not—I pray every night for him—and the reports are encouraging, or at least most of them, but there is that possibility. Are you prepared for it?"

Katherine was already getting to her feet. "I don't know what you think I am, but I'm no child and I resent being treated like one. I'm fully aware of Stanley's neurasthenia and fully prepared to do anything I can to see him improve. It's not as if he's—"

"Yes? Not as if he's what? Crazy? Is that what you mean to say?"

"Of course not," Katherine said, but even as she said it the idea was there in her head, ugly as a scab that refuses to heal. "I meant it's not as if his behavior is cause for alarm, not to me, anyway, because I know him in a way you never will. He's my husband, don't you understand that? He's not yours anymore—he's mine."

The old woman in the armorial hat just stared at her out of two eyes that were exactly like Stanley's. It took her a moment, and then, in a voice so low it was barely audible, she said, "Yes. That's right. He's yours."

They stayed a month in Paris, occasionally making overnight motor excursions in the Renault Stanley bought, and they switched hotels at Katherine's whim—from the Elysée Palace to the Splendide to the Ritz. "I need a change," she would tell Stanley as he staggered through the door with the bundle of string-bound parcels and hat boxes that represented the day's removable offerings, but she never gave him a reason beyond that. The reason, of course, was Nettie. She was entrenched in her suite of rooms at the Elysée Palace like a fat swollen tick, sucking the blood out of everyone, and Katherine only wanted to get away from her—and to get Stanley away too. That was the important thing. That was essential. Because they'd be all right if she would just leave them alone, Katherine was sure of it.

But Nettie was tenacious. She insisted on lunching and dining with them daily and consulting on every purchase they made, from the andirons, vases and oil paintings that would grace their future home to the white fox tippet and muff and tourmaline bracelet Stanley picked out for his bride, and Katherine's only recourse was to use her own mother as a buffer every step of the way. It was like a game of checkers: Nettie advanced a square and Katherine countered with Josephine. "Should we go to the theater this evening?" Nettie would propose at lunch, and Katherine, looking up languidly from a book or catalogue, would say, "Why don't you and mother go?—Stanley and I are exhausted, aren't we, Stanley?"

Stanley was a prince through it all, though he refused to hear any criticism of his mother—he wouldn't even allow Katherine to mention her without bunching up the muscles of his jaw till they began to shift beneath the skin like some sort of abnormal growth. He was dutiful and patient, the soul of propriety, and never once did he let a thought of socialism or Eugene Debs come between him and the determined campaign of acquisition Katherine had embarked on: they did have a house to fill, after all. Or would have soon. There was only one thing in which he continued to fail her, the biggest thing, the ultimate thing, the thing all the creatures of the earth did as naturally and unconsciously as they drew breath and ate and gamboled in the fields, and there was no fulfillment without it, no security, no consummation, no hope.

Each night was a repetition of the first. He was busy. He was worried. The Harvester Company. Correspondence. Accounts. Bills. If she would just give him a minute, just a minute. . . . Alone, in their rooms, just before retiring, he would take her hand, bend to her with a formal kiss and excuse himself, and no matter how seductive she tried to be, how suggestive or shy or elaborately unconcerned, he sat at his desk in a sea of paper until she gave up and found her bleary way to bed. That was her hidden affliction, that was her sorrow, and she blamed Nettie for it—the proximity of Nettie, Nettie's face and image and her fierce emasculating will: if she couldn't have her son, then no one could.

Finally, in desperation, Katherine hit on the idea of a motor tour to the south of France, a tour that would be certain to deflect both mothers, what with the dust and mud and sheer barbarity of the lurching, fuming, backfiring monster of a contraption they would be expected to immure themselves in for days at a time, and hadn't Nettie sworn she would never set foot in an automobile as long as she lived? Yes, of course: a motor tour. What could be better? Katherine woke with the inspiration one crisp morning in October and let it incubate while the maid laid out her clothes and she brushed her hair and studied her face in the mirror. She waited till the waiter had brought their breakfast and Stanley was poking idly through the newspaper, and then she let out a little gasp and clasped her hands together, as if the notion had just come to her. "Stanley," she exclaimed, "I've just had the most wonderful idea!"

But yet again, Katherine had underestimated her adversary—and her own mother, for that matter. Both women greeted the plan enthusiastically, and when the morning of their departure arrived, Nettie and Josephine appeared at the Ritz in identical motoring costumes, a sort of pale dust-colored webbing that covered them from crown to heel and suggested nothing so much as beekeeping or an escape from the seraglio. Stanley climbed into the front seat beside the chauffeur and took the wheel himself, while Katherine and the cocooned mothers jostled for position on the narrow rear seat. They got no farther than Montrouge before the first tire blew, and after languishing beneath an unseasonably warm sun for an hour and a half while Stanley and the chauffeur patched it, they made two brisk miles to Bagneux before mechanical failure forced them to call it a day.

Naturally, the inn at Bagneux was considerably less than what they might have hoped for, and Stanley's mother, crusty and outraged, was the principal soloist in a chorus of complaint. Katherine was testy herself, and at dinner that night, after they'd staggered up three narrow flights to rooms that were like pigeon coops, she found herself drawn into a ridiculous argument with her mother-in-law over the French pronunciation of "orange." They'd all changed and freshened up and settled themselves in the dining room with a decent sparkling wine and a consommé madrilène that was really quite refreshing, and the waiter had just taken their orders, when Nettie, grimacing sourly under the baggage of a bad day, leaned toward Katherine and said, "You pronounce that like a foreigner."

Katherine looked to Stanley, but he was studying the wine list so earnestly you would have thought he was going to be quizzed on it, and then looked to her mother, but Josephine could only shrug. "Pronounce what?"

Nettie drew herself up, her tongue working behind her teeth to produce a nasty mincing parody of Katherine's French: "Canard à low-ron-zheh."

"And how, pray tell, am I supposed to say it?"

"Like an American. Because that's what you are, despite all your Geneva airs, and you should be proud of it, like Stanley is—aren't you, Stanley?"

Stanley gazed up from the wine list. He looked mystified and vaguely guilty, as if he were being punished for something he hadn't done. "I—well—I, yes," he said in a low voice.

"I'm sure it's just a matter of—" Josephine began, but Nettie cut her off.

"Decent people," Nettie hissed, "do not talk like"—and here she paused to glance round the table, stern, pampered, autocratic, an empress of money, McCormick money—"*Frogs.*"

Katherine was so outraged she wanted to smash every bit of crockery on the table and walk out the door and never come back, but she restrained herself—for Stanley's sake. "Yes," she said, barely able to conceal the contempt in her voice, "and how do you pronounce it then?"

All eyes were on the old woman in the adamantine hat, and she savored the moment, held it just a beat, and said: *"Auwrenge."*

So it went for the three and a half weeks it took them to get to Nice. They were constantly thrust together, exposed to all sorts of weather and every conceivable type of roadway, from cobbled village streets to cartpaths that began in the middle of nowhere and wound up at the end of it. Everyone was irritable, even Katherine's mother, who was the gentlest, most even-tempered woman alive, and by the end of the trip they were taking their meals in a brooding silence broken only by the occasional murmured request for salt or vinegar to rub into their wounds. It was an unmitigated disaster. Hateful. Utterly hateful. And Katherine, the scientist, always alert for unusual specimens, was ready to write all the major journals and testify that she'd discovered the single most horrible and irritating member of the human species, and to name her too so there would be no mistake about it: Nettie Fowler McCormick.

And then, miraculously, Nettie threw in the towel. She'd had enough. Her kidneys were scrambled, her sinuses clogged with dust and dander and dried horse feces and all the rest, her feet were dead to all sensation and both her legs and the small of her back were separate crackling bonfires of unadulterated pain. At Nice she announced that she would be boarding a liner for London and thence for the United States of America and Chicago, Illinois. She made Stanley suffer for it, there was no question about that, and they were closeted for hours at her hotel before she decided to go, and on the day she left he was so consumed with guilt and fractured loyalty he could barely speak, but to Katherine's mind it was worth it: she was gone. The ogre was gone. And now the rest of their lives could begin.

"Mother," she said, sitting with Josephine in the hotel lobby the day Nettie left, "I don't know how to say this—and I hope you won't take it the wrong way—but I wonder if you might not be feeling a little home-sick yourself? For Prangins? Or Boston, maybe?"

Josephine was in her late fifties then, a compact lively woman dressed in her eternal black, her hat mad with feathers, her eyes too small for her face. She cocked her head and smiled. "I understand you, dear: you need time alone with Stanley. I can take the train for Geneva tomorrow."

"You don't mind?"

Josephine shook her head. "No, of course not. I remember how it was with your father"—and she looked down at her hands and then gave Katherine a guarded look—"on our honeymoon, I mean. You know, we had a big wedding—half of Chicago was there—and when we finally got off on our own, that first night in the hotel . . ."

Katherine had been leafing through a book of poems, but now she quietly closed it and gripped its leather covers as if it were alive and wriggling in her lap. Her heart was pounding. "Yes?" she said.

"Well, it was a real adventure for us both, because we'd never been alone together in that way, and your father was"—she looked down again—"he was very amorous."

There was an awkward silence. After a moment, Katherine cleared her throat. "I've been meaning to ask you about that, Mother, just that subject—about marital relations, that is—because Stanley, well, he—"

"Oh, dear," her mother cried, "will you look at the time? It does fly, doesn't it?" She looked as if she were about to leap from the chair, dash across the strand and plunge headfirst into the sea. "I did want to get up to my room for a nap before dinner—it's all this sun, it's positively draining."

"Just give me a minute, Mother," Katherine persisted, "that's all I ask. Will you, please?"

Her mother's head moved just perceptibly, the faintest nod of that feathered hat. Her eyes were pinpricks, her mouth a slash of distate and disapproval.

"Stanley doesn't seem—" Katherine began, and then faltered. "He doesn't act as if he—" She reddened. Her voice wadded up in her throat. "Intimacy, I mean."

Josephine looked startled, and her face had colored now too. She made as if to get up, then thought better of it. "Katherine," she said finally, in the tone of voice she might have used to scold the servants, "there are things one just doesn't discuss—or one isn't comfortable discussing."

"But I need to discuss them, Mother," Katherine said, and all the pain and confusion of the past weeks stabbed at her, goading her on, "because Stanley isn't my husband, not, not the way I thought he would be, the way everyone . . ." She trailed off.

"Not your husband?" Josephine had put a hand to her mouth, and she shot a quick glance round the room. "What are you talking about?"

Katherine was miserable, she was abject, she was a little girl all over again, and all her scientific training, all her understanding of what men thought and knew about the systems of life and reproduction availed her nothing: her mother knew what she didn't. "He won't . . . perform."

It took Josephine a moment. She sat there rigid in the chair while the Mediterranean moved luxuriously beyond the windows, and she had the look of a torture victim, a woman whose nails were being prised from the flesh, one after the other. "Get him out of doors," she said finally. "Fresh air. Meat. That sort of thing." Another pause. "Why not take him skiing?"

The place Katherine chose was St. Moritz, in the Rhaetian Alps, not far from the Italian border. They booked rooms at the Grand Engadiner Hotel Klum, an immense and charming old place with snow-sculpted roofs, great roaring fireplaces and a Viennese quartet playing at dinner and tea. In the mornings they went for long walks through the snow-bound village, all the houses and shops decorated for Christmas, the air fragrant with woodsmoke and the smell of roasting chestnuts, and after a leisurely lunch they took to the slopes. Katherine was an accomplished skier, but Stanley was nothing short of magnificent. Graceful and adept, he moved across the unblemished hills like a line drawn across a blank page, tackling even the most daunting trails with a confidence and élan that bordered on recklessness. She'd never seen him so exuberant. Or physical.

By the end of the first week he was a new person altogether, utterly reborn, and Katherine kicked herself for not having gotten him away sooner. He laughed at the slightest pretext—an open, cheerful sort of laughter and not the startled hyena's cry that seemed to burst out of his mouth when his mother was around. He grew reminiscent over dinner. He was soft-spoken and confidential. He anticipated his wife's every need. This was what Katherine had been waiting for, the slow sweet unfolding of the days, each one opening on the next like a vase of budding roses . . . and yet still the nights remained problematical. And chaste. Maddeningly, insufferably, heartrendingly chaste.

But what to do? She had plenty of time to turn it over in her mind—a surfeit of time, nothing but time—lying awake at all hours, sitting over breakfast, lunch and dinner with her grinning husband, schussing down the slopes while he cavorted round her, launching himself dizzily over every hummock and mogul as if his legs were coiled springs, the silence of the mountains absolute, the sky a vast empty ache. Her muscles firmed. Her appetite grew. She felt vigorous and young and so wrought up with frustrated desire she couldn't have slept if she'd wanted to.

The solution came to her one afternoon just before Christmas—the day before, in fact—and it was so clear and self-evident she almost gasped aloud. They were skiing the runs at Pontresina at the time, high above the village, out of sight of their guide, the peaks rising up around them like the white walls of the earth, and she'd broken the heel binding of her left ski and Stanley had knelt before her in the snow to repair it. Even through the integument of his gloves and the insensible thickness of her boots, she could feel his touch. That was what set her off, that touch, that lingering humble subservient gesture of love, her husband there at her foot, and in that instant she knew what she had to do: *she had to take charge.*

It was so obvious it was ridiculous. Though it violated every notion of the woman's role—the pure vessel, the passive partner, sex an onus—she had to take charge, seize the initiative, go where no wife had gone before her. Stanley was a special case, and no one would know what happened between them in the privacy of their bedroom—and there was no shame in that, none at all. She was determined. She would come to him in the night—that very night—and use her hands, her mouth, any means necessary to excite him to his duty. Of course. Of course she would. It was either that or die a virgin.

They dined that night in a restaurant not far from the hotel. Katherine had made herself up, a red-and-green bow in her hair, a new dress, the tourmaline bracelet Stanley had given her sparkling on her wrist. She encouraged him to drink—a Grignolino that smelled potently of the earth— and she drank two glasses herself, for courage. When they got back to their rooms, she submitted to his stiff nightly kiss and then told him she was worn out from skiing and thought she'd retire early—if he had no objections. "Oh, well, yes—sure," he said, jerking each word out as if it was fastened to his teeth, his eyes running up and down the wall behind her. "Well," he said again. "So. Happy Christmas to all and to all a good night."

She waited till the light had gone out in his room—the very moment; she didn't want him drifting off—and then she padded across the floor, perfumed and naked, and she could have been anybody, any wanton, any whore, and tried his door. It was unlatched. And she pushed it in with the breath caught in her throat and every nerve strung taut. "Who is it?" he said, and she could see the dark form of him sitting up in bed in the cool blue light the snow threw at the windows.

"Hush," she whispered, "it's just me. Katherine. Your wife."

"What are you—?" he began, but then she was on the bed, naked in the frigid light, the springs jostling, the mattress giving, naked and on all fours, the chill sweeping over her breasts and her navel and groin till she was all gooseflesh.

"Don't talk," she said, "don't say a word," and she found his face and his lips and she kissed him, a wet kiss , a true kiss, the heat of their bodies conjoined, she poised there atop the covers and Stanley forced back into the headboard and no place for him to go. He fought away from her mouth and came up sputtering like a diver, his nightcap knocked askew, the blue light in the window as solid and tangible as a block of ice. "I'm not," he said, "I—I—I—"

"Shhhh," she hushed him again, and in the next moment she was beneath the covers with him, her toes seeking his, her breasts tender against the fabric of his nightshirt, her head cradled under his arm, and she just held him for a long while, an eternity, till she felt him relax—or begin to. She kept kissing him, kissing the side of his face, his throat, his fingers, and then, after another eternity, she worked an expeditionary hand up under his nightshirt till she found what she wanted.

His penis was limp. Or not limp, exactly, but by no means was it stiff either. It was the first penis she'd ever held in her hand and she was amazed at how small it was, at how she could cradle the full length of it in her palm, but she knew enough to rub it, stimulate it, make it swell, and all the while she was kissing his throat and breathing hot endearments into the collar of his nightshirt. At first he stiffened—in every place but one—and tried to move away from her touch, but after a time (five minutes? ten?) she began to feel something, a definite movement, a twitching, a palpable thickening. Encouraged, she brought her other hand into play, rubbing furiously now, rubbing Stanley's awakening member between both palms with all the intensity of a red Indian rubbing two sticks together to produce fire.

And she did produce fire—of a sort. He was erect now—or nearly erect; she was no expert—and she lifted his nightshirt and rolled atop him, rubbing now not with her hands but with her own groin, and the sensation was intoxicating, like nothing she'd ever known, except maybe for Lisette and her precocious forefinger, and "Stanley," she whispered, "Stanley, I'm ready. Make a baby for me, Stanley, make a baby."

But he didn't make a baby. Didn't even try. As soon as she spoke he shrank away to nothing, less than nothing, the softest, smallest, most irritating little thing in the world, all coiled up in its nest, and when she reached for him again he pushed her away—and with more force than was necessary.

There was a shock of cold air, a great flapping of the covers, and suddenly he was standing over her in the glacial light of the room, and she could just make out his face, the lips curled in a snarl, the wild glint of his eyes. He was trembling. "You whore!" he shouted. "You dirty whore!"

3.

ON SHAKY GROUND

Dr. Kempf's time began in 1926, but the need for him—for direct action, for hope, for change—had been a long time coming, as O'Kane would have been the first to admit. And it wasn't just that everything fell to shit and ruin under Brush and the new estate manager (a grubbing incompetent multiple-chinned little fraud of a man by the name of Hull), it was Mr. McCormick himself. Very gradually, day by day, in a way you might not even notice, he began to withdraw into himself again, as if he were slipping back into the catatonia of the early days, and O'Kane was afraid they'd have to break out the sheet restraints and the feeding tube all over again. Mr. McCormick was torpid and morose, barely articulate, and there were days at a stretch when he didn't want to get out of his pajamas—even the prospect of a drive in the country didn't seem to get much of a rise out of him. And of course it was always unpleasant to have to force him to undress and get into the shower bath, much less try to get him to put his feet into the legs of his trousers if he was fundamentally opposed to it.

O'Kane was no psychiatrist (even if he did have more experience in the field than half the headshrinkers running around the country with their dabbed-on beards and Krautish theories), but he was finely attuned to Mr. McCormick's moods and he was worried. As far as he could see—and he'd discussed it with Mart time and again—Mr. McCormick's present decline was traceable to a series of traumatic events over the course of the past few years, the first and most devastating of which was the loss of his mother. That was in 1922 or '23, and it was followed by his brother Harold's divorce and remarriage and the hullaballoo the papers made over it, which to Mr. McCormick's mind was a shame and a blot on the whole family and the Harvester Company too. Then came the news that Dr. Brush finally had to commit his wife because she was parading naked through the streets and setting trashcans afire; this seemed to disturb Mr. McCormick on all sorts of counts, from his sheer horror at the notion of aggressive female nudity to the sad contemplation and reevaluation of his own hopes for cure and release into the world of men and women. And finally, just when it seemed as if he were coming out of it, making his little jokes and eating his meals calmly and nicely, there was the earthquake that knocked down half the city of Santa Barbara and gave Riven Rock such a rattling that all the windows broke out, the piano wound up on its back in the middle of the music room and the garage fell away into a random-looking heap of stones with a dozen cars crushed like salmon tins in the middle of it. Any man would have been hard-pressed to remain cheerful and forward-looking in the midst of all that, but for a man in Mr. McCormick's state of mind it was like putting up walls on top of walls.

Indeed, when the old lady died, O'Kane braced himself for a major outburst at least equal to the business with Dr. Hoch and the gopher, but if Mr. McCormick was anything, he was unpredictable. He barely blinked, and officially, for Dr. Brush's records, he said all of seven words. He was playing a game of solitaire when O'Kane broke the news to him. (Brush had thought it would be best that way, for the main and simple reason that Mr. McCormick was more comfortable around his head nurse, who had, after all, known him longer, and the news was bound to be traumatic, for the main and simple reason that Mr. McCormick was so pathologically attached to his mother, though of course he hadn't actually seen her since nineteen-ought-seven, and he was very likely to give vent to his grief in a volatile way and to resent the bringer of the news, which for obvious reasons shouldn't if at all possible be his attending psychiatrist for the main and simple reason of the risk of alienation.)

"Mr. McCormick, I'm afraid I have some bad news," O'Kane had announced, Brush concealed behind a closet door on the landing, Mart looking on as placidly as if they were discussing a change in the luncheon menu.

Mr. McCormick glanced up quizzically from his cards. "B-bad n-news?" he echoed in a kind of bray.

O'Kane steeled himself. "I'll come right to the point, sir: your mother's died. Last night. Peacefully. In her sleep." He paused. "She was eighty-eight."

For a long while Mr. McCormick merely sat there, looking up at him out of a neutral face, the last card arrested in his hand. He cleared his throat as if he were about to say something, then turned back to the table before him and laid the card at the head of one of the four neatly aligned rows. After a while he glanced up again, and he had a sly secretive look on his face, as if he'd just gotten away with something. "I won't be going to the funeral," he said.

Outwardly, he showed nothing, but you could see he was grieving, as he had for Dr. Hoch, and O'Kane kept waiting for some sort of manic episode, especially when the news of Mr. Harold McCormick's divorce broke. The first O'Kane heard of it was when he came into work one morning and all Mr. McCormick could talk about was the subject of divorce — divorce in all its legal, historical and anthropological ramifications, how so-and-so had divorced his wife of thirty years and what King Henry the Eighth had done and how the Trobriand Islanders would kill and eat their wives on divorcing them and offer the choicest morsels to their in-laws, if savages could be said to have in-laws, and how did he, Eddie, feel about the subject? He'd been divorced, hadn't he? From what-was-her-name, Rosaleen?

O'Kane had to admit that he hadn't.

That stopped Mr. McCormick cold. They were outside at the time — they'd just come back from hurtling aimlessly round the property at a pace that varied from a jog to a sprint — and Mr. McCormick blinked at him in incredulity. "You mean you — all these years — and she, she — all by herself? Or maybe, maybe even with, with other *men*?"

Mart, still heaving for breath, was looking on. They were at the front door and Butters was there, his nose in the air, holding the door stiffly open for them. "I, uh, I guess I never told you—remember when she had to leave to go back and nurse her mother? And her brother, the one that had brain cancer?"

Mr. McCormick gave him a blank look. He probably didn't recall much from those days. In fact, O'Kane was amazed that he'd remembered Rosaleen's name.

"Well," O'Kane said, painting the picture with his hands, "sad to say but she caught the brain cancer from him and died. So I'm a widower, really. A widower—that's what I am."

Mr. McCormick seemed satisfied with the explanation, but when they got back upstairs and settled into the parlor, he became agitated all over again. "Here," he said, "here, look at this," and he thrust a pile of newspaper clippings into O'Kane's lap, clippings that hadn't actually been clipped, since he wasn't allowed access to scissors, but which he'd painstakingly creased and torn out of the papers.

The first headline read HARVESTER PRES TO DIVORCE ROCKE-FELLER HEIR, and there were half a dozen more of that ilk. It seemed that Harold, who was now president of International Harvester since Cyrus Jr. had retired, was divorcing Edith, to whom he'd been married for twenty-six years. She'd spent the last eight years in Switzerland as a devotée and disciple of Karl Jung and his school of psychoanalysis, and Harold, who was the playboy of the family, fond of fancy clothes, expensive cars, airplanes and women, had fallen for the Polish diva, Ganna Walska. A dark and fleshy beauty, Madame Walska was once widowed and twice divorced at thirty, and she was twenty years Harold's junior. And she couldn't sing, not a note—or not enough to keep people from stampeding for the exits, anyway.

After O'Kane had read through the articles and handed them to Mart for his perusal, he looked up into Mr. McCormick's expectant face and shrugged. "It happens sometimes, Mr. McCormick," he said, "you know that. It's nothing to get excited about."

"No, no," he said, rapid-fire, and the floor turned to magma suddenly and he had to hop from foot to foot, "no, no, you don't, don't understand. He's the president, he's the *president*, and he could, I could—Katherine. I could divorce Katherine."

The idea remained fixed in Mr. McCormick's brain for some time, and when he wasn't debating its finer points in a high ragged voice, he was brooding over it in a chasm of silence. If Harold could divorce, then so could he. But if he got divorced, then he wouldn't have Katherine, and if he didn't have Katherine who would be his wife and run his affairs for him? And he loved Katherine, didn't he? Even if she was running around with other men and that Mrs. Roessing? On and on it went, round and round, like a dog chasing its tail.

Meanwhile, Harold's situation only got worse. Because after his divorce was granted and Edith got custody of the children and the better part of their joint property, including their Lake Forest mansion, the Villa Turicum, which she would convert into a "Mecca for devotées of psychoanalysis," Ganna Walska turned around and married an American millionaire by the name of Alexander Smith Cochran. Harold was devastated and the press howled with delight. But then, a year later, Madame Walska jettisoned Alexander Smith Cochran and married Harold, but only on condition that he finance her operatic tour of America, replete with the finest choruses, orchestras, costumes and staging money could buy. Again the press howled in derision and howled so vociferously and at such length that Harold was forced to step down as president of the Harvester Company in the wake of the scandal.

All this Mr. McCormick seemed to absorb with a growing sense of despair and gloom till the day came when he wouldn't get out of bed. O'Kane arrived to find Dr. Brush and Mart trying to reason with him. Wouldn't he like to get up now and have a nice shower bath? No, he wouldn't. Wouldn't he like breakfast? No. A drive? A movie? A concert with Mr. Eldred? No, no and no. Well, and what seemed to be the problem? He wouldn't say. But after Dr. Brush and Mart had gone out in the hallway to consult, Mr. McCormick reached into the breast pocket of his blue silk pajamas and handed O'Kane a newspaper clipping folded so rigorously and so repeatedly it had been reduced to the size of a matchbook. "Go ahead," he said. "G-go ahead, Eddie—read it. Out loud."

O'Kane unfolded the pellet of newsprint, smoothed out the wrinkles on the table, and began to read:

EX-HARVESTER PRES TO HAVE
MONKEY GLAND TRANSPLANT

Mr. Harold McCormick, former president of International
Harvester, whose sudden marriage last year to the Polish chanteuse,

Madame Ganna Walska, rocked the company and scandalized the nation, has gone into hospital in Chicago for urologic surgery. His surgeon, Dr. V. P. Lespinasse, known as "the dean of gland transplantation," is said to be experimenting with the use of monkey glands to improve Mr. McCormick's chances of fathering children with his young wife. Madame Walska had no comment, except to say that her husband was "insatiable in his search for the realization of the physical demands of marriage — insatiable because they were unattainable for him anymore."

When he looked up, Mr. McCormick was wearing the strangest expression on his face, as if he'd just pulled himself up onto solid ice only to have it give way and plunge him back into the dark chilling waters all over again. "Monkeys," he said bitterly, "why does it always have to be monkeys?"

And then there was the earthquake.

It struck just before seven on June 29, 1925, and it flipped O'Kane up into the air above his bed, where he'd been sleeping off the effects of several boilermakers and a woman whose name he couldn't remember, turned him over and dropped him back down again as neatly as an omelet flipped in a pan. Everything in his field of vision was alive, just like in his hallucinations the last time he'd given up drinking, but this was no hallucination. The painting over the bed came down on him, impaling one of the gamboling kittens on the bedpost, the wardrobe skittered across the room and toppled with a crash, plaster rained down, and still everything shook and danced and jittered as if the floor was electrified. It was exactly like being on a train coming into the station and the engineer hauling too hard on the brakes.

After pulling on his pants and shoes, O'Kane rushed headlong into the hall, where dust infested the air and the banister on the landing had given way in a conspiracy of splintered wood. Below, in Mrs. Fitzmaurice's immaculate parlor, a welter of bricks and lath lay scattered over the carpet, and he could see where the building next door had poked its elbow through the wall. Like the hero he was, O'Kane assisted all the ladies out into the street and then spent the next ten hours running from one place to another, rescuing a child here, battling flames there, mad with the adrenal rush of it, soot-blackened and bleeding and hatless and shirtless, galvanized in the moment.

When the dust cleared, it was found that most of the older buildings in town were destroyed or severely damaged—the Fithian Building, the Mortimer Cook Building, St. Francis Hospital, the Potter Theater, the Diblee Mansion on the mesa to the south of town, the old Spanish Mission itself—and that three people had been killed (two of them when a sixty-thousand-gallon water tank crashed through the roof of the Arlington Hotel) and more than fifty injured. President Coolidge ordered the USS *Arkansas* up from San Diego to give medical aid and detach a squadron of marines to patrol the streets against looters.

Telephone lines were down, of course, and it was past five before O'Kane was able to get news of Riven Rock. He could picture the whole place in ruins—there was no way in the world that rigid rock structure could have survived such a shaking—and he thought about Mr. McCormick, sure, but it was Giovannella he was most worried for. Giovannella, who'd been in command of the kitchen four years now without incident, Giovannella, his sworn enemy who shrugged off his every advance and yet threw up the children to him constantly—yes, *children:* the infant girl she gave birth to in the summer of 1920 was named Edwina and had the same glaucous Dingle Bay eyes as little Guido. He loved her. He worshiped her. Mooned at her from the kitchen doorstep (he was forbidden to set foot inside), wrote her impassioned letters (which she never opened), begged her to—yes—marry him. That Giovannella. Giovannella Dimucci Capolupo, the most stubborn woman on God's green earth, mother of his children, the love of his life—"You had your chance, Eddie," she said, "and you wasted it"— he was worried for her.

He was battling a blaze in a lunchroom down near the foot of State Street with an army of boys and men and soot-blackened women in kerchiefs—the bucket brigade, up from the sea, hand over hand—when he saw O'Mara limping up the street toward him. "O'Mara!" he shouted, dropping the bucket at his feet and rushing across the shattered pavement to grab the man by the narrow wedge of his shoulders. "What happened out there? Is anybody hurt?"

O'Mara gave him a distant look, as if he didn't recognize him, but that was because of his wandering eyes, which you never could pin down. "The garage collapsed," he said, shaking out a cigarette and putting a match to it, "and all the cars got crushed. Fucking destroyed, every one of them."

"And the house?"

"Still standing. There's nobody hurt but Caesar Bisordi's wife out in the cottages—the roof fell in on her—and I'm the one Hull sent into town to fetch a doctor, as if I could find one in all this mess."

O'Kane turned directly away from him and started out on foot, and all those paradisiacal hills and beaches were turned hellish, fires everywhere, cars wrapped around trees and standing up to their skirts in ditches, and everything so absolutely hushed and silent you would have thought the word had gone deaf. He reached Riven Rock by six-thirty and found Mr. McCormick, preternaturally excited, out on the lawn in the company of Mart and Dr. Brush and one of the huskier laborers, surveying the damage. "Eddie!" he cried out when he saw O'Kane coming up the drive, "we've had a terrible big pounding here, worse than anything you ever saw. It—it blew out all the windows and look there at where the stone facing came loose. . . ." He paused to catch his breath. "But you—you're naked, Eddie. And you've got no hat—"

"I'm all right, Mr. McCormick, don't you worry about me—I'm just glad to see you're safe and well. It was pretty bad down there," addressing them all now. "You should see it—the city's pretty well destroyed, streetcars lying on their sides, houses tumbled into the street, fires everywhere. And dust—Jesus, I had to clamp a rag over my mouth to keep from choking on it. I got here as soon as I could—and I had to walk the whole way."

Brush began to bluster out some nonsense about the milk cows and roosters sounding the alarm just before the tremor hit, and everyone began talking at once. O'Kane turned to Mart. "How's Giovannella?" he asked, but before Mart could answer, Mr. McCormick came right up to them, looming and twitching. "And you're, you're bleeding—you know that, Eddie? You—you're naked and you-you're bleeding—"

"It's nothing," O'Kane said, and he looked into his employer's face and smelled the rankness of his breath and saw the frenzy building in his eyes and gave Mart a nod: this was when he was most likely to bolt.

"Eddie, you're bleeding, you're bleeding—"

"She's okay," Mart said, stepping back a pace to avoid Mr. Mc-Cormick and giving O'Kane a look that could have meant anything. "She's in the kitchen."

"Yes," Brush boomed, closing in on them with his arms spread wide just as Mr. McCormick shied away, "the house stood up pretty nicely, considering the magnitude of this thing—they're saying it's the worst earthquake since the one that hit Tokyo two years back or even the ought-six quake in San Francisco, for the main and simple . . . but go ahead, Eddie, go on in there and get yourself cleaned up and see to the cook. We didn't want to bring her out here, of course," he said, lowering his voice, "because of Mr. McCormick—and don't worry about him, we've got Mr. Vitalio here to see to his needs." He glanced up to where Mr. McCormick was now pacing up and down the sward in front of the house, as agitated as he'd been over the gopher, and then he glanced at the laborer, a big black-haired wop with muscles you could see through his shirt. "Isn't that right, Mr. Vitalio?"

The wop glanced uneasily at Mr. McCormick's manic figure, as if he was expected to wrestle him to the ground at any moment—which he might well have to do before the day was out—and then he turned back to Dr. Brush and folded his arms across his chest. "That's right," he said.

"Okay, then"—O'Kane was already turning away—"I'm going to go in and see about Giovannella."

But before he could escape, Brush caught him by the arm. "Oh, Eddie, I almost forgot: we might have to move Mr. McCormick into the theater building—just till we have somebody come out to see whether the house is safe or not—and I'll want you to stay here tonight, for the main and simple reason that it'll help calm him and we can't really expect to see Nick or Patrick anytime soon, can we?"

O'Kane just nodded, and then he broke away, trotted up the drive and went round back of the house and into the kitchen. The place was shadowy and dark—the lights were out, of course—and there was litter everywhere. All the pots and pans had come down from their hooks, the cabinet drawers had disgorged their contents and jerked themselves out onto the floor, the stove was shoved out from the wall and the big meat locker in the back was tilted crazily against the doorframe. "Giovannella?" he called. "Giovannella? Are you there?"

At first there was no response, and he waded into the gloom, kicking aside saucepans, cheese graters and broken crockery, glass everywhere. "Giov? You here?"

Just then an aftershock hit the place with a sudden wallop, as if the earth were a long raveling whip and the house and kitchen riding on the business end of it. Things fell. Plaster sifted down. There was a clatter

and a boom and then everything was still again. That was when Giovannella cried out—and it wasn't a shriek of terror or a plea or a cry for
help so much as a curse of frustration and rage.

He found her in the broom closet, trembling, her eyes climbing out
of her head, and her clothes—apron, dress, stockings, shoes, all of it—
steaming and wet with what he at first took to be blood. His heart froze.
She looked up at him, her legs folded under her, her clothes saturated
not with blood, he saw now—and smelled, smelled it too—but marinara sauce, and every emotion was concentrated in her eyes. "Eddie,"
she said. Just that: "Eddie."

He wasn't wearing a shirt, his chest and arms filthy, a crust of blood
like a badge over his right nipple; she was crumpled in the closet, as wet
and redolent as a meatball. She'd cleaned up the kitchen three times already, working like a slave, like a maniac, and three times the after-
shocks had brought everything down again, including the big pot of
sauce she was making to feed everybody, because there was nothing,
nothing to eat, and the poor people in the cottages with their stoves collapsed and their iceboxes smashed, what were they going to do? He
saw it all in an instant, and if he needed the details to complete the picture, he would get them later, when night had fallen and there was no
light but for the kerosene lanterns and Mr. McCormick was settled in
the theater building and everybody on the estate had eaten sandwiches
with fresh-squeezed orange juice and he took her deep into the big deserted stone house and found a bed and lay in it with her till the light
came and he never wanted to get up again.

As for Mr. McCormick, he adapted readily enough to the theater
building while repairs went on in the main house (after a short but violent period of adjustment, that is), but all the spirit seemed to have gone
out of him when the earth stopped shaking. There was no novelty anymore, nothing new, and he sank back into the morass of his hopeless
and stultified mind, so that by the time Dr. Kempf came to redeem him
he'd regressed so far that O'Kane and Mart had to drag him into the
shower bath each morning, force the deadweight of his limbs into his
clothes and spoon-feed him at the table. And that was no pleasure at all.

Dr. Kempf didn't rush into things the way Brush had, and he didn't
bluster or boom or pin Mr. McCormick to the floor—better yet, he

wasn't a Kraut and he didn't have a beard. He was forty-one years old when he took over for Dr. Brush in the autumn of 1926, the author of two books (*The Autonomic Functions and the Personality*, 1918, and *Psychopathology*, 1920) as well as innumerable learned papers, and he'd most recently been a clinical psychiatrist at Saint Elizabeth's Hospital in Washington, D.C., before setting himself up in private practice in New York. He was of medium height and build, the hair on his crown was so sparse and so severely slicked and pomaded it looked painted on and he had a dazzling full-lipped smile that was the key to his success on the interpersonal level. That and his eyes, which were a sympathetic and liquid brown—and perfectly round, as round as twin monocles set in his head. The McCormicks wanted to make him rich—or so it seemed to the amazed nurses when they discovered how much he was making per month: a cool ten thousand dollars. Mart, who had no great head for sums, was nonetheless quick to point out that that added up to $120,000 a year, more even than the King of Abyssinia could expect to make. If there was a King of Abyssinia.

He settled himself, along with his wife, Dr. Helen Dorothy Clarke Kempf, at Meadow House, a princely stone-and-frame dwelling the McCormicks had erected on the southern verge of the estate for the comfort of the physicians, who could thus be near at hand in the event of an emergency. Dr. Brush had lived there for a time, and Dr. Hoch too, but Brush had opted eventually for town life and Hoch had moved on to less roomy accommodations, six feet underground. O'Kane tried to get some sort of fix on the new doctor—he didn't want to get his hopes up too high and yet he couldn't help himself—and during Kempf's first week he attempted to read one of the doctor's learned articles in the *Journal of Abnormal Psychology*. It was called, promisingly enough, "A Study of the Anaesthesia, Convulsions, Vomiting, Visual Constriction, Erythemia and Itching of Mrs. V. G.," but it was dry as the stuffing of an old mattress and O'Kane nodded off twice just trying to get through it. In fact, in later years he kept a copy of it at his bedside as a soporific in case he couldn't get to sleep.

The man himself was easier to read, thank God, and O'Kane liked him right from the start, from the first minute he walked into the room with his uncomplicated smile and took O'Kane's hand in a good dry firm honest grip. Brush was there at the time, hearty and big-bellied and roaring, but Kempf had been closeted with his predecessor all

morning and made it clear that O'Kane was the man he wanted to talk
to. They were in the office in the theater building, three in the afternoon, day one of Dr. Kempf's regime, Brush packing his books and effects in cardboard containers, Mr. McCormick napping quietly in the
stone house under Mart's semi-watchful eye. Kempf asked a few questions about Mr. McCormick's present state, but Brush kept interfering,
so finally he took O'Kane by the arm and steered him out into the theater itself, a cavernous high room with the chairs all set out in rows,
acoustic panels on the walls and a deep mid-afternoon hush hanging in
the air. They sat in two folding chairs under one of the big iron-girded
windows, and Dr. Kempf leaned forward confidentially. "So tell me,
Eddie," he said, and his voice was like Dr. Hamilton's, smooth and hypnotic, "can it really be true that Mr. McCormick has had no contact
whatever with a woman since, what was it, 1907? 1908?"

"Contact? He hasn't even *seen* a woman, not even on our drives,
which we've been very careful about, back roads and all of that."

"And why is that?"

"Too dangerous. In the old days, in the beginning, when we first
came out here, that is —"

"Yes?" Kempf was intent and concentrated, the annular eyes, the
shining smile, as fixed on Eddie O'Kane as the needle of a compass.

"Well, he would attack them —women. Beat them. Maul them."
O'Kane was remembering that girl on the train, the one going home to
Cincinnati with her mother, and the way Mr. McCormick had pinned
her down and forced his hand up her privates —and how he'd brought
his tongue into play and licked her throat like a cow at a salt lick. Or a
bull. A rutting bull.

"Did anyone ask him why he had all this hostility toward women?
Dr. Hamilton? Dr. Meyer? Did you?"

O'Kane shifted in the chair. The seat was narrow and hard. "It was
a sexual thing," he said, "very disturbing for all concerned. I was embarrassed, to tell you the truth. And besides which, he went catatonic
about then, and nobody could ask him anything —or you could ask all
you wanted, but he wouldn't answer."

"But that was a long time ago," Kempf said.

"Eighteen years. Nineteen. Something like that."

Kempf leaned back in the chair, the hinges creaking under his
weight. He had his hands wrapped behind his neck as if he were bask-

ing in the sun and he closed his eyes a minute, deep in thought. "He hasn't made much progress, has he?" he said finally, snapping open his eyes and bringing the chair back to level again.

O'Kane could hardly deny it. He shrugged. "He has his periods."

"I've been studying this, Eddie," the doctor said, handing him a manila folder with several sheets of bound typescript inside. It was a year-by-year account of Mr. McCormick's condition, from the onset of his illness right on up to the present, and as O'Kane glanced over the entries he had the uneasy feeling that he was reading a shadow biography of himself—he was the one laboring just off the page here, he was the one living, breathing, drinking, shitting, sleeping and whoring through all those compressed and hopeless years:

> In 1908, when the patient was seen by Drs. Kraepelin and Hoch, he was diagnosed as suffering from the catatonic form of dementia praecox. At that time he was tube-fed and refused to walk.
>
> In 1909, there occurred some mental clearness, then delirous excitement, after which he became dull. He continued to be spoon-fed and refused to move his bowels, but began to walk with the aid of his nurses.

They were just words on a page, clinical shorthand, as cold and indifferent as a news report of carnage in China or the eruption of a Peruvian volcano, but O'Kane felt himself oddly moved. The poor man, he was thinking, the poor man, and he wasn't thinking only of Mr. McCormick. He skipped ahead and read on:

> In 1916, music became a regular activity. He talked more coherently and had more purposeful activity. He continued to wet the bed, was restrained during certain hours, was mixed and incoherent in his ideas, impulsive, and at times drank his own urine. He was diagnosed as suffering from dementia praecox by Dr. Smith Ely Jeliffe, who now agreed with Drs. Hoch and Meyer.

And then again:

> In 1924, he pursued endless corrections and endless substitutions for Christmas cards. He had impulsive outbursts, began to

stammer. He slumped in his seat while riding. He fussed about a calendar, about his father having received undeserved credit for the invention of the reaper.

In 1925, he read infrequently, was less willing to discuss his impersonal problems. The oddities of gait persisted and for a period he had to be spoon-fed. Because of an earthquake he had been removed to the theater building, on which occasion he tried to batter down the door.

When O'Kane handed the folder back to Kempf, there were tears in his eyes. He had to pause to dig out his handkerchief and dab at them, and then he blew his nose in a long lugubrious release of phlegm and emotion. "No, doctor," he said finally, "there hasn't been the kind of improvement I—we all—hoped for, not at all."

Kempf was watching him closely, eyes glistening, the hair glued to his scalp. "You know what I find missing here, Eddie?" he said.

O'Kane looked up, took a deep breath. He shook his head.

"Treatment. That's what's missing. The patient has had all the finest minds here to examine him and diagnose his condition, quite accurately I'm sure, but his treatment has been almost purely custodial to this point, am I right?"

O'Kane could only blink. What was he suggesting—monkey glands? The talking cure?

"I think I can help him, Eddie—through intensive daily sessions, two hours at a sitting, seven days a week. I treated upward of three thousand cases at Saint Elizabeth's, applying Freud's analytic methods to patients suffering from hysteria, neurasthenia and a whole range of other neuroses, and to cases of schizophrenia too, and Mr. McCormick's guardians have brought me here at great expense to devote myself solely to him."

"You don't mean the talking cure, do you?" O'Kane said, and he couldn't hide his astonishment. "Because Dr. Brush tried that back in the teens, and let me tell you, it was a disaster."

Kempf had begun to laugh—he didn't want to, you could see that, but now he gave up all pretense of sobriety and threw back his head and howled. When he came back to himself in a flurry of breastbone pounding and head shaking, the room seemed much smaller to O'Kane. He felt the blood come to his face. "I don't see the joke," he said.

"I don't mean to—" the doctor began and then had to break off again and suppress a final chuckle. "Listen, Eddie, I know what you're thinking, and I don't mean to be critical, but psychoanalysis has come a long way since then—and it isn't just a parlor trick or a kind of psychological compress you squeeze on one day and forget about the next. It's an ongoing and dynamic process—it may take years. And it may seem as if the patient—Mr. McCormick, in this case—is becoming yet more disturbed before he begins to improve, because of the repressed material we need to bring to the surface, deep fears and anxieties, sexual matters, the whole construct of his personality. We're going to open up all his old festering wounds and we're going to sew them up and bandage them right. Do you understand me?"

"Sure," O'Kane said—what else could he say?—but he was doubtful. Doubtful in the extreme.

"His wife will be the first," Kempf was saying, "that's only right. Of course, that's sometime in the future yet, but our goal is to normalize his relations across the board with—"

"You don't mean women, do you?"

Kempf gave him a look. "Yes, of course. What could be more *abnormal*, for any man, than to be shut away from half the population of the world? Good God, he didn't even get to see his mother before she died—how can you expect a man to improve in a situation like that?"

"You can't," O'Kane heard himself say, and he'd known it all along, they all had, he and Nick and Pat and Mart: give him women. Women. Women would cure him, sure they would.

4.

I'VE SEEN YOUR FACE

While Dr. Kempf was at Riven Rock, quietly revolutionizing Stanley's treatment, Katherine and Jane Roessing were in Europe, beating the drums for Margaret Sanger and the birth control movement. As 1926 passed into 1927 and she made her fruitless annual visit to Riven Rock and Stanley's voice on the phone seemed weaker and less steady and ever more distant—the voice of a stranger, a phantom, someone she'd encountered in a reverie so long ago she couldn't recall even the vaguest blurred outline of his face—Katherine was already planning for the Geneva Population Conference, to be held that August at Prangins. And why birth control? Because without it a woman was chattel and nothing more, a breeder, a prize mare or sow, and why educate a sow? Why hire one? Why teach her science and maths and the workings of the world? Pregnant and bloated every year of her life from sixteen to forty and beyond, every woman was handcuffed by her husband's sexual urges, and where was the hope of advancement in that? Besides, as Jane was quick to point out, it seemed axiomatic that the more igno-rant and degraded you were, the more you bred—the Irish, Italians,

Swedes and Bohemians whelped ten babies for every one a woman of their class had. And where would that leave the race a generation hence if it kept on in that direction?

All right. So she stood in line at customs in Boston, her heart thundering in her ears, and smuggled in two steamer trunks and a handbag full of diaphragms for free distribution to women at Sanger's clinics, and she petitioned congressmen and used her influence in Washington and spent Stanley's money—and her own—on the clinics, the literature, the fight. It was all she had. Because she had no husband and no baby of her own and the Dexters would die with her—she would be the last of her line; she had no illusions about that.

She began to intuit as much all those years ago, after the headlong disaster of her honeymoon (it was like jumping off a bridge, over and over again, day after day, night after night), but she wouldn't admit it, not even to herself. She could have divorced. She could have accepted the McCormicks' terms and had the marriage annulled. She could have faded away and emerged into another life altogether, her own life, remarried and secure, a life of babies and diapers and wet nurses, perambulators, primers and little lifeless porcelain dolls with little lifeless smiles frozen on their faces. But she didn't. She couldn't. She'd made her choice and she would live with it.

She and Stanley had taken separate cabins on the *Brittania* on their return to the States in the spring of 1905, and she was as close then to giving up on him as she'd ever been. It was a rough crossing, the Atlantic black and jagged, the whole great shuddering steel liner thrust up out of the water like a feather in a fishpond and then shoved back down again till the steel decks were awash and the wind snatched the boiling spume into the air. She was sick the entire time. So sick she could barely crawl to the head and heave up a wad of nothing into the sea-stinking vacuum in front of her face. Stanley burst in on her at random—two in the morning or two in the afternoon, it was all the same to him—and he was white to the roots of his hair, his feet riding the deck beneath him as if he were a fly stuck to a windowpane. She smelled of herself. She was embarrassed. One minute he would be solicitous, helping her to her bunk, dabbing at her face with a warm washcloth, and the next he would be shouting "Whore! Whore of Babylon!" Screaming it, howling it, his whole face swollen and his fists beating at the air.

When they landed she went straight to her mother's—and there was no mention of the house they were planning in Marion, no mention of a life together at all—and Stanley went home to Chicago. To the Harvester Company. To his duties. To his mother. Katherine didn't get out of bed for a week. She cried till there was no fluid left in her body, her mother and the housemaid plying her all the while with broth, tea and ginger ale. That was the worst. That was the low point—lower even than when she'd broken off the engagement. She was separated from her husband after only six months of marriage, no smiling tall handsome figure of a man to show off at the theater, parties and teas, Abigail Slaney with three adorable children already and Bessie Dietz with four, her schoolmates all grown matronly and plump in their adventitious fecundity and she a withered root, a failure. A failure, after all.

And then the telegrams started arriving. A blizzard of telegrams, a spring storm. So many that she got to know by face, name and footfall every Western Union delivery boy in the Back Bay, and when she fell off to sleep at night bicycle bells jingled through her dreams. Stanley missed her. He hated his job. He hated the whole enduring concept of reapers, tractors and harvesters. He hated his mother. He wasn't feeling well. Cyrus was president and Harold was vice president, but Katherine was his wife, his only wife, and he loved her, wanted to fall at her feet and worship her, wanted to quit his job and come to her in Boston and build a house for her in Marion and fill it full of things and live happily. Ever after.

He came in on the train this time, less than two months after they'd parted, and this time it was she who met him at the station, flushed and expectant. And when she saw him there in the crowd, the face of him, the brooding masculine beauty and power, Stanley Robert McCormick, the genius, the artist, the millionaire, she fell in love all over again. He took her in his arms right there on the platform and they embraced for all the world to see, shoe-shine boys and porters and peanut vendors and silly little women in silly little hats, and she didn't care a whit. She held him, just held him, for what seemed like hours.

Josephine couldn't disguise her pleasure. And she couldn't have been prouder and noisier and more excited if Stanley was Teddy Roosevelt himself, returned triumphant from Havana all over again and plopped down in her front parlor. The ensuing month was one fête after another, the Stanley McCormicks toasted and congratulated from one house to the next, bluestocking Boston getting a look at the groom at last. All seemed well, and Stanley seemed to be enjoying himself, his nervous twitches and irritable moods all but evaporated, until one night they attended a dinner party given for them by Hugh and Claudia Dumphries on Beacon Hill and Stanley got it into his head that Butler Ames was among the guests.

They were eighteen at dinner, and Hugh, an old friend of Katherine's mother and a celebrated landscape artist, stood to propose a toast. He was a fatigued-looking man, skeletally thin, with a gray tonsure and rectangular spectacles that distorted his colorless eyes; his preferred topic of conversation—his sole topic—was art and art history, and Katherine had thought Stanley would find him amusing. "To Katherine and Stanley," he proposed, lifting his glass at the head of the table.

Stanley was sitting to his immediate right. He'd been complaining all day about dogs and looking glasses, muttering under his breath in the cab on the way over, and Katherine should have seen it as a sign. "I won't have it," he said, bolting up from the table as sixteen guests froze in place with their wineglasses stalled in midair.

Hugh looked as puzzled as if the ceiling had cried out in pain or the walls begun to speak. He hunched his thin shoulders and gazed out myopically from the prison of his spectacles. "What?" he said. "What do you mean?"

"Stanley," Katherine warned, her voice tight in her throat.

Stanley ignored her. He was transformed, huge and threatening, looming over the table like a tree cut and wedged and about to thunder down on them. He pointed a finger at an innocuous-looking young man at the far end of the table whose name Katherine hadn't quite caught when he was introduced at the door. "Not while he's here," Stanley roared.

"Who?" half a dozen voices wondered.

Stanley trembled, tottered, swayed. His face was red. His finger shook as he pointed. "Him!"

The man he was indicating, ectomorphic and pale, with a fluff of apricot hair standing up straight from his head, looked over first one shoulder and then the other, utterly baffled. "Me?" he said.

"You!" Stanley bellowed, and Katherine got up from the table now to go to him, to calm him, to stop him. "You, friend. *You!* You're, you're a *wife-stealer*, that's what you are!"

Nothing was broken that night, not the innocent man's head or their hosts' Wedgwood plate, but the dinner was a fiasco; after Katherine had got Stanley into the other room and calmed him and explained separately to the guests that her husband was suffering from nervous exhaustion as a result of overwork at the Harvester Company, dinner went on, but Stanley didn't utter a word more all evening, eating with a silent furious rectitude that made them all — even his wife — cringe.

That was the end of the social whirl, and no matter how hard Katherine and her mother tried to put the best face on it, they had to admit that Stanley's eccentricities had gone beyond the pale. Certainly everyone was eccentric to a degree, especially the most sensitive and artistic — Katherine's Aunt Louisa never removed her boots, for instance, even to go to bed or to bathe, and Mrs. London, who lived two doors down from her mother, spoke of her aspidistras as if they were sentient beings with informed opinions on taxes and the municipal elections — but neither was a danger to herself or others. And then there was Stanley's family history to take into account, his sister Mary Virginia and his mother, who if she wasn't actually unbalanced, was as close to the edge as normalcy would allow. Katherine agonized for days before deciding to call in a doctor — a *psychiatrist*, and she could hardly bear to pronounce the term aloud — but she remembered the look on Stanley's face the day he hurled the vase across the room, the same look that came over him when he denounced her on the boat or ruined Hugh and Claudia's party, and she went ahead with it.

Discreet inquiries were made — no one in their set had ever needed a doctor of *that* sort, and if they had they would never have admitted it — and on a leafy bright day in early August a very young-looking man with galloping palomino mustaches and two dull brown lidless eyes came up the walk of the house they'd taken in Brookline while their permanent residence awaited construction. His name was Dr. Jorimund Trudeau, and he'd had eleven years' experience at the Rockport Asylum for the Criminally Insane after taking his degree at Johns Hopkins. The maid showed him into the room.

Stanley was seated at a table by the window, poring over the plans for the new house, and Katherine had been pretending to read a magazine while the carpet crawled across the floor and the minute hand of the clock on the mantel advanced with a mechanical unconcern that made her want to scream aloud. She rose to greet the doctor, and Stan-

ley gave him a quick startled look, though she'd been preparing him for
this visit for days and they'd both agreed that he needed to consult a
physician about his nerves, which were still—they both agreed—a bit
overtaxed from all the recent change and excitement in their lives.

Introductions were made, Stanley rising gravely to take the doctor's
hand, and after an exchange of pleasantries about the weather and the
season and the amount of fur the woolly bear caterpillars were carrying
into the fall, Dr. Trudeau said, "So tell me, Mr. McCormick, how you're
feeling today—any nervous agitation? Anything troubling you? Business worries, that sort of thing?"

Stanley kept his head down. He had a T square in his hand, and he
was making penciled alterations to the architect's plans. "I feel slippery," he said.

The doctor exchanged a look with Katherine. "Slippery? How do
you mean?"

Stanley turned his face to them, a pale hovering handsome face that
hung like a moon over the world of the table and the ceaselessly altered
plans. "Like a salamander," he said. "Like an eel. And all this room—
you see this room? It's like a big sucking f-funnel and I'm too covered
in, in, well, *slime* to get a grip, do you know what I mean?"

The doctor's voice slid up the scale and he took on another tone
altogether: "Do you happen to recall what day it is today, Mr.
McCormick?"

Stanley shook his head. He grinned beautifully, heraldically.
"Tuesday?"

"He's been out of sorts lately," Katherine put in. "Really quite
flustered."

"And what month?"

No response.

"Uh, could you tell me, generally, where we are at this moment—
this house, I mean? The neighborhood? The state?"

Stanley looked down at the plans. It took him a moment, and when
finally he spoke he addressed the table. "I—the Judges told me not to
talk to you anymore."

It was at this point that Dr. Trudeau turned to Katherine. "Mrs.
McCormick, I'm afraid I'm going to have to ask you to leave the room
now, and I hope you won't mind, but Mr. McCormick and I will need to

consult in private from here on out—if you would, please?" And he rose
to show her to the door of her own parlor.

Dazed, she left the room, the unread magazine rolled up like a
wand in one hand, and dazed, she mounted the stairs, entered her bedroom, pulled back the covers and slid herself between them. It was the
first time she'd been excluded, as if she could be of no help at all to her
husband—as if, far from being a help, she might even be a hindrance—
and it hurt her, hurt her all the way down to a place so deep inside even
the biological sciences would have been hard-pressed to identify it. It
was the first time, but it wouldn't be the last.

Three days later, after having examined her husband for several
hours each afternoon, Dr. Trudeau asked to have a minute alone with
Katherine. Since Stanley was in the sitting room, blackening both sides
of the plans with a freshly sharpened pencil, she took the doctor into
the library. She was impatient with the man, because he'd cut her out
like that right from the start, and she was apprehensive too, because of
Stanley's extremely odd replies not only to the doctor's preliminary
questions but to the more intimate and domestic ones she put to him in
the course of a day, and as soon as they were settled she crossed her legs
and demanded, "Well?"

The doctor pulled at the long cascading mustaches that were meant
to distract the eye from his receding chin and parsimonious little mouth.
He looked directly at her. "About your husband," he began, clearing his
throat.

"Yes?"

"I'm afraid it's more than nerves."

For Stanley's part, he knew something was wrong, deeply wrong, dog-
in-the-mirror wrong, Mary-Virginia wrong, and it so terrified him he
felt the pain of it in every fiber and joint of his body, in the pulp of his
teeth, singing out, pain, pain, pain, in his brain and his fingertips, can-
cerous pain, killing pain, and he wanted to cooperate with the doctor
and find a way out of it, he really did. But the Judges were strict and
implacable, they were captious and shrill, and they wouldn't let him. He
heard the doctor's voice clearly enough, heard the questions addressed
to him, but there was static all around him, a noise of grumbling and

dissent, and it sometimes drowned out the thin piping psychological voice as if it were the dying gasp of those pinched and hairy lips. Still, Stanley was fighting it, a ritualistic fight no one would understand, two steps up and one step down, don't step on the cracks, hold your breath for sixty seconds and the Judges will vanish with an obscene flap of their black robes, and when the doctor advised him to go off somewhere and live a simple stress-free rustic life for a while, a life of hiking (how they loved hiking, these doctors), wood chopping, long walks and meditation, he said yes, yes, of course, we'll leave tomorrow.

Katherine found the place. It belonged to one of her mother's bridge partners — or maybe it was her mother's bridge partner's mother — and they were able to lease it for two months without any fuss or trouble. It was in Maine, deep in the woods, a modest cabin of fourteen rooms and fourteen baths overlooking a lake, the leaves exploding all around them, simple tastes, simple fare, just Stanley and his wife, the chauffeur, the cook and two housemaids. Stanley chopped wood, and it was very therapeutic. He beat hell out of that wood, utterly destroyed it, and yet he was creating something too — the fuel for their fire. And every morning he built the fire, the Judges carping over his shoulder, no you idiot, that's not how you do it, you don't stack the logs like that, it'll never catch, where's your sense, more kindling, more kindling, and he took his time, sometimes hours, but then the moment would come, triumphant and complete, and he'd apply the match and watch the whole thing blaze up. And Katherine. She was there. White-faced. Sweet. His wife. He loved her, joked with her, cut the Judges right off — and so what if she was a slut, so what if she was all white underneath and her body a weapon of destruction and she as capable of that disappearing trick, that vaginal sleight-of-hand, as the whore in Paris? So what?

Some days he wouldn't speak to her, not a word. He'd fling himself out of bed, dress in casual clothes (shirt, collar, tie, sweater and sport coat) because this was the wild rural backcountry woods of Maine, after all, and then come to breakfast and there she'd be, full of white smiling cheerfulness, and the Judges would be at him, a game really, could he, would he, did he have the resourcefulness today to ignore her every word and gesture and shut her out completely? Of course he did. He was a man of iron. A man of steel. Inflexible. Inexorable. A walking trap, serrated teeth, snap, shut, game over. On other days, the game reversed itself, and he couldn't stop talking to her, all sorts of silly non-sense about love and holding hands and sweethearts and the poems of Robert Herrick. She was there, right there with him, his wife, his love, Katherine, and that made him feel better.

One afternoon—there was a nip in the air, every leaf singed with it—he went down to the lake to find an old man perched there on the end of the boat dock, fishing. He didn't remind Stanley of his father, really, this old man, but he was about the age of his father when he died, and he did have his father's bellicose beard and unforgiving eyes and the boxy giant's build, but that wasn't it, that didn't affect him at all. "Good afternoon," Stanley said, his feet leaping away from the cracks between the boards as he made his way up the dock. The water gleamed all around him in a sick watery way.

The old man—he wasn't like Stanley's father at all—glanced up from his pole and his bait and the float that bobbed in a liquid dream at the end of the line. "Afternoon," he said.

Stanley had reached the end of the dock now, a boat tethered there, beardy reeds, a smell of muck and decay. He loomed over the man, who was dangling his heavily shod feet over the lip of the gently quaking wooden structure, his feet lolling there, just lolling there, inches from the water. Stanley was very erect, very proper, the tight clasp of the collar, his beautifully brushed hair, his shoes glowing at the nether end of him like toeless hairless impervious new and improved feet—or better yet, hoofs. Hoofs of iron, hoofs of lead, hoofs of indestructible horn. "What are you doing," Stanley said, "fishing?"

"Ayeh," the old man replied.

"I fished once," Stanley said. "In the Adirondacks, when I was a boy. The guide said I should be proud."

The old man said nothing. He spat in the water, a circle of concentrated spittle, minuscule bubbles, floating there on the unbroken surface like something else altogether, like jism, sperm, spunk. The float twitched at the end of the line, plunged suddenly, and the old man snatched it back with a whip of the rod, the line hissing through the sunlit air, but there was nothing there, not even a fish's disappointed lips, no bait fish either, just a hook. "That one," Stanley observed, "got away."

A look, that was all: the old man gave him a look. "Ayeh," he said, fishing a minnow from the bucket beside him and impaling it on the wickedly curved device of the hook, where it wriggled in its pain, fishy pain, a pain not worth mentioning, dumb animals and dumber. And then the float shot through the air and slapped the water like the flat of a hand — *thwap!* — and in that moment Stanley's mind failed him.

What happened next is entirely from the fisherman's point of view because Stanley was no longer, in a sense, there. But the fisherman got wet, tattooed by those hard horny shoes and then lifted right out of his collar and flung into the cold clean enveloping water. And he damned near drowned too, what with the cold and the weight of his clothes and boots, but it was his own two arms and legs and the McCormick money that saved him and hushed him and made him comfortable in the declining years of his old man's life.

Katherine was upset — no, distraught would be more accurate. For days on end she had no one to talk to but the servants, Stanley haunting the place like a revenant, as silent as if he'd had his tongue cut out. They were together, yes, and he seemed calmer (but for the single terrifying incident with the fisherman at the boat dock), and yet he was more remote than ever. There would be nothing from him, no spark, no animation at all, and for hours he'd be gone in the forest or obsessively chopping wood — wood enough for a village — and he'd pass right by her as if she didn't exist. That was the hardest thing. That made the breath catch in her throat and it darkened the room and put out the sun in the sky.

And then the next day he'd walk into the room completely transformed. "Katherine," he'd say, "do you remember that woman with the funny little dog in Nice?" and go off on a fascinating reminiscence of all the dogs in his life — and hers, because hadn't she had dogs too? He would be attentive and affectionate, taking her arm when they went in to dine, rowing her round the lake for hours — no, no, she wasn't to touch an oar — getting up from his reading to adjust the pillow behind her head. Sometimes this would go on for days and her hopes would leap up. The long face was gone, the muttering, the halting walk, the whinnying laugh: he was Stanley again, her Stanley, Stanley of the charm and sweetness and concern. She reveled in his smile, his dimples, the way his eyes seemed to reach out and hold her. He was hers. All hers.

"What do you think of Jack London?" he asked one morning when they were lying on a blanket in a meadow, the sun palely warming, the season crashing down all round them. He was lying on his side, his head propped up on one hand, a stalk of yellowed grass between his teeth.

Katherine had been reading desultorily in a book of Wallace's — *The Malay Archipelago*— that one of her professors had particularly recommended. She was planning to begin graduate research during the winter semester, once Stanley had recovered. Her hand was clasped in his. She looked up from her book and into the blue sheen of his eyes. "Oh, I don't know," she said. "I certainly like him for his social consciousness, but as for his adventure stories . . . well, I guess I prefer stories about proper people, Edith Wharton, that sort of thing. You know I do."

"He's a real he-man," Stanley said.

She looked at him, looked into his eyes, his grin. "Yes," she said, "I suppose he is."

"Chasing after gold, mushing dogs, risking everything." He glanced away from her, at the line of trees at the edge of the meadow, one flame of motionless color. "I'm not like him at all," he said, dropping his voice. "I'm — I'm — I've been pampered and coddled all my life, up to my ears in my father's m-money. I haven't accomplished a thing, not the smallest thing, not even on my ranch. I'm not a he-man. I'm not even a man."

"Oh, Stanley, you are, you *are*—"

He couldn't look at her. "Not to you I'm not."

She slid a hand up over his shoulder and gently, very gently—hold your breath, Katherine, hold your breath now—laid her cheek against his. "I love you, Stanley," she whispered.

"I feel—" he began and trailed off.

"You will be a man to me, Stanley, I know you will. You just need to . . . relax."

Cheek pressed to cheek, the sky all around them, the trees, the silence. "I feel better now," he said.

She lifted her head so she could look into his eyes, the softest fragmentary wisp of a smile playing across her lips. "Do you think we could—?" she whispered.

A trace of panic. "Here? Out-outside?"

She held him to her.

"In the light?"

It wasn't ideal. It wasn't even natural. And it was a failure, absolute, unmitigated, beyond hope or repair. He managed, after an eon and a half of fumbling and apologizing and kissing her ear so assiduously it ached for days afterward, to pull her dress up and her bloomers down and to work himself out of his trousers, but when it came to the blind impulsive moment of insertion, of becoming one with her after all, he shrank back and she felt nothing but a premature wetness and a grasping yearning sucking drain of emptiness that would never, in all her natural life, be stopped or plugged or filled.

So the years went by, years of abstinence and denial, a withdrawal from the world of men so complete that Katherine became a kind of prisoner herself, Mrs. Stanley Robert McCormick, married and yet not widowed, attached to a man and yet detached from him too. Jane helped. Her mother helped. NAWSA and the American Birth Control League and the War Service Department, they all helped. But the fact was, she turned fifty-two years old in 1927, and as far as men were concerned she might as well have been a nun. Sexual love—heterosexual love, procreative love—was a thing she would never experience, she was resigned to that, but beyond sexual love there was dutiful love, a platonic and idealized love, and when her activism flagged, when the speeches became repetitive and the speakers crabbed and insipid, she thought of Stanley. Still. After all these years. Was it even love at this point, she wondered, or just curiosity? She managed his affairs with the fierce uncompromising zeal she'd brought to NAWSA and the birth control movement and saw that he was provided with the best of everything, and she wrote him and spoke with him on the phone, but it was all an abstraction. She wanted to see him, just see him, and that was what Kempf had promised her.

Dr. Kempf. The new man. The Freudian. The profligate who cost as much as any six doctors combined, and yet she'd gone along with the other guardians (Stanley's brother Cyrus and his sister Anita, Favill having passed on and Bentley retired, thank God) and hired him. Anything was better than stasis and cynicism, even at ten thousand dollars a month.

It took him over a year, but finally, in the fall of 1927, after she'd sent all the delegates home, closed up Prangins for the winter and smuggled her trunks of diaphragms through customs, he wired her to say that the time had come. Stanley had undergone a radical transformation through analysis, his hatred of his tyrannical father and fear and mistrust of his emasculating mother out in the open, his misogyny examined from every perspective, his knowledge of himself and his phobias brought into line, and he was now ready, if not to take up ballroom dancing or reinvigorate the International Harvester Company, at least to entertain and comport himself as a gentleman with members of the opposite sex. He was ready. But Dr. Kempf—*Edward, call me Edward*—felt it only right that she, Katherine, should be the first woman in two decades her husband would lay eyes on—see, that is—and perhaps even, if conditions were right, touch.

When she received Kempf's telegram and then spoke with him via long distance, she was in Boston, at her mother's, seeing to the affairs that had piled up in her absence, and Jane had gone on to Philadelphia to look after her own concerns. Katherine called her that night with the news, and they arranged to leave for Santa Barbara two weeks hence—just after the Thanksgiving holiday. Katherine engaged a private car for the two of them and when the train made its Philadelphia stop Jane was there with her hair all aflame and her face opening like the petals of a flower. "I don't believe it," she said, once they were settled and she had an illicit drink and a cigarette in her hand and the station had begun to move and the tracks took them in a rush through the artificial canyons of the city. "Do you?"

Katherine gave her a wry look, took the cigarette from the embrasure of her fingers and drew deeply on it. "What choice do I have?" she said, exhaling.

The servants were shuffling around, getting things settled, and the train, lurching around a long bellying curve, began to pick up speed. The lights flickered. Jane sipped her iced gin—good Bombay gin smuggled in amongst the prophylactic devices—stretched her legs and kicked off her heels. "Twenty years," she murmured. "It's going to be like seeing someone raised from the dead."

Roscoe was waiting for them at the station in Los Angeles, and by the time they made the long drive up the coast to Santa Barbara it was dark and they were both exhausted, and so they decided to wait till morning before going out to Riven Rock. They dined quietly in their cottage at the El Mirasol, just across the street from the place where

Katherine would eventually build a house for herself, replete with a gymnasium for Stanley, and then she telephoned the estate.

Butters answered, and she could hear him calling up the stairs to Nick so that Nick could have Stanley pick up the extension. She heard a click, and then Nick's voice, saw-edged and abraded: "Mrs. Mc-Cormick, ma'am? It'll be just a minute. He's been sitting up late tonight, waiting for you—he's very excited—and he's just been doing his, you know, his ablutions and his teeth, . . . Oh, but wait, here he is—"

"Katherine?"

"Hello, Stanley: it's good to hear your voice."

"You too."

"I'm looking forward to seeing you."

"Me too."

"It's going to be such—it's been such a long time. I feel like a girl on a first date, I'm so excited. And I can't tell you how pleased I am to hear of your progress with Dr. Kempf. He tells me you're your old self again."

A pause. "I have my slippers on."

"Yes, so Nick told me—you're getting ready for bed. I hope we didn't keep you up, the train was late getting in and then with the long drive and whatnot we both just felt, Jane and I, that tomorrow, when everyone's fresh, would be better for the big event."

"One is you and one is me."

"Hm? What do you mean?"

"The slippers. Two souls: Katherine and Stanley. Two soles, two souls—get it?"

She gave a laugh, not so much because she was amused but because she was bewildered and because this was Stanley, Stanley working through the convolutions of his mind. "Yes," she said, "yes, yes, I do—that's very good. Two souls." A pause. The fraught silence of the wires. "Well," she sighed, "I won't keep you. Till tomorrow, then?"

A hiss, a sound as of two wooden blocks rhythmically pounded, and then Stanley's voice, full of grain and sand and silt, so far from her he might have been on the moon: "Tomorrow."

Katherine was a bundle of nerves as the car took her out to Montecito the next morning, her stomach sinking through the floor, her skin horripilated and her breathing shallow. It was the way she felt just before she had to give a speech, stretched taut as a rubber band and then snapped back into place again. She lit a cigarette, set it down in the ashtray, and then lit another. Palms flashed by the windows and she didn't even see them, let alone attempt to categorize them. But Jane was there. And Jane took her hand and leaned across the seat to give her a kiss on the corner of the mouth. "It'll be all right, Kat," she breathed. "You'll see."

Then they were skirting the high stone wall that hemmed in the property, and Roscoe, gray-haired now but as jumpy and energetic as ever, turned the wheel sharply and let it slide back through his fingers again, and they swung into the familiar drive. That was when Katherine came to attention. She couldn't help herself. She saw where Hull and his crew had been busy among the rhododendrons and saw that the ground cover needed cutting back at the edge of the drive. And there, the house, rising up out of the dense landscape like a stone monolith, like a fortress, like a prison.

"Well," she said, turning her face to Jane, "wish me luck," and while Jane waited in the car with a magazine and Roscoe stood motionless at the buffed and flashing door, she stepped out into the drive and went up the broad stone steps at the front of the house. The door opened as if by magic and there was Butters, rigid as a corpse, saying, "Morning, madame, and welcome back," through the stiffest of formal grins. The entrance hall was the same, a severe high deep-ended room softened with tropical plants, tapestries and the statuary she'd bought in Italy for Stanley's edification and enjoyment; on the wall of the staircase going up to her husband's quarters hung the two Monets and the Manet they'd selected together, on their honeymoon. The door closed soundlessly behind her, and then Butters, his face like a shying horse's, all pinched in the nostril and wild in the eye, said, "I will inform Mr. McCormick that you're here, madame." She stood there, in her hat and gloves and furs, and watched the ghostly form of the butler recede up the stairway.

She found herself pacing: three steps this way, three steps that. Should she wait for him in the library? The drawing room? Or here, here where she could see him coming down the stairs—and more importantly, he could see her—and they could gain those extra seconds to prepare themselves separately for what was to come? She pulled off first one glove, then the other—Stanley would want to take her hand and draw her to him for a kiss, and it wouldn't do to offer him a glove as if he were just anyone she'd happened to meet on the street. There. That was better. She held her hands out before her, fingers spread wide, to examine them, steady hands, attractive hands still, her nails done just that morning, the wedding ring in place, right where Stanley had put it twenty-three years ago. And there, glittering on her wrist, the tourmaline bracelet, for equally sentimental reasons.

Her heart raced. Would he find her attractive still? She was a girl the last time he'd seen her, or a young woman of thirty-two, nearly the age of Christ when they nailed him to the cross, and she wasn't a young woman any longer. She was fifty-two years old. Fifty-two and still well-preserved for all the passage of the years. Jane thought so, and her mother too. She still had her skin and her eyes—and her hair was dark yet, for the most part. The hairdresser at the hotel had helped—she just hoped Stanley wouldn't notice. Of course, he'd gone gray himself. At least he appeared to be gray the last time she'd seen him, but that was through the flat distorting lens of her binoculars.

There was a noise from the landing above, and her heart stopped. The clank of the iron door, a murmur of voices, male voices, deep and true. She moved toward the foot of the staircase to intercept him, to get the very first look at him at the top of the stairs . . . and there they were, three of them, three forms, and then the ghost that was the butler. Stanley was in the middle—ashen, towering, his hair streaked silver and white—and O'Kane was on one side of him, tight to his shoulder, and Martin on the other. They came down the stairs that way, three abreast, shoulder to shoulder to shoulder, as if this were some sort of military maneuver, each step a hurdle, halfway down now, O'Kane's left arm locked against Stanley's right, Martin's right against his left, their hands clenching his sleeves in the long jacket of his cuffs.

Then he saw her, and the procession halted. Three right legs were bent at the knee, three right feet arrested in their polished shoes. Stanley stopped and his eyes seemed to rivet her, nail her, drive holes right through her flesh and out the other side. He stopped. O'Kane and Martin stopped. The three men regarded her, Stanley with a panicky look now, a look she knew from the days that led up to his breakdown, and O'Kane and Martin drained and white, their eyes seeking anything but hers. And then, as if it were all just a momentary hitch, all three looked to their feet and came on down the stairs.

They halted at the bottom, not three paces from her, one step more and then out onto the marble floor. Stanley was staring down at his shoes. "Stanley," she said, "Stanley, darling. It's all right. It's me, Katherine. Your wife. I've come to see you."

He lifted his eyes then, but his head was cocked to one side, as if he didn't have the strength to raise it. "They," he said, his voice unnatural and high, "they wo-won't let me go. Eddie and Mart. They think . . . They've got my sleeves. My sleeves!"

Katherine wanted to touch him, lay a hand on his cheek, hold him in her arms and comfort him, poor Stanley, poor, poor Stanley. "Let him go," she said.

Immediately, O'Kane and Martin released their grip and took a step back from him, and there he was, all alone before her, his shoulders slumped, his hair slicked, his head canted to one side—and who was that, up there at the top of the stairs, watching from the shadows? Kempf. Of course. Kempf. Well, it was quite an intimate little gathering, wasn't it? The husband and wife reunited in the presence of one butler, one psychiatrist and two apelike nurses. She tried again. "Stanley, Stanley, look at me," and she moved forward to touch his arm.

It was then that he broke. Straight for the door. A scramble of his feet, fifty-three years old and you would have thought he was eighteen, the door a quick slice of light, O'Kane and Martin leaping forward, and he was gone. Katherine was suddenly in motion herself, no time to think, out the gaping door and onto the front steps, and there he was, Stanley, her husband, leading the nurses twice round the drive in a burst of speed before making for the car, Roscoe locking the doors against him, Jane's startled face, and then O'Kane had him in a bear hug and Stanley was whinnying "No, no, no, you don't understand, you don't—"

Katherine came forward as if in a trance, no thought for Jane or herself or anyone else but Stanley, and Martin had joined the fray now, all three men flailing on the ground in a confusion of limbs, gravel crunching, dust attacking the air. She came forward, bludgeoned by her emotions, and stood over them until her husband was subdued and panting and the nurses working to improve their grips, one pinioning his shoulders, the other clamped to his legs. "Stanley," she begged, pleading now, her eyes wet, everything confused and hurting, "it's only me."

He flashed his eyes at her then and jerked his head as far as O'Kane's straining limbs would allow. "I've—" he began, and there was wonder on his face, the wonder of discovery, epiphany, eureka, eureka, "I've seen your face," he said. "I've seen your face!"

5.

IN THE PRESENCE

OF LADIES

"No, you wouldn't call it auspicious," O'Kane said. "Not exactly. But it's a start, and I think Kempf deserves some credit." He was in the upstairs parlor, the door secured, a fire snapping complacently in the marble fireplace, Mr. McCormick off in dreamland, and he was feeling expansive and generous, full of seasonal good cheer—not to mention rum—and as far as goggle-eyed Dr. Kempf was concerned, he'd been a skeptic and now he was a believer. Mr. McCormick had made enormous progress over the course of the past year and a half and what had happened out there in the drive this afternoon was nothing more than a minor setback, he was sure of it. The brothers Thompson, Nick and Pat, who'd come on duty an hour ago, were struggling with the concept. They weren't convinced. Not at all.

"From what I hear, from Mart, anyway, the whole thing was a farce," Nick rasped in his burnt-out voice that was like the last scrapings of the pot, irritating and metallic. "He just ran for the door, couldn't even look her in the face. And Roscoe says he tried to get hold of the car, for Christ's sake."

Pat gave a low whistle. "Imagine him behind the wheel? What would it take to stop him—the whole Santa Barbara police force? The army? The navy? Hey, call out the marines!"

It was Christmas, or just about, and the place was bedecked, sprangled and festooned for the season, Mr. McCormick having been especially fixated on the decorations this year, and O'Kane had lingered to have a cup or two of Christmas cheer with his colleagues (he was going to quit drinking, absolutely and finally, the day after New Year's). He was also temporarily stranded, because Roscoe was out ferrying Mrs. McCormick and Mrs. Roessing around somewhere.

Nick was sunk into an overstuffed chair in front of the fire, his feet propped up on an ottoman, his hands nested over his stomach. Like Pat—and to a lesser extent, Mart—he'd accumulated flesh over the years, steadily and inexorably, but the funny thing was they'd all three finally achieved some sort of mysterious physical equilibrium, having grown into their heads like crocodiles. "I don't know if auspicious or not auspicious is the word for it—to me it's just more of the same, with or without Kempf."

O'Kane shrugged. He gazed round at the streamers and popcorn chains, the clumps of mistletoe and endlessly replicated effigies of Father Christmas and snowmen hanging like cobwebs from the ceiling. "At least he didn't attack her."

Pat snorted, burying his nose in his drink—a real drink, American style, mixed and heated in the kitchen by O'Kane himself while Giovannella frowned over the dough for tomorrow's bread and the scullery maid they'd hired to keep her company and deepen the presence of women in the house hummed a jazz tune and ran a wet cloth over the supper dishes. It was a toddy O'Kane was making, from a recipe his father had taught him—the only thing his father had taught him, besides a left jab maybe, followed by a swift right cross. Lemons, oranges, sugar, a stick of cinnamon, boiling water and what passed for rum these days. It had the right smell and it warmed you, though how much warming you needed when it was three hours past dark on the twelfth of December and still sixty-four degrees out was debatable.

O'Kane could feel the rum like lead in his veins—he didn't know how many he'd had thus far, but it was more than four, he was sure—and felt he'd better sit down. Nick and Pat seemed content to watch the fire, but the subject of Mr. McCormick's initial meeting with his wife had been broached, and O'Kane wanted to chew it over a while. "It'll get better," he said. "Tomorrow and the next day and the day after that. No more talking on the phone—she's due here tomorrow for lunch and she and Dr. Kempf both expect she'll be eating it downstairs in the dining room with Mr. McCormick at her side."

"I'd like to see it," Nick said.

"Me too," Pat put in.

"Kempf says she's going to stay this time. Indefinitely."

Nick sighed, bent to retrieve his cup from the floor and took a long ruminative sip. "She never gives up, that woman, does she? Twenty years she waits, and he bolts right by her like a runaway horse. Doesn't she know it's hopeless?"

"She's looking old," Pat said. "Like a little old lady. Like a widow. But that one with her, Mrs. Russ or whatever her name is, she's a piece of something, isn't she?"

"I don't know," O'Kane said, "—you've got to have hope. Anything can happen. People like Mr. McCormick have just snapped out of it, miraculously—I've seen it myself. And look at what they're doing with gland feeding and these hyperthyroid cases."

No comment from either of the Thompson brothers. They pulled at their cups, their eyes sunk into their heads. They could figure the chances on their own.

"Look how far Mr. McCormick's come already—he was right on the verge of going back under before Kempf came and you know it. He's coming back to life with this talking cure, he is—I can see it in the way he holds himself and his walk is better and he's hardly stuttering at all anymore."

"Yeah," Nick said, "and he still pisses his bed."

"Kempf says he needs women around him, and maybe he's right—it makes sense, doesn't it? We've tried everything else, from apes to sheet restraints to Brush's colossal fat arse—you remember how he pinned him to the floor that first day? 'Compression is what they need,' isn't that what he said?" O'Kane couldn't help laughing at the memory of it. "Or maybe you guys weren't there—you weren't, were you?"

"Shit." Nick sat straight up in the chair and cranked his head round to give O'Kane an outraged look.

"What? He's older now—he's settled down. He can be with women—he should be. As long as he's monitored."

"Didn't we—all of us—say that years ago? And we're not getting paid half what the mint in Washington prints up each month either," Nick growled, his voice scraping bottom. "I still say you go down to one of these hootch parlors on De la Guerra or Ortega Street and find him a willing little piece once a week and let him take out his urges like any other man. It's all that spunk clogging his brain." And he laughed, a fat rich braying laugh that made O'Kane want to get up out of the chair and poke him in the face a few times, good cheer or no.

"Well, he jacks off enough, doesn't he?" Pat said, rolling his cup between his hands; he was standing by the fire now, one elbow resting on the holly-strewn mantel, his face flushed with the drink. "I don't look at you and Mart's reports, but I'd say he's going at it four or five times a week on our shift—and Lord help us if we don't note down every little wad for Dr. Kempf, who in my opinion is half a pervert himself."

O'Kane wasn't listening. He was thinking about that—Mr. McCormick with a woman—and whether they'd get to watch. He'd have to be restrained, of course, and the woman would have to know her business—and no syph or clap, thank you, or they'd all wind up losing their jobs.

"I think they're lesbians," Nick said.

"Who?"

"Your sweetheart Katherine and what's her name, Mrs. Russ. You know, Eddie, cunt-lappers."

Well, sure. He'd suspected as much himself, way out on the periphery of his mind, but he wouldn't dignify Nick with a response. And so what if she was, which he doubted. It was better than going off and getting herself involved with a man—that was adultery—and she must still have had the itch, even if she was getting up in years, practically the prototypical old maid in her dowdy long skirts and outsized hats . . . but what he would have given just to touch her when she was younger, and he thought of that day in Hamilton's office when she bowed her head and let the tears come. And why was she crying? Because she couldn't see her husband. Well now she could, now that it was too late to matter.

He got up out of the chair, the fire jumping off Nick's big face and hands and winking metallically from the strings of decorations. "Anybody for another?"

Downstairs, in the kitchen, Giovannella was still busy with the dough—enough to make Guinea loaves and hot muffins for the twenty-two regular staff who had to be fed twice a day and a little extra to sell on the side and maybe take home to her mother and father. And her children. Never forget the children. They were her shield and her badge and the whole reason she was alive on the earth and pounding away at a corpselike lump of dough in the grand environs of the McCormick kitchen. And she *was* pounding, hammering away at the dough with both fists as if it were something she'd just stunned and wanted to make sure of.

O'Kane eased into the kitchen. Ever since their rapprochement during the earthquake two years back she'd tolerated his presence in the kitchen, but he could never tell when she'd lash out at him, not only verbally, but with any instrument, blunt or sharp, that came to hand, their entire history together bubbling and simmering in the stewpot of her eternally resentful peasant's brain, from the time she was seventeen and a virgin and he'd seduced her, right on up to this morning, this afternoon and this evening. If Mr. McCormick had his problems with women, so did he, so did Eddie O'Kane, and they started and ended here, right here in this kitchen.

"You still at it?" she said, pounding the dough. The maid, a girl of twenty with no chin and an overripe nose but with a spread and bloom to her that more than made up for it, started slopping a mop around. It was quitting time. The kitchen was still redolent of dinner, a roast of pork with rosemary, brown gravy, mashed potatoes and green beans, with apple turnovers for dessert.

"It's Christmas," he said.

She looked up from the dough, just her eyes, and her eyes were little pre-prepared doses of poison. "With you, it's always Christmas."

He sidled up to the chopping board, where he'd left his cloven fruit and the bottle, keeping a wary eye out for any sudden movement. She wasn't his wife, Giovannella, though he'd given in and in so many words asked her to be after the night of the marinara sauce and the big bed in the deserted and still subsiding house, but she carped and caviled at him as if she was. And that was strange too, utterly inexplicable, because that was what she'd wanted all along — for him to marry her — and then when he came for her and they were in bed and they'd had that sweetness and pleasure all over again, she'd refused him. "No, Eddie," she'd said, the house crepitating round them, the dark an infestation, a dog howling in duress somewhere off in the shattered distance, "I can't marry you—you're already married, remember? Isn't that what you told me? And besides, I couldn't expect you, a man like you, to raise another man's children, could I?"

"Just one more," he said. "For good cheer. You want one?"

Nothing, not even a glance.

"How about you, Mary? You want one?"

"Get out of my kitchen," Giovannella said. Her voice was low and dangerous and the blood had gone to her ears, her beautiful coffee-and-cream ears with the wisps of black hair tucked behind them and the puckered holes punched in the flesh for the gypsy earrings she sometimes wore. He loved those earrings. He loved those ears. And he was feeling sentimental and vague, full of affection for the world and everything in it, and for her, especially for her, for Giovannella.

She stepped away from the breadboard and picked up the first thing she saw—a flour sifter, peeling green paint over the naked tin, a sprinkling of white dust.

"What?" O'Kane protested. "Come on, Giov. It's only a little drink. It's not going to hurt anything."

"Get-out-of-my-kitchen," she said, raising the sifter ominously.

"You'd think I was a criminal or something."

"You are," she said, and there it was, that edge in her voice, as if she were about to cry or scream. "You are a criminal. Worse—you selfish stinking big prick of a man!"

He ignored her, slicing lemons, squeezing oranges, his elbows busy, the knife moving in his hand. He was angry suddenly, the generous all-embracing mood boiling off into the air like vapor. Who did she think she was? He'd had the run of the house since she was a girl in her mother's kitchen. "Besides," he said over his shoulder, "Nick and Pat want one. They're up there waiting for me—and lest you forget, I'm stranded here myself. You want me to look like an idiot and go back up there empty-handed?"

He would have said more, working himself into a state of real rhetorical fervor, but for the fact that the sifter suddenly ricocheted off the back of his head, and here she was, coming at him with a wooden spatula the size of a bricklayer's tool, cursing in Italian.

The tin had gouged his head, and it was bleeding, he was sure of it, and though he had absolutely nothing to regret or retract and was just spreading a little Christmas cheer and not even drunk yet, he couldn't help catching her by the wrist, the right wrist, just by way of defending himself. The left was another proposition all together. He'd caught the hand with the spatula, but she'd snaked away from him, as if they were doing a tarantella, everything a whirl, and snatched up a big wooden implement that looked like a mace, and already she'd managed to connect with two savage over-the-shoulder blows to his left forearm, and why, why was she doing this?

He always felt bad when he had to hit a woman—he felt like a dog, he did—but if she was going to get familiar with him (and over what?), then he was going to get familiar with her. A pot clattered to the floor. Mary, hand to mouth, vanished. They danced away from the stove, his fingers still hooked round her wrist, the mace flailing, the breath exploding from her clamped lips in short ugly bursts—uhh-uhh-uhh—and he just got tired of it, very tired, tired of the senselessness and her barometric moods and the way she went after him all the time, and he slapped her. Just once. But it had enough force behind it so that when he simultaneously released her arm she went hurtling back against the breadboard with a sharp annunciatory crack as of a stick being snapped in two, everything sailing out into the bright kitchen void and the pale laid-out corpse of the dough upended unceremoniously on the floor.

There was no sequel. Nothing at all. No apologies or recriminations, no battle rejoined or tears shed. Because at that moment—Giovannella slapped, the dough ruined, O'Kane half-drunk and outraged and cursing and swollen up to the full height and breadth of him—there came a sudden single excoriating cry that froze them both in place: *"Mama!"* O'Kane looked to the door, the open door, and there stood little Guido, eleven years old and already thick in the shoulders, and what was in his eyes besides shock and terror and rage? Three o'clock. Three o'clock in the afternoon.

Lunch was a success, everyone agreed. O'Kane lingered in the dining room with Katherine, Dr. Kempf and Mrs. Roessing while Mart escorted Mr. McCormick up to bed for his postprandial nap, and the feeling of relief and self-congratulation was palpable. It was as if they'd all gone through a war together, or a battle at least, and now here they were, all intact and no casualties. "Well, Katherine, Jane, didn't I tell you?" Kempf crowed, stirring a lump of sugar into the black pool of his coffee.

O'Kane was stationed at the door, hands in pockets. He'd been about to retreat, along with Mart and Mr. McCormick, when Kempf signaled him with his eyes. He knew what his role was. Moral support. The nurse in evidence.

Katherine was glowing. Her lips were pursed with pleasure and she sipped at her coffee as if it were an infusion of new blood and new life. "It was wonderful, it really was. Stanley was so . . . so much like his old self."

And what was so wonderful? That she'd sat down to a meal with her husband for the first time since 1906 and he hadn't attacked her, dumped the soup over his head or jumped out the window? Small victories, O'Kane was thinking. But it was a start, one step at a time, just like when they'd had to teach him to walk all over again. It had happened. It was a fact.

"What did you think, Jane?"

Mrs. Roessing must have been in her mid-forties, by O'Kane's calculation, but she looked ten years younger, what with her makeup and her clothes and her bright red marcelled hair. She gave Katherine a look, all eyes and teeth. "Well, I can't really say I'm an authority on the subject, since I never knew Stanley's old self, but his new one, at least as I saw him here today, was absolutely charming, don't you think, Dr. Kempf?"

The doctor drew himself up, the neat slightly puffed pale little hands, the painted hair and shimmering skull. He was a puppeteer, a ventriloquist, the mad scientist showing off his creature, Svengali with his Trilby. "My word for it exactly," he said with a polished grin. "Charming."

O'Kane had been amazed himself, especially after the previous afternoon's performance — Mr. McCormick had been a model of behavior, exactly like the man he'd golfed with at McLean, genial, courtly, haunted by neither demons nor judges. He'd been up and about when O'Kane arrived, full of smiles and little jokes, and he was very precise and efficient with his shower bath — he didn't squat on the tiles to soap his toes or rub himself raw with the towel. And he whistled, actually whistled in the shower, like a man on his way to work, "Beautiful Dreamer" echoing off the walls, followed by a spirited rendition of "Yes, We Have No Bananas." He breakfasted with perfect comportment and good humor, joking over the toughness of the ham (which wasn't really tough at all, if you had a knife and fork to hand, which he didn't, and he was acknowledging the absurdity of his predicament in his own sly way) and teasing Mart over his expanding girth ("Excuse me, Mart, but is that a life preserver you're wearing under your jacket?").

After breakfast, he took a stroll to the theater building and back, and then twice round the house, and he walked very nicely, not bothering with the cracks between the flagstones and hardly dragging his leg at all. Then there was his daily two-hour session with Dr. Kempf, from which he often emerged very upset and confused, sometimes speechless, sometimes with tears in his eyes or in a rage, but not today. Today he was perfectly composed, smiling even.

She was seated in the grand entrance hall, dressed all in gray, and O'Kane could see she'd put some time and thought into her outfit—she looked good, very good, better than she had yesterday or a year ago even. Mrs. Roessing was a middle-aged flapper in ultramarine and a silver wraparound hat, and those very fine and shapely legs exposed all the way up to her thighs in white silk stockings you could have licked right off her. O'Kane stood there like part of the décor.

"Katherine," Mr. McCormick said in a pleasant, muted voice, coming right up to her and taking her hand, which he bent to kiss, glove and all. And then, grinning till you'd think his face would split open, he turned to Mrs. Roessing. "And this must be, must be"— and here he lost himself a moment, understandably, twenty years and all that leg, and O'Kane braced himself for the worst— "Jane," he said finally, all the air gone out of him. Amazingly, he took her hand too, and bent to kiss it as if he were playing a part in a movie.

Butters took the ladies' wraps, Mart slunk out from behind the statue, and after a few inconsequential remarks about the weather— And how lucky you are, Stanley, to have this heavenly climate year-round and you should just *see* Philadelphia this time of year, snow up to, well, snow up to here—the whole party made its halting way into the dining room. The table could seat eighteen in comfort, but Butters had instructed Mary to set four places at the far end of it, Mr. McCormick to sit at the head of the table, as he was the host, his wife on his right-hand side, Dr. Kempf on his left, and Mrs. Roessing to the doctor's left. Mart and O'Kane were to stand guard and watch them eat.

Essential to all this was Giovannella, stalking round the kitchen with her left arm in a sling—no, it wasn't broken, only sprained—her eyes breeding rage while Mary and one of the houseboys scuttered round like scared rabbits. O'Kane had brought her flowers and a box of candy, and he'd actually crawled through the kitchen door on his hands and knees at eight-thirty A.M. to beg her forgiveness, but she wouldn't speak to him, wouldn't even look at him, and that was the end of that, at least for now. Butters would be serving at table, and they would start with caviar, large gray grain caviar from Volga sturgeon, served on little glass plates set down airily between the big yellow Arezzo dinner plates, and wine, real wine, decanted from an enigmatic green bottle.

There was soup—minestrone, one of Giovannella's specialities—followed by financières aux truffes from Diehl's, a salad and Italian food for the main course, very Continental. Mr. McCormick's veal had been cut up for him in the kitchen, so as not to cause him any embarrassment vis-à-vis the six silver spoons of varying size laid out at his place, and O'Kane had been instructed to particularly watch that he didn't snatch up a knife or fork from one of his fellow diners' settings. They chatted. Ate. Sipped at their wine. O'Kane watched, his back to the wall, and he felt the prickings of his salivary glands and the tumultuous rumblings of his stomach—this was when he hated his job most, this was when he felt his place, one more servant in a sea of them.

Mrs. Roessing praised the grounds—Had Stanley really had as much of a hand in laying them out as she'd heard?

Dr. Kempf: "Yes, Stanley, go ahead."

Mr. McCormick: "I, well, I—yes."

Mrs. Roessing (leaning in to show off the jewels at her throat): "It's such a talent, landscaping, I mean—I just wish I had it. Really, my place in Philadelphia is going to the dogs, if you know what I mean."

Katherine: "Stanley's always been clever that way—with drawings and architecture too. Haven't you, Stanley?"

Dr. Kempf: "It's all right. Go ahead."

Mr. McCormick: "My mother . . . she always said I was, but then she wouldn't . . . And I stud-studied in Paris, sketching, I mean, with Monsieur Julien. At his studios."

Dr. Kempf (by way of explanation): "Julien was very big at the turn of the century, practically doyen of the Paris art world—Stanley produced some very unique sketches under him, didn't you, Stanley?"

Mr. McCormick: "I, well, yes. In pencil and charcoal too. I sketched the Pont-Neuf neuf times. But no nudes, never any nudes. And what do you think of that, Mrs., Mrs. Jane?"

Mrs. Roessing: "Marvelous. Simply marvelous."

It went on like that for two hours, through the successive courses, the desserts, the fruits and now, finally, the coffee. "And what's your assessment, Dr. Kempf," Katherine asked all of a sudden, and a chill had come over her, the Ice Queen showing her face. "Can we expect more of this self-awareness and lucidity? Or is this a sort of act you've trained Stanley up to perform, like a dog jumping through a hoop?"

Kempf set down his cup, bowed his head, rubbed his eyes and shot a look at O'Kane, all in the space of a second. "I did talk to him, yes. Yesterday he was afraid of you, afraid you wouldn't recognize him—or love him still. We went over that this morning and we agreed that there was nothing to be afraid of, that you were his wife and would always love him. You see, the idea is to reeducate him, resocialize him, and introducing him into social situations, particularly in the company of women, is essential. In fact, I'm thinking of hiring on a female nurse."

This took O'Kane by surprise. Women, yes, but a female nurse? Upstairs? Locked in with him?

Katherine said nothing to this. The specter of the female nurse hung in the air a moment, just short of materializing, and then it dissolved. Mrs. Roessing asked for the cream. Kempf looked as if he were about to say something, but held his tongue.

"And what about his teeth?" Katherine suddenly demanded. She glanced at Mrs. Roessing. "And his body odor?"

"He bathed just this morning, didn't he, Eddie?" Kempf said, swinging round in his seat to address O'Kane.

"Yes, sir, he did, and very nicely too. He bathes every day, without fail."

"His teeth are another matter," Kempf said, "and we're all very concerned about their condition, but as you know, your husband has an aversion to dentists and it's been difficult—"

"Body and mind," Katherine said. "Mens sana in corpore sano."

"All things in time," the doctor said. "The mind and body are one, as you suggest, and by treating the mind I *am* treating the body. You wait and see. As his mind becomes free of its impediments, his teeth will improve spontaneously. And then, if we still feel we need to consult a dentist, we'll bring one in—once he's well enough—just as we've brought you ladies in today." He paused a moment to brood over his cup. "You should be gratified, Katherine, after Stanley's performance today—and I hope you'll give me a little credit for it."

"But that's just it—it *was* a performance. I want my husband sane and sound, and I'm worn out with waiting. And I don't see that psychoanalysis is the ne plus ultra—as you well know. I've been in contact with Dr. Roy Hoskins, of Harvard, and he's had great success in cases like Stanley's by correcting glandular irregularities and I see no reason why he shouldn't be called in to examine my husband to see if there isn't some somatic solution to all this. After all, you can't deny that he shows certain features of hyperthyroidism—his height, the disproportionate length of his digits and other appendages, which on seeing him today seem to me to have grown, and quite noticeably, and I really feel—"

Kempf cut her off with an impatient wave of his hand. "I couldn't disagree more. Psychoanalysis got him into this room to sit down at table and conduct himself as a gentleman in the presence of ladies, and psychoanalysis will provide his cure—if we can speak of a cure at all in these cases. He is *not* a hyperpituitary case, and gland feeding will accomplish absolutely nothing, I assure you."

The Ice Queen wouldn't let go of it. "It wouldn't hurt to try, would it? I really wish you would at least consider—"

"I'm sorry, Katherine," Kempf said, bringing the cup to his lips and giving her a long steady look. "Though I take note of what you're saying and I'm willing to try anything short of witchcraft to improve your husband's condition, believe me, the analytic approach is the best one, and as long as I'm in charge you'll have to let me make those decisions. He's improving. You've seen the result of it today."

Katherine leaned into the table, both her elbows stabbing at the cloth so that it bunched up around them. "Yes," she said acidly, "and I saw it yesterday."

"At least you're seeing him," Kempf shot back. "Isn't that something?"

"Yes, yes it is, doctor—Edward," she said. "But I expect more, much more. And I intend to stay right here in Santa Barbara for as long as it takes to see my husband's health restored—both mental and physical. That's my mission, that and nothing else." She looked to Mrs. Roessing for approval, and Mrs. Roessing, smoke streaming from her nostrils over her pursed and pretty lips, gave her a wink.

"What's more," Katherine went on, the Ice Queen, all buoyed up now and never satisfied, never, "let me remind you that *I* am the one who will make the final decisions here. All of them."

Katherine was true to her word. Every day at one, through Christmas and the New Year, on through the soft stirring close of winter and the advent of the spring that was just like the winter, fall and summer that had preceded it, she and Mrs. Roessing came to have lunch with Mr. McCormick and to sit with him as late as five or six some afternoons, playing at cards or reading aloud to one another or simply sitting there in a swollen bubble of silence. O'Kane was present for all of it, and so was Mart. Mr. McCormick's improvement had been dramatic and he was making new strides every day, but he was still dangerous and unpredictable, still a threat to his guests and himself, and when he'd made his good-byes—always bowing and scraping and kissing the women's outstretched hands in a drama of self-effacement and servility that made O'Kane queasy to watch—his nurses escorted him back upstairs to the barred windows and the iron door.

He had his bad days still, days when he would stagger out of Kempf's office in the theater house with his eyes streaming and his lips drawn tight, and then he'd try to run or take out his anger on some innocent shrub the gardeners had been attentively nurturing and shaping for years. Once, when O'Kane gave him a gentle nudge toward the house after he'd begun to stray, he bent down, pried up one of the flagstones and chased both him and Mart all round the lawn with the thing held up over his head like a weapon. Another time, for no reason at all, he kneed Mart in the privates and boxed O'Kane's right ear so savagely it buzzed and twittered for days, like a dead telephone connection.

"What'd you do that for, Mr. McCormick?" O'Kane protested, clutching the side of his head while Mart blanched to the roots of his hair and sat himself awkwardly down in the daphne bed, right atop a gopher's mound. "Be-because," Mr. McCormick stammered, his face clenched like a fist, "because I—I hate, I hate—" He never finished the phrase. Not that day, anyway.

Still, he was improved, vastly improved, and being with women— seeing them, smelling their perfume, touching their hands with the driest fleeting caress of his lips—seemed to be working wonders for him. Katherine began to bring Mr. McCormick's twenty-year-old niece, Muriel, with her on occasion, and at Dr. Kempf's suggestion, they began to take Mr. McCormick on outings. At first they confined themselves to the estate, picnicking amongst the Indian mounds or taking advantage of the views from the upper reaches of the property, but before long—under supervision of Kempf, O'Kane and Martin, of course—they began having beach parties. Katherine rented a cabaña on one of the splendid south-facing beaches in Carpinteria where the waves broke in gentle synchronization and you could ride them in like a dolphin, the water as warm as a bath. It was comical to see Mr. McCormick in his bathing costume, his limbs pale as a Swede's, crab-walking up to the quavering line of foam and seawrack and then dashing back like a grade-school boy as the water washed over his toes. Comical, but healthy. It stunned O'Kane to think of it as he sat there on his beach towel, eyes riveted on Mr. McCormick while two men hired for the day hovered just beyond the breakers in a rowboat against the darker potentialities, but in all his years living here in the paradise of the world, Mr. McCormick had never once touched the ocean nor had it touched him.

It was a good time. A happy time. A time of hope. Everyone, even Nick, began to feel that something extraordinary was happening, and they were all of them almost afraid of speaking of it for fear of jinxing it. Mr. McCormick was experiencing life again, out of his cage, reintegrating himself into the grander scheme of things, particle by particle, and for his nurses, that promised—maybe, possibly, eventually—an end to their labors, and a reward. And who knew?—perhaps it would be a substantial reward, a lump sum, every punch and kick and smear on the sheets accruing interest over the unwieldy course of the years.

But it wasn't to be. If McCormick's constricted life had miraculously dilated during that amazing summer, opening and opening again as if there were no longer any limits, any judges, any fear or despair or self-loathing or sheer immitigable craziness, there came a day in September—and O'Kane could name it—when things began to close in again. It started with the beach. An ordinary day, the sun high and white, Mr. McCormick in good spirits, the ocean rolling and rolling all the way out to the islands that were wrapped in a band of silver fog. There was the picnic luncheon. The cabaña. Young Muriel was there, daughter of a Rockefeller and a McCormick, her legs browned from the sun and her hair turned golden, and Katherine and Mrs. Roessing too, the latter daring in a skirtless bathing suit. Everything seemed fine, until Mr. McCormick, waist-deep in the surf with O'Kane to one side of him and Mart to the other, suddenly cried out shrieking in a way that made you think of men murdered in a dark alley, slit throats, the bayonet in the gut. He was shrieking suddenly and hopping on one foot till he lost his balance and plunged his face into the water and the wet sand beneath, the surf relentless and O'Kane and Mart dragging him out of the water by his arms.

What was the matter? What had happened? Was he all right? Was he hurt? Kempf, Katherine, Muriel, Mrs. Roessing, Mart, O'Kane and even the two men from the boat all crowding round, and Mr. McCormick just clutching his foot and screaming. "The Judges!" he bawled. "I knew they'd get me, I knew it!" His hair hung in his eyes and his face was twisted and wet, the black of his throat and the jagged craters of his rotten teeth, sand like a hairshirt all over his prickled body. Later they discovered the cause—it was legitimate and real: he'd been lacerated by a stingaree—but that was the end of ocean bathing, and of the beach.

It was also the end of Mr. McCormick's positive phase, because overnight he became mistrustful and paranoic again, and no amount of reasoning—the stingaree lives in the sea, it meant you no harm, it was an accident, these things happen—would convince him that the whole episode hadn't been planned as a punishment for him. And he seemed, finally, to blame the women, their presence, for what had happened. If it weren't for them he wouldn't have been at the beach—were they trying to kill him, was that it? Was Katherine after his money? Did she want to see him dead? The next day he wouldn't come to lunch, though Katherine and Mrs. Roessing were waiting in the dining room for him;

O'Kane and Mart were prepared to drag him down the stairs, but Kempf said no. When he wanted to see women again, he would. On his own terms. Give him time, Kempf said.

Two days went by. Three. A week. And still Mr. McCormick refused to come down those stairs, and when the rumor reached him one afternoon that Katherine was coming up, he threw one of his fits, replete with the smashed furniture and the deranged raving and the foam on his lips. Katherine had become impatient and began to nag at Kempf, in O'Kane's presence, threatening and storming like a madwoman in her own right: she was used to seeing her husband again, seeing him daily, and now she'd been cut off from him once more. It was intolerable. She'd have Kempf's head—or his job at least, all ten thousand dollars a month's worth.

It was then, right at the end of September, that the nurses decided to take matters into their own hands. "It's a dirty shame," Nick said one night when both O'Kane and Mart had stayed behind their time because Roscoe was otherwise occupied and wouldn't be back till nine. They all agreed. Mr. McCormick had come so far and now he was spiraling back, two full turns a day, and no one to reverse his direction. "What about what we discussed, back around Christmas of last year, remember, Eddie?" Nick said. "Getting him a woman, I mean. If his wife can't do it for him, some—what would you call her?—some consulting nurse could. Right?"

O'Kane was elected, because of his reputation with women—a reputation long since obscured by Giovannella and little Guido and Edwina and the business end of the bottle, but never mind that. He went down to Spanishtown the next night—and it had changed, squeezed and reduced by the grand new buildings going up in the wake of the earthquake—and asked around a few of the joints he knew. It was all underground, speakeasies, triple knock and codeword—"Clara Bow"; "Big Bill"; "Dixieland"—but anybody who knew anybody or anything could get in and no questions asked. He found her at the third place he tried, a cramped downstairs space so full of people, noise and smoke there was no room to breathe, let alone enjoy a drink of whatever shit they were selling behind the bar. O'Kane sampled a few anyway, leaning into the bar as if it were a bed, a pillow, Giovannella with her dress up and a smile on her face, and when he turned his head, there she was.

She was sitting alone at a table in the middle of the room, people

dancing and jostling all around her and nobody even giving her a second glance. She had a compressed, angry look about her, bad luck and
worse news all the way round, and she was clutching a cigarette as if
she were trying to strangle it. Smiling Eddie O'Kane, pimp to the Mc-
Cormicks, moved in. "Hi," he said. "Mind if I join you?"

She glared at him.

He sat down.

"Buy you a drink?" he offered. The music was furious, clarinet, piano, drums, people doing the shimmy and the Charleston, the very table shaking with the thump and roar of it.

Her mouth softened. She'd been holding it very tightly, as if it
might fall off her face and shatter if she wasn't the carefulest girl in the
world. She couldn't have been more than twenty. "Sure," she said, and
her lips fell back in what she probably thought was a smile.

They agreed on a price—it was dicey, real dicey, because all the
way up the stairs, out the door and into the big blue-black Pierce Arrow
limousine she thought she was going to bed with him, Eddie O'Kane—
but when he explained the situation to her somewhere between the Salt
Pond and Hot Springs Road, she began to balk, especially seeing the
car and its appurtenances and Roscoe up front in his monkey cap, and
he had to double the price to keep her quiet. Twelve-thirty in the morning, the night watchman, the iron gates, the house like a chunk of the
night cut away with a serrated knife and blackened in India ink. Lights
on upstairs, though, and Nick and Pat waiting on tenterhooks. "He
won't hurt me, will he?"

"No," O'Kane assured her, "no, he won't hurt you. Besides, we've
got him restrained."

Her voice, so thin and frightened it sickened him and he almost
backed out of the thing right there: "Restrained?"

O'Kane didn't know what to say. He led her up the big staircase
and opened up the barred door himself, her thin cold elbow quailing
under the grip of his hand, and she was trying to be brave, trying to get
through with this, he could see that. "Jesus," she whispered, turning
her head to get a look at the bars as they passed through the doorway,
and O'Kane held her there a minute while he turned the three separate
keys in the three separate locks. And then, Nick and Pat gouging her
with their eyes, she hesitated at the bedroom door and the thought of
what lay behind it, the bed bolted to the floor and the barred windows

and Mr. Stanley Robert McCormick, Reaper heir, lying there on his back, wrists and ankles bound up tight—double tight—to the bedposts. "You better give me the money," she said, her eyes shrunk to pinpricks, the mouth a misshapen hole in the middle of her face. "Give it to me now."

Nick and Pat both watched, silent presences in a darkened room, no light but what the stars gave and the moon—it was their duty, after all—but O'Kane couldn't do it. He should have been exhilarated, should have felt good, should have rejoiced in Mr. McCormick's happiness, the need and thrill and privilege of every man—sex, just sex—but instead he went out onto the upper patio and hung his head over the drain in the corner and threw up everything he'd drunk that night, and the taste of it, full of bile, was bitter and lingering, a sharp unallayable sting of the lips and tongue that was like the very kiss of despair.

Kempf was perplexed. "I can't understand it," he said, getting up from behind his desk and pacing up and down while O'Kane sat in a chair so comfortless and hard it might have been designed for the witness stand at the county courthouse. "We were making such progress, and now nothing: Pffft! I throw the usual bugbears up to him—his parents, his wife, the experience in Paris—and he won't respond at all. Even free association's a dud. I say 'boxer dog' and he just stares at me. All he'll say is 'one slit, one slit,' over and over again." He knotted his hands behind his back, shaking his head, dapper and narrow-shouldered, with the bleeding eyes and precise hair of a screen idol. "I thought we were past all that."

O'Kane didn't respond. The doctor was talking to himself, really, as he did nearly every afternoon in the wake of his session with Mr. Mc-Cormick; O'Kane was merely a sounding board. Holding himself very rigid, hardly breathing, he let his eyes crawl round the room. The décor wasn't substantially different from that of the Hamilton and Brush eras, but for the fact that Hamilton's neurological molds and Brush's Hawaiian scenes were gone, replaced by a single massive reproduction of a painting that was affixed to the wall of Dr. Freud's office in Vienna, or so Kempf claimed. "Le Leçon clinique du Dr. Charcot," a plaque beside it read, and it showed a white-haired doctor—presumably Charcot—supporting a young hysteric by the waist while twenty bearded students looked on and her nurse stood ready to catch her should she fall. The woman was wearing a low-cut blouse that had slipped down over her shoulders, and though she was standing, she appeared to be unconscious—either that or faking it. The significance of it all escaped O'Kane, except that the woman was a real looker and Charcot obviously had her in his power. So what was the attraction for Kempf—wish fulfillment?

"That stingaree was a damned unfortunate thing," Kempf mused, still pacing, "rotten luck and no two ways about it. But I thought Stanley was getting over it, I really did, and now he's blocked again, no more sensible or responsive than a stone. Something has set him off, no doubt about it—you don't know anything that might be troubling him, do you, Eddie?"

O'Kane, rigid, just his lips: "No, nothing at all."

"It's funny," Kempf said, pausing now in front of O'Kane's chair. He was looking down at him, furrowing his brow, squinting those rounded eyes till they were no more than slits. "Really odd. Nothing happened last night, did it? While you were here—or after? That you might've gotten wind of, that is?"

"No, nothing."

The doctor made a feint with his hand, as if he were trying to snatch something out of the air. "I just thought that Nick or Pat might've—"

"No. Uh-uh. They didn't say a word."

"Well, something has happened. I'm sure of it. He won't say, but I'll get it out of him. You watch me. I just hope it won't . . ."

"What?"

Kempf let out a sigh. "I just hope it won't compromise the progress we've made with his wife and the others—and you know, I've already hired on the new nurse. Mrs. Gleason. She worked under me at Saint Elizabeth's."

And now O'Kane was stammering, just like Mr. McCormick: "I don't think—well, it's not my place to say, but is it really advisable to bring a woman in—I mean, at this juncture? When he seems so disturbed? Over the stingaree, I mean."

Kempf's face fell open like a book, only it was an unreadable book—a psychology text, written in German. "Why, yes," he said, "of course. That's the whole idea. To show him that women are no different from you and me, from men, that is, and that they're as natural a part of living in the world as trees, flowers, gophers and psychologists. The more women we introduce him to, the more—"

He was interrupted by a knock at the door. It pushed open partway and Butters' face, flushed and startled-looking, appeared in the aperture. "Mrs. McCormick to see you, sir. And Mrs. Roessing."

Katherine stalked into the room then, her heels punishing the floorboards, Mrs. Roessing following languidly behind. "I just can't stand it," she announced, addressing Kempf, who'd stopped his pacing and was posed in front of the painting in the exact attitude of Charcot. "And frankly, Dr. Kempf, I don't care what your opinion or advice is on the subject, but Jane and I have come to take my husband out to luncheon—a proper luncheon—at our hotel."

The doctor blanched. He looked like Valentino facing down a bull in *Blood and Sand*—sans the mustache and excess hair, of course. "I can't allow it," he said. "Not today, of all days."

Katherine was in a state, all her Back Bay debutante's ire aroused, the crater visible between her pinched brows, her eyes incinerating all before her. She wouldn't be denied, not this time—O'Kane could see that, and he began to feel very uncomfortable indeed. "What you will or will not allow is beside the point, Edward," she said, "because I'll have you out of here in two shakes if you continue in this obstinate—"

"Your fellow guardians may have something to say about that."

"Well, do you hear that?" Katherine huffed, looking to Mrs. Roessing for support; to her credit, Mrs. Roessing merely seemed embarrassed. "The insolence of the man. I'll see Cyrus and Anita in court—and you too. It's high time I had the guardianship of my own husband, and we've come this far, with our lovely beach parties and, and"—here she faltered, the voice gone thick in her throat—"and Muriel and all the rest, and I won't see it spoiled now, I simply won't." She shot a look at O'Kane, as if to see if he was going to offer any protest, and he dropped his eyes.

"All right, Jane," she said then, her voice brisk and businesslike, "let's go fetch Stanley."

There was a moment of hesitation, Kempf giving O'Kane a sour look as the two women slammed out the door and down the steps to the path that led to the main house, their shoulders squared, hats marching in regimental display, and then he said, "Come on, Eddie, we'd better get over there and see that Martin doesn't open that door—or if he does, well, I won't answer for it."

They weren't more than two minutes behind the women, but by the time they reached the main house, with its door flung open wide and a faint cool breath of lemon oil and furniture wax emanating from somewhere deep inside, Katherine and Mrs. Roessing were already at the top of the stairs, on the landing, and Katherine was shrilly demanding that Martin open the door. Mr. McCormick was bent over the table in the upstairs parlor at the time, rocking back and forth and chanting his mantra—*one slit*—over and over, while he worked at drawing a continuous line down the center of a hundred or so sheets of the finest handmade cotton-rag sketching paper, front and back. He was still in his robe and pajamas, having refused to dress that morning, an act of insubordination Kempf overlooked because of Mr. McCormick's highly discomposed state. O'Kane was just coming up the stairs at this point, and all he was able to see at first was some sort of commotion, but Mart later filled him in on the details.

The moment the women had appeared on the landing, Mr. McCormick snapped to attention. He stopped rocking, stopped chanting, threw down his pencil. "Martin," Katherine demanded, "open this door at once. Jane and I are taking Mr. McCormick out for a proper lunch."

In the absence of Kempf and O'Kane, Mart was slow to react, a farrago of conflicting loyalties—he knew perfectly well that Mr. McCormick wasn't himself and he knew what had happened the night before and what it meant, and that opening the door would lead to trouble, he was sure of it. On the other hand, Mrs. McCormick was the ultimate authority here, the president, Congress and Supreme Court of Riven Rock all rolled in one. "I'm coming," he said, though she could plainly see through the grid that he wasn't, that he was delaying, pretending to fumble in his pockets for the keys, and she became impatient and began to rattle the bars. There she was, in her tailor-made clothes and half-a-melon hat, her slim gloved fingers wrapped round the impervious iron bars, tugging in impatience as if it were she who was locked in and her husband roaming free.

The bars rattling, his wife's fingers and her white throat, the petulant crease over the bridge of her nose, the pique of her eyes and the set of her hat: suddenly Mr. McCormick came to life. In two bounds he was at the door, and though she drew back instinctively and Mrs. Roessing cried out and Mart rumbled up out of the chair, Katherine was caught. Mr. McCormick had her by both wrists, all the incensed, aroused, preternatural strength of him, his rotten teeth and his close and personal odor, and he drew her to him, Sam Wah all over again, and then snatched a hand to her throat, clamped it there like a staple, forcing her head back, and he was whinnying in his excitement: "A kiss! A kiss!"

O'Kane was the one who broke his grip and then he was pinioned there in Katherine's place, Mr. McCormick like the tar baby, stuck fast now to *his* wrists, Katherine staggering back from the door, the wreck of her bloodless face, Mrs. Roessing already wrapping her in her arms and Dr. Kempf's voice gone high with agitation: "You see? You see what happens when you interfere?"

And all of them—O'Kane and Mart, Mrs. Roessing, Kempf and even the furiously tugging and whimpering Mr. McCormick—looked to her for a response. She held tight to Jane Roessing, her hat askew, the red marks of her husband's fingers melting into the chalk of her throat. "I blame you for this," she said finally, all threat and defiance, glaring at Kempf as if to incinerate him on the spot. "You're alienating my husband's affections, that's all you're doing with your, your precious psychoanalysis—and that's just what the McCormicks want, isn't it? Isn't it?"

Kempf held his peace. Mr. McCormick dropped O'Kane's wrists and worked his arms back through the bars—he looked dubious and bewildered, as if he'd just gotten off a streetcar at the wrong stop. Mrs. Roessing reached up to straighten Katherine's hat and mumured something to her, and then the two of them were receding down the staircase, their hats in retreat.

"You know what's wrong with that woman?" Kempf said as soon as she was out of hearing. Mr. McCormick stared wildly through the bars. Mart hovered helplessly in the background, undecided as to whether he should tackle their employer from behind and bind him up in the sheet restraints or just let it go and settle back into the personal hollow he'd eroded in the pillows of the couch over the course of the stultifying months and obliterative years.

"No," O'Kane said, and he was interested to know, vitally interested, "no, what's wrong with her?"

"It's a prescription I'd give her, really—one of Freud's." Kempf tugged at his sleeves and then brushed down his jacket with a flick of his fingers, as if to rid himself of the residue of what had just transpired. "Do you know Latin, Eddie?"

"I was an altar boy."

"Good. Then you'll appreciate this. Freud said it of a female hysteric whose husband"—he lowered his voice, out of Mrs. McCormick's hearing—"was impotent. And I'd say it fits Mrs. McCormick to a T."

"Yes?"

The doctor lowered his voice still further. " 'Penis normalis, dosim repetatur.' "

6.

SICK, VERY SICK

stanley knew what was going on he might have been sick but he wasn't retarded and he wasn't blind or deaf either and it was the women the women yet again because they weren't content to sit at lunch with him or make conversation over iced tea in the cabaña don't you think it's just outrageous what the french have done to the hemline this year no they weren't satisfied that he was a gentleman bred by his mother and held himself just so and made the smallest talk and didn't punish them and give them what they needed and deserved and wanted no they had to come to him in the night ghostly and white in their skin with their wet tongueless mouths and the smell of their heat a bitch in heat like a bitch in heat and take hold of him down there where he was most vulnerable and how he hated that because there was nothing nothing nothing he hated more than that and the Judges had warned him and lashed him and beaten and pummeled him and yet here it was all over again and she didn't even have a name but she wasn't katherine oh no not katherine never katherine he was sure of that because she was some slut and whore and degraded filthy streetwalking prostitute who could have her way with him any way she liked and he'd almost felt it almost almost thrust back at her and showed her what it was to be a man a real man a he-man like his father the president and his brother the president and harold the vice president with his two wives like a pasha and his monkey glands and his beautiful little adorable little child woman daughter muriel . . .

almost . . .

but almost wasn't all the way home almost didn't win the race or drive the ball over the fence or invent the reaper out of nothing or the stingaree either which was gods reaper lurking there in the water and who knew better that it was there and what it liked to do and was likely to do than katherine who was the scientist after all the biologist who would sing out the latin names of every animal and plant and bounding squirrel with the breeze of the car in her face her beautiful face katherine dexter and he thought about that and brooded and picked over it all through the day of the stingaree and the day it melted into because she'd done it because she wanted to see him dead and drowned because she wanted to be a widow like mrs. jane two of them widows because she wanted his money and he could see right through her because dr kempf the free associa-tor and inkblot man — "Tell me, Stanley, when I say 'boxer dog,' what do you think of?" *— had taught him to control himself just as if he were wear-ing the harness again an invisible harness no straps or wires or restraints but that was the end of katherine no more katherine no sir never again not after that stinking filthy animal of a whore and what was her scientific name he'd like to know she'd brought into his very bedroom to debase and humiliate him while nick and pat breathed in the dark and yes he'd heard them there and felt them but no more no more and never again make me a baby stanley make me a baby . . .*

Katherine couldn't know what her husband was thinking—she never knew what he was thinking, even when he was sitting there on the car-pet they brought to the beach discussing the Malemute Kid with Muriel and fastidiously nibbling round the edges of a smoked salmon sandwich Giovannella had prepared at first light. All she knew was that he'd come so far, come all the way back to who he was, her Stanley, Stanley of the retiring mien and shining eye, and now he'd fallen away from her again—and she would be damned twice over if she was going to be cut out of his life this time. That was why she'd hired Newton Baker, her old friend and colleague from the War days and the Women's Commit-tee of the National Defense Council, to petition the Santa Barbara Su-perior Court for sole guardianship of her husband:

T. Coraghessan Boyle

IN THE MATTER OF THE GUARDIAN- SHIP OF THE PERSON OF STANLEY MCCORMICK, AN INCOMPETENT PER- SON:	No. 7146 PETITION FOR REMOVAL OF CERTAIN GUARDIANS

TO THE HONORABLE, THE SUPERIOR COURT OF THE STATE OF CALIFOR-
NIA IN AND FOR THE COUNTY OF SANTA BARBARA:

COMES NOW KATHERINE DEXTER MCCORMICK, AND RESPECTFULLY SHOWS:

That Kempf was alienating the affections of her husband on behalf of
Cyrus and Anita and refusing him the endocrine treatment that could
well provide a cure for him, and that she, as Stanley's wife, knew better
than his brother and sister what was good and proper for him and was
better able to provide it without their interference. That all they cared
about was keeping the McCormick fortune intact. That she, Katherine,
his wife, had through all these splayed and tottering years managed her
husband's estate despite their automatic two-to-one vote against her on
any matter of real importance, as for example spending ten thousand
dollars a month on a psychiatrist who believed that psychoanlysis could
repair rotten teeth, and she wanted redress and wanted it now.

Jane backed her. And her mother too. And though she hated the
publicity and dreaded the thought of what the papers would do with
this, she could hardly wait to take the stand and give them all a piece of
her mind. And why? Because of Stanley, nothing more. Stanley was all
that mattered—and her guilt for having neglected him over the course
of the years, all her loyalty notwithstanding, because she *had* neglected
him and she'd allowed herself to be badgered and pigeonholed by the
Favills and Bentleys and Hamiltons of the world and now by Anita and
Cyrus. But she wouldn't give in. Not anymore. Because she alone knew
how wrenching and terrifying it was to lose Stanley the first time, the
time he floundered and splashed and finally went down, and no one
there to throw him a lifeline, no one but her. . . .

It all came to a head after their return from Maine, the ongoing and
unrelieved nightmare that was Maine, in the fall of 1905. Everything
she'd tried—patience and understanding, firmness, reason, love—was a
failure, that was clear, and Stanley was caught in a downward spiral
that threatened to suck her under too. "Sexual hypochondriachal

neurasthenia and incipient dementia praecox" was Dr. Trudeau's chilling assessment, and all she could do was try to insulate Stanley against anything that might cause him undue stress—his mother, in particular, the Reaper Works, and, sad to say, marital relations. She'd pushed him too far, moved too quickly, and now she had to draw back and assuage and nurture him all over again.

On their first day back in Boston—the twenty-first of November—they went down to the harbor to meet her mother, who was just then returning from an extended stay at Prangins. The day was gloomy and cold, with a scent of rain on the air and a low scrolling sky stuffed full of gray clouds that unfurled in procession out over the sea. The liner was just docking as the driver let them down from the carriage and they hurried up to the gate that gave on to the pier, hardly noticing the others in the crowd or the man in a cap and loden jacket trimmed with gold piping standing to one side of the entrance. Katherine was intent on her mother and on Stanley, who'd been stiff and incommunicative all morning, and never gave the man a second glance, never dreaming that they needed passes to enter the dock area and that this man was stationed there in an official capacity to check those very passes.

There was a cry at their back, rude and insulting, and here came the man—an Italian, she believed, swarthy and black-eyed—rushing down the pier to intercept them. "Hey," he shouted, addressing Stanley, "where the hell you think you're going, mister?"

Katherine felt the blood rush to her face. She could scarcely believe her ears. At the same time, her arm was looped through Stanley's, and she could feel him stiffen. He gave the approaching guard a wild look, and then the man was there, out of breath, and he reached out to seize Stanley by the arm.

He couldn't have known what he was doing. Because in that moment all Stanley's frustrations came to the surface in a molten swelling rush—Maine, his mother, the farce of their honeymoon, his failure in bed—and he erupted. He shook the man off as if he were an insect, sending him careening across the planks in a clutch of spinning limbs and flailing hands. And when the man picked himself up with a curse and came at him again, Stanley brought his umbrella into play, slashing away at his adversary's face and head until the umbrella was nothing but rag and splinter and the dazed guard, blood wadded in his hair and bright down the front of his jacket, staggered off in retreat.

They were both upset, both she and Stanley, and she held tight to his arm as they made their way through the awestruck crowd, which parted automatically at the sight of Stanley's grim bloodless face and the shredded trophy that had been his umbrella. "The impudence of that man," she said. "The first thing I'm going to do when we get home is write a letter to the steamer line — if they can't hire a gentleman to accommodate the public then they shouldn't hire anyone at all. You're not hurt, are you?"

He shook his head, his lips pressed tight.

"Good," she said, "thank heavens," but she could feel him trembling and recoiling like a plucked string. They were almost at the boat now, the vast field of it blocking the horizon from view, the crowd closing ranks behind them. Was that her mother, up there, leaning over the rail and waving a handkerchief? No, no it wasn't.

"I can't," Stanley said suddenly, pulling up short. "I — I've got to go back. They'll have the police."

"Don't be ridiculous. The man attacked you — there were witnesses. If anyone need fear the police, it's him."

"No," he said, trembling, and there was that look, the eyes sunk into his head and his lips jerking away from the skirts of his teeth and his teeth clamped and grinding. "They-they'll put me in jail, I'll be ruined. Bars," he said, "iron bars," and he pulled away from her in a single clonic spasm, turned his back on her and started up the pier in the direction of the gate.

"Stanley!" she called, but he was beyond hearing, already swallowed up in the milling crowd, already lost.

She didn't see him again till late that night — past ten — and all through her reunion with her mother and dinner and the unwrapping of the little gifts Josephine had brought her back from Paris she was sick with worry. She was sure Stanley had gone off and got himself in some sort of trouble (she thought of the old man at the lake and what might have happened if he hadn't been able to swim) — trouble no amount of money could get him out of. He was seething. Out of control. Ready to lash out at anyone who got in his way, however unknowingly or innocently. And while her mother nattered on about Prangins and Madame Fleury and how the wedding was still the talk of the village, all Katherine could think of was the police. Should she call them? But what would she say — that her husband was lost? That Stanley Robert

McCormick, with all his savoir faire and talent and wealth, couldn't be trusted on the public streets? That he was mad and disoriented and suffering from sexual hypochondriacal neurasthenia?

She broke down in the middle of one of her mother's stories about Emily Esterbrook, of the Worcester Esterbrooks, who'd had the stateroom across from hers on the passage back and could whistle the second violin part to Beethoven's Harp Quartet—all the way through—without missing a note. "Emily's daughter is engaged to the nicest man," her mother was saying, when suddenly Katherine began to sob and she couldn't seem to stop, not even when Stanley finally came banging up the stairs.

"Stanley," Josephine cried, rising from her chair to greet him, "how nice to see you again," but then she faltered. Stanley stood there in the middle of her mother's parlor with the strangest look on his face, as if he didn't recognize the place at all—or the people in it. There was a smudge of oil or grease on his forehead and the flesh round his right eye was puffy and discolored, as if just that smallest part of him had begun to decay. His jacket had suffered too, the left sleeve hanging by a thread and the right gone altogether. What looked to be blood was crusted round the elbow of the exposed shirtsleeve.

"But Stanley, what's happened?" Josephine exclaimed, crossing the room to take him by the hand, and she was thinking of her own son, her own dead son, all sympathy and maternal solace, and Katherine's heart went out to her. As for Stanley—her own reaction to him, that is—she was paralyzed, utterly paralyzed. She couldn't say What? or How? or even open her mouth. "Here," Josephine was crooning, "let me see. Here, under the light."

At first, in the first moment her mother touched him, Stanley seemed to acquiesce, bowing his head and relaxing his shoulders, but then all at once he jerked his hand away as if he'd been bitten. "You stupid old woman!" he shouted, every cord of his throat flexed and straining. "You stupid interfering old woman, don't you touch me, don't you dare touch me!"

"Stanley!" Katherine gasped, and suddenly she'd found her voice, angry now as she watched her mother's face collapse—the kindest woman in the world and she meant nothing but kindness—sore and angry and ready to put an end to this . . . this insanity. "Stanley, you apologize this instant!"

But he turned on her now, out of control, out of anybody's control, even his own, his face a whipping rag of rage. "Shut up, you bitch!"

In the morning, early, before anyone was stirring, they went out to Brookline in a private carriage, Stanley sunk so deep in the cushions he was all but invisible from the street, his long legs tented before him, his head and shoulders slouched at the uncomfortable level of Katherine's buttocks. Both his cheekbones had swollen overnight—he'd been beaten, beaten savagely, she could see that now—and it gave him a look of squint-eyed inscrutability, as if he'd been transformed into a Tatar tribesman while he slept. He said nothing. Not a word. No explanations, no apologies. As soon as they got home, she put him to bed and he slept all through that day and the night and morning that followed.

Then came the procession of psychiatrists, neurologists and pathologists, an unending parade of them marching through the parlor of the Brookline house, tapping, probing and auscultating her shrinking husband, holding up pictures and geometric forms for his comment, questioning him closely about current events and throwing their arms over his shoulder and suggesting a nice walk around the garden. Katherine was frightened. Stanley seemed to be getting progressively worse, slipping away from her, and no one seemed capable of touching him—each physician who came to the door undermined the opinion of his predecessor, as if it were all some elaborate medical chess match. She needed a plan of action, a line of inquiry and therapy to pursue, but all she got was confusion. Outside, the trees stood in tatters, winter advancing, the light fading, the wind gathering, and nothing settled. She wasn't sleeping well. Meals were a torment. She couldn't exercise, couldn't read, couldn't think. In her desperation, she wired Nettie, hoping for some insight, some shred of wisdom, sympathy, anything. The reply was curt: YOU'VE MADE YOUR BED STOP NOW LIE IN IT.

The last of the doctors, a leonine general practitioner with white hairs growing out of his nose and ears, was the only one able to reach Stanley—at least at first. Dr. Putnam had been recommended by a friend of Josephine, and though he didn't know Charcot from Mesmer or Freud from Bloch, in his forty-seven years in the medical profession he'd encountered just about everything, including dementia in all its forms and the secret hysteria that made women hang themselves in closets. He came up the steps jauntily enough, considering he was in his seventies, and before he had his hat and gloves off he'd challenged

Stanley to a game of checkers. The two of them played wordlessly through the afternoon and into the evening, and the next morning at eight the doctor appeared with two iron posts and a set of horseshoes under his arm. All morning the posts clanked as he and Stanley studied and released their shoes, and the only other sound was the low murmur of their voices totting up the score.

The next day, the old doctor didn't appear till nearly three in the afternoon—he'd had to make the rounds of his other patients, he explained, and Mrs. Trusock had kept him with her shingles—but Stanley had been out all morning in a cold wind, flinging his horseshoes at the unyielding stake, over and over again. They played till dark, and then the doctor, warming himself by the fire with a cup of tea before heading home to his wife and supper, called Katherine into the room. She found the two of them drawn up to the hearth in a pair of straight-backed chairs, their knees practically touching. "Stanley," the doctor said when Katherine had settled herself in the armchair across from them, "you're as crafty a checkers player as I've seen and a deadeye shot at horseshoes. My advice to you, sir, is to find yourself a hobby and pursue it— does wonders for the nerves. Tell me, what do you like, in the way of hobbies, that is?"

Stanley made no reply.

"Nothing?" The old man canted his head, as if listening for a response from the next room. "Well," he said, smacking his lips over the tea and giving Katherine a quick penetrating look, "I'd prescribe German and fencing lessons. Something you can sink your teeth into. And useful too. Nothing more useful than German in today's world, and the fencing, well, it will give you some discipline and rigor, and that's just what you need to take your mind off your troubles. Business troubles, isn't it? Yes, I thought so." He set down his teacup with elaborate care and rose from the chair. "I'll stop in to see how you're doing in a week or so—and I'll bring my sabre along too. . . . Well," he said, smacking his lips again and looking round the room as if he'd just healed all the lepers of Calcutta in one stroke, "what can I say but auf Wiedersehen!"

For the next several days Stanley was very quiet. Twice Katherine found him out in the yard, brooding over the extemporized horseshoe pit, but when she asked him about it—if he'd like her to play him a match—he wouldn't give her the courtesy of a reply. One night, soon after, it snowed; Stanley hung the horseshoes on a nail in the basement and never mentioned them again. Christmas came and went—Stanley's favorite season—and he hardly seemed to notice. He didn't send out cards, he was so unenthusiastic about the decorations that Katherine and the maid wound up trimming the tree, and their exchange of presents was perfunctory to say the least. They spent a quiet New Year's mewed up in the house, barely talking to one another, while everyone else was dancing and visiting. Stanley brooded. Katherine was miserable.

At the end of the first week of January they went into Boston, Katherine to see about her research work at the Institute and Stanley to locate and purchase the foils he would need for fencing. They had a late breakfast with her mother and Stanley didn't have two words to say the whole time, but at least he was tractable and outwardly calm, and then they took a walk down Commonwealth Avenue, just as they had when they were lovers two years before.

Stanley was very solemn and he held himself with a kind of fanatic rigidity, his chest thrust out so far the buttons of his overcoat seemed ready to give way. She tried to make small talk, more as a way of reassuring herself than anything else, but after a while she gave it up and made do with the morning, the briskness of the air and the gentle pressure of her husband's arm in her own. German and fencing, she was thinking. As ridiculous as the idea had first sounded to her, she'd now begun to warm to it—maybe it would help focus Stanley in the way the checkers and horseshoes had. Maybe the old ghost of a country G.P. knew more than the experts, maybe he was right, maybe he was. Just then, just as she began to feel that things might turn out right after all, Stanley began to drag his foot—his right foot—as if he'd been shot in the leg. She tried to ignore it at first—it was a passing quirk, she was sure of it—but after they'd gone a block, people staring, his foot scraping rhythmically at the concrete, the pressure ever greater on her arm till it felt as if she were supporting his entire weight, she had to say something.

"Stanley, dear, are you all right?" she asked, slowing her pace to accommodate him. "Are you feeling tired? Or cold? Would you like to go back now?"

He pulled up short then and looked at her in surprise, as if he didn't know how she'd become attached to his arm. His face was working and she had the strangest fancy that he was drifting away from her like a helium-filled balloon and that if she let go, even for an instant, he'd recede into the clouds. "I can't," he said. "You see, I've got—got to find a German teacher. That's where I'm going."

"But your leg—?"

"My leg?"

"Yes. You were limping. I thought you'd got a stone in your shoe, or—"

He gently disengaged himself from her arm and tipped his hat. "Auf Wiedersehen," he said, and he went off down the street in a peculiar slouching hobble, dragging his right foot all the way.

It was a repetition of the scene at the pier and she was afraid for him—anything could happen—but she knew enough to understand that she couldn't stop him now, short of putting a collar and leash on him, and she still fanned that dim little coal of a hope: *the German teacher*. Of course. Why not? She went on to MIT and at two she took a cab to the restaurant where they'd arranged to meet for lunch, but no Stanley. No Stanley at two or two-fifteen or two-thirty either. She waited until three and then she left a note with the maître d' and went back to the Institute.

It was dark by the time she returned to her mother's, only to discover that Josephine was out, and she settled into a chair with Wallace and read about natural selection amongst the mammalian species of Borneo and watched the clock. Sometime later—at seven or thereabout—the bell rang downstairs and she heard the maid tripping through the hallway to answer it. This was succeeded by a confusion of voices—Stanley's, she recognized Stanley's—and a thunder of footsteps coming up the stairs. She rose from her chair and her heart was flapping like a sheet in the wind: what now?

A moment later Stanley appeared at the parlor door, a slight embarrassed-looking man in a gray overcoat and gold-rimmed spectacles at his side. Stanley had his hand on the man's upper arm and he wore a look of transport on his face, of rapture, as if he'd found the very key to existence. "My—my German teacher," he announced.

The man in his grip seemed to shrink away from him. "I'm very sorry," he said through the impediment of a heavy accent while lifting his eyes to Katherine's, "sorry to intrude on you this way." He looked to Stanley, but Stanley was oblivious. "My name is Schneerman, and I teach at the Deutsche Schule, and, uh, this gentleman, your husband,

I take it, well—he was very persuasive. I give him my card. I tell him that I am expected home to dinner with my wife"—and here his voice cracked—"and, and my children, but he is very insistent."

"Deutsche Schule," Stanley repeated. "Das Bettchen. Der Tisch. Ich bin gut. Wie geht es Ihnen?"

Katherine moved across the room and tried to separate her husband from the German teacher, who'd gone white and begun to breathe rapidly and shallowly, as if he were having some sort of attack. She laid a hand on Stanley's arm and said, as casually as she could, "You must be exhausted, both of you. Here, sit down, won't you, Mr. Schneerman?"

Stanley was in a sweat; he neither moved nor relaxed his grip. The German teacher looked as if he were about to faint.

"How about a nice cup of tea, Stanley?" she said. "We can sit here with Mr. Schneerman and have a chat about your lessons—perhaps he'll even give us some tips as to our pronunciation of some of the more difficult configurations, the umlauts and such. Would you like that, Stanley? Hm?" She turned to the German teacher. "Mr. Schneerman?"

"Yah," the little man said. "Yah, sure. We have a lesson now."

Still nothing. Stanley seemed to be in some sort of trance, his eyes fixed on the lamp across the room, his hand so tightly clamped to the German teacher's arm she could see the tendons standing out like wires beneath his skin. She was afraid suddenly. Very afraid. What if he hurt the man? What if he had one of his tantrums? It was then that she hit on the expedient of asking Stanley's help with the furniture—as a gentleman coming to the aid of a lady, and that was the true and invincible core of him, she knew it, civility, decency and goodness. "Stanley," she said, "would you help me move this end table so we can settle Mr. Schneerman here by the fireplace?" And she bent to remove the lamp, doily and bric-a-brac from the table, then lifted it with some effort and held it out before him in two trembling hands.

Stanley's eyes came back into focus. He gave her that searching, bewildered look and then automatically dropped the German teacher's arm and took the table from her. Immediately, the little man backed away from him, ducked his head and shot out the door, Katherine on his heels. "Just a minute, Stanley," she called over her shoulder, "I'll be right back."

She caught up with Mr. Schneerman at the front door. "Please," she begged, and she thought she was going to cry, "please let me explain. It's my husband, he—"

The little man spun round to finish the sentence for her: "—he should be locked up. The man is a menace. I have in my mind to sue, that is what!" If he'd been meek and cowed in the parlor, he was self-possessed now, storming at her, all the fear and embarrassment of the situation released in a rush of anger. "You, you *people!*" he cried, and he might have gone further but for the fact that Stanley appeared suddenly at the top of the stairs, the end table still cradled in his arms. "Where did you say you wanted this, Katherine?" Stanley called, and the man shrank into himself all over again, flung open the door and disappeared into the night.

Clearly the situation had become impossible. There was no fooling herself anymore—Stanley had become a danger to himself and to others and he needed to be watched around the clock, watched and protected. She wasn't equal to it, she knew that, and the charade of domestic life had to end, at least for the present. Stanley needed help—professional help, institutional help—and he needed it now.

She was able to calm him that night by having him rearrange all the furniture in the parlor, even the heaviest pieces, which he was capable of handling without the slightest evidence of strain. He worked at it with the obsessive attention to detail he brought to any task, shifting a chair an inch here or an inch there, over and over, till he got it right, but after an hour or so he began to flag, moving automatically now, until finally, at her suggestion, he took a seat by the fire. The maid brought up a light supper and Katherine put him to bed. When she looked in on him an hour later, he was in a deep sleep, the covers pulled up to his chin, his face as relaxed and still and beautiful as if it had been carved of marble.

When her mother came home, they sat up over biscuits and hot chocolate and discussed the situation. "Oh, I liked him well enough before he changed," Josephine said, pursing her lips as she dipped a biscuit into her chocolate. "That's the way it is with marriage sometimes—once they've got you they lose all respect for you. The things he said to me in this house, well, I just hope I don't have to hear anything like that again as long as I live. To think I'd be called a stupid old woman in my own parlor—and by my own son-in-law!"

"He's sick, mother," Katherine said. "Very sick. He needs help."

"I wouldn't doubt it. Look at his family. His sister. His mother. They're all of them three steps from the madhouse, and if he keeps on like this, I must say I'm going to very much regret your having married him."

The room was very still. But for the hiss of the coals in the fireplace and the low persistent ticking of the clock there wasn't a sound. Katherine cradled the cup in her hands. She was thinking of her wedding night, of the scene on the boat, of Maine, of Doctors Putnam and Trudeau and the sick pale terrified face of that poor little German teacher. She looked up at her mother, at the paintings on the walls, the furniture, the draperies. There she was, her mother's daughter, safe in the familiar room, surrounded by the shapes and colors of the life she'd led up till now, but it seemed different somehow, barren and cold as some Arctic landscape.

"Mama," she said, reverting to the diminutive she hadn't used since she was a child. "Mama, I'm afraid of him."

7.

THREE O'CLOCK

At first, when O'Kane saw the four men standing there in the alley out
back of Menhoff's, he didn't think anything of it—there were always
men there, milling around in the shadows and perpetuating various
half-truths and outright lies while passing one of the fifths of hooch
Cody sold on the sly. He wasn't even especially surprised when he recognized one of them as Giovannella's father, Baldy Dimucci, and another as her brother Pietro, the runt he'd had that minor disagreement
with a lifetime ago in the driveway at Riven Rock. Pietro was now in
his forties, and there wasn't much more to him than there'd been twenty
years ago—he was scrawny as a chicken, not as dark as Giovannella,
but with her shining hair and fathomless eyes. O'Kane had run into him
any number of times over the years—out on State Street, in Montecito
Village, in the drive of the Dimucci house when it was raining and
Roscoe gave Giovannella a ride home before taking him and Mart on
into town—and though he couldn't say he liked the man, there was no
animosity between them, not that he knew of. They typically exchanged
a few words, mainly of the hello-how-are-you-fine variety, and went on

about their business. But here he was, out in the alley with his father and two other guys, big guys, O'Kane saw now, big guys with ax handles clutched in their big sweating fists.

O'Kane had been drinking with the projectionist from the Granada, a whole long night of drinking, and it had been so long since his little altercation with Giovannella—a year or more now—that he'd forgotten all about it. Up until now, that is. "Hi, Baldy," he said, but his feet couldn't seem to work up the volition to usher him on past this little Dago confabulation. "Nice night," he added uncertainly.

Baldy was an old man now, with a potbelly and a fringe of white hair that stood straight up off the crown of his head like a nimbus of feathers. "You're the bad man, Eddie," he said. "You're the very bad man."

O'Kane wanted to deny it, wanted to hoot and caper and tease the old man's hair right up off his head, but he was drunk and he knew what was coming. He knew it, but somehow he couldn't seem to muster the energy to care.

"You hurt-a my daughter, Eddie, and now you gonna answer to me."

That was when the two goons moved in close with the ax handles and started chopping away at the fragile tottering tree that was Eddie O'Kane. He went down after the first couple of blows, and he stayed down, cradling his head, even as the tempered oak sought out his ribs and his knees and the tough little fist of bone at the base of his spine. The last thing he remembered was Pietro cursing him and the soft wet kiss of the spittle on his cheek.

He came out of it right at the end of his first day in the hospital, a smell of hot food, the rattle of a cart, a dapple of light on the ceiling as the sun sank out of sight. There were flowers on the table beside him—sent, he would later learn, by Katherine, the Ice Queen herself—and he was in a room that had two beds in it. He didn't feel a whole lot of curiosity about who was occupying the other one—his head ached too much— but later, after the tide of nurses had ebbed, he saw that it was a child, a little boy, all wrapped up like King Tut and with his leg in a cast suspended from a hook over the bed. That was when O'Kane began to wonder about the extent of the damage to his own bodily self, and he ran a reluctant hand—his left hand; the right was pinned fast to his chest—down one side of his rib cage and up the other. He felt pinched and constricted, as if he couldn't fill his lungs and take a breath of air, and he knew that he was all wrapped up too, and he was wondering about that in a drifting remote sort of way—his ribs, they'd broken his ribs—and then he was running through the streets of the North End with some lady's pocketbook in his hand and a whole horde of people chasing after him, and wasn't Mr. McCormick one of them?

When he woke the next morning, there was a doctor standing over him, or at least he looked like a doctor, white jacket, clipboard and regulation smile. "How are you feeling?"

"Scrambled," O'Kane managed, and he tried to lift his head but couldn't. "Three eggs in a pan."

"It could be worse." The doctor's smile was eerily serene. "You'll walk again—in three to six months—but you'll very likely carry a limp the rest of your life. You've shattered your right patella and there's a hairline fracture of the femur, just above it, in addition to a compound break of the tibia—the shinbone. You've got three broken ribs on the right side, a fractured wrist—also on that side—and oh yes, as you've no doubt noticed, your arm is in a cast too. The right ulna is fractured—your elbow, that is." He paused. "Do you remember anything of the incident? The identity of your attackers, for instance? The police want to know if you can provide a description."

O'Kane looked into that fixed smile and tried on a smile of his own, albeit a weak and evanescent one. "No," he said, "I don't remember a thing."

The next day they wheeled his bed out the door and all the way down the corridor to the admissions office: Mr. McCormick was on the line. "Hello? Ed-Eddie? Are you all—are you okay?"

"Sure," O'Kane said. "I'll be up and about in no time."

Mr. McCormick's voice was high and excited, sticking on the consonants and ratcheting up over the vowels. "I w-wish I'd been there with you, to—to fight, I mean. I would have given them something to think about, you know I would—"

O'Kane, miserable, broken in half, reaping his own sour harvest, tried nonetheless to placate him—it was his job, after all. "I know you would. But don't worry, don't worry about a thing."

A pause. Mr. McCormick's voice, pinched almost to nothing: "You-

you're coming back, Eddie, aren't you? Back here with m-me and Mart?"

What could he say? Of course he was coming back, coming back like a convict to his ball and chain every time he tries to lift his foot from the floor. It was sad to say, sadder even to admit, but Mr. Mc-Cormick was his life. "Yeah," he said, "I'll be back."

On the third day, Giovannella appeared. He was dozing at the time, drifting deliciously in and out of consciousness while the mother of the boy in the next bed read aloud from a book of children's stories in a soothing soft mellifluous voice: " 'Pooh always liked a little something at eleven o'clock in the morning, and he was glad to see Rabbit getting out the plates and mugs, . . .' "

"Eddie?"

The story faltered, just the smallest pebble in the path of that smooth onrolling voice, and then it picked up again: " '. . . and when Rabbit said, "Honey or condensed milk with your bread?" he was so excited that he said, "Both" . . .' "

"Eddie?"

He opened his eyes. The ceiling was there, right where he'd left it, and then a glint of the boy's mother's blondness combed out over her shoulders, and finally, Giovannella. Her face hovered over him, an anxious look, the ends of her hair so close he could smell the shampoo she'd used that morning. He smiled, one of the smiles his mother had no name for because it was spontaneous and true: how could he blame Giovannella? She'd provoked him, sure, but he had no right to touch her, never, and he'd had it coming to him for years now, a debt of violence accruing.

"I talked to my father," she said, and he watched her eyes and her ringless fingers as she tucked the hair behind her ears. It was January of 1929 and she was thirty-eight years old, ripe in the bosom in a white blouse and yellow cardigan, her face getting rounder by the day and the flesh settling under her chin. "It's going to be a small wedding, just the Dimuccis and the Fiocollas and maybe Mart, Pat and Nick, if you want—but in the church, with a white gown and rice and everything else."

He didn't know what to say, but he felt it, something stirring in the deep yearning root of him, inside, beneath the sixty yards of gauze and tape and the rock-hard plaster and the flesh that was as tender and yielding as a—as a bride's. Or make that a groom's. He was going to marry Giovannella, adulterously and bigamously, and legitimate his two surviving children, Guido of the heavy O'Kane shoulders and Edwina with the green eyes in her sweet vanilla face, and this was it, this was what he'd been waiting for all his life: his three o'clock luck. It wasn't money or orange groves or a fleet of cars, but this woman hanging over him in a moment of grace and poignancy and the children waiting in the wings. Okay. All right. He was ready. He tried to nod his head and winced.

Giovannella was smiling down on him, the strong white teeth, the everted lips, the faint hairs trailing all the way down her temple to the hollow at the base of her jaw. "As soon as you can walk, of course," she said, and her voice was every bit as sweet and assured and anodynic as that mother's in the next chair over. "We don't do anything till you can walk. Okay, Eddie?" He felt the soft pressure of her hand on his.

"Okay," he said.

The wedding was in April, on a fine blue-scraped day with every flower in creation bursting all around them, and after the ceremony at Our Lady of the Sorrows, O'Kane and Giovannella and Guido and Edwina and all the Dimuccis and Fiocollas and half the Italians in Santa Barbara (*Italians*, not wops, most definitely not wops anymore) piled into the McCormick automobiles and had their reception on the front lawn at Riven Rock, Mr. McCormick looking on from the high barred windows of his room. They'd hoped to have him right down there amongst the guests, but Kempf vetoed it—after the incident with Katherine, not to mention the complication of the professional girl, which Kempf had never found out about, thank God in His Heaven, Mr. McCormick had to be isolated from women again. Except for Nurse Gleason, that is, and she gave him a wide-enough berth, at least at first.

But still, it was a real celebration, and with enough food prepared by the Dimucci girls and their mother and aunts to feed everybody twice and enough left over for all the millionaires and their starved-looking racehorses too, if they'd had the sense to show up and toast the true match of the year. O'Kane got along pretty well on his crutches, and everybody said he looked as handsome as one of God's angels, and Giovannella filled out her satin gown in a way no rumpless flapper could ever have. After the ceremony, after the toasts and the *gnocchi* and the *intercostata di manzo* and the *palombaccia allo spiedo* and the *millefoglie* and the wedding cake that was as tall as little Guido, Roscoe drove O'Kane and Giovannella up to San Luis Obispo and a three-day honeymoon in a blue-and-white clapboard inn by the sea. And then O'Kane, moving well enough and with his seminal parts in an advanced state of relaxation, went back to work at Riven Rock.

Mr. McCormick was glad to see him. Very glad. Ecstatic even. The minute O'Kane appeared on the landing outside the upper parlor door, his crutches extended like struts, Mr. McCormick sprang up off the sofa and rushed him. "Eddie, Eddie, Eddie!" he cried, "I knew you'd be back, I knew it!" The keys turned in the locks, Mart hovering over Mr. McCormick's shoulder, Nurse Gleason a frowning presence in the background. "Sure I'm back," O'Kane said, and he was touched, genuinely touched, he was. "Just because I'm married you think I'd desert you? We're in this together, aren't we? Till you're well again?"

Mr. McCormick didn't say anything. He stood there inside the door and waited patiently as O'Kane fumbled with his keys and the crutches and his arms that were stiff with the strain of doing two things at once; Mr. McCormick had something in his hand, a trophy of some sort, bronze, with an engraved inscription. It looked like a bugle with two bells.

"So what's this?" O'Kane asked, maneuvering through the door while Mart secured it.

Mr. McCormick gave him a big grin, rotten teeth, faraway eyes and all. "F-first prize in the orchid show. For—for our cymbidiums, the Riven Rock cymbidiums. Mr. Hull entered for me, and Kath-Katherine said it was a real coup. She, she—"

But that was it. The rest of the story, whatever it was, was locked up inside him and he couldn't get it out. Normally O'Kane would have coached him, the way Kempf did, but he'd just stepped through the door for the first time in three and a half months and Nurse Gleason was giving him a fishy eye and he didn't know her from Adam yet and he just didn't feel up to it. Instead, he stumped right by his employer, putting some good weight on the right leg now and walking through the crutches every other step, and settled himself at the table. Mr. McCormick was already at the bookshelf, making a place for the trophy amongst the eight others he'd won in previous years. He was a while at it, getting things just so, and from his posture and the attitude of his shoulders and the way he ducked his head and muttered to himself, O'Kane could see that his judges were very likely looking on and commenting on the arrangement.

Nurse Gleason, who'd nodded a curt hello at O'Kane as he entered, passed between them now, making a show of straightening the cushions of the sofa and beating out and folding the pages of Mr. McCormick's newspaper. She was a big-beamed, fish-faced pre-crone of a woman, fiftyish, and as close to being sexless as you could get—short of hermaphroditism, that is. Kempf's thinking was that Mr. McCormick would be predisposed to accept her more readily than someone like poor what-was-her-name from McLean, the one with the locket between her breasts—or if not accept her, then at least refrain from any sort of sexual impropriety. O'Kane had heard she was a good clinical nurse who took no nonsense from anybody—she'd been at the Battle Creek Sanitarium for years, wielding nozzle and enema tube, before going on to Saint Elizabeth's—and so far Mr. McCormick had tolerated her presence.

After twenty minutes or so, during which no one said a word, Mr. McCormick finally seemed satisfied with the relative positions of his trophies and came over to sit down across from O'Kane at the table. O'Kane had a magazine spread out before him, but he wasn't reading anything in particular, just leafing through the pages as if they were blank on both sides. He looked up and smiled. Mr. McCormick did not smile back. He seemed unusually tense and his face was running through a range of expressions, as if invisible fingers were tugging at the skin from every direction. "You're looking well," O'Kane said automatically.

"I'm not."

"Is something the matter? You want to tell me about it?"

Mr. McCormick looked away.

Nurse Gleason entered the dialogue then, her eyes very close-set and her lips puckered fishily. "He's been out of sorts lately, because of the doctors."

O'Kane lifted his eyebrows.

"You know," she said, "the trial and all. And I don't blame the poor man, what with one after the other of them here poking and probing at him so he hasn't had a minute's peace these last two weeks."

O'Kane looked to Mart, but Mart, sunk into himself like some boneless thing washed up out of the sea, had nothing to add.

"They, they—" Mr. McCormick said suddenly, his face still going through its calisthenics, as if the muscles under the skin couldn't decide on an appropriate response, "they want to take Riven Rock away from me, in the courts, Kath-Katherine and, and—"

"No, no, Mr. McCormick," Nurse Gleason chided, interposing her bulk between them as she scurried over to lean into the table on one stumplike arm, "nobody's going to take Riven Rock, that's not it at all—"

Mr. McCormick never even glanced at her. "Shut up, cunt," he snarled.

She flared then, Nurse Gleason, but only briefly, like a Fourth of July rocket sputtering on its pad. "I won't have such language, I tell you," she spat, leaning in closer, but then Mr. McCormick kicked back the chair and leapt to his feet and she faded back out of reach, her face flushed and crepuscular. O'Kane, bad knee and all, came up out of his chair too and caught his employer by the wrist; for a moment both of them froze, looking first into each other's eyes and then down at the intrusive hand on the trembling wrist. O'Kane let go. Mr. McCormick righted his chair, and after a moment's fussing, sat back down. "It's all right," O'Kane said, but clearly it wasn't.

A trio of doctors appeared that afternoon, just after Mr. McCormick woke from his postluncheon nap. O'Kane didn't catch their names, not that it mattered—there was the lean one, the heavyset one and the one with the bandaged nose. Dr. Kempf wasn't present, because they were examining Mr. McCormick with a view to supporting Katherine's contention that psychoanalysis alone was not the proper treatment for her husband and was in fact having a deleterious effect on him. Other doctors would come on other days to examine him in support of Cyrus and Anita, who wanted to retain Kempf—look at the progress he'd made, women in the immediate environment and their brother as fit and rational as ever, or almost—and maintain their two-to-one advantage on the board of guardians. But these doctors were for Katherine, and they gathered solemnly in the upper parlor to await Mr. McCormick's emergence from the bedroom.

Did they want anything? Nurse Gleason wanted to know, fishily solicitous. Tea? Coffee? A soft drink? She only had to ring for it, no trouble at all.

They didn't think so.

When Mart led Mr. McCormick out into the main room, O'Kane could see immediately that the meeting wasn't going to be a propitious one. Mr. McCormick was actively engaged in a debate with his judges as he came through the door, and his face was still going through its permutations.

The Lean Doctor: "Good afternoon, Mr. McCormick. I'm Dr. Orbison, and this is Dr. Barker and Dr. Williams. We've come to chat a bit, if that's convenient."

True to form, Mr. McCormick said nothing, but his face spoke volumes to O'Kane. He positioned himself on the arm of the sofa, propped up on one crutch, ready to fling himself forward at the first sign of trouble.

The Lean Doctor (settling himself into one of the three folding chairs set up in anticipation of this visit, while his colleagues followed suit): "Well, pleasant day, isn't it?"

Mr. McCormick: "Blow, winds, and crack your cheeks!"

The doctors exchanged a glance. The one with the bandaged nose craned his neck to look out the window, as if to be sure the sun was still there and shining.

Mr. McCormick: "Be-betrayed by his daughters."

The Bandaged Doctor: "Who?"

Mr. McCormick: "Lear."

The Heavyset Doctor: "Leer?"

Mr. McCormick: "First name of King."

The Lean Doctor: "Oh, yes, I see. Of course. Lear. Do you, uh, think much about Shakespeare then, Mr. McCormick — I take it you're an aficionado?"

Mr. McCormick (his face working): "Kath-Katherine . . ."

The Lean Doctor: "Katherine?"

The Bandaged Doctor: "His wife."

The Lean Doctor (puzzled, drawing at his chin with two lean fingers): "Your wife reads Shakespeare?"

Mr. McCormick said nothing to this, and though he was alert and struggling with his facial muscles and rapping his long fingers on the twin pyramids of his knees, he had very little to say to their subsequent inquiries, which ranged from his knowledge of the Peloponnesian War to the Declaration of Independence, American banking customs, the mechanism of the reaper and his feelings about Dr. Kempf, women and dentists, to his recognition of various celebrated individuals in the public eye, both by name and likeness: Babe Ruth, Al Capone, Calvin Coolidge, Sacco and Vanzetti. If it was a test—and O'Kane knew that it was—then Mr. McCormick had flunked it badly. There was only one point at which he rose to something like coherence, and that was right at the end, when the distinguished doctors had filled their notebooks and begun to shoot glances at one another out of the corners of their eyes. The Lean Doctor said "Riven Rock" and Mr. McCormick looked up alertly.

The Lean Doctor: "Tell us about your home, if you would, Mr. McCormick, about Riven Rock—how did it get its name?"

Mr. McCormick (sunshine at first, and then increasing clouds): "I—well—it's because of a rock, you see, and I—well, my mother, she—and then I came and saw it and it was, well, it was—"

There was a long hiatus, all three doctors leaning forward, the day drawing down, Mart snoring lightly from the vicinity of the couch, Nurse Gleason silently dusting the plants, and then Mr. McCormick, his face finally settling on a broad winning ear-to-ear grin, at last spoke up. "It beats me," he said.

As a family man, O'Kane wasn't exactly an overnight success. His experience of children was limited and sad, infinitely sad, and he was used to the peace and sterility of Mrs. Fitzmaurice's rooming house (reconstructed after the quake to look exactly as it had before, or even more so). He was used to the speaks too and to eating at the drugstore or not eating at all if he didn't feel like it and to doing any damn thing he pleased any time he pleased. And now, in the spring and early summer, he found himself living amongst the olive-pressing garlic-chewing Valpolicella-quaffing turmoil of the Dimucci household, a place rife with screaming barefooted children, dogs, pigs, chickens and Italians. Baldy had fixed up one of the outbuildings for Marta and her husband, and when they'd moved to their own place downtown on Milpas Street, he let the unsteady O'Kane and his new family move in temporarily—"Just," he said, "till Eddie can get back on his feet," and there wasn't a trace of irony in his voice.

Edwina turned nine in June and Guido would be thirteen in October, too old to be fooled by anything O'Kane tried to do to ingratiate himself, though they took the candy and games and dolls and penknives he pressed on them readily enough. He wasn't their father, not in their eyes—their father was Guido Capolupo, and he was dead, like the saints in heaven. With Giovannella it was different. He'd made the ultimate sacrifice for her, giving up his body and soul both—not to mention committing bigamy—and she came each night to worship at his altar. In the beginning, before he could walk without the aid of crutches, she gave him sponge baths in bed, spoon-fed him to keep his strength up, every stray drop of soup or sauce lovingly blotted from his chin with a carefully folded napkin, and once he was getting around again, she spent hours massaging his cramped muscles or depressing the skin around the cast on his leg and gently blowing into the aperture to relieve his itching. She made love to him with all the fierceness of possession and when they were done and sweating and still breathing hard she would straddle him and run her hands through his hair again and again. "You're mine now, Eddie," she would say, her lips puffed and swollen with all they'd done, "all mine."

He couldn't say that he forgave the Dimuccis (not exactly—he was no pacifist and he would as soon crush Pietro as look at him), but he accepted the rightness of what had happened and he was content, or at least he thought he was. But once he was back at work and putting in his twelve hours a day at Riven Rock, free of the chaos of the Dimucci dominion and the incessant demands of the children—*Read me a story; Fix this; You don't like me, I know it; You're not my father anyway*—he knew the time had come to move on. The first order of business was a car. Baldy had been dropping him off at Riven Rock in the morning and Roscoe swinging by in the evening, and that was all right—or no, it was intolerable—and he scanned the want ads till he found a ten-year-old Maxwell just like the one Dolores Isringhausen used to drive, only older and slower and noisier, the spark of life in its greasy automotive heart all but extinguished. Roscoe helped him get it going, tuned it up for him and drove him down to State Street to invest in a new set of tires.

Two weeks later he and Giovannella found a place for rent in

Summerland, just to the east of Montecito and an easy drive both to her parents' house and Riven Rock. It was a bungalow, with a low creased roof that climbed way out over the front porch and two palm trees set into the ground on either side of it like flagpoles. You could see the ocean from the far right-hand corner of the porch, and best of all, there was a private citrus grove out in the backyard, three grapefruit trees, two oranges and a Meyer lemon. O'Kane stood out in the street and took six snapshots of the house—dead-on and not a soul in the picture—to send home to his mother.

He was fit enough to carry Giovannella over the threshold and play husband and wife with her through one whole afternoon, evening and night while the kids made their grandparents' lives miserable and the pelicans sailed across the patch of sky defined by the bedroom window and the sound of the old man next door watering his roses invited them to slide down into the dreamless embrace of sleep. Baldy dropped off the children late the next morning and Giovannella made bruschetta and spaghetti and the house grew smaller and noisier till O'Kane felt he needed to get out for a drive—"Don't worry about me, I'll be back in a couple hours"—and he found himself at Riven Rock, Sunday afternoon, his day off, shooting the bull about one thing and another with Roscoe out in the reconstructed garage.

"How does he seem to you?" Roscoe said, leaning into the front fender of one of the new Pierce Arrows with a chamois cloth. "Because as far as I can see he's getting more and more worked up about this trial business, which from what I hear isn't even scheduled yet."

"I'm not sure if it's a trial, exactly. There's no jury or anything like that, just a judge. From what Kempf says, anyway."

"What's the difference? The point is, Mr. McCormick thinks she wants to take everything away from him, and that's why he's been so jumpy lately, just like years ago when we first started to take him out for his drives and he'd think every other tree was going to fall on the car. You know what he did the other night? He came out here with Nick and Pat—and why they let him out is a mystery to me—and he spent I don't how many hours rearranging the back seat because it wasn't comfortable enough . . . here, take a look, see for yourself what he did." The panels of the rear door grabbed the light and then released it and there was Mr. McCormick's handiwork, the seat pried right out of its frame and meticulously customized with fifteen or twenty pillows appropriated from the couches in the main house.

"She already has," O'Kane said, leaning in for a closer look, "—he just doesn't know it."

"What?" What're you talking about?" Roscoe was wringing the wet cloth over a bucket, the sun painting two long white oblongs on the concrete floor where the bay doors stood open.

"Yeah, that's a real mess," O'Kane said, straightening up, "but no real harm done—at least he didn't carve up the upholstery like last time." He paused to pinch the crown of his hat and run a spit-dampened finger over the crease of the brim. "I mean Katherine, Mrs. McCormick. She already has everything—she got that back in ought-nine when she had him declared incompetent."

Roscoe turned back to the car, the pliant wet cloth swallowing up the beads of water as he flagged it across the fender. "Then what's she want now? Aside from Kempf's head on a platter, which I think's a crying shame, I really do. . . ."

O'Kane gave it some thought, watching the chauffeur with his quick elbows and jerky movements, the little monkey cap and his flapping crimson ears, his body heaving out over the hood and the reflected glory of the deep-buffed blue-black steel. "Him," he said after a while. "She wants him."

One hand braced, the other moving in a clean, circular sweep, Roscoe glancing over his shoulder. "Kempf?"

"No, not Kempf—her husband."

"Hmpf," Roscoe grunted, rubbing now, really digging into the moving cloth. "Why doesn't she get herself a lapdog instead?"

The year ticked by, the summer soft and compliant, and then came the fall, spread like margarine across the corrugated sea and all the way out to the soft and melting islands. On a rainy Thursday afternoon at the end of November, O'Kane put on a clean shirt and his best suit and went down to the county courthouse to testify at the trial, Katherine's lawyer—Mr. Baker—raking him over the coals of Mr. McCormick's condition, one searing step at at time. Has there been any improvement, in your view, Mr. O'Kane, over the very lengthy course of your service—coming up on twenty-two years now, isn't it?—and did Dr. Kempf do this and did he do that? The attorney for the McCormicks— Mr. Lawler—seemed to wrap himself over O'Kane's shoulders like a warm sweater on a cold evening. Wasn't it a fact, Mr. O'Kane? and Isn't it so? and Wouldn't you say that Mr. McCormick was much improved as evidenced by his association with women—even to the extent of employing a female nurse? And hadn't the previous physicians been merely custodial with regard to Mr. McCormick's care—that is, all but useless?

Together, they called eighteen doctors to the stand, including Dr. Meyer, Dr. Brush, Dr. Hamilton (his hair gray now and his eyes spinning out of control) and most of the headshrinkers and pulse-takers who'd tramped through the house over the course of the past eighteen months, and they called Dr. Kempf and Mr. Cyrus McCormick, and Mr. Harold and Mrs. Anita McCormick Blaine, Nurse Gleason, Nick and Pat and Mart, and eventually even the Ice Queen and Mrs. Roessing. O'Kane caught only two days of it, his testimony split between Thursday afternoon and Friday morning, and then he pushed through the crowd of reporters in the courthouse hallway and drove himself back to Riven Rock and Mr. McCormick.

The proceedings had been going on for a week and a half when O'Kane arrived at the estate one morning to find a letter waiting for him on the table in the entrance hall. His name had been typed neatly across the front of the envelope—EDWARD JAMES O'KANE, RIVEN ROCK, MONTECITO, CALIFORNIA—and in the upper left-hand corner, in raised black letters, was Jim Isringhausen's name, over the legend ISRING- HAUSEN & CLAUSEN, STOCKS, BONDS, REAL ESTATE. Mr. McCormick was sleeping still, but Nick and Pat would be anxious to leave—and to- day, since Mart was due to testify, it would be only O'Kane and Nurse Gleason upstairs—so O'Kane brought the letter with him and waited till the Thompson brothers had departed and Mr. McCormick was up and preoccupied with folding and refolding his toilet paper before he slit open the envelope.

Inside was a check drawn on the Chase Bank in New York. It was made out to him, Edward James O'Kane, and it was in the amount of $3,500. A note was attached to it with a paper clip, and O'Kane found that his hand was trembling as he shook out the single sheet of white bond and began to read:

November 24, 1929

Dear Eddie:

Enclosed please find my check in the amount of $3,500, your share in the proceeds of the sale of our Goleta property. The orange trees never prospered as we'd hoped, but I and my partners were able recently to sell the property to a housing contractor, at a small profit.

But Eddie, I want to tell you that this is nothing compared to what you can make in stocks and bonds. Don't pay the slightest attention to all these scare stories in the newspapers, men jumping out windows and etc., because the big stocks, the Blue Chips, have never been a better bargain. American Can, Anaconda Copper, Montgomery Ward, United Carbide and Carbon, Westinghouse E. & M., these stocks are sure to rise through the roof on the next buying surge, and believe me, the Great Bull Market isn't dead yet, not by a long shot.

Enclosed for your convenience is a self-addressed, stamped envelope. Just put that check inside and send it on back here, and I guarantee you I'll triple that $500 profit of yours in six months' time or my name isn't

Jim Isringhausen

O'Kane had to take a minute to catch his breath. Married and a father, with a bungalow and a car, and now this, smiling Eddie O'Kane's three o'clock luck come home to roost for good. And what Giovannella wouldn't do to get her hands on that check — *three thousand five hundred dollars,* and the five hundred of it pure profit, for doing nothing more than sitting on his hands. And what was Mart's share in that, for the hundred he'd invested? Something like what, seventeen dollars? And of course he'd give it to him, right out of his own pocket, unless . . . well, unless he reinvested it for him, and nobody the wiser. No one knew about this check but him and here was the envelope to seal it up and send it right back to make another thousand dollars profit by June. Sure. And hadn't Jim Isringhausen steered him right the first time?

It was at that moment, O'Kane contemplating his future as a Wall Street savant and the letter stretched taut in his amazed hands, that Mr. McCormick emerged from his bathroom and strode into the parlor, naked as the day he was born. But he wasn't simply naked, he was naked and erect and advancing on Nurse Gleason, who despite her rigorous asexuality was nonetheless, technically, a woman. O'Kane had been expecting something like this ever since the day she walked through the door, and though she was tough, Nurse Gleason, hard as nails, he doubted she was anything like a match for Mr. McCormick, and so he hastily stuffed letter and check into his breast pocket and jumped up to intervene. "Mr. McCormick," he called out to distract him, "you've forgotten your clothes."

O'Kane had long since recovered from his injuries, but the right knee was still a bit tricky and recalcitrant and he did walk with a pronounced limp, as the doctor had predicted, the right foot forever half a step behind the left. It ached when it rained, and sometimes when it wasn't raining too, and he had a hell of a time keeping up with Mr. McCormick when their morning walk turned into a footrace. Still, he was reasonably fit for a forty-six-year-old former athlete, and he was able to intercept Mr. McCormick just as Mr. McCormick, his arms spread wide, had managed to back Nurse Gleason up against the barred window beside the sofa. O'Kane came in swiftly from the rear and got him in a headlock while Nurse Gleason shooed at his stiff red member as if it had a mind and life of its own, which apparently it did.

Immediately, the frenzy came into Mr. McCormick's shoulders and he took O'Kane for a wild ride round the room, a four-legged jig, furniture flying and Mr. McCormick pulling the air in through his nostrils in deep whinnying snorts. "No, no, no, no!" he cried, his usual refrain, trying all the while to throw O'Kane off his back and work his jaws round to bite the inside of his arm. Two minutes, three, they kept whirling and grunting, both of them, O'Kane gasping out truncated pleas and reproaches, Nurse Gleason maneuvering on the periphery, till finally they both tumbled onto the couch, O'Kane never relaxing his grip and Mr. McCormick's erection pointing staight up in the air. It was then that Nurse Gleason moved in, her face like a big granite block crashing down on them both, and she performed an old nurse's trick with a hard repeated fillip of thumb and index finger that wilted Mr. McCormick's erection like a flower starved of water.

No one was hurt, nothing broken that couldn't be fixed, and when Mr. McCormick, gone lax and sheepish, promised to behave himself, O'Kane let him go. And that was it, that was the end of it. Bowing his head and mumbling an apology, he limped off into the bedroom, dragging his right foot, and a moment later O'Kane got up and went into the room to help him dress.

Nothing was said about the incident, and Mr. McCormick did a creditable job with the breakfast Giovannella sent up, but he was fretting over something, that much was evident. He kept repeating himself, something about Dr. Kempf, but wouldn't respond when O'Kane questioned him, and after breakfast he began to pace up and down the room, jerking his head and arms out to one side as if he were trying to pull an invisible garment over his head. This went on for an hour or so, and then he came over and sat beside O'Kane on the couch, a flux of emotions playing across his face. "Ed-Eddie," he said, "I—I want to, because they're taking Riven Rock and Doctor—Doctor Kempf too, I—" And he broke off, looked O'Kane dead in the eye and lowered his voice. "Eddie," he said, all trace of a stammer gone, "I want to get out of here. Let me out of here. Use your keys. Please. Use your keys."

O'Kane had been looking over his letter again, electrified with the idea of it—sure the market was going to go up, sure it would—and he'd just sealed the check in the envelope when his employer stopped pacing and sat down beside him. They were two millionaires sitting there—or one millionaire and a millionaire in potentio, because with Jim Isringhausen the sky was the limit. "You know I can't do that, Mr. McCormick," O'Kane said.

"B-but Dr. Kempf's not, not here, I mean—today. Be-because—"

"Because he's on vacation. He explained that to you last week. You remember, don't you?" In fact, Kempf was tied up at the trial, defending himself and Freud in front of a roomful of lawyers, reporters and McCormicks, but Mr. McCormick, on strictest orders, was to know nothing of that. Each morning Nick went through the newspapers with a pair of scissors and excised any reference to what was going on in the courtroom downtown.

"Don't—don't you bullshit me, Eddie. I'm not crazy and I'm—I'm not stupid. I know what—I know what's going on. Let me out. For a d-drive, I mean, just a drive. I'm—I'm nervous, Eddie, and you know how a drive always calms me. Please?"

And here was where O'Kane's judgment let him down. They were shorthanded, and so a drive would involve just Roscoe up front and himself, Mr. McCormick and Nurse Gleason in back, and there was risk in that, especially given Mr. McCormick's mood that morning. But it would be nice to get out, the day grainy and close and pregnant with something—rain, he supposed, more rain—and they could stop for sandwiches to go and maybe a little pull at a bottle of something to speed up the future of his thirty-five hundred bucks, which he could also slip into a postbox because it wasn't doing one lick of good sitting in his pocket. Kempf wasn't there. Mart wasn't there. The Ice Queen wasn't even close.

O'Kane gave him his richest smile. "Sure, okay," he said. "Why not? Let's go for a drive."

It was raining by the time they swung through the gate, the mountains just a rumor in a sky that started at the treetops, everything heroically glistening and the road a black wet tongue lapping at the next road and the next one beyond that. Mr. McCormick, his eyes bright and his lips tightly tethered, sat between O'Kane and Nurse Gleason in a yellow rain slicker, the hood pulled up over his head. Nurse Gleason wasn't saying anything—she didn't like this, not one bit—but to Roscoe, exiled up front, it was business as usual. And here was the rain, fat wet pellets bursting on the hood of the car and trailing down the windows like the tears of heaven, as O'Kane's mother would say, the very tears of heaven.

They got soft drinks and sandwiches at a drugstore downtown, Roscoe doing the honors while O'Kane and Nurse Gleason sat stiffly in the car on either side of their employer, and what the hell, O'Kane was thinking, better to get him out than keep him cooped up in that parlor all day and him feeling the way he was, so agitated and disturbed—and it was Kempf who was nuts if he didn't think Mr. McCormick knew exactly what was going on. They ate in the car, windows steamed, Mr. McCormick going through two tuna-salad-on-ryes and a bottle and a half of ginger ale, O'Kane unwrapping his own sandwich—roast beef and horseradish sauce—with a maximum of show and crinkling of waxed paper to mask the fact that he was surreptitiously spiking his ginger ale with a good jolt from the pint bottle Roscoe had picked up for him.

Lunch seemed to improve everybody's mood, and they drove east of town toward Ojai for a while and then swung back along the coast road, the rain slackening and then picking up again before falling off to an atomized drizzle. "Let-let's drive by the B-Biltmore," Mr. Mc-

Cormick said, and then, "Turn left here, Roscoe," and Roscoe obeyed because Mr. McCormick was the boss. In a sense.

The Biltmore was on Channel Drive, just off Olive Mill, and it had been erected two years earlier to cater to the tastes of the itinerant tycoons in the wake of the Potter's incineration and the New Arlington's destruction in the quake. It was quite the place, a hundred and seventy-five luxurious rooms, ballroom, dining room, tennis courts and all the rest—and right on the ocean too, for ocean bathing and lolling richly and idly on the confectionery beach. Mr. McCormick had never of course been inside nor had he even set foot on the grounds, but he often asked to drive slowly by it and get a look at who was passing through its portals, women included—especially women. And that was all right, as long as he didn't try to get out of the car, but on this particular day they found their way blocked by the train heading south to Los Angeles, the crossguard down, the rain misting around them, the trees and succulents and sharp-leafed exotic shrubs all shining with it, eight cars in the line ahead of them. The train creaked and rattled, brakes whining, the slow backward illusion of the wheels caught in suspended time.

That was when O'Kane saw the postbox, right there across the street, not twenty paces away. "I'll just be a minute," he said, feeling for the envelope in his pocket, and then he was out on the glistening street and smelling the rank wet insistent odor of the eucalyptus buttons crushed into the pavement. He crossed the street and dropped the envelope in the box and had turned to hustle back to the car when he saw the dog, pale brown with a white star on its chest, trembling and wet, raising the black shining carbuncle of its nose to the slit of the window— and there was Mr. McCormick's hand, extended, the last bits of tuna salad and rye descending toward the dog's yearning pink mouth. And that was all right, no problem, no trouble, no hurry, even the thunder of the train something to hold and consider on a mild wet close-hung afternoon away from the cage of Riven Rock that made you wonder half the time who was the prisoner and who the keeper.

Sure. But then O'Kane watched the dog jerk suddenly back and away as the door flung itself violently open and Mr. McCormick's left shoe appeared beneath it on the pavement, and then the other shoe, the creased legs of his pants, the door gaping now and Mr. McCormick half-in and half-out, turning briefly to flail his fists at the shadow of Nurse Gleason's desperately clinging form. O'Kane broke for the car, but it was too late, Mr. McCormick out in the street with a wild look in his eye and his hat on the ground like a dead thing and the yellow slicker already flapping behind him. He was gone, running in the spastic ducking canter O'Kane knew so well, elbows flying, his head hanging there above his shoulders like an afterthought, but what did he want—the dog? Yes, the dog, skittering away from him suddenly in the direction of the train, the gleaming steel back-whirling wheels and manufactured thunder, and "Here, doggie, here, pooch, come here, come here."

O'Kane gave it everything he had, no time to think of the danger or the consequences, intent only on that loping mad twisted form he'd followed one place or another for the better part of his life, wedded to it, inured, stuck fast, but his knee wouldn't cooperate. Mr. McCormick was running flat-out, dipping and feinting to grab at the dog, past the line of cars now, staring faces, a man with a cigar, lady in a hat, right up to the crossguard—and then, without hesitating, a simple compression of the spine, heartbeat and a half, he was under it.

It was almost inevitable that the dog would die. A brown streak shooting through the gap of the grinding wheels, the cars rocking, the slowest train in the world, and here was the dog's last and final moment in this time, no sound at all but the screech of the wheels, and when O'Kane reached Mr. McCormick, there was one long stripe of blood painted down the front of him, from his sorrowful stricken eyes to the yellow waist of the rain slicker.

"Eddie," he said, but he jerked his arm away when O'Kane tried to take it, and the train was right there, as loud as the very end of everything, "Eddie, I want to die," he said. "Eddie, let me die."

That was a moment O'Kane would remember for the rest of his life, the life he would spend breathing air and eating food and sharing the sofa with Mr. Stanley Robert McCormick, a life he had no flake of choice in, because he didn't let Mr. McCormick die under those ratcheting wheels, already blooded, already released, but seized him in his arms and hugged him to him with a fierceness no force on earth could ever hope to break.

8.

COME ON IN, JACK

Katherine McCormick sat stiffly on one of the high-backed wooden benches of the Santa Barbara County Courthouse and studied the muraled walls with a vehemence of concentration that obliterated everything around her. Her clothes were flawless, her face neutral, her hair pinned up tightly beneath the brim of her hat. Her mother, looking sweet and determined, perched protectively on one side of her, and Jane on the other. Above all, she kept telling herself, she mustn't show any emotion. These people were like hounds, a whole yammering pack of them, the world of men arrayed against her yet again—the jostling rude loudmouthed reporters, the twanging hayseed of a judge, the McCormicks and their hired guns and even Bentley, her old nemesis, looking on from the wings with a mocking grin. But this time she had Newton Baker on her side, and if there was any man in America with more presence in a courtroom or a bigger reputation, short of Clarence Darrow himself, she'd like to know it. This was a fight she wasn't going to lose.

So she studied the murals as if she were in the Prado or the

Rijksmuseum, and tried to control her breathing and the wild fluttering surges of her heart. The courthouse was newly built, a replacement for the old structure that had fallen victim to the earthquake, and it was a grand high-crowned edifice in an ersatz Moorish-Iberian style, with hand-painted tiles from Algeria, half a mile of wrought iron, a flurry of arches and broad stone steps and a white watchtower that would have made Don Quixote feel right at home. The murals had been rendered by a Dutch set designer more usually employed by Cecil B. DeMille, and there was no danger of mistaking him for the reincarnation of Rembrandt. The one Katherine was fixed on at the moment depicted a group of noble savages and their dog looking suitably impressed as a group of halberd-wielding Spaniards descended on them from a galleon glimpsed mistily in the distance. The legend beneath it read: *"1542. Fifty years after Columbus Juan Rodriguez Cabrillo lands at Las Canoas with the Flag of Spain."*

Well, it was a distraction. And she needed a distraction, because Oscar Lawler, the McCormicks' attorney, backed by his three assistants and the resources of two Los Angeles law firms, was leading some miseducated, misguided and thoroughly self-satisfied fool of a physician through his paces vis-à-vis the dangers of endocrine treatment. "Moreover, in the cases of quiescent catatonia," the doctor droned, "it is now generally recognized that they do not depend on thyroid, pituitary or gonadal insufficiency. . . . In some instances the administration of thyroid substances has been followed by an exacerbation of the symptoms and in more than one instance an actual acute frenzy has developed. . . ." And blah, blah, blah. Why didn't Newt stand up and object? Why didn't he slam his fist down on the table and put an end to this charade? When would they ever get to cross-examination?

After lunch, it seemed. The doctor, a true by-the-rote man who spewed up everything the McCormicks had crammed down him, came back to court with a smear of mustard on his collar, and Newton Baker stood up and went to work on him. "Isn't it true, Dr. Orbison," Newt wanted to know, "that to expect a cure for a man in Mr. McCormick's condition through purely psychoanalytical means is an exercise in futility? Especially when, as a number of your distinguished colleagues in the medical profession have testified in this court, he is clearly dyspituitary and could be immeasurably helped, if not even cured, by feedings of the extract of the thyroid gland?"

Dr. Orbison, the smear of mustard in evidence, denied it. He felt
that the patient had improved markedly under Dr. Kempf's regime and
he reiterated that gland feeding was dangerous and irresponsible in a
case like Mr. McCormick's.

"But isn't it the case, doctor, that Dr. Kempf's 'treatment' consists
in nothing more than telling dirty stories for two hours each day, and
this under the cover of medical authority, which makes it all the more
detrimental, not to say reprehensible, and has had the effect of arousing
in the patient an antipathy toward women—and toward his wife in
particular?"

Mr. Lawler objected. Mr. Baker was leading the witness. Judge
Dehy sustained the objection and the question was stricken from the
record, but not before the doctor denied it.

"All right then, sir," Newt intoned, all solemnity and barely suppressed indignation, "deny me this: isn't it a fact that Mr. McCormick is
hopelessly insane and that his present physician's treatment amounts to
nothing more than so much hocus-pocus?"

Katherine gave a start, and all the courthouse saw her, the smug
McCormicks, the scribbling reporters, and three assistants to Mr.
Lawler and the stewing mass of whey-faced gawkers and hangers-on
who only lusted after the most degrading details of her and her husband's private life: Newt had gone too far. Yes, she understood he was
trying to make a point, trying to suggest that psychoanalysis had its limits in cases like Stanley's, but *hopelessly insane?* He didn't believe that,
did he? The doctor, the McCormicks' man, might have believed that the
sun revolved around the earth and that God and his angels had set up a
summer camp on Pluto, but he denied that her husband was hopelessly
insane, and for a minute she forgot which side she was on.

There was more of the same the next day and the next and the day
after that, doctors and more doctors, doctors for Lawler and the Mc-
Cormicks, doctors for her and Newton Baker, and none of them had a
thing to say you couldn't have written on the back of a penny postcard.
Then she had to endure the testimony of the nurses—Edward James
O'Kane, sinfully handsome even in his decline, taking the stand to say
that yes, Dr. Kempf had done wonders, and how was that for grati-
tude? And worse: Lawler called witnesses to impugn her character, as if
she were unfit to have the guardianship of her own husband. She was a
radical, a feminist, a member of the American Birth Control League,

and more than that they could only imply, because they wouldn't dare, and it took everything she had in her to sit on that leather-upholstered bench and listen to them try to cast their filthy aspersions on Jane Roessing when there wasn't a man or woman in that courtroom fit to wipe her feet. . . .

Yes. And then they called her, Katherine Dexter McCormick, to the witness stand.

Did she swear to tell the truth, the whole truth, and etcetera?

She did.

And she looked out over the courtroom with a calm and steady gaze, sweeping the tentative faces of Kempf and Cyrus and Harold and Anita, the twittering crush of reporters and curiosity seekers, the lawyers and expert witnesses huddled in their separate corners like teams out of uniform, before settling finally on Jane and her mother, drawn together now in the space she'd vacated. She gave them the briefest tight-lipped smile and then raised her eyes to Newt Baker's. *Now,* she thought, *now* they would hear the truth, now they would hear how a greedy and vengeful family tried from the beginning to isolate her and cut her out and how their only intent was to separate her from her husband and preserve the McCormick fortune at all costs and how Kempf was simply the latest in a long line of quacks and charlatans hired to exclude her not only from her husband's care but from his rooms and his house and the very sight of him. And who was the loser in all this? She was. And Stanley, never forget Stanley, deprived of her support and physical presence through all these cruel, inexorable, downwinding years. Oh, she had a story to tell.

Newt Baker led her through it step by step, as well as he could, but of course motive wasn't admissible here except by implication and every time she began to tell the whole truth and nothing but the truth Oscar Lawler popped up like a jack-in-the-box to object. Still, Newt was able to guide her toward a thorough airing of the central question at issue here: Kempf's competence.

"When did you first suspect the efficacy—or lack thereof—of Dr. Kempf's methods, Mrs. McCormick?" Newt asked in the gentlest wafting breeze of a voice.

"When he informed me, in all seriousness, that my husband's teeth, which are in a deplorable state, would be somehow miraculously repaired through the effects of Freudian analysis."

"His teeth?"

"Yes, you see my husband has an unreasoning fear of dentists because a dentist was involved in an altercation with him on the day of his
breakdown, his final breakdown, that is. And this is quite clearly a case
of the patient leading the physician, as if words alone could rectify a
physical ailment — one that is well within our scope and means to repair
through the expedient of dental surgery. This is a matter of tooth decay,
not mental manipulation."

Newt gazed at the judge a moment, then leaned in close to the witness stand. His hair was silver now, not a trace of the color she remembered from the War years, and he carried himself with the exaggerated
care that hinted at fragility, the first ineluctable whisper of old age —
though he couldn't have been more than sixty, if that. "And that," he
was saying, "was when you first began to suspect that Dr. Kempf's
treatment, though we've heard it irresponsibly lauded here in this court,
might be akin to mental healing or Christian Science even?"

"That's correct." Katherine drew herself up, sought out Kempf's
eyes, gave the judge a look as if to be sure he was listening, and then
came back to Newt, who was waiting there like a catcher crouched behind the plate at Fenway Park, and she the pitcher all wound-up and
ready to let fly. "I told him it was utter nonsense, unscientific and inef-
fective, and that there were physical treatments available to treat physical problems like my husband's — thyroid feeding, for instance. He
proceeded to give me a long account of his new theory, which he's em-
bodied in a monograph called 'The Autonomic System' or some such.
He sees himself as very big in the field and explained to me how this
new theory of his was being gradually accepted and how widely it
would affect the position of psychoanalysis. But no amount of talk,
whether it be therapeutic or merely harmful and alienating, is going to
cure a physical ailment."

"And Dr. Kempf persisted in applying this 'theory' to your husband, despite the fact that noted physicians like Dr. R. G. Hoskins of
Harvard found your husband 'indubitably endocrinopathic,' I believe
the term was?"

"Yes."

Newt took a moment to stride from one end of the raised platform
in front of the box to the other. This was his moment, and he seemed to
swell himself in proportion to it. "And that was when Dr. Kempf, who

had been engaged above your objections by your husband's other two guardians—Cyrus and Anita McCormick—at the staggering sum of ten thousand dollars a month, turned on you and banished you altogether from your husband's house?"

Mr. Lawler rose to object. Judge Dehy, who seemed either to be asleep or in a state of suspended animation, made a show of rustling about in his seat before murmuring, "Objection overruled."

Katherine turned her face to the judge, all the hurt stabbing at her eyes, the crime of it, the abuse, the indecency and injustice. She felt her voice quaver. "Yes," she said, "yes. That's it. That's exactly it."

Then it was Lawler's turn, and he couldn't make her so much as flinch, though to a man like that no accusation was too scandalous or irresponsible, no scab too thin to pick, and he went after her with everything in his mercenary's arsenal. He questioned her competency as a guardian, her scientific background, her attachment to "radical" causes, her friendship with Mrs. Roessing, but nothing, nothing could make her waver. It was "Yes, Mr. Lawler," and "No, Mr. Lawler," throughout the afternoon and into the next morning.

—And wasn't it the case that her husband had improved dramatically and that it was Dr. Kempf who was responsible?

—No, she insisted, no it wasn't. Her husband had simply settled down with age.

—But she wanted his money, didn't she, to devote to her radical causes and Mrs. Margaret Sanger's godless movement to prevent natural conception?

—No, she didn't want money. She wanted control of her husband's care because of the mess the McCormicks had made of it. She loved her husband. She wanted to see him well.

And then, eleven o'clock in the morning and with Juan Rodriguez Cabrillo and his Indians and their fawning dog all lit with the glow of the day advancing beyond the windows, Oscar Lawler rested his arms on the rail of the witness box and drank her up with his hateful liver-complected eyes. There was dandruff on the shoulders of his brown suit, dandruff in his eyebrows; his nails were bitten to the quick. He was so close she could almost smell him. "Then you believe," he said, his voice rich with irony, "in contradiction of your own attorney and his string of 'expert' witnesses, that your husband is *not* hopelessly insane. Is that correct?"

"Yes," she said, her voice nothing more than a whisper, "yes, I believe it," but Newton Baker was rising to object or request an adjournment or dash outside to climb the flagpole and howl at the sky, but she wasn't really there, not any longer. The phrase Lawler had used—the phrase Newt had used, just to make a point—came back at her, beating at her like a rising sea, *hopelessly insane, hopelessly insane,* till she felt herself letting go and she wasn't in the courtroom anymore staring down at that chittering little rodent of a man in his litigious brown and his sleek lawyerly shoes . . . no, she was in Boston, twenty-three years ago, and it was the morning of the day Stanley went out of her orbit for good and ever.

The night had held, a dense fabric of the familiar and the usual, Stanley stretched out like a corpse across the bed in the guestroom, Katherine lying awake and staring into the darkness of her room down the hall. She awoke to the smell of bacon and came down to breakfast feeling as drained and exhausted as if she'd been up a hundred nights in a row: the German teacher had gotten away unharmed, but who was next and how would it end? Stanley was already up and dressed, seated at the table in the dining room with the newspaper folded neatly at his elbow and a pyramid of sausages, bacon, eggs and fried tomatoes all mounded up in the center of the plate before him. He looked, of all things, *crisp*— crisp and fresh in a new shirt, collar and cuffs, his face newly shaven, his hair still damp and fastidiously combed away from the sweep of his brow and the tight plumb-line of his parting. "Good morning, Stanley," she murmured, and he glanced up quickly, frowned, and went back to his newspaper.

Josephine wasn't down yet, and Katherine took the place across from her husband and rang for tea and a toasted muffin and jam. She didn't have much of an appetite, not after what she'd been through the night before, but she'd always believed in exercise and vigor and the fuel to sustain it, and she felt she'd force herself to have something at least. The maid appeared, a little curtsy, face of stone, the door swinging once and then twice and here was sustenance set out before her. She buttered her muffin in silence, waiting for Stanley to take the lead, and then made a pass at the jam and poured a dollop of cream into her tea, stirring all the while. Her heart was pounding. She had to say something. "Looks to be a pleasant day," she said, "for January, I mean. I just don't think I can stand any more of this gloomy weather, and at least the sun's shining for a change. . . ." She trailed off.

Stanley looked up then, and his eyes seemed to be swollen, leaping right out of his head, as if there were a corpse nailed to the wall behind her. "I—Katherine," he suddenly blurted, "about the, uh, the German teacher—"

"Yes?"

"I've decided not to study German, not—not now, anyhow. Maybe later. Maybe next month. Or the month after that. It—it's my teeth, you see, I mean my tooth, you see, I—well, it aches and hurts me and I think, my mood yesterday—"

She softened. And she hoped, still and foolishly, because wouldn't that be something if it was all just a kind of poisoning of the system and hadn't she just yesterday remarked to her mother about his breath being tainted? "You poor thing," she said. "Do you want me to have a look?"

"No."

"Well, what about a dentist then? Shouldn't you be seeing a dentist if it's bothering you, especially in light of your nerves and the sort of thing that took place in this house last night?" And here she couldn't stop herself. "Really, Stanley, I don't mean to lecture but you can't just go around brawling with people on the docks and, and *kidnapping* German teachers. It's gone too far. It has. You need help, Stanley, professional help, and you've got to let me take you someplace where you can get the kind of care and rest you need . . . just till your nerves are settled." She tried on a smile. "Wouldn't that be the best thing to do?"

He stood abruptly, in the same motion snatching a fistful of food from his plate and forcing it into his mouth. He was shaking his head back and forth automatically, his cheeks bulging, his eyes sinking all the way back down to nothing, pitiful starved eyes that seemed to beg for help and intervention, and she got up too and reached out to him.

The table lay between them, the cold eggs, the sausage and bacon subsiding in a pool of congealed fat. His jaws were working and yet he winced with every downward thrust. "My, my *tooth*," he said, spewing bits of partially masticated food, "I—I've got to f-find a dentist—"

"I'll call mother's dentist—he's really quite good and I'm sure, if it's an emergency, he'd be—"

"No, no," Stanley cried, still chewing, food down the front of his shirt now, "I—I have to go," and he shot out the door, through the hall and down the stairs, where he snatched up his hat and overcoat before plunging into the cube of light that stood there in place of the front door.

All right, fine, she was thinking, trying to calm herself, trying to stop quaking and fuming every time he entered or left the room. He'd gone to the dentist to have a bad tooth seen to. What could be more normal or prosaic? She shook her head as if to clear it, squashed all her worries and presentiments, and went back up to bed.

When she woke it was past ten and she saw that she was going to be late for her appointment with Professor Durward, who was in the process of setting up a very intriguing set of experiments into the nature of simian sexuality with a young Harvard psychiatrist by the name of Hamilton. She was hoping to get some direction from him regarding her own future at the Institute—she very much wanted to work with larger animals, rats, rabbits, apes and monkeys, rather than the microbes or fruit flies everyone seemed to prefer. But she'd have to call and reschedule—if she could even get through on the phone—or maybe she could make it after all, if she hurried.

In the end, she chose to take a cab to the Institute and she did manage to catch Professor Durward, who seemed to have forgotten all about her, and she stayed on through the afternoon and examined some of his charges with him—a shipment of twelve rhesus monkeys from India. They stared out at her from their cages in a dull yellow bundle of limbs and parodic faces, their toes and fingers so human-like as they gripped the wire or groomed themselves and their babies. There were two babies among them, she remembered, sparse clinging things that had been born on shipboard, or so Professor Durward claimed.

It was late in the afternoon by the time she got home, and she found Stanley waiting for her on the front steps, highly agitated. His collar was torn, there was a gash over his left eye and his lower lip was yellow and crusted. He'd had a fight with the dentist or the dentist's receptionist or a man in the waiting room or the taxi driver who brought him there, she could see that in a minute, one of a thousand fights, fights that would go on till he was stopped. Or killed. She took one look at him and wanted to walk right on by, sick to death of him, ready to call it quits, send him back to his mother, anything, but the choice wasn't in her hands, not this time.

The minute he saw her he leapt to his feet and grabbed her arm. "You—you can't leave me like that," he said, breathless, the veins swollen in his neck above the slashed collar. "Who was it," he demanded, forcing her up the steps and against the slab of the door, "one of your boyfriends? But-Butler Ames? Huh? Tell me!"

"I've been at the Institute," she said.

"Lies!" he spat. "All lies!"

She told him he was hurting her—and he was, the strength of him, his hand like a ligature right there above her elbow—but he just kept repeating "Who was it?" over and over again. Then she took her key out and they were in the hallway, fighting away from one another, the maid's stricken face lost somewhere behind the plants, and then she was free of him and dashing up the stairs, his feet thundering behind. Up and up, no time to stop or reason, down the hallway and into her room, the door shut and bolted and him out there on the runner pounding and pounding. "Let me in!" he cried, and he was furious, pounding, "let me in!"

After a minute he stopped, and the fury had gone out of his voice. "Please," he begged, "please let me in. I-I'll be good, I will." He was sobbing now, hot and cold, and where was the tap to turn it off, where was it? "I-I love you, Katherine. Don't leave me."

She clung to the door, and she found that she was crying too, a dry rasp of the throat and the water stinging her eyes. This was it, this was her life, this was her marriage, a madman in the hall and an inch-and-a-half thickness of mahogany between her and harm, yes, harm, because all of a sudden he'd begun to rage again, hammering the door with his shoulder, the bolt shivering, the frame heaving and protesting. "Go away!" she screamed.

There was no answer, not for the longest time, and she held her breath and listened, listened so hard she could hear the thoughts colliding in his head and the blood bolting through his veins, and then there was a sudden crash and the wood gave way where it was thinnest, right in the middle of the center panel, and she could see his face through the snarling hole, nothing but eyes, all eyes, seeking her out. "I'll k-kill you, you bitch!" he roared.

She backed away from the door, all the way across the room to the bed, and he began shouting out to someone only he could see. "Jack!" he cried. "Jack London! Come on in, Jack, and we'll both have her!"

That was when she retreated to the closet, the last place she could go, the key on the inside of the door and the door shut tight, and nothing but darkness now and fear, fear and hate, because he was what she was afraid of and that made her hate him beyond all forgiveness or consolation. Stanley. Stanley Robert McCormick, the madman, the lunatic, the nut, the sexual hypochondriacal neurasthenic. And that was what she was left with when they came and got him and they put him in the straitjacket and the sheet restraints and used all their outraged male muscle to hold him down.

But that wasn't how she wanted to remember him, not now in the stairwell of the courthouse with the reporters shoving their faces at her and Newt Baker guiding her by that same abused elbow with a grip as gentle and tactful as it was firm. That wasn't right. That wasn't Stanley. No, she remembered him the way he was that night in Chicago, the ground frozen hard and his mother looming beside them in the carriage like some excrescence and demanding that they take Miss Dexter directly home: "Rush Street? Have you lost your senses?"

He'd fought for her. Stood up to his mother and made his choice. And when he came back to the carriage he was ten feet tall, her Stanley, all hers. A hush, the door pulled to, that intimate space all ordained, hot bricks for their feet under the fur robe, the pale light fading, the horses moving now through the richest haze of possibility. He was shy and awkward and he wanted to talk about Debs, "About Debs and what he said in the paper the other—the other, well, day. It was the most significant thing I've—"

He never got to finish the thought, as if it would have mattered, because Debs could only take you so far, and Debs didn't matter now and he never would again. She put her hand on his chest and felt his heart living there beneath his coat, his jacket, his shirt. "Hush, Stanley," she said, and she felt her face move toward his through the heavy atmosphere and complex gravity of love. "You don't need to talk now," she whispered, "not anymore. Just kiss me, Stanley. Kiss me."

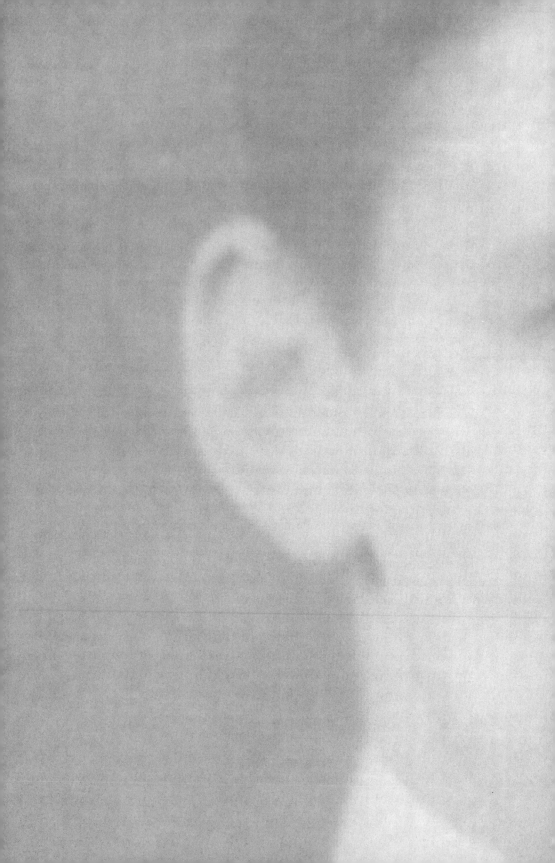

EPILOGUE

1947,
World Without Walls

And so he died a prisoner, Stanley Robert McCormick, seventy-two years old and his hair white as bone, handsome, tall and bereft till the last. Nurse Gleason was gone, along with her stalwart charms, and Muriel gave up visiting for her own life, and though the new doctor — Dr. Russell — had a shining golden buttercup of a secretary and there was a dietician with two breasts roaming around somewhere in the depths of the house and the Italian woman, Eddie O'Kane's wife, cooked on in the kitchen, Stanley never got to touch any of them or hold them in his arms the way his mother had held him or the way Katherine had. She came to visit almost every day, Katherine, or every other day, because sometimes he didn't want to see her, just refused, flatly and absolutely, and no one to make him say different, and she came haunting the streets all the way from her house in downtown Santa Barbara with the grand modern rooms and the gymnasium she'd built for him to use when he came visiting, but he never came visiting.

He couldn't touch *her* either, because he'd been up in the Yukon Territory with Sitka Charley and the Malemute Kid and whole considerable teams of dogs and she wasn't woman enough for him—no, she was an old lady, of the very properest and stiffest sort, and she sat and read to him from the paper and made him kiss her on the cheek every time she came and went. Then he became ill with pneumonia and all the florid faces and vivid formless things came back to him again and inhabited him and raised an unholy yowl of voices inside him, and the Judges were there too in their flapping black robes and no surcease. He was thirty-one years old when he was blocked the first time and he was worth six million dollars and he knew all about that because he was the comptroller and could add up two columns of figures as well as any man or mathematician alive. And when he died finally and was finally released into a world without walls or bars or restraints, he was worth thirty-four million and more, because it wasn't his money they'd locked up—it was his body. And his mind.

Katherine inherited that money, all of it, and everything else too—the properties in Chicago that were minted of gold, the securities and stocks, Stanley's eight grades of underwear and the house at Riven Rock with the bars on the windows and the eighty-seven acres with their views of the stunned and scoured islands and the nurses who were all through with nursing now. She sold the estate to pay the inheritance taxes and she took what was left to seed the causes and institutions she believed in—MIT, the League of Women Voters, the Santa Barbara Art Museum and Dr. Gregory Pincus, an old friend of Roy Hoskins, who developed a little yellow progesterone-based pill that would free women forever from sexual constraint. All that was to the good, but she lost the court case, despite what the newspapers said. Kempf was sent packing, that much she'd accomplished, but the McCormicks were still there in all their obstinacy and immovability and the judge had added three whisker-pulling male physicians to the board of guardians and all the wrangling went on and on. It was a partial victory, she supposed, but there was little consolation in that. Because she never did get the thing she wanted most—her husband—not until he was dead.

And by then it was too late.